A Cassandra Jones Book

OF CAMPUS
SCHEMES, HOPES
AND

Dreams

Of Campus Schemes, Hopes, and Dreams

The Extraordinarily Ordinary Life of Cassandra Jones

Tamara Hart Heiner

paperback edition
copyright 2024 Tamara Hart Heiner
cover art by Tamara Hart Heiner

Also by Tamara Hart Heiner:
Guardian Angel Academy
Year 1: Renegade (Tamark Books 2021)
Year 2: Redemption (Tamark Books 2021)
Year 3: Rebellion (Tamark Books 2021)
Year 4: Revolution (Tamark Books 2021)

Perilous (WiDo Publishing 2010)
Altercation (WiDo Publishing 2012)
Deliverer (Tamark Books 2014)
Priceless (WiDo Publishing 2016)
Vendetta (Tamark Books 2018)

Goddess of Fate:
Inevitable (Tamark Books 2013)
Entranced (Tamark Books 2017)
Coercion (Tamark Books 2019)
Destined (Tamark Books 2019)

Kellam High:
Lay Me Down (Tamark Books 2016)
Reaching Kylee (Tamark Books 2016)
Considering Margaret (Tamark Books 2023)

The Extraordinarily Ordinary Life of Cassandra Jones:
Walker Wildcats Year 1: Age 10 (Tamark Books 2015)
Walker Wildcats Year 2: Age 11 (Tamark Books 2016)
Southwest Cougars Seventh Grade (Tamark Books 2017)
Southwest Cougars Eighth Grade (Tamark Books 2018)
Southwest Cougars Freshman Year (Tamark Books 2019)
Springdale Bulldogs Sophomore Year (Tamark Books 2020)

Springdale Bulldogs Junior Year (Tamark Books 2022)
Springdale Bulldogs Senior Year (Tamark Books 2023)
Of Life, Love, and Other Noble Pursuits (Tamark Books 2024)

Tornado Warning (Dancing Lemur Press 2014)

Eureka in Love Series
Shades of Raven (Tamark Books 2020)
After the Fall (Tamark Books 2018)
#

Table of Contents

EPISODE 1 :

Ending a Chapter

CHAPTER ONE

Killing Time

Eighteen hours after leaving Arkansas, my plane sets down in Recife, Brazil.

I'm bone-weary. I finished my freshman year of college just days ago. Yesterday I permanently deleted my ex-boyfriend from my contact list. My heart is heavy, and I need sleep.

Instead I'll be expected to smile and be polite while I greet Tiago and his family, who are putting me up for the next month.

I have no idea how this month will go. Tiago and I dated when my family hosted him as an exchange student. We were close, but the time and distance forced us apart. Other than a few emails and phone calls, we haven't talked much these past few months.

Coming here seemed like such a good idea when I bought the ticket. I'm studying Portuguese at Preston Yarborough University, and spending a month in Brazil with one of my dearest friends sounded like an exciting adventure.

Maybe I'm just tired, but it doesn't sound that way now.

I trudge through the line of other weary travelers, blinking against the grit in my eyes. I went through customs in São Paulo, so now all I have to do is exit through the doors and collect my baggage. I remember where to go from the last time I was here. The air is thick with moisture, a salty, mildewy scent clinging to the walls. I inhale, and the scent takes me back in time.

It smells like Brazil.

People come to life around me when they spot their loved ones waiting for them on the other side of the doors. They brighten, teeth flashing as they shriek, scream, gasp, or stand in place and cry. My heart pounds a little harder as the reality breaks through my exhaustion: as soon as I get through these doors, I'll see Tiago.

What I feel is a frightening combination of dread and anticipation.

Will he recognize me? My hair is longer than the last time he saw me, but I have it up in a ponytail. I'm nineteen now and ten pounds heavier but still have a baby-face.

Will I recognize him?

I push through the doors and keep moving, taking deep breaths to keep calm as I scan the faces.

I see him the same time he sees me. Even though Tiago has also put on weight and grown his hair longer, it's the same face, the same dark eyes, the same high cheek bones and thick lips. Our gazes meet across the room, and then a smile splits his face. He crosses over to me, parting the crowd to get to my side, and I smile back, but my heart hasn't stopped racing. In an instant he wraps me up in a hug, but he's only a few inches taller than me and his hug doesn't swallow me whole.

Not like Owen's hugs.

Why am I thinking of Owen? We broke up months ago. I might not be over him, but I've moved on. Why is he haunting me now?

Because of Tiago. Because of the drama that occurred between those two boys. Because they are the only two I've ever loved.

Tiago pulls out of the hug and kisses both of my cheeks, which is a customary Brazilian greeting and calms my nerves because he's treating me like a friend.

"I can't believe you're here," he says, and his accent is much thicker than I remember. "I can't believe it. After all this time."

"I know." I lick my lips, surprised I found my voice. "It's been a long time."

He steps away from me and heads to the luggage piling up by the exit door. "Which one is yours?"

I point it out. "The blue one." I take a deep breath and hold it, slowly exhaling. It's going to be okay. This trip will be good for me.

He gets my bag and comes back to me, and then he can't seem to help wrapping me up in another hug. I let him, and it feels so nice to be touched, I find myself fighting tears.

"Your hair is long," I say, laughing as he steps back. It's long enough he has it in a ponytail at the nape of his neck. I reach back and tug it, teasing. "You look like a girl."

"You don't like it?" He takes out the ponytail holder and shakes his head, letting the thick black hair fall around his shoulders. "Isn't it sexy?"

"No." I laugh harder, relieved. I'm not attracted to him. We are not the same people we were two years ago. "Not at all."

"I'm wounded." He grins at me to show he's teasing, and my defenses break down. He's a friend. Just a friend.

I follow him to the curb.

"Who's driving?" I ask. I glance up at the dark sky, the palm trees lit by the overhead street lamps. Like last time I was here, it's winter in Recife. It gets dark early. But the streets are crowded with honking cars and squealing brakes.

"My dad. His car is there."

Tiago points, and then he takes my hand to pull me across the busy street. He opens the back of the car, and I climb in.

"Hello, Cassandra!" Tiago's father turns around to grin at me from the front. He hasn't changed at all. His thick dark hair matches Tiago's, but he wears it short. They have the same darker-toned skin, as opposed to Tiago's mother, who is fairer, lighter than I am. Tiago's father also wears glasses, and he adjusts them now as he looks me over.

"How was flight?"

"It was fine. I'm tired. *Estou cansada.*" I throw in some Portuguese because I know he doesn't speak English, and one of my goals here is to improve my Portuguese.

"Ah." He nods. "You want eat? Or sleep?"

"*Pai,*" Tiago says, and then he proceeds to rattle off several sentences so quickly that I don't catch another word.

I sigh in disappointment. Getting all As in a Portuguese class didn't make me fluent.

His dad nods and pulls the car into the flow of traffic. He's a much calmer driver than Tiago's grandpa.

Tiago turns to me. "We'll stop and get food, then we'll go back to my grandpa's house. We have a room ready for you."

"Thanks." My stomach growls in appreciation. "It's kind of your family."

"Your family took care of me for nine months. My family is happy to take care of you for one."

Traffic lessens as we move away from the airport. We park at a cafe with tables and umbrellas.

"You sit," Tiago says, pointing out a table. "I'll get food."

"All right."

"What would you like?"

I shrug. "Anything. I'm not a vegetarian anymore."

"You're not?" He blinks at me in surprise. "Cool. Okay."

I sit down at the table and release my hair. My head aches, and I massage it. Tiago's dad doesn't join me, so I assume he's staying in the car and waiting for us.

Tiago returns with several fried items, and I sit up taller, excited.

"*Coxinhas!* And *pasteis!*" I pick up the deep-fried ball of dough and chicken and groan as I bite into it. "Oh, I've missed this," I say around a mouthful of food.

"I missed it too when I was in the U.S.," he says. "There's one pastel of cheese and ham and one of just cheese."

"Which one is just cheese?"

He points to it, so I grab the other one and put it on a napkin in front of me. He laughs.

"It's good to see you eating. And enjoying meat."

"It was a good experience." I take a bite and stop talking for a moment to enjoy the flavors. Tiago places a can of *guaraná* in front of me, and I happily chug the Brazilian soda before speaking again. "I tasted foods I never would have tried if I hadn't been a vegetarian. But I couldn't go back. I enjoy meat too much."

"And how is the other food thing?"

I take my time with the next bite, pondering my words. Tiago lived with me during an extremely volatile time in my adolescence, when I was battling two eating disorders. "I'm careful. I don't overeat and I exercise so I don't feel bad about myself. I'm doing well."

He reaches out like he's going to touch my face, and then he thinks better of it and squeezes my hand. "That makes me so happy."

"Thank you for being there for me," I say, catching his eyes so he'll know I'm sincere. "Thank you for being my friend. I wrote an essay on the experience in my freshman

English class, and it made me realize how much you influenced me, how much you helped me overcome it."

He blinks and drops his gaze. "Sometimes I felt such guilt because I wasn't the nicest person to you. Sometimes I worried I made it worse for you."

There had been some of that. Dating Tiago was a roller coaster of ups and downs. But I don't point that out. "I always knew you loved me."

He glances up, meets my eyes and then looks away again, and I'm glad because suddenly I'm afraid of what I might see there.

If he still loves me, I don't want to know.

I finish the pastel and crumble up my napkin. "Thanks for the food. I didn't realize how hungry I was." I cover a yawn as sleepiness overwhelms me, my eyes throbbing with the need to shut. "I'm so tired."

"Come on." He stands up and places a hand at my shoulder blades when I stand also. "Let's get you to bed."

The drive from the cafe to his grandpa's house is less than ten minutes, but I lean my head against the window and doze off and on for those brief moments. I can barely pry my eyes open when we arrive. I shoulder my purse and get out of the car, and Tiago stops me when I start for the trunk.

"I'll get your bag," he says, his tone gentle. "Go to bed."

I nod. I turn to the house before remembering my mom. I spin back to him.

"Oh. I promised my mom I'd tell her I got here. Can you show me how to call the U.S.?"

Tiago waves me off. "I'll call her."

I hesitate. I need to make sure this happens, but my body tells me to accept his offer and get to bed. "Promise you won't forget?"

"I promise."

I believe him. I shuffle toward the house with its door in the brick wall. Tiago's dad holds it open for me, and Grandpa greets me when I come in. He points to the flight of stairs leading to the two bedrooms.

"Your room," he says, indicating the one on the right.

I force each foot to lift up the stairs. The lights are dim and the house is dark, but I know my way around. Tomorrow I'll admire Grandpa's house with his indoor garden in the small courtyard, but tonight I can't think of anything.

I pause in the bathroom to remove my contacts, and then I flip off the lights and tumble into the twin bed.

CHAPTER TWO

Arrival

No one wakes me. My room is toasty from sunlight floating over my bed through the open window when I finally stretch and kick off the thin blanket over me.

I blink up at the ceiling fan, and it dawns on me that I'm in Brazil.

By myself.

I'm not alone because Tiago is here, but still—I made an international trip by myself. A rush of pride and excitement invigorates my limbs.

I check the time and see it's almost eleven in the morning. Eleven! I can't believe they let me sleep that long.

I hear voices in the kitchen and get dressed before I head downstairs. I'm not surprised to see Tiago there with his grandfather, his longer hair concealed by a baseball cap. He glances at me, and I feel a surge of affection for this boy. I smile at him, and he smiles back.

"Good morning," Grandfather says in his highly affected English accent.

"Almost afternoon," I answer.

Tiago laughs, and then he yells something in Portuguese toward the kitchen.

I expect the maid to appear—it seems everyone has one here—but instead it's his mother, Martha, who steps into the doorway, wiping her hands on a rag.

"Cassandra!" she exclaims, and her nose turns red. "I miss you so much!"

I go to her and hug her, and I think she might be crying. She's an inch or two taller than me and much rounder, and so sweet.

She pulls away, sniffling, and pats my arm. "*Minha filha Americana. Voltou para mim.*"

I understand all of her words, and that fills me with pride. Her American daughter, returned to her. I hug her again. "*Sim. Voltei.*"

She laughs in delight. "*Estás falando português!*" she says, and that's all I get before she rambles off so quickly that it sounds like one long run-on word.

I must look lost.

"Come sit down and eat," Tiago says, gesturing back to the table. "And we can talk

9

about what you want to do today."

I sit down and pour myself a glass of orange juice. Martha brings out a tray of cheese and meat and small loaves of bread. I can appreciate the beauty of this house now with its open-concept floor plan and painted tiles and the exposed strip of roof where the rain can enter and water the indoor garden.

"I can't believe I slept so late," I say, a little sheepish.

Tiago shrugs. "I do it all the time. It's fine."

I bet he does. I remember countless arguments where I disapproved of his late night party habits.

It was none of my business, anyway.

"Your hair is long," he says. "It's very pretty. I like it."

"Thank you." I butter a loaf of bread and add honey to it.

"And you look great. Healthy. Eating is good for you."

I have to laugh at that. "Yeah. It's good for most of us."

"Was there anything you wanted to do today?"

"Can we go somewhere with internet? I need to check my grades and email my friends."

"Yes. And then what?"

"Well . . ." I trail off. My goal here is to learn Portuguese, to improve my understanding of the language. But I also want to immerse myself in Brazilian culture. "Would it be all right if we went to the beach? I haven't been since the last time I was here."

He gives me a look that can only be described as pity. "Yes. Of course."

Martha drives us to the public library to use the internet, and I tease Tiago as we walk toward the entrance.

"How old do you have to be to get your license?" I say.

"Eighteen," he says.

"And you turned eighteen when?"

"I know, I know," he says, grabbing the door and holding it for me. "But it's not that easy here."

"Yeah, driving here is crazy," I agree, leading the way to the computers in the back. "I'd be scared also."

"I'm not scared!" he protests.

I just laugh and sit at one of the computers. He sits beside me.

I check my grades first and give a whoop of joy. "I got all As in Portuguese!"

He leans over to examine my screen. "Congratulations. That's better than my grade."

I smirk at him. "It raises my GPA, also. It was an eight-credit class. Now I'll keep my scholarship for sure."

"Good job." He scratches the top of my head, a gentle touch on my scalp. He always used to do that. I called it the "Tiago-scratch." "Soon you'll speak Portuguese better than I do."

"Or at least, I'll know the rules better than you do."

He removes his hand, and I open my email program next.

"Who are you emailing?" he asks.

It's a nosy question, but it doesn't bother me, coming from Tiago. He knows almost everyone I know. "My family. Riley. A few friends from college."

"How is Riley?"

"She had a baby last week. It was amazing."

"Wow!" His eyes bug out. "She's a mom? Is she married?"

"Yeah, they got married."

"I can't believe it. Do you have pictures?"

I pull out my phone and hand it to him. "Here."

He starts with my pictures in Arkansas while I send emails. I know he's going through all of them when he doesn't give the phone back, but again I don't care. I'm astonished at how easy it is to talk to him, to feel close to him, after all the time we spent apart and all the hurt we caused each other.

He puts the phone between us and begins asking about people, pointing to their picture. "Who is this?"

I finish sending an email and pivot to give him my full attention. "These are my roommates." I take the phone back so I can point them out. "That's Camila. She shared my room. That's Iris, she's Canadian. That's Layne, she caused *sooooo* much trouble last year, but she's awesome. She's leaving on a mission to Guatemala next month."

"That's amazing."

I keep going, pointing out the kids from college who have made up my hours and days for the past few months. "That's Stirling, he's watching my fish for me until I get back, that's my cousin Jordan, that's Jared—" I pause.

I have a picture of me and Jared.

I didn't know I have it. The whole group of us are at Abby's house playing volleyball, but I have one picture where I've turned away from the volleyball net and I'm facing Jared, laughing while he grins at me.

I wonder who took this picture. Someone who knew there was more between me and Jared than either one of us let on.

"Who is Jared?" Tiago asks, suspecting he's someone important.

"He's—he's someone special."

"Did you email him?"

I shake my head. I want to but— "I won't. He's leaving on a mission in a few weeks also. It's better if we don't stay close."

"Was he a boyfriend?"

I glance at Tiago, trying to ascertain if there's any jealousy in his words. If there is, he conceals it behind a mask of benign curiosity. "No. But more than just a friend."

"What about Owen?"

I smile, but it's tight, and I avert my eyes, not able to quite hide the pain in that name. "We broke up months ago." I try to say the words glibly. To show it's no big deal, that's part of life, I'm over it. Or at least okay with it.

"I'm sorry," Tiago says. "I know how much he meant to you."

Hearing these words from Tiago nearly undoes me. He, more than anyone else, should be gloating over the fact Owen and I are through. But he has enough compassion for me that he sees the pain I'm in. And he's sorry.

I look away before I cry and repeat the facade I'm trying to portray. "It's fine. It's life. Happens to everyone."

His hand comes up under my hair and squeezes the back of my neck in a miniature version of a hug. I go back to my emails and take comfort from his touch.

By the time we head to the ocean a few hours later, I've successfully put my sadness behind me. The aqua-blue water, sandwiched between the sand and the coral reef Recife is named for, is grand in its wide expanse leading out to the edge of the world, waves crashing like thunder on the shore.

Martha sees a hot dog vendor and insists we go buy one.

"I don't love hot dogs," I say to Tiago as we stand in line.

"Because you've only had American hot dogs," he says, wiggling his eyebrows. "Brazilian ones are much better."

My eyebrows rise as Tiago gives instructions to the man behind the cart, adding tomato sauce, peas, corn, eggs, raisins, and string potato chips to his hot dog.

"That can't possibly be good," I say.

"Try it," he urges.

I'm not as brave. I fumble through the words, using my fingers to point out the food items I want. Tomato sauce. Corn. Potato chips. Mayonnaise.

We step out of line, and Tiago waits for me to take my first bite. It falls apart when I do, the bread soaked by the tomato sauce, and I understand why the vendor served it in a cardboard tray with a fork.

"It's really good," I admit, mopping my face with a napkin.

"See?" Tiago grins at me, and then his expression sobers. "I still can't believe you're here."

"Me neither," I say. "I can't believe I bought that ticket." It was an impulse by with my new credit card right before my high school graduation.

"I'm so glad you did. I missed you so much." He studies me, that half-hooded expression I remember so well. "You're my best friend. You mean the world to me."

I hold his gaze, for once not uncomfortable by his bold statements of affection. "You're a lot kinder to me now than you were last time I was here."

He winces. "I was young. Stupid. I'm sorry."

"I forgave you already." But if he's hoping for a second chance . . . That's not happening.

We head back to Tiago's house, and nostalgia pushes up against my brain when I enter the front room. I stand by the kitchen and sigh, remembering being here two years earlier, when I was so in love with Tiago. We ate here, we fought here, we made out here. I flash back to those moments, and for an instant I feel seventeen again, transported to the past, to the hopes and fears and hurts of that time.

I turn when Tiago comes in behind me, and I see him through the lens of the past also, only sixteen and so confused about his place in his world and mine. I resist the urge to hug him, because the me that I am now does not feel what the me of then felt.

But briefly, the two merge, and I struggle to know what is real and what is memory.

I turn away from Tiago and follow Martha into the kitchen to put away the groceries. She continues chattering at me in Portuguese, and I find it very helpful. I'm forced to search my Portuguese vocabulary for words to talk to her, and it stretches me. It's only been two days, but already my brain is forming new pathways, connecting dots. I'm excited to see how much I know after thirty days.

Tiago walks me back to his grandfather's house after dinner.

"We will come pick you up for church tomorrow," he says.

He unlocks the gate for me, and I step through.

"See you in the morning," I say. "Thanks for such a fun day."

"See ya," he echoes.

The door closes behind me, and I let myself into Grandpa's house. I hum as I go past the kitchen and up the stairs.

We are still friends, Tiago and I.

I can almost forget that Owen and I are not.

CHAPTER THREE

Friendly Recap

Tiago's whole family comes to pick me up for church in the morning. I wear the brown floral dress Martha bought me last time I was here. She recognizes it immediately and tells me how wonderful it looks. I squish into the back of the car with Tiago and his brothers. We don't fit, but I won't complain because I'm pleased they're coming.

"Last time you didn't come to church with me," I say to Tiago. I'm wedged between him and his brother Rafael.

"I told you I was pretty stupid last time," he says.

His hair is back in its ponytail, lending him a sultry vampire look. I bite my lip to keep from laughing.

"What?" he says, seeing it.

"Nothing."

He touches his ponytail. "You really don't like it?"

I shrug. "What do you care what I think?"

"I will cut it if you want."

"No." I say the word sharply enough that his mom glances back at us and his brothers lean forward. I soften my tone and lower my voice. "Don't do anything for me, Tiago. Do what you want for you."

Even though its winter, the temperatures here in Recife are sweltering. I pull my hair up as we enter the chapel, cooled not with A/C but with open windows and large ceiling fans over the pews. I forgot how tropical it is here.

I forgot how much I love it.

The rain comes, like it has every day since I got here, like it does all winter. I imagine it raining on Grandpa's garden in the courtyard in his house. It sprinkles for a few minutes, and then it stops. Like magic.

Last time a young girl who spoke English led me to each class and translated for me. Today I stick with Tiago, and a number of people remember me when he introduces me. He starts to translate for me, but I brush him off.

"I understand most of it. I need to learn the rest."

He nods and lets me try to decipher the language.

Reading scriptures I'm familiar with helps. I know what they say in English, so I'm able to put more meaning into the Portuguese words.

The moment we step into the house after church, I smell food, and I take a moment to inhale with anticipation. Their maid kept busy while we were gone.

"Lunch almost ready," Martha tells me, then she disappears into the kitchen.

Tiago gets out his guitar, but Rafael snatches it from him hard enough that it bangs into the wall, and suddenly the two of them are fighting. Yelling at each other, getting in each other's faces, popping their necks and trying to show off who is more manly.

It happens so fast, and I feel like a cat stuck in a dog fight.

I expect them to calm down, but instead they circle each other like rabid wolves, hands in fists and pupils dilated. They yell at each other, spitting insults and hurling words I don't understand, stretching their necks to make themselves look taller and glaring down at each other.

And then they pounce, and I can't speak as they grapple with each other, my heart racing in my throat.

Martha gets in the middle of them, telling them to stop, and Tiago turns on her, gesturing angrily and speaking in the same tone as he did to his brother.

Somehow I find my voice, and I jump in beside her.

"Don't talk to your mother that way!" I yell at him.

"Cassandra, *não entra nisto, vai lá, fique fora,*" Martha says.

I don't need to speak Portuguese to get the gist of what she's saying as she tries to shove me from the room, but I won't budge. "Tiago won't hurt me," I say, and I catch his eye. I'm shaking, but I'm not sure if it's fear or anger. "Grow up. Now. STOP IT."

The fury in his eyes dissipates, his pupils returning to their normal shape. He strides from the room, and I collapse on the couch, shaken. Martha sits beside me and babbles in Portuguese, but I can't make out a single word. Turns out I have to be emotionally stable to understand.

Rafael grumbles and leaves the house. Martha stands up and goes after him.

"Hey, I'm sorry."

Tiago comes back into the room, and I look up at him with glazed eyes. He sits by me on the couch.

"I know that upset you, and I'm sorry you had to see it," he says.

"You're sorry I had to see it?" I say, firing up again. "How about being sorry you let it happen?"

"I had to defend myself," he replies.

"You had to show you were the tougher one," I bite back, angry enough not to mince words. "It was a stupid immature display of aggression toward your younger brother and YOUR MOTHER. There's no excuse for it."

"She should not have gotten involved."

I want to slap him. But I've done that before and know it won't go over well. "I hated watching you act that way. I felt like I don't know you after all."

I see from the way he flinches that my words hurt.

"Everyone gets angry," he says.

"That wasn't normal, Tiago," I say. "It scared me. I was afraid you would hurt someone."

"I won't. I'm in control."

"That makes it worse. You chose to act that way."

"It's how men act, Cassandra."

And there it is: the cultural differences between us. Here in Brazil, he might be right. But in America, that behavior is not acceptable. I won't accept it. "Anyone who treats their mom that way, the most important woman in his life, will do the same to his wife."

The words strike him exactly as I hope they will. His eyes flick over mine, searching, a flicker of fear in them.

"I won't," he says. "I promise I won't."

"There's no way to know until after you're married, is there?" *But I won't take that chance.*

I leave the words unsaid. But they hang there. I know he feels it.

His mom comes back in, her face weary and streaked with tears, her nose red. Tiago rises and goes to her, then folds her in a hug. I don't know what he says, but my jaw unclenches as she hugs him back. Her shoulders shake, and he holds her. She goes into the kitchen when he releases her, and he returns to me.

"I won't treat her that way again," he says. "You're right."

"It's easy to say that," I say. "But will you follow through?"

"I will. My mom deserves better." He meets my eyes, a quick glance before he looks away.

For a second, I thought I saw it. Blatant hope. The desperate prayer that we can be together again.

But I must have been mistaken. Tiago knows I only feel friendship for him. He knows we can't be anything more.

❧◈❧

The days flow together gently as I settle in. Brazilians like to take life slow. We eat, play games, and sit around. Usually I go to Tiago's house because there is not much to do at Grandfather's house. But today he surprises me by coming over to Grandpa's while I'm eating breakfast.

"What do you want to do today?" he asks.

"Not sit here," I say. "I've been here five days and don't feel like I've done anything."

"We can go to the beach," he says.

I make a face. "We did that yesterday." I peel down the shoulder of my shirt and twist my neck to look at the exposed skin. "I think I'm burned." There's a redness to the brown color.

"Looks like it. Like raw meat."

I scowl at him. "Thanks. That's appealing."

He laughs. "We can walk to the park."

Walking sounds good. "How far is it?"

"About twenty minutes."

I push away from the table. "Let me get my shoes."

We walk side by side down the cracked sidewalk, stepping over dog poop and around piles of trash brushed off the cobblestone street. All of the houses are concealed behind concrete walls with broken glass stashed along the top to deter intruders.

"I want to live in one of those someday," Tiago says, pointing out the high-rise apartments in front of us.

"An apartment?" I wrinkle my nose. "I'd much rather have a house."

"The condos are clean and big and safe. Better than houses."

"I suppose." It's hard for me to imagine an apartment beating your own private residence.

"They are very expensive, though. I have to get a good job to buy one."

"What will you do?"

He shrugs. "I think I'll go to university to study engineering. And then—I don't know. What did you study?"

"Lots of things. But I'm majoring in English."

"What will you do with it?"

I get this question a lot, and it uneases me because I have no answer. "I don't know. Everyone expects me to be a teacher, but I don't like little kids, so I don't think so."

"I thought you did like kids."

I shake my head. "They're stinky and sticky and annoying. I liked the ones at Kids First, but they were special."

"So will you have kids?"

"Oh, yes. Of course. One day." I picture Riley as she held her new baby, the maternal expression on her face, the softness of that new life. "I was there when Riley had her baby, Tiago, and it was the coolest thing. So amazing. It made me excited for someday."

"You will be a great mother."

"I hope, right? No one knows until they actually become one." I glance at him and find him looking at me. He looks away as if caught doing something inappropriate, and I pretend not to notice.

I wonder what else I'm pretending.

I remember talks like this we used to have, only they involved us as a couple, our children. Wondering who they'd look like.

It was a conversation like this that made Owen break up with me in high school. He found the chat where I talked about little Isaac from the daycare, and how he looked like a mixture of me and Tiago. What I pictured our children would have looked like.

If we'd stayed together.

Which we didn't. And that part wasn't clear to either boy, because Owen thought I was cheating on him and Tiago thought I wanted to get back together.

I was younger and stupider then, but at this moment, I don't feel any wiser.

"Tell me more about school," he says, filling the silence that fell between us. "Which roommate were you closest to?"

"Camila," I say without hesitation. "We met at church camp when I was still in high school, so we were already friends when we went to school. She understood me the best and she knew a lot about my life already, which was nice not to have to give a backstory every time something happened."

"I remember you talking about her. Then who was next?"

"Hard to say. Maybe Abby, but also maybe Iris. I was the least close to Layne, but I still love her."

"Was she the wild one?"

"Depends on your definition. Abby's the one who wanted to party all the time, but Layne's the one who always had boys over."

"Isn't that what college is for?"

"Maybe some. Not PYU. The whole point is to help kids get outside of themselves. They really encourage mission trips and have a strict honor code about alcohol and co-ed sleepovers."

We turn the corner, and there's a park up ahead. I wrinkle my nose as we walk past an open canal that reeks of sewage. A man covered in dust and not much else stretches out in front of the gate leading to the park, and Tiago takes my elbow and steers me around him.

"No raging parties where you got drunk, then?"

Tiago leads me to a bench beneath a giant tree with long branching arms and dangling tufts of leaves that remember hair more than plants.

I cast him an amused look. The idea of me touching alcohol . . . "Nope. Still an alcoholic virgin."

He smirks. "I gave that up a long time ago."

"Oh, I know."

He settles back on the bench, resting on his hands, the overhead sun dappling his face as he blinks up at the sky.

I wait for it. I know the question is coming.

We're both curious about the other's sexual experiences since each other. And he's about to ask.

I'm not sure how I'll respond.

CHAPTER FOUR

Sharing a House

"If you didn't break the drinking rule . . . Co-ed sleepovers, then?"

I shrug. "On occasion."

"At least you had fun."

"I did." I don't regret it, not any of it.

"Did any of them mean something to you?"

"A few." I pull out my phone again and flip through the pictures until I find another of Jared, this time in our kitchen, sitting on the couch by the fish tank. Justin and Iris sit beside him, grinning at the camera. I point to him. "Jared."

"You dated?"

"We did. But we stopped when I realized I liked him."

"Why?"

"Because of Owen." His name whispers out of me, hushed, reverent, afraid of the injury it might cause upon its serrated exit.

There's a long silence, and I sense it's Tiago giving me space more than anything awkward. I blink at my phone, willing back any evidence of emotional damage.

"Do you want to talk about it?" Tiago finally asks.

I exhale and straighten my shoulders before looking at him. "It's weird that you're asking."

"Why?" But he must know, because he grins. "I was there through your whole break up."

His grin breaks my mood, and I laugh, shoving his shoulder.

"You caused our break up!"

"It didn't work." He shrugs. "You got back together."

I turn back to my phone, but his teasing about such painful subjects makes me feel close to him, he who was a friend and confidant. "Owen and I got back together, and we broke up, and we got back together, and we broke up, and we got back together, and we broke up. I lost track of how many times. The last time we got back together, Owen tried to make the distance between us disappear. He wanted us to be committed, to keep an eye on our future. But that didn't work either. Maybe it made it worse, because the next time he broke up with me, it was for good. We are not getting back together."

I say it so stoically that I almost manage to get it out with no reaction. But my voice hitches in the last sentence.

We are *not* getting back together.

I'm still trying to convince myself.

"When was that?" Tiago asks.

"February." My heart throbs as if swollen, and I look down at the dirt beneath the bench as the memory of that break up flashes through me. "I went to Louisiana to see him for his birthday."

"And he broke up with you?" Tiago sounds ready to be angry on my behalf.

I lift my face. "It was more complicated than that. He got his mission call and knew he was going to leave for two years. He wanted to be friends, but I—" I shake my head. "I was done. I told him I couldn't be friends. Having a little bit of contact, in my mind, was worse than no contact. That was the last time we talked."

"You didn't speak again?"

"I blocked his number and then deleted it."

Tiago takes both of my hands and cradles them in his own, gently. His dark brown eyes meet mine.

"I know what you felt. About the contact. It's how I felt after you left Brazil."

I pull my hands away and turn my gaze to the trees. I keep talking as if Tiago hasn't spoken.

"I wasn't a super pleasant person to be around after the break up. But Jared stuck by me. Then—" I smile wistfully. This memory is sweet. "He kissed me goodbye."

"Do you hope to see him again?"

I shake my head. "I have zero expectations of doing so." I focus on him. "And you?"

He hesitates, and then he gives a strained smile. "Yeah. I've gone on dates."

"Anyone special?"

"Maybe." He shrugs. "Not yet. We will see."

⌒⌒※⌒⌒

After the park, Tiago and I walk to a bakery and buy *sonhos*, a delightful fried confection with soft dough, custard filling, and powdered sugar.

"I'm in love with these," I tell him as I wipe sticky whiteness from my face.

"*Casal lindo*," the woman behind the counter says, nodding at Tiago. "*Muito lindo*."

"*Obrigado*," Tiago says.

I wait until we've left the shop before asking. "What was very beautiful?"

"Us."

"Us?" I raise an eyebrow.

"She said we are a beautiful couple."

"Ah." I nod in understanding.

We walk the ten minutes back to his grandfather's house. Tiago's aunt has returned with her two small children, and they've taken up residence in the room across from mine. Tiago heads back to his house to see if his mom needs anything, and I go upstairs to my room.

The little girl, who looks to be about six or seven, follows me. She's darling with a head of thick black curls, large black eyes, and the perfect nose.

"Hi," I tell her, and she runs off. I think I've frightened her until she returns with a music player. She sets it up on the other bed and loud, happy Brazilian music pumps through my room.

"*Vamos pular!*" she shouts. She jumps around on the floor and the bed, then comes and grabs my hands and jumps around with me, shouting along with the chorus until I catch on enough to sing also.

"*Vamos pular, vamos pular, vamos pular!*"

It repeats the same words over and over, which is lucky for me. *Vamos* is let's, and I'm guessing *pular* is jump or something like that. I collapse on the bed when the song finishes, hot and sweaty, and she collapses beside me, giggling.

"What's your name?" I ask her in Portuguese, one of the phrases we practiced enough in class that I have it down pat.

"Ana," she replies. "*E tu?*"

I give a mental fist pump. She understood me! "Cassandra."

"Cassandra, *vamos—*"

I lose the rest, but I hear the inflection at the end and know she's asking me a question. I shake my head. "*Não entendo.*" I don't understand.

She takes my hand and hauls me from the bed, then leads me over to the window in the bedroom. It overlooks Grandpa's terrace and the swimming pool, which yesterday was green with filth. Today, though, pool workers clean the grime from the surface. Ana points down to it and says again, "*Vamos nadar?*"

"*Piscina?*" I say.

She nods vigorously.

Pool. Okay. Why not? "*Claro que sim,*" I say, smiling, parroting another phrase I learned in class.

Communicating with Ana is exhausting. I didn't know my brain could feel stretched and pulled, but after half an hour in the pool, I'm mentally worn out. She chatters nonstop and I try to pick out words, but I feel like I'm at a shore getting sucked under water every time I try to catch my breath. I plead for a break forty minutes after we start, pointing to my sunburned skin and using that as an excuse. Ana looks disappointed and starts to follow me out, but I dissuade her by miming sleep.

I escape to my room and pull out a novel. It's written entirely in English, and I caress it like an old friend before laying down in bed with it. My brain needs a break.

☙ ❀ ❧

I'm Ana's new best friend.

She wakes me in the morning and takes me to breakfast. She talks at me and I nod along, remembering just yesterday how I longed for something to do besides sitting in the house.

Her mom tells her to leave me alone, but Ana looks hurt when she turns her large eyes on me. She asks me something, and I guess at the content of the question.

"No, no, it's fine. *Está bem,*" I say.

Ana's face lights up.

We take a walk to a playground, and I wonder what Tiago is doing. Does he wonder why I haven't showed up at his house? Or does he think I'm still sleeping?

I ring the buzzer to the gate when we get to Grandpa's house because I don't have a key, and Tiago comes to open it. He looks at me holding Ana's hand, her other clasped around an ice-cream cone with at least half of it smeared on her face, and he laughs. He bends down and says something to Ana, and she releases me to throw herself at him. He wraps her up and stands with her cradled in his arms.

"Do you want to stay and play with Ana, or do you want to come to my house?" he asks.

I exhale, trying to hide my relief. "Let me get my book."

He goes inside with her and delivers her to his aunt while I run up the stairs.

"Ready," I say, coming to his side and interrupting his conversation with Ana's mom.

We turn to leave, and Ana shouts, "*Espera!*" She throws herself at me and then smears my face with ice-cream kisses. "*Tchau, te amo!*"

I know those words, and my heart melts at her declaration of love. I decide I can handle her incessant chatter and exhausting energy. "*Também te amo,*" I say, returning her kiss on each cheek.

Tiago chuckles as we head outside. "She adores you."

I shake my head. "Buy a girl an ice-cream . . ."

"Is that all it takes?"

"Well, maybe not."

"You seem to be understanding a lot more."

"She doesn't stop talking. And besides, I already knew *te amo*. Those were the first words I learned in Portuguese." Oh, crap. I accidentally tiptoed right up against the line of forbidden subjects.

I hold my breath, afraid of what he'll say next, but he says nothing, thankfully.

But I'm sure he's remembering.

CHAPTER FIVE

Moving Day

I settle into the computer room in Tiago's house, which also has a twin bed, and begin to read. His brothers are fighting in the kitchen and I tense, ready to intervene if it gets ugly. But instead it calms down, and nobody bothers me.

The phone in the hallway rings. I pay it no attention until Tiago's brother calls my name.

"Cassandra!"

Is it my mom? I leave the room and find Rafael in the hall.

"For me?" I ask, forgetting to use Portuguese.

He understands anyway and nods.

I take the phone. "Hello?"

"Cassandra?" Little Ana's voice carries through the line.

"Ana!" I reply. "*Como vai?*"

She responds excitedly to my greeting, a happy babble of familiar sounds with words I can almost make out. I shake my head, laughing.

Tiago appears in the living room, and I gesture him over.

"It's Ana and I have no idea what she's saying to me!" I whisper.

He leans in close, his chest bumping my shoulder as he listens to her piping voice. "Nothing important," he says. "You can say, *Okay, tá bom.*"

I nod and insert those words every time she pauses, which isn't often. Tiago stays by me, and I turn to him when she asks a question.

"She wants to know when you'll be back," he says.

"Okay." I search for words so I can respond to her. "*Voltarei hoje à noite,*" I tell her in slow, precise Portuguese.

Tiago grins, and Ana says, "*Tá bom, tchau!*" and hangs up.

I go limp with relief when the call is over. "Well. That was interesting."

"You did great." He takes the phone from me and presses against me as he hangs it on the wall behind me. He takes a step back, his eyes flicking over my face. Then he kisses my forehead and says, "*Também te amo,*" just as I said to Ana when we left the house, and leaves me.

I stand there for a moment, my heart racing, frozen.

I also love you.

What does he mean by it?

Surely not romantic love.

And yet I've always suspected he never got over me.

Should we talk about this? He knows I don't feel the same.

I slip from the hallway, moving quietly as a ghost, and enter the computer room. This time I close the door, wanting privacy. I sink into the twin bed, letting my feet dangle off the edge, and replay the scene.

The soft touch of his lips on my forehead. *Também te amo.*

I close my eyes, and I'm not here anymore. I'm sixteen in Arkansas, hanging out in Tiago's bedroom, our exchange student, my best friend. We're sitting on the bedroom floor working on my Spanish homework, laughing, joking, scribbling out poor translations and making fun of each other's handwriting.

"Te amo," he says.

"What does that mean?" I ask.

"I love you in Portuguese," he says.

"Cool," young, naive, little me says. "This is I love you in sign language." And I shape my hands into the signal, with the two middle fingers bent into the palm and the other fingers extended.

He makes the signal back to me.

We finish our homework, and he stands with me when I do.

"Good night. See you in the morning," I say.

He surprises me by stepping closer and planting a kiss on my forehead. "Good night. Te amo."

"Te amo," I repeat, and I say it in sign language.

He does it back to me.

I go to bed, upstairs to my room, completely unaware of what just started between us.

⟨ ⟩

Grandpa calls that night and talks with Tiago's dad, then Martha comes into the room where I'm still reading so she can talk to me. She tries to explain something to me, but I don't understand. She switches to English.

"You stay here?" she says, pointing at the bed.

I put my hand on it. "Today? For a few hours."

"Okay? To stay here?"

"Sure, it's fine."

She shakes her head. "Tiago!" she shouts.

He comes into the room. I study him while she explains something. He's wearing a baseball cap again, which emphasizes his high cheek bones. From the profile I see his lashes, so thick they kink in the middle, forming a perfect crown around his eyes. He glances at me, and I notice with a start that he's attractive.

I didn't think so a few days ago.

"So," he says, unaware of my scrutiny, "my aunt has decided to stay at my grandfather's house for a few months. He asks if it's okay if you stay here with us."

I blink in surprise. "He's kicking me out?"

"He needs the space. But if you're not comfortable staying here, we can find somewhere else . . . Maybe a family from church . . ."

I look from him to Martha. It would be ridiculous of me to stay with another family, someone I don't know, when they have the space and desire to put me up. But still . . . staying here in the same house as Tiago . . .

It makes my heart race with uncertainty.

"Where would I be?" I ask, trying to mask my sudden anxiety.

"Here." Tiago gestures to the room I'm in. "This would be your room."

I glance around it without seeing it. I've been here all day, I know what it looks like. And I decide not to cause this family any more trouble. "Yes. That's fine. I can stay here."

He tells his mom, and she says something else, and he says, "My dad will take you there after dinner to get your suitcases."

Then he leaves me with his mom.

❦

We move me in that night. Tiago keeps himself scarce, appearing only when summoned to help move something. I wonder if his declaration earlier weirded him out or if it's having me in the same house.

I can't stand the suspense.

It is strange to close my bedroom door and know that Tiago is down the hall. We're under the same roof once again.

I'm up before anyone else in the morning. I go to the dining room when I hear voices and find Tiago's brothers eating breakfast and watching TV, but not Tiago.

So I head back to his bedroom.

The door is ajar, and I give a tap before pushing it open further. "Hello?" I say, poking my head in.

Tiago stands by the dresser, wearing only a pair of shorts, arm lifted as he applies deodorant. And my eyes are drawn to his torso, the same one I saw the other day at the beach but failed to fully notice. Or appreciate. He's not as slender as he was when we were younger, but he still has a set of nicely tanned, defined abs above his waistline.

"Hey," he says, dropping his arms. He grabs a shirt and pulls it over his head before approaching me. "Do you need something?"

"Are you avoiding me?" I pleat my fingers in front of my stomach, forcing myself to maintain eye contact.

He opens his mouth, then closes it. "Maybe a little," he admits.

"Why?"

"I know you don't like it when I talk about my feelings. And I was afraid I made you feel awkward yesterday."

"What exactly are your feelings, Tiago?"

He studies me, his eyes somber, and shakes his head. "Nothing."

"Nothing?" I feel a surge of frustration. "Or do you just not want to tell me?"

He turns away from me and walks out of the room.

I can't believe he walked away from me.

"Tiago!" I zip out after him and grab his arm. "I'm talking to you!"

"What do you want me to say?" he says, spinning toward me, his voice harsh. "You

25

don't want me to feel anything for you. I'm not allowed to. You made it clear that for us to be friends, I can't see you as anything but that."

"So you're pretending not to feel something for me?"

"Do I have any choice?"

He's angry. I see it in the dilated pupils, the rise and fall of his chest.

"Of course you do," I breathe, trying to calm my own emotions. "I want you to be honest with me."

"But only if my honesty puts me in the box you want me to be in. The box that says, 'someone you used to love but now is just a friend.'"

"I thought you said there was someone you like—someone you might have feelings for—"

"I lied to you! Because you want me to like someone else! But how can I when I still love y—"

And he cuts himself off. He pivots away from me.

I stand there catching my breath, shaken from the emotional spin cycle, trying to piece his words together, when he pivots back to me. He grabs my shoulders and he kisses me.

There is nothing soft about this kiss. It is anger and hurt and fear and loneliness and despair, all crashing into me as he presses me up against the wall and crushes my lips with his.

And it's also hungry and passionate and voracious, and it stirs me awake like a sudden jolt of electricity. My arms go around him, and we've been here before, this is not new territory. He pushes me right back into his bedroom, back onto his bed, and he climbs on top of me.

He still turns me on. He still knows exactly how to touch me.

This can't be happening. It can't be. Somewhere my logical brain is in complete denial. I swore this wouldn't happen, I swore I felt nothing for him, I swore I wouldn't do this—

It's happening.

I utter a groan because I don't want to stop this, but I'll hate myself if I don't. I push his chest, hard enough that he can't mistake my meaning, and then as he sits up, as he pulls away from me, I see the haze clear from his eyes too as he realizes what we did.

"Cassandra, I—"

I hold up a hand to stop him. I don't want to hear anything right now. I bite my lip and break the skin, the pain and taste of blood knocking some sense into me.

I don't speak. There will be a reckoning later, but right now I can't think of anything to say. I stand up and leave the room.

I'm trembling when I close the door to my little room. I lock it and lean against it, then slide down to the ground. I grab my suitcase and dig around until I find my journal.

But I don't write.

What does this mean? Was I caught up in a lustful exploration of feelings? Or do I feel more for Tiago than I've wanted to believe?

CHAPTER SIX

Getting to Know You

I can't stay in my room all day, as much as I want to. I recall those days in Arkansas when Tiago and I were going through a rough patch and he would spend his days in his room. I know how he felt now. He just wanted to get away for a minute, not have to face me and our tormented relationship, but there was nowhere to go.

I feel that now.

I pretend to be sleeping at lunch and no one bothers me, but by the time dinner rolls around, I'm too hungry to stay in my room. I come out as the maid sets the table and find Tiago at the front door, sliding on a pair of shoes and grabbing a bag.

"Where are you going?" I ask, and I'm suddenly seized with the fear that he's escaping me.

"I have class tonight," he says. He looks toward me but doesn't meet my eyes.

If he worried I'd feel awkward because he told me he loved me, right now he must be terrified.

I turn around and go back to the room and get my shoes. I'm not thinking, just acting. I come back out and say, "I'm coming with you."

"To my class?" He blinks in surprise.

"Yes. Should I get my book?"

He gets over his shock and nods. "Yes."

I grab my book and he yells bye to his mom, then we head out the door.

Neither of us speaks for a long moment as we walk down the street. I follow him because I don't know where we're going. The sun is setting, lending a pink hue to the cracked sidewalk and piles of trash along the street.

"I'm sorry for earlier," he says finally. He sounds tired, defeated. "I didn't mean to. I'm not sure how it happened. I've dreamed of kissing you for so long, and now you're here and I—I couldn't stop it."

I take my time pondering a response. "I wish you didn't love me."

"Me too."

I snort at his admission. "I've done nothing but hurt you for the past two years."

"Yes. But it's my fault."

We walk in more silence, accompanied by honking horns and screeching tires as we get closer to the city center.

"I don't know what I feel for you," I say finally.

He glances at me as we stop at a cross walk. "You said you feel nothing for me."

"I thought I didn't. But kissing you—confused me."

The light turns green to walk, but he's holding my gaze solemnly and doesn't see it. "In what way?"

I shrug, and suddenly I feel close to tears. "I feel more than I thought I did." I blink, and the tears slip free.

Tiago grabs me and hugs me. "Then I'm not sorry. I'm glad I kissed you." He releases me. "I think we need to talk."

I nod.

His eyes are steady on me. "I can skip my class."

"No. Go to class."

"How will I be able to concentrate now?"

"It's fine. I'm still figuring out what to say, anyway."

He finally notices the light and takes my hand to cross the busy intersection. He releases me at the other side, but I flex my fingers.

Everything about him is familiar.

I sit in a chair in the hall while he does class, and I borrow paper from someone so I can try to organize my thoughts. But they are a jumbled mess that keep going to one big question mark: what do I feel for Tiago? Followed by: are my feelings for other people relevant? Or is Tiago all that matters right now?

His class is four hours long. He should have warned me. I finish my book and wander the halls, and I think I've settled on an understanding by the time he's done.

He finally comes out, pulling his bag over one shoulder. "Are you hungry?"

"I'm starving," I admit.

"Come on."

He takes me to a quiet place on the beach with a few tables set up on the sand. He orders *carne e fritas*, a delicious dish of fries covered in cut steak, grilled onions, and *au jus*.

But now I can barely eat because I feel the weight of everything that needs to be said sitting on my shoulders. I take a few bites and settle back in my chair.

"I feel like, to understand all this, I need to go back to the beginning," I say.

"Back to the beginning?"

"When this started between you and me." I gesture between us. "I'm not myself right now. I've gone back in time and stepped into the skin of that girl I used to be. And she's fragile." I rub my arms. "I feel fragile."

"Tell me what you are thinking."

"I—The girl I was, she loved you. You were her whole world. But that week in Brazil with you hurt her. She started to think you never really cared for her at all."

"I'm sorry," he says, but I wave him off. It's my turn to talk.

"When she came back to the States, she waited for you. She checked the mailbox every day. She caught her breath every time the phone rang. Her heart belonged to you, and she would do anything to keep you. She was yours."

I see the shame in his eyes. He flinches but holds my gaze.

"You—" I'm there in those moments, a senior in high school and devastated at the loss of the boy who I thought loved me. I search for the right word to describe what he did to me. "You *crushed* her. Every day with no word from you killed her a little bit more. You could have saved her heart with a word here or there, a note, a phone call. She was *devoted* to you. And you took that devotion, that loyalty, that *love,* and crumbled it up and spat on it before throwing it away. And you let that love rot in a gutter." I'm not remembering the pain. I'm in it. My lips tremble, my teeth chatter, and I wrap my arms around myself.

"I'm so sorry." He gets up like he would hold me, embrace me, but I shake my head.

"She found you untrustworthy. But she got over you, Tiago. She never got you out of her heart, but she found a safe place for you. In the 'friendship box.'" I make air quotes around it so he knows I'm referencing what he said earlier. I lean closer to him and say, "Do not ask me to undo all her hard work and let you out of that box."

Tiago settles back in his chair and scrubs a hand over his face. "There has been so much hurt between us."

"Yes." I nod. "We can't seem to help hurting each other. We need to respect each other and not get romantically involved."

He drops his hand and reaches across the table. His fingers find mine, and he squeezes.

"I'm not that same person. I'm ashamed I did that to you. I regret so much. Don't you think it keeps me up at night, the knowledge that maybe we would be together now, maybe you never would have loved anyone else?"

My mind hasn't gotten that far. I'm still stuck in first semester of my senior year, still wracked in the pain he gave me. But now I follow his thoughts and realize what I would have lost if he hadn't done that to me.

Being free to date. Owen.

My mind seizes on Owen, because he's still the light of my life. Maybe he always will be, even if we're never together again.

Suddenly I'm looking at everything differently. If Tiago hadn't abandoned me, I never would have loved Owen.

I owe Tiago a huge debt of gratitude.

"You're not that same person," I say. "You're not him. And I'm not her." I laugh suddenly. I feel the weights and shackles of the past falling away. "We are not them, Tiago."

He watches me, trying to read me, but I haven't settled on what I'm feeling.

"So who are we?" he asks.

"New people. We carry the memories of those people, but we aren't them."

It's liberating, to see Tiago this way.

CHAPTER SEVEN

Reality Hits

I awake in the morning expecting to feel guilty. But I don't. I haven't done anything wrong.

Martha has friends over to work on tile pieces. She asks me if I want to make one, but I decline. Not a crafty person. Then she sets me to work sorting the colored pieces into boxes, and I sit at the kitchen table, the fan overhead blowing wisps of hair around my face, and sort each glass square into the appropriate place.

"Good morning."

Tiago comes out of the bathroom freshly showered, toweling off his shoulder-length hair. I look up at him, and I'm glad it's long. This Tiago looks older, acts older, than the boy I knew.

"Morning, friend," I say. Never mind that we had a heavy make-out session yesterday that was more than friendly. I pat the seat beside me. "Want to help sort tiles?"

He comes over, but then his mom calls him to her table with her group of friends. The ladies tease him and poke at him and he takes it with a smile. Then his mom says something and he nods. He returns to me.

"My mom needs more tile glue," he says, leaning over the table where I sort. "I have to go to the store and get some. Want to come?"

Better than doing this. "How far is it?" I ask.

"Pretty far. Maybe a thirty-minute walk. We can take the bus, but it will take twenty minutes."

"Walking is fine. I like walking."

I get my purse, and we head outside.

"I hate walking," he says. "It takes forever to get anywhere."

"You could drive, then."

"We only have one car. Even if I had my license, I couldn't."

"Oh." I hadn't thought of that. "We could take a taxi."

"Yeah. Maybe if it were night. But daytime, this is easier. I still hate it."

"What physical activities do you like?"

"Soccer, jujitsu—" he steals a glance at me. "Sex."

I'm so startled I stumble. He catches my arm, but I pull free and turn on him with rounded eyes. I don't mean to be surprised and it's absolutely none of my business, but I got the impression from our conversations that he hadn't gotten serious with any girls since me. "Have you—"

He starts laughing. He shakes his head. "I couldn't help it, I wanted to see your face. For a second, you thought—"

I slap his forearm. "Tiago, you jerk! That was mean. So you haven't . . ."

He shakes his head. "I haven't had sex."

I study his profile, and I see him as the handsome man he's becoming. "It would be okay if you had, you know."

"Oh, I wanted to. But I just—couldn't." He casts me a sideways look. "And you? If you feel like telling, I mean."

"I haven't either."

"What about—I mean, have you had any serious boyfriends?"

"Yes, a few."

"How serious was your last one?"

I chuckle at how cleverly he asks about Owen. "Really serious. We talked about marriage. But it turns out talk is talk, because now we're broken up and definitely not married."

"Do you miss him?"

"Yes."

"Do you think you'll get back together?"

"I do not," I say, very quietly. "But I still want to."

He surprises me by putting an arm around my shoulders and hugging me into his side. "I'm sorry. I know that pain. It sounds like you're not ready to move on."

"I'm not, and I appreciate you understanding that." I exhale.

"What do you think is the number one thing that ruins a relationship?"

"Dishonesty," I say, without hesitation. "It ruins everything."

"Yeah. I think you're right."

He doesn't release my hand as we walk to the shop.

Martha's friends have all gone but one by the time we get back from the store. The two of them are huddled together over a tile, arranging colors on top of it. Martha glances at us when we come in and then barks an order at Tiago.

He sets the bag of glue down and says to me, "She wants us to find the box of small green colors out of her shed."

"Her shed?" I follow him around the side of the house, and sure enough, there's a small building in the back. "Wow. I never came back here."

"Yep. She keeps her craft things here."

It's cramped inside, not much bigger than my bathroom. I bump into a chair and hit my hip on a table when I spin away from it. Tiago goes to a pile of boxes against one wall and starts opening them. He points to another pile near me.

"Can you check those? Looking for little green squares."

"Ow." I scrape my elbow along the bumpy interior wall. Then I squat and begin going through boxes. "Wires. Magnets. Purple squares." I move boxes out of the way to get to more in the back. "More magnets."

"You don't have to tell me," he says.

I roll my eyes, but of course he can't see me. Just for that, I begin calling out what I find in a loud voice. "Glass bottles. Colored tape. Chicken wire?" I stand up, forgetting I moved inward and there's a beam, until I smack it with my head. The box tumbles from my hands.

"Ow!" I almost swear, but I bite it back.

"Cassandra!" Tiago scurries around the table and comes to my side, moving my hand away from my head to check it. "Are you—" He looks down at the spilled box at my feet. "You made a mess."

"It's your fault!" I say. "You told me to check this side."

"Somehow I didn't know you are so accident prone."

"I'm not! It was just—" I whack his shoulder because he's still laughing. "This feels unfair."

I go to whack him again and he grabs my wrist, preventing me. I lose my balance, tripping over the box and chicken wire and taking him with me. Several other boxes crash around us, and he grabs me by the waist before I topple into them.

He can't stop laughing. He pulls me into a hug and then rears back as if startled he got this close to me, his face inches from mine.

He could kiss me. I catch my breath in expectation, heady from the feel of his arm around me.

But he doesn't. Instead, he starts to release me. I feel his arm go slack, and I tug him closer, wrapping my arms around his torso and holding him in place.

His heart races beneath his shirt. Is mine going that fast? I turn my face up and push up on my toes to meet his mouth.

He's cautious, returning my kiss slowly, as if afraid I'll change my mind and bolt or leave him feeling like he took advantage of me. But this time there is no way for me to separate the boy from the past from the boy in front of me, because his mouth is the same and dang, he's a good kisser.

He grows more confident, his arms tightening around me, his lips opening against mine, and I pay attention this time as I feel his tongue slip inside. My mind is awake as I taste him, lingering on the feel of his lips, feeling the heat between our bodies.

I move my mouth from his lips to his jaw, the stubble rough against my lips, and he exhales, closing his eyes and arching his neck. He yanks on my shorts, pulling me to my toes as he crushes me against his pelvis.

I still turn him on also.

This feeling is powerful.

My hand comes down to his jeans, rubbing the length of him with my palm, and his hand follows mine. For a moment I think he will stop me, like Owen did every time I tried to take it this far, but Tiago does not. He undoes the clasp of his jeans and guides my hand inside, under his clothing.

I open my eyes, stunned. What am I supposed to do now?

But I forget my question entirely when Tiago undoes the clasp of my jeans and slips his hand inside. I cling to him, gasping from the intense feelings of his fingers on my flesh.

And then the guilt hits me.

I pull my hand from his pants and fight the urge to sit down and cry. I button my jeans and can't meet his eyes.

I miss Owen with a sudden fierceness. We fooled around, we took things a little too far, but Owen never let it get this far. And now I'm so angry at myself because I'm the weak link.

It turns out I'll go as far as the guy wants to go.

Tiago's hands grasp my shoulders, and he holds me at arm's length, head tilted to study my face.

"Are you okay?" he asks, and I hate that I've stolen away his confidence also.

"Yes." I nod. "I'm sorry, I—I shouldn't have done that."

"Oh, Cassandra." He sighs and then he hugs me. "I thought I'd have more control around you."

I let him hold me and formulate my own thoughts. "I think we shouldn't kiss."

"Ever?" He pulls his head back and peers at my face.

"I—I'm still not sure what I feel, and—I hate to feel like—like I'm using you." My face burns with shame as I say the words, but it's the truth. Tiago has always known how to turn me on, how to get me off, and I wanted it right then, and I knew how to get it.

He sits down on the floor, in the mess of spilled boxes, and he pulls me down with him. "You know that I love you, don't you?"

"Yes." I nod. I can't pretend otherwise.

"Do you think you could love me?"

I don't answer. I wish he hadn't asked. The truth is I do love Tiago, but not the way he wants. I don't know if I can. But I feel a lot of affection for him, and clearly attraction.

He does not speak, and I force myself to say something.

"I don't know. I told you I'm not over Owen." How can I love someone else when I still love him so much?

"But you feel something for me."

"Of course I do." I lift my eyes to his. "You were my first."

He gives a soft smile and taps my knuckles with his. "You still are. You are the first girl to touch me that way."

"You too," I whisper. "The first person to touch me."

And that makes me infinitesimally sad.

I wanted it to be Owen.

But I can't go through life putting off experiences just because I want it to be Owen, or I'll be a virgin forever.

I still want it to be Owen.

Tiago watches my face. He knows me well. The person I used to be, and the person I am now. Somewhere they merged, and I can't keep us separate anymore. I'm an open book to him.

"Maybe you should talk to him," he says. "Tell him how you feel."

I let out a choking laugh. "Sure." Write him on his mission and tell him my ex-boyfriend felt me up and it made me sad because I wanted Owen to be the one to do that. Oh, and I grabbed his cock, too. "That would go over real well."

"Or." Tiago shrugs. "We can sleep together and get it over with."

I roll my eyes and slug his shoulder.

He grunts and rubs it. "Do you want to go home?"

"Home? You mean—" He means Arkansas. I give him a puzzled look. "Why?"

"Because of what's happening between us."

Do I? I shake my head. "I'm happy for this chance to talk and reconnect and put aside the hurt feelings between us." I look up at his face. "Can you help me not do that again?"

"You're the one who kissed me," he says. "I wasn't going to. Not after—"

Yesterday. Was it only yesterday? There is so much chemistry between us, and so much history, so many flesh memories.

And the memories set my blood on fire, wanting to replace the experiences of two years ago with current ones.

I'm in trouble.

"No kissing." I stand up. "We have to be strong, Tiago."

There are footsteps outside, and I turn as Martha steps into the shed. Her eyes widen as they take in the mess of spilled boxes.

"*Gente!*" she cries. "*Que aconteceu?*"

I understand every word but lack the vocabulary to explain, and I'm so grateful she didn't walk in ten minutes earlier when her son and I were feeling each other up. I shrug and point to Tiago.

"*Ele fez,*" I say, casting the blame on him.

CHAPTER EIGHT

What Comes Next

Martha wants to take me shopping, so we head to the mall.

Tiago comes with us. We have not touched each other in two days, not even to hug or hold hands.

But things are different. It's impossible not to look at him and remember where his fingers were, where my hand was.

We know each other more intimately than we know anyone else.

I need space. I'm frightened by this development. He seems to instinctively know it.

Martha buys me a beautiful, sleeveless orange dress with green embroidery, and I want to find a sweater to go with it. She says she's tired and sits on a bench, so Tiago and I go off together.

"Did you listen to that CD?" he asks.

I have a list of songs he gave me to download when I get back to the states, Brazilian music, starting with "Vamos Pular." But since I have no data and can't do it yet, he bought me a CD yesterday.

"Yeah, I did." I nod. "It's interesting. Sounds like music my dad would like."

He snorts. "Can't please you. You hated the music I listened to in Arkansas, and now you don't like this either?"

"The music you listened to in Arkansas was heavy and angry."

"Yeah. I was sad a lot."

"So why would I like it?"

"But you should like the one I gave you yesterday."

In truth I thought the lyrical ballads a bit boring, but I see that he chose it especially for me. "I do like it. I'm just teasing you."

"What's your favorite song?"

I can only remember the first one, so I begin to sing, "*Quando o sol bater na janela—*"

He joins in and finishes the lyrics with me. "*. . . do teu quarto.*"

I don't know the rest of the song, but Tiago does, and he sings it as we walk through the mall. He shakes his head when he finishes.

"You remember the artist, right?"

I pause at a shop with an orange sweater on the mannequin. "Barão Vermhelho," I say. "Which means, the red baron in English."

"Good job."

I go into the shop and attempt my limited Portuguese on the employee. "Can I try this sweater? I want to see if it. . ." I can't remember the word for "goes" or "works," so I fall on a close synonym. " . . . functions with my dress."

I hold up the dress Martha bought me.

The woman looks at me strangely. "It functions, yes," she answers me.

Over her shoulder, I see Tiago laughing. I glare at him. "Thanks," I tell her. "I'll take it."

Tiago contains his mirth until we're out of the store. "It functions, yes," he quotes her Portuguese. "The sweater functions. It does exactly what it's supposed to do."

"Shut up," I growl. I pull out the skirt and hold it to the sweater. "Yes, they will *function* quite well together."

"It looks good. I want to see you wear it."

"Maybe to church on Sunday. I have two more weeks." Two more weeks. How quickly a month goes by.

Tiago's expression changes, the smile wiping from his face. "So soon you'll be gone."

"Yeah."

"Do you think we will see each other again?"

"I don't know. There are a lot of people in my life that I don't know if I'll see again." I fold the sweater and the skirt and put them back in the bag, not looking at him.

"Is it that easy for you? To let people go?"

I lift my face, holding back a sigh. "I have watched literally everyone I care about walk out of my life in the past year. From my parents to my roommates to Jared to—" I stop short of saying Owen's name. I can't heal if I'm constantly bringing him up.

It doesn't help that he's constantly on my mind. One day, he won't be, right? I'll wake up and realize I haven't thought of him in weeks.

That doesn't make me feel better.

"I knew when I came here that I'd be saying goodbye to you shortly after," I say. "It's not that I don't care. I just know it's part of life."

"I suppose you're right." He sits down on a bench, and I settle in beside him. "I didn't think about how you've been letting everyone go already."

"The only constant in my life is God."

"Do you want to see me again?"

"Of course I do. You're one of my dearest friends."

"Even if I see you as more than a friend?"

I lean closer and whisper, "Just don't tell my husband."

He laughs, but it cuts off too soon. "You don't think I could be your husband?"

I look away. "I don't know. I can't picture who it would be. I'm tired of trying to figure it out. Someday I'll get married, and that person will be my husband."

"Then it could be me."

"Sure, why not?" I shrug.

"Would you be happy with me?"

I tilt my head and examine him, giving the question the sincere attention it deserves. Tiago makes me laugh. He's funny, he's considerate, he gives me space to think and make my own decisions. He respects me.

I remember that was a big one previously, that I didn't feel he respected me. He does now.

He's willing to go to church, or at the very least, let me go to church.

And there's plenty of sexual compatibility.

He loves me. And if I married him, it would be because I love him also.

"Yes," I say. "I would be happy with you."

"I would make it happen, Cassandra. If you wanted to be with me, I would find a way for us to be together, no matter what it took."

Would he? My heart beats a little faster at the thought of someone loving me enough to do that.

Even if it's not the person I want it to be.

"Thanks, Tiago."

⦿ ⟶⚹⟵ ⦿

The whole family rides together again to church on Sunday. I sit by Tiago. His hand brushes mine in the pew while we listen to the preacher, and then his fingers twist around mine.

My heart stirs ever so gently. His kindness and attention are winning me over.

In Sunday School, the teacher talks about missionary work, the kind the early apostles of the church did. After, I sit with Tiago outside the chapel while we wait for his mom to stop chatting with people.

"What do you think of missionary work?" I ask.

"It seems like something people do a lot in the States, when they have money and time. It's not so easy here."

I nod. I can't judge the truth to that statement. I'm not fully aware of how finances are here in Brazil. "Is it something that interests you?"

"To go away from my family and talk about God? Not really. I already spent time away from them, and I hated it."

"You hated your time in Arkansas?"

"No, silly." He bumps my shoulder. "I hated being away from my family. I don't want to go again if I don't have to."

"I plan to go on one."

"I know. When do you think you'll go?"

"I want to finish college first. So when I'm twenty-one or twenty-two."

"Where did Owen go?"

"Chicago. The day he got his call was the day he broke up with me."

"Have you considered that maybe you're not meant to be with him?"

I turn to Tiago, more irate than I should be. "Well, that's fairly obvious, isn't it? That's what it means when people break up. They're not meant to be together."

"Sorry," he says, and I back down, ashamed.

"No, I'm sorry. He's just . . . A sore spot."

"Is he in Chicago now?"

I check the date on my phone. May 21. "In less than two weeks."

He puts his arm around my shoulder and hugs me.
I lean into him, accepting his comfort.

CHAPTER NINE

Unsupportive

Tiago and Mario get in a fight as soon as we walk in the door from church. A stupid one over who left the phone off the hook so it didn't charge.

"Tiago," I say, getting between him and Mario before they come to blows, "let's take King for a walk."

He looks like he wants to bust his brother's head into the wall, but he won't deny me. I have some kind of super power over him. He says something cutting to his brother, who says something back, and then I manage to get him out the door with the dog.

I struggle with the leash. The dog is bigger than I am, and I'm half trotting while I pull on the collar, trying to slow him down. "It really bothers me the way you fight with your family," I say.

He shrugs and takes the leash from me. He's already calmer, his body more relaxed. "We're not really fighting. Just disagreeing. It's fine."

"It's not fine. It's not normal."

"It is here."

"I guess it's a good thing I don't live here, then."

He doesn't respond to my snide statement. We get King all the way around the block before he says, "I haven't fought with my mom, at least."

"That's awesome," I say. "That means you can control it. So stop fighting with everyone."

"Sometimes you have to fight. People don't listen otherwise."

"I know there's a time and a place for it. I get angry too. But you're getting angry over stupid stuff."

"It's kind of important to charge the phone!"

I deadpan and give him my best "are you serious?" expression. Tiago relents.

"It seemed important at the time."

I laugh at his acquiescence. "I hate when people fight."

"I'm a fighter. I was raised that way. It's how it is here. If you're a man, you fight."

I chew on my lip as I internalize that cultural difference. It might not be something he can yank from his psyche.

"But I don't like to fight with you," he adds.

"Me neither. We used to fight a lot."

"Not now."

Only because we're not as close as we used to be.

He takes my hand as we walk. I don't object. Sometimes everything about Tiago feels so comfortable, so familiar, that I think we've already been married for a decade. This is one of those moments.

We reach his house, and he turns me slightly and meets my eyes. He holds my gaze as if asking permission as he tips my chin up. I don't deny him. I don't pull away.

I close my eyes as he gets closer, and I assume he takes that to mean he has my permission, because he kisses me.

It's lovely. His lips are soft and warm, plying mine with gentle pressure. Something light flutters in my chest. He doesn't pull me against his body, and the kiss is one of the most tender I've ever received. When he pulls back, I open my eyes and see a depth of emotion in his.

"I love you," he whispers.

My heart stirs, but I don't know what I feel. So I won't say anything.

He takes my hand and leads me back into the house.

His dad is in the kitchen arguing with Mario. He turns on Tiago when Tiago walks in and immediately starts berating him. I don't know what they're saying, but Tiago jumps right in. All the calm he acquired on our walk vanishes as they yell at each other.

Martha gets in between them, putting her hands on her son's shoulders and pushing him back.

"*Vamos comer*," she says, guiding Tiago to the dinner table. "*Venha*."

She collects her other son next, bringing him to the table and then going down the hall to get Rafael. She doesn't say anything to her husband. I watch as an outsider observing while the maid sets the table.

She has no input to what her husband does. She has no say. She can act on her sons, but her husband is the one with the voice.

It is the way things are.

I sit down between her and Tiago and spoon the customary beans and rice on my plate before adding salad and chicken and farofa. We bless the food, and I think we're past the negative discussions until Tiago's dad turns to him and starts up the argument again. I can't catch a word, it's too fast, but I press my hand against Tiago's thigh, willing him not to engage.

I see him trying not to. He keeps his eyes on his plate, chewing, listening to his dad, but his eyes get narrower and narrower. He swallows, his jaw tightening.

Stay calm, I think, holding onto his leg and watching him from the peripheral.

Martha interjects, gently, saying something to her husband, but he brushes her off with a wave of his hand and raises his voice, and it sounds like he's demanding an answer.

Tiago answers. His voice is low, curt, the response to the point. But then his dad stands up, and Tiago stands up, their chairs screeching across the tile as they shove them back. My heart pounds in my throat, and I want to run away and hide.

"Sit down!" his father roars, Portuguese words that I understand loud and clear.

"*Vou não!*" Tiago yells back.

Before his dad can say another word, Tiago moves away from the table and leaves the room. A door slams down the hall.

For a second I think his dad will follow him, and I don't know what I'll do if they continue to fight. I'm terrified of them getting physically aggressive with each other. But then his dad must decide he won the argument, because he sits down and resumes eating like nothing happened.

I suppose we are to do the same. I spoon beans over my rice, but I'm shaking so bad I'm afraid I'll be sick.

What chance does Tiago have of learning to manage his anger if this was the behavior that was modeled?

Dinner is quiet without him. I wait for him to come back, but he doesn't. The maid clears the table and his brothers leave the kitchen. I hear a guitar playing deeper in the house.

His dad gets out a set of dominoes and lays it out over the table.

"*Vai lá buscar Tiago,*" he tells Martha.

"*Vai lá tu,*" she replies.

Neither of them moves. Neither of them intends to get Tiago. I stand. "*Vou,*" I say.

Martha turns anxious eyes on me. "*Não, não,* Cassandra, *eu vou,*" she says, and she stands up also.

She doesn't want me to see that side of him. I sit down and take my domino pieces and listen to her talk to him in the hall.

Playing his guitar hasn't calmed him down. His voice is loud, the pitch of his tenor voice higher than usual as he yells at his mom. She returns a minute later, alone and with her lips pursed. She offers a curt smile as she sits across from me.

"*Vamos jogar.*"

He won't come. We begin to play, but my head is preoccupied. I don't want to play games with Tiago's parents.

We play for an hour before I decide I'd rather sit alone in my room and read a book than sit here with his mom and dad and feel isolated. I thank them for the game and leave for my room.

I pause outside the door when I realize the guitar music is coming from within. Great, Tiago took sanctuary in the same place I intended to. I open the door and the guitar stops. I don't look at him as I move around him to get my book from the suitcase by the bed.

"Are you mad at me?" he asks.

I shrug. "Well, you aren't talking to me," I say.

"You aren't talking to me!" he retorts.

I spin to him. "You're the one who got up and left the table and wouldn't come back when your mom asked you to! You left me there! What do you want me to do, beg you to come back?"

His dark eyes study me for a moment, and then he looks back at his guitar and begins strumming the chords again.

Ignoring me.

Fire shoots through my chest, anger, hurt, indignation.

I almost laugh. This is how he fights me. With coldness and silence.

I take my book and leave the room, and I want to go back to Grandpa's house so I won't face Tiago again today.

I feel it deep in my soul. I can't beat this.

We avoid each other the rest of Sunday, and it's even harder in his tiny house than it was in my home. As soon as he vacates my room, I go back into it and close the door, and I recluse myself for the rest of the evening.

I'm sure the whole family knows we're fighting.

It's been a difficult but revealing day.

No matter what I might feel for Tiago, it would never work out. There's too much of this macho culture ingrained in him. And while I hate fighting, I'm not a pushover.

If he treated me or one of our children the way his dad just treated him, I'd get in the middle of it.

And then we would fight. Like we are now. Except when the newness wore off, when he wasn't trying to win me back, when we were old and tired and impatient, he would get angry at me also.

I can picture it clearly.

CHAPTER TEN

Moving Boundaries

Tiago knocks on my bedroom door in the morning before I've gone to the bathroom. I run my hands through my hair and open it, then lean my head wearily against the door jamb and wait to hear what he has to say.

"I feel bad for yesterday," he says. "I don't know why we are fighting. I'm not upset with you."

"I know," I say. I'm not sure what else to say, and I think it probably doesn't matter.

I don't need to tell him what I've realized. I've got two weeks left in this country, and then it's goodbye. For good.

"Are you still upset with me?" he asks.

"No. Let's not waste our time that way."

"Agreed." He dips his head and presses a quick kiss to my lips.

My heart squeezes when he does. Whatever I feel for him will never be more than this.

I come out to the table when I'm dressed and ready for the day. Martha is excited because tomorrow she wants to take us back to Itamaracá. We went to the island when I was here two years ago, and I'm a little leery because I got terribly sick from the seafood last time. But it was a beautiful location, idyllic and isolated, and I love the thought of going again.

Rafael and Mario sit watching TV when suddenly the screen goes black. At the same time, the fan whirring above the table stops. Martha and I lift our heads to look at it.

"*Que foi?*" Rafael says. He gets up and messes with the TV, and I turn to Tiago.

"Did we lose electricity?"

"Maybe." He says something to his mom, and they wander through the house before returning.

"Yep. No power."

"Does that happen a lot?" I fan myself with my hand. His house doesn't have air conditioning, but with the windows open and the fan on, the heat is tolerable.

Not now. Now it's stifling.

43

"Let's sit outside," Tiago says.

Rafael and Mario grumble but there's nothing else to do, and it's hot. Tiago grabs his guitar and we settle in the chairs on the porch. Even though we're shaded, at first all I notice is the still air and the sweat gathering uncomfortably in the folds of my skin.

But then Tiago winks at me and starts singing, "*Quando o sol bater na janela . . .*"

I grin and join in, singing the next line because it's all I know. But his brothers know the rest of the song, and they belt out the lyrics. Tiago moves from that to another Brazilian song. I don't know the words but it's catchy and fun. Soon I've forgotten I'm hot and uncomfortable.

We spend two hours outside, singing song after song, moving from Brazilian music to classics like John Lennon and then familiar reggae tunes by Bob Marley. Tiago grins at me while he sings, and I'm flooded with so many beautiful memories of being in his room in high school, listening as he played his guitar and sang to me. I put my hand on his thigh and sit close to him.

The electricity announces itself when the TV begins to blare in the sitting room behind us. We whoop and jump and run to Tiago's parents' bedroom in the back of the house, the only room with an AC unit. Martha turns it on high and closes the door, and we are a mess of bodies crowding on the bed. I bury my face in Tiago's shoulder and giggle.

It might be my favorite day yet.

☙❦❧

Itamaracá is as beautiful as I remember it, but Tiago keeps fighting with his mom. It's the three of us, and one time after they argue in front of the beach near the old fort, he walks off huffy and moody.

She pretends like nothing is wrong and I don't know how to ask her what they're fighting about, so I ignore it. But it bothers me how he treats her.

She and I climb the stone ruins of the fort by ourselves, walking over the ramparts at the top and taking pictures by the cannons. Tiago finally comes back and joins us. Martha says a few words and then takes the stairs down. I turn to him.

"Why are you fighting with your mom?"

He shrugs. "She says I spend too much time at home. She wants me to get a job. Isn't it enough that I go to school?"

"She's looking out for you. She doesn't want you to get fat and lazy." I poke his stomach.

"I'm not doing either of those things." He rolls his eyes and shoves my hand away. "It's none of her business what I do, anyway. I'm eighteen. Almost nineteen. I can do what I want.

"Treat her with respect, even if you don't agree with her. She's your mom."

"She treats me like a child. I deserve space."

"Well, you still live at home, you still eat her food, you still let her clean up after you. It sounds like she's treating you the way you act."

He turns his gaze on me, the irritation apparent in his furrowed brows. "Just because I live with her doesn't mean she's in charge of me."

"Doesn't it?"

"In Brazil, we live with our parents until we get married. It doesn't mean we're still

44

kids."

"That's an odd tradition."

"Not to us. We think it's heartless that your parents kick you out at eighteen and expect you to make your own way in the world. To pay for the rest of your life when you're just getting on your feet. They should be taking care of you, setting you up for life."

"No." I shake my head. "They're teaching us independence. We still rely on them for help while we learn to struggle and overcome challenges on our own. So that by the time we get married, we're fully capable and functioning adults."

"And completely broke, too. Americans get into crazy amounts of debt going to school and getting married. Your system is broke."

He's insulting me and my country, and I'm angry now. I fire right back.

"Says the boy from the country where the majority of the people have no education after high school and live below the poverty line. Who's helping them?"

He tenses his jaw. "You are the same as always. Judging what you don't know. Believing that your narrow perspective is the only one. Unable to see that there are multiple ways to be."

"And you're as immature as you were in high school. You think you can treat people poorly and it doesn't matter because they're your family, and they're always going to be there. But listen up. Your mom might put up with it, but your wife won't. You can't talk to her or your kids that way. Or she'll be gone."

"You'd be gone, you mean," he says.

Fine, if he wants to take it that way. "You got it. I refuse to be in a picture where someone treats me that way."

"Well, you aren't—"

He stops and takes a deep breath. I try to guess what he intended to say. Something insulting. Maybe something about how I'm not who he wants to marry anyway.

Something he knows will cause damage and he won't be able to undo.

He pushes off the rampart.

I should let him go. But I'm tired of this. "You can't walk away from me, you know!" I follow him. "Just because you don't like what I have to say. Just because you want me to shut up."

He turns around. "You are making me angry. So I'm walking away. Now let me go."

His words are precise and clear and intentional, and I take a step back. Why am I pushing him? Almost as if I'm goading him? If he were Owen, I'd let him go, I'd understand his need to cool off and I would give him space.

I don't treat Tiago with the same respect, and I feel a flash of shame.

"I'm sorry," I say. "Of course."

I suppose it's a good sign. It's better that he walk away from his wife when he's angry, rather than get angrier and take it out on her.

But even better would be if he could control his anger enough to sit down and talk with her.

I'm expecting too much.

I follow his mom's steps and find her in the gift shop. I peruse the purses made of coconut and the carved figurines, pretending to be interested.

He's waiting for me when I exit.

"Our cultures are different," he says. "I didn't mean to imply that mine is better or yours is worse."

I know what he meant, and I know his opinion hasn't changed. I know he also thinks I have a superiority complex.

Just like he always has.

He's trying so hard to keep the peace. So hard to not be angry with me.

"It's all right," I say. "I'm sorry I didn't give you the space you needed to cool down."

I don't say anything else.

More and more I see the conflict between us. If I thought we'd be together for real someday, if I thought I was going to marry him or we might spend our lives together, I'd fight harder. I'd fight for change. I'd fight for him to understand what it is I don't like. I'd fight for him to see what he needs to do differently.

But I'm not going to.

Some other girl can fight with him if she needs it to be different.

⌒〜✳〜⌒

I wake in the morning when something bumps the bed. Outside the sun hasn't woken, and a dark shape looms over me, blocking out the white oscillating arms of the fan overhead.

It's a man. My heart skips a beat, and I let out a gasp when he climbs onto my bed. Fear turns me to liquid, and I open my mouth to scream.

"Shh, it's me."

Tiago's whisper fills the space between us, and I close my eyes, exhaling and relaxing in relief.

"Tiago!" I reach for something to hit him with but I have nothing, so I slap his arm. "You scared the tar out of me."

"Sorry. I couldn't sleep, and I knew you were here." He bends forward and kisses me.

I'm still drunk with sleep and not in my best state of mind. I sink into the bed, pulling him down so his weight lies on me.

He settles himself against me, breathing with me, getting closer to me with every moment.

I'm too tired to think. Instead I just feel. He pushes my legs apart and slides between my thighs, and I run my hands down his bare chest. He wears nothing but his underwear.

He kisses me again and then fingers the buttons of my pajama top.

"Can I undo this?" he whispers.

There are a million reasons why I should say no and I can't think of a single one why I should say yes. I feel a shiver of fear at the thought of a boy seeing my breasts, small lumps of underdeveloped tissue that fill me with shame.

I'm afraid no boy will love me once he sees them.

Maybe that's why I say yes. Tiago will be the test.

"Yes," I whisper.

He undoes the buttons and peels back my top. My nipples pop out and not much else. My heart pounds and I hold my breath, watching him. I'm nearly concealed in darkness, but I know he can see that much from the budding light coming through the

46

window.

Outside the sun is rising. The soft orange light fills the room.

"You are so beautiful," he murmurs.

"You really think so?" I murmur back. "They're not too . . . ?"

"They're perfect." He turns away from my breasts and hugs me, lifting me up and cradling my bare chest to his. Then he lays me back down and pulls my pajama top closed over me.

"Put this back on," he says quietly.

He's not going to take this further. I'm completely surprised, but my mind is catching up to my body now, and I realize how impaired my judgment has been. I button up my pajamas and wonder if I should be insulted.

"You don't . . ." I shouldn't ask. "You don't want me?"

He sucks in a breath. "I want all of you. If you want to have sex right now, I'm ready. Do you?"

"No." I shake my head.

"I know. So I'm stopping."

"For me?" I finish with the buttons and sit up on the bed, leaning against the wall. He settles in beside me.

"For you. For me. I don't just want to experience an orgasm. I could go to the bathroom and do that myself."

I snort.

"I want to be connected to you. To your body, your heart, your soul. So this has to happen on your time. Or it won't be what I want."

I take his hand and lay back on the bed. He curls up behind me.

But I'm sad. I'm sad that he loves me, and that a part of me loves him, because that connection is never going to happen.

I don't know yet who it will happen with, but I feel like I'm giving pieces of myself to every boy I meet. To Owen, to Tiago, to Jared. Who else will get a piece of me? It's unfair.

I'm tired of dividing myself. I want to find the person I will be with forever and give myself to them and never go through loneliness and uncertainty again.

CHAPTER ELEVEN

New Look

On Monday we take Martha to get her hair cut.

"You should get yours cut too," I tease Tiago as we watch the hairdresser trim and chop his mom's hair.

"You should get yours cut," he returns.

I look in the mirror at my long brown hair. It's shiny and straight and so boring. I finger the edges and wonder what I'd look like with a pixie cut.

The idea of doing something so drastic seizes me. "I think I will."

"You will?"

I go to the couch and open one of the magazines on the coffee table. Tiago sits beside me, and we thumb through it, looking at styles.

"This is pretty," he says, pointing to one of a girl with an A-line cut dipping below her shoulder blades.

I shake my head. "No. If I'm cutting it, I'm going extreme."

"Like what?"

I keep thumbing through until I find it. The girl is European, with white blond hair and pale skin and way too much dark eye makeup. But her hair is a darling Tinkerbell cut, full of fun layers on top and choppy pieces around her face.

"Oh my gosh. This."

Tiago looks at it and then looks back at me with big eyes. "You wouldn't do that."

I give him a grin and stand up, my thumb in place in the magazine.

He follows me as I go to the receptionist.

"Can I get my haircut here now?" I ask her.

"Yes," she answers, and I'm so pleased she understood my Portuguese question that I fail to hear what else she says.

Tiago asks her something, and the conversation continues without me. He takes the magazine from me and shows the picture. She studies it and then smiles at me and says something.

"What was that?" I ask as she walks away with it.

"She said it will be very stylish on you. Very chic."

Tiago leaves me to go talk to his mom, and a moment later the woman is back. She gestures me forward and puts me in a chair in front of the mirror. Tiago grabs another chair and sits down beside me.

"Are you really going to do this?"

"Yes!" I'm excited. "I've never done anything like this before."

"What if you don't like it?"

The man who cut Martha's hair comes over with her in tow. "Ah, *que bom!*" he says, his eyes lighting up when he sees me. He runs his hands through my hair, lifting it up and letting it fall. "*Pronta?*" he asks, meeting my eyes.

Am I ready? I nod.

Martha is wide-eyed as she pulls a chair up next to Tiago, and they both watch like this is a suspenseful movie. The hairdresser pulls my hair back into a ponytail, gets out a pair of scissors, and cuts it off.

I gasp. I can't help it. He puts the ponytail with my long hair on a tray and fluffs up what remains.

Suddenly I'm not sure I'm ready. But it's too late now.

He talks to me in Portuguese as he cuts and snips, and I nod along with him but I'm not hearing anything. I don't dare look at Tiago or Martha.

The man runs his hands along my cheeks and says something about my beautiful face. He doesn't consult the picture once he's gotten started, and his style is slightly different, but my worry falls away as he frames the layers around my face, highlighting my cheekbones.

I don't look fourteen anymore. He just aged me to at least eighteen.

He finishes and takes a step back. "*O que você acha?*"

"I love it," I say, so ecstatic that I forget to answer in Portuguese. "It's amazing!" I turn to Tiago and Martha. "What do you think?"

"It's different," Tiago says, his expression uncertain.

But Martha's face is lit up. "*Tão tão tão tão lindo. Adorei.*"

I smile. She loves it.

I can't wait for everyone at school to see.

The hairdresser hands me a small mirror, and I stand to examine my reflection from all angles.

What would Owen say?

He would love it. I know immediately that he would.

I have this terrible fear no one will ever love me as much as he did.

Did. Past tense. It doesn't matter how much he did. I have to take what someone else can give me.

⁓⁂⁓

Tiago's brothers stare at me when we come in the door like they aren't sure who I am.

"It's me!" I exclaim, and Mario turns to Tiago. He mimes cutting his hair and jabbers away so fast I catch nothing.

But I know what he said.

"It should be fairly obvious I cut my hair, right?" I say jokingly to Tiago.

He laughs, and I leave them in the hallway. I settle down on my bed with my book, but then I hear Tiago and his brothers laughing in their room and decide to join them. I bring my book and sit on Tiago's bed. The boys laugh and sing songs and mess with each other. I wonder what it was like for the three of them, growing up in this little room, in this little house.

Then Rafael and Tiago start to argue. It begins small, disagreeing over something, and grows louder, with the two of them standing up and getting in each other's faces. I don't understand enough to know what they're arguing about. I expect Martha to barge in as they shout and get in each other's faces, but maybe she's used to this. I probably should be; it happens almost daily. But I'm not.

"Tiago," I say, trying to get his attention.

But he doesn't hear me. He puts both hands on Rafael and pushes him.

I jump to my feet, and Mario grabs my arm.

"*Não!*" he yells, barring me from getting closer.

Rafael stumbles back but regains his footing, and he charges Tiago, smacking into his torso like a football player. Tiago slams backward, his back crashing into the tile flooring and his head cracking against the closed door.

"Tiago!" I exclaim.

He lies there, stunned, and I finally break free of Mario. I collapse in front of Tiago, grabbing his shoulders, touching the back of his head.

He shoves me off. "Get off me, I'm fine."

He's trying to get to his feet. His eyes are glossy, unfocused, but rage darkens his face. I know what will happen if he gets back up.

"No!" I exclaim. "No, I won't!" I punch his shoulder, getting his attention. "You're such a stupid idiot, all of you are! Grow up and stop treating each other like rutting pigs!" I stand up and grab the door, and if he hadn't slid out of the way, I would have banged his head again when I yanked it open. That's when I realize I'm crying.

Silence reigns behind me.

I don't stay to see if they'll resume the fighting. I don't go to my room, where I know Tiago can find me and tell me he's sorry I had to see that but that's the way it is here. I move right out the front door.

Now what? I'm in the courtyard between the house and the wall that keeps out intruders. The garage is to my left and the shed is behind the house. Neither offers a good place to sit and mope.

So I open the gate and leave the yard.

I stop when I get outside. I've never been out here by myself before.

But I've walked these streets plenty of times. Grandpa's house is to my left and around the corner. The park is ten minutes down the diagonal path from there. The grocery store is twenty minutes to my right, and the city center is half an hour away.

I don't know where I'm going, but I start walking.

The tears leak out as I walk. I turn down streets and hope I don't get lost because I didn't bring my phone in my rush to escape. I suspect there will be hell to pay. I accused Tiago of immaturity, but I'm the one who ran out of the house like a crazy lady.

I stop on a bridge overlooking a stinky, filthy river, and I know where I am. There's a restaurant not far from here where Tiago and I ate on one of my first nights in Brazil. I lean over the railing and take a deep breath.

I desperately want to talk to someone about the painful web of emotions whirling around inside of me.

I want my mom.

I want to leave. I can't be around Tiago anymore and realize every day that I could love him quite desperately if I let myself, but I won't let myself because if he and I ended up married, it would be a disaster.

I would not be happy. I didn't mean to lie when I told Tiago I would be, but I didn't have all the facts.

Love is not all you need.

CHAPTER TWELVE

Mother-in-Law

I don't leave the bridge. I'm certain Tiago will come looking for me. I tick off the days I have left in my head. Five.

Owen will be on his mission in three.

My heart is broken and I'm tired of hurting. I want to forget them both.

It's not always meant to be and it's not always up to me.

I hear him coming before he reaches me. He's out of breath, his face red, and I like to imagine he's been running through the whole city trying to find me. He slows when he gets near me, and then he stands beside me, resting his arms on the railing and looking out over the water.

I don't look at him or acknowledge him.

We stand that way for a few minutes before he says, "I ran past you three times before I realized it was you. I was still looking for long hair."

He's trying to break the ice, but it's not working.

"I want to go home," I say quietly.

"Come on. I'll walk you back."

I don't move. "Not your home. Mine." Tears prick my eyes again, and I thought I was done crying.

He looks at me. I feel his eyes studying my face. "Why?" he asks, matching my tone.

"If I tell you, I will only hurt you," I answer.

He's quiet a long moment. Then he says, "Okay. I'm ready."

I give a half smile and finally turn to face him. "Are you sure? When I finish, you'll want to put me on a plane and never speak to me again."

His gaze flicks over me. "It was just another stupid fight, Cassandra."

I roll my eyes. "Yes, I know. Just another one. And you're sorry I had to see it. But it had to happen. That's how it is when someone is disrespectful and you're laying down the law."

"Well—" he begins.

"I'm not here to change your mind. I tried that. I accept things the way they are."

"You sound like you are still mad at me."

I shake my head. "I'm not. I'm tired, that's all."

"Come on. Let me take you back. You can sleep."

I give up. I don't know how to explain what I'm feeling, anyway. I let him take my arm and pull me from the bridge.

He starts talking as we walk. "When I realized you'd left the house, I was so worried. I didn't know you were that upset. I didn't tell my mom because I was afraid she'd call the police, but I came right out to find you. And Rafael and Mario, they are out also. Or they were. I texted them and told them I found you, so they went home."

Shame stirs in my core. "I didn't mean to cause a scene. I just wanted to get away and be by myself for a bit."

"I know how you feel." His arm goes around my shoulder, pulling me into his side. "You worried us. Are you okay?"

Five more days. Five more days until I leave him.

I'm dreading it and anxious for it.

I stop walking. He needs to be able to move on with his life also. But is this the right time? Should I wait?

Suddenly I know how Owen felt when I showed up at his house for his birthday. He knew we were going to break up, but with me there—it changed the timing. He wanted every last minute with me before he did it.

I decide I want it also.

"I'll be okay." I stand up on my toes and kiss his cheek.

It's okay to love this boy also. It's a different kind of love. And it's okay.

❦

I'm startled when I walk into the bathroom the next morning and see my hair. It sticks out in different directions, and I laugh. I look like a little boy.

Luckily it's easy to tame with water and a comb.

The boys are still sleeping, but Martha greets me when I come out.

"*Quer ir comigo à piscina hoje?*"

I tilt my head, wondering if I understood her right. Did she ask me if I want to go to a pool with her? Does she mean the pool behind Grandpa's house? "*Piscina?*" I repeat.

She nods, and I shrug. "Sure."

She smiles. She knows that English word, because I accidentally say it a lot.

I think she will get Tiago, but she doesn't. We go just the two of us.

I take a deep breath when we're alone in her car. I've needed space. This is good.

She takes me to a country club with a pool. We fall into a conversation that's a mix between her broken English and my broken Portuguese, and we laugh at some of the difficulties, but we manage to get by.

"You and Tiago are so beautiful together," she says.

She's not the first person to say that. "Thank you."

"He is so lucky to have someone like you."

Her praise makes me uncomfortable. I can't mislead her. "I don't know if he and I will stay together after I leave."

Her smile is sad but her eyes are understanding. "It is too hard when you are apart, isn't it?"

"I wasn't looking for a boyfriend when I got here," I say. "I didn't plan to have one when I left."

She nods. "Yes, yes. But if you come back one day, and he is still here . . ." She shrugs.

I have to laugh. "Yeah, maybe."

"But I love you. I always will, no matter what."

I kiss her cheek. She's a great lady.

The boys are glued to the television when we get back.

"Hey," Tiago says when he sees me. "There's a birthday party tonight. All my friends are going. Want to go?"

I've heard about Brazilian birthday parties. How grand they are. How much food there is. "Sounds like fun. What should I wear?"

I head for my room, and he follows me.

"Something nice, like a dress. Girls dress up for these parties."

"Like a fancy dress?" I sift through my suitcase. "I don't have anything."

"That is good." He points to a short jeans dress in my bag. "It's nice."

"Very American." I pull it out. "No one wears things like this here."

"Which is cool."

"All right. What time?"

"Late. Like nine o'clock. But it's good because I have class before that."

"Ah." I nod. "Should I come to class with you again?"

"If you want. Or I will come back and get you."

I remember how boring his class was last time. "I think I'll stay."

"Don't you want to know whose party it is?"

The question catches my attention enough that I straighten and look at him.

"I don't know any of your friends," I say. "So what difference does it make whose party it is?"

"There is one you know," he says. "Or kind of know. Know of."

His grins holds a hint of mischief, but I can't read it. I rifle through the names I know from church but come up empty.

"I'm at a loss. Should I be nervous about this party?"

"I think it's someone you've been wanting to meet."

"Who?"

He shrugs. "Maybe you don't remember her."

Her. It's a girl's party. That narrows the contenders down by quite a bit, and suddenly I'm certain who it is.

"Mariângela?" I guess.

CHAPTER THIRTEEN

The Ex

"You do remember her!"

I can't believe it. "It's Mariângela's birthday?" I say in a tone of disbelief. "And we're going to her party?"

He lifts both eyebrows. "I seem to recall you were jealous of her."

Jealous of her. To put it mildly. Mariângela was his girlfriend in Brazil when he came to the States, and she was quick to contact him again when he got back to Brazil.

I was insanely jealous of her.

"You wish," I smirk. I go over to the bed and push him back, then climb up next to him and sit on his stomach. "You used her to make me jealous." I poke his chest with my finger.

"I did. I'm sorry."

"You dated her after I left, didn't you?"

He rolls his eyes. "Yes. But that's when I knew for sure I didn't like her anymore. She has a loud laugh, and her mouth is big, and sometimes I wanted to tell her to shut up."

"Tiago," I admonish. "That's so rude!"

"You will see when you meet her. You had nothing to be jealous of."

"I'm not jealous anymore." He doesn't want her. If he did, I'd let her have him. I want him to be happy. To love someone else.

"Can I ask you about Owen?" he says, very quietly.

I freeze where I sit on his stomach. There's no reason why I should tell him about Owen. It's in the past. The information will hurt me to divulge, and it will hurt him to hear it.

But maybe it will help him understand why I cannot love him like I once did.

"I will tell you anything you want to know," I say, my soft pitch matching his.

"When did you start liking him?"

I slide off him and pull over the chair behind the computer desk. Then I sit down on it and pull my legs up so I sit cross-legged on the seat. "Summer was nearly over before my senior year when I noticed something change between me and Owen. I started to notice him more, and I would be happy when he was around me." I keep my voice steady and try not to get lost in memory lane.

"But you didn't start dating?"

I shake my head. "Even though I felt something for Owen, my heart belonged to you. Owen didn't want to date me when I was hung up on someone else. We tried a few times, but he didn't like sharing my heart, so it didn't work."

"So you had to get over me first."

"I had to reach a point where I believed there was no hope for you and me." A wave of deja vu washes over me.

It's hard to believe Owen was once second choice.

"What happened for you to reach that point?"

"You gave me hope and then crushed it, and I gave up on you."

"What did I do?"

"I emailed you about my foot surgery. And you responded, with concern, with care, and for the first time in months, I thought I'd reached you. I thought it might be what brought us back together. I emailed you back, eager to keep the conversation going, waiting to see what would happen—and I waited. And waited."

"I remember your surgery. I remember emailing you. But I don't remember after that. What did I say?"

I blink at him. This was a pivotal moment in my life, and he doesn't remember. "You didn't respond."

"No, of course I did."

"You didn't." I say it emphatically. "You broke my heart. But for the last time. I told Owen you and I were through, and he asked me out, and I said yes."

"You didn't love him before that?"

"No."

"But then you did fall in love with him."

"Yes."

"How long did it take?"

"About two months for me to know I loved him."

"And you and I were talking by then?"

"Yes."

"But you didn't love me anymore."

"I did not."

"Did he love you?"

I give a wistful smile. "Owen loved me before I loved him."

"Do you still love him?"

I don't mince words. "Yes."

"Do you think you will ever stop?"

"No."

"But you didn't think you would stop loving me, either, and yet you did."

I don't quite agree with his assessment, but I don't know how to disagree with it, either. "That's not exactly accurate."

"Which part?"

I shrug.

"How far did you guys go?"

I consider the answer to that question. I replay various steamy make-out sessions in all their glory, and my chest squeezes with longing. "We didn't go all the way."

"But you fooled around?"

"Yes."

"But not as much as you and I."

That's not a question. Tiago already knows the answer to it. "No," I say, and I hate the answer.

I hate that Tiago and I have done so much.

And I hate that Owen and I didn't.

"Do you remember, I told you once, if you were my girl, I wouldn't be able to keep myself from having sex with you?" Tiago says.

"I remember. I was highly offended by that."

"This is me, trying not to have sex with you."

I smile slightly. "I appreciate your efforts."

"What I don't understand is how you and Owen didn't."

I'm lost in thoughts of Owen for a moment. How Owen loved me, how he respected me, how he wanted me. "We were older than you and I were when we started dating. We had more control."

"What does he think of you being here with me?"

I shrug. "Owen let me go. He knew when he broke up with me that I would date other people. Develop feelings for other people. It could happen here or anywhere, and he knew that. He accepted it."

"Have you accepted that he will?"

"That Owen—" I cut myself off.

I've pictured him like a celibate monk in Tibet for the foreseeable future.

But not forever.

He's not going to build a shrine to me in his heart and love my memory until he dies.

"Is there anything else you want to know about Owen?" I ask, my voice cool and collected.

"No, just that—I hope you can love someone else like you loved him, Cassandra. I hope you won't let someone in your past be the love of your life. You deserve to have that in your future."

They're kind words, and not the ones I expected. I expected a plea for his own case. Even disparaging remarks about Owen.

I cannot imagine meeting someone else who would fit me better than Owen did.

"Thank you, Tiago," I say. "That's a very good thing to hope."

Maybe I won't have to tell him what I feel for him after all. Maybe he already knows.

⊙~֍~⊙

Even though I say I'm not jealous of Mariângela, I find myself paying more attention than usual to my appearance. I frame the short pieces of hair around my face and feel insecure about my new haircut for the first time. I line my eyes with black and hope they can make up for my lack of hair. Then I pull on the sleeveless denim dress. At least my tan goes nicely with the dark jeans.

I'm restless while I wait for Tiago to arrive from class. He finally lets himself in and

57

comes to my room, and his eyebrows rise when he sees me.

"Wow," he says. "You look hot."

"Do I?" I pat my short hair and shove up my push-up bra, trying to give my non-existent breasts some help.

His friends will be there, and I feel silly for it, but I care what they think of me.

"Let me change my clothes and we can go."

I check my time. "We'll be late."

He waves me off. "That's not a thing here."

I don't tell him how anxious I am. I stand and go to the window and look out at the tall wall lined with broken glass bottles. I can just see the roof of another house next to it.

Tiago returns a moment later. He wears an off-white button up shirt with blue embroidery on the edges with his jeans. He comes to me where I stand and places his arm around my waist.

"You look beautiful," he says, and he turns me to kiss him.

He takes my hand and leads me to the street, where we wait while he calls a taxi. Though the sun has set, the muggy heated air sticks to my skin.

"She lives too far away to walk?"

"Yeah, an hour on foot. And we would be wet with sweat by the time we got there."

"I'm a little nervous," I admit.

"You are?" He casts a glance at me. "Why?"

"What if they don't like me?"

"Of course they will."

The taxi arrives, and we stop talking as we get in. He sits in the back with me. We take the ramp that leads to the busy highway roads criss-crossing over the city. From here I see the city lights, and I see the spot in the distance where they disappear into the blackness that must be the ocean.

"Your city is so big. It's so beautiful."

"I love my city. And my country. I don't know if I can live away from it ever again."

I love Brazil also, but could I live here? "I miss Arkansas."

"Did you like Colorado?"

I shrug. "It's fine. Super dry and cold. It's not my home. Just a place to stay for a bit. I can stay anywhere if I know it's short term."

We come to a downward ramp, and the city sprawls outward in front of us, high rise buildings stretching along the coast and bending inward. Even in the dark, I can tell these buildings are nicer, newer, more expensive.

"Mariângela lives here?" I ask.

"In one of these. You'll see it."

Tiago pays the taxi, and I wait on the sidewalk. The building rises in front of us, the lights winking on each floor. A man sits inside a cubby in front of the first level, which looks to be a parking garage. Tiago approaches him and speaks. I hear his name and Mariângela's name. The man looks over a long list, and then presses a button on his side.

The metal gate in front of me buzzes. Tiago pushes it open, thanks the man, and leads me through.

CHAPTER FOURTEEN

Dearly Departed

"He's the security guard?" I ask as we step past the gate into the building.

"Kind of. He's the *porteiro*. All nice apartments have one. He knows the residents and he lets people in and out."

We climb the granite steps to the lobby. My sandals clack against the tile flooring, and Tiago guides me over to the elevators.

"It seems you've been here before," I say, a bit sardonically.

"A few times."

The elevator closes behind us, and Tiago turns to me. He's not wearing a baseball cap tonight, and his hair is pulled into a ponytail at the nape of his neck.

"Is it odd to you that your hair is longer than mine?" I say.

"I wasn't thinking about your hair."

"What were you thinking about?"

"The last time I kissed you in an elevator."

The doors open as the elevator grinds to a halt on the thirty-second floor, but I feel the smile that softens my features at the memory. "My grandma's apartment."

"When we were just getting to know our feelings." He traces the length of my arm with one finger, down from my shoulder to my elbow.

"Those days were magical." I hold his gaze.

He takes my arm and pulls me close, and I close my eyes as his lips fall on mine. It's an exquisite feeling of reliving a memory, but it's not quite the same, because in my memory we were still a bit shy, still uncertain around each other.

He bends my body to his and I wrap my arms around his torso, and there's no shyness now. His hands go around my back to cup my butt, and I let out a sound that's between a sigh and a moan as he yanks me against his groin.

The elevator doors close. It jolts as it begins to descend, and he releases me.

"My gosh," he breathes. "You are so hard to resist." He presses the button of the floor we need again.

I step back to the opposite corner, a bit sheepish. "Same." This is what Tiago and I

59

are good at. Sexuality. We developed that part of our relationship before the rest of it, and it's our foundation.

"Stay over there until we get to Mariângela's apartment," he instructs.

I laugh and obey.

Another couple gets on the elevator on the first floor, which helps keep us apart. We don't look at each other, and they probably think we don't know each other. They get off on the seventeenth floor, but Tiago and I maintain our distance, staring at the wall until we arrive. The door opens and we step off into a hallway with only one door in front of it.

I glance around and spot no others. "This is her apartment? It takes up the entire floor?"

"Yes. Some apartments get two floors."

"Really?"

He presses a doorbell, and laughter and voices carry closer to the door until a woman with long sweeping dark hair and beautiful skin beneath a blue halter pants suit opens it.

"Tiago!" she cries and she kisses both of his cheeks.

She's too old to be Mariângela, but she's exotically beautiful.

She takes his hands and they converse before they both turn to me.

"Cassandra," Tiago says.

She kisses both of my cheeks also. "*Prazer*, Cassandra," she says.

"*Prazer é meu*," I answer.

"*Entrem, entrem*," she says, and Tiago pulls me through the kitchen, past a table laid out with two cakes and dozens of finger foods, into a living room. The balcony doors are thrown open, revealing the black ocean in the distance, and kids mill about in all directions.

They spot us as we come in, and simultaneously voices call out.

"Tiago!"

A girl in a long sparkly pink dress sits on an ottoman, pulling a gift from a bag. Her head is tilted so her long dark hair, exactly like her mothers, falls in gentle waves past her exposed shoulders. She tosses her head when she hears Tiago's name, and her brown eyes light on him.

She's as beautiful as her mother, with her dark skin, luxurious hair, and sculpted features.

Then she smiles, and her lip dips in the middle at the same time the edges curve upward, giving the impression of a bow across her face.

I know why Tiago said her smile is weird.

She stands up, and she's as flat-chested as I am. But she's not cheating with a bra.

It's petty, but suddenly I see she's not perfect either. And I feel better.

Tiago introduces us, and her eyes go wide as she looks at me. "Tiago, *ela é tão linda!*"

I'm so beautiful.

"*Sim, ela é*," he agrees, and I smile now.

"*Obrigada*," I say.

There is no more ice. I'm not jealous and I'm not uncomfortable. I need to stop comparing myself to other people. The kids include me, each one of them wanting to practice their English on me. And I eat as many of the chocolate caramel balls, *brigadeiros*, as I can, because when I leave here in four days, I don't know when I'll see them again.

❦

My eyes flutter open the next morning, and the first thought that enters my mind is, *Owen has left on his mission.*

It must have been there in my subconscious. I didn't know I was thinking about it. But I lay there on my bed, staring at the fan oscillating above me, feeling the short hairs on my head wave in the breeze, and I miss him.

Does he think about me? I turn sideways in the bed and focus on the wall, a montage of photographs of Tiago's family through the years.

I want to talk to Owen.

I regret deleting his contact info. I should have sent him a message yesterday. Just a simple, "Good luck! You're going to be amazing!"

But that's why I deleted it. So I wouldn't do the sappy pathetic things that most exes do while they try to maintain any sort of link.

I want to write him. I'm already drafting a letter in my head, but it's a mix of "I believe in you" and "I'm never going to find anyone like you again."

Even in my head I know it's not appropriate.

Still, I let myself draft it. Tears slide out the corners of my eyes. My heart cries as I tell him my thoughts, my regrets, my longings. I consider putting it down on paper, but that will only make it more real.

I get dressed and dry my face and take King for a walk. I'm outside with the dog when Tiago finds me.

"Three more days," he says.

I nod.

"You ready to go home?"

"I think so," I say. I am. There's no reason to prolong the inevitable end of our relationship.

Tiago leads the way to a park, and King and I follow. The big dog tries to chase down every smaller dog he sees, and Tiago ends up taking the leash from me. He sits on a bench, and I join him.

"Are you glad you came?" he asks.

"Yes. Absolutely."

"Why?"

I laugh. "You're asking me to verbalize the thoughts that run through my head all night long?"

He grins back. "The ones you write in your journal every night."

He knows I'm a journaler.

I sit back and think about the answer. "This has been really great for me to work on my Portuguese. I'm not fluent, but I know a lot more."

"You've done a good job with the accent, at least."

"At least. And some vocabulary."

"Yeah."

"I love Brazil. I know I want to come back and spend more time here."

He nods and leans forward to rest his elbows on his knees, his eyes steady on me.

61

"And seeing you was amazing," I say, letting my voice go soft. "I wasn't sure what it would be like, after two years. And after all that's happened in between. But you are still so dear to my heart. I—" My voice chokes, and I shake my head.

How can I tell him that now I know for sure we'll never be together and I've gotten closure on our relationship?

"You what?" he asks.

"I love you," I whisper. The admittance makes me shake. I know what he will think.

He reacts exactly the way I expect. His eyes light up, his face brightens as if the sun came out from behind a cloud and shone on him.

"You do? You know you do?"

I shouldn't have told him. I regret it now.

He tries to hug me, but I hold him back.

"I do," I say. "I realized it. It's impossible not to love you, after everything, everything we've shared. But that makes it so much harder because—I also know this is all we'll ever have."

"It doesn't have to be." He's quick to disagree, quick to come up with other solutions. "We can make plans. Cassandra, I love you, I'll do anything to be with you."

I'm already shaking my head. "It won't work."

"Yes, yes it will." His voice rises in pitch, and he scoots forward, agitation visible in his hands as he moves King's leash back and forth over his knees. "You can come to school here, or I'll go there."

I laugh. "You said you don't ever want to leave Brazil."

"But I will. I will to be with you."

"You're not thinking logically. You have school, I want to go on a mission, neither of us wants to live away from our families—"

"None of that matters!" He blows off my concerns with a wave of his hand. "That's nothing. I'll wait for you. I'll work. We can live where you want. We can get married now, today, I'll go back with you to the U.S.—"

"That's a fantasy. It's not real."

"Stop letting your head do all the talking! Let your heart speak up!"

Tiago cups my face in his hands and kisses me hard, with much the same urgency as the first time he kissed me here in Brazil. I grasp his wrists, but I don't pull him away. Instead I lean into the kiss, my mouth opening against his, feeling the strength of not just his desire for me, but his love.

He breaks away and presses his forehead to mine. "We can do this if we want it," he whispers to me.

My breath shudders. My heart is shredding and bleeding. I squeeze my eyes closed.

I don't want it.

This is the moment where I should be honest with him.

But I can't.

I can't rip his heart out and leave him to bleed out across the bench in this park here in Recife.

"It won't work," I whisper.

"Why not?" he demands, shaking me.

I opt for the reasons behind my belief. "Because we're too different. Because we don't see eye to eye on important things. Because one of us would have to give up too much to make the other happy. Or both of us."

He's silent, and then he says, "I will do it. Whatever it is."

"Then you would resent me forever. You wouldn't be you anymore."

"Don't you understand, Cassandra? You are all I want. My life is nothing without you in it!"

"Tiago!" I snap my head up and squeeze his hands. The tears are hot in my eyes again. "I'm not it! I'm not the girl for you! There's going to be some girl, some amazing, kind, beautiful Brazilian girl who gets you and agrees with you and understands all the small nuances of your culture and who you are in a way that I never can! I'm not her! I can't be!"

I see the understanding dawning in his eyes. He pulls his hands away and leans back on the bench.

"How do you know you are not her?" he asks.

"Because I feel it in my heart!" The tears break free, and I'm crying openly. "I feel it every time we disagree. I'm not wrong, but you're not wrong, and it's not fair, not fair to you to feel judged, to feel misunderstood, and for me to be angry about things I don't agree with."

He hugs me again, holding me while I cry.

"We can fix those things," he whispers.

"We can't." I cling to him, hating this pain. I can't tell what's mine and what's his. We are both wounded hearts. "And we should stop trying. You need to be open and ready for when she comes along. The girl who will fit you."

He inhales harshly, and I realize it's a sob. "What if you're wrong?" he whispers, his voice breaking.

I know he's in so much pain, he'll cling to any desperate hope he can find. I can't give it to him.

"I'm not wrong. When I leave here, it's goodbye."

He cries openly, holding me, and I sob right along with him.

CHAPTER FIFTEEN

Final Closure

I expect after that excruciating tear-fest, after the awful things I had to say, that Tiago and I will spend the next three days in awkward silence. But instead, when we finish crying and decide we've had enough of sitting on the hard bench with King whining at our feet, we stand up, wipe our faces, and hold hands the rest of the way home.

A huge weight is lifted from my shoulders. While we will always have emotional ties, memories and firsts that bind us together, our journey ends here. The expectations and worry and disappointment will be severed, and for me, that's a relief.

Martha takes one look at our faces when we return and bursts into tears herself. Which Tiago and I find humorous. We spend ten minutes comforting her while looking at each other over her heads and sharing amused smiles.

After dinner he brings a big box into my room and places it on the bed.

"I've been meaning to organize these for years," he says. "But I'm too lazy. Can you help?"

I put my book down and pull the box over, intrigued. I take the lid off and pull out an envelope, and then I gasp when I see my handwriting. "These are letters I wrote you."

He nods. "Can you put them in date order?"

He gets his guitar and sits in the corner of the room, singing and strumming, while I thumb through a dozen letters.

Of course I have to read them.

The first letters are sappy and cloying, but full of expectation and joy. I dig through to find the next one, but then I see the desperate pain behind the words of a seventeen-year-old girl who just left her boyfriend behind, a boyfriend who didn't instill her with confidence when she visited him. I see her begging for a reassurance that he still loves her, that he still wants her.

The next letter is cringe-worthy in its desperation. *Just contact me,* she begs. *So I know you're alive.*

Huh. I remember those days.

The next is short. Almost cold in its perfunctoriness.

But it's better than the one after, which borders on rage. Anger seeps through every veiled hint of abandonment, of falsehood, of never actually caring. I smirk and look up at him. "Do you ever read these?"

He shakes his head, and he matches my smile, but it's tinged in sadness. "Once."

"When?"

"Right before I called you after Christmas."

The phone call that put us back in contact. "Just got curious and decided to reread them?"

"I thought it would make me stop missing you. Instead I saw how you grew more and more distant until you seemed to despise me. And I knew what an idiot I'd been."

"You've not read them since?"

He shakes his head. "I can't bear to remember that idiot."

I turn back to the letters, placing them in careful chronological order. "I don't blame you. You were a kid. I think we took the journey we were meant to take." I hand the box to him. "Will you keep those?"

He accepts it from me. "Always. You will always be my first love."

I'm Tiago's first love. I'm Owen's first love. I'm Jared's first kiss.

I've been collecting hearts even if I didn't mean to.

⚬᷍᷍᷍᷍᷍᷍᷍᷍᷍᷍᷍᷍᷍᷍᷍᷍᷍᷍᷍᷍

I spend the next day packing. It's harder than I expect it to be. After nearly a month in Tiago's house, I've left my things everywhere. I find clothing in the bathroom, pens and books in the living room, make up in Tiago's room.

Tiago is with me at almost every moment. He'll follow me around to carry my things, then put everything down and grab me in a hug, just holding me. Then he'll put things in my room and disappear for a moment, only to return in my shadow, snagging my belt loop and hanging off me as I go through the house.

I turn to him once, ready to tell him he doesn't have to be everywhere I am, but before I can speak he's pulling me close, crushing me against him, and then he's kissing me slowly, delicately.

Our kisses are numbered. I don't know how many there are to go, but I'm not inclined to decline a single one.

Martha throws a goodbye party for me. Grandpa comes with little Ana and her family, and half the kids I've met at church show up. A few of Tiago's friends come, and lots of cousins I've never met who I assume only came for the food. I gorge myself on *coxinhas* and *brigadeiros* until I fear I'll be sick.

Brazilians love to party, and as the time slips closer to midnight, I'm afraid I might need to leave my own party early.

But Martha catches me falling asleep at the table and has the good graces to shoo everyone out. I stand and force a smile even though most of these people won't remember me when I leave and I won't recall their names.

I try to help her clean up, but she sends me to bed.

"*Até amanhã, minha filha,*" she says, kissing each cheek.

Tomorrow. Tomorrow I leave.

Where is Tiago? I wander the small house until I hear voices outside. I step onto the

65

patio and find him conversing with friends and uncles. I touch his arm, and he turns to me.

"I'm going to bed," I say, quietly, and he hugs me.

"I'll come say goodnight," he says.

I nod and slip back into the house. I rub my arms and glance around the small living room, the kitchen to the side and the washing bucket in the alley outside the bathroom.

I'm a different person than I was a month ago when I arrived.

I ready for bed and turn on the lamp by the computer before putting out the bedroom light and climbing into bed. I'm drowsy but not quite asleep when Tiago comes in. He closes the door behind him, and I scoot over on the twin bed because I already know he's coming to me. He tugs my body against his, his arms going around my back so we're chest to chest, and he kisses me slowly.

We've reached the end of the countdown. These are our final moments.

His hand comes around to the front of my pajamas, and he undoes the buttons, one by one. He's already seen me, so why should I stop him? His eyes are dark as he studies me in the soft lamplight. He bends to kiss me again, and his hands slide down my flesh. He strokes my exposed breast.

"Are you okay?" he asks.

A short laugh escapes me. "Yes." I might feel differently tomorrow, but right now, I feel my swollen emotions filled to the brim, and I'm close to him, as close as I can get, as close as I'll ever be.

I can't give him anything more than this.

"Can I see you naked?" he asks.

I draw back, startled by the request. "What?"

"One thing that helped me keep control around you was the thought that someday, we wouldn't have to stop. Now I know, that's never going to be. I will never make love to you." He catches my gaze, and I swallow hard. "Can I at least see you naked? One time? I want to see you."

I sit up and finish pulling off the sleeves of my pajama top. He scoots off the bed and over to the computer desk chair and watches as I slide my pajama bottoms off.

I hesitate at my underwear. Am I really doing this? No one has ever seen me naked. Other than when I was a baby.

I take a deep breath and slide the underwear off. Immediately I feel exposed, and I wrap my arms around my torso.

"Don't," he says, his voice husky. "Don't cover yourself. You're so beautiful. Every part of you."

He swallows hard, and I know he's close to tears again.

"You're turn," I say.

He lifts an eyebrow. "You want to see me?"

I nod.

He stands and removes his shirt. This I've seen hundreds of times. But I watch with keen interest as he pulls his shorts down, revealing black briefs with a slight bulge. He keeps going, sliding the briefs down his thighs, and his penis lies against his sack in a mass of black hair.

I'm fascinated. I've never seen a male's body before. The color, the size, it's not what I expected.

He comes back to the bed and sits down. I run my fingers down his navel.

"You are turning me on again," he says. "That's what happens when there's a beautiful naked woman touching you."

I smile slightly.

He fingers the pearl necklace nestled against my chest, and a pang of sadness spurts in my heart.

"Do you ever take this off?" he asks.

"No." I've tried. But I don't feel whole without Owen's necklace. We might not be together, but I keep a piece of him there.

I'm afraid he'll ask why, and that would be awkward to explain. But he doesn't. He presses a kiss to my forehead and hugs me.

We hold each other, one hundred percent naked, until he stirs and says, "I need to go."

I already know. I feel him hardening against me.

He rises and pulls his clothes back on. Then he kneels at the bed, his dark eyes staring into mine.

"Never forget how much I love you," he says.

I shake my head.

I will never forget any of this.

CHAPTER SIXTEEN

Shut the Door

I take Tiago's entire family out to lunch the next day and spend the rest of my *reais*. The Brazilian money will do me no good in America. Then Martha takes me and Tiago to the airport.

He holds my hand in the car and stares out the window.

A lump lives in my throat. It hurts to swallow. It hurts to breathe.

We get me checked in for my flight. I watch my luggage get carried away and know it's time. I turn to say my goodbyes.

Martha hugs me, already sobbing, her tears soaking the neckline of my shirt. I blink and will the tears to stay back. I look over her shoulders and meet Tiago's eyes.

His jaw is clenched, his eyes narrowed, and he sucks in a breath when we make eye contact.

I release Martha and move to him. He grabs me and hugs me so tight I can barely breathe. His shoulders shake, and I sob right along with him.

"Goodbye," I whisper, and I kiss his cheekbone.

He kisses my mouth. It's so wet it's hardly a kiss.

I have to break away. I have to leave. I slip from his grasp and turn to the passenger doorway.

I intend to go through without looking back, but I don't make it. I glance back once. He's holding his mom, and both of them are crying. He's still watching me. I give a small smile and a wave, and then I go through.

Ice Cave

Soft fallen snow
Bury my heart
In delicate warmth
From the drifting cold
And let me freeze

I sob through the announcement on my flight from Recife to São Paulo. By the time the plane reaches full elevation, my tears have dried up, however. I feel fragile, but a sense of calm falls over me as my plane moves farther from Recife.

Farther from Tiago.

That chapter is done.

I do feel a flush of guilt when I remember yesterday. I shouldn't have let that happen, especially knowing we were walking away from each other.

But I can't bring myself to regret it. A part of me loves him, and I sacrificed a piece of myself by leaving him. My tiny consolation prize for carving him out of my life is the physical pleasure we took and gave to each other last night.

And that's the end of it.

I pull out my notebook and start that letter I've been drafting in my head, but now I'm not as desperately emotional.

Owen,

I pause. Should I say "Dear"? It's a customary English greeting. Does it seem rude if I don't?

Will he read too much into it?

I continue.

If my calculations are correct, you're out on your mission now. I'll have to get your address from your mom, but I assume you're in Chicago. Congratulations.

You asked me if you could write me, and I said yes. At the time, I wasn't sure it was a good idea. I wasn't sure how to separate "Owen the boy I loved" from "Owen the missionary."

I think I've figured it out. And since I said you could write me, I'm also assuming it's safe for me to write you.

I'm on an airplane right now, on my way home from Brazil. It's been a crazy month, and I've learned a lot, a lot more than just Portuguese.

I stop again to consider my words. This is not a confession. I'm not going to tell him how close Tiago and I got. For one thing, it won't help him focus on his mission. And for another, it's none of his business.

But I do want him to know Tiago and I are not back together.

And while I know these are not subjects you wish to talk about as a missionary, it's important for me that you know, right from the get go, that I remain unattached. I suspect my love affair with Brazil is just beginning, but it's time for me to explore that relationship on my own, with no ties or connections to the past.

I am excited for my future.

I would love to hear from you. No matter where you are in the world, or what you are doing, or who you are with, you are inextricably woven into my life.

I'm your biggest supporter. Go and do what you need to do, be who you are meant to be. Hold nothing back but serve and love with all your soul. You have the brightest light I've ever seen.

Sincerely,

Cassandra

I very intentionally do not write "love." He said I was a distraction. He said he worried he wouldn't be focused on the mission because he'd be thinking about me. I'm already worried this letter will be too much and he'll ask me not to write him again.

I fold it in half in my notebook. I'll buy an envelope in the airport.

My flight is delayed, however, and by the time I land, there's no time to stop at the store and get an envelope. As the dozens of passengers exit the plane and head for their connections, a security guard greets me as I turn down the hall for the flights to the U.S.

"Cassandra Jones?" he asks me.

I blink at him, startled. "*Sim.*" I answer in Portuguese without meaning to. I'm so used to communicating that way.

"They're holding the plane for you. Hurry, this way."

He starts off at a death march, and I run along after. We get to another set of doors and he takes me to a counter out front where a man in a uniform waits. They converse quickly, and the second man turns to me.

"*Passaporte, por favor,*" he says.

I fish my passport out of my bag and hand it over.

He flips through it and looks up. "*E seu passaporte Brasiliero.*"

I blink at him in confusion. Did he ask me for a Brazilian passport? "Uh," I say, not sure how to respond.

He lifts an eyebrow, and I squeak out, "I don't have one."

The other brow lifts, and he glances down at my passport in his hand, then back at me. "You are one hundred percent American?" he asks.

I laugh. "Yes."

"Oh." He hands it back. "Go on, then."

The security guard takes me back in his care, and we run down the next hall.

"Do you speak Portuguese?" he asks me.

"*Um pouco,*" I answer.

"You do, you already have a Brazilian accent."

"I'm learning." My face grows hot. I hope he won't ask me to say anything else, or he'll see how little I do know.

"There is the plane, do you see? The gate is still open," he says, pointing down the hall.

A woman stands in front, beckoning me forward.

"I see," I say. "*Muito obrigada!*"

"*Adeus!*" he says, and he stops running, leaving me to make the last ten yards alone.

"Cassandra?" The woman checks my passport and then shoves me through the gate. "*Pressa!*"

I am hurrying! I'm out of breath by the time I crash into my seat, and I barely get my seatbelt on before the plane begins taxiing. I close my eyes as I lean back against the uncomfortable seat, knowing I won't get much sleep tonight.

Home. I'm on my way home.

CHAPTER SEVENTEEN

The Best of Friends

My mom picks me up from the airport. We hug, but I'm too tired to do much else. I remember wanting her desperately a week ago, but now my head throbs, my throat is tight, and all I want is my bed.

"Was it a good trip?" she asks as she puts my suitcase in the trunk.

"It was amazing," I say.

"Are you planning to go back?" She sneaks a glance at me.

She thinks she's being so sly. I know she really wants to know if Tiago and I made plans for the future.

I play coy. "I'll definitely go back. I can feel Brazil's in my future."

"Oh? It was that good?" She smiles, but the knot of worry furrows itself between her brows.

"Um-hm." I'm too tired to play more. I pull out my phone and text the person I've been dying to contact since the first plane ride.

Me: Hey, it's Cassandra! Would it be all right if I got Owen's address on the mission?

Owen's mom responds before we've left the airport parking lot.

Mrs. Blaine: Oh my goodness, I'm so glad you contacted me! How are you? Where are you? I know he would love to hear from you. Here's his address.

She types out the necessary info, and I text back: *thanks!*

And then I reread her first message and over-analyze it.

She knows he'd love to hear from me.

She could be just saying that.

Or she could know. Because maybe Owen said something to her.

Or she thinks she knows. Because moms think they know everything sometimes.

I look over at my mom, who I'm certain is worried I'm planning a future elopement, and bite down on my lower lip to keep from smirking.

Sometimes they're so much fun to mess with.

But I stop dissecting her words.

My youngest sister Annette greets me when I get home, but she's the only one here.

Scott and Emily, my other siblings, are both gone to summer camps for the next two weeks. I won't see them before I head back to college.

I sleep thirteen hours straight. When I check my email the next morning while still lying in bed, I find two worthy of consideration: one from PYU, telling me my summer classes start in two weeks and tuition is due before then, and one from Tiago.

I open the one from Tiago.

Hi Cassandra,

I just want to make sure you made it home safe.

Thanks for coming to see me.

I love you

Tiago

A lump forms in my throat. We did not discuss maintaining contact, but I assumed we would not. I would prefer we do not. Reading his note brings back all those painful feelings, followed by doubts and uncertainties about my decision.

I should not email him back. He'll get the hint.

No, this time I will. But if he emails me again—

I type out,

Got in last night. Slept for hours.

I'm safe.

You changed my life, and meeting you will always be one of the greatest things that ever happened to me.

Thank you for everything.

Wishing you nothing but joy

Cassandra

I reread it before I send. It's nice but not very personal. Almost cold.

But I can't be personal. I already told him.

I'm certain he won't email me again.

I hit Send, and I cry again, and I pray it's the last time I have to say goodbye to him.

To make myself feel better, I address Owen's letter and pop it in the mailbox.

And then I try not to think about it. In less than a week, he'll have my letter.

Will he write me back?

I return to my room and pull up the university page and make sure my classes are correct. I wince as I pay the tuition bill. My bank account was seriously depleted by this trip to Brazil. I'm going to need to find a job like yesterday, as soon as I'm back in Colorado.

Harper calls me while I'm working on this. I snatch the phone up so fast I nearly drop it. I haven't talked to her, or anyone, since I left for Brazil.

And I'm desperate to talk to someone.

"Harper!" I exclaim into the phone once I have it safely in my hands. "I'm so so so so happy to hear from you!"

She cackles, and it's so like her that I laugh also. Harper's been my best friend since my sophomore year of high school. We only see each other when I'm home from college these days, however.

"You're back from Brazil!" she crows.

"I'm definitely back," I agree.

"I'm dying to know *everything*. When can you come over?"

I glance around the room, the one I'm sleeping in but I don't consider mine anymore. My home is at college. "Now. Anytime."

"I get off work in four hours. Want to spend the night after?"

"Yes, but you'll have to come get me. My car is safely parked at Camila's house in Colorado."

She clucks her tongue. "No problem. See you in a few!"

I kill time by unpacking and sleeping a few more hours while I wait for Harper to arrive. I'm still laying on my bed when she comes bursting into the room, full of flamboyance and Harper-energy.

"I'm here!" she announces, tossing her long blond hair behind a shoulder.

"Hey, my lovely friend!" I say. I rise from the bed, and she comes to my side and hugs me super tight.

"Come on, let's get some food," she says while I gather a few things for staying the night. "When was the last time you went to Vicenza's?"

"Years." I straighten up, all kinds of fond memories of the restaurant where I worked in high school flooding my mind. "Maybe senior prom."

"Oh, you're due. Let's go."

She slides her arm around my waist and we crash into each other as we try to walk to her car hip-to-hip, giggling like a bunch of second graders. I hug her super hard when we reach the car.

"I'm so happy to be here with you," I tell her.

She gives me a tight squeeze and hops in the car. I get in on the other side.

"I'm sure you have loads to tell me," she says. "Want to get started?"

I shake my head. "I'm not sure where to start. So you go first. How are you and that high school kid you're dating?"

She throws back her head and laughs, that particular Harper-sound. "Oh my gosh, high schoolers are so immature!"

I laugh with her. "And you, robbing the cradle."

We pause at a red light, and she glances at me. "Actually, that's the number one reason we haven't had sex."

"Say what?"

"Yeah." She nods. "He asked me to, and I was seriously debating it. But then I realized it's illegal because I'm nineteen and he's seventeen!"

I shriek and whack her forearm, and I'm laughing so hard it sounds like I'm yowling. "Harper, he's a baby!"

"I know!"

We can't stop laughing. We're still giggling when we walk into Vicenza's, where the staff immediately recognizes us, and everyone from the owner to the cook to the wait staff comes over to hug us.

My earlier funk evaporates. I smile at everyone, joy seeping through my veins and flushing out the sadness.

Harper and I sit and order, and I sip from my lemonade and sigh.

"Why do boys have such a big impact on our lives?" I ask.

"Strange, isn't it?" she says.

"Like, they're on my mind every moment. My moods and my days fluctuate based on my thoughts and interactions with them. No other relationship affects everything I do like my connections with the boys in my life."

She plays with her straw and focuses her eyes on me. "Tell me about Tiago. How old is he now?"

"He's eighteen, but only for another month. Then he'll be nineteen."

"So no statutory rape." She wiggles her eyebrows.

I smirk. "No, that rule doesn't exist down there, I'm sure. Thirty year olds marry thirteen year olds all the time."

"Did you, then?" She leans closer. "Did you do it?"

I look away from her. I want to tell her everything, but this doesn't feel like the place. And if I give the simple answer to that question, she'll consider the matter closed. "Let's talk about it later."

"It's a yes or no question, darling!"

"I don't want to talk about it right here!"

"Hey, if you're willing to let someone in your pants, you can't be nervous about talking about it."

That makes me laugh. "Fine. He did get in my pants."

She's too smart to make assumptions. "Did he do anything while he was in there?"

Her question brings up a flood of emotions, from guilt that I let Tiago touch me to remorse that it wasn't Owen to sadness that I'm without them both. When my eyes flood with tears, she backs off.

"Oh, honey, I'm sorry," she says, her voice quiet. "Okay. We'll talk about it later."

I sniff and blink back the moisture and push away the lingering sadness. My heart aches. "See?" I take another sip of lemonade. "They impact everything. It's not fair."

"No. No, it's not."

She doesn't bring it up again as we eat, instead asking me about Portuguese and what foods I ate, which I gladly talk about. My spirits brighten again. From there she takes me to the mall, and I can't help but talk about how different malls in America are to malls in Brazil.

"Let's see a movie. When was the last time you saw one?" she says, pausing outside the theater.

"I saw a few in college at the dollar theater. That's where the poor college kids hang out."

She lifts an eyebrow. "Today you're paying full-price at a fancy theater."

She pays for both of us and gets a big thing of popcorn and soda. I'm still satisfied from lunch but can't say no to the greasy popcorn.

"You must be making good money," I joke as we climb into our seats.

"Yeah, it's great. They actually promoted me to manager. I'm loving it and I have some control over my hours."

"That's awesome. I'm jealous. I'm so broke."

"Says the girl who just spent a month in a tropical country with a hot guy." Then she squints at me. "Is he still hot?"

"Yes." I feel that tug in my heart again. For how long will this sadness linger at the edges of my vision?

"You didn't send me any pictures."

"Later." I don't want to look. This goodbye is still tenuous. I'm still fragile.

But the movie is wonderful escapism. For two hours, I'm not me but the ditsy girl in the film who can't figure out how to make it to a second date. I laugh until my belly hurts.

"It's sad that I can relate to so much of her pathetic life," I say when we leave. "Either guys think they want to marry me, or it's *adios* after one date."

"We all feel pathetic sometimes."

We drift into silence in the car, and I imagine we're each reflecting on our pathetic natures.

"This kid in high school, are you waiting for him to graduate?" I ask as we park at her house. "Is it serious?"

"No way. It's a summer fling. I'm waiting to find someone I can get serious with."

She unlocks the door and flips on lights. No one else is here. I don't question their absence but make myself comfortable on the couch. She sits down across from me.

"Are you ready to talk now?"

I nod and pleat my hands together. I'm desperate to talk.

CHAPTER EIGHTEEN

Ready for It

"I'm not sure where to begin."

"Are you and Tiago back together?"

"No. We are through. One hundred percent." My eyes well with tears in spite of the confidence in my voice. "It's the right thing. I know it. Part of me is so glad to be done with that confusing chapter of my life, but the other part is absolutely aching that I let go of him."

She reaches over and hugs me. "It's okay. It's okay."

I cry into her shoulder and pull back. "I'm still a virgin."

She smiles at me. "Whew. If you weren't—it was going to make it a lot harder for me to resist."

"Virgins together." I giggle and choke back a sob at the same time, which makes a noise like a drowning cat.

She holds out her pinkie finger, and I clasp it with mine, and we press our foreheads together, laughing.

"So tell me what happened."

I take a deep breath and go back to the beginning. "My heart was closed when I got to Brazil. I was determined not to let anything happen between me and Tiago. And for a few days, it worked. We were just friends with a history. But I guess we have too much history, because it didn't last. One morning we got in a fight—we were always fighting—but this fight turned into making out."

"I like those kinds of fights," Harper says.

I smile. "Yeah. But I didn't expect it, and what it showed me was that I could still love him. I could still feel things for him. I just had to let myself."

"So you did."

"Not at first. I tried to fight it, but he's such a good kisser!" I groan and put my face in my hands. "And we know each other. We know how to affect each other. So he would turn me on, and I would turn him on, and things got crazy."

"That's how he got in your pants."

I nod. "I'm struggling with this. Because he's not my boyfriend, he wasn't my boyfriend then either, there's no commitment between us, yet I let him do that to me. And the first time it happened, all I could think of was Owen and how I wanted him to do that and he never did. How terrible does that make me, thinking of one boy while I let another touch me? And—what would Owen say if he knew?" I feel a rush of shame. "I've tried so hard not to think about that because Owen's gone and we're not together. There are no promises between us."

"You're punishing yourself over an imaginary scenario," Harper says. "Do you really think this is a conversation you will ever have with Owen?"

"Honestly?" I close my eyes. "I want it to be. Because it means Owen and I got back together."

She takes my hands and squeezes them, which forces me to look at her. "Listen, babe," she says. "If you and Owen get back together, awesome. That's fantastic. But you will owe him no explanations of what went on after he broke up with you."

"I know I won't owe it to him," I say, pushing back my frustration. "But just like I wanted the truth from him about what he did with Lacey Gregg—" I stop. "Did I tell you that?"

"No." She shakes her head. "We can get to that later. Keep going."

"Right. Anyway, what happened between them was before he and I dated, and he still felt I deserved to know. I feel that way. Even if what happened between me and Tiago was when he and I weren't dating, he deserves to know."

"Because it's Tiago, or because of what you did?"

"Both, I think." I sigh. "It's not something I want to tell him."

"Okay. So let's explore this future conversation between you and Owen when you tell him what happened. What is the worst thing you think can happen?"

"Owen decides he doesn't want to be with me anymore."

"You think he wouldn't want you after that?"

I consider it. "No. But it would hurt him. He might not look at me the same." I can't bear the thought of being "less than" in Owen's eyes.

"So Owen's never done anything sexual with anyone else?"

She lifts an eyebrow. I roll my eyes.

"You know he has."

"He did sleep with Lacey Gregg, didn't he?"

It was only a rumor for us in high school. But Owen confirmed it for me last year.

"Yes." I bite my lip. "And that still hurts. Which means this would hurt him."

"But you didn't sleep with Tiago."

"No."

"Did you want to?"

I consider it. "Not really. I liked the intimacy, the physical closeness. I knew it wasn't going to be him."

"So he doesn't have anything to be upset about."

"Maybe." I'm not sure Owen would see it that way. "It's a moot point. I'm torturing myself over nothing."

"Yeah, you are. You can't keep framing your life around Owen."

"Does it make me a slut? That I did that with Tiago knowing we were ending things forever?"

"Oh, honey." Harper reaches over and rubs my shoulder. "Not at all. It wasn't just a booty call. It was a boy you loved once who will always be a part of your heart."

I nod. "I have a theory."

"What's that?"

"That once you love someone, you never stop. You can put them from your mind, lock up the piece of your heart where they live and move on, but that love is still there. If you unlock that piece, it comes floating right up to the top of your brain. I didn't know I still loved Tiago until I saw him, and if I saw him again, I think it would be very easy to nourish that part."

"You're not in love with him?"

"No, thank goodness."

"Do you think you'll see him again?"

"No." I shake my head. "I'll never see him again."

She rubs my back. "Then get ready for the next grand adventure, babe. There are more boys for you to love out there."

I laugh. The aching pain of being alone squeezes my chest like a constricting band. "I don't think I want to let any more boys into my heart."

"Oh, there's room. Let's see what this next year of college brings you."

⟳∾҉∾⟲

I spend the next five days with Annette, since Scott and Emily are both gone at summer camp. I help my mom throw a big party for her thirteenth birthday, and it's fun to hang out with her. We start planning a trip for her to visit me in college.

"I'll take you to do so many things," I say. "We can go camping, hiking, swimming. Colorado is beautiful!"

"I want to go to class with you, see where you live."

"Of course!"

My mom thinks it sounds like fun, so we set a date for a few weeks after my summer term gets going.

Annette and I go to the lake so many times we get bored with it. We take a trip to the water park an hour away but don't stay long because it starts raining on us. Instead we go out for Chinese food. She spills her soda across the floor and I tease her mercilessly, which is immense fun because she can't stop laughing.

"The lake was better than the water park. If it weren't raining we could go again," I say. I unlock my mom's van, the car I use to drive us around, and we climb inside. "Maybe tomorrow."

"Oh, not tomorrow, I've got church camp," Annette says.

"You do?" I turn to her in surprise. "I fly back to Colorado in two days."

"I forgot." She screws up her eyes. "So tomorrow is goodbye."

I thought I'd have more time with her. I'm sad about this. "Yeah."

My mom comes into Annette's bedroom that evening where the two of us are playing with our cat, Baby Meow. She's pregnant and spends a lot of time grooming herself. We've had this cat for years, and she's probably too old to still be having kittens, so we're anxious for their arrival.

"Cassandra, I have to run a few errands tomorrow morning when Annette needs to be at the chapel to leave for camp. Could you take her?" Mom asks.

"Sure," I say.

"Perfect. Thanks for helping out."

I'm up early to help Annette finish packing. She grabs her pillow and sleeping bag, and I take the duffel and smaller bag. Then I grab the keys from the rack and head out the front door.

I draw up short when we step outside.

My mom's van is gone. The only car in the driveway is my sister Emily's red Honda. And it's a standard.

"What's wrong?" Annette asks behind me.

"Oh, crap," I say.

"What is it?"

I point. "I can't drive that car."

She looks at it, furrowing her brow in confusion. "Why not?"

"I can't drive a stick shift."

Annette blinks, and then her eyes lighten in understanding. "Oh! You don't know how?"

"Well." I lick my lips. "I learned on one when I was fifteen. But I never got great at it, and I switched to an automatic after Daddy wouldn't stop yelling at me."

Annette shields her eyes and looks across the street. "I can see if one of the neighbors can take me."

I look down at the keys in my hand and debate my options. Then I shake my head. "I can do this."

"You're going to drive?"

She follows me to the trunk of the car, where we throw her overnight stuff.

"How hard can it be?" I say.

CHAPTER NINETEEN

Antsy to Leave

I get in, my heart racing, and run through what I can remember for driving a stick shift.

Which is almost nothing.

I put my feet on both the clutch and the brake and start the car. To my relief, it fires up. I slide it into reverse and exhale as the car rolls back.

"So far, so good," I say.

"Yeah," Annette says. She looks anxious.

I turn down the gravel drive, still in first gear. I have to switch into second, but I can't remember how. My heart races as we turn onto the street. I move one foot to the clutch and switch it into second, and the car roars with appreciation, only lurching slightly as I make the transition.

"You're doing it!" Annette says, starting to relax.

"Yeah," I breathe.

It's not so bad if I just have to push the brake and gas. We get up the hill and around the bend, and my shoulders loosen up also.

Then we reach our first stop sign at the bottom of the hill. I down shift rapidly, hoping that's the right thing to do, but we're still going too fast. Panicking, I slam on the brake. The car stops, sputters, and chokes.

"It's okay, it's okay," I say. "We can do this." I start it up again and make my left turn.

We putter along before I find the courage to get back into second. I hold my breath at the next stop sign, but this time I manage to push the clutch in at the right time, and the car doesn't die. I smile brightly at Annette and we keep going.

I get nervous as we approach the railroad tracks. Already I see a line of cars, so I slow down. The tracks sit on a hill, and there's a stop sign right before them. I have to get up the hill and then hit the clutch and come to a stop. My heart is racing as I anticipate all the steps I have to do correctly.

I can't get up the hill in first gear, so I switch to second. Up, up, up we go, and—clutch and brake!

I don't hit it right, and the car dies.

"That's okay," I say. "Let's get going again." I push in on the clutch and the brake and turn the key.

The car makes a choking sound but doesn't start.

I furrow my brow and stare at it as if concentration will fix the problem. Then I try again.

Still nothing.

I glance in the rear view mirror and see the line growing behind me. Sweat beads on my brow and makes my underarms sticky.

"What's wrong with it?" Annette asks.

"I don't know." I press down on the clutch only and try. Nothing. Then the brake. Nothing.

I'm helpless.

"Come on, come on," I gasp out, turning the key one more time.

Annette emits a nervous giggle.

An old man in overalls gets out of a red pickup several cars behind me. I roll the window down as he comes over.

"Do you need any help?" he asks.

I give him my best sheepish grin. "I can't get my car started again."

He leans his head in my window and peers at the stick, then back at me. "Put it in first gear."

Put it in first.

What an idiot.

"Oh, right," I say, my voice shrill to my ears. "Of course." I make the shift and turn the key, and the car starts right up. "Thank you!"

I wave and drive away, my face hot, and Annette can't stop laughing.

"Shut up," I growl.

"First gear," she says. "Put it in first gear."

I huff. We're almost to the church, but I'm so rattled now I can't think. I stall at the next stop sign and again at the red light and barely manage to limp the car into the church parking lot.

"I got you here, all right?" I say as Annette springs from the car and makes a show of kissing the ground.

"I can't wait to tell everyone," she says.

I roll my eyes, but I'm also smiling. "Go on and have fun." I open the trunk and get her bags out.

We hug, long and hard.

"Have fun in college," she says.

"Have fun in eighth grade," I reply, sticking my tongue out at her.

She grins, but I see the shimmer in her eyes, and I hug her one more time and kiss her face.

"I'll see you in a few weeks when you come out to visit me!" I say.

She squirms away from me. "Good luck getting home!" she crows, grabbing her stuff and running off.

I groan. I forgot about that part.

I'm a visitor in my own house.

I'm antsy to leave, especially since I'm the only kid here. I bid my mom farewell in the airport and then hurry to my plane, counting down the hours until I land in Colorado.

I text Camila as soon as I do. *I'm here. Taking the shuttle to your house to get my car.*

She responds: *No, come straight to the apartment. My parents brought your car here yesterday.*

Oh. That was nice of them.

I call her as soon as I'm in the shuttle, taking the half hour ride back to PYU. "How's the new place?" I ask.

"It's great! It sleeps six people, so we always have new roommates coming in and out."

"Is that weird?" We knew it was an option when we decided to get that many rooms, but it weirds me out now to think of strangers living with us, coming and going.

"It's fine. You'll like everyone. Iris and Layne are here too."

So four of us will be together. "Where's Abby?"

"I don't think she'll be here until the fall."

I nod. "So who are the other roommates?"

"We have one other right now, this girl named Tracie. She rooms with you."

"Me? Why me?"

"Well, because Iris and I are rooming together and Layne will be with Abby."

"What? I thought I was rooming with you or Layne." I feel a slight panic attack coming on.

"We had to rearrange things."

"Why?"

"I'll explain when you get here."

"Okay." I hang up, but I feel less settled about my college situation now.

The airport shuttle drops me off in front of the three-story brownstone condos we picked out last spring. I haven't seen it since then, but standing in front of it with the dry, warm air of Colorado tickling my exposed skin, I get a keen sense that I'm a different girl than I was then. I tilt my head back and study my home for the next year.

Two identical buildings face each other across a courtyard, and a stairwell in the middle of each building divides the condos into four sections. I turn to the right building, the one housing women, and climb up the stairs to the second floor. I take a deep breath past the trepidation building in my chest and knock on the door.

It flies open, and Iris stands there, looking a little more tan than the last time I saw her, her black hair as long as ever. She looks at me, her almond-shaped eyes sliding right over me, before they widen in recognition. She gasps.

"Cassandra!" she exclaims. "You cut your hair!"

"Iris!" I drop my bags and throw my arms around her. We topple into the apartment behind her, laughing, and Camila and Layne soon appear from down the hall and join us in a group hug.

What was I afraid of? These are my people. We fit together, the four of us. Layne is the outgoing, boy-crazy one, Camila's the runner and the brains, Iris is the musician and film student, and I'm—just me.

They exclaim over my hair, complimentary and stunned, touching and telling me how amazing it looks.

"I like it," I say. "I wanted something different."

"It's very different," Layne says. "I love it."

"Maybe I'll cut mine," Camila says.

"You would look good with short hair too," Iris says.

They follow me to my room, which is the one in the back with a big window overlooking the street. I decide they gave me the best room, and I let go of any other misgivings. The three of them chatter at me nonstop as I begin the arduous process of unpacking my suitcase. The rest of my stuff is in my car, which Camila's family so graciously left here for me. But moving goes quickly with my three roommates helping me lug stuff from the car to my room. A swamp cooler churns noisily in the hallway ceiling, gifting us with a blast of cool air every time we walk under it.

I pause every once in awhile to hug them. "I love you guys. I'm so happy to be back with you."

"How was Brazil?" Iris asks.

"Unbelievable. I love that country."

They don't know about Tiago. All they know is I'm minoring in Portuguese and decided to spend a month in Brazil to immerse myself.

Except Camila. She's been my friend since high school. She saw how wrecked I was after Tiago stopped speaking to me. She gives me a knowing side-eye, and I give her a half-grin. We'll talk later.

"Where do you guys sleep?" I ask once my bed is made and my laptop set up on the desk.

"Iris and I are over here." Camila leads me from my room to the one across the hallway. I nod as I examine their things separated into two sides. Two beds, two desks, two closets, two computers.

"I'm in this room by myself right now," Layne says, and we move to the third bedroom in the same hallway. "I was with Abby when she was here, but it's just me now that she's gone."

"It will be empty soon," Iris adds. "Because Layne is leaving for the rest of the summer tomorrow."

Tomorrow! I turn to her, and I very much want to sit and talk to her. "You're going home?"

She nods. "I rented a room, but my mom wants me home. I'll come back when school starts and spend a week here before I leave for Guatemala."

My head spins, trying to categorize the information. "Are you excited?"

"So excited. I've been studying Spanish and trying to speak it at every opportunity."

"You'll be so great. But then who will be in here next semester?" I look at Iris and Camila.

Camila shrugs. "The landlord sticks people in here even if it's for one month at a time."

"And Tracie is getting married," Iris adds. "So she won't be your roommate for long."

"So we'll be getting two new people?" My anxiety rises.

"No, because I paid for my room all year," Layne says. "I wanted to make sure it's available to me whenever I want it."

"You did?" Iris turns to her. "So we won't get another roommate after you leave?"

"Nope."

"Sweet!" Iris says.

"So I'm the one who has to switch roommates every few months?" I say.

All three of them look at me and nod. Like, duh.

I can handle this.

"Okay. Awesome. Cool." I go back to my room and distract myself with unpacking. I glance at the bed across from mine, the pastel pink covers and the lamp near the head board. "Where's Tracie now?"

"Probably at her fiance's apartment. He lives across the courtyard. You'll love the balcony. It's so much fun to talk to the boys!"

"The boys, huh?" I smile.

Boys are fun.

I'll deal with the rest.

CHAPTER TWENTY

Reunited

Tracie's nice but distant. She's a few years older than me but just as tiny, with long blond hair she keeps parted down the middle. Her fiance lives across from us, and she spends most of the evening on our balcony, talking to him on his balcony.

"What time do you leave tomorrow?" I ask Layne as we clean up the dishes from dinner. Layne washes, I dry, and Abby puts them away. The small kitchen sits opposite the living room and has a sink catty-corner to the stove. The round table in the middle is stained and chipped, and I bet my roommates found it at a garage sale.

"Around four in the morning," Layne says. "My mom will be here to get me and we'll drive home to California."

"Oh. I was hoping we could go to breakfast or something."

"You were?" She gives me a side hug. "That's sweet of you."

It's not because I'm trying to be sweet. It's because I wanted to talk to her about things I think no one else would understand. Like, physical intimacy. "I'll miss you."

"It's a month. I'll be back for a few days after school starts. Then I'll leave for Guatemala."

That's a long time to wait for a talk.

Layne's mom and her mom's boyfriend show up an hour later, and they take us out for dessert, except Tracie, who opts out. We go in my car and follow Layne's mom, since the five of us can't fit in her sedan.

"We have a hotel room," Layne's mom says to her as we eat our gelato outside of the shop. "You can stay with us. It will make the morning easier."

"You can't drive the extra five minutes to my apartment to get me?" Layne hooks her arm through mine. "I'm about to leave my girls. Tonight I stay with them."

I squeeze her arm. The four of us haven't always gotten along, but when it comes down to it, we love Layne. She's one of us.

We thank her parents for the ice cream and say goodnight, then I give us a ride back to our apartment. We put on a movie and spend the evening making fun of it and laughing until we nearly burst, and I can almost ignore the aching hole in my heart left by the boys no longer in my life.

I'm not going to analyze which one I'm missing the most.

We fall asleep in the living room. I wake up to Camila cooking in the kitchen. Iris sits at the kitchen table munching a bowl of cereal. I look over to the spot on the floor where Layne slept rolled up in her fluffy blanket.

She's gone.

I stumble to the bathroom and wash up, then take a moment to study my reflection. I feel so old, but the girl peering back at me glows with youthful innocence and exuberance.

Ha. Appearances can be deceiving.

I return to the living room and stand in the middle of our apartment, surveying the old green couch, the beanbag, and the TV set up on a dresser. "Where did we get these things?"

"Second-hand store," Iris says, not looking up from her bowl of cereal.

That explains why everything looks shabby and nothing matches. "We need to move the TV."

Iris lifts her head as I grab the dresser and grunt with the effort to pull it away from the wall.

"Why?"

"So I can put the fish tank here." I gesture beside it.

Her eyebrows lift, and she laughs. "Of course. I forgot about them."

She dumps her cereal bowl and comes over to help me move it. "What will you put the tank on?"

I wipe my brow. We have the balcony doors open, but it's hot with little breeze. And so dry. I miss the Brazilian humidity. "I'll stop by the store and get a little table."

"Go to Goodwill. Don't pay full price."

"Sound advice."

I grab my purse and head for the door. "Do you think—" and then I halt, cutting my sentence in half.

"What?" Iris asks.

"I was going to see if anyone wants to go with me," I say slowly.

I was going to ask if Jared might want to go with me.

I miss him quite suddenly. I hadn't known I would. But Jared was more than just my friend. He was my companion, my supporter. My confidant.

My almost-boyfriend.

"You could ask any of the boys on the other side," Iris says, unaware of my thoughts. And I can't tell her, because she crushed on Jared most of the year and probably doesn't know he kissed me. "Several of them have mentioned being eager to meet you. They thought you looked hot." She points to the pictures from last year taped on the wall. I have long hair in them and look quite different.

"Okay," I say, but I'm not bold enough to wander over to the houses of unknown boys and ask one to come along with me.

So I drive by myself to Goodwill and pick out a small table and then head to Stirling's apartment.

Stirling is safe. I can be assured that he feels nothing for me, and I know I feel nothing for him.

I wonder after I park if I should have called first. Stirling and I worked together last year, and he coerced his roommate into caring for my fish while I was in Brazil. But Wyatt and I barely know each other. What if Stirling isn't there and I'm forced to communicate with Wyatt?

Wyatt answers the door when I knock. His blond hair stands out like it needs a cut and hasn't been combed in days, giving him an eccentric-student look. He blinks like he's not sure who I am, and then recognition crosses his features. "Cassandra, hey!" he says. "How are you?"

He steps back to let me in, and I close my eyes as we walk into the cool entryway. Ah, air conditioning. Not something our cheap apartment has. But Stirling lives a more posh life, his condo roomier, more updated, and more expensive.

"Great! I've come for my fish."

"Right, right, this way." Wyatt leads the way to the kitchen, and he takes a deep breath before entering it. "I'm sorry to tell you this, but one of them died."

He casts me a guilty look, but I brush it off.

"Only one? That's great!"

"Really?" He brightens with relief. "Oh, good, I was so nervous about it."

"No." I laugh. "Those suckers are so hard to keep alive." I smile when I see the tank. These annoying little fish make me happy. The tetras swim around, their neon colors bright under the lamp. And the sucker fish are fat and keeping the walls clean. We still have Moby . . . "Dick died."

"Huh?"

"Dick." I gesture to the tank. "That's the fish that died."

"Oh. You named him Dick?"

"Layne did. You had to know her." I smirk.

"Ah." He nods.

"But Jared and Justin are still alive." We named the fish after the two boys who haunted our apartment, and again I miss Jared. Who am I going to call on to hang out with now? I wonder if I should write him, but I dismiss the idea. I don't need to pursue another quasi-romantic relationship with another boy who isn't here.

"Do you need help?" Wyatt asks as I set my supplies on the counter.

"No. I've got this." I brandish the small net and baggies I brought for capturing the fish.

"Gotcha. Just let me know."

I realize then I haven't seen Stirling. "Is Stirling here?"

"No, I think he went camping with some friends. But I'll tell him you came by."

"Thanks." Maybe I'll hang out more with Stirling. My cousin Jordan will be back for fall semester, but that's three months away.

Unless he decides to leave on a mission trip before then. He thought he might go this year, but last I talked to him, he hadn't filled out an application yet.

The little fish are sneaky, hiding behind rocks and disappearing into the tall fake grass every time I try to capture them, but eventually I get them. Once they're safe in their plastic baggies, I dump out the fish water in the kitchen sink, which is gross and Stirling might not appreciate, but he's not here to discourage me.

I wash my hands and clean his counter and notice a beautiful frame of a nearby church by the sugar canister. It's a white-washed, simple building that reminds me of one I used to visit in Arkansas. I swallow past the emotion rising in my throat and focus on the yellow canister behind it.

Seriously. Who has sugar canisters in college?

I take the frame. I find a pen and paper in a drawer and scribble a message.

Hey, Stirling!!! I came by and got my fish. I also took your picture of the church. Thanks!!

Half an hour later I have the fish loaded up in my car and ready to go.

"Bye!" I call to Wyatt. I wait for an answer, but when there is none, I let myself out. All the baggies of fish are inside the waterless tank, and I carry it very carefully to my car. I don't want to lose it.

The process of setting them up again in my apartment brings back a sense of security and control. I stand back to look at them once I have the tank arranged on the small table, the little fishies swimming in their clean water. I stick the frame of the church behind the tank so it looks like they'

re swimming through it. I love it. "Welcome home, guys," I whisper to them, and I sigh.

I'm home too.

My phone rings. I dig it out of my pocket while I pull a chair over so I can sit in front of the fish tank. I check the caller before I answer.

Monica.

CHAPTER TWENTY-ONE

The Hottie

Oh, Monica! How long has it been since I've talked to her? She's one of my dearest friends, but she's also Owen's sister. She and I didn't have a falling out after Owen and I broke up, but talking to her became more painful, and I avoided it.

I'm past that now. I answer immediately. "Monica!" I exclaim. "I'm so happy to hear from you!"

"Yeah?" She gives a delighted laugh. "Would you be happy to see me?"

"Are you kidding me? Of course I would be! Are you here?"

"I switched schools. I'm going to the community college near you."

"What?" I'm astonished. "And you didn't tell me?"

"It was a last-minute decision."

"Where are you?" I go to the big window in my room, half expecting to see her outside my apartment. But she doesn't know where I live.

"I'm still in Utah. I'll be there in a week, though."

"Are you looking for housing?" I think of the vacant rooms in my apartment.

"No, a friend of mine from high school is out there. I'll be staying with her. Probably about ten minutes from where you are."

I pace the worn carpet in my room. "I can't believe it. This is awesome. We'll get to hang out!"

"Yeah, it's going to be great. I can't wait to see you!"

We make plans to meet up, and I set to work unpacking from Brazil.

Time to find out who I am now.

I spend a few days readjusting to living on my own, the responsibility that comes with maintaining a house, cleaning, accommodating people. I go to the bookstore to get my books and a new backpack a few days before summer term starts, but my mind feels ill-prepared for the coming stress.

The first day arrives with unexpected speed. I'm only taking three classes. I thought it would be easy, but by the end of the day, I know I once again underestimated the rigor of the classes at PYU. It's invigorating to sit at a desk, but the classes will be demanding.

I feel the tension building in my veins.

I'm also broke and refuse to live off ramen like I did last year. I stop by the employment center and begin the arduous process of applying for jobs. I know I could go back to the call center and get hired, but I'm done with that. No more calling people and bugging them for money, even if it's for a good cause, like the scholarships that help pay my tuition. It's someone else's turn.

I fill out eight different applications. Most are meaningless, jobs in any department I can find, something to pay the bills.

But there is one I would like to get. The receptionist job at the Department of Students with Special Needs. I've done a lot of volunteer work with kids and special services, and my heart burns with the desire to know them, to meet them, to help them.

I hope that's the job I get.

Then I put my backpack on and begin the walk home.

Our apartment is much farther from campus than the dorms were. I thought I had it bad last year when it took ten minutes to get to campus. Now it's anywhere from twenty-five to thirty minutes, depending on the traffic lights.

"I have to get used to this," I grumble to myself as I walk. At least my short hair isn't clinging to my neck.

My phone beeps with a text, and I pull it from my pocket at the light. It's from Monica. She moved in four days before the term started, but we haven't seen each other yet.

M: almost there. What's your address?

I type it out for her and quicken my pace. I don't want her to beat me home.

She doesn't, luckily. I walk into the apartment and find it like it usually is: Iris cooking while Camila studies at the table, and Tracie standing on the balcony talking across the courtyard to her fiance. I greet them and troop back to my room, where I turn around backward so my heavy backpack can slide onto the bed.

One problem of being an English major is the books are fatter than my waist.

The doorbell rings, and then Camila yells, "Cassandra!"

I bolt out of the room, already smiling in anticipation of seeing Monica.

Except it's not Monica. It's Stirling.

"Stirling!" I exclaim in complete surprise. "I didn't expect you!"

"You took my church," he says, his eyes crinkling in a smile. "I figured that meant I could track you down." His eyes flick to my hair. "Wow, you chopped it off."

"I did." I gesture him in. "How'd you get my address?"

"The student directory."

"Smart." I updated my info yesterday. "I hope you don't want your picture back. I'm using it."

He follows my gaze to the fishtank and gives an appreciative laugh. "I see it's been put to good use."

I study him while he studies the fish. Stirling is only slightly taller than me and has dark brown, slightly wavy hair. His skin is fair, and he has a smattering of freckles across his nose I don't recall from last spring. He's not unattractive, but there has never been any chemistry between us.

A knock comes on our open door, and this time when I turn, it's Monica who stands there.

Behind her is one of the hottest guys I've ever seen. Skin tanned to a golden hue, high cheek bones and light brown eyes peering directly at me.

I cut my eyes from Hottie back to Monica before he catches me staring.

"Monica!" I dart past Stirling to hug her, but she catches me before I do and holds me out in front of her.

"You cut your hair!" she gasps.

"You noticed!"

She lets me hug her. She's much taller than me, approaching six foot, which is only slightly shorter than her brother.

"Stirling," she says, giving him a wave when she releases me. They met once last fall. "You're the one they call Grandpa."

That makes him laugh. "I felt a bit old when I hung out with the freshmen."

"You don't seem so old now that we're not freshmen," I say.

"Hey, I know you," Stirling says to the boy behind her. "We were in the same apartment complex a few years ago. Mitchell, right?"

"Yeah, I remember," Mitchell says.

Even with his T-shirt on, I see that he's ripped. Like, rippling forearm muscles, corded neck muscles. His arms bow away from his sides like they're swollen and can't touch his waist.

"Good to see you again," he says.

"Yep." Stirling turns to me. "I'll leave you to your company. Give me a call later."

"Sure." I grab Monica's arm and haul her inside. Mitchell follows. I thought he was her boyfriend, but now that I see their height difference, I'm not so sure. He's about five inches shorter than her.

"And this is?" I shoot her a questioning glance.

"Oh, sorry!" she exclaims. "I forgot you don't know each other! Mitchell, this is Cassandra, my best friend from Arkansas."

"Hi, Mitchell." I barely refrain myself from lifting up to kiss both his cheeks, a custom I picked up in Brazil after introductions are made.

His cheeks are very kissable.

I move over to the couch and curl up in the corner, and they settle on the other end. "How do you guys know each other?" I ask.

"I'm so bad at introductions," Monica says. "Mitchell's my cousin."

I lift an eyebrow. Cousin.

"And he lives here in your apartment complex!" Monica adds.

"Here?" I glance out at the balcony where Tracie still chats with her fiance.

"Yeah, on the other side," Mitchell says.

"That's so cool!" And he's so hot. I turn my eyes to Monica and level her with a stare. How could she withhold this information from me?

"Monica says you just got back from Brazil," Mitchell says, directing my attention back to him.

"Yes."

"Was it fun? What were you doing there?"

"Visiting some old friends and working on my Portuguese. I'm minoring in it."

"That's awesome! I'm minoring in French. I served a mission in France and I love the language."

He speaks another language? He just got hotter. "I'd love to hear all about it."

Monica clears her throat. "Mitchell, it's been so great to see you, but I'm going to take Cassandra back to my apartment now."

We both look at her, and I blink to hide my surprise. This is the first I've heard of that. I thought she wanted to hang out at my place.

"Yeah, of course. I'll let you guys catch up." Mitchell stands. "Great to see you, Monica, can't wait to spend time together. Cassandra, I'll see you around."

"See you," I echo.

He can bet he will. I'll make sure of it.

"You don't have anything right now, do you?" Monica says. "My place is twenty minutes from here. I could use help unpacking."

"No, my evening's all yours!" I say. "I don't have a job yet. Just school."

"School, ugh. A necessary evil."

"In total agreement with you there. Why did I think I needed further education?"

"Right?"

We laugh and head out of my apartment together. I smile at the sight of her little Toyota parked out front.

"So what made you decide to come to school here?" I ask.

"I needed a change of pace. My school was too small and after my boyfriend and I broke up, it felt crowded. Almost claustrophobic. My friend from high school is out here, and she invited me to room with her. And of course I knew you were here, and Mitchell, and it sounded like a good opportunity, so I said yes."

"I'm so happy you're here!"

"Yeah, I hope life doesn't get so busy we never see each other."

We climb into her car, and Monica does a u-turn to take us back to the main road.

"Pssh." I wave that off. "I've got nothing going on."

"No boyfriend?"

"No. No boyfriend."

"How was Brazil?"

I settle back in my seat. "Brazil or Tiago?"

She smiles without looking at me. "Tiago, I suppose."

"He was good. He's a wonderful person, but we are so different. We could never make it work."

She exhales. "At least you know."

We fall into silence as I contemplate my next questions. I'm not sure how to ask, if I'm even allowed to. But she doesn't provide the information for me, so I finally say, "How's Owen?"

"Oh, are you asking about my little brother?"

I ignore her jibe. "Did he get off to Chicago okay?"

She nods. "Yes. He finished out his semester and left a few days ago for Chicago."

I don't tell her I know. "Did he seem happy?"

"Very. He's excited."

"Good. He'll be an amazing missionary."

"Yeah, he will. He gets people."

I run out of things to say about him. Except . . . "I miss him."

Monica shoots me a glance. "Do you?"

I give her an incredulous stare.

She laughs. "Don't look at me like I'm stupid for asking."

"You know how I feel for him."

"You cut him out of your life, Cassandra. You wouldn't take his calls or answer his texts—"

"He called me?" I interrupt.

"Well, yes—"

"When?"

"Your birthday."

I remember the message she delivered to me on his behalf. "When else?"

"The day before he left."

I turn to her, and my heart swells. "He did?"

"He knew you wouldn't answer. That's what he said when he hung up. And he acted like it was no big deal, but I knew he really wanted to talk to you. Just to hear your voice before he left."

I don't say anything. Not only was Owen blocked, but I was in Brazil with my cellular data turned off.

He never would have reached me.

Unless I knew he was trying to.

My experience in Brazil would have been very different if Owen and I were still together.

"Do you know how our break up happened?" I ask.

"I know Owen broke up with you. But he thought you'd still be friends."

"I couldn't be friends. Not after what he did."

"What did he do?" She says it in a hushed tone, like she's afraid of spooking me.

"He made me promises for the future, promises about us. And then he broke them all."

"And now you'll never be able to talk to him again?"

"I wrote him," I say quietly.

She brightens. "You did?"

"I hope it's all right. He told me he wanted to be able to focus. I hope I didn't screw that up by writing him."

"He'll be so relieved!"

"You said he was happy."

"Yes. Happy and excited."

Without me. He's doing fine. Great, even.

"I'm glad he remembers me," I say.

Now she's the one who gives me a look like I'm stupid.

"If you thought he'd forget you, you don't know Owen."

I keep quiet.

I want to think I knew Owen. But I'm not sure.
And if I did know him, I don't know who he is now.
People change a lot in a few months. More in two years.

EPISODE 2 :

Fish in the Sea

CHAPTER TWENTY-TWO

Learning Things

I stand at the far side of the soccer field, my hands on my knees while I pant for breath.

It's only a practice, but I'm dying.

The ball comes my way, and I dart out to get it. My feet remember these maneuvers from my grade school days, and I successfully intercept the ball and pass it to my teammate, Sara.

And then I wheeze from the effort of running to get it as I head back to my position in front of the goal.

When practice is over, we stand around chatting, and I go over to Iris.

"Why," I groan, "did we sign up for soccer?"

"It was your idea," she says. Her long black hair is pulled into a ponytail at the nape of her neck, and her cheeks are red and flushed. "You said soccer would be fun."

"Soccer *is* fun. When you're in shape. Not when you just spent a month in Brazil doing nothing except eating rice and beans and chocolate candy."

She laughs with me. I splash water from my bottle on my face, and we fist bump the other kids on our way out. There's a few cute guys on the team. I eye them as we leave.

Iris elbows me. "Stop checking out every guy we see."

"I'm seriously shopping," I reply. "I have to figure out what my options are before I buy anything."

"Just remember, some things you can't return."

I grunt. "Hence why I'm being careful."

We start down the south side of campus, which will lead us to the street we need to get home.

"Not going to the library tonight?" she asks.

"No. They switched my Portuguese class and now I can't take it." I scowl in displeasure. "So I threw in a religion class, but I haven't been yet, so I don't have homework."

"And you're caught up on English?" She looks at me like she doesn't quite believe me.

"For today. I just have to—" I stop walking. "Oh, crap. I forgot I have an outline due tomorrow."

She salutes me. "See you at home."

I groan as I turn for the stairs and climb to the upper part of campus where the library is.

The library closes at ten, but I finish my outline a little after nine. By the time I get to my apartment, it's past nine-thirty. But I can tell as I climb the stairs that no one's in bed. Apartment doors are wide open, letting the bugs in, and the lights and sounds of laughing students flood the corridor. I'm not surprised by the cacophony that greets me as I step into my apartment, though it does add another layer of exhaustion onto my already overworked brain. Chatter surrounds me, and I have to stand there for a moment to take it in.

The social hub of Preston Yarborough University is right here in our living room. Or maybe that's an exaggeration. But it certainly feels like it tonight. Twenty people are crammed into our living space, sitting on every available surface and the carpeted floor, while others congregate at the counter where they can reach the bowl of popcorn.

"Cassandra!" Camila cries out from somewhere behind the hordes of bodies as she spots me in the doorway. "Come join us! We're watching 'The Bachelor.'"

"That's what got you guys riled up?" I ask with raised brows.

She waves her hand dismissively. "The show is lame. It's the watch party we love."

I weave my way through the maze of legs and bags and bottles until I find Camila perched on the arm of a chair. There's no more room left on the couches, so I slip into the two-foot by three-foot square directly in front of her where nobody else has ventured yet. She grins down at me.

"I swore I was going to stay away from these things," I say.

"Well, look at you now." Her eyes sparkle as she leans forward.

"Aren't you glad you stayed, Cassandra?" says a voice from beside me, and I turn my head to see a pair of khaki shorts-covered legs. They move aside, which intrigues me enough to follow them upward until I can put a face to the body.

Mitchell.

He's as hot as I remember from last time, with his bronzed skin, high cheekbones, and light brown eyes. The shirt can't hide the bulge of his biceps beneath the sleeves.

Monica introduced him to me last week. He's her cousin.

He scoots over on the couch, making a space between him and Camila, and pats it. "There's room for you up here," he says.

I'd rather sit there than on the floor, so I climb into the space. Now I'm squished hip to hip next to them. "You remembered my name," I say.

He grins, showing me both dimples. "Of course I did."

"Wouldn't you rather watch this show in your apartment?"

"And miss out on your sharp wit? Why would I do that?"

Now he's got me smiling too. My heart rate accelerates, but I force myself to remain calm. He probably talks like this to everyone.

"What's your major?" he asks.

"English with a Portuguese minor."

"Wow," he says, blinking. "What grade are you in?

"I'm a sophomore."

The television show blares in front of us, completely forgotten. The Bachelor makes some critical decision, throwing the room into temporary chaos while everyone shouts in outrage or approval, depending who they were rooting for before this moment. I ignore it and focus on the boy next to me instead.

"What about you?" I ask, swatting his knee lightly. "Why are you here?"

"I ran into Camila in the hallway and she invited me."

"One more girl for you to juggle, huh?" I don't know where I get the courage to say that. Or the audacity.

He doesn't bat an eye when he says, "Nah, she's not on my list."

Is he joking? Against my better judgment, I decide to push. "How many girls are you juggling?"

"None, at the moment."

He holds my gaze, and for a moment I can't remember what I was going to say.

"What's your maximum number?" I ask.

"Of girls to juggle?"

"Yes."

"Are you making a list for me?"

"Maybe."

"Three."

"Why that number?"

A shrug. "I can handle three dates in a week. Four gets exhausting."

I snort. "So after four weeks, you drop one and pick up someone new?"

"Depends on the girl. Some need five weeks. Others only last two."

I have no idea if he's serious. "So you're a player."

"No. I'm a human being figuring out what I want."

"And those poor ladies thought you loved them when all you cared about was how much longer you had to endure their company."

He bursts into laughter, clutching his chest as though to keep his heart inside. People turn to stare at us, but neither of us cares. "Can't let an innocent young woman fool me," he says.

"Nope. Can't do that. Women are unpredictable creatures."

"You can say that again." He leans toward me. "Here's a secret, brave crusader. Those innocent young women break more hearts than you would guess. It's the boys you should be protecting."

And now I know that behind all the joking, we've gotten to the truth.

He's got heartache in his past.

Well, so do I.

⊙〜❀〜⊙

Sunday is probably the first time I've ever called church fun.

I enjoy going to church. It's a place of solace, of refuge, of acceptance, no matter where I am in my life.

But today, as the entire congregation is made up of the two halves of my apartment complex, fifty percent female and fifty percent male, church is fun.

We meet in a small theater attached to the music building. Before the sermon starts, we crowd together in the aisles and pews, laughing and joking in voices that my mother would call irreverent.

Nobody silences us. The fact that a hundred college kids chose to get up and come to church today makes up for the fact that we're noisy.

"Excuse me. Excuse me."

I hear a girl pushing her way through the boys around our chairs, bumping into others as she tries to cut a path. I slide my head out to catch a glimpse of her. She's my height with short, stunning red hair, and a perfect face with dimples that appear on either cheek when she smiles, which is often because she can't seem to speak without smiling.

"Abby!" I cry.

Iris and Camila turn as well, and then the three of us rush her and embrace her.

"I didn't think you'd be here for a few more weeks!" I say, pulling back to study my beautiful, vivacious friend.

Abby rolls her eyes. "Let me tell you, there's nothing to do back home. It made a lot more sense to come out here, get settled, get a job."

I nod. "I agree. Though I've had three interviews and no job offer yet." I make a face.

She reaches over and cups the bottom of my hair. "You did not tell me you cut off your hair!"

"She told no one," Iris says.

"Surprise." I shrug. "It was an impulse buy."

"I love it! It's so sexy."

"Tiago thought so too," I say, which is more than I meant to say. My face grows hot as I remember how sexy he thought it was.

Only Abby catches it, throwing me a questioning look as we file into our seats. "Isn't that the friend you visited in Brazil?"

"Yes," I say, working hard at my poker face. "But that's all he is."

I say it too quickly, and I can tell she wants to ask me more, but then the preacher gets up.

That calm reverence I was expecting settles over us. There it is. I'm amazed how quickly everyone quiets, and the sweet spirit of worship and devotion replaces the congenial joviality of earlier.

I love the change. I love how we can be both rambunctious and spiritual.

⟡

Monday night I drive out to the airport to pick up my little sister. She had to fly with an airline companion since she's so young, but I have the proper identification when I arrive, and they release her to me. We hug and then I take her hand and pull her from the airport.

"The mountains are so grand!"

Annette keeps dancing around in a circle, staring at the mountains, and I laugh as I tug her over to my car.

"You're going to see lots of them this week."

"Can we go hiking? Maybe see a waterfall?"

"We can definitely do that."

First I take her grocery shopping. We pick out foods she'll enjoy, and she gets excited when she sees the fresh cherries. I buy a pound, but she wants more, so she uses her own money to buy two more pounds. We munch on them while I drive and spit the pits out the windows.

"This is your apartment?" She gawks when I park. I can almost see the stars in her eyes.

"Yeah. Cool, huh?"

To make it cooler, a dozen boys lean out their balconies, peering into the courtyard as we walk by. They call out to me.

"Hey, Cassandra! Who's that?"

"Is that your sister, Cassandra?"

"Did you get me food, Cassandra?"

I wave at them and call out, "This is my little sister, Annette!"

A chorus of hellos and her name rises around us, and her mouth is hanging open when I pull her into the stairwell.

"Do they all know you?"

"We know everyone." But still, it made me look pretty cool when they called out to me. I send them my mental gratitude.

"Hi, guys!" I say when I enter my apartment. My roommates look up from the couch. "This is my sister, Annette!"

"Hi!" Iris says. "Nice to meet you!"

"Hi, Annette!" Camila hugs her. "You've grown!"

Abby waves from the kitchen table. "You're sharing a room with me."

"Fun." Annette stands there beaming, soaking it in. She gets to live like a college kid this week.

We treat her like one of us. We eat, goof around, then watch TV with Annette chilling there. A parade of boys comes over after dinner, like always.

"I'll wake you when I get up in the morning," I say. "If you want to go to class with me, that is."

"I do." Annette nods vigorously. "This is so fun."

I grin. "Yeah, it is."

CHAPTER TWENTY-THREE

Sister Visit

Annette rises early in the morning and walks with me to campus. We see people I know everywhere we go, and everyone stops to ask me who she is. She preens with the attention. She brings along a backpack and reads a book through my English class.

"Please get out your class supplies," my teacher says. Her round glasses and frizzy hair make me think she escaped from Hogwarts. "Put your two notebooks on your desk."

Two? I fumble through my bag, but I know I only bought one.

"What if we only have one?" a boy across the room asks.

She scowls at him. "Then you better have that rectified before our next class period."

Crap. I'm glad he took that bullet for me. I place my one notebook on the desk and put on my best apologetic expression as she walks around the room, checking out our supplies like we're in kindergarten. I hold my breath when she gets to my desk. She gives me the evil eye but doesn't say anything else.

Annette misses the entire exchange as she reads her book.

"Where's the bathroom?" she says when we leave class. "We do so much walking and I really need to go!"

"Come on, there's one in the cafeteria," I say, leading the way. "I need to get something from the bookstore."

I drop her off and then run upstairs to grab another notebook.

"Just one notebook?" says the cashier as he rings me up.

"Yeah. I missed one, somehow, and my English teacher wasn't pleased with that."

"Ah. English classes are important ones for notebooks. We sell a lot to them."

"And as an English major, I'm afraid I'm taking way too many English classes." I roll my eyes and take the notebook from him. "No bag, thanks."

"Hey, I'm an English major also," he says, turning toward me and keeping me from leaving. "It's not all it's cracked up to be."

"No, it's not," I agree, and we both laugh.

"Where are you off to now?" he says. "I'm off work in ten minutes. We could meet for lunch and bemoan the faults of our major."

Up to this point he's been another face in the masses to me, but I pause to really see him now. He looks much older, mid-twenties, at least, with dark brown hair and a round face and a slender physique.

"My sister's visiting me. I have to go now because I dropped her off at the restroom and told her I'd be right back."

"By all means, don't ditch her! But hey." He grabs a leftover receipt from his register. "Let me get your number, I'll call you."

"Sure." Just because there's no initial attraction doesn't mean it can't build.

"I'm John, by the way. So you know when I call."

"Of course." I give him my number, wave, and dash off, not wanting Annette to freak out when I'm still not there.

She's waiting outside the bathroom doors when I run up. "Sorry about that!" I huff. "Some guy wanted my number and I was trying to hurry."

"Did you give him your number?" Her eyes are wide.

"It's nothing." I shrug. "Guys ask all the time. It's like a hobby or something. They never call."

"Oh." She looks disappointed.

"Guys are weird. You'll get used to it. Come on."

I lead her down the hallway toward the cafeteria, following the scent of sliced meat and frying foods.

"There are so many places to eat," she says. "It's like the food court of a mall."

"It's exactly like that." I find a place for us to sit. "I used to eat lunch with Jordan, but he's not here over the summer."

"That's so cool! Maybe when I come here some of our cousins will be here also."

"You want to come here?" I'm so proud of my little sister.

"Yeah! Seems like a fun school."

"Hey! Cassandra. We meet again."

We both look up as a shadow crosses the table, and I give a start when I see Mitchell.

"Mitchell, hey! How are you?" Even in a simple blue T-shirt, he's hot. I watch Annette's eyes go buggy as she takes him in.

"I'm great." He grins and pulls out the third chair at our table. "Mind if I sit here?"

"No, go right ahead!" I gesture him forward. Please.

He turns to Annette and extends his hand, all formal. "Hi, I'm Mitchell. I take it your Cassandra's little sister?"

"Annette," she says, and she giggles, her face flushing pink.

I can't help but smirk.

"Nice to meet you. You look just like her."

I glance at Annette. She's a miniature version of me, though she got our dad's fairer coloring. Her skin is light and her hair a lighter brown.

Annette smiles. "I hope so." Her cheeks turn peek.

Mitchell keeps talking to her like he didn't notice. "So you came to spend a few days with your sister?" Annette nods. "Do you miss her while she's away at school?" She nods again. "What do you think of college so far?"

Annette looks at me like she wants me to answer for her. I purse my lips.

"You've taken away her ability to speak, Mitchell," I say.

He laughs. "Call me Mitch, Annette," he says, winking at her. "All my friends do."

"Mitch," she squeaks out.

He looks at me. "You too. Anyone who's Monica's friends is my friend."

Annette perks up at that. She glances from him to me, and I hold her gaze. Please, please don't say anything about Owen.

"And you can call me Cassandra," I say, which makes him laugh again.

He sits with us through lunch, getting food when we do and teasing Annette because she giggles at everything he says.

"It's not you," I tell him. "Don't start thinking you're really witty. She laughs at everything. Or cries. Or both."

Annette laughs so hard I think she's going to cry, and I gesture at her.

"Like now."

Mitch stands up, checking his watch. "You know what, I've got to get out of here. But let's do this again sometime, shall we? How long are you here, Annette?"

She whispers something, then lifts the collar of her shirt to hide her mouth as her face goes bright red. Oh, brother. She's pathetic.

"Through Sunday," I say.

Mitch offers me his fist. "See you before then."

I bump his fist with mine, and then he leaves.

Annette recovers, dropping the edge of her shirt. "He's *sooo* cute. Do you like him?"

"He's cute," I say. "And I might."

"So he knows Monica? Does he know Owen?"

"Yes." I lift my eyebrows. "They're cousins."

⌒〜✳︎〜⌒

The next few days keep me busy with classes and homework, and I feel bad I'm not doing anything fun with Annette. Friday I'm done with class by ten, so I take her out for Chinese food for lunch.

"So what happened with Owen?" she asks as we use chopsticks to pick at our orange chicken.

My stomach tightens, but I wondered when she was going to ask. Annette might be young, but Owen was a part of everything in my life, and subsequently a part of hers.

I shrug. "We broke up."

"I thought you were going to marry him." There's no mistaking the wounded tone of her voice.

"Oh, honey." I put my chopsticks down and look her square in the face. "You know this is how life goes, right? We fall in love, we break up, we fall in love, we break up. And each time we fall in love, we think we're going to marry that person. We can't imagine life without them. Until that's what life makes us do."

"But you loved him so much." Her eyes actually well up with tears.

"I'll tell you a secret," I say, lowering my voice. "I still love him. I probably always will. But that doesn't mean I get to be with him."

"You still love him?" She looks mildly appeased at my admission. Like she worried I'd discarded him as easily as a used tissue.

My heart squeezes at the very idea. "Yes. But life is forcing me not to be with him."

"So you're waiting for the next person you'll fall in love with."

I make a face. "Not exactly. Falling in love is fun but also sucks. Dating is fun without the suckage part. So I'm keeping it casual and having fun."

She nods. "Okay. That makes sense."

We both pretend like I have control over who I fall in love with. Maybe she thinks I do.

I eat so much I feel sick, and I whisper kind words to myself at the restaurant, my own gentle affirmations so I don't overreact because of how much food I put in my stomach. I fight the urge to run to the bathroom and purge the contents from my body.

It's been three years since I last made myself throw up, but I still feel like a recovering addict. The shadows of my past will always haunt me.

An unknown number calls me while I'm paying the bill. It's a local number, so I answer it as we walk to the car. "Hello?" I climb in the car and turn it on so Annette and I don't roast.

"Hi, is this Cassandra?"

It's a boy's voice, but I can't place it. "Hi, yes."

"This is John. We met at the bookstore a few days ago when you were buying a notebook?"

"Oh, hey!" I laugh. "I didn't think you would actually call."

"Really? Yeah, we have to talk English major stuff!"

"So exciting." The sarcasm doesn't come through across the phone. The car has cooled off enough that I roll the windows up and back us out of the parking lot.

"What's your emphasis?"

He really does want to talk about school stuff. "I haven't picked one yet."

"Oh. What year of school are you?"

"Sophomore. What about you?"

"I'm a senior."

"Nice! Almost done."

"So what are you doing tomorrow night?"

I search my brain. "Nothing, I don't think."

"A bunch of my friends are getting together for a barbecue and yard games. Want to join us?"

"If my sister can come." I grin at her.

"Your sister?" It's an odd request, but he goes with it. "Sure. What year is she?"

"She's in eighth grade. She's visiting me."

"Oh." He laughs. "The one you left by the bathroom. Yeah, of course! That'll be fun."

We make plans for him to pick me up tomorrow, then we hang up.

"So you have a date tomorrow?" Annette asks.

"We both do."

"Tomorrow's the third. Are we doing anything for the Fourth of July?"

"Someone will set off fireworks."

July third. Tiago's birthday. And I have a date.

I do not regret my decision to end things definitively with him. But I wish him a happy birthday with all my heart and wish there was some way for him to know without me contacting him.

July third is more than a month since Owen left on his mission.

I check the mail at my apartment when we arrive and tell myself not to be disappointed when there is nothing from him. It's only been three weeks since I sent the letter.

Maybe he won't write me after all.

Maybe he feels like I do toward Tiago. Some things are better left in the past.

CHAPTER TWENTY-FOUR

Guys Everywhere

Camila gets home from school a little after five, as I'm pulling food from the fridge to make dinner.

"I'm so hungry!" she exclaims. "Coach has us running doubles!"

"I don't know what that means, but it sounds terrible," I say. "I'm about to cook dinner. Want me to make something for you also?"

She eyes the canned chicken and dried noodles I've put out on the counter and wrinkles her nose.

"I've got money," she says. "Let's go to Applebee's."

"You want to eat out?"

"I'm treating everyone. Who's here?"

I nod my head down the hall. "Iris and Abby."

She goes down the hall to get them, and someone knocks on the front door.

"Can you get that?" I ask Annette. I open the cupboards and put away my food offerings.

Annette hops up and opens the door. "Hi, Mitch!" she says, and I spin around.

Sure enough, Mitch stands in the doorway. He grins at her.

"Told you I'd see you before you go."

He holds out his fist and she bumps it, and I come over, wiping my hands on a rag.

"What's up?" I push the door open wider. "Come on in!"

Camila reappears in the hallway, this time with Iris and Abby in tow.

"Hi, Mitchell!" she says, and she tilts her head, sending a sideways glance my way. "We're about to go to dinner. Do you want to come?"

"You're all going out?"

"Yeah. To Applebee's." Camila counts our heads. "Except if you come, we'll need another car."

"I can squish four in the back," I say. I'll happily do so if it means Mitch comes with us.

But he backs out of the apartment. "This looks like a girls' night, and I don't want to intrude. What time will you be back?"

He turns to me when he asks, and I look at Camila, who shrugs.

"We don't have a set time," she says.

"Well, I'll call you," he says. "My friends and I are hanging out. We might see a movie. You can come."

"That sounds fun," I say, wishing my roommates weren't standing around us gawking.

"Great. Bye."

He bails, and even though we're about to leave, Camila closes the door and busts out laughing.

"That was so awkward!" she says.

"It wasn't that bad," I say.

"He practically invited himself to dinner with us," Iris says, and she looks annoyed.

"We invited him," I say, annoyed that she's annoyed.

"But only to be polite," Abby says. "We didn't want a boy with us."

"Which he picked up on, luckily," Camila says. She opens the door, and we troop down the stairs to my car. "Poor guy."

I don't say anything, but I wish Mitch had come. I hope he didn't pick up on any awkwardness.

My roommates want to go to a movie after dinner. I keep checking my phone to see if Mitch has called, but he hasn't. The night is young. We might be able to hang out still, but not if I go to a movie.

"I've got homework," I say. "I need to get back."

"You study too much," Abby says with a sigh. "Fine."

"We can watch a movie on the couch," Camila says.

"I can do that," I say.

We head back to our apartment to sift through our streaming options. We're too poor to have our own cable account, but all of us have parents who have generously donated access to their accounts, which leaves us with a plethora of choices. Tracie, my engaged roommate who spends more time at her fiancé's apartment than over here, is outside on the balcony, and I take my leftovers to her.

"Hungry?" I ask, offering the rest of my chicken quesadilla. "You weren't here when we went to dinner."

"Oh, thanks!" She accepts it, and I lean against the balcony railing, blinking up into the evening sunshine above us.

"Have you guys set a date?" I ask. Even though she's my roommate, she's like a ghost, rarely in the apartment.

"For the wedding?" She shakes her head. "Maybe late summer."

"But that's only weeks away."

She shrugs. "Once you decide you want to be together, why wait?"

I ponder that. I suppose there's truth in the statement. I can recall various moments in my life when I was ready to forgo fancy extras and beautiful gowns and long guest lists just for the chance to put a ring on our fingers and permanently seal the connection between us. "But you only get married once, right?"

"That's the plan," she agrees.

"Hey! Up there on the second floor balcony!"

It takes me a moment to realize that means us. The words hit Tracie at the same moment, and we both lean over the edge.

A man stands on the sidewalk in the commons, in his early twenties and clearly of Latino descent. He's thicker in the neck and chest with tanned skin and dark brown hair. He tilts his head, looking up at us.

"Yes?" Tracie asks.

He points at me. "What's your heritage?" He speaks perfect English, but with that crispness to the vowels that indicates it's not his only language.

"Me?" I put my hand on my chest.

"Yes, you!"

He didn't ask my nationality, which means he's more politically aware than most people. I'm American, and it's what I tell everyone who asks that question.

But he wants my ethnic background, because I, like him, have a darker coloring that makes me just different enough to stand out in a place like Colorado, USA.

So I give him the answer he wants. "Colombian. You?"

His face lights up. "I'll be right up!"

He disappears from the courtyard, and Tracie and I both turn from the balcony with an air of curious expectation.

The front door is open, like usual when we're hanging out at home. Our open-door policy makes it so people can come and go as they please, and the frequent, unannounced visitors is one of my favorite parts about living off campus. My other roommates have settled on a movie, and they barely glance up when he pops in.

"Hi!" he says, bypassing the living room and joining Tracie and me on the balcony. He extends his hand. "I'm Victor. I'm half-Guatemalan, and I don't see a lot of Latinos on campus."

"Hi," I say, taking his hand.

He squeezes my fingers and uses his grip to pull me in and kiss both cheeks, Latin-style. "I had to meet you. Hopefully I'll see you around campus. What's your name?"

"Cassandra," I say.

He releases my hand and bends his head in a pseudo bow. "Cassandra, *mucho gusto*."

Oh, Spanish. This is a language I haven't used much lately. "*Igualmente*," I say.

He grins and leaves, and I'm amused and perplexed by the strange interaction.

"You must get tired of it," Tracie says.

I look at her. "Tired of what?"

"Guys fawning over you all the time."

I tilt my head. "Actually, this is new. It doesn't usually happen."

But it's definitely been a theme since I got back from Brazil.

I flash back to last summer and remember with a sharp pang Owen's prediction that this would happen. That I'd get to college and suddenly be noticed. He predicted it would catch me by surprise.

And he predicted I'd get back together with Tiago.

So far he's been right.

He also said I'd probably get married.

I hope he won't be right about everything.

Mitch doesn't call, and I spend the evening hanging out with my roommates and sister, who all seem to think I'm some kind of guy magnet. It's like they didn't live with me last year.

Annette comes into my room a little after eight on Saturday morning. I sit at my desk working on an English essay. She plops onto my bed, eating a bowl of cereal and kicking her feet like she's ten instead of thirteen.

"What are we going to do today?"

I pause mid-sentence. "Well. Saturday is usually when I catch up on homework."

"What are you doing *this* Saturday?"

I laugh at her obvious implication. Doing homework might be acceptable when it's just me, but when my little sister's visiting, I better find a more suitable Saturday activity. "What would you like to do?" I ask, turning to face her.

"Get outside. It's so beautiful. Let's go on a hike."

I shrug. "All right." I did some hiking last year as a freshman, but I know there's much more in the area I haven't explored. I pull up a website with local hikes. "There's a hike an hour from here that goes up one of the mountains to a cave. Want to do that?"

"Absolutely! I'll get my shoes."

She bounces away, and I call after her, "I have to finish this essay!"

Thirty minutes later I drive us out of the parking lot, heading toward the canyon.

"How many dates do you go on every week?" she asks.

"I don't, really. My first date since I got here is tonight."

"But there are always guys talking to you."

"Yeah, but usually nothing happens. It doesn't pan out. So you have to talk to lots of them."

"You seem to like Mitch."

I bob my head, keeping my eyes on the road. "I find him intriguing."

"He's cute."

"He's hot." I say the words without thinking, and then I blush. "And he's nice."

Annette laughs, and I ask, "Have you had your first kiss yet?"

She shakes her head. "No."

"No boyfriends?"

Another head shake. "No. Not so far."

She's only thirteen. Boys didn't begin to shape my life until high school. I never could have imagined at her age the trouble they would cause me.

"Don't rush it," I tell her. "It's so much simpler before you get one."

I don't expect the hike to be hard.

I wear hiking sandals, but it's their inaugural run, and half a mile into our hike up the mountain, I feel blisters at my heels and on the sides of my feet where the leather rubs. We wind up and up and up, taking sharp switch-back curves on a paved path made specifically for visitors coming to these caves.

"In the middle of a mountain!" I gasp out, pausing to wipe sweat from my face. "Why are there caves in the middle of a mountain?"

"It's really just the base," Annette says.

I glare at her. Devil's advocate. "Two miles up isn't the base."

She lifts an eyebrow. "It is when the mountain is sixteen miles tall."

"Why do you have to be right?" I grumble.

Benches line the path, and I stop to sit and rest as we pass the mile mark. Little chipmunks dart into our path. Annette throws scraps of her sandwich at them, even though I point out a dozen signs saying, *Please don't feed the wildlife.*

"How are you going to justify that one?" I say mockingly.

She shrugs. "They're not wild anymore."

It's true. When she bends down with the scrap of crust in her fingers, the chipmunk races right up to her, grabs the crust, and bolts away.

"That doesn't make it okay," I quip, but there's no real bite to my words.

We pause again at the one and a half mile mark. I sip water and pant as the sweat drips down my face.

"It must be hard to be old," Annette says, straight-faced, not winded at all. I grunt in affirmation.

"Half a mile left," she adds with an insipid, encouraging smile.

"I don't know how you talked me into this," I say.

"You promised me hiking and waterfalls," she says.

I did. There better be a waterfall on this hike so we can check off that promise.

I stand up and take ten steps, and then my phone rings. I'm glad for the excuse to stop again.

It's another unknown local number. Not John, because I saved his contact info last time. It could be anyone, thanks to the student directory that allows students to look each other up.

"Hello?" I answer, trying not to sound too winded.

"Cassandra! It's Mitch."

His cheerful, friendly voice fills the speaker, and my spirits lift immediately.

"Oh, hey!" I say.

You didn't call last night.

I don't say that. A lesson I learned late in life is guys don't like needy, desperate girls. So I have to act nonchalant, like I don't care.

"Did you have fun with your friends last night?" I say instead.

"Yeah." He laughs. "Sorry I intruded on your night out with the girls. I didn't mean to."

Curse my roommates, they did make him feel awkward. "You totally didn't. It was a last minute activity."

"All the same, I'll call ahead next time."

"Looks like you found my number."

"Guilty as charged."

I grin. Talking to him is fun. "Well, Mitch, I'd love to chat, but I'm actually hiking a mountain right now with my sister, so . . ."

"Annette! My favorite person. How are you, friend?"

I put the phone on speaker and hold it out. "He wants to know how you are," I say.

"I'm great," Annette calls toward the phone.

I take it off speaker. "So anyway, I should go now."

"Yeah! There I go, intruding again. What time do you think you'll get back?"

"Well, I'm slow-going up this mountain," I say. "So maybe another two hours of hiking, then an hour to get back . . . I'm thinking we'll be back before one."

"Want to do something tonight? Get some ice-cream?"

My heart somersaults.

Mitch is asking me out.

And I have to say no. Because I have my first date since last semester tonight.

CHAPTER TWENTY-FIVE

Boys and Church

"Hey, I'd really love to," I say, putting as much sincerity into my words as possible so Mitch will know I'm not blowing him off. "But I've already got plans."

"No worries. Don't stress it. Have fun on the mountain, okay?"

He hangs up before I even respond.

"Dang it!" I say, shoving my phone into my back pocket.

"What? What happened?" Annette asks.

"He wanted to go out tonight," I say. "And I can't, because I already have a date!"

"Oh," she says. "I guess you can't cancel one for the other."

"No." I shake my head. "And now he thinks I blew him off. I don't know if he'll ask again."

"If he does, you have to tell me."

We finish hiking the last half mile up to the blasted caves, with me cursing the sun and the heat and my burning calves with each step.

But once we get inside, the cave is colorful and cold.

"Was it worth it?" Annette asks as we stand in the mouth of the cave, the refrigerated air inside soothing our hot bodies.

"I'm glad we came," I admit. "Though I don't know if I would do it again. At least, not anytime soon."

Annette laughs at me.

The hike down is nothing like the hike up. It takes us less than half the time, and even though my knees buckle with the impact of each step, it doesn't hurt my body like going uphill.

There's a gift shop at the bottom of the mountain, and we both get ice cream.

"That was fun," I say. It's a lot easier to feel that way now that I'm not drenched in sweat and we're at the end of our journey.

"But we never saw a waterfall," Annette says.

I groan.

I want to call Mitch when we get back to my apartment, or even head over to his apartment, something I've never done before. But it feels wrong, seeing as how I'm going on a date with another boy in a few hours. So I don't call him.

"What should I wear tonight?" Annette asks when I tell her to get ready for our outing.

I shrug as I peruse my closet. "John said it's a barbecue. I'm guessing a T-shirt should be fine. Maybe some jeans because it gets cold at night."

"Oh. I wouldn't have thought of that. It doesn't get cold back home."

I think of the warm humid summer nights in Arkansas. And then I'm thinking of a particular warm humid night in the back of Owen's truck, and the flesh on my arms pops up. I should not let my thoughts go that way.

When will I be over him? And why doesn't he write me?

Are those thoughts contradictory?

It's best not to think too much when it comes to affairs of the heart. Logic gets in the way.

Annette puts her hair in a ponytail, but mine is too short for that. I secure the side with a pretty butterfly clip, and hope I didn't age myself down to eight years old.

John knocks at my door at precisely five-thirty, and I congratulate him on his punctuality when I open it.

"I've learned the importance of making a good impression," he says.

"Not something to be underestimated," I agree.

"Like you. You made an excellent first impression."

My face warms under the compliment, and then he adds, "The second impression is going well too. I like the butterfly."

"Thank you." I smile and hope I don't look as nervous as I feel. I always get anxious on a first date.

His car is a small blue Volkswagen. He opens the back door for Annette, and I see he already cleared one side of the car so she would have room.

"Here you go," he says to her.

"Thanks," she says, her face flushing pink.

I try not to giggle. My little sister is enamored with the boys.

He drives us into the foothills of the mountains ten minutes away where the permanent residents with more money than college students make their homes. A number of cars are parked outside one house overlooking the valley. He joins the line of cars, and then he hops around to open my door. I get out and wait while he lets Annette out also.

"How well do you know these people?" I ask.

"Really well. I grew up with their son."

That's good. I won't feel like we're hanging out at a stranger's house.

He leads us around the side of the house.

A large table has been set out on the lawn and decorative lights strung over the backyard. At least twenty other college kids mill about the area, laughing, talking, eating. John puts his hands on my shoulders and gives them a squeeze before steering me in the direction of his friends.

"Guys, this is Cassandra. She's an English major also."

They turn toward me, a mixture of boys and girls who look a few years older than me, but they smile warmly and greet me.

"Hi, Cassandra."

"Nice to meet you, Cassandra!"

"You're both English majors, huh?" one boy says.

"Did you try the macaroni and cheese yet? It's so good."

"Mac and cheese?" Annette's eyes light up, and she moves away from us toward the table.

"Is that your little sister?" a girl asks me.

I nod. "She's visiting me from Arkansas. I didn't want to leave her alone."

"That's so cute. I'm Alisha."

"Arkansas!" a boy says. "I didn't know people actually lived there!"

I keep my smile in place, but I feel it straining. People think they're hilarious, always making fun of Arkansas. It's like they don't realize they're insulting the people who live there and like it.

"I'm going to take Cassandra to try that amazing mac and cheese," John says, and he pulls me away.

"You all right there?" he asks as we leave. "It felt like you got a bit tense."

I'm surprised he noticed. "It gets old, everyone making Arkansas the butt of their jokes."

He purses his lips and looks thoughtful. "I never thought about that. I'll make sure I never do that."

"Changing the world, one person at a time," I joke, but I'm not really joking. Hopefully every person I meet at college will think differently about Arkansas after knowing me.

We find Annette at the serving table. She has her plate loaded with one hotdog and probably three helpings of macaroni and cheese. I laugh and tell John, "Annette has a thing for mac and cheese. Every time we go to a restaurant, she avoids the Chinese food or the Japanese food or the Mexican food and always asks for macaroni and cheese."

"It's good stuff," John says, and he offers her his knuckle.

She bumps it with her own, and I feel a surge of gratitude that these college kids are so willing to include my little sister.

I consume macaroni and cheese and the better part of a hamburger until I can't get anything else in my belly. A few people leave as the sun goes down, and those of us who remain draw our chairs close together in a circle. I'm not very conversational around people I don't know, but I'm content to sit and listen to the jokes and stories everyone shares.

The crickets come out, their happy chirping filling the twilight air. I miss the throaty hum of the cicadas.

"Who's up for night games?" a tall, thin boy with light blond hair named Kent asks.

"What kind of games do you have in mind?" Alisha asks.

"You know, games like kick the can, hide and go seek."

A flurry of excited chatter breaks out among the kids, and John leans over to ask me, "What's your favorite night game?"

I think about it for a second and shake my head. "I'm not sure I've ever played any."

He draws back to stare at me. "No?"

"No." Running around in the dark is a sure way to make sure someone ends up wounded in a hospital.

"Oh, you are in for a treat."

Raising his voice, he says, "Let's play kick the can! Cassandra's never played."

It's decided. We pile into cars and drive over to John's house because he has a large flat backyard.

It's pitch black. The middle of the yard slopes down toward the wooden fence that surrounds it. The slightly darker outlines are the only indication that the yard has trees.

"Okay, here are the rules of the game," John says. "It's like hide and seek, but in the dark. The point of the game is to get everyone in jail, so whoever's It has to find people. Once you're found, you sit right here." He points to a concrete porch behind the house. "And you're out. But you can get free if someone gets to the can before whoever's It does and kicks it over." He holds up a giant can of beans and places it in front of the "jail." "Got it?"

Not really. I understand that there's running and hiding right away because I'm terrible at both.

John's up first. He begins to count while the rest of us run and hide. I think it will be difficult to hide with so few trees and no outbuildings, but when I trip over a body lying on the ground, I realize it's much easier than it appears. I drop down beside them, and it's Alisha.

"Sorry!" I rasp. She grabs my hand to silence me, but we're both giggling.

John runs past us to a tree. I know it's him because his neon green shoes glow even in the dark, reflecting what little light there is. Someone yells by the tree, and John yells back, but I don't hear what they say because Alisha grabs my hand and jerks me up.

"Come on!" she says. And then she half drags me as we run for the opposite end of the backyard, where several people already sit in "jail." I yell as we arrive and Alisha kicks over the can of beans. Somebody grabs me and hugs me, fake sobbing, like a freed prisoner of war, and I can't stop laughing.

I'm not 100% certain on the rules of the game, but I have a lot of fun.

It's more than an hour later before John takes me and Annette home.

"Thanks for tonight," I say, unlocking the door to my apartment and letting Annette go inside. "I had tons of fun."

"Yeah, it was great," he says as he bends toward me. Like he might hug me. Or worse.

And I'm suddenly terrified of being touched, of leading him on, of making him think there might be a reason to pursue this when, as fun as it was, there are no sparks between us.

So I duck into my apartment as quick as I can and say, smiling brightly from the other side of the threshold, "Have a good night!"

Then I offer an enthusiastic wave before closing the door.

CHAPTER TWENTY-SIX

Wanting to Crush

I have two more job interviews on Monday, but as I walk home with Annette from the second one after school, I feel the pinch of stress creeping up my shoulders and into my neck. Why hasn't anyone hired me? I'm well-qualified. I even showered and put on deodorant this morning.

I try not to show my alarm to my sister, but not having enough money is like wearing a pair of jeans that are too small. No matter how you move, it pinches and rubs and is uncomfortable.

My apartment door is open when we arrive at home. I walk right in and see Mitch standing at the kitchen table, talking with Abby and Iris. A smile pushes its way onto my face, and I say, "Mitch!"

He turns around, and at the same time, I berate myself. He was talking to my roommates. Maybe he came over to see one of them. My heart sinks slightly as I see the big grin on Abby's face, one cheek dimpling.

But a smile spreads across his face, and he says, "Cassandra!" He moves around the table and hugs me.

I'm caught off guard because I thought it would feel like one of Owen's hug, but it doesn't. Mitch's arms are strong, but he's a lot shorter, and his embrace doesn't swallow me up like Owen's did.

Stupid girl. Stop comparing every boy to Owen.

It will stop, right?

He releases me and moves over to the couch. Annette goes to the kitchen for a snack, but I follow Mitch to the living room.

"Sorry I couldn't do something with you Saturday," I say, sitting down on the cushion and leaning into the armrest. "I already had plans, but I would've preferred hanging out with you."

He favors me with another smile. "You probably say that to all the guys."

I laugh. "I never reveal my secrets."

He taps my thigh with his knuckle. "You might be able to make it up to me."

I lean toward him, drawn by his touch on my leg. "I'm intrigued. Tell me how."

"A bunch of us are going out to the reservoir tomorrow. Want to come?"

"The reservoir?" I haven't heard of it. "To do what?"

"To swim, of course!"

"The reservoir has water?" He hasn't given me enough context clues to figure out what it is.

"You bet! It holds the water from the snow run off before the dam. It's a giant lake, and it's pretty deep this time of year!"

How have I never heard of this big lake? Oh, right. I forget it's my first summer here.

Hard to believe a year ago I was at home, getting ready to move away for college.

"Well, sure. Where is it?"

"Not far from here, just up the canyon a bit. Do you have class tomorrow?"

"I do, but I'm done at ten."

"If I give you the address, can you give me a ride?"

"Sounds like a fair exchange to me." I try not to show how delighted I am he wants to ride with me.

"Great!"

I stand when he does, shoving my hands in my pockets. "Awesome. See you tomorrow!"

He waves and ducks out of the apartment, and I bite my lip to keep back my grin. Immediately I turn to Abby and Iris.

"Do you like him?" Abby asks before I can get a word out.

I blink. "I was about to ask you guys the same thing. He was talking to you when I got here."

Abby shakes her head. "He came over to see you. As soon as you arrived, he dropped us like hot potatoes."

"So neither of you is interested?" I hold my breath, because I know from experience, I can't turn off my feelings for him, even if one of my roommates likes him.

It will just make things complicated.

But Iris shakes her head. "I know better than to get between you and a boy."

My face grows hot. She also knows from experience. She crushed on Jared all last year, and I did my very best not to encourage him, but Jared and I struggled to control our feelings.

I still don't think she knows he kissed me.

"Well, great! I'm glad we got that worked out!" I take my backpack and head to my room, and Annette jumps up from the table to scurry after me.

"So is that a yes?" Abby calls after me. "You like him?"

I close my door without answering, but I hear their laughter.

⚘

Annette has had enough of my early morning college classes. I leave her sleeping in my apartment the next morning and head off to school. The moment my English class ends at ten, I call her.

"Hello?" Her voice is groggy when she picks up.

"Good morning, sleepyhead!" I say. "You ready for this day?"

She mumbles something back incoherently.

I laugh. "Does that mean you don't want to go swimming with me and Mitch anymore?"

"No!" She perks up. "I definitely want to!"

"All right. I'll be home in about twenty minutes. Get ready."

I hang up and hold my phone in my palm, pausing in my walk. My heart rate quickens. I take a deep breath before calling Mitch. Somehow this feels more personal. And I can't remember the last time I called a guy.

I wouldn't be so nervous, except this one means something to me.

It rings twice, three times, and I think it will go to voicemail when suddenly Mitch answers.

"Hey there, Cassandra!" he says, Mr. Cheerful Ray of Sunshine himself.

I grin. His enthusiasm excites me. "Hey! I'm on my way home. Still up for swimming at the reservoir?"

"You bet! I'll see you when you get here."

"Sounds perfect."

I start walking again, but there's an added pep in my step. I don't bother tamping down the excited energy pulsing through me. I take back my weekend frustration with the male species. They keep life unexpected and fun and it would be very boring without them.

Mitch and his roommate, Isaac, are in my apartment when I walk in the door. They're standing around the kitchen table where Annette sits, eating a bowl of cereal. I pause in the doorway. "Hey, guys," I say.

"Hey!" Mitch comes over and hugs me. He wears a T-shirt over board shorts, and I feel the warmth of his skin through the soft material. He smells like aftershave and coconut. Did he already put on sunscreen?

"How was class?" he asks, stepping back but leaving an arm around my shoulders.

"Astonishingly boring and equally enlightening," I reply. He laughs. "Give me a moment to change."

I slip out from under his arm and head down the hall.

Iris pops out of her bedroom when I walk by. "Where are you going?"

I lift a shoulder. "Swimming in some reservoir up the canyon."

"I want to come."

I take a quick mental count of the people I can cram into my car. "Sure. Let's go."

She disappears back into her room.

I analyze the swimsuits in my drawer. The one-piece is my favorite, but it doesn't have enough chest padding and I'm self-conscious in it. On the other hand, the two-piece adds a little bit to my breasts but exposes my rib cage, which also makes me self-conscious.

I decide on the two-piece, but I bring a shirt to wear over it.

It takes longer to get out the door than I want because Iris decides it's a good idea to pack a lunch, and then I find myself in an assembly line, making sandwiches next to Mitch and Iris. Annette slices apples since snack food is not something we have a lot of. Then we fill up bottles of water and finally get out the door.

The drive out of the city and into the canyon never fails to take my breath away. Steep mountains flank us on either side, and though the foliage lacks the deep luscious green from back home, there is a rugged handsomeness to these looming rocks.

Mitch directs me. We go farther into the canyon than I've gone before, past the turn off to popular hiking places. We swing around the bend, and suddenly a dam looms to my left.

"Whoa," I say, staring at the large concrete structure.

"Drive over it," Mitch says. "The reservoir's on the other side."

I follow the road over the bridge, and a wide open lake appears to my left. "I never knew this was here," I say, staring at the crystalline blue lake standing between us and the base of the mountain.

"Yeah," Mitch says. "It's formed from the melting snow every year."

It takes me a second to put that together. I think of how the snow covered the mountains last winter and how it only recently melted away. "So the water should be really warm," I say, as straight-faced as possible.

Mitch looks at me as if to ascertain if I'm serious, and then he laugh. "Yes. Really warm."

He directs me to a small parking area off the side of the road. The shore is neither sandy nor soft dirt, but instead laden with large, sharp pieces of gravel. A boat weaves back-and-forth across the wide lake, JetSkis bumping over the wakes left behind.

I notice the people on the JetSkis are wearing wet suits.

A portion of the shore has been built up as a volleyball pit. This is where Mitch decides to put down our towels, on the soft sand surrounding the volleyball game. Annette puts her towel next to mine, and we peel off our layers. The sun is hot, and I close my eyes, enjoying the radiating feel of heat on my skin.

Mitch touches my shoulder. "Where do you get your brown skin?"

"From my mom," I say. I smile to let him know I'm playing with him. "I'm half-Colombian."

"I thought people in Colombia had lighter skin."

I raise an eyebrow. "I'm impressed. Most people don't know one Latin American country from the other. It's true that Colombia was heavily colonized by Europeans, but there were enough remnants of the Muisca people and other indigenous peoples that some of us were lucky enough to get darker coloring."

I'm proud of the knowledge I've acquired about my heritage in the past year. My mother was very hush-hush about her origins, and I only recently discovered her family came from Colombia.

"Makes sense. I don't actually know that much, either. But you say Colombia, and I think Shakira."

"Again, impressed. Most people don't know where she's from."

"I feel like I have to come clean with you." Mitch leans down toward me and whispers, "I used to have a huge crush on her."

I laugh, both at his confession and at the imagery of a young Mitch, crushing on the beautiful singer.

"And what about you?" I poke the flesh of his inner arm and feel the thrill of my own bravery. "Where do you get your golden coloring? I know for a fact your cousins don't have it."

For some reason, saying this makes my face grow hot. Like there's something vulgar in the relationship between Mitch and my ex.

I refuse to think about it.

"That comes from my dad's side. I'm one-sixteenth Cherokee."

"One-sixteenth, huh? Impressive." I study his light brown hair and blue eyes more closely. Other than the skin coloring, I don't see my much evidence of it. Maybe in the high cheekbones and tall forehead?

"That's three times I've impressed you today," he says.

I look out toward the lake glistening in front of us. Iris and Isaac are perched on large rocks by the shore, with Iris cautiously dipping a toe into the water. Annette has not bothered to move from the towel where she sits reading a book. I turn back to Mitch.

"I'll be much more impressed if you get into the water."

He looks at it and sucks in a breath before looking at me again. "You know how to make a man feel small."

I fight another smile. "Well?"

He shakes his head and pulls off his T-shirt, revealing the most finely honed torso I've ever seen. Muscles ripple across his chest as he tosses the shirt on the sand, and his biceps bulge as he inhales and clenches his fists.

I'm not generally impressed by muscles. But even I can't help noticing how ripped he is.

That's four times he's impressed me.

He was smart enough to wear water shoes, and he takes off running, calf muscles flexing as he sprints over the rocks. He barrels straight past Iris and Isaac and launches himself into the water. He doesn't stop until he has completely submerged himself. Then he gets out, turns around, and runs straight back to me.

I shriek as I realize what he's about to do, but there's no place to hide. In an instant Mitch has reached me and wrapped his freezing arms around me, icy water cascading from his hair, bleeding from his soaking body into my clothing.

"Don't you tell me you're cold," he says, laughing as I struggle in vain, trying to push him away. "I jumped in there for you. The least you can do is accept my sacrifice."

It's useless to fight him, his arms are like steel wires covered in flesh. I give up, going still in his embrace.

"You did that to prove you're a man?" I say.

"For you." He finally takes a step back, and I shudder as the wind whispers over my wet body. "To prove it to you."

I'm suddenly cold without his arms around me. I hug myself, shivering, and say, "I believe you."

He glances back toward the lake. "Now you have to get in."

"No. I already know how it feels. I'm going to stay right here, thank you."

He settles down beside me on my towel, goosebumps popping up over his skin as the breeze blows across it. "We should've invited Monica. She would enjoy this."

"Yeah." But my stomach twists uncomfortably, and I realize I wouldn't want her to be here, watching me flirt with her cousin. I feel traitorous. "Maybe next time."

CHAPTER TWENTY-SEVEN

Mountain Climbers

Annette won't leave me alone about the waterfall.

She whines at me as we walk to class. She whispers to me while we sit at meals. She mentions it to my roommates while we watch TV.

"Haven't you had enough adventures?" I say, and I tick them off my fingers. "A barbecue, playing kick the can, going to class with me, swimming in the reservoir, hiking to the caves."

She stares back at me, unfazed. "I was promised a waterfall."

My roommates laugh and I groan. I'm not getting out of this one.

It's been three days since we went to the reservoir, and I've only seen Mitch once, on campus and in passing. But as much as I want to worry about it, I haven't had time between my classes and soccer and endless job interviews.

Still no job. Too bad you don't get paid for applying.

"I know a hike with a waterfall at the end," Camila says. "We could go tomorrow."

"I have a soccer game tomorrow evening," I say.

"We can do it in the morning," Annette says. "Right, Camila? It won't take too long."

"It's totally doable in the morning," Camila says.

Now I know I'm doomed. This hike is going to happen. "How far away is it?" I ask, as if that makes a difference.

"Not far. It's the same road through the canyon, only you turn off into a park before you get as far as the reservoir."

"And how hard is the hike?" I'm thinking of that wretched two-mile hike up to the caves.

She shrugs. "It's not too bad. I've run parts of it with my cross country team."

She says that like it must mean the hike is easy, but I know how hard those cross country runners work.

I look at Annette, whose eyes are wide and hopeful, her fingers clasped together. I only have a few more days with her. "Fine. We'll hike to the waterfall. But Camila, you have to come."

"I'm game. Sounds like fun."

I'm not so sure.

But it's settled in Annette's eyes. So the next morning I make cheese sandwiches, fill up our water bottles, and load up backpacks so we can go hiking to the waterfall.

Camila directs me as we take off through the canyon, a route I'm becoming increasingly more familiar with. But before we reach the dam, she tells me to turn off to the left, and then we wind up a smaller road until we reach an unexpected parking lot to what looks like a state park. It's already full of cars and people picnicking, or walking their dogs, or playing frisbee golf.

"Wow, this is a thing," I say.

"Yeah, it's awesome. I'm sure you'll like it."

I park the car and Camila leads the way. At the entrance to a trail leading deeper into the woods is a sign with a map on it.

"See these different trails? You could spend hours up here." She runs her finger along various dotted and solid lines. "We're taking this one." She taps a broken blue line that winds around the side of the mountain. "Here are the waterfalls."

"Let's go!" Annette says, bouncing up and down giddily.

"Lead the way," I say, gesturing Camila forward.

The incline is gradual at first. Once we're beneath the canopy of the trees, the temperature isn't as hot, and I barely notice we're climbing upward. The aspens around us reach toward the sky, forming nearly a solid wall of gray-white trunks.

"This is a beautiful hike," I say.

"It is. It does get harder," Camila says.

Of course it does.

I don't fully appreciate Camila's warning until we're half a mile along our path. The mountainside begins to fall away steeply to our left, and then our trail winds to the right. As it does so, the incline becomes much more aggressive. My calves begin to ache, followed by my knees, then my ankles.

"This is beginning to feel familiar," I huff. I pause to hold onto a tree trunk and catch my breath.

"I could run up this trail," Annette says.

"I have," Camila says.

"Not this part!" I say. "You guys don't run all the way up here, do you?"

"Yeah, sure. Just for fun, usually in between hard training days."

This isn't considered hard training? I glance at her askance as I puff up the mountainside but say nothing.

"It's easy for me," Annette says.

"You should join the cross country team," Camila says.

"I might. I made the track team last year, but they said I couldn't be on it because I was already on the varsity soccer team."

"That's not fair!"

The two of them launch into a tirade of the unfairness of athletics in Arkansas schools. I feel my heart racing at the base of my neck, and my legs ache. The morning, which started out so pleasant and cool, is warming, and I relish the breeze as it whispers through the trees and cools my face where sweat gathers along my hairline.

Just when I think I'll have to beg for a break, I hear it: the roar of the waterfall.

"Do you hear that?" Camila asks, stopping.

"The waterfall!" Annette gasps.

Camila and I exchange smiles, and then the three of us break into a run, my backpack bouncing up and down behind me as I chase after Camila and Annette. They crow as they go around the bend up front, and the trees fall away, revealing a deep canyon. To our right, falling over a rock outcropping on the other side of the canyon, is the waterfall.

We take a moment to revel in the stunning scenery and snap pictures like great conquerers, the pine trees and waterfall forming a backdrop behind us.

"No more running," I say as we resume our hike, keeping the waterfall in our sights. "It's a lot more narrow and steep here."

"Truth," Camila says. "We don't run through here as a team. We usually turn back before the rock, actually."

I take the lead, keeping my sights on the cliff in front of us. The roar of the water grows louder as we approach, and we see people a hundred feet below us wading in the creek formed by the waterfall.

"How do we get down there?" Annette asks.

"I'm sure the trail takes us there," I say.

"I'm hungry now," Camila says. "We should eat lunch at the base of the falls."

"Starving!" I agree. "Getting here was hard work!"

"And you barely worked at all," she teases.

"Hey! I walked as far as you did!" I say. "I probably worked harder because my legs aren't as strong!"

"Good point," she says. "All right, you can have my sandwich also."

"Not mine," Annette says.

Our spirits are high as we follow the path. There's a split by a tree root, with one path curving upward and hugging the mountainside, and the other, a smaller, rockier path, continuing down. I take the one going down, since I can see the waterfall and know we're trying to reach the creek beneath us. Camila and Annette follow me. It's slow-going now, and I frequently have to use my hands to grip the rocks around me as I step down. Hand-holds become less frequent as the trees give way to shrubs. The path flattens out, looking less like a footpath and more like a gravel wash. I hesitate as I step onto it and my foot slides.

"What's wrong?" Camila asks behind me.

I look out in front of me. The trail seems to vanish into the steep rocky terrain, but I see people milling about, playing in the cave behind the waterfall. I glance behind me at the narrow path we climbed down to get here.

"Is this the right way?" I ask.

"We followed the trail," Camila says.

"We have to get across that white patch," Annette says, pointing at a chalky stretch of ground in front of us.

I survey the rocks in the chalky white area. "It's what, twenty feet across?"

"Maybe less," Camila says.

The white rocks sit tightly together on the downward slope. They look like a strong rainstorm would wash them down the mountain. On the other side, people sit on large granite outcroppings, eating their lunches and taking photos. Beyond them, hikers move cautiously up and down a variety of trails reaching to the creek.

It must be safe. I'm just being nervous.

"All right," I say.

I step out onto the rocks and pause as they shift under my feet. I hold still in a crouch, catching my balance, and then take another step. Then another. I make a slow step after another, glancing back to make sure Camila and Annette are with me. I take one more step, and the rock slides beneath me.

In an instant I'm being carried down the mountain-face. I turn slightly and throw my body hard into the side of the slope, hugging the rocks, my heart hammering in my chest. The slide stops, but I don't move, my breath coming in small, panicked gasps. I hear Annette calling my name and look up to see her and Camila only five feet above me.

"Are you okay?" Camila asks, her eyes wide with panic.

"Yeah," I pant. "Yeah, I'm okay."

This isn't the correct path. It can't be. We went the wrong way.

"You've got to keep going," she says, her voice tight. "We can't cross until you move."

I nod. She's right. If they send rocks tumbling my way—I push away from the wall and look over my shoulder. This sheet of loose rocks vanishes over a ledge, and I don't want to find out what's beneath it.

Nobody speaks as I inch my way across the rocks, still trying to get to the other side. I freeze every time they jostle. It's much steeper than it first looked, and I'm certain it's more than twenty feet across. The slide levels out enough for me to get back into a crouch, but I don't stand. I scoot on my butt, ignoring the scrapes and scratches on my legs as I make my way off the slide.

I take a deep breath when my feet settle on solid ground on the other side. I swivel to watch Camila and Annette. They're sliding, pausing to get their balance, mimicking my posture of scooting. Annette is farther behind Camila, and my heart slams a triple beat in my throat as I watch her.

Camila reaches me first, and I give her my hand and pull her to safety. Then I turn my attention back to Annette.

"You got it, girl!" I say. "You're almost here!"

Annette takes another step, and then the rocks shift. She squeals and throws herself backward as the slide moves her downward.

"Annette!" I scream.

CHAPTER TWENTY-EIGHT

Rock Slide

I make a move to get back on the rock slide, but Camila grabs me.

"It stopped," she said. "She's okay. You'll make it worse."

My head is pounding. "Come on, Annette!" I cry. I hold my hand out toward her, but she's still a good ten feet from me. I can't reach her, I can't help her even if she needs me. I swallow past a lump in my throat. I want to cry but I won't. "Just get to my hand!"

"Turn onto your stomach," Camila calls. "Use your legs."

Annette lifts her face and meets my eyes. I see the fear in them, and I smile and nod.

"You've got this," I say.

She takes a deep breath and moves her foot, then the other, inch by inch, like I did. She's lower than us, and I climb down my side until I'm at her level. It's flatter here, but I don't get on the slide. I might think I'm helping, but one of us needs to be on solid ground.

She's so close. Three feet away. I feel Camila beside me, and she grabs my arm as I lean toward Annette, stretching out.

"Get my hand, girl," I breathe. "Just take my hand." I'm shaking with anxiety.

Annette gets closer and reaches for me, but the rocks shift and she hugs the mountainside again, not moving until they settle.

"Almost here," I say. I push closer to her. "Come on, come on." She's inches away from touching me, and I'm terrified I'll lose her now.

She shifts enough that she could reach me, and my heart soars. But she doesn't lift her hand. She turns her head to face me, her cheeks stained with tears.

"I'm afraid to let go," she says.

"It's not as bad here," I say. "It's not as steep. You can let go. You won't fall."

She takes a deep breath and throws her hand toward me. I grasp her wrist and yank hard enough to pull her arm from her socket. But she has her feet working now, kicking away from the rocks, and Camila is beside me, reaching for Annette and grasping her shoulders when she gets close enough.

We collapse into a huddle, the three of us, hugging and holding each other. Annette cries and I squeeze her tight, adrenaline racing through my veins.

"We're okay," Camila says. "We're okay."

I squeeze my eyes shut, hardly believing the dangerous situation I got my little sister into. "One wrong step on a mountainside," I murmur.

No one says anything else. We don't need to.

Once we reach the other side of the slide, getting down to the waterfall feels like a walk in the park. We follow other hikers along a much wider path, safe in the knowledge that we're not traveling a strange, uncharted trail.

"It must have been a run-off trail," I muse. My adrenaline is receding, and I'm removed enough from the situation to analyze it dispassionately. "Created from rain or snow melt."

Camila nods. "Yeah, it seemed awfully steep and narrow for humans."

This seems so clear now. But at the time, the path looked like a logical option.

Camila drops her backpack on a rocky outcropping a few feet from the waterfall. "This way my things don't get wet."

"Oh, great idea." I tuck my phone into my backpack and toss it at the rock with hers.

But I miss. My backpack sails right past it, into the oblivion beyond, and then disappears from view.

"Nooooo!" I cry, my hand reaching out as dramatically as the forsaken hero in an adventure movie.

The three of us creep to the edge and peer down. The river is about thirty feet below us.

My backpack sits in the middle of it.

Camila laughs. "So much for not getting wet."

"So much," I agree with a sigh. I hope my phone isn't ruined. "I'll go get it."

"I'll come with you," Annette says, probably afraid I'll take a wrong turn somewhere and fall and break my neck.

I wave her off. "Go enjoy your waterfall. That's why we're here."

She glances at it, less than ten feet away, and I know she's envisioning standing beneath the rushing water, exploring the cavern behind it, maybe anticipating the cold shock of snow runoff.

"Are you sure?" she says, looking back at me.

"Yes. I'll be fine."

"Want me to come?" Camila asks.

"No. Stay with my sister."

They both watch me begin the descent with worry in their eyes. I know my track record so far isn't great, but as long as I don't try to jump to a rock and miss, I'm not in any danger here.

I scoot down, keeping my center of gravity low, and use my hands to balance myself against the rocky ground. It takes less than ten minutes to get to the river, and I stand up straight as a I jog over to the bank.

It's a creek, less than twenty feet across and moving at a slow, leisurely pace once it makes it off the mountain via the waterfall. My backpack hasn't moved. A few branches clog the creek and hold the canvas bag in place. I step in and yelp as the frigid water fills my shoes and burns its way up my ankles.

"Don't think, just go," I whisper, and I plunge into the creek.

The water creeps up to my calves, and I bite my lip to keep from whimpering. The large slippery rocks slide beneath my feet, and I topple forward several times but manage to catch myself before I fall face-first into the creek. I imagine Annette and Camila up on the ledge above me, watching me. I refuse to look up to find out.

My backpack comes within reach, and I bend over and grab the straps and pull it from the water. Small rivulets stream off it. I carry it by the top loop, holding it away from my body, and trudge toward the shore, wincing with each step. My legs have gone numb from the calf down, but somehow the cold still stabs into my skin. I emerge from the water, but the air jumps in to take the place of the creek, stinging my exposed flesh.

The rocks on the shore are warm and sunbaked. I drop onto one of them and take off my shoes and socks, laying them on the hard granite surface to dry. The sun soaks into my shoulders, warming my upper half while my lower extremities still complain about the ice bath. I heave a sigh and unzip my backpack, wincing as I see the water-logged canvas sides.

My phone sits on top, face-down on a pile of granola bars and a sweater. I remove it, holding my breath as I flip it over.

It's dry! And not cracked! I laugh with relief. My feet aren't as cold now and the rock is comfortably warm beneath my legs. I turn on my camera and snap pictures of the terrain, and then of Annette and Camila thirty feet above me at the waterfall. They spot me and wave, and I wave back.

Annette grins as they join me, her wet clothes clinging to her, displaying the yellow swimsuit she wears underneath.

"Anything broken?" she asks.

"No." I brandish the intact phone. "I got lucky."

"That is lucky!" Camila exclaims. "Now let's see if we can be as lucky getting off this mountain."

"Did you get enough waterfall in?" I ask Annette.

She twists her hair over one shoulder and wrings it out. "This was perfect. Thank you so much for bringing me here."

"Then let's go." I shoulder my backpack and stand.

The most exciting thing that happens on the way down is seeing a baby groundhog that runs off into the woods when I try to pet it.

⚬⁓※⁓⚬

Mitch comes over to our apartment after dinner, when we've showered and no longer feel on the brink of death.

"We still doing a soccer game?" he asks.

I beam at him, pleased he remembered. "Yes, we are!"

"Can I get a ride?"

He has his own car, an antique BMW, but I like that he prefers to ride with me. "Of course."

I change my clothes, and then Annette, Iris, Camila, and Mitch pile into my Toyota and head to the soccer fields behind campus. Annette sits up front with me while the other three sit in the back.

"I like your car," Mitch says. "Toyotas are nice."

"They are," I say absently, running my palm over the logo in the middle of the steering wheel.

I can't help thinking of a certain beige Toyota Tacoma that belonged to my ex-boyfriend.

Of course I can't tell Mitch what I'm thinking.

Camila and I regale Mitch and Iris with stories of our near-disastrous hike to the waterfall, which has them both simultaneously laughing and shaking their heads at our stupidity.

"Next time you go hiking, take me with you," Mitch says.

"I will if you promise not to think less of me," I say.

"That's not possible," he says, in a tone that makes me glance at his face in the mirror. He grins, and my face warms.

No one else is at the soccer fields when we get there, but we're early, so I don't expect anyone to be here yet.

"We can be one team," Iris says. "Cassandra's pretty good."

"Annette plays on her school team," I say. "We'll win for sure."

"How many people do we need for a full team?" Camila asks.

"We can play with five," I say. "If we put one in goal and two on defense and offense. But eight is ideal."

"So we need five more people."

"Yep."

We putt around with the soccer ball I brought, passing to each other and practicing field kicks. As the minutes tick by, I check the parking lot more often.

Where is everyone else?

Ten minutes after the time I set, I'm forced to admit no one is coming.

"I'm so sorry," I say, chagrined. "What a lame turnout. You guys want to head back?"

"No way," Mitch says. "You promised us a game. I say we play."

"With only five people?" Iris says.

It will be a lousy game. "How? Playing two on three?" Even one more person would make this more enjoyable.

Mitch shrugs. "Sure. Or two on two with a sub."

We're here. There's nothing else to do. And I appreciate Mitch's attitude. "All right."

We decide to play on one half of the field so we don't have to run back and forth as much. I join up with Annette and Mitch joins with Camila. Iris volunteers to sit out.

It's far more fun than I expect and painfully hilarious. I'm winded after a mere five minutes and pause with my hands on my knees, watching Mitch and Camila gang up on Annette. The two of them attempt to get the ball from her, but her fancy footwork out dances both of them, and she feints left. When they both turn that direction, she goes right, and I laugh in amusement as they spin around to stare as she dribbles her soccer ball to the goal line.

"Playing without us?"

I swivel to see Hayden, Mace, and Javier, three boys from my soccer team, walking to the field. It's Hayden's British accent that rings out across the field.

"Hayden!" I run to greet them and give him a hug, though Hayden is at least eighteen inches taller than me, which makes the gesture more awkward than friendly. "You made it!"

Mace surveys us. "We have eight people? How are we supposed to play?"

"We were managing with five," I say. "It just got a lot easier."

"Four on four," Hayden says, holding his fist out to me. "I like it."

Mitch jogs over to join us, his face red from the physical exertion. "Fresh blood!"

Iris and Camila come over as well.

"All right," Mace says, counting our numbers. "We should play boys on girls."

"Is that meant to be suggestive?" Camila says, raising her eyebrows.

I elbow her, embarrassed at her brazenness, but Mitch laughs.

"Good one," he tells her.

"All joking aside," Mace says, not the least bit amused, "we have four girls and four boys."

"You'll lose if you split us that way," I warn.

He blinks at me as if surprised to notice I'm standing here. One eyebrow lifts, and he all but sneers.

"You think?"

"They're pretty good," Mitch says.

"We have Javier." Mace claps the shorter man on the shoulder. "He's good enough to go pro."

Iris snorts, unable to hide her derision. I bite my lip. No one good enough to go pro would be playing on our college soccer team.

"Actions speak louder than words," Annette says, and all eyes are drawn to my thirteen-year-old sister, standing off to the left with the soccer ball under her arm. "Let's play."

Javier shrugs. "If you insist."

That does it. He's going down.

CHAPTER TWENTY-NINE

On the Prowl

It's decided. We split into teams, two on offense, two on defense, and no goalie, and then we play.

Iris is a good decoy. She always looks like she's going to stop the ball but fails at the last moment. Luckily I'm good back-up defense. What I lack in stamina, I make up for in tenacious sprints. I get the ball and shoot it down the opposite side of the field before I have to bend over and grab my knees, wheezing for breath. Camila outruns the boys every time, beating them to the ball and tapping it away before they get close.

But it's Annette who steals the show. She's ready every time Camila passes. She outmaneuvers anyone who gets close, and she has the skill and speed to keep the ball tucked in close to her while she zips around every intruding foot.

We call the game half an hour later, and we win five to three.

"It was a close game," Mace says, unwilling to accept defeat.

"You lost by two points," Camila says, snorting. I've never seen this challenging, competitive side of her, and I feel bad I've yet to watch her run in a meet. "Hardly a close game."

"They beat us." Javier holds out a hand to Annette. "You've got skills. Maybe someday we'll see you play on this field."

"Maybe," she says, her cheeks turning pink. But there's no mistaking the pleasure on her face.

We pile back into my car, thirsty and slick with sweat, and Mitch directs me to the gym where he works.

"There's a smoothie bar inside," he says. "I'll get us drinks. On me."

"You work in a gym?" I glance at him in the mirror, but I don't need to see his reflection to know the bulkiness of his biceps and thighs, which I saw in full working efficiency this evening.

"Yeah. I'm a body-builder."

"Are you a trainer?" Camila asks.

"No. But I compete."

"Compete how?" Iris asks.

"In like, you know—weight-lifting competitions."

"Do you wear skimpy underwear?" Iris asks.

I can't help glancing back at him again, and his tan skin turns a lovely chartreuse.

"I wouldn't call them underwear—" he begins.

"You do!" Iris shrieks.

"Pictures. We need pictures," Camila says.

Mitch shakes his head. "I don't have any."

"Oh, that's so not true." She digs her phone out of her pocket and talks to herself while she types into the search bar. "Mitchell . . . Henry . . . Body builder. Ha!" She crows and holds the phone out to Iris. "Found him!"

They hoot and holler together, leaning over his phone, while I cry, "I want to see, let me see!"

Poor Mitch is bright red, but we are merciless. As soon as I'm parked at the gym, Annette and I swivel around in the front seat to look at Camila's phone.

There's Mitch on a stage wearing nothing but what looks like a man's thong, smiling his charming, friendly smile while he flexes his arms. He's bulkier in the picture than he is now, and I snatch Camila's phone from her to read the caption, astonished.

"First place?" I glance up at him. "You won first place?"

"I compete," he mumbles, not quite able to meet my eyes.

We can't stop laughing. The girls get out of the car and head into the gym, but I stand by my door and wait for him. I hook my arm through his and grin up at him.

"We're just messing with you."

"I know."

"You set yourself up for it, wearing those underwear."

The red deepens across his face again. "It's not underwear," he says, staring at the sidewalk.

I laugh again and squeeze his arm. There's something delightful about seeing this big man so timid and embarrassed, and I have the feeling it's not the last time we're going to tease him about it.

"Invite me the next time you compete," I say, pulling him into the smoothie bar. "I want to see."

"You do?" He finally meets my eyes.

I can't help myself. "Yes. I need to see these non-underwear for myself."

Then I laugh and release him so I can dart inside, leaving the mortified body-builder to come in behind us.

⊙෴⊙

After smoothies, we drive back to the apartment. I expect Mitch to part ways with us at the commons and go to the men's side of the complex, but instead, he follows us to our apartment.

"So what's next?" he asks as we step inside, and I'm delighted he considers himself one of us and wants to spend the rest of the evening with us.

"I've got nothing planned," I say.

"How about a movie?" Iris says.

We watch a lot of movies. It's cheap and easy.

131

There's literally not much else we can do without leaving the apartment. None of us has invested in any games, other than Uno, which we veto.

Which means we find ourselves seated on my couch and watching sitcom reruns.

I squish onto the couch next to Iris and Annette. Camila melts cheese on chips in the microwave and brings them like they're nachos. We pass the large platter from lap to lap, and Mitch stands and asks if anyone's thirsty. When he returns with plastic cups of water to hand out, he changes up the seating arrangement and seats himself between me and Iris. Iris gives me a side-eye. I can't begin to imagine what she's thinking. I sip from the water Mitch gave me, aware of his body next to mine, of the bare skin of his forearm against me. I lean forward to put the cup on the carpet in front of me, and he lifts his arm and drapes it over my shoulders when I sit back.

It's a bold move and doesn't leave a lot of room for ambiguity. It could just be a friendly gesture, except he doesn't put his arm around Iris. I settle into the crook of his arm, resting my head against his shoulder. His fingers tighten around my forearm, his bicep flexing beneath my cheek.

He's so strong. I've never dated anyone as muscular as he is. I'm not sure what I think about it.

There's no denying how nice it feels to be held, though.

⚬〜✿〜⚬

I finally, finally, finally get a job interview.

"I'm calling in regards to your application to the School of Engineering," the woman on the other side of the phone says. "Are you still looking for a job?"

"Yes! Yes, yes, I am." I'm not sure how many times I said yes, but I wince, realizing I must sound desperate.

I don't remember this application. By this point, I've submitted almost thirty. If I don't get one, I've resigned myself to return to the telefund, the call center where I worked last year.

"How about Friday at two?"

It's Thursday.

"Yes," I say. "That will be perfect." It's not like I have a work schedule to contend with.

"Great! We look forward to talking with you more."

I hang up and refrain from doing a full on happy dance in the quad outside the library. There aren't a lot of people out, though, so I allow myself a small celebratory fist pump.

My phone rings again, and I look down to see the name "John" flashing on my screen. Who's John? I must know him, because the contact is in my phone. So I answer.

"Hey, Cassandra! How are you?"

"I'm good. How about yourself?" I'm generic with my response, not about to let on I don't know who this is.

"I'm great, really great! How are your classes going?"

"Fine. Busy. Lots of essays." I don't recognize his voice. Is he someone from church?

"Oh, I know how that goes. The bane of being an English major!"

And just like that, it clicks. John. The English major. The one I met in the bookstore. He took me to a barbecue, and then we played kick the can.

132

"Yeah." I laugh, instantly warmer now that I know who I'm talking to. "Sometimes I question my life choices."

He laughs with me. "Don't we all? Hey, what are you doing this weekend?"

"As in, tomorrow or Saturday?"

"As in, both."

I tilt my head, intrigued. "I have a job interview tomorrow at two. But I'm done with classes at ten, so I'm good otherwise."

"Awesome! Want to go camping?"

Both eyebrows rise simultaneously. Camping? That's a new one. No boy has taken me on a camping date yet. "With you?" Even I hear the caution in my voice.

"Yes, but not just me, of course not! It's a whole bunch of us."

I relax with that. "I have to bring my sister. She's still with me."

"That's no problem, you can bring a roommate if you want! It's a whole bunch of friends getting together. Do you have a tent? You can use one of mine if you don't."

This sounds less like a date and more like a youth activity. "Yeah. Yeah, that sounds great. I'll invite my roommate." Maybe both of them.

"I'll text you the details and pick you up tomorrow, then, if that works."

"Fun! I look forward to it."

I bring it up to my roommates as soon as I'm home. Camila can't come, but Iris is all over the idea.

"But I thought you liked Mitch," she says. "Why are you going camping with John?"

"I totally like hanging out with Mitch," I say. "But I don't know what I feel, and we're not in a relationship, so there's nothing wrong with going out with other boys."

"But it's a little unfair."

"What's unfair?"

"Well." She wrinkles her nose. "It's just, every time we go somewhere, all the boys like you."

I raise my eyebrows, amused at the assessment. "It seems to me they all like Abby."

Iris considers that. "That too. It's a good thing she doesn't go places with us very often."

We giggle, but I'm surprised Iris feels that way about me. I remember having friends in junior high who always seemed to attract the boys, so I was secretly relieved when they couldn't join certain activities because that meant I might be noticed.

Am I that girl now?

Her question also has me thinking about Mitch, whom I haven't seen in two days since we played soccer.

I finish my homework and walk across the common courtyard to his apartment.

Mitch's apartment is on the opposite side of the complex. I wander through the hallway to the building on the far side. The apartment door is open, which is standard around here. Two girls sit inside on the couch, one on the cushion and one on the armrest. I don't see any boys, so I knock on the open door frame and say, "Knock, knock."

The girls turn to look at me, a brunette with long brown hair and a blond with a short bob haircut.

"Hi," the blond says.

The couch and TV are set up opposite my apartment, with the back of the couch to the front door and the TV on the opposing wall. I don't realize there's someone on the couch until Mitch sits up, coughing, one hand over his ear. He takes one look at me and jumps to his feet. "Cassandra!"

"It's me," I say.

He lets go of his face and takes a step, then groans and grabs his head again.

"Are you okay?" I ask, startled.

"Here, sit back down," the blond says, and she guides Mitch back to the couch.

I tilt my head, curious. Is she someone important to him? "Hi, I'm Cassandra," I say, hoping to get an introduction out of her.

"Cassandra, this is Sheryl." Mitch flutters a hand in the blond's direction, though he doesn't release his face with the other. "She lives in the apartments across the street. She's a really good friend of mine. And that's Robin, her roommate."

I turn my attention back to him. "What happened to you?"

He groans, and Sheryl and Robin laugh.

"He side-flopped into the pool," Sheryl says.

"What pool?" I ask. "What's a side-flop?"

"The pool at their complex," Mitch says. "And it's like a bellyflop, but on your side."

"And he busted his eardrum," Robin says.

I focus on Mitch, envisioning the scene where he falls sideways hard enough into the water to bust his eardrum. "For real?"

He nods, then hisses, squeezing his eyes together.

"Lie down, lie down," Sheryl says, maneuvering him back onto the couch and depositing his head on her thigh.

"Want to try something else for the pain?" Robin says.

I want to be at his side also, crooning over him, making him more comfortable. But it looks like they've got it covered.

Mitch shoots Robin a dark glare. "Like the rubbing alcohol you poured into my ear?"

"You did what?" Even with my lack of medical training, that sounds like a bad idea. So maybe they don't have it covered.

"Oh, it hurt so bad, I thought I was going to cry." Mitch cups his other hand over his ear, looking as if he were blocking out a repulsive noise.

"I'm so sorry," I say. I'm not sure what else to say. I didn't expect Mitch to be in the care of two other women when I popped by.

Maybe he reads my mind because he says, "I'll come by your apartment later."

"Think you can handle the pain?" I say dryly.

"For sure. I just need to recover here a little bit longer."

I look at Sheryl with his head resting on her leg, her fingers patting his curly locks, and I feel a flash of jealousy that it's not me. But all I say is, "We'll see if you can manage." And I turn around and walk away.

Visiting him did not go as planned.

CHAPTER THIRTY

Camp Out

Mitch doesn't come by.

Annette has bailed on college classes. I have two job interviews scheduled on Friday, one before class and one after, so I leave her at home while I walk to campus. I stop at the inventory warehouse and answer the questions with a bright smile, hoping I'm giving off the vibe of positive and capable. *Choose me, choose me!* runs through my head.

I'm still thinking about it through my teacher's English lecture. The interview went well, but that's no guarantee I'll hear back from them.

Another unknown number calls me while I'm sitting there stewing. I can't take it until I'm out of class, so I watch it light up in my backpack and don't touch it.

When the two-hour English seminar finally ends, I dash out the door into the hallway to take the call.

"Department of Students with Special Needs, how can I help you?" says a friendly and perky voice.

I applied here for a job also. I stand up a little straighter, hope firing through me.

"Hi, I missed a call from this number."

"Let me see... What's your name?"

"Cassandra Jones."

"Just a minute."

Hold music plays, and then a moment later, another voice gets on, this one more mature and female. "Hi, Cassandra, I'm Ms. Kate. Are you still looking for a job?"

"Yes, ma'am, I am."

"We'd love to schedule an interview with you. Are you available this afternoon?"

Wow, they are not wasting any time! "I'm unavailable after two, but I have time between now and then."

"Just a moment."

The hold music is back, and I bob my head from side to side, tapping my fingers along my thigh and trying not to show my anxiety.

The music stops, and her voice comes through the line. "We could do an eleven.

Does that work for you?"

Eleven. As in, less than an hour from now. I glance at my clothes, grateful I'm dressed appropriately because of my other interview. "Yes, I can do that."

She tells me where to go, and I put my phone away, feeling more productive than I have in weeks. Three interviews in one day! I cross my fingers and say another prayer that something will come of this. I'm running out of money fast, and I hate feeling broke.

Normally, I do homework in the library, but my interview is in the student center, so I go there instead. I'm hard at work drafting an essay on my computer when the table jolts as someone sits down. I look up, only mildly surprised because it happens a lot here; people sit down with strangers either because they need a seat or want to get to know the other person.

But this is not a stranger. I smile, my face lighting up when I see Mitch.

"Hey! How's the ear?"

"Oh my goodness." He rolls his eyes. "I felt like such an idiot. And then when Robin poured rubbing alcohol in my ear—"

I nod sympathetically. "That was probably the worst part."

"That girl is not a nurse."

I'm burning with curiosity, and Mitch has given me some pretty good openings. "So, who is Sheryl? You guys seemed really comfortable with each other."

He's no dummy, he knows exactly what I'm fishing for. "Oh, we're not close like that. No, no. We met a few weeks ago and she's a really good friend, really funny. She's Robin's friend, and Robin's Isaac's friend, so we hang out all the time. But yeah, there's nothing else between us."

I suppress a smile. He could not make it clearer if he wrote it out in bold letters: "I am not interested in her." But I pretend like that's not what I was asking and that's not what he said. "My favorite part of college is the friends we make everywhere we go."

"Right? This is my new family."

"I know exactly what you mean. My roommates are my sisters."

He taps the table with one hand, but I notice how he keeps his head cocked, the injured ear tilted upward. "What are you working on?"

"English. Are you sure your ear's okay?"

He shrugs. "It will be, as long as I don't go swimming or anything until it heals."

"So you went to the doctor?"

He grins. "The internet and I are well acquainted."

I snort. "Typical college student."

He laughs. "What are you doing tonight?"

My heart skips a beat and batters hard against my chest. "Well, I have two job interviews this afternoon, and then tonight I'm going camping with a bunch of friends."

A bunch of friends. Iris would snort if she were here.

"Oh yeah? Who's going?"

"Some people I met at a barbecue a few weekends ago, and my sister and Iris." I get the impression Mitch would like to invite himself along, which, somehow, I think would be horribly awkward. "I'm not the organizer, or I would've invited you for sure."

"Totally understandable. Maybe I'll plan a camping trip one of these weekends. I'll make sure to invite you."

"Oh, thanks for the consideration." I wrap my hand around the back of my neck and rest my elbow on the table, grinning at him.

Mitch Henry is even more pleasant to look at than I remembered.

⁂

Both interviews go remarkably well, in my opinion. But the job I want is the one working with special needs students.

I'm not even home from school before I see the number from the School of Engineering calling on my phone screen. I waver. My interview with them finished less than an hour ago. I can only think of one reason they would be calling me. I desperately want a job, but I'd rather have the other one. If I answer and the School of Engineering makes an offer, can I ask for more time? Or will they move on to the next candidate?

I don't answer. If I haven't heard back from the student advocate office by Monday, I'll call the School of Engineering back.

The call finishes and a voicemail dings on my phone. My heart races when I see it. When I play it back, I hear:

"Hi, Cassandra, this is Jan from the School of Engineering. We had an interview about an hour ago, and I wanted to ask you a few follow-up questions. Please give me a call back at your earliest convenience. Thank you."

That's it. The whole message. But I get this gnawing feeling in my gut telling me the follow-up questions include a job offer.

John comes by a few hours later to pick us up for the campout. We throw our bags into the trunk of his car and wave to Abby as we drive away. I don't see Mitch, and I'm glad. Thinking about him seeing me with another boy makes me feel guilty.

John is funny and talkative as he drives us up a mountain road toward primitive campsites. Partway up the mountain is a small lake with a raft out in the middle. We're the first to arrive at the site, so we claim a flat spot and set up our tents next to each other. John is there with his friend Kent. Once the tents are set up, we change into our swimsuits and jump into the lake.

It's warm, but long, stringy grass-like stalks creep up from the bottom and grab at our legs, causing us to squeal and hurry to the raft in the middle. The raft is anchored somehow, and Iris gets on first, then me and Annette.

The boys come out to join us, and I can't help comparing John's face and slight frame to Mitch's tanned, sculpted abs. It's hardly fair, I know, but I can't help it. It turns out I'm more carnally minded than I want to admit.

Another dozen kids arrive over the course of the next hour. Some start setting up their tents, while others toss their gear on the ground and jump in the lake with us. Some of the guys are cute, but my thoughts drift back to Mitch more often than I expect. I find myself wishing he were here, and not because he's eye candy, but because I enjoy talking with him.

Once the sun sets, the guys light a large bonfire. I sit close to Annette and Iris.

"I'm the s'more master." John comes over brandishing marshmallows and roasting sticks. "Want me to make one for you guys?"

"I won't say no," I say.

"Sure," Iris says.

"I'll make my own. It's fun," Annette says. She bounds up and away to find her own marshmallow stick.

John's back a minute later with my s'more. He sits himself in Annette's vacated spot, wedging in between me and Iris.

"What English classes are you taking this term?" he asks.

"I've got Professor Douglas' British lit class," I say.

He makes a snoring noise, then adopts a British accent and says, "How very dull."

I shrug a bit sheepishly. "I'm kind of enjoying it. I'm fascinated by Thomas Hardy's fatalist mentality."

"Yes, if you're into the depressing sort of stories."

I laugh. "They are depressing. It makes me appreciate my life more."

"I can see that."

I take a bite of the s'more, and the gooey chocolate spills over my fingers, marshmallow sticking to my lip. "Hey, you did a great job with this. It's hard to get the chocolate to melt."

He puffs out his chest, preening. "I pride myself on my marshmallow skills."

I smirk. "For good reason." I glance over at Iris, who hasn't said a word since he came over. If she wants people to talk to her, she needs to talk to them.

"Ever notice how bright the stars are out here on the mountain?"

John's voice directs my attention back to him, but it's someone else I hear, someone else's voice and words.

"Do you know your constellations?"

Owen. On our last night together before I left for college.

It stirs a memory I had almost forgotten. Hanging out in the back of his truck while he showed me the different constellations he remembered from his childhood. The ache of missing him catches me so off guard I almost can't breathe. I cough and wipe my face, and John says, "Smoke get in your eyes?"

"Yes. Really bad. Excuse me."

I stand up and go to the tent. It's completely dark inside, with only the flickering campfire light casting a glow on one wall. I take out my contacts, but it doesn't ease the burning in my eyes. My throat still aches.

The smoke is not the culprit.

I lay down on the sleeping bag and bury my face in the soft fabric and cry like I haven't cried in weeks. I miss him, dammit. My soul aches for him. Is he not even going to write me?

A sense of déjà vu falls over me, and I realize I've played this record before, only last time it was Tiago I was longing to hear from. I don't want to play it anymore. I'm ready to smash it for good.

And that's when I decide it's time to start dating Mitch.

CHAPTER THIRTY-ONE

Not Dating

Camping is not my forte. I wake with the sun, groggy, but unable to stay laying down on this rocky ground any longer. I smell campfire and sweet bread. Outside the tent, someone is playing a guitar, the music mixing with the morning air. Annette is sprawled across her sleeping bag next to Iris. Annette came in last night during my cry fest and stayed with me, but I was asleep before Iris appeared.

It's a primitive campsite, so I exit the tent and go as far away from the tents as possible to take care of business before returning. The morning is crisp and chilly despite it being July, and I shiver as I sit down next to the fire, where the boys are up and stoking the flames.

John looks up at me and grins over the Dutch oven. "Good morning! We're making blueberry pancakes."

"Sounds lovely."

He retrieves a blanket from his tent and wraps it around me, then returns to the Dutch oven and pours batter in with a plastic spoon. "You didn't come back last night."

"I had to take my contacts out, and then I couldn't see very well because I forgot my glasses, so I stayed in the tent." I did forget my glasses, but I didn't realize that until this morning when I was forced to put my contacts in first thing.

"You should've said something. We would've happily guided you around."

I laugh. "A dark campsite with only smoke and firelight to lead the way sounds like the beginning of a Gothic novel."

"Or a horror novel."

I warm to the banter of literary genres. "Or it could be the beginning of an inspirational novel about someone's climb from darkness to light."

His lips quirk up, and he shakes his head. "And that is the beauty of literature. All of us can hear the same first line and write an entirely different story."

I ponder that statement. It's more profound than he realizes. "I think we can say the same about life. You can give all of us the same first line, and we will all make a different life."

He rocks back on his heels. "Now it's gone too deep. We're turning into philosophy majors."

I laugh with him. "Time to step aside."

Annette comes over and joins me, and I wrap the blanket around us both. "You fly home tonight," I say. "Are you ready?"

"Yes." She doesn't hesitate. "I miss home."

"Of course you do." I rub her arm. She's only thirteen; she's not meant to live away from Mom and Dad yet. "I sure enjoyed having you here."

She sniffles, her nose turning a delicate shade of pink while her eyes get glossy. "It's been really fun."

I hug her tighter. It must be really different to be the youngest and watch all of your siblings leave the house. As the oldest, I couldn't wait for that moment. But nobody left me behind.

Kent gets up, and even though it's only dawn, nobody complains when he pulls out his guitar and begins strumming.

Half an hour later, everyone is awake, and John pulls the Dutch oven from the fire.

"Breakfast is ready!" he calls.

The boys are prepared. They put paper plates and utensils on the picnic table, and they haul out containers of orange juice and cartons of milk from a cooler.

"Don't forget the maple syrup," John says to Kent, who gets out not just a bottle of pancake syrup but a legit bottle of pure maple syrup.

I'm not sure I've ever had maple syrup before.

John removes the lid from the Dutch oven, and we all lean forward to inhale the scent of blueberry pancakes.

But it's the scent of burning plastic that fills our noses.

"Oh, no!" John says. He uses a metal serving spoon to pull out the stringy, melted remains of the plastic spoon he used to stir the batter. "I left the spoon in there!"

I start laughing. All that effort to make breakfast—getting up early, making the fire, preparing the batter—and he left the spoon in there.

"We can eat around it," Kent says, and he takes a huge spoonful of pancake from the opposite side of the Dutch oven.

Even from three feet away, I can smell the plastic.

Kent is brave, and we watch him pour maple syrup over the top before taking a bite. His cheeks rise, his eyes squint, and he grimaces, shaking his head as he tries to swallow.

"I'm sorry," he says. "It's ruined. The whole thing has the essence of plastic."

"I'm so sorry," John says.

We think it's a riot. We can't stop teasing the boys. But it does bring an abrupt halt to the campout, as we're all starving. Take-down goes faster than setup, and then I wish I had my own car because we have to wait for John to finish helping everyone else. Finally, he loads up his car with our things, and we leave.

"I hope that wasn't too much of a disaster," John says.

"It was not. We all enjoyed it. And the pancake incident was probably the most memorable."

He allows himself to laugh with me.

But I know as he drops us off at my apartment that this is the last time I will go out with him. If he were looking for friendship, we could be friends, but that's not what he wants. And while speaking with him is easy, there's no chemistry.

He helps us unload, gives me a hug goodbye, and says, "See you later."

Later sometimes means never.

⌒〜✳〜⌒

Annette cries when I drop her off at security in the airport. She throws her arms around me and hangs on me.

"I had so much fun with you! I'll miss you so much!"

I squeeze her tight. "I loved it." I don't know what it's like for her. I do know as much as she misses me when I'm at school, she misses our mom more. She's still a little girl who needs her mama, even though she's taller than me.

I plan the order of my homework assignments during the half-hour drive back to my apartment. I'm grateful Mom spent the extra money to have my sister fly out of the airport near me, avoiding a six-hour round-trip journey to Denver. That was not in my plans today.

There are four boys in my apartment when I walk in: James, Dave, Matt, and one I don't know. They're here for Abby, who can't help stealing the show with her bright smile, dimples, and show-stopping red hair. They circle around her like bees, basking in her attention as she laughs and giggles. I'm not in the mood to compete and disappear to my room to do homework.

That's the one problem with your living room being social central.

Iris's door opens and she calls out to them as she goes down the hall. Then she joins them in the kitchen, and it gets even louder. I'm about to give up on my homework.

Abby pops into my room. "We're gonna go swimming at the lake and then ice skating. Want to come?"

"You guys are leaving?" I should be happy. I'll be able to concentrate better when they're gone.

"Just for a few hours. Come on, it'll be fun."

"What lake?" I swam in a lake yesterday and the weekend before. Lakes in Colorado are freezing. Not like the ones in Arkansas that feel slightly cooler than bath temperature.

"One up by the reservoir. It has a rope swing."

"And where's the ice skating? The water's cold but not that cold."

Abby laughs, flashing those dimples. "There's an indoor rink ten minutes from here."

I consider it. I look at my homework, and I want to play, not sit here and analyze literature. Then I think of my empty bank account because I still don't have a job. "I'll come to the lake, but not ice skating."

"Why? That will be the best part."

"Because I don't have a job yet and I have lots of homework." I close my English anthology and climb off my bed.

Abby follows me to the kitchen, already trying to convince me to do more. "It's not that much money. Ice skating is like five dollars. For an hour."

"What's wrong?" Matt asks as I join the group. He's my age, nineteen, and super tall, yet somehow he still strikes me as a teenage boy barely out of high school.

"Nothing's wrong. I'm coming swimming at the lake, but not ice skating."

"She doesn't want to pay the money," Abby says.

"I'm broke." I open the cabinet and search for a box of crackers. "What time are we going?"

"We're going in about twenty minutes," Dave says.

"I'll pay for you," Matt says, surprising me enough that I look at him over the box of crackers.

"You don't need to pay for me."

He shrugs. "Will you come if I do?"

It feels like a trick question. "It might be a good idea if I came home and did homework."

He waves that off. "It's Saturday. You shouldn't have to worry about homework today."

The very idea makes me laugh. "Tell that to every teacher on campus. The weekend is when I catch up on assignments."

"So is it homework or money holding you back?"

"Both," I say.

He grins. "So you'll go if I pay for you?"

He completely sidestepped my argument about homework.

"I might," I say.

Abby cheers. "That's better than what she said before!"

We negotiate the driving situation next, and I'm amused when I end up being one of the drivers. Now I have to stay the whole time. This feels like a trap. I hop back into my room to change into a swimsuit.

Mitch calls me just as we're pulling into the gravel lot in front of another glacial mountain lake with pristine mountains behind it and sparse bushes around it. Iris and Matt make a beeline for the rope swing dangling from a tall oak tree, but I sit in my car and wait for everyone to leave so I can take the call. Except the other passengers take forever to get out, so the call hangs up before I get to it.

"Are you coming?" Dave asks.

"In a moment," I say.

Dave gets out, and I'm finally alone. I call Mitch back.

"Hey!" he says.

"I missed your call," I say.

"Yeah! A bunch of us are getting together to play soccer tonight. I wondered if you want to come."

I look at the cold water and the rope swing and wish I were available. "I'd love to. I can't. I'm down the canyon swimming in a pond."

He makes a clicking sound with his tongue. "It seems like you've always got something going on."

"If you want on my calendar, you might have to ask sooner," I tease.

"Looks like it. Put me down for next weekend."

I smile, warming to the banter. "What day?"

"I don't know. Block off the whole weekend. Write on your calendar in great big letters, Mitch."

That makes me laugh. "I don't know if I can give up that much time to one person."

"I see. I'm going to have to earn it. Fine. Give me Friday. And maybe I can get Saturday too, if I'm on good behavior."

"It's entirely possible." The flirtatious dialogue feels good. It warms my heart. I want to do it in person.

My friends are yelling my name, even though I would rather stay on the phone in the warm interior of my car. "I better go. But I'll see you tomorrow at church."

"See you later, Cassandra."

I get out of the car, reluctant to pull my shirt off and reveal my bony upper half, but I know the T-shirt isn't really hiding anything. Iris and Matt are in the water, and Abby swings out on the rope swing before letting go and plunging into the cold depths. Dave turns to me, grinning, and holds out the rope.

"You're up."

"Me?" My voice comes out as a squeak.

"Yup."

I don't touch the rope. "How do I do this?"

"You hold onto the rope and push off the rocks. When you're at the farthest point out, you let go. If you don't, the rope will bring you back here."

In other words, if I chicken out, it'll be okay.

"Don't let go at the rocks," he adds. "Either let go over the water, or hold on until you get back."

That's an added dimension I didn't need to worry about.

I finally take the rope, and everyone cheers.

I can imagine how that frigid water will feel when I fall into it. And I'm afraid of how the rope swing will feel as I arc out over the water.

I grip the rope in both hands and kick away from the shore.

For a brief, exhilarating moment, I'm flying. The breeze blows through my hair, whipping it up around my head, and then I reach the highest point. I know I'm supposed to let go, but my nerves freeze, and I don't. The arc heads back to the rocks, and Iris shouts, "Jump!"

My heart hammers faster in my chest. My window of opportunity is closing. I'm swinging fast towards the rocks.

Iris screams, and I let go.

The icy water hits me like a slap in the face, and I plunge into the depths, cold fingers rushing past my ears and neck, bubbles erupting with the force of a volcano in my ear. I kick my legs and push up until my head breaks the surface, and then I gasp as I draw in the cold air.

"Are you okay?" Iris asks, her expression anxious.

"I didn't think you were going to make it!" Abby says.

"That was amazing!" Dave hollers from the shore.

I grin. "Let's do it again!"

CHAPTER THIRTY-TWO

The Invitation

Monday afternoon arrives, and I still haven't heard back about the job at the student center. The School of Engineering hasn't called again either. I want to wait a little longer, but I don't want to lose the job option I have in hand. I could call the student center and ask if they're going to offer me a job, but that seems so presumptuous. Instead, I call the School of Engineering.

"Hello, this is Jan Martin," an elderly woman's voice answers.

"Hi, this is Cassandra Jones. I'm returning your call from Friday."

"Oh, Cassandra!" Immediately, her voice turns enthusiastic. "Thank you for calling me back! We were very impressed with your interview on Friday, and we would like to offer you a job, if you're still looking."

There's no legitimate reason for me to turn this down. I want a job, I *need* a job, so I take a deep breath and say, "I am! That would be great!"

"Fantastic! I know you'll love working here in the department. If you can swing by later today, we can fill out your paperwork and talk about your start date."

"Sure. I'll swing by after class."

I hang up and immediately start to compose a text to Owen to tell him—

And then I remember. Owen's gone. We broke up. I haven't talked to him in six months, and I deleted his number, so why the hell do I want to talk to him now?

Sometimes I hate boys.

I refocus. Who can I text? My mom, I guess. I send her a happy text with a bunch of emojis: *I got a job!* And then I text my roommates because I want to tell somebody and get a reaction.

For a moment, I think of Tiago. I haven't forgotten him, the boy I left in Brazil, the boy who first stole my heart and knows me more intimately than anyone else. But I don't speak to him, and I won't start now. When you're as bound up together as we were, there's no place for friendship. It's all or nothing.

After class, I go to the office to fill out the required paperwork with my student information, and Jan makes a photocopy of my driver's license.

"Our current secretary found out she's pregnant and she's not feeling well," Jan says. "So she's quitting next week."

"Oh." I try to absorb this information.

"We would like her to train you before she leaves. It'll take me a few days to process the paperwork. Could you start on Thursday?"

I flip through my schedule and nod. "Yes, I only have class in the morning." Luckily, I planned my schedule that way. Most of the jobs I applied for required me to have either a morning or an afternoon shift, and my class schedule last year didn't make that possible. I learned from that and only scheduled morning classes this term.

"Great. That will give her five days with you before she's done. We'll see you Thursday."

I leave with a pep in my step. I don't care anymore that this wasn't my first choice. I'm excited to have a job to fill my time and earn money. My bank account is woefully low.

I have a little bit of homework, but not so much that I'm stressed out, so I decide to go home instead of going to the library. I'm standing at the intersection, waiting for my turn to walk in the crosswalk, when someone calls my name.

I turn and shield my eyes against the sunlight, then smile when I recognize Mitch walking toward me, his hand in his pocket, backpack on his shoulder.

"Hey! I didn't know you were taking classes right now," I say.

He shrugs. "I'm not. But my brother asked me to return a few books to the library for him."

"Your brother is a big reader?"

"Yeah."

"Me too."

"You'll have to meet him sometime. I bet you guys would get along."

The light changes, and we cross the street together.

"Have you seen much of my cousin lately?" Mitch asks.

The question catches me off guard, since I was thinking about his cousin a few hours ago. When does he think I would have seen him? Does he know something I don't know? "Excuse me?" I stutter.

He tilts his head and furrows his brow. "Monica. Have you seen much of her?"

"Oh, no." My face grows hot. Of course, he meant Monica. "No, I think we've both been busy."

"Yeah, I haven't seen much of her either. We should hang out with her later this week."

"That sounds like so much fun!" I hope he doesn't know me well enough to tell when I'm lying.

I can't hang out with Mitch and Monica at the same time.

"Hey, I know I talked about wanting to go camping sometime, and I still want to do that. But my friend Robin—you met her at my apartment when I busted my eardrum—"

"Yeah, how's that?" I glance up at him. I don't have to look far because he's only a few inches taller than me.

He waves me off. "Oh, it's totally fine. But anyway, Robin's parents own a house on Lake Powell, and she invited a bunch of us to go down this weekend. Want to come?"

I'm floored. I can't believe he asked me. It's a five-hour drive, a weekend away on the lake with Mitch.

"Yes! I'd love to! That sounds like so much fun. What day do we leave?"

His face lights up in a big grin at my enthusiasm. "We were thinking Thursday night so we can be there Friday morning and spend all day Friday, Saturday, and Sunday boating. We'll come back Monday afternoon in time for evening classes."

"It sounds amazing!" I can't believe he invited me. That means something, it means I mean something—

Wait a minute.

Thursday.

"Oh," I say, deflating. "I just got a job."

"Hey, that's great!" He holds his hand out for a high five, which I give him, but he notices my lack of enthusiasm. "It's a good thing, right? You've been wanting one."

"It's totally a good thing. But—I'm supposed to start Thursday."

He furrows his brow as he considers this. "We don't leave until Thursday evening. You should be able to go to work."

"But Friday..." As badly as I want to go, I won't risk losing a job over this.

"Talk to your boss. Maybe they'll be understanding. And if not, hey, we'll still go camping in Grand Junction sometime."

I nod. But now I really, really, really want to go to Lake Powell with him and his friends.

And then I think of something. "Is Monica going?"

"Oh, no, I didn't invite her. You know, it's a bunch of my college friends and . . . She doesn't know anyone except you . . ."

I smile. He only invited me.

That knowledge makes me somewhat giddy.

❦

"Oh," Jan says when I call the Department of Engineering to talk to her about it. "Actually, this could work out well. Lara said she's feeling better and asked if she could stay on one more month. I hate to ask you to wait, but are you okay starting at the end of August instead?"

That's two weeks away! I bite back my first hasty words. I want to start next week and put money in my bank account. But since that's not going to happen, I say, "Yeah. I can do that."

I hang up, feeling a sense of frustration. I get to go to Lake Powell with Mitch, but I've delayed my employment by weeks. If I hadn't called her, I would've shown up on Thursday, started work, and they would've had two employees.

I have to deal with it. It's too late now. I try to focus on the happy news that there are no obstacles keeping me from going to Lake Powell.

I stay up late getting ahead on my homework since I'll be missing two days of classes and an entire weekend of study. Just as I'm about to shut my computer down, an email comes through. I hesitate when I see the name.

Tiago.

Seeing his name brings a flood of nostalgia, memories, and sadness. I truly did love him, and a part of me will always hurt because he's not with me. I tell myself not to read the email, but even I am not that strong. I open it and read his words.

I know you don't want to hear from me. I just want to talk to you, even if you don't respond. I need to talk to you. To know you're receiving my words. I miss you. I love you.

I should not have opened it. My heart hurts worse, and my eyes burn. Responding to him will only prolong this pain. I delete the email. Nothing good can come of our continued communication.

I put my computer away, go to bed, and dream of Brazil.

☙✽❧

Mitch comes to my apartment door at six o'clock Thursday evening.

"Ready?"

"Yeah."

I grab my duffel bag with everything I need for the weekend. I yell at my roommates, "Bye!"

Iris and Abby are in the kitchen, and they look up and grin at me.

"Have fun!" they yell back, and I don't miss the way Abby wiggles her eyebrows at me. They're hoping I might get some action this weekend.

I have to admit I'm not opposed to it.

I don't reveal any of that as I turn back to Mitch. "Ready."

He leads the way down the stairs and out the complex to the four-door sedan parked outside. Isaac and Robin sit up front with Isaac driving, and they both swivel around when Mitch opens the back door of the car.

"Hi guys, this is Cassandra, remember her?"

I wave as I slide in, and Isaac waves back.

"Hi, good to see you again!" Robin says, smiling. "I'm so excited Mitch invited you to come with us!"

"Yeah, it was really kind of him."

Mitch climbs in the back next to me, and Isaac turns on music while he drives.

There's no quiet moment. He fires questions at Mitch as we head out of town, and Mitch gives brief, one-word responses. Isaac then turns his attention to me, asking about my family and school. Then a song comes on the radio that he likes, and he says, "Oh, I love this song!" and turns the music up. He and Robin sing along together from the front seats.

I turn to Mitch. "You okay? You're a little quiet."

He shrugs. "I'm fine. Just tired."

It's a classic response everyone gives when something is bothering them and they don't feel like talking about it. I want to touch him to show my compassion, but I'm afraid he'll think I'm hitting on him. "I'm sorry," I say, and then I gather up my courage to pat his shoulder.

It's a shoulder, but it's hard as a rock, and I feel the corded muscles between the roundness of the shoulder. I forget myself and squeeze his bicep, just to feel for myself how strong he is.

He laughs and pulls his arm away from me. "That tickles."

"Sorry." My face heats with embarrassment. I've already managed to make a fool of myself. I tuck my hand into my lap and move to the other side of the car, leaning against the window.

But Mitch reaches over and puts his arm around my shoulders, pulling me into his side. I rest my head in the nook between his shoulder and collarbone, and he tilts his head so it rests on mine.

It's a five-hour drive to Lake Powell, and we're exhausted. My head starts to bob as I fall asleep, and Mitch scoots to the other side of the car and lowers my head to his lap. He rests his hand lightly on my waist. I glance up at him to see his eyes closed, head leaning against the window, and I shut my eyes.

My chest is full of a warm, gooey feeling like the insides of a freshly baked chocolate chip cookie. It's so nice to be touched.

CHAPTER THIRTY-THREE

Lake Trip

It's late when we arrive, and we stumble into the five-bedroom lake house Robin's parents own without much more than a good night. Robin and I take one room. I get my contacts out and crawl in the bed, sinking into the cocooning white sheets.

Much nicer than the ones on my own bed.

Robin's dad, Stan, wakes us with donuts and orange juice in the morning. There are more people coming, but they couldn't leave Thursday, so they won't arrive until this afternoon. Robin's dad doesn't want to wait.

"Can't waste a day!" he says. "Come on, come on, let's get out on that blue water!"

"Better hurry," Robin tells me in our bedroom as we change into swimsuits. "He gets impatient."

Eek. I tangle the straps in my rush but manage to get a sundress over my swimsuit before Robin leaves the room.

Mitch catches my gaze when we step into the kitchen, and his eyes crinkle in a grin. I grin back, wrapping my arms around my torso with a sudden bout of shyness.

It feels like I'm a trip with my boyfriend. And yet, that's not what we are.

Stan drives down to the dock where the boat waits, and I get my first glimpse of the lake and the canyons surrounding it. My breath catches at the steep, red rock walls, layers of stratified earth, reminiscent of the Grand Canyon I visited when I was younger. At the base of the rock walls glistens a sparkly turquoise lake as far as my eye can see. The canyon's structure forms fingers of water leading to inlets that break up the large water mass. A few other boats are already out, leaving white-tipped wakes behind them as they glide through the lake.

"It's so beautiful," I breathe, staring out the window.

"Wait until we're on it," Robin says with a big grin.

"Have you gone boating on a lake before?" Mitch asks me.

"We have a big lake back home. We used it for church activities a lot."

"Can you water ski?"

"Oh, no." I shake my head, grimacing as I remember the one time I tried. I fell flat on my butt so hard that the water shot up places it never should've gone. "But I can handle a tube." I smile widely.

Mitch laughs. I study his profile as he looks out at the view. He seems in a better mood today, quicker to smile, the glimmer of light back in his brown eyes. He's very pleasant to look at.

Robin's dad parks the car and leads us down to the dock, and then we strip out of our clothing, revealing swimsuits. I can't help staring when Mitch removes his shirt. The muscles on his tanned torso tighten when he lifts his arms over his head, and his abs have abs. A breeze blows by, sending a whisper of goosebumps across his flesh and puckering his nipples, and I look away so he won't see me staring.

He's definitely causing a physical reaction in me.

Robin looks cute and sexy in her plaid two-piece. I'm not comfortable in a two-piece, but I hope I don't look too girlish in my new blue-and-green houndstooth one-piece. It's the kind with a shelf bra, which I appreciate. The small amount of padding helps me not feel nearly so self-conscious.

The boys wear board shorts. Stan hands out sunscreen and warns us about the dangers of the sun over here, so we lather up.

Then he says, "All right, who's tubing first?"

Not me, I intend to say. But Robin pipes up and says, "The girls get to go first, of course." She looks at me for accordance.

Suddenly I'm terrified. But I smile as if this is a great plan. "Sure!"

We pile onto the boat from the dock, a decent-sized vessel with a cabin and bathroom underneath the seating area. Robin's dad has food and drinks, and I grab a bottle of water and guzzle it quickly.

"Life jackets," he says, opening a bench and throwing them into the middle of the boat.

I choose a small purple one and cinch it up as tight as it will go. He lets the boat idle while he pulls the tube up to the back.

"You know how to do this, right?" Robin asks me.

"I've done it before," I say. "But it's been a while." Like, seven years.

"Okay, you'll catch on, no problem. The goal is to not fall off the tube."

She climbs down the ladder at the back of the boat, and I follow her. We jump from the ladder into the water, and I'm surprised at how pleasantly warm it is. Nothing like the lake I've been swimming in near campus.

The giant tube is only a few feet from us, and we paddle over. We giggle as we begin the awkward climb over the side of the tube, clawing, pulling on each other's hands, and throwing our legs over until we finally get around and on top. We lie on our bellies, legs splayed out on the inflated rubber, faces close to each other, hands gripping the handles. Mitch and Isaac take their seats at the back of the boat and lean over the edges, grinning at us.

"Don't fall off!" Isaac calls to Robin.

"Your turn is coming!" she hollers back at him.

The boat engine revs, and then it takes off so fast the tube lifts out of the water and crashes back down to the surface when the rope pulls taut. I squeal and grip my handlebar, not about to fall off in the first three seconds of being on here.

The wind blows through my hair, softening the sun's rays that beat upon us. We bounce and jostle, making figure eights on the water.

"Wake!" Robin shouts at the boat.

Isaac turns around and says something to her dad, then the boat picks up speed. Stan turns at a sharp 180-degree angle, and I gasp as a spray of water hits me in the face.

And then I see what we're aiming for. The boat cuts a smooth wake into the water with multiple ripples flowing toward us, and then the boat doubles back and slices across them, creating waves only moments before we follow. I can't help screaming as the tube goes up and over such a large wake that we are airborne, the tube flying like a kite behind the rope, my legs lifting off the tube, while I hang on for dear life with both hands as everything soars.

Robin is laughing and screaming, and as the tube punches back into the water and soaks us with spray, I have to admit this is exhilarating.

Robin holds one hand out in front of us and lifts her thumb. "Faster, faster!" she shouts.

The boys must understand her message because they pass it on to her dad, and then somehow we're going even faster, the wind rippling at the skin of my face, and I narrow my eyes, afraid my contacts are going to fly out.

Stan pummels us over a wake and then whips the boat around again so that we're forced to go over the one he just made.

It's the biggest one yet, and I know, as we go over the crest and my hands lose their grip, that I'm done for.

I manage to close my mouth as I fly off the tube and smack into the lake. I go underwater for a split second, but the life jacket pulls me to the surface an instant later, and I gasp in a breath of air before I start laughing. I'm still laughing when the boat swings back around to pick me up. Mitch takes my hand and pulls me up.

"You stayed on that tube for seven minutes."

"Is that good?" The short hair at the nape of my neck drips water all over me.

"It's awesome."

"So am I going alone or what?" Robin calls from the tube.

"I can't believe you didn't fall off," I say.

Mitch leans toward me and whispers conspiratorially, "She may have had more practice than you."

I laugh and nod.

"I'm coming!" Isaac says. He peels off the shirt he was wearing in the boat and jumps off the side, not even bothering with the ladder.

The wind whips up as the boat takes off again, and I shiver as it rolls over my wet skin. Mitch grabs me a towel, but he's still shirtless, and his chest brushes my forearms before he gets me wrapped up in a towel.

His skin is hot. I want to take the towel off and let him wrap me up.

I don't.

We sit at the back of the boat and cheer for Robin and Isaac.

"So, tell me about yourself, Cassandra," Mitch says, poking my thigh with his finger. "Other than being Monica's friend, I don't know much about you."

My heart rate ratchets up at the question. It sounds so innocent, but it usually means people want to know about past relationships.

I don't want to go there.

"Well, you know I'm majoring in English. I love words. I love to read. I like poetry."

"I love poetry," Mitch says.

I laugh. "Boys don't like poetry."

"Says who? Half of the world's famous poets are male."

"True," I concede. "But I don't actually like to read poetry. I like to write it."

"I'd like to read some of your poems," he says, genuine interest in his open expression.

"Do you write poetry?" I ask.

"Only in French," he says, and his face lights up in a grin.

His grin is infectious. I can't help returning it. "Where did you learn French?"

"I did a mission trip to France."

"You did?" I can feel myself falling harder, leaning into him while my soul sighs with longing. "That's so awesome!"

Our conversation gets interrupted when Robin lets out a whoop, and we turn our eyes back to the tube to see Isaac bobbing in the water and Robin laughing.

"Wearing out yet?" she says, throwing both arms in the air. "Mitch! You up?"

He accepts the challenge, jumping over the side of the boat to swim to her, and this time, Isaac comes to sit by me.

"So, you and Mitch." He grins at me in a friendly way.

"Oh, we're just friends," I say quickly.

"Ha ha." He winks. "I can tell."

"Has he said something?"

"Ha!" Isaac smirks and takes a sip from his drink. "So you do like him."

"He's really fun and nice," I say, not ready to be vulnerable to this guy I barely know.

"He's one of the most sincere people you'll ever meet. He's really passionate about the things he cares about."

It's an intriguing comment. "What is he passionate about?"

Isaac shrugs. "French. God. Weight lifting."

He grins at the last, and I laugh.

"That last one is pretty unique," I say.

"Yeah, he's really into it. I've never met someone else as into it as he is."

"Me neither."

We end our conversation as Mitch and Robin get back on the boat, and Mitch looks over and flashes a smile while he towels off his hair. My heart flips. I feel a little guilty for talking about him, but sometimes it's the easiest way to find out about someone.

I've got two more days with him. And I suddenly know that I want him to be mine before this is over.

CHAPTER THIRTY-FOUR

Making him Mine

We spend the next hour taking turns on the tube, and then Stan pulls out the water skis. I'm the only person who declines to try them, and no amount of persuasion changes my mind. I remember very clearly my butt pain from the previous experience.

I don't mind making small talk with the others while Mitch mans the skis. And he looks like a Greek god on the water, his bronze skin shining and reflecting the sun, his hair brilliant with rays of light, every muscle rippling as he uses his forearms and core, holding tight to the skis.

He's an inspiring sight.

Stan takes us to a small rocky island for lunch. The cooler comes out, and we sit down to feast on ham and cheese sandwiches Robin's mom made for us. Robin eats a salad, and Mitch asks her, "Are you gluten-free?"

"No. I'm a vegetarian."

I perk up slightly and swallow my bite of food. "I was vegetarian through high school."

"Really?" Robin says, and we engage in an excited conversation about eating habits. I don't tell them I used to have an eating disorder; that would be oversharing.

"So, Cassandra," Isaac says.

He sits so close to Robin that their thighs are touching. At the risk of looking idiotic, I say, "Are you guys dating?"

They share a grin.

"Yes," Robin says.

"I guess you could say that," Isaac adds.

"How long have you been dating?" I ask.

"Officially?" Robin tilts her head. "About three weeks. Unofficially..."

I laugh. I know how that goes also.

"Now ask her how many guys she was kissing in that unofficial stage," Isaac says, pretending to look put out.

"Hey, you wouldn't make a commitment," Robin says.

"I did now," Isaac says.

"Then I guess the strategy worked." Robin winks. "And it was a lot of fun."

Laughter erupts out of all of us.

Isaac looks at me. "Are you dating anyone, Cassandra?"

All eyes turn toward me, and my face grows hot, though that could be the sunshine beating down on it. "No."

"And how many guys are you kissing while you're not dating anyone?" Isaac says, wiggling his eyebrows.

"Hey!" Robin says. "That's private. She doesn't have to tell you that."

I shrug. "I don't kiss if I'm not dating."

Isaac leans back, his expression shrewd. "Ever?"

I consider the question. "Well, there was that one guy..."

They laugh again, and I sneak a glance over at Mitch. He's laughing too.

"So how many guys have you kissed?" Isaac asks.

"Tell him to screw off if you don't feel like answering, Cassandra," Robin says.

"I don't mind," I say. It's fun to go through those memories. I count them out in my head. Josh, my horrible first kiss, right before ninth grade. Then, the first boy I actually liked, Ben. Does Oliver count? It was a barely-kiss, but even now, I get tingly remembering it. Then Tiago, of course, followed by Owen, and finally Jared. "Six."

Isaac nods. "A respectable number."

"I'm not sure why you're interrogating her about her love life," Robin says. "It's none of your business. How many girls have you kissed, you man-whore?"

I would not have believed it possible for Isaac to blush, but his face flames bright red now. He mumbles something, and Robin laughs, poking his side with her toe.

"Louder. Say it so everyone can hear."

"I don't keep track," he says.

"Since when?" Robin goads, obviously familiar with this refrain.

"Since high school."

"Because?" Robin prods.

He sighs. "Because I lost count after twenty."

Robin throws her head back and crows with laughter. I'm embarrassed for Isaac, but not particularly astonished. Owen's numbers would be similar. He kissed at least four our senior year of high school. Eddie, Susan, me, and Kristin.

There I go, thinking of him again! How long before he falls out of my mind?

"I got a bit carried away in my younger years," Isaac says.

Robin rolls her eyes. "I think it's a man thing."

"We're not all like that," Mitch says, his tone a combination of joking and seriousness.

Of course, our attention turns to him.

"So, tell us your numbers, Mitch," Isaac teases, a gleam in his eye.

He must already know the answer.

I tilt my head, very curious. Mitch is so stunningly beautiful. Certainly, he's had some experience.

"Two," he says.

"Two what?" Robin asks.

"I've kissed two girls."

His statement is met with stunned silence. Suddenly my six feels like a cavalier number.

"They must have been special," I say.

Mitch looks at me. "I should hope so."

There's not much I can say in response to that. Robin and Isaac start talking about something else, but I study Mitch's profile a bit longer as he turns away, and I can't help the way my eyes are drawn to his lips, given our conversation.

I would like to make myself number three.

☙ ❦ ❧

Sheryl, the third girl in our group, and two more boys arrive that evening. I stand slightly behind Robin as Isaac introduces everyone. I wish they hadn't come. I got quite comfortable in our quartet and resent that the dynamics are about to change.

But I'm not the outsider, and the three of them include me as if they've known me as long as they've known Robin. Robin's mom makes us a big pasta dinner, and then she tells everyone to put on swimsuits because we're getting in the hot tub. She leaves no room for disagreement. Since my suit is already on, I waste no time filing out the door to the hot tub by the pool.

We sit in a circle around the bubbling hot water, and the conversation consists of mercilessly teasing Isaac, who, it turns out, is a cheerleader for the PYU football team. This is news to me and fuel for endless banter from the other boys. I can do nothing but laugh. I'm sitting next to Robin and Lewis in the hot tub, and I've never felt so comfortable in my skin. I'm not a freshman in college anymore, I'm not a newbie, and I'm not a kid. I feel like a woman, like an adult.

It's about time.

Robin's mom comes out with popsicles, and we climb out of the hot tub like a parade of five-year-olds, water streaming off our bodies. Isaac takes the opportunity to grab Robin and haul her away, shrieking, and the rest of us climb back into the hot tub with our popsicles in hand, shaking our heads as the two of them disappear back into the condo.

We rearrange our seating positions, and I'm not surprised that Mitch ends up next to me. We settle into the steaming liquid, and the conversation becomes quieter now that Isaac and Robin are gone.

"What year of school are you in, Cassandra?" Sheryl asks.

"Sophomore," I say.

"And how did you and Mitch meet?"

Mitch and I glance at each other, sitting shoulder to shoulder, hip to hip, and I know I'm not imagining the connection between us.

"Church," I say. "And living in the same apartment complex, I guess."

"Actually, Cassandra is really good friends with my cousin."

He has no idea how good of friends I am with him.

"She introduced us."

But of course he means Monica. He doesn't know about Owen. And I'm so tired of always thinking about Owen. Owen, Owen, Owen. He needs to stay in the memories of nostalgia as my high school boyfriend. Nothing more.

155

Even that thought of him being nothing more hurts.

☙ ❈ ❧

Saturday we sleep in. There was some talk the night before about getting out on the lake to watch the sunrise, but in the morning, nobody stirs. Least of all me. I hate mornings. I finally open my eyes when Robin gets out of bed and heads to the kitchen, where I hear the sizzle of bacon.

I check the time: a little after nine. I sit up, startled. The blackout curtains hid the sun from our view. Sheryl yawns and murmurs something when I pass her bed on my way to the bathroom, but I don't catch it.

I go through my morning routine, and five minutes later, I'm in the kitchen with Robin and her mom. They put me to work setting out paper plates and plastic utensils. By the time the eggs and bacon hit the table, the rest of our party has woken and come to join us.

Mitch gives my shoulder a squeeze when he walks by. "Good morning," he says.

"Morning," I respond, my flesh warming at his touch.

I'm certain he likes me.

We finish breakfast and change clothes to head out for another day at the lake. I expect we're going to do the same things as yesterday but with a bigger group. We fill every seat in the boat, with two guys sitting on the edge. Nobody wears a life jacket, which makes me nervous, but I keep it to myself.

With this many people, the tubing takes longer, but we all get a turn. Robin goes over to her dad and says something, then comes back to us and says, "He's going to take us to the cliffs."

The boys whoop and cheer with joy, but I don't know what that means.

The boat zips across the lake. I marvel at the tall red rock walls towering over the sparkling water.

Now I know what she meant by cliffs.

We approach one, and Stan angles the boat parallel to it before cutting the engine.

"Okay, here we are."

We're still at least fifty yards from shore. Robin stands up, and she says, "Who's with me?" before her lithe figure dives off the boat.

How deep is it here? I peer over the side, but she's already surfaced. She takes long freestyle strokes for shore.

"She's hot," Lewis says to Isaac.

"Don't I know it. She's the whole package."

"Any guy would be lucky to get her."

I pretend not to overhear them. But I know if I dive off this boat, it will end in a spectacular belly flop at best and me drowning at worst. Nobody will admire my tall, athletic form, and someone might have to swim in after me when my dog paddling gives out before I reach shore.

"I'm staying," I say.

Silas, Lewis, and Isaac dive in after Robin, and I inch closer to the edge of the boat.

"Really? You're not coming?" Mitch asks.

I gesture out at the water in front of us. "I barely swim. I took a swimming class last semester to help me learn how, but I'm not comfortable with it."

He raises his eyebrows and jacks his thumb toward the boat's life jackets. "You can keep the life jacket on."

I look at Robin, already on the shore, and the boys behind her. They can touch now, and they're standing, splashing each other, their bare torsos glistening in the sunlight.

Nobody is wearing a jacket.

"I think I'll pass."

"You don't want to go cliff jumping?"

My gaze snaps back toward him. "Cliff jumping?"

CHAPTER THIRTY-FIVE

Spiritually Inclined

The words squeak out of me. I take in the tall, red rock cliff wall and look back at him, my eyes going wide. "You're not actually going to jump from those, are you? They're like a hundred feet tall!"

Mitch laughs. "No, they're not. Only thirty feet, at most."

"It's not safe!" I know I should act chill and totally cool with this, but my anxious self gets ahead of me. I can't keep quiet. "There could be fallen trees in the water that weren't there last time, you could hit the water wrong and hurt yourself!" I have a better understanding now of how he busted his eardrum.

Mitch reaches over and gives my bare shoulder a squeeze. "We're going to be okay."

He lets himself fall off the back of the boat, and I'm left gaping after him. I feel like a total idiot for going off like that and wish I would've kept quiet. Now he probably thinks I'm a worrywart and afraid of everything.

He wouldn't be terribly far off.

"I'm staying too," Sheryl says beside me, giving a visible shudder from her shoulders all the way down to her hips. "Cliff jumping? No way. If I'm jumping from a ledge that high, it's because my life is in danger."

I turn toward her, my anxiety lessening. At least I'm not the only one.

"There are other things I would rather do for kicks," I say.

"Yeah. Like decide which pair of shoes goes better with my new dress."

I laugh with her, although that's not what I would choose either. I have a better sense of fashion after working in a clothing store through high school, but I would still rather decide between books at a used bookstore or the latest hardcover release in my favorite series.

That's a good dilemma to have.

"There they are!" Stan calls from the front of the boat.

Sheryl and I turn to look at the cliff in front of us. I shield my eyes against the high afternoon sun and see the boys at the top of the cliff.

"How did they get up there?" I ask.

"There's a path that winds up behind it," Stan says.

Robin appears next to the boys, looking perfect with her slender, toned figure and bikini that fits her like lingerie. She jostles Isaac, who pushes her back, and she shrieks and grabs his arm to keep from falling off the cliff.

My heart rate picks up. "This looks so dangerous."

"It's really okay," Stan says. "We've been coming here and doing this since she was ten."

That doesn't make it okay. But nobody likes a worrywart, so I say nothing.

Lewis lets out a yell, and then jumps off, tucking himself into a cannonball before he hits the water. The splash is magnificent, and I stand up to watch him surface.

He comes out crowing and yelling challenges to the remaining figures on the cliff.

Robin follows. She doesn't cannonball or dive but makes herself as straight as a pencil. She barely makes a splash as her toes guide her body into the water.

We cheer for her when she emerges. It was so beautifully done.

And then Mitch jumps, letting out a boyish yell that brings a smile to my lips. He hits the water and emerges seconds later, tossing his head and sputtering. He turns around and waits for Isaac and Silas, then swims back out to the boat while the others return to the shore to climb again. He hauls himself up on the ladder and sits on the rung, resting on the boat and catching his breath.

I lean over the edge next to him.

"That was mighty impressive," I say.

"Are you sure you don't want to go?" he asks. "It's really fun."

I shake my head. "I don't like heights." It's not precisely true. Heights don't bother me; falling from them does. But it's easier not to explain.

He shrugs and drops off the ladder back into the water. "Well, if you change your mind, you know where to find me."

I watch him swim back, hoping he doesn't think less of me now. Robin's out there taking the world with both hands, and here I am, hunkering down in the safety of a boat. But Sheryl doesn't seem to think anything of this, and she's able to carry the conversation for both of us pretty much one-sided.

We spend at least an hour cliff jumping, and then everyone who jumped is exhausted. We find spaces along the boat and stretch out for a siesta. My legs look a little pink, so I slather on more sunscreen.

I think Mitch will come sit by me, but he doesn't. He lays on his stomach between Lewis and Sheryl, then rests his head on his hands and closes his eyes. I stretch out on the bench along the edge of the boat and wonder if I'm reading too much into this. Maybe Mitch treats me the same as he does every other girl here. Maybe I'm imagining there being something between us.

Stan lets us rest for twenty minutes, and then he asks if anyone wants to swim again. But we're all waterlogged, and we vote instead to head back to the condo for a barbecue dinner at the pavilion. Robin pulls on a spaghetti-strap sundress she brought with her on the boat, and somehow she looks even more beautiful than she did in her bikini. She sits by Isaac and threads her fingers through his. She's on the bench adjacent to me in the boat.

"That dress is lovely on you," I blurt. "I could never pull off something like that."

"Thank you, it's one of my favorites," she says.

"Don't sell yourself short," Mitch says, his eyes on me. "You would look great in that dress too."

I turn my gaze to him. "My shoulders are too big. They're pretty broad for my frame."

He snorts and rolls his eyes. "You don't know what you look like. You could put on sack cloth and ashes and still outshine anyone around you."

I flush at the compliment, but Robin meets my gaze and smirks.

He thinks I'm pretty.

⁘

Robin's family takes the Sabbath very seriously, insisting we find a local congregation to go to church, which reminds me of my own parents. They were so strict about Sundays that I wasn't allowed to sing with my choir at Carnegie Hall when we took a trip to New York City. I'm devoted to God and believe in the power religion can have in one's life, but I don't feel the same strictness I was raised with.

I wear one of the dresses Martha, Tiago's mom, bought me in Brazil. It's sleeveless and orange, a two-piece set of a skirt and a blouse with colorful embroidered flowers on it. I feel a rush of nostalgia as I put it on. For a brief moment, I allow myself to wonder what Tiago is doing, but there is only pain in that line of thought. I hope he's happy, but he will never be a part of my life.

The sermon is inspiring, and the members of the congregation are friendly enough. We leave after the sermon, not staying for Sunday School. Instead, Stan drives us out to the Hoover Dam Museum and overlook. There's a picnic area, and his wife brought sandwiches. We settle around the table and munch on chips while discussing the things the pastor said in the sermon.

"I just have to say," Mitch says, "how much I feel God's presence in my life. So many times I feel discouraged or incapable, and He picks up the slack. He's my rock, my strength, and I can't help but feel grateful for each breath I take, grateful when I look around at this amazing world He created, that I get to be a part of. I'm amazed at what He does for me."

I stare at Mitch, stunned by his impassioned speech. I'm not sure I've ever heard someone speak so fervently about God. I'm moved by his sincerity and devotion. How does that shape his life? How does it change the decisions he makes, the paths he chooses to follow? What would it be like to walk that path beside him?

I'm more intrigued by Mitch than ever, and I didn't think that was possible.

Mitch's impromptu declaration sets off a chain of declarations from the other kids. It's not hard to find something to say as I look out over the splendor of the canyon and the river below, marveling at the beauty of this mortal life.

This place might be one of the most beautiful I've ever seen, and I feel a serene contentment with this group of kids, and the fact that I get to be here with them.

"Group picture!" Robin's mom says.

She moves us over to one of the bridges spanning a chasm across the Colorado River. I get put in front, which is par for the course, thanks to my height. Mitch comes and stands behind me, then surprises me by wrapping his arms around my waist, pulling me up against him. I place my hand over his and smile big for the camera, pleased that he finally initiated physical contact.

I turn around when we finish with the picture. "Thank you for your words. They touched me more than you can know."

He puts his arms around me and hugs me, and I sink into it because being wrapped in a man's arms is both comforting and stimulating.

"You're welcome. I know sometimes I can be sappy, but I can't help expressing what I feel."

"I think it's great." I squeeze his hand. "Don't ever stop."

We spend the rest of Sunday cleaning the condo and packing.

"We never did see the sunrise on the lake," Lewis says.

"Was that a real goal?" Sheryl says, raising an eyebrow.

I laugh because I echo her sentiment. I have no desire to wake up early for the sun.

Lewis is not put off. He empties the trash into a giant garbage bag and says, "We should do it tomorrow. Let's get up at five. It's our last chance."

I admire his enthusiasm, even if I disagree with his goals.

He turns to Mitch for backup. "Mitch? You in?"

Mitch looks up from where he's sweeping. "Yeah. Let's do it."

"Well, that clinches the deal. Five A.M?"

They nod in agreement.

I shake my head. "Somebody owes me for this."

Isaac laughs and hugs me. "You'll be singing a different song when you see that sunrise tomorrow."

I expect we'll go to bed early since we're getting up for the sunrise, so around eight I change into my pajamas. I'm brushing my teeth in the bedroom when Mitch comes in. He stands in front of the full-length mirror by my bed and picks at his forehead.

"I'm already peeling," he says.

I come and stand next to him and examine the spot on his face where the skin is peeling, revealing pink, fresh new skin underneath. "I didn't know you got sunburned." I check my shoulder. "I'm not peeling."

"That's because you're blessed with naturally dark skin. I'm one of those people trying to fake it."

"So your tan is fake?" I tease him.

"It's a real tan, but I have to work extra hard for it, and I can lose it easily. One sunburn and it's gone."

"Guess I'm blessed to have Colombian blood."

"I think my cousin dated a girl from Colombia."

I nearly choke as lean over the sink to spit out my toothpaste. Is he talking about Owen? Did Owen mention me to his cousin? I'm still trying to work it out, wondering how to ask, when Isaac bounces into the room. He looks over at me in my pajamas and says, "Why are you ready for bed?"

I gesture to the bed behind me. "I'm going to bed."

"But we're putting on a movie."

"But you said we were getting up at five."

"Yeah, and?"

"So those two things don't go together."

"We can make them go together."

I laugh. "That's not how the universe works."

"Watch and see. We're turning on the movie. Mitch, come on."

Mitch turns back to me. "It looks like we've been summoned."

I wave at him. "You go on. I'm off to bed."

"For real?"

I nod. "I'm really not a morning person."

He shrugs. "Okay. See you tomorrow then."

I feel a big ache of disappointment when he leaves. We were alone in the room, and he didn't try to kiss me or even hold my hand.

CHAPTER THIRTY-SIX

Perfection

I've only been asleep for a few hours at most when the bedroom light turns on. I pull a pillow over my head and hope Robin and Sheryl get into pajamas quickly. The bed bounces, but not the way it does when Robin crawls in beside me. Instead, it bounces as someone puts an arm on either side of me and purposefully shakes the mattress.

"Wake up, Cassandra!" Robin's voice cuts through my grogginess.

I move the pillow away from my face to see her inches away, grinning.

"What's going on?" My voice is groggy. I know it's not morning. I don't feel rested but have that slow buzz of lethargy in my head as if I was woken from a nap.

"We're going to Denny's."

"What?" Her words don't make sense to my sleep-addled brain.

She flies off the bed, taking my pillow with her. Sheryl pokes her head in. "Are we ready?" she says.

"Just about," Robin replies. "I've almost got Cassandra up."

Isaac steps into the room. "Come on, Cassandra! You can even come in your pajamas."

I sit up in bed and fish around for my glasses on the nightstand. "I don't understand. What time is it?" I grab my phone and groan. "It's twelve-thirty in the morning!"

They cackle like this is insanely funny.

"Denny's is open twenty-four/seven," Robin says.

"The boys are going," Sheryl adds.

I climb out of bed, my glasses settled firmly on my nose. I check my reflection quickly. I've only been asleep for a few hours, so my hair hasn't had a chance to make itself stand up. Robin hooks her arm through mine and hauls me from the bedroom as if she's afraid I'll climb back into bed otherwise.

The boys are standing around in the living room, talking and laughing, none of them showing any signs of tiredness. Silas spots me and Robin and claps his hands, rubbing them together. "Ready?"

"Ready," Robin says for me.

I don't feel ready. I feel groggy and sluggish and like I want to go back to bed. But as we stuff ourselves into two separate cars, my grogginess transforms into goofiness. By the time we get seated at a large booth at Denny's, it's one in the morning, and I find everything hilarious.

"Would you like coffee with your eggs?" the waitress asks me after I place my order.

"No, thank you. I prefer my eggs dry," I say with a straight face.

The waitress furrows her brow in confusion, and Robin and Sheryl giggle behind their menus.

"But I will take a hot chocolate," I add.

"With your eggs?" the waitress asks.

"Separate. The hot chocolate in a mug, the eggs on a plate."

The girls bury their faces in each other's shoulders, writhing with laughter.

"Okay." The waitress draws out the word and looks at me like I'm the one not making sense. Then she takes the menus and walks away.

Mitch sits on the other side of me, and he elbows me. "You confused her," he says, laughing.

"She confused herself," I say, nonplussed. "Who puts hot chocolate on eggs?"

The girls laugh harder, and the boys shake their heads, amused smiles on their faces.

My hyper energy only lasts for forty minutes. I'm half asleep, dragging my feet when we leave. Mitch puts an arm around me and helps me to the car, and I want to snuggle into his embrace. But while I'm aware of his arm around me in the car, I'm too sleepy to enjoy it.

"Remember, five a.m.!" Isaac says as we stumble into our beds.

Is he crazy? I thought going to Denny's at one in the morning would make him rethink the sunrise thing. A quick glance at my phone shows it's after two.

"We may as well stay awake," Robin whispers.

I might agree with her, except I'm so tired.

It seems like I only close my eyes for a second before the bed is jostling again. I open my eyes to see Isaac waking Robin. "It's ten to five," he whispers. "If we're going to do this, it has to be now."

"I don't want to anymore," Robin groans.

Sleep pulls at my eyelids, weighs down the front of my head. I'm annoyed at whoever came up with this idea and fight the urge to tell them so.

But it's the sleep talking. I get up with her, and we're silent as we change out of our pajamas into comfortable clothing. I put on shorts and a T-shirt and then a sweater over the top because I'm freezing.

Stan waits for us. We climb into cars and head to the dock, still as silent as a group of burglars busting into a house. I lay my head against the window, my arms around my torso, and sleep.

I wake when the car stops moving. We're at the dock, and the sky is beginning to turn that deep blue shade as the coming sun lights it up. The lake is placid, quiet, a black space between the cliffs.

We pile into the boat, but as the engine sputters to life and we move out across the dark lake, I start to wake up. The sky changes from dark to light blue with shades of pink and lavender on the horizon. It's chilly enough that I'm grateful for my sweater, and Stan passes around a thermos of hot tea. Mitch sits beside me and surprises me by putting an arm around my hips and tucking me into him. I rest my head against his collarbone, warmer with his body heat beside mine. I close my eyes for a moment, tempted to drift off to sleep, but into the stillness of that moment, someone whispers, "Here it comes."

I open my eyes and sit up straight, pulling away from Mitch. Isaac gets to his feet, and I follow suit because now he's blocking my view.

It's not the best view, in my opinion. The tall cliff wall above us shields us from the first rays of light, but we see the sun winking over the top of the cliff. The sky is lighter, brighter, blue, with layers of orange and pink rippling on the horizon.

It's not what I expected, but it's still beautiful. How can it not be? It's the sunrise of another day. A new day.

⟲〰✦〰⟳

Eight hours later, Mitch deposits me in front of my apartment with my things. Before I open the door, he reaches over and gives me a big hug.

"Thanks for coming. It was so fun having you there."

"Thanks for inviting me."

I don't pull out of the embrace. I enjoy being held. But then Mitch steps back, and I lift my face. My heart skips a beat with the anticipation of finding his face tilted toward mine, but it's not. He moves out of the embrace.

"Enjoy the rest of your day," he says with a wave.

"You too," I murmur, and then I let myself into my apartment.

I'm confused. Mitch seems absolutely perfect for me. And I think he likes me. We spent the five-hour drive cuddled together in the car, his fingers playing with the strands of my short hair, making me wish I hadn't cut it. I tried to take a nap but couldn't stop shivering, and he wrapped his hand around my arm and told Isaac to turn the AC down.

And yet, in spite of these signs that I'm certain indicate his affection for me, he hasn't tried to hold my hand. He didn't try to kiss me.

There's a pile of mail on the table, and I pick it up and sift through it. There's no denying my attraction to Mitch. And he admitted he's attracted to me also. Is he so shy he doesn't know how to make a move? I'm mildly frustrated by that because I don't want to be the one to be the instigator. Why can't he just—

My thoughts come to a stuttering halt. I don't even know what I was thinking as I stare at the envelope in my hand. The return address.

Owen Blaine.

Owen wrote me.

I drop my bags on the kitchen floor.

No one's here. It's Monday afternoon, and everyone's in class or out doing something. But I still want the privacy of my room.

I crawl up onto my bed and arrange my pillows just right behind me, savoring every moment, letting the suspense build before I tuck my knees up to my chest and slide my finger under the flap of the envelope, moving slowly, carefully, my heart pounding hard in my chest with each breath.

The flap opens, and I turn the envelope upside down to pull out the letter. Several photos fall out, and I pluck them up.

It's Owen, looking fit and proper in a suit before a church service. Then Owen again, in slacks and a nice shirt, standing beside several other similarly attired boys, wearing backpacks and standing on a busy street. Then another one, sitting in folding chairs in what looks like a church building with several other missionaries, holding a cake in their hands and leaning forward to smile at the camera.

He looks amazing. He looks happy. I fight tears because it warms my heart to see him doing so well, and it breaks my heart that it's been six months since I've seen him. Talked to him.

My hands are shaking when I turn back to the letter. What will he say?

Cassandra Jones,

I was so happy to hear from you. I was afraid you would never talk to me again. I was afraid you hated me.

It took a while for your letter to get to me. It got delivered to the mission home, but I wasn't there. The administrators forwarded your letter to the city where I was staying, but by the time it got to me, I had switched cities. The missionaries who got it kept forgetting to forward it. Finally, somebody realized it was important, so they sent it back to the mission home, and it got sent to the correct city where I was. So, before you think it took me two months to write you back, I wrote you the first free day I had.

Anyway, I'm glad you're home safe from Brazil. I bet that was an interesting trip.

I snort and roll my eyes. He has no idea.

Or maybe he does.

I turn back to the letter, anxious to devour his words. Longing to feel a connection to him.

I'm here in Chicago. I sent you a few pictures of me and the guys I've been serving with. It's a whirlwind of activity, and at first, really overwhelming. I'll admit, I got out here and thought, is this what I signed up for? There's a lot of crime here, a lot of poverty, and a lot of need.

But it's just been a few weeks, and I'm finding a good rhythm. The people I meet are kind. The bottom line is, all people everywhere want the same thing: love and security. So I'm going to do my best to help those around me find it.

I hope you'll write me again. I promise I will always answer. I want you to know, Cass, that every word I ever said to you was the truth. Life did what it does, and we're along for the ride, and sometimes that means we get pulled in different directions. But I will, forever and always, love you.

Forgive me for letting you go.

Owen Blaine

My heart clinches at his last words. His letter slashes me to pieces. I bury my face in my hands and sob. I don't know how to forgive him for letting me go. I feel like we could have stayed together, we could have kept going. I don't want to write him again. Hearing from him is like getting a glimpse of paradise and being told I don't get to enter.

I prefer not to see it.

CHAPTER THIRTY-SEVEN

Wanting More

I don't see Mitch the rest of the day on Monday. Tuesday I go back to school and try not to think about Owen's letter, which for some reason is in my backpack, not that I need it, because against my better judgment, I've read it enough times to have it memorized.

I distract myself with thoughts of Mitch. How nice it felt to be held. How fun it was to tease and play. How beautiful his torso is.

I need to see him. I need to remind myself how perfect he is.

Luck is on my side, because I run into him when I'm coming home from school.

"Hey!" he says, spotting me at the light to cross the street. His expression brightens, and I smile back, pleased at the eruption of flutters in my stomach.

"Long time no see," I say, and we walk across the intersection together.

"Yeah, it's been a whole twenty-four hours," he says. "I was starting to panic."

I laugh. We walk beside each other, elbows nearly touching but not. And I feel that frustration again. Why doesn't he make a move?

"I'm glad I saw you," he says. "I was going to stop by your apartment anyway."

"Oh, yeah?" I stuff my hands in my pockets to convince them they don't want to reach for him. "Good. I missed seeing you."

It's about as open as I can be about wanting him more involved in my life. I'm afraid he'll drop the hint, but he picks it up and runs with it.

"You missed me?" His light brown eyes dance toward me, a dimple showing in his cheek when he smiles. "I'm sorry to tell you you'll be missing more of me."

"Why is that?"

We've reached the commons of our apartment complex now, and we pause because this is normally where we go different directions.

"Want to come over to my place?" he asks.

That's what I was waiting for. I shrug like it wasn't. "Sure."

He keeps talking as we move across the lawn and up the stairs to his apartment near the back.

"I have a competition in California this weekend. So we're driving over there."

"Driving? Not flying?"

"My dad likes to drive. Says it's good family time."

"How far of a drive is it?"

"Twelve hours, if we go slow. Which my dad does."

I laugh. "Okay, not so bad."

We get to his apartment and I stop in the living room. Per the honor code that I signed before coming to PYU, boys and girls are not allowed in each other's rooms.

It hardly matters that we spent the weekend together.

Mitch disappears down the hall but then returns with a suitcase. "I'll pack out here so we can chat," he says.

I plop myself down on the couch and watch as he brings out an armload of clothing. He lines the suitcase with it, and I say, "Is this where you wear one of your tiny swimsuits?"

"Well—the judges have to be able to see your form," he says. "Not that big a deal."

And yet, to him it appears to be. I try not to giggle. "Show me pictures from you last competition."

"You don't want to see."

"Come on, I already saw the one online."

"Well—okay. If you really want to see."

He disappears back down the hall, and I bounce on my hands.

He returns with a framed, color photo of three smiling, buff men standing on a podium, arms held away from their sides while they flex, veins popping on their corded muscles above the speedo-style bottoms clinging to their hips.

With a jolt, I realize the one in the middle is Mitch.

Even though I spent three days with him at the lake, I never saw his body ripped and bulging like this.

"That's you?" I say, and my voice squeaks.

"That's what we have to wear. It's a body-building competition."

He sounds defensive, and I'm quick to allay his concerns. "It's totally fine." I hand the picture back. "You should be proud."

I can't get the image out of my head. Mitch standing there in almost nothing.

"Yeah. I am proud. I'm just not sure what other people might think. Especially around here."

"I think you look great." The words pop out of my mouth before I can censure them. Suddenly it's my face getting hot. "Nothing to be ashamed of."

I'm saved further embarrassment when the door opens and Isaac comes in with Mitch's other roommate. They greet me and turn to Mitch, and I stand up, grateful for the convenient excuse to leave.

"Good luck, Mitch," I say, waving as I back out the door. "Can't wait to hear how it goes."

I like being around him. I get giddy, excited, anxious to see him. But while he's incredibly attractive, seeing that picture should have made me feel something more. Something deeper.

It will be good to have a few days a part so I can figure out what's real.

I expect it to be quiet with Mitch gone, but it's not. The same constant flow of guys moves in and out of our apartment.

Only this time I can't blame my roommates.

"Hey, I met you on a campout a few weekends ago," one boy says after coming over with Thomas and Jake, two guys who live across the way from us.

I look up from my laptop, where I'm furiously working on my English term paper. Iris is making dinner for us, something Chinese, judging from the aroma. I offer a courteous smile. "Oh, yeah?" My eyes turn back to the laptop. I don't mean to be rude, but I've got to get this done.

"Yeah. You must know John. He organized it?" The kid doesn't pick up on my ice and sits down next to me. "I'm Rick."

"Oh, right," I say, trying to be nice. "Yeah, I was on that campout."

"Are you and John dating?"

I laugh. I can't help it. "No. Just friends." Come to think of it, I haven't heard from him since the campout.

"Cool. Want to see a movie tonight?"

I stare at my computer screen, willing the paper to write itself. A movie would be nice. Distract me from everything else. I want to go.

I shake my head and meet Rick's eyes. "I can't. I've got to get this term paper done. Maybe some other time."

"Yeah, awesome." Rick stands up, not looking the least bit discouraged by my rejection. "What's your number? I'll call you."

Movement in the kitchen attracts my attention, and I glance over to see Iris and Abby whispering together, heads bent near each other, glancing at me. I turn back to Rick and give him my phone number.

"Great. Good luck on your paper."

He waves and leaves, and I scowl at my roommates.

"What?" I say.

"Do you have a date every weekend?" Abby asks.

"No," I say. "I don't have one tonight."

"Because you said no," Iris says. "And tomorrow hasn't happened yet."

"I'll be busy tomorrow too," I say. "Have to write this paper."

But now I'm thinking.

Somehow, I've become a serial dater.

I finish my term paper Saturday afternoon after being locked to my computer screen for sixteen hours. I emerge from my bedroom anxious to get out and do something. Mitch has been gone three whole days, and I've not heard anything from him. No texts. No calls. No emails.

I pop into the living room and find Iris and Abby curled up together, watching TV.

"Let's go out!" I exclaim. "It's Saturday!"

Abby checks the time. "I told my parents I'd come over this weekend. I'm heading out in an hour so I get there before it gets dark."

This is the problem with living close by. Camila has the same issue; her parents always want her to come home. But Iris is from Canada, so she and I are frequently the weekend warriors holding down the fort.

How many idioms can I fit in one sentence?

I turn to her. "Iris? Want to do something?"

"Hayden did ask when we want to play soccer again."

Hayden's the British kid on our soccer team who I think has a crush on Iris, but she's oblivious to it. Even when I tried to point it out to her. "Brilliant!" I say, borrowing one of his words. "I'll start calling people."

Half an hour later we have enough people invited for a full scrimmage. I fill up water bottles and munch on saltine crackers at the kitchen counter.

"Your phone's ringing," Iris calls from the couch.

I pounce on it. Hopefully it's one more person wanting to play soccer with us. "Hello?" I say, answering.

"Hey, is this Cassandra?"

"Yes, it is." I return to the kitchen and begin twisting lids on bottles.

"This is Rick."

"Hi, Rick." I run through a mental list of kids in my apartment complex but come up short. "Are you coming to play soccer with us?"

There's a short pause, and then he says, "Am I invited?"

Crap, I've missed something. I realize I don't know who this is, and now I don't know how to uninvite him. I plunge onward, sweat beading along my forehead, hoping Rick's identity reveals itself soon.

"Yeah, we're heading out the door now. Meeting at the soccer fields below the athletic complex."

"Dang, that sounds like fun! I didn't know you're a soccer player."

"Only for fun." *Who are you, Rick?*

"I've got something else right now, but if you're free later tonight, I'd love to catch a movie with you. Did you finish your paper?"

Just like that, it comes together. Rick. The kid I met on the campout. The one who asked me out yesterday and took my phone number.

I'm so relieved to have a face to the name that I blurt, "Yeah, sure! That would be great."

"All right, awesome! Call me when you're done with soccer and we'll make a plan."

"Great," I echo, at a loss for anything more coherent.

I finish with the water bottles, sifting through my feelings to get to the bottom of my unease. My life only has a few options right now. I can either date or not date. Not dating would make college really boring.

Do I want a boyfriend? I think of Mitch with another twinge of uneasiness. Am I ready for commitment?

When we were at the lake together, I thought so. But I'm not so sure now. And I don't want to live like a nun, either.

Which means dating. Maybe lots of dates.

Life did what it does and we're along for the ride, and sometimes that means we get pulled different directions. But I will, forever and always, love you.

Owen's words recite through my head. He's right. Our separation is a consequence of life. It's not his fault. He did what he thought he had to do.

And he still loves me.

That's significant.

I find I can forgive him after all.

CHAPTER THIRTY-EIGHT

Figuring Things Out

Dear Owen,

I was so glad to hear from you! I didn't consider that my letter might take weeks to get to you, so I was a bit sad when I thought you hadn't responded. I'm happy you're doing well on your mission. The people around you are blessed to have you. They don't even know what a special person they have working with them.

College is hard. I'm only taking a few classes for summer, and one of them is a dance class! I didn't expect to be this busy. But at the same time, I don't feel as overwhelmed as I did last year. I feel confident. Sometimes school sucks, but I've got this.

And summer might be my favorite time to be out here. There's so much to do outside. And even at school, my teachers seem more relaxed. We are enjoying the amazing weather and the beautiful nature.

I finally got a job! All summer I looked for one, and just when I thought it wasn't going to happen, I got one. I start tomorrow. It's office work this time, at the college of engineering. I'm excited not to have to call people and ask for money!

How is your family? You probably know Monica moved out here, and I feel a bit guilty admitting I haven't seen much of her. Things have been busy. But I'm going to make more of an effort to spend time with her. My family is doing well, Emily is a senior in high school this year. So is Richard, huh?

Oh, I forgot to tell you! I chopped off my hair! Like, pixie cut. It's so short sometimes I look like a boy when I wake up!

I miss you. You're an amazing person. I love you dearly, and I pray constantly for your success and happiness.

Love, Cassandra.

I put my pen down and reread the letter. My eyes burn from holding back tears, but that's par the course where Owen is involved. I hold back on expressing the deep feelings of my heart to him. He doesn't want to hear them. That's why he initiated this intense separation.

I also don't tell him I've been hanging out a lot with his cousin. One more thing he doesn't want to know.

It's a good letter. It's personal, it's genuine, but it's not weepy, sappy, or needy.

We can be friends.

I put it in an envelope and address it so I can mail it tomorrow.

⟡

We have our final soccer game this Friday. The rest of our games have been scrimmages against each other, but this week we're preparing for the real thing: a game against another team. I hope our grade doesn't depend on us winning. We're an enthusiastic group, but most of us are not very skilled.

Practice goes well. We break into two teams and scrimmage against each other. I try to get the ball from an opposing teammate but end up taking an elbow to my forearm before falling face-first into the grass.

"I'm so sorry! I didn't see you!"

The scrimmage pauses as Hayden helps me to my feet. The rest of the team can't stop laughing. It's not the first time Hayden has clobbered me to the ground.

"I know I'm beneath your line of sight," I tease, spitting out dirt and brushing off my knees. "But the guys in my apartment complex are starting to think they should call the police if I show up with more bruises."

The kids around me chuckle, and Hayden's face turns bright red. "I'm terribly sorry," he says in his British accent.

I wave him off, but my arm throbs when I shake it. I know I'll have another shiner to add to my collection. "Just make sure you do that to the opposing team on Friday."

Now that we're certain I'm not dead, play resumes. We end up tied, two to two, and our instructor is pleased.

"You guys are playing well," he says. "Neither team had the upper hand. That's a good sign you'll hold your own on Friday."

I nod at his words. Maybe. If the other team is as unskilled as we are. If not, we can expect more clobbering.

I join Iris on the grassy field to drink water and wipe the sweat from my face. Even though there's a definite lack of humidity here in Colorado, I sweat enough at soccer to have a very dewy countenance.

Hayden comes over to where Iris and I are stretching and plops down next to us. "I have a gift card to a local pizza place that expires in two weeks. I thought I'd use it tonight. Want to come with me?"

I perk up. "I'm always up for pizza! Iris?" I elbow her, trying to hint at Hayden's interest.

"Just us?" she asks.

"Well, unless there's someone else you want to invite," Hayden says, his cheeks turning pink.

He's probably wondering if Iris has a boyfriend. "We'd love to," I say. "Do you want to go home and shower first, or head straight there?"

"I'll shower here," he says, gesturing toward the athletic building beside us. "It has everything you need."

Iris and I exchange a look. Neither of us brought a change of clothes or shampoo, but when in Rome... I shrug. "Yeah, we can do that."

We chat with the rest of the team for a few minutes before heading to the girls locker room.

As we walk, I nudge Iris. "It's no surprise he wanted to take us to dinner, hey?"

She shrugs. "He feels bad because he knocked you to the ground."

"How can you be so oblivious? He likes you!"

She flicks her long black hair over her shoulder. "Nobody's interested in me. You're the one everyone likes."

"Not this time."

We find the shower stalls that still have curtains on them and shower quickly. Neither of us brought a change of clothes, so we have to put our sweaty soccer clothes back on. I finish first and cringe as I pull my damp clothes over my newly cleaned skin. The water is still running in Iris's stall.

"Iris," I call, "want me to run home and get us a change of clothes?"

"Yes, please!" she replies.

That's all the permission I need. I sprint out of the locker room, feeling worse than disgusting with my showered body in these sweat-soaked, muddy clothes. It's a twenty-minute walk home, but we drove, so in less than five minutes, I'm at our apartment. I take the stairs to the second floor, but as soon as I open the door, I halt in the entryway.

There's a note scribbled on our whiteboard in my section. In neat handwriting, it says, "Hey there, you with the olive complexion, it's Mitch. Sorry I missed you... Hugs, Mitch."

Mitch! He's back! And he came over to see me. Warm fuzzies spread through me, and I want to run across the commons straight to his apartment. But Iris is waiting for me in the locker room with no clothes! There's no time!

I deliberate for half a second before dashing to my bedroom. I change quickly, grab clothes for Iris, and head back out the door.

I also grab her a towel.

When I return to the locker room, it's only been fifteen minutes, but I'm surprised she's still in the shower. "Are you almost done?" I call to her.

"Oh, I've been done for a while!" she says. "But I didn't want to stand out there freezing, so I stayed in here!"

I get it. She turns off the water and I hand her the towel, then tell her all about Mitch's note.

"Wow, I guess he really likes you," she says.

"I don't know," I say cautiously. "I think we're building something. It's a really good feeling. I want to see where it goes."

She tactfully avoids asking about Owen. None of my roommates have asked about him since we broke up in February. Maybe they think I'm over him. I didn't tell any of them about the letters. It's better to let them think he's part of my past.

We drive over to the Italian restaurant a block from the athletic complex as soon as she's dressed. We spot Hayden inside when we walk in, and he waves from a booth in the back. I nudge Iris forward, and both of us scoot down the aisle to join him.

"What's good here?" I ask as I slide in on the outside while Iris takes the middle.

"They're famous for their pizza," Hayden says. "But I'm curious about their lasagna."

I scan the menu. I worked at an Italian restaurant in high school, so I'm a bit of a connoisseur and more picky than most when it comes to Italian food.

"They have pesto but no gnocchi," I complain.

"So get something else," Iris says. "I think I'll try the Alfredo."

I'm a little worried about how great their food can be if they don't have gnocchi, but I take a chance and choose another favorite, shrimp scampi.

Iris chatters away while we wait for our food, and Hayden is quiet at his end of the table. I widen my eyes at her, then nod toward him, and she finally notices. But her attempt at making small talk is telling Hayden he shouldn't feel bad for elbowing me during soccer because everyone else does it.

I do a literal facepalm.

Hayden takes it in stride, though. Now that he has her attention, he takes the conversation and runs with it. He asks Iris if she finds it weird living here in the U.S. after Canada, and they start talking about the differences between their home countries. Our food arrives, but they don't stop chatting. I listen to them, feeling satisfied that the two of them are finally connecting.

"Your lasagna looks really good," I say, eyeing the hot lasagna boat in front of Hayden.

"It sure does," Iris agrees.

"Mind if I try it?" I ask. "Here, have a shrimp."

"I wanna try the lasagna too," Iris says.

We dig into the end of his lasagna boat and make appreciative noises as we taste his food.

"This is really good," Iris says.

"As good as the lasagna at the restaurant I worked at in high school," I add.

"Yes, yes, we all know that was the best Italian restaurant ever," Iris says.

"I guess I talk about it a lot."

"We've heard it a few times."

I glance over at Hayden and notice him carefully trimming off the edge of the lasagna where we took bites.

It dawns on me that he didn't give us permission to try his food. Iris and I just assumed and took over. "Wait—are you okay that we took some of your food?"

He lifts his fork from the lasagna boat, his cheeks pink. "Oh, yeah, it's totally fine!" he says in his adorable British accent.

I gesture at his lasagna, drawing Iris's attention there as well. "But you're cutting off where we touched it."

His face turns even redder. "It's to avoid, you know, cross-contamination."

I arch both eyebrows. "Are you a germaphobe?"

"No!" he insists. And then, "Maybe a tiny bit."

"Oh my gosh!" Iris says. "And we dug into your food and contaminated it!"

"I'm so sorry!" I say, but now my mind is conjuring images of tiny germs jumping from my fork into his lasagna, and I can't stop giggling. "Really! So rude of us!"

I'm one-hundred percent serious in my apology, but now I can't stop laughing.

Hayden's ears have turned the same color as his cheeks. "It's not a big deal. I'm not that concerned about it. Here, I'll prove it." He reaches over and steals a piece of chicken from Iris's plate, then stuffs it in his mouth. There's a choking sound in the back of his throat, and he quickly grabs his water to take a drink.

I can't help myself. I shriek, "You've been contaminated!"

"Cassandra!" Iris says, shoving her elbow into my ribs.

But Hayden is laughing too. He knows I'm teasing. He grins, and I'm relieved he has a sense of humor. Iris laughs as well, then she sections off a portion of her chicken Alfredo.

"This part is for you," she says, pointing at it with her fork but not touching it. "Nobody else has touched it."

"Oh, thank you. I feel better already."

Hayden might be good for Iris.

CHAPTER THIRTY-NINE

Building Something

When I get home, I swing by Mitch's apartment, but he's not there. I could text him, but instead, I decide to copy his communication style and leave a note.

Hey!! Sorry I missed you. I can't wait to hear about your competition. Hope I catch you later! Cassandra.

They don't have a whiteboard for messages like we do, so I grab a discarded envelope from the kitchen table and write the note on that. I stick it to the fridge with a magnet and head back to my apartment, curious to see what happens next.

But I don't hear from Mitch that evening, or the next day. As my anticipation grows, my excitement dwindles. I shouldn't have to guess if he's interested. I don't play games.

We have our final soccer game the next evening, our first match against a real team. As we warm up on the field, Iris nudges me. "The other team is arriving."

Something in her tone makes me turn to look. My stomach tightens when I see them. They look more like volleyball players than soccer players. A quick survey reveals they have only one female player.

"What are they, professionals from the Amazon?" Hayden jokes as he dribbles the ball between his feet. "It won't be so bad. We have tall people too."

He towers above Iris and me, but we both barely reach 5'2" on our tiptoes. Honestly, everyone towers over us.

"We can do this," another teammate says, offering us a fist bump.

"Okay, guys!" Our instructor gathers us together. His face is flushed, and for the first time, he looks more like a coach than a teacher, with his tracksuit, stopwatch, and clipboard. He seems more nervous than I've ever seen him.

"I don't want anyone to stress too much," he says. "Use the skills we've worked on in class and give it your maximum effort." He pauses, then adds, "But if we win, I can guarantee an A for all of you."

It's an enticing promise. I lick my lips and lean forward, my shoulders tense, ready to give this my all.

I'm assigned to defense, my preferred position. I can sprint fast for brief periods, but then I need recovery time, and our instructor knows this. I take my position in front of the goal, opposite Sara, another girl on our team.

The whistle blows, and the game starts.

In a heartbeat, the other team takes possession of the ball. My heart skips a beat as they skillfully maneuver around our offensive players and head down the field toward our goal.

I didn't expect to be playing so soon!

Taking a deep breath, I charge as they approach. One of their players fakes a pass, but I don't fall for it. He's not quick enough to get around me, and I kick the ball away.

"Yes!" I whisper under my breath, giving myself a mental fist bump.

But my victory is short-lived. I kicked the ball away, but it went straight to another one of their teammates. Seconds later, they're back, barreling toward our goal. I rush to intercept, but this time, the player gets around me. I spin, my heart sinking as he continues down the field. I scan for my defending teammate, but she's on the other side of the goal, too far away to help.

Hayden is in goal, but though he has the height, his skill is lacking. He jumps a second too late, and the ball flies over his head, past his outstretched arm, and into the net.

I groan as the other team cheers. The goal isn't unexpected, but so soon?

Play resumes, but the game doesn't improve. We manage to score one goal before halftime.

One goal to their five.

We are utterly defeated. The game ends eight to two, but I suspect their coach told them to stop scoring out of pity.

We show good sportsmanship by high-fiving the other team at the end of the game, but we're crushed when we gather around our instructor.

He puts on a good face, refusing to let us wallow in our defeat.

"That was a great game! I saw all of you using the skills we practiced. They were a tougher team—"

"A better team," someone grumbles, and we all laugh.

Our instructor smiles. "Yes, a better team. But you still managed to score two goals on them. I'm proud of your efforts, and you should be too."

His words lift our spirits, and we're a little more enthusiastic as we gather our water bottles and walk away from the field. Hayden keeps pace with Iris and me.

"It's no skin off his back," I say about our instructor with a shrug. "He gets a new team every semester."

"And it's literally the luck of the draw," Iris says.

As she and Hayden banter about the pros and cons of getting a new team each term, my phone rings. I glance at it but don't recognize the number. I consider letting it go to voicemail, but it's a local number, so I take a chance and answer.

"Hello?"

"Hi, Cass!"

"Hey!" I say, trying to sound friendly yet questioning. I don't want to flat-out ask who it is, but I have no idea.

"It's Mitch. I'm calling from work."

Mitch! I want to smack my forehead. How did I not recognize his voice? "Hey!" I respond again, adding a lot of enthusiasm this time. "How are you? It's been a bit!"

"Yeah, I feel like we keep missing each other!"

"How was California? Did the competition go well?"

"Yeah, it did." His voice turns sheepish. "I took first in my division."

I may not know much about weightlifting or bodybuilding, but I know that taking first in anything is a big deal.

"Oh my goodness, that's amazing! Congrats!"

"Thanks." He still sounds a bit sheepish. "Hey, I'm getting ready to leave for a week-long camping trip, but I wanted to see you before I go. Wanna join us for ice cream tonight?"

I immediately latch onto the fact that he wants to see me. That's a great sign. "Who's 'us'? Do you mean Robin and Sheryl?"

"My family, actually. We're all going out for ice cream, and I thought it would be fun to have you there too."

He's introducing me to his family? Goosebumps rise on my skin. This is good. Maybe a bit sudden, but good.

"I'd love to. I just finished a soccer game, so I need to change first."

"Nice! Did you win?"

I force a laugh. "Quite the opposite. But it was fun."

"Well, at least it was fun! I'll pick you up in an hour?"

"Yes."

I hang up the phone and allow myself a brief squeal. "Mitch asked me out!"

"As if asking you to Lake Powell wasn't enough evidence that he likes you," Iris says dryly.

"You're not understanding the importance of this moment!" I say, exasperated. "He hasn't spoken to me in days, and he's so hard to read. He's nice to everyone. This is the first clear sign that he actually likes me."

Iris gives me a deadpan look. "Besides asking you to Lake Powell and the cute messages on the whiteboard, you needed more proof?"

"One message," I correct her.

But she's right. I should be more confident.

⁓⁂⁓

I wonder how I should dress to meet Mitch's family. There's not much I can do with my short hair, so I part it on the side, frame it around my face, and add a cute hair clip.

I head into the kitchen as Camila pulls a tuna casserole from the oven. She makes it at least once a week.

"Eat something before you go," she says.

I'm not really hungry, but I oblige her. Mitch mentioned it was just ice cream, so I grab a plate and serve myself some noodles and cheese. Still, I'm too anxious about my date to eat, so I pick at it while listening to my roommates chat about upcoming school activities and who's asking out whom.

"Hello!" Mitch taps on our open doorframe, and my roommates turn to him with smiles.

"Mitch! Come on in!" Camila says.

"Good to see you," Iris adds.

I quickly dump my plate in the sink. "Catch you guys later."

We step out of my dorm, and Mitch gives me a side hug.

"How have you been?" he asks, his hand rubbing my arm just beneath my shoulder.

"Pretty good. I got beat up in my last soccer game."

He pauses to take me by the shoulders and examines my arms, wincing at the new bruises. "Ouch, girl."

"Yeah. And you? Feeling good about L.A.?"

He lights up as he tells me about the competition, speaking with a humility that suggests he's proud of how well he did but doesn't want to brag.

"That's amazing," I say. "First in the lightweight division. Wow."

"Yeah, it's pretty neat."

"Own it, Mitch. You did awesome."

He beams. "So what are your plans after summer term? Are you going to stay at the Brownstone?"

I glance back at the apartment building as I get in his car. "Yeah. I signed a contract for the year. Didn't you?"

"No, just spring and summer. I'm moving into a house with some buddies when school starts."

"Oh." I sit in stunned silence for a moment. He's leaving the complex? "I didn't know that."

"It's not far from here. Still within walking distance of campus."

Of course it is. But he won't be right across the commons anymore. He probably won't even be in my church congregation.

I feel a twinge in my chest but shove it down. Just because it won't be as easy to see each other doesn't mean we won't.

"Ever been to a frozen yogurt place?" he asks as he turns into the business district of Glenwood Springs.

"When I was a kid," I say, flashing back to the yogurt place my parents took me to after recitals. "Been a while, though."

"This place is one of my favorites." He parks in front of a frozen yogurt joint. I open my door before he can, but he waits for me when I step out. "That's my dad." He points inside, then grabs my hand and pulls me along.

"Dad!" Mitch releases me in the shop and waves. A few people in the line turn around, but only one of them nods at Mitch.

I focus on the man with graying hair. He's about the same height as Mitch, which is, on the shorter side. But where Mitch's eyes constantly crinkle in a smile, his father has a stern expression as he lowers his chin and glowers at us.

Or maybe it's just me.

Mitch puts his hand on the small of my back and urges me forward, and I force back the sudden bout of anxiety as I step forward to meet his dad.

CHAPTER FORTY

Interrogation

We bump past people and join his dad in the line of people holding cardboard cups of pastel-colored swirls of yogurt.

"Hi, guys!" Mitch says. "Dad, this is Cassandra. Cassandra, meet my dad, my brother John, and my sister, Heather."

John looks a few years older than Mitch but not any taller. He smiles and jerks his chin in greeting. Heather is small, maybe eight or nine years old, and she studies me with her head tilted.

"Hello, Cassandra," his dad says, extending a hand. "You can call me Nate."

My heart races as I offer what I hope is a firm handshake. "Thanks," I sputter.

No way am I calling him by his first name.

"Go get your yogurt," his dad says, nodding at the array of churning flavors.

We step out of line to get our frozen yogurts. Mitch hands me a cardboard bowl, and I look at the myriad of self-serve flavors on the wall.

"All right," I say, "it's been too long. I'm not sure what to do here."

"Oh, hey, this is the fun part," he says, grabbing several small paper cups. "You can try any flavor you want. Then put however much you want in your bowl, sprinkle on your toppings, and put it on the scale."

He demonstrates by pouring some yogurt into his little sample cup.

"I can try any flavor I want?"

"All of them, if you want."

I see why he likes this place. I taste every flavor before deciding on Greek yogurt and blackberry sorbet. Then I follow him through the toppings line, choosing fresh raspberries and hot fudge to pour over my frozen treat.

Mitch leads me to the table where his family sits. It doesn't have enough chairs, so he grabs one from an adjacent table and pulls it over for me. We sit, and I take my first bite of the yogurt.

"Oh, this is good," I say, leaning toward Mitch because, for some reason, I feel shy around his family.

He grins as he scoops up his own concoction of salted caramel and peanut butter. "Beats the creamery on campus, huh?"

My mind flashes to the creamery. Last year I lived on campus and went there almost weekly. Toward the end of the year, I spent a lot of time there with Jared, the boy I never dated but kissed. My heart warms at the memory. I shake my head. "I don't know. The creamery is pretty good."

"You need to get out more." He nudges my foot with his.

"So, Cassandra," Mr. Henry says, pulling my attention away from Mitch. "Mitchell tells me you're from Arkansas?"

"Yes, that's right," I say.

"And what do you think of Colorado?"

"I like it," I say diplomatically. "It's different, and I miss the green of the trees—"

"We have green trees here," Mr. Henry interrupts.

"Yes, of course," I say, my face warming. "It's a different color green, though. And a lot drier."

"Ah." He nods. "Yes. A lot easier to live here."

That's debatable. I don't get nosebleeds and alligator skin back home, but I simply nod and take a bite of my yogurt.

"And what's your ethnic background? You have a darker skin tone."

I sneak a glance at Mitch, wondering what he thinks of his dad's interrogation, but he gives me an encouraging smile. Maybe this is normal. "My grandmother is Colombian," I say. "So I was blessed with Latino genes."

"Wow. That's pretty unique." His dad settles back in his chair with his frozen yogurt and proceeds to eat it while studying the interior of the cup.

Is the interrogation over?

The conversation shifts to the upcoming family camping trip. Heather is excited to go kayaking and caving, but Mitch's dad is most excited about the fact that there's no cell service out there.

"All of my children, unplugged and unable to use their devices for eight whole days," he says.

Mitch and John exchange amused glances. I wonder if they're laughing at their father or if they have a secret way to get service he doesn't know about.

I try to conceal my relief when Mitch stands and says he'll take me home. It was a short date—if it could be called that—but I don't wish to spend any more time with his father. We say our goodbyes, and everyone says it was nice to meet me. I respond with the same sentiment.

"Well. That was fun," I say as we get into the car.

Mitch laughs. "I can't tell if you're joking or not."

I smile and shrug. "It was really good ice cream."

"Frozen yogurt."

"Exactly."

Mitch shoots me a grin. "I hope my dad didn't come across too strong. He's a history professor, and he likes to get all the details."

"He's a history professor?" Mitch didn't mention that before.

"Yeah, he actually teaches at Preston Y."

"He does?" My anxiety spikes in hindsight, but I realize it's a good thing Mitch didn't tell me.

"Yes, but he only teaches upper-level history classes, so unless you're a history major, you'll probably never have him."

I nod, somewhat reassured. "So I guess I won't see you for a bit when you leave on the family campout."

"It's like our last big thing together before school starts. But I'll see you when I get back."

It's sad, knowing Mitch will be moving out soon. We won't be able to bump into each other—it will require effort.

I guess I'm about to find out how much effort we're both willing to put into it.

I clasp my hands together and keep my negative thoughts to myself.

⊙━✻━⊙

We've just pulled into the parking lot at the Brownstone apartments when Mitch's phone rings.

"It's Isaac," he says, putting the car in Park. "Mind if I answer it?"

I remember his fun friend from Lake Powell and shake my head. "No, go for it."

"Hi, Isaac!" he says, holding the phone to his ear. "How's it going?"

Isaac's voice echoes in the tinny space in the car. "Hey! A bunch of us are gathering at Robin's place to play video games. Want to come?"

"Fun!" Mitch says. "I've got Cassandra with me, though."

"You're with Cassandra?" Isaac's excitement is evident though the speaker. "Bring her!"

"Are you sure?"

"Yeah, of course!"

"Hang on." Mitch covers the phone with his hand, like that's going to make a difference, and turns to me. "Mind if we go to Robin's place for a bit?"

I shake my head, happy to prolong this outing. "Not at all."

Robin's apartment is a block away. We leave Mitch's car at our complex and walk over. We laugh and talk the whole way, our hands swinging next to each other, fingers almost brushing. But he doesn't take my hand.

The door to Robin's apartment is open, and my anxiety spikes when we get near. I hear lots of voices. How many people are in there? I remind myself that I know most of them.

Except we get inside, and I don't. I recognize Robin and Isaac, and that's it. Mitch ditches me almost immediately, going to the front to claim a controller and settle in front of the TV. What kind of power do video games have over boys, anyway? I sit on the edge of the couch next to a bunch of chatty girls. Robin introduces me, and we wave hi before we proceed to ignore each other.

Isaac hands his controller to another guy, and then he spots me hanging out on the couch. He pulls up a chair and sits next to me.

"Hey!" he says, handing me an open bag of chips. "What's up, girl?"

"Not much." I take a handful of the salty crisps.

"You were on a date with Mitch?"

I shrug. "Yeah, I think so."

"Not sure?"

"He invited me to get ice cream with his family."

Mitch glances over his shoulder, as if remembering he came with someone. His eyes fall on me talking to Isaac. He smiles before turning back to his game.

"Dating and kissing is so nice, isn't it?" Isaac says.

I arch an eyebrow. "Happy with Robin?"

He grins. "I wasn't talking about me."

"I'm not dating or kissing anyone."

"That's a crying shame. I know someone who would be perfect for you."

His gaze swings toward Mitch, who hollers gleefully when his video game avatar accomplishes something amazing.

"Why do you say that?" I turn to him. "Has Mitch said something about it?" *About me*, I want to ask. I feel like we're playing mind games, and I want to cut to the chase.

"No . . . but you both have similar personalities. You're sweet and sincere and so is he. And you both have gorgeous complexions so you'd make beautiful babies." He starts making kissing noises and wraps his arms around himself, loud enough to draw the attention of others in the room.

"Stop that." I grab his arm and force him to hold still, but I'm laughing.

He waits until the eyes in the room turn away from us, and then he says, "Are you interested?"

"A bit," I admit. "We're great friends, and I really respect him. He's an awesome guy."

Isaac nods, and he's all seriousness now. "You two should be together."

"How long have you thought this?" I ask.

"Since I saw you guys together at Lake Powell." He nudges my leg with his knuckle. "Is it going to happen?"

"Maybe," I say.

I don't have much control over these things.

But Isaac must think I do. He lets out a whoop and hugs me, and Mitch glances back at us. Again.

"Don't say anything," I warn Isaac as he lets go.

"I won't. But I'm hoping for you."

CHAPTER FORTY-ONE

Good Plan

I spend the next day trying not to think about Mitch. I can't figure him out. Just when I think he likes me, he seems to pull back. He asked me on a date, but then he didn't try to hold my hand, and I got nothing except a hug when he dropped me off at my apartment.

I'm not sure how to categorize him.

He doesn't call me or text me, and I'm grateful for my new job. The computer training and learning how to handle the professors keeps my mind occupied.

Camila has dinner waiting when I get home. It's her signature dish, tuna casserole, but I'm not one to complain. She left me a note on the white board:

"We're across the way at apartment 313! Come join us!"

Maybe I will. Tracie is on the balcony chatting with her fiance. I rarely see her, and we're only acquaintances, even though we share a room.

I've just scooped myself up a huge bowl of casserole when a tap comes on the open door.

"Knock knock."

I look up. "Mitch!"

"Hi," he says, giving me a wave from the hallway.

Again, he's surprised me. I didn't hear from him all day.

"Come on in! I'm about to eat dinner. Want some?"

He shakes his head. "I'm on my home from work and thought I'd say hi."

"You accomplished that." I laugh. "You need to eat, right?"

He gives a sheepish grin. "Sheryl and Robin invited me over for dinner, so I'm headed that way."

"Oh." I arch an eyebrow. He's eating dinner with other girls . . . More mixed signals. "Okay. Have fun."

He lingers in the doorway. "If they decide to do something tonight, I'll call you so you can come. Sound good?"

There it is. A vague invitation. "Yeah, great. Sure you don't want to come in a for a bit?"

"I'd better not. They're waiting for me."

"All right."

I don't rise from the table, and he doesn't come closer. He waves as he heads out the door, and I'm left feeling . . . perplexed.

Before he leaves on his campout tomorrow, I should sit down with him and figure a few things out.

⟳∿※∿⟲

My phone rings in the middle of my English class the next day, startling me. I forgot to put it on silent because no one ever calls me. All the heads in the classroom swivel toward me, and my face burns as I bat at my backpack, trying to find the pocket with the offending sound.

I manage to silence it. I hold still for a heartbeat, letting my adrenaline recede, and when I sit up again the class has resumed without further attention on me. I check my phone, hoping it's Mitch. He leaves on his campout tonight, but I'm certain he'll want to hang out before then. He never got back to me last night, and I need to know what's happening between us.

The missed call is from Stirling.

For the first time I can remember, I'm excited to hear from him. Stirling was my first guy friend freshman year, and even though we went on several dates, we finally accepted there was no romantic tension between us, no chemistry. Instead, he might be the only guy I can genuinely call a friend. If my cousin Jordan were here, he would be that friend, but he's in Texas with his family until fall term.

I sit back and rattle off a text.

Me: hey!! I'm in class. What's up?

S: oh sorry! Didn't mean to interrupt. I'm looking for a ride from the airport tonight, but I don't want to bother you.

I quickly play back my schedule.

Me: no bother, I'm free! What time?

S: eight.

I'll call Mitch when I get home. We can hang out before then, maybe get dinner together.

Me: I'll be there!

Stirling gives me a thumbs up.

I only stay on campus until around two in the afternoon, and then I head home to study.

The door is locked when I arrive, which means no one's home. I unlock it and throw the door wide open, leaving the clear invite for anyone to drop by. My eyes turn to the white board to check for messages.

There's one, in big script taking up my entire square.

Cassandra—sorry I've not been too talkative lately. It's been a rough summer. I'll see ya when I get home. Mitch

Wait, he's gone? He left already? I step into the living room and deposit my backpack on the couch, my heart sinking in disappointment. I didn't think he was leaving until later.

I'm seriously dying to have a talk with him. To get to the bottom of what's going on between us.

I pull out my phone and send him a text.

Me: I'm so sorry I missed you! I thought you'd be here tonight and we could hang out. Have such a great time on your camping trip!

I wait for a moment, but it doesn't show delivered. I don't know what time he stopped by or where his family is now. He might already be in an area with no service.

I have to wait eight more days before I can clear things up.

⟲⟳⟲

I pick Stirling up from our tiny airport in Eagle Ridge a few hours later. I text him from the curb, and then when he comes out, looking fresh and tan from his summer in California, I hop out to meet him.

"Stirling!" I exclaim, surprised at how happy I am to see him.

"Hey, Cassandra!"

He grins at me and we hug. Stirling's short of stature, only a few inches above my five-two height. But that's been my summer. Tiago and Mitch are both about the same height.

I pull back and muss with his wavy hair, lighter than usual. "Been on the beach much?"

We get into the car together, and I heave a deep sigh before I pull out of the airport terminal onto the main highway.

"What?" he asks. "Been a crazy summer?"

I groan. "I don't even know where to start."

"Start with Brazil. That was a big trip, right?"

He makes it sound like that's an easy place to begin. My mind flashes back. Was it just a few weeks ago that I was there, in the hot humid South American country, spending my days with Tiago?

No one except Camila knows Tiago exists.

"Yeah," I say, a sigh escaping my lips. "Brazil was amazing."

"That's great! So you feel good about the language?"

"Terrible!"

We both laugh.

"But I want to learn it," I say. "It's a beautiful language."

Stirling narrows his eyes at me. "There's something else different about you. Did you meet someone?"

My face grows hot, and I don't answer.

"You did!"

"You could say I had a summer fling," I admit. "But we agreed not to stay in contact. So that's all it was."

He lets out a whistle. "Sounds like a doozy."

I'm not sure how he got that from my words, but he's not wrong, so I don't correct him. "You? Meet anyone special in California?" Stirling dated a girl seriously a few years ago, but I don't think he's been with anyone since she got married.

He shakes his head. "I guess my head's not in the right space. Every time I think I might like a girl, I decide it's too much effort and I'd rather have a chat buddy."

187

I arch an eyebrow. "Chat buddies are nice," I agree. "But sometimes I want more than that."

"Hence the summer fling?"

I bite my lip. "That one I was actually trying really hard to avoid." I continue on before he can ask more questions about Tiago. I'm not ready to divulge any of that. "There's a guy I'm interested in now but I'm really confused about him."

"Oh?" Stirling settles back in his seat, but I see from his body language that he's curious. "What's confusing?"

"Well, I think he likes me. Sometimes I think he really likes me. He invited me to Lake Powell a few weekends ago, and I thought we connected during our time there. But since then, he's been hard to read. He went out of town and didn't contact me the whole time."

"Ouch."

"Right? I literally spent the weekend telling myself to stop obsessing over him because he wasn't interested."

"What happened when he got back?"

"Well, he contacted me right away. Asked me out to meet his family."

"Sounds like he's interested in you."

"He keeps giving me mixed signals. He'll ask me out but not touch me, walk me home but only give me a hug. Maybe all he wants is a chat buddy also."

Stirling laughs. "Maybe. You guys might need to have The Talk."

The Talk. Everyone dreads that conversation. "I thought we might need to, and I planned on bringing it up yesterday when I saw him. But then he went out of town again, and I won't see him for eight days. Not only that, but he's going out to the boonies where they don't have signal."

Stirling whistles. "That's a long time to sit and stew in your thoughts."

"I know!"

"Did he say anything before he left?"

"Actually, yes. He went to my apartment when I was at school and left a note saying bye. He said he was sorry he missed me and we'd talk when he gets back."

Stirling points at me. "That's huge. He must have been so disappointed when he got there and you weren't there. I bet he left your apartment thinking, 'suck. Eight whole days without talking.'"

I want to believe that. "You think so?"

"How much do you like this guy?"

I lift one shoulder. "Just a little right now because he feels so flaky. But I could like him a lot. Everything about him is pretty much perfect."

Stirling grins and rubs his hands together. "I'm excited to see where this goes for you! He sounds like he could be the real deal but nervous to plunge in."

"I suppose that makes sense," I say. A shiver of anticipation runs down my spine. "Eight days before I can explore this!" I groan.

"I'll help distract you. Wyatt invited me to go river rafting Saturday. Want to come?"

It's perfect. I have nothing else to do. "Yes! I'll be there."

EPISODE 3 :

In Between Moments

CHAPTER FORTY-TWO

Suspicions

It's not even nine o'clock by the time I get to Stirling's apartment. The evening's still young, but the guy I'm interested in is out of town.

Interested in? I'm certain Mitch is about to ask me to be his girlfriend. The relationship is headed for commitment. I can feel it.

"You coming inside?" Stirling asks when I park. He glances over at me, his face half-concealed by a baseball cap.

Stirling's cute, in a boyish sort of way, with dark hair and dark eyes and a slender face. But although we attempted dating last year, there's no chemistry between us. He's another one of my boy friends.

I'm collecting them like charms for a bracelet.

"Just long enough to say hi to Wyatt," I say. His roommate took care of my fish all summer, so I feel some obligation to be friendly with him.

I say hello to Wyatt and give an update on my fish, which are thriving nicely. Stirling gives me a hug goodbye, tells me we'll talk soon, and then I leave.

My thoughts are still all over the place, but there's now an underlying current of excitement. Stirling says Mitch and I are both feeling the same thing. And he's a guy. I trust his judgment.

I greet my roommates when I walk in the door, but there's a crowd of boys I don't recognize. I disappear into my room.

I've just settled with my laptop across my thighs when my phone rings. I pick it up, and Monica's name flashes on the screen. I feel a rush of anticipation, followed by guilt. She's one of my best friends, practically a sister, and in the weeks since she moved out here, I've only seen her once.

I pretend not to know why.

I answer the phone. "Monica! How great to hear from you!"

"Long time no see!" she says. "How's life going?"

"Great!" I reply.

We make small talk for a few minutes. Then she says, "My roommates want to go hiking up to a cave this Saturday, but I can't stop thinking about how long it's been since I saw you. Do you want to come? It would be a good chance to hang out."

I think of the long hike up to the caves I took with my sister earlier this summer, and I don't want to. "I already have plans. I'm going river rafting with a few friends. You should come! It would totally be a chance for us to catch up."

"I'm game," she says immediately, with no hesitation. "That sounds like more fun. When and where?"

I grin. "Meet me at my apartment, and I'll drive you. We're starting at the top of the dam and floating down."

"Do I need to bring a raft?"

"Do you have one?"

"No, but I could ask around."

I shake my head. "I think the boys organizing it have it taken care of."

"If boys are organizing it, we'll see about that."

We have a good laugh and talk a little more. I hang up and push down the slightly anxious, uneasy feeling I have about spending time with her. I don't want to talk about boys, dating, my summer in Brazil, or her brother.

That's why I've been avoiding her.

But I can't avoid those subjects forever.

⁂

I'm in the living room eating a bowl of cereal and watching my fish swim around their tank when Monica arrives. She knocks on the door just as I receive her text.

M: I'm here!

I jump up to get the door before Iris or Abby move from the table. Camila is already gone to cross-country practice, as she is most mornings now.

I open the door and squeal when I see Monica. She's wearing a yellow tank top over light-colored jean shorts, her dark blond hair falling in soft waves around her face. Her eyes light up when she sees me.

"Cassandra!" She throws her arms around me, and we rock back and forth.

"Come on in, I'm about ready." I guide her to the kitchen table and put my bowl in the sink. "Meet my roommates, Abby and Iris."

Iris waves from her bowl of rice, and Abby mumbles a "hi" around a mouth full of toast. None of them know Monica is Owen's sister, and I let out a tiny breath of relief as I rush back to my bedroom to grab my backpack.

When I come back out, Monica is standing in front of our whiteboard, reading the messages. She turns around when I enter the kitchen, a funny look on her face, her brows furrowed. "Is this from my cousin?"

She points at the message Mitch left me.

Cassandra—sorry I've not been too talkative lately. It's been a rough summer. I'll see ya when I get home. Mitch

"Oh, yeah, he stopped by before they went out of town." I try to sound casual.

"Oh, I was here when he came by!" Abby chimes in, suddenly interested. "He was so disappointed to miss you. But he said he'll call you as soon as he gets back."

Monica lowers her chin, leveling her gaze at me. "You guys have gotten to be pretty good friends?"

"They're basically dating," Abby says unhelpfully. "Right?"

My face warms. "I wouldn't say that."

"Wait." Now Iris is looking at Monica, and I can tell by the set of her brows that she's putting the pieces together. "Did you say you're Mitch's cousin?"

"Yes." The word comes out clipped and annoyed. "And I'm Owen's sister."

There's nothing I can do but watch the detonation happening in front of me.

Abby turns to Monica with renewed interest. "Oh!" she exclaims. "You're Owen's sister!"

"You mean Owen is . . ." Iris looks at me as if to confirm before finishing her thought. "Owen is Mitch's cousin?"

Could this be any more awkward? "All right, see you guys later." I grab Monica's arm and pull her from the apartment, but she's staring at me, almost glaring, her blue eyes like ice as we head down the stairs. I try to ignore it, pretend she's not looking at me like that, but I feel the chill from her intense gaze on my skin.

"What?" I say, unable to help myself.

We reach my car, but Monica doesn't get in. She stands by the passenger door and asks, "You're dating my cousin?"

I shrug off the accusation in her voice. "We've gone out a few times."

"You're dating my cousin?" she repeats.

The tone makes me feel guilty, and I'm irritated by it because I have no reason to feel guilty. I get in the car, which forces her to do the same if she wants to continue the conversation.

She keeps talking as she gets in. "I never thought when I introduced Mitch to you that you guys would start dating."

I feel myself getting defensive. "We're not dating."

"Do you like him?"

Her tone is adamant, and my words flutter like a dying fish. "Why does that matter?"

"You do! What about Owen?"

Her question makes me flinch, and then I'm angry. This isn't fair. "Owen broke up with me. We're not together."

"And you're not going to wait and see what happens when he gets back?"

"He made it clear we're both going to date other people. When he gets back from his mission, I'll be on mine. And we all know how fast Owen moves. He'll be married before I see him again!"

I say the words with more anger and emotion than I mean to, but my feelings are jagged and raw where Owen is concerned. I lower my voice, making a concerted effort to calm down.

"Owen and I had a good run. But we are over."

She sits in silence for a long moment, and I wonder if this will permanently impact our friendship.

"But dating his cousin?" she says. "Did you think about how that would look if you ever show up at a family function together?"

I didn't think about it. And I don't want to, but of course, now that's what I'm thinking. Mitch and I showing up at a family reunion, and Owen is there with his woman while I'm there with Mitch. It's all kinds of unbearable.

But I lie and say, "I don't see how it matters."

She doesn't say anything else. I spend the next ten minutes trying to get my emotions under control, feeling like she's wounded me, but all she's done is expose a festering sore in my soul.

She finally speaks as I pull into the parking lot by the dam. "I'm sorry, Cassandra. I shouldn't have said anything. I reacted without thinking. What you do is really none of my business."

She reacted as Owen's sister rather than my friend. But I can forgive her for that. "It's okay. I understand. None of this has been easy for me either, you know."

"I know."

I put the car in park and give her a tentative smile. "Are you okay?" What I really mean is, are we okay?

She smiles and squeezes my hand. "Yeah."

We get out of the car, and I see Stirling and his friends with a bunch of tubes and rafts in a shallow part of the river near the dam. The sun beats down on us hotly, and I try to ignore the ache in my chest. I don't want to feel this way, missing the part of me that was Owen.

Stirling waves. He grins at Monica, who he met last fall when we both went to Utah.

"Hey," he says.

I examine the river flow and look over the tubes and rafts. "Does it matter which one I pick?"

He gestures at an inflatable raft. "If it's for two of you, I'd take that one. It's the most spacious."

Monica gives an agreeable smile, as if we had a very pleasant drive out here. "That'll be perfect, thank you."

I nod and smile as well, eager to put our conversation behind us.

Monica puts the raft in the water and holds it still from the shore. "You get in first, Cassandra. I'll hold it steady for you."

"I can hold it steady for both of you," Stirling says, coming over to secure the raft. He nods at Monica. "Go on."

She shoots me a look. "You're coming, right?"

"Of course I am!" I say.

Monica turns back to the river and puts one foot in. Her eyes widen, and her lips curl up toward her nose. "It's cold!" she exclaims as she gets inside the raft. It's not big enough for her to get her legs inside it, but she tries.

Stirling laughs. "Of course it is. It's fed from the snow runoff."

I remember how cold the water was when we went to the reservoir. I think I'm prepared, but when I step into the ankle-deep water at the bank, the chill fires through me, making me yelp and jump back.

"It's like ice!"

Around us, the other boys are jumping into their tubes and already heading downstream. Stirling glances at them, and I know he doesn't want to be left behind with us. He looks back at me.

"Get into the raft. It gets warmer once you're only half in it."

"Are you getting in?" I ask him.

"Not with you guys. I'm getting in my own tube."

"That's not as fun," Monica says.

I give her a startled look. Is she actually flirting with him?

Stirling gives the raft a push toward the river center and then goes to get his own tube.

I planned on getting in from the shore, but the current tugs the raft downstream, and I'm forced into the water to keep up with it. I take three steps and grab hold of it.

"Get in, get in, get in!" Monica yells.

I'm afraid of tipping it, but the water is rapidly getting deeper, up to my thighs. Monica grabs my forearm, and I throw myself over the edge. I hardly notice the biting temperature of the water now as I kick and she pulls, and somehow we get me into the raft. I lay there on my belly, gasping and laughing.

She's laughing too, and she hugs me, and I know our earlier disagreement is behind us.

"The water is frigid," I say. I roll onto my back opposite Monica so both our legs dangle past the raft's edges. Except she's much taller than me, so the water goes up to her knees, while only my ankles hang over the edge.

"Yup. It's cold," she agrees.

Even though the raft has a plastic bottom, it's still wet and flooded from me climbing in. I shiver at the water under my hips and creeping over my belly.

"Stirling lied," I say, a bit peevishly.

"The boys did this in Arkansas, too. They were always getting into the coldest rivers they could find, and then they'd float them. Or raft them."

"Why?"

"'Because it's exhilarating.'" Monica deepens her voice, attempting to mimic Owen's tone. We both laugh. I rest my head on the side of the raft, tilting it back to gaze up at the blue sky.

Monica does the same, and soon we're floating down the river, bobbing gently along with the current, letting the natural flow take us.

I close my eyes and spread my arms, feeling the warmth of the sun and imagining it's heating the cold water pooled at the bottom of the raft. Then I suddenly realize something and open my eyes. My toes, dangling from the raft, stare back at me, revealing chipped toenail polish from the last time I painted them, probably last spring.

"I lost my shoes," I say, somewhat surprised by the realization.

"When you got in the raft?"

"It must've been. I was wearing them when I stepped into the river. I would have noticed if I'd been walking on these bumpy rocks."

"What do they look like?"

"Pink, with ankle straps."

"They're probably floating with us. Let's keep an eye out for them."

For a while, we survey the river around us, but I don't see them. I dip a hand into the water and am surprised by how strongly it pushes against my fingers.

"The current is stronger than I expected," I say.

"It's snow runoff moving down the mountain. We're lucky it's not whitewater rapids."

"Yeah, probably right. We must not have gotten that much snow last year."

The river is quite shallow in some places. I wince as the raft bottoms out on some rocks, scraping along, digging into the back of my thigh. Another scrape hits my back.

"This river probably changes a lot with the seasons," Monica says.

I pull my hand out of the water because my fingers are going numb, and I ponder her words. Maybe I'm like this river, changing with the seasons, too.

The water takes us around a bend, big rocks jutting up from the shallows. "Ouch," I say, wincing as another rock digs into my leg, up my butt, and into my back. The raft jostles with me.

"That hurt," Monica agrees. "Felt like a knife."

I lift my leg to examine the back of my thigh and see a long red welt on the skin. Cold water rushes around my hips, and Monica shrieks.

"We're taking on water!" she says.

I look beneath me and gasp. The boulder sliced the raft open, and water is spilling inside.

Monica squeals as her butt falls through the hole in the raft.

"We have to treat it like an inner tube," I say. "Hold onto the sides."

We try. We let our legs fall into the middle and wrap our arms around the outside. But it doesn't work. The sides of the raft aren't insulated like a tube, and they sink beneath our weight.

The bank closes in, narrowing the waterway. The river picks up speed as it deepens. Boulders and tree branches rush past us, and I feel the first stirrings of panic in my chest. "We should've worn life jackets."

Monica scoffs. "For this little river float?" But both of us are struggling to stay within the raft as the bottom gives way.

We may as well be holding onto a piece of plastic wrap.

The boys are nowhere in sight. We're all alone on this part of the river, which is twisting and turning its way down the mountain.

We come around another bend, and my heart stops.

There's a bridge ahead with four pillars supporting it over the river. The pillars force the water to flow through narrow channels, and the water rises nearly to the top of the bridge under each pillar, white caps frothing as it churns through.

There's no other way.

CHAPTER FORTY-THREE

Water Troubles

I suck in a gasp, and then another. Did the boys go through that? Really? No one's dead?

I look at Monica and shake my head. "I can't go through there!" My voice is shaking. I'm breathing too fast, my heart racing.

Monica looks over my shoulder at the water rushing under the bridge, then back at me. "Let's try to get to the bank before we reach it."

I turn around and see we're only a few yards from the steep incline on either side. I lean over the raft and paddle, letting my legs dip into the freezing river. I kick, my heart pounding because what if we don't make it to the bank before we reach the bridge?

I don't want to die on this river today.

We speed toward the bridge, carried along by the current. I put my bare feet down on the rocks, trying to walk us toward the shore, but the current rips my feet right out from under me. Neither of us speaks as we move in a slow diagonal, aiming for the rocky bank. My heart races in my throat.

I don't know if we're going to make it.

We're only a few meters from the bridge when our fingers claw onto the dry shore of the bank. It's steep and rocky, painful as we haul ourselves onto it. We crawl upward on our knees and hands, my toes scraping along the rocks, dragging our broken raft with us. The shore levels out near the road, enough for me to stand, and I pause to catch my breath.

The river looks so calm from here. I can see it rushing under the bridge, but it doesn't look life-threatening like it did a moment ago. I look at Monica, and she meets my eyes before she starts laughing.

I do too. We stand there, laughing and hugging, weepy with relief.

The adrenaline fades as we continue climbing the hill to the road, and now I feel every pointed rock under my bare feet.

We make it up to the asphalt, and I breathe a sigh of relief to be off the jagged rocks. But as soon as I step on the blacktop, I yelp and jump back.

"What is it?" Monica asks.

"It's hot. Really hot." The expression, "hot enough to fry an egg," comes to mind, and suddenly it makes sense. That's how this road feels.

But it's better than the rocks. I let different parts of my feet take turns on the heat, curling my toes, walking on the outside edges, walking on my heels. It's excruciating, but after several minutes, my feet go numb. Though I still wince with every step, I think I've burned off the flesh and can't feel anything anymore.

Ironic, how I'm longing to dip them in the icy cold river.

It takes us ten minutes to walk down to where the boys have exited the river.

"We wondered where you guys were!" Stirling says. Then he takes in our condition: dragging a ripped raft behind us, bruises on our legs, and me barefoot.

"You guys okay?" Wyatt asks.

I sit down on a bench and lift my feet, pricks of pain and heat sparking through the soles. "We may have had more of an adventure than we bargained for," I say.

"And yet, it looks like you fared better than my raft," Stirling says.

I look at the shredded raft in my hand, then over my shoulder at the long line of purple bruises arcing up from the back of my knee to my glutes. "Debatable," I say.

⁂

I take Monica back to my place after our wild river adventure. We relive every harrowing moment, laughing until our sides hurt. At my apartment door, I give her a tight hug.

"I loved spending the day with you," I say.

"Me too," she replies. "Let's get together again soon."

"Anytime," I say, and I mean it. We get along so well. As long as we avoid talking about boys or her family, our conversations are easy and natural.

Of course, that does limit what we can talk about.

I drop my backpack in my bedroom and head to the bathroom to shower and check my bruises. I wince when I see the long purple stripe running down the back of my leg. Ouch. Those rocks really did a number on me.

The warm shower feels amazing, and I step out clean and refreshed. Camila is the only one home, sitting at the kitchen table sifting through our mail when I come out.

"You got a postcard," she says, glancing up at me with a look I can't quite decipher—something between curiosity and mischief. She sets the postcard on the table between us, picks up her pile of mail, and disappears into her bedroom.

Her reaction piques my curiosity. I pick up the postcard. The front shows a beautiful cathedral, wrapped in flowing vines under a deep blue sky. At the bottom, it reads Andohalo Cathedral, Madagascar.

Madagascar! No wonder she looked at me like that—I only know one person in Madagascar. My heart races with anticipation as I flip it over to read the postcard.

Cassandra, I hope this postcard reaches you. I'm here in Madagascar. It's incredibly beautiful.

Don't you love this cathedral? I thought you might. I got to visit it. It's in Antananarivo, the capital city, where I've been for the past four weeks. I love the Gothic architecture, and the views are breathtaking!

It made me think of you.

Have a great summer! Stay amazing. Your friend always, Jared.

P.S. I hope this is a piece of mail that makes you happy.

The last line flashes me back in time. I remember him walking me home to my dorm, crying to him over my boy problems, and counting mailboxes with him as he tried to cheer me up.

He did cheer me up. He'll never know how much.

There's no return address. I want to write back and tell him how much I miss him, how much I miss our deep talks and our easy friendship.

But I suspect the lack of a return address is intentional.

I take the postcard to my room and slip it into my journal. I'll have to content myself with knowing that he's happy. Even though our lives only intersected briefly, we enriched each other.

⟳➳ ⚜ ➷⟲

My English teacher assigns a forty-stanza poem for us to memorize and analyze. I walk around campus muttering to myself, reciting lines while cooking dinner, constantly checking my open book because I can't seem to remember the second line.

"Are you coming to my concert tonight?" Iris asks, interrupting my monologue as she bursts into my bedroom.

"I have to recite this stupid poem tomorrow," I reply.

"Your mind will work better if you take a break."

Her words sound logical, even if I'm not sure there's any scientific backing. But who am I to argue?

"All right," I agree.

We go through the apartment, rounding up our roommates and inviting them to her concert. Camila and Abby decide to come. Tracie, our almost invisible roommate, politely declines—she's heading out to spend the evening with Tom.

Of course. Not that I blame her. If I were seriously dating a guy, that would take priority over a concert of someone I barely know.

Actually, I'd probably still go, but I'd make him come with me.

We drive to the music building, since we dressed up in concert attire and don't feel like walking twenty minutes in the hot Colorado sunshine. My roommates and I settle in the front row and watch Iris set up her cello. I wasn't sure which instrument she'd play today—she's versatile and can play the viola, violin, and cello. For all I know, she can play even more.

Her music director comes out and says a few words to her, and then Iris sets everything down and walks off the stage. I watch her, puzzled, especially when she locks eyes with me and makes her way down the aisle toward me. She crouches beside my seat and asks, "Can you turn my sheet music for me?"

My eyebrows shoot up. "I've never done that before."

"But you know how to read music."

I feel like she's overestimating my abilities, but I glance around at our group, realizing I'm probably the best option.

"Okay," I agree, somewhat reluctantly. "I'll try."

"You have to do more than try. You have to turn the music for me."

I gather my confidence and follow her onstage, feeling the eyes of the audience on

198

me, probably wondering why I'm up there. At least I'm wearing a long dress.

My heart races as she shows me the music. Since she's the only one playing, it's more straightforward than the music I'm used to reading when I sing. She goes over the score with me, pointing out where to flip the page for the coda and what notes to listen for as cues to turn the page. I nod along, then give her a reassuring smile.

"I can do this."

I stand beside the music stand and listen while she's introduced, then start my job as she begins playing.

For the next half hour, I'm on my feet, turning pages as she moves through song after song. Iris gets to sit behind her cello, standing only at the end of each piece to take a bow.

I don't sit at all.

I breathe a quiet sigh of relief when she finishes the last song and I can finally drop into my chair. As the audience claps and a few people cheer, I know nobody was watching me—but my skin still crawls with the paranoia of being observed.

The concert ends, and Iris moves over to her music teacher. I'm not trying to eavesdrop, but as I fold my chair and put it away, I can't help overhearing.

"How was it?" Iris asks.

"Well, you weren't as precise on some of the higher notes as I'd like, and a few strings sounded flat."

Iris's face falls, and I resent her teacher's critique. It sounded amazing to me.

I tell her as much as she's packing up her cello, slinging it over her shoulder. "You were incredible. Thanks for making me come and letting me turn your music."

She shrugs her slender shoulders. "I appreciate it."

We head back to the audience to rejoin our roommates. Everyone congratulates Iris and she perks up, not letting her music teacher's words get to her. I reach into my purse and pull out my phone, checking my notifications—several texts, emails, and one missed call from Idaho.

I'm about to delete the notification, but I notice they left a voicemail. It's rare for anyone to do that anymore, so I click over to listen.

"Cassandra! Sorry I missed you. That seems to be happening a lot lately, huh? Anyway, it's Mitch, in case you didn't know. Calling from a payphone at the campsite. I don't know if I'll be able to call again—do you know how hard it was to scrape up change for this? Anyway, I'm rambling, but I hope you're having a great week, and I'll talk to you when I get back. Bye."

I gasp when the call ends, then squeal, "He called me!"

My roommates turn toward me, and I clarify, "Mitch called me! From Idaho!"

☙❀❧

None of my roommates are as excited about the phone call as I am. They walk ahead with Iris toward the car while I linger behind, trying to call the payphone back. It rings and rings, but no answer. I try a few more times before giving up—Mitch isn't hanging around the payphone.

But I'm still elated. He called me. He didn't call me when he was in L.A., even when he had service.

We've crossed into the next realm of our relationship. Mitch clearly likes me.

I catch up to my roommates and link my arms with Iris and Camila. They both give me sunny smiles, and I smile back.

I can't wait to see what happens when Mitch gets home.

CHAPTER FORTY-FOUR

The Check List

I don't hear from Mitch the next day, but I can't expect him to call me from the payphone every day—he probably doesn't have enough coins, anyway. The thought of him rummaging through pockets and cupholders just to call me makes me giggle.

Most of my day revolves around my English exam. I turn in my paper, recite my poem, and then sit down to take the exam with the rest of my class. It's definitely a British English overload, but I only missed two words on my poem, so unless I bomb the test, I should have an A in the class.

I try not to think about Mitch as each day turns into the next, but as the time gets closer for his return, I'm anxious. What will happen if we start dating for real? Things could get serious fast, if we decide to commit to each other. There wouldn't be any reason not to—except that I'm only nineteen. And I've always wanted to go on a mission trip.

Do I still want to?

The day before Mitch comes home, I write a small note for him: "Hey! Welcome back!" I sign it with my name and a smiley face and leave it on his car windshield at the apartment complex. Then I write another, longer note.

I can't wait to hear how your week was! I didn't do much besides get bruised on a river rafting trip, make a fool out of myself turning pages at Iris's concert, and recite a forty-stanza poem for my English class. I'm sure Idaho was more exciting! I'll talk to you soon!

I hope that between the two notes, Mitch will realize I like him too. I want to encourage him to make a move and instill confidence in him.

His roommates let me into his apartment, but they won't let me go down the hall to his bedroom. They deliver it instead, promising to place it on his pillow where he'll see it when he gets home. Part of me is annoyed, but another part respects the fact that they follow the rules even when no one is watching. I remember the trouble we had with Layne last year when we caught her bringing boys back to her bedroom.

And sleeping with them. At least, with one of them.

There's nothing to do now but wait for Mitch to come home and see the note. I don't want to hide out in my apartment, sneaking glances at the the parking lot ever few minutes to see if he got home a day earlier than expected. Instead, I go to the library to kill time. I knock out my English essay and get through a full chapter of classic civilizations.

Have his feelings grown during this time apart? Is he thinking about me as they drive home, imagining what he'll say to me? Will he be ready to solidify things?

I finish the chapter and realize I haven't retained any of the information.

Giving up, I pack up my school supplies and head home. I'll find a good book to distract me until tomorrow.

❦

I wake up Saturday morning with flutters in my chest. I imagine Mitch's face lighting up when he sees me, like it did the time I visited him after he busted his eardrum. Will he hug me, or will he be shy again? Where should I be? Should I wait at his apartment or accidentally bump into him in the parking lot? Or chill at my place as if I don't care?

I don't know what time he's coming home, but I don't want to leave in case I miss him. So I sit at the kitchen table, working on homework while my roommates watch TV. The door is open, an invite for anyone who wants to pop over.

People do pop over, but not Mitch.

I fix myself lunch, but I barely have an appetite. I feel foolish for sitting here doing nothing. What if he doesn't come home until tonight?

I clean the house, then go outside to get the mail.

His car is gone.

At first, I'm startled. It's been here the whole time he was out of town, which means he came home and got it. He was here, and then he left? But I calm myself. He probably had to go somewhere with his family, so they grabbed his car and left again.

But now I have something to watch for. When the car comes back, so does he.

I can't see the parking lot from my apartment, so I have to get up and take a little walk down the stairs, where I can peek over the banister and check. I feel quite stupid doing this every ten minutes.

It doesn't stop me.

The afternoon turns into evening.

Sometime between my five p.m. vigil and five-thirty, his car reappears.

My stomach flips, and my heart does jumping jacks.

I know he saw my note on the car—that one was impossible to miss. But maybe he hasn't seen the one in his bedroom yet. I picture him in his room, unpacking, glancing at his bed and seeing it.

One note might just be friendly, but two?

I'm sending a message. I sit on the couch and chew on my nails, imagining his smile, that dimple, the brightness of his eyes, and wait for him to come see me.

The minutes tick by.

Half an hour later, Abby collapses next to me on the couch.

"Want to get something to eat?" she asks.

My roommates have tactfully kept silent, pretending not to notice my behavior. But now, there's no way to ignore how I'm curled in the corner of the couch, hands around my knees, staring at the fish tank in despondency.

202

I blink and nod. It's better than sitting here. "Yeah, let's go."

My eyes drift over to Mitch's car as Abby and I climb into mine. He hasn't called me, hasn't texted me, and he didn't come over to see me. I set my jaw.

Well, I won't either. I feel stupid. Foolish.

I'm so sick of these mind games.

⁓⸙⁓

Stirling calls me the next day.

"Have you recovered from river rafting last week?" he asks.

"I can still see the bruises." I stand in front of my bathroom mirror in nothing but my underwear and examine the back of my thigh. The dark colors have faded to streaks of yellow, the only reminder of what the river put me through.

Nothing compared the bruising Mitch has caused on my heart. I can't believe he hasn't said a word to me. I dread going to church, where I'll have to face him in my shame.

"And how's your raft?" I ask, bringing my thoughts back to the conversation at hand.

"Terrible shape. Afraid we couldn't patch it. We're calling it a total loss."

I laugh in spite of my dismal mood. "Sorry."

"How about another adventure?"

I arch an eyebrow at my reflection. I need to get out of the apartment, and skipping church sounds appealing. But I don't know if I can handle another river ride. "Like what?"

"Come play racquetball with me. They have courts in the athletic center."

"I've never played. And I'm horrible at sports."

"Sounds fun."

I consider it. "Yeah, okay."

"Great. Wear shorts and a T-shirt. Pick you up in an hour."

"All right."

"Hey, it's your turn to do dishes," Iris says when I appear.

I make a face and head to the sink. She scoots over to make room for me. She wears a form-fitting, sheer black dress with small roses embroidered on it.

"You look nice," I say.

She glances over my attire. "Want toast?" she asks as she butters hers.

She doesn't mention how I'm obviously skipping church. I'm grateful.

"Sure," I say.

"Me, too." Abby plops down at the table, bright red hair pulled into a ponytail. She's also not dressed for church. "Cass, I need a ride into town today. My friend's getting married and she scheduled me a fitting for my bridesmaid's dress. Can you take me?"

"Sure." May as well fill up my schedule. "I'm going out with Stirling in an hour, though."

"What time will you be back?"

"Maybe around noon."

"That's perfect. Let's go after lunch. Does that work?"

I shrug. "Yeah, that's fine."

"All right."

Iris hands us both plates with buttered toast, and I pause my dishwashing to eat it while it's warm.

"Where are you going?" Iris asks Abby as she ties on her tennis shoes.

"For a jog," she says.

Like that's normal. Like she does it every day.

Camila's the only one of us who consistently exercises.

"With who?" I say.

Abby just smiles and shoves the rest of her toast in her mouth. "See you later!"

She flounces out the door, and Iris says, "Why doesn't she tell us?"

"Probably because it's a different guy from yesterday," I say, and we cackle.

It's not unusual for Abby to be kissing multiple guys at once.

I eat my bread and finish the dishes, then spend my time wiping down the counters waiting for Stirling. Abby left the door open, and the knock on the open frame has me turning. For the briefest second, my heart leaps, and I hope it will be Mitch.

But it's Stirling.

"Ready?" he says, waving at Iris.

"Yep. Do I need anything?"

He shakes his head. "I've got gear for you."

We head out to his car, and he asks, "So, did home boy come back?"

Dang. I forgot I told him all about Mitch. I scowl and say, "Yeah, and he hasn't said one word to me. So let's not talk about him."

"You got it," he says, and he promptly starts talking about the terrible movie he saw the night before. I laugh at his play-by-play and appreciate him not mentioning my pathetic love life again.

We drive down to that athletic center. I stand by Stirling's car as he gets out rackets and a small blue ball. He pulls out two sets of goggles and hands one to me.

"You can rent this stuff here," he says. "But I prefer to bring my own."

"I need goggles?" I eye them suspiciously and follow Stirling into the building.

"Never played before?"

"I'm what they call athletically disinclined."

"Me too. You'll like this one."

CHAPTER FORTY-FIVE

Eye Protection

Stirling signs us in at the desk and leads me down a hall. Immediately a noise like cracking and thunder radiates around us. I look through a hazy window into a square room, where two people pelt the ball into the walls. Each time it smacks the wall or a racket, it rebounds with a loud crack, and the two people inside crash like elephants into the walls of the small room as they chase it down.

Stirling continues down the hall past several rooms until we reach an empty one. The door is short. He squats to go through it, and I follow.

"Goggles on," he says, placing his own over his face.

"Why?" I ask, feeling ridiculous as I slide the plastic plates over my eyes.

"To protect your eyes," he says.

I roll them, but he misses the effect. "How do we play?"

"Basically, one of us serves to start. You have to hit the ball off the front wall and make it over this line." He toes a piece of tape that cuts the court in half horizontally. "The other person has to hit that serve after it bounces or the point goes to the server. Got it?"

"Not in the least," I reply.

He grins. "I'll serve first. You'll catch on."

I do. It takes about three starts before I get the hang of it, and Stirling explains more rules as we go along. Fouls and using the walls and how many bounces.

We only play for half an hour because after that I'm wiped. My arm twitches and trembles from the exertion, sweat drips through my hair and down my face, but more than that, I enjoyed it. We step out of the hot and humid court and drink water.

"What did you think?" he asks.

"Honestly? I don't think I've ever had so much fun playing a sport. We should do it again."

"You were pretty good at that one. You should try others sports. You might find others you enjoy."

I nod and pat my face with the hem of my T-shirt. "Sounds like a plan."

But my mind is already back on Mitch. He'll be in church now, with Iris and Camila and whoever else decided not to skip today.

I want to think he'll notice I'm not there and ask about me.

It hurts to think he might not.

I need to shower when I get home, but Abby's standing at the kitchen table waiting for me.

"There you are!" she says, looking up from her phone. "Ready?"

She's definitely had the chance to shower. She wears a flowy skirt with a blouse, and her red hair is in soft waves. A fragrant floral scent drifts off her.

"Ready?" I repeat. "I just walked in the door. You want to go now?"

"Well, yeah, we said noon, right?"

I glance at the clock. It's 11:56. "I didn't mean on the dot."

Abby shrugs, her green eyes wide and innocent. "We can go, right?"

I can't say no to her. "Yep."

She gives me the address while I grab another drink of water, then we're off to my car. I follow the GPS, and she talks about the dress.

"It's my best friend from high school getting married, and she wants me to be the Maid of Honor," Abby gushes.

"Your best friend?" I glance at her. "From high school?"

"Yes."

"So she's like . . . nineteen?" The thought of getting married now sends a tremor of horror down my spine.

"Yeah. Her fiance is five years older than her, and I can't believe how fast she's getting married."

"Or how young," I can't help adding.

"But he's got a job and a house and he's so good to her. And she loves him."

"I hope it's enough," I say.

Abby pinches my arm. "You're just a cynic. Right person, you'd do it too."

"No. Has to be the right time, also." I'm not just saying it. I went through this with Owen. We weren't ready to get married.

"That's what we tell ourselves because we're afraid to commit."

I don't agree, but I bite my tongue. "Have you seen the dress? I hear they're always awful."

"Oh, I hope it won't be. She said it's light blue."

I pull up to a long driveway leading through a fenced-off cow pasture to a single-story rambler at the end of the drive. "This it?"

"Um." Abby consults her phone. "Not sure. She said it's got a brick mailbox and yellow shutters."

We both crane our heads around to the passenger side and look for a mailbox. I spot it first. It's a standard black box on a stick, red flag up and waiting for the mailman.

"Right address?" I ask.

"Well, it's what she sent me," Abby murmurs, furrowing her brow. She shows it to me. "That's it, right?"

"It's what I typed in," I confirm. "Want to try knocking?"

She chews on her lower lip and looks apprehensive. "Let me call."

I sit back and wait while she dials the number.

"Oh, hey, this is Abby! Diane's friend? Yeah, I'm supposed to be getting sized for the bridesmaid dress. . . . Well, I followed the address and I'm not sure this is the right house . . . We're at the end of the driveway. . . No?" Abby covers her phone with her hand and says to me, "She looked out the window and doesn't see us." Then she removes her hand. "What's the address again? Maybe I have it wrong. Seven sixty-three East Sycamore . . . Yep, that's where we are. Wait. New Castle?"

My head turns toward her as her eyes dart my direction.

New Castle is a small town west of the university. Except I drove the opposite direction from there, south toward Aspen.

"Oh, yeah, I didn't realize. So sorry. I'll be a bit late."

I narrow my eyes, and Abby mouths an apology.

"Yep. We're on our way now!" she says cheerily. Then she hangs up and shoots me a brilliant smile. "Did you catch that?"

I groan and roll my head against the back of the chair. I reprogram my GPS and groan again. "It's half an hour away!"

Her grin gets wider. "I'm so sorry, Cassandra."

What else am I going to do? Take her home and tell her someone else has to take her? I heave a sigh to make sure my exasperation is known and pull away from the house. Abby reaches over and hugs me.

"You're the best!" she says.

"Yeah, yeah." I wave her off, but I relent a bit. It might be her fault, but it's a mistake anyone could make.

She chatters about everything and nothing for the next half hour, wearing away at my irritation until I'm begging her for a moment of silence, and even my dismal mood over Mitch disappears. We find the driveway, and it matches the given description exactly.

"We made it!" Abby says, ducking out of the car.

"It helps when you have the right city," I grumble, but I'm not annoyed.

The dress is indeed light blue, but as I watch the woman measure Abby and pin sleeves and waist pieces together, I think there's a reason bridesmaid's dresses have a reputation. It doesn't fit Abby, and the cut makes her slender form look blocky.

"What did you think of it?" she asks when we finally get back in my car.

"The color was nice," I say. "Did you like it?"

"Not really. It's someone else's idea of romantic."

I nod and check my text messages for the hundredth time.

Why do I keep looking? I should give up. Mitch isn't going to contact me.

"Makes sense," I say. "The bride gets to decide how everyone's going to look."

"Yeah, but I'm the one who has to pay for that two hundred dollar monstrosity," Abby says.

I shoot her a startled look before pulling onto the highway. "You?"

"Who else do you think is going to pay for all of us?"

"Well." My mouth gapes open and closed. "I guess I assumed the bride." But that doesn't make sense, does it, especially if the dresses are two hundred dollars a pop.

"No way! She's got so many other things to pay for. This one's on us. And it's an honor to be asked."

I grunt and keep my disdain to myself. It's an honor I suspect I'll never have.

❧

Luckily New Castle is less than twenty minutes from our apartment. I breathe a sigh of relief when we're finally home. That excursion took more than two hours out of my day.

I open the fridge and peruse for food, leftovers, anything, but it's the end of the week and I haven't gone grocery shopping yet.

"I made rice," Iris says, opening her rice cooker. "There's lots of it."

I spoon rice into a bowl, then sprinkle her Chinese flavorings over the top. "Thanks." I grab a pair of chopsticks and sit down to eat. I won't starve as long as we have rice.

A sound like skidding shoes comes from the hallway outside our apartment, and then a little blond-headed girl pokes her head into the living room.

"Hello?" she says, glancing right then left. She spots Iris and me. "Is Cassandra here?"

Iris looks at me, and I arch an eyebrow and wave a chopstick. "That's me."

She grins and prances into the kitchen, then leans on the back of Iris's chair. "I'm Elyssa."

"Hi, Elyssa," I say, stealing a confused glance with Iris. "Did you need something?"

"No." She bounces away and plops onto our couch. "Does your TV work?"

Iris turns around to watch her. "Elyssa, do we know you?"

"No." She turns on the TV with the remote. "You know my brother. He sent me over."

Iris shoots me a questioning glance, and I shrug.

"Who's your brother?" I ask.

"Mitchell Henry," she says.

Like I haven't been waiting to hear from him all day.

My stomach does a funny flip. I immediately go into calculated cool mode.

"Oh? Mitch is your brother?" I move the rice around in my bowl and keep my eyes on the small white grains. "Is he here?"

"Yes. He's coming over here too. He sent me first."

Iris is watching me, and she looks unimpressed by this. I keep fiddling with my rice, but now I can't eat.

I'm waiting.

Elyssa found a show to watch, so she ignores us, laughing out loud at the antics on television. I stir my rice.

"Hello?"

I nearly drop the bowl when Mitch pokes his head into the apartment. He spots Elyssa on the couch before turning to me and Iris.

"Hi," he says, a grin splitting his face.

Oh my word, he's adorable.

"You got some color," I say, circling my face to indicate his tan.

"Left over from Lake Powell, I think." He crosses into the kitchen and gives me a hug, squishing my bowl between us. "It's so good to see you!"

My insecurities melt away, and I don't care why he didn't come earlier. All that matters is he's here now. I smile when he steps back. "You too." I add, almost shyly, "I missed you."

He play-punches my forearm and swivels to the living room. "Good job, Elyssa! You found Cassandra!"

"I did. Can I stay here and watch TV?"

"No. Dad said we only had a few minutes. We have that wedding reception to get to, remember?"

She hauls herself from the couch with a theatric eye-roll. "It's another one of his students. They're always getting married."

"Yeah." Mitch laughs.

He turns to me, and I blink wide eyes at him.

"You're leaving?" I say.

"For a bit. I'll be back." He stretches his fingers out and brushes the back of my knuckles with his thumb.

A shiver tickles my belly.

"Want to do something later?" he says. "In like, two hours?"

I nod. I don't ask what he wants to do. I don't care. I want some time alone with him, and this time I hope it goes somewhere.

"Great." He turns to Elyssa. "Let's go, you've pestered them enough."

"I pestered no one," she says, hauling to her feet.

"She's adorable," I say, leaning close like it's a secret.

Mitch grins and touches my arm again.

That's three touches. Plus his hug.

Then he's herding Elyssa out the door, and I call after him, "Bye!"

"See you soon!" he calls back.

I wait until I hear their steps thundering down the metal stairs before letting out a sigh and sinking into the chair next to Iris.

"That was lackluster," she says.

I turn to her, blinking in surprise. "Are you kidding? He came over to see me. And there was definite chemistry between us."

She grunts. "He barely said hi. And he didn't explain why he hasn't come to see you before now."

"He doesn't owe me an explanation!" I protest, though I'm dying to know also. "I'm sure he and his family were busy!"

"For someone who called you from a payphone at a campsite, he could be a little more eager."

"Oh, he's fine." I take my bowl of rice and go to my room. I won't let her rain on my parade.

But my doubts whisper to me. What if she's right? What if Mitch came over just to be nice?

CHAPTER FORTY-SIX

Emotional Anguish

I leave my bedroom door open as I study, trying not to listen too closely as people come and go from our apartment. Every time the deeper timbre of a male voice crosses our threshold, I hold my breath and tilt my head without meaning to. None of them are Mitch.

Until one is.

Almost three hours later, he comes into the open apartment and says, "Hey, Abby! Looking for Cassandra."

"Hi, Mitch," Abby replies warmly, and I'm glad she's the one out there on the couch greeting people now instead of Iris. "Cassandra! Mitch is here!"

"Be right out!" I call. I take my time closing my laptop, carefully shelving my English book and placing everything neatly in its place. Then I pause by the bathroom mirror and check my hair. It's getting longer, slightly unruly as it pushes past my ears into a cut that isn't quite a bob but isn't a pixie anymore either. I still look cute, though, so I add a clip on one side and pop into the hallway, smiling brightly. "Hey!"

"Hey." Mitch gives me a side hug. "Ready to get out of here?"

"Sure." I turn to Abby, who sits cuddling on the couch with some guy I've never seen before. "See you later."

"Have fun."

Mitch shoves his hands in his pockets as we cross the parking lot, and I clasp my fingers together. Somehow, it feels like there's space between us that wasn't there before, and I want to bridge it.

"How was your camping trip?" I ask as I open the passenger door and get in.

"It was a blast. The weather was perfect during the day but freezing at night. We were in this weird climate where we had to sleep in parkas, but pants were too hot by noon."

"Wow!" I nod along to his words, keeping my eyes on him. "And you had fun with your family?"

"Yeah, we get along really well."

I wait for more, but there isn't any, so I ask, "How many of you are there?"

"I have one brother and two sisters, John and Elyssa and Heather. I'm the one in between. And my mom, of course."

"Cool. And your whole family went camping?"

"Yep. One big happy party."

The conversation tapers, and I feel myself panicking, trying to find something to fill the silence. A question comes to mind, and I blurt it out without thinking about it.

"What did you eat while you were camping?" Who cares? Why are we talking about meal plans?

"Lots of fish. We're the fishing type of family."

I laugh before I can stop myself. "Of course."

He shoots me a quick look. "Of course?"

"Of course, because you're . . . Monica's cousin." Then I add, somewhat lamely, "And they love to hunt and fish."

Silence blankets the car again. Then he says, "She gets that from her dad's side of the family. We don't hunt, but we like to fish."

And then he's quiet again. There's an awkwardness between us that I don't understand. He hasn't said anything about the phone call, so I bring it up now.

"Thanks for calling me while you were gone," I say, trying to inject warmth into my voice. "It really meant a lot to me that you thought about me enough to reach out."

"Oh, yeah," he says.

That's it.

I'm at a loss. This hardly seems like the same person who came over to my apartment a few hours ago. I lean back into my seat and tumble through my list of small-talk topics. Nothing sticks, so I settle on the practical. "Where are we going?"

"Oh. I guess I should tell you, huh?" He smiles, but he keeps his eyes on the road. "We're going to the drive-in movie with Sheryl, Robin, and Isaac."

Friends from Lake Powell. I should be excited, but for some reason, I'm not. "Cool."

"Do you like drive-ins?"

"I don't remember the last time I went to one," I admit.

"They're a lot of fun. Nobody cares if you talk through it because you're not sitting close to anyone except your group. And it's perfect weather for it."

I nod. I wonder who orchestrated this and how I got invited. "When did you talk to Sheryl?"

"I've been with her and Robin all day."

He delivers the line casually, but I feel stung. "You weren't with your family?"

"Oh, no, we got back last night. I spent the day over at Sheryl's apartment playing volleyball, and we got together and watched a movie at her place last night."

Each word is a sharp dagger to my chest. The message is very clear: he got home last night, saw my messages, and made sure to spend his time elsewhere. And it feels like he wants me to know it.

He hasn't said one word about my notes, and I don't bring them up. I settle back into my seat, a mixture of unsettled and rejected emotions swirling in my chest. I don't want to be here anymore. I don't know why I am. A lump in my throat and burning behind my eyes tells me I'm shockingly close to tears, but I absolutely will not cry—not right here, not right now.

How did I misread everything?

We don't speak again until we get to the drive-in. I hate to say I'm relieved when we get there, but the car ride was tense, at least for me. He pays the fee and then drives through the rows until we find the spot where Sheryl, Robin, and Isaac are waiting. His whole demeanor changes when he gets out, and he walks over to give them high-fives and hugs.

I stuff my hands in my jeans pockets and meander behind him. The ache in my throat makes it hard to swallow, and there's a corresponding pit in my chest.

Sheryl and Robin turn to greet me, and Isaac grabs me in a big hug. They are more enthusiastic about my arrival than Mitch was.

The hood of Mitch's car is long and sturdy, so the five of us pile on, everyone giggling, touching, and laughing—except me. Robin sits next to me, with Isaac on her other side. Mitch squishes next to Isaac, and Sheryl is beside him. They talk through the first twenty minutes of the movie. I focus on the screen and watch the first quarter of the movie, but I flinch whenever someone bumps me. I'm on edge. The edge of the car, actually.

I have no idea what we're watching. I don't believe Mitch is interested in Sheryl—I've seen them together too often, and it looks like friendship to me. But this feels like a deliberate message: *I'm not interested in you. Don't take it personally.*

I can't stay here. Halfway through the first movie, I get up and leave. I'm tempted to call Iris and have her come get me, but she'd have to use my car, and I don't let people drive it.

Instead I go into the concession stand area. There's a bench inside the building. It's warm and it smells like popcorn. I settle myself down with a book on my phone and read. But it's hard to concentrate. My chest hurts like I fell and got the wind knocked out of me. I feel like someone told me the light was green, but then I got run over when I tried to cross. Unexpectedly. Suddenly.

They lied to me.

I didn't see this coming.

I slip back out when the credits start. Mitch spots me as I approach the car.

"Hey," he says. "Where did you go?"

So he noticed. But he didn't text or try to find me. Jerk. I hate him.

"Bathroom," I say. "My stomach started hurting."

He lifts both eyebrows, immediately concerned. "Oh, no! Need me to take you home?"

"Isn't it over?" I look at the credits rolling over the big screen. I'm so ready to go.

"There's another movie," Isaac says. "It's a double-feature."

I turn to Mitch, and I'm sure there's ice in my gaze. "Were you planning on staying?"

"Hey, it's no problem. I'll run you home and come back."

"That's all right." I pull out my phone. "I'll ask Camila to come get me." It's worth letting someone else drive my car for this.

"Oh, no, Cassandra." Mitch hops off the hood and shoos everyone else off also. "Come on. I'll take you home."

He leans in and starts the car before I can protest further.

"Sorry you don't feel well," Robin says, and Isaac gives me a hug goodbye before the two of them crowd into his car.

"See you later," Sheryl says, and she gets in with them, leaving me alone with Mitch.

I get in beside him and say nothing.

He doesn't speak either. We drive in silence until we near the apartment.

"So your stomach hurts?" he asks.

"Yes." Among other things.

"Something you ate?"

Someone I talked to. "I don't know."

We pull into the parking lot, and I grab the door handle. "Hope you make it back before the next movie starts."

"I'll probably stay here, now that I'm home."

"Oh. Then sorry you had to leave early." I push open the door.

"Wait, Cassandra," he says, and I turn to glare at him. I'm clenching my jaw to keep my face rigid because I'm about to freaking cry.

How did he so thoroughly ruin this?

He hesitates. He doesn't meet my eyes, and it dawns on me.

He *knows* what he's done. He knows something was building between us and he's left me hanging on the line. Did he decide he doesn't like me after all?

He knows he's hurt me.

"Thanks for coming," he says, and I exhale.

"Yeah," I say. "Good night." I get out and close the door, proud of myself for not slamming it.

I won't give him the satisfaction of seeing my emotional anguish.

Abby and Iris are cuddling on the couch watching a movie when I come in.

"Hey, girl!" Abby calls. "Come join us!"

"How was your date?" Iris asks.

I push the biggest smile on my face that I can. I'll tell them all about this tomorrow and we can hate on Mitch together. For now, I can't bear it. "Great. We saw a movie. Now I'm really behind on homework. Catch up with you guys later!" Then I make a beeline for my room.

They might know something is amiss. I hold my breath for ten seconds to make sure no one's following me. Then I throw myself on my bed and sob into my pillow.

⁙

Existence

To feel the flower run
Or see the bees unwind
Or smell the purple sun
Existing if I find
That I do without fear.
To exist is to be
For the lilac I hear
Only when the sweet tree
Exfoliates the air.

I am what you expect
The injustice you bear
In the feelings you kept

My arm aches so badly Monday morning from my racquetball activities that it's hard to get dressed for school.

My heart hurts worse.

I spend the morning telling myself I don't like Mitch. I don't care. He's stupid.

The only comfort I take is in knowing it's Mitch's last week in our apartment complex, and then I never have to talk to him again.

But I feel angry. I want an explanation. What happened between him leaving me notes and calling me from Idaho and him arriving in Colorado after his camping trip?

Work is the perfect distraction on Monday. Summer term ended and Fall semester hasn't started, so I'm in between classes. I meet all the professors, and they're patient with me as they show me how to work the space-age copy machine that can do everything except replicate food.

I don't care about Mitch anymore. I don't care that we didn't speak again yesterday. Or that he won't talk to me today. He should have stayed in Idaho.

Was it the notes? Was I too clingy? What did I do to make him back away from me?

Ugh.

CHAPTER FORTY-SEVEN

Why the Change?

Monica pops over to my apartment Wednesday afternoon.

"Hello!" she calls, poking her head in.

"Hey!" I'm sitting on the couch, propped up by pillows. "Don't make me move," I beg. "I never knew working at a computer all day could mess up your back."

"Poor baby." Monica smiles and sits beside me on the couch. "Other than your aching back, how's it going?"

"Meh." I shrug. "It's fine."

"Ready to go back to school?" she asks.

"Are you kidding? I've been enjoying the break! Does anyone actually like school?"

"Well..." she starts, then laughs.

I chuckle too. "So, what brings you over here? Came to see me?"

"Oh, I was helping my cousin move some things."

"Mitch?" Even I can hear the displeasure in my tone.

She glances at me, curious. "So, what's going on with you two?"

"Nothing," I say, my voice tight. "He's barely spoken a word to me since he got back from camping."

"Oh, really?"

I shrug. "Guys are stupid. I'm better off being single. At least my roommates like me."

"And I like you." She smiles brightly, but her expression makes me wince. I'm still too annoyed by the unpleasant turn of events to appreciate her kindness.

"I don't get it," I say, venting. "I thought we were friends. We hung out, talked, invited each other over, and then, all of a sudden, he stopped."

"All of a sudden?" she echoes.

"Yeah, well." I sigh. "I hate to think this has something to do with it, but maybe I scared him away."

"How could you have scared him away?"

I shrug again. "I was starting to be honest about how I felt. I didn't want him to be in the dark, so I put myself out there and let him know I was interested. And it backfired—

like it always does. When it comes down to it, guys like the idea of me, but they don't actually like me."

"Oh, Cassandra." She leans over and gives me a side hug. "You know that's not true. I can think of one boy in particular who really likes you."

I give her the evil eye. This is exactly why I avoided hanging out with her for so long. "We're not talking about him. Or are you trying to tell me that he's the only boy on the face of the earth who finds me tolerable? Because, if you recall, he broke up with me. Which means I'm doomed to a life of loneliness unless someone else decides I'm likable."

She bites her lip, looking torn. "You're adorable. Of course somebody else is going to like you. And you know that's not why he broke up with you."

I turn back to the television, pretending she's not there.

"Look, I'm sorry. Sorry for bringing him up."

I say nothing.

Monica stands up. "Well, I guess I'll see if they need any more help. I'll call you later. Let's do something."

"Sure," I say, not taking my eyes off the TV.

She hesitates, but then she leaves, and immediately I feel guilty for being so petulant. But I don't want to talk about what can't be every time I see her. Until she realizes that, we won't be able to hang out.

❧

I spend the morning at work, learning spreadsheets and file merges and even basic design concepts. All things I need when working in the engineering department. My brain's a little frazzled by the time I get home, and I'm feeling the desire to open a can of soda and veg in front of the television.

Camila sits at the table studying, and Iris waves from the couch. I move to join her, when Camila says, "There's a letter for you."

My eyes slide from the TV to the table, and all other desires snap away when I see the letter.

It's from Owen.

It does not matter how my life moves on, how my thoughts get filled with other people, everything about him draws me like a magnet, and I circle back to him in an instant.

I'm starting to hate that I can't get past him.

I grab the letter and bolt to my room. I sit on the bed and breathe in the envelope, closing my eyes and imagining him writing my name, my address. Then I rip it open and read his words.

Cassandra Jones,

   I cannot believe you cut your hair. But more than that, I can't believe you told me and sent no picture. Where's the proof? I don't believe it. You'll have to show me.

I laugh out loud. It's like I can hear him beside me, shaking his head, tsking his tongue and saying, "Nope. Nope. Didn't happen. I don't believe it."

I think it's also his sly way of asking for a picture of me. And that makes me happy.

I'm working hard with the people here. We spend a lot of time helping the homeless, working in shelters, serving in soup kitchens. And we spend a few hours every day at a literacy school. Inner city Chicago is rough, Cass. Sometimes I can't believe I'm still in

America. My heart goes out to these people. It makes me see how privileged my life was, and I took it for granted. I didn't even appreciate how lucky I was.

My roommate right now is nice, kind of weird. I don't think he ever lived away from home before here and sometimes he gets this wide-eyed scared look like he just wants his mom. I'm trying to be patient. Okay, I'm not so good at it.

Yeah, Richard's a senior. Mom says he's giving her a hard time. Almost as hard a time as I did. I wasn't the greatest example to the people around me. I sure wish I could have a do-over. If it weren't for you, I would have squandered my entire high school years. I owe you a debt I can never repay.

Good luck with your new job, you'll kill it. Tell Monica I said hi. Pray for me always because some days I'm dead on my feet, not sure where I'm going to find the energy to slap out another ladle of soup or staple another shingle to the roof, and I also don't want to seriously injure my roommate for being a total idiot.

That was a very un-missionary thing to say. Pretend I didn't.

Write me soon.

I love you,

  Owen.

I read it and reread it, just like the last one. It fills my heart with joy. He still loves me, I feel it in every word. And I love him. But now it's different. There's a deep, steady connection, so rock-solid I'm certain we'll be friends forever.

I slide over to my computer and pull up a few of my more recent photos so I can print them and send them in my next letter.

I don't pay any attention to the voices in the living room until Iris shouts, "Cassandra! Someone's here for you!"

I want to sit down and write Owen back. I want to tell him how happy it makes me to hear from him, but not in a romantic way, and I'm 100% okay with it.

Except I'm not sure I can say all that, anyway.

"Coming," I call back. I place the printed pictures on my bed and wander out into the kitchen.

Mitch is standing in the entryway, leaning his head against the wall. He straightens when he sees me and gives me a wan smile.

I blink at him. What is he doing here? We haven't spoken in days.

"Hi," he says. "Want to sit outside for a bit?"

I almost snort. I bite back the response, "Not really." I don't want to be where he is, period.

He must see it on my face, because his smile drops, and he heaves a sigh. "I want to talk to you."

I turn to my roommates without answering him. "I'll be outside." Then I step past Mitch to the stairwell and trot down the steps, not waiting for him.

He catches up to me in the courtyard as I move toward the front of the building.

"Where did you want to talk?" I ask.

"Somewhere private. Where everyone's not sitting and watching."

"Not our apartments, then." I wonder what he's going to say. I'm annoyed, I'm angry, I'm hurt. I gesture to the grass in front of my building. "Let's sit there."

He leads the way and sits down on the green grass. I follow, tucking my legs under me and resting my weight on my hip. Then I wait.

He glances at me and looks away and clears his throat, then plucks at the blades of grass in front of him. "So, how are you?"

"Fine." I keep my tone curt. He's not my friend.

"Ready for classes?"

"Sure."

"How are you?"

"I'm fine, Mitch." *What do you want?* I want to say.

"I've been wanting to talk to you," he says.

And then he stops.

I watch him as he plucks at the grass. He flattens his lips and exhales through his nose, then blows air out his mouth. The whole time, he doesn't look at me.

"Say what you came to say," I say.

He looks at me, his brows pinched. "You're angry with me."

I lift a shoulder, feigning indifference. "You haven't spoken to me in days. I thought we were friends." I let the rest of it dangle there. That I don't think so anymore.

"We are friends," he says.

I don't even roll my eyes. I don't care. "Okay."

"Is everything okay with you?" he asks.

Like he *cares*.

"Everything's fine with me," I say. "I was a little bit sad a few days ago, but I'm fine now."

His eyes trail over my face, his gaze astute. "Because of me?"

He *knows*. "Partly, yeah." I can't bring myself to bluntly cast the blame on him.

"You know I think you're a great friend," he says. "You can talk to me anytime. And if you have any questions for me—you can ask."

I raise an eyebrow. "What questions should I ask?" Questions like, why have you given me the cold shoulder? Or questions like, were you ever interested in me?

"I don't know," he says, looking away again.

Fine, if he's going to play that game. "There's nothing I want to ask."

"Where did you go during the movie Saturday?"

"I told you. I went to the bathroom."

"For half the movie?"

I shrug. "I wanted to read my book."

Mitch puts his hand on my knee and catches my eyes. "Cassandra, are you being completely open with me?"

Why the heck would I do that? I want to yell. But I say, "As honest as I care to be."

"Okay." He bobs his head and looks away, and it's almost in resignation. He hardly seems like the same person I talked to before his camping trip.

And then I can't help it. I blurt out, "What happened? Before you left, I felt like we were friends. More than friends, since you want my honesty."

"We are—we are," he says, jumping into my tirade. "We are friends. Close friends."

I laugh. "No. No, we're not."

"Of course we are," he says, and his eyes flit over my face. "I care about you. I enjoy being around you."

"You hurt my feelings," I say. "I don't *trust* you. Something *changed* between us, and you're pretending like it didn't. So when you're ready to be honest with me, we can try to talk again."

I stand up, shaky from my outburst but proud of myself for being *honest.*

Mitch stands behind me, wiping grass from his legs. "Cassandra, hey. Look, I'm sorry. I just—" he sighs.

I squint my eyes at him. "What is it you're not telling me?"

He looks away again, and I feel a shiver of triumph. I have him pegged.

Something did happen. Maybe he found another girl. Maybe he discovered something about me he can't stand. Whatever it is, he turned a switch from liking me to not.

"Own it," I say.

"Own what?" he says.

That you liked me! I want to scream. *That you led me on and dropped me like a hot potato! You played me!*

But I can't say that. I would be admitting how much I liked him. That I did, indeed, fall for him.

I won't give him the satisfaction of knowing that.

"Great talk," I say, and I'm so full of anger even I flinch at my tone. Then I turn around and walk back into my apartment.

CHAPTER FORTY-EIGHT

Hot then Cold

I carefully follow a recipe from a beginner's cookbook in my kitchen after classes Friday. I don't want to open another can of soup or prepare another box of pasta for the rest of my life. That might change someday, but for now it's how I feel.

Tonight's dinner is chicken with mozzarella and marinara sauce. I've got the chicken simmering in the frying pan when I hear a voice behind me. "Knock, knock."

I turn around to see Mitch standing there. What he's doing here? I thought I made it clear yesterday that we're not friends. Unless he's changed his mind about keeping things from me.

"Hi," I say.

He glances into the living room, where the TV is on, but nobody's there. Iris opens the bedroom door and pokes her head out at the sound of voices, but when she sees Mitch, she quickly retreats.

"I was hoping we could talk a little more," he says.

I blink at him, not sure what to say. He gestures toward the stove. "Smells good."

"Thanks. My goal this year is to learn how to cook."

"Oh, yeah, that's an important life skill."

"Yeah, it is," I agree.

So is learning how to communicate and be genuine with people.

"Need any help?"

He's trying to be friendly, but I'm unsure of his intentions. Two weeks ago, I thought we were building something. Now it feels like we can't even talk to each other.

"Hello?"

A female voice calls out from the open apartment door, redirecting our attention moments before Monica walks in.

Oh. That's why he's here.

Monica's eyes flick between Mitch and me, her smile freezing on her face. There's a brief, intense, nonverbal exchange between the two of them where she lowers her chin and narrows her eyes. I can't quite read Mitch's expression, but before I can question anything, Monica turns her bright smile back to me.

"What are you doing tonight? Want to watch a movie at my place?"

"Sure!" I say, sliding a portion of the chicken onto my plate. "I'm eating dinner. Want some?"

She shakes her head. "I'll watch something on your TV while I wait, if that's okay."

"I can give her a ride to your place," Mitch offers. "Assuming I'm invited to watch the movie too?"

Monica shoots him a glare, making it clear he wasn't invited, but then she forces a smile and says, "Sure, of course!"

"So you don't have to stay if you don't want to," he says. "I'll give Cassandra a ride over."

Monica shrugs and turns back to the television. "We can leave at the same time."

I continue eating, but I'm subtly aware of the tension between them. Their cousin dynamic is strange. I have a cousin I'm close with, and that's not how we communicate.

If only he were here—he's so good at helping me think through things.

I finish eating, rinse my plate, and put it in the dishwasher. Then I dry my hands. "Okay, we can go. Do I need anything?"

Monica hops up. "No, let's head out." She dangles her keys on her finger. "Are you riding with me or Mitch?"

I glance at Mitch, then back at Monica. I want to ride with him because I'm curious about what he has to say, but I get the feeling Monica doesn't want me to. "I'll ride with you," I say.

She smiles, and I avoid looking at Mitch. Is there some kind of battle going on for my attention? It doesn't make any sense.

Monica is parked on the street, and I climb into her car. Immediately, she starts talking about the classes she signed up for and her new job at a tea shop with a really hot guy who works there.

I expect her to ask about Mitch. Or even Owen. I'm prepared to tell her about his letter.

But she doesn't ask me anything.

She only lives a few blocks from me—maybe a fifteen-minute walk. But it takes us seven minutes to get there because of the slow speed limits. She parks along the side of the road, and Mitch pulls in behind her.

"Come on," she says, taking me by the elbow and pulling me into the house.

We enter through the kitchen, a small room set off by itself. I follow her into the living room, which feels more like a long, rectangular hallway with three couches lined up in front of the television. Four girls are already sprawled across the couch cushions.

"Hey, guys, this is Cassandra, one of my best friends from back home," Monica says, introducing me.

"Hello," one of the girls says, waving.

Monica proceeds to introduce them to me as well.

"So, you're from Louisiana too?" Sandy, a girl with strawberry blonde hair in pigtails asks as I sit down next to her.

Mitch enters through the kitchen doorway, and I try not to turn my attention to him.

"No, actually, I'm from Arkansas," I say, but she's not listening. She's already spotted

Mitch.

"Oh, it's your cousin!" she exclaims, bouncing off the couch to greet him with a hug.

The girl on the end stops filing her nails. "Hi, Mitch," she says.

Mitch falls into a couch cushion several spots away from me. Monica turns on a foreign film with subtitles, and the conversations around us don't stop, even as the movie begins. I've seen the movie before, but I still think it's rude no one stops talking. So I comment, "Good thing we don't have to hear it to know what's going on."

I don't think anyone is listening to me, but Mitch laughs from a few seats over. "You can pretend you're hearing it in surround sound in a language you don't understand," he says.

Sandy laughs like he said something incredibly witty, and I lean forward slightly, tilting my head to catch his eye. He grins at me, and I grin back. I settle back into the couch cushion and try not to think about it anymore.

When the movie ends, Mitch stands up and says, "I better head back—I've got work early in the morning. Coming, Cassandra?"

I stand as well, but Monica interjects. "I'll take Cassandra home. I just need to grab a snack first. All right, Cass?"

The use of the nickname feels deliberate. While Owen isn't the only person on earth to call me that, he's the one who did it most often. I'm not sure I've ever heard Monica use it. It's like she's reminding me of the depth of our friendship.

I glance at Mitch. I want to ride with him. I get the feeling there's something important that needs to be said between us. But he's not looking at me. Instead, he locks eyes with Monica, and they have another silent stare-down before he shrugs and says, "Okay. See you later."

I don't push it. At least, not at this moment. I stay and eat tacos, getting to know Monica's roommates better before finally asking her to take me home because I'm exhausted.

I'm fully prepared to bring up Mitch myself, but as soon as we're in the car, Monica asks, "So, what's going on with you and Mitch? I thought he was ignoring you or something."

I'm somewhat startled by her directness. "Yeah, that's what was happening. He hurt my feelings pretty badly. But now he's trying to make up for it, I guess."

"Which means what? Are you guys starting to date?"

"I don't know. I think right now we're trying to be friends. I was pretty mad at him and didn't even want to talk to him again."

"Well, I think you might find that Mitch is a bit flaky like that," she says. "He seems to run hot and then cold. I've noticed it a lot over the years. He gets really excited about something, but then he moves on to something else."

This conversation is odd. It's not how I would describe Mitch at all. But Monica has known him much longer than I have, so I don't say anything.

"Anyway." She gives me a big smile as she pulls up to my apartment. "Something to keep in mind, you know, in case he gets weird again. It's probably not you. Want to come over tomorrow and spend the night? I have some glow-in-the-dark stars I want to put all over my ceiling." She beams at me.

"Sure," I say, slowly, because her words have left me reeling.

But it will be nice to spend time with my friend.

⚬⚬✿⚬⚬

I head over to Monica's the next evening. This time, I take my own car.

When I pull up and park along the curb, I'm surprised to see Mitch's car in front of mine. What is he doing here? Why is he everywhere right now?

I slip into the house quietly through the kitchen door, making no sound. For some reason, I'm in stealth mode.

As I step into the living room, I hear voices coming from Monica's bedroom. Angry, whispered voices. I move closer, and I have to admit—I'm intentionally eavesdropping.

"You promised me," I hear Monica say.

"I know what I said," Mitch replies, "but it's not that simple."

"You're making it complicated." Her words are sharp, almost hissing. I inch closer, enough to catch a glimpse of them in her doorway. Monica, a few inches taller than Mitch, is glaring down at him, jabbing her finger into his chest. "You said you wouldn't —"

Mitch's head turns slightly, and he sees me. He takes a step back from her, his face flushing. "Cassandra," he says.

Monica swivels around. "Cassandra!" she echoes.

They clearly didn't expect me to be here.

Which is weird, since she invited me over.

"What's going on?" I ask cautiously, not a hundred percent sure this conversation is about me.

But I'm ninety percent sure.

Neither of them answers. Mitch turns and strides out of the bedroom, brushing past me. "I better go."

Oh no. Not until I get to the bottom of this. I rush after him.

"Wait!"

"Cassandra!" Monica calls, but I ignore her and follow Mitch. He's already at the curb, unlocking his car, about to get in when I reach him.

"Were you guys talking about me?" I demand.

He shakes his head quickly, then says, "Maybe."

CHAPTER FORTY-NINE

Adulting

My mouth drops open. "What the heck?"

Mitch glances back over my shoulder. Monica is standing on the sidewalk, biting her lower lip, hugging herself. Her expression is unreadable. My gaze shifts between the two of them. I'm suddenly tired of being left in the dark, of no one giving me answers. Of the two of them having secret conversations around me. I turn and head to my car.

"Cassandra, wait!" Monica starts toward me.

I get in and start the engine, slamming the door and locking her out. Then I back up, pull away from the curb, and drive around the corner, out of sight.

I'm shaking. I have a tiny suspicion about what's going on, but I won't allow the thought to fully form in my mind.

My phone dings with an incoming text. I check it.

Monica: Come back, please. I can explain.

Another text comes in. This one from Mitch.

Mitch: Talk?

Yes. That's what I want. I respond.

Me: Where?

Mitch: My new place.

He sends me an address. I plug it into my phone and turn left, heading that direction.

It's not three minutes later when I pull up to a single-story old house. Headlights brighten over my car as Mitch pulls in behind me.

He gets out and heads to the front door, so I follow. It's dark inside when he unlocks it.

"Are we the only ones here?" I ask. It's not that I don't trust him, but I don't want to be alone with him.

"No. My roommate's in his room, but he's kind of reclusive. We won't see him."

Mitch doesn't look at me as he speaks. He flips on the light and steps into the living room, which has a small kitchen in the corner.

"Want anything to drink?" he asks, moving to the kitchen.

I shake my head and sink into the green couch, wrapping my arms around myself. I'm still shaky, my nerves on edge, and I just want to sit down and figure out what's happening.

Mitch dumps ice into a glass and pours water over it. The ice rattles as he walks over and sits next to me, still not speaking, still not looking at me. He stares into his glass of ice water instead.

"What were you guys talking about?" I finally ask.

He looks at me, his brow furrowed slightly, a troubled expression in his eyes—so different from the jovial, open person I knew at the lake.

"Tell me," I say quietly, my heart pounding. This is it. I know it. I'm going to find out why he's been acting this way, why he hurt me.

"What's happening between you and my cousin?" he says.

My mind flashes to Monica and the obvious tension between us, even though I didn't argue with her directly. "I don't know. She's keeping something from me. I feel like—"

"Not Monica," Mitch interrupts. "Owen."

My eyes widen. I catch my breath. That's not the name I expected to hear. Although, I guess I should have.

Because now it makes sense.

I meet Mitch's gaze. "What did Monica say?"

He shakes his head. "I want to hear it from you."

A trickle of anxiety runs through my veins, but I remind myself that I've done nothing wrong. "Owen and I dated."

"When?"

I lower my eyes. There's a sting in my chest. Something about this conversation hurts. "Last year."

"Why didn't you tell me?"

His tone is gentle, almost soft, but firm.

I lift my eyes. "I didn't know I needed to."

Mitch frowns and leans back to look at the ceiling. "He's my cousin."

"I know."

He looks at me again. "I was about to date you."

Those words send an electric thrill through me.

He liked me.

We were almost dating.

And now we're not.

"So... if it weren't for Owen, we were going to date?"

He leans forward and drops a hand on my knee. I flinch at the touch but don't move.

"I like you. But he's my cousin. No matter what I feel for you, I can't date his girlfriend. Not even his ex-girlfriend."

Even as I open my mouth to argue, I know he's right. It's like Monica said. How would it be at family gatherings? What kind of wedge would it put between Owen and Mitch? How would I feel seeing the two of them together?

A relationship could never go anywhere.

And I don't want one.

I realize it even as the thought tangles through my head. I did like Mitch. I was willing to date him and see what might happen. But I'm still not ready.

Mitch must see some of this on my face because he pulls his hand back and asks, "Do you still love him?"

I nod. I can't lie.

"I'm sorry if I hurt you," I say. "I did like you. I do."

"And I'm sorry. I know I hurt you."

It's all falling into place. "Who told you?"

"Monica. She told me when we were unloading from camping. I heard her, but I had a bit of a tug-of-war with myself because, yes"—he lifts his eyebrows— "you're the kind of girl I want to be with. But then I went to the wedding reception, and all of my family was there, half of my cousins, including Monica, and I imagined what it would be like. And I couldn't do it. I can't put that wedge in my family. So I knew we had to end this thing before it got bigger."

I pull my knees up to my chest and tuck into the corner of the couch, turning my gaze away to stare at the kitchen. It makes sense, everything, and it doesn't hurt as badly as I thought it would.

But I'm pissed at Monica. She had no right to tell him without my permission. If she thought it was something Mitch needed to know, she should have told me to tell him.

"I'm sorry I wasn't open with you right away," he says. "Monica didn't want me to tell you."

I give a short laugh. "Because she knew I'd be angry."

Mitch pulls out his phone. "Yeah, well..." He taps a few keys. "I just told her I told you. So now you guys can deal with it."

I arch an eyebrow. "Oh, we will."

"I really do think you're amazing. I hope we can be friends."

I look at Mitch, and while I want his friendship, I see a repeat here of Jared, of Tiago, of every boy I've friend-zoned, and I'm wary.

"Yeah," I say. "We can still be friends."

I'm glad he moved out. I won't have to see him in the mornings, walking home from school, at church.

I stand. "Thanks for telling me. I'm going home now."

Mitch stands too, and he reaches over to hug me. I allow it for two seconds before I pull out of the embrace because suddenly I feel fragile.

I leave without another word.

My plan was to drive straight back to Monica's house and confront her, but I'm too achy. I need someone else to talk to.

I text Stirling.

☙ ❈ ❧

Stirling's car pulls up beside mine in the parking lot of Canyon Park. I stay in my car, so he hops out of his and slips into the passenger seat.

"What's wrong?" he asks.

I take a deep breath, trying to steady myself. My conversation with Mitch has left me shaken, and Monica's betrayal weighs heavily on me. On top of that, I'm grappling with my unresolved feelings for Owen.

I'm a mess.

"Remember that guy I told you about?" I begin.

"The one who called you when he was camping?" Stirling asks.

I nod. "And then ghosted me after?"

"Yeah, I remember."

I proceed to tell Stirling the whole story, concluding with how upset I am over Monica meddling in my life without talking to me first. I leave out any mention of my feelings for Owen, but I can't hold back the emotion, and tears spill over. Stirling gives me a side hug and says, "Let's go hike the Y."

I glance in my mirror at the mountain behind us, where the whitewashed Y is visible two-thirds of the way up. "Now?"

"Why not?"

The fact that it's almost midnight crosses my mind, but I push it aside. "Yeah, let's do it."

The path starts off easy enough, a long switchback trail with a gentle incline. We use our phones for light, sweeping the beams back and forth across the trail to watch out for rocks. We talk about Stirling's family, mine, and how he has to fly home tomorrow for his cousin's wedding.

"I think my mom booked me on the first flight out," Stirling says. "Five-thirty in the morning."

I let out a sharp laugh. "Five-thirty? You have to be there by four?"

"I'll be happy if I make it by five. I'm not checking any bags."

I shake my head. "I don't envy you. At least you have a car."

"The funny thing is, I don't want to drive it, but I can't figure out who I could sucker into taking me at four in the morning."

I glare at him. "No."

He glances at me, wide-eyed and innocent. "No what?"

"I'm not taking you to the airport at four in the morning."

He raises both hands in surrender, the light of his phone briefly blinding me. "I wouldn't dream of asking."

I sigh. "Fine. Just make sure you're ready, and I'll pick you up at four."

He laughs. "Deal."

The trail grows steeper as we ascend, with the switchbacks getting tighter.

"The Y didn't look that far from the parking lot," I say, panting and leaning forward to power through the climb.

"Yeah, it's deceptive."

"I'm glad I wore tennis shoes."

It's not a long hike, only about twenty minutes from start to finish, but it's vigorous. We finally reach the giant whitewashed Y and climb up to sit on its base. I lean back on the rocks, arms stretched out, chest heaving as I catch my breath. Stirling sits beside me, wrapping his arms around his knees.

"It's pretty nice from here," he says.

I sit up and take in the view. The buildings below are specks of light, and the few cars on the road twinkle like stars as they wind through the city. The night air is cooler, and I welcome the breeze that brushes across my sweaty face.

"Yeah, it's beautiful."

"How are you feeling about Mitch now?" Stirling asks.

"I don't know." I chew on my lower lip, my feelings still bruised and tender. "I really did like him."

"Enough to make it a long-term, serious relationship?"

I nod slowly. "Everything about him drew me in. I thought I was ready for something serious."

"And now?"

"He said some things that made me realize maybe I'm not. But it still hurts. I let him in, you know? And Monica—"

"Yeah, she crossed a line."

"Way past being a good friend, way past being my ex's sister. She jeopardized a relationship I was building. She had no right to do that."

"Has she tried to talk to you?"

I shake my head. "No, actually. And Mitch told her I knew."

"About her role in it?"

"Yeah. I think I'll wait for her to contact me, and then we'll figure this out."

"Do you think you'll be able to be friends after this?"

I consider the question. There's been serious damage to our friendship, but I also understand where Monica was coming from. She's practically a sister to me. "I think so. I think we'll be okay."

Stirling turns on his flashlight and shines it under his face like we used to do before telling scary stories around a campfire. "If you need me to take care of her... or him..."

I laugh. "You look ridiculous." I snap a picture of him.

We spend the next ten minutes taking silly photos and selfies at the top of the Y. By the time we hike down, even though my heart still feels tender, I'm not as distraught.

CHAPTER FIFTY

This Is Why

When my alarm goes off at 3:30 the next morning, it takes me a moment to remember why. At least I don't have to worry about waking my roommate, since Tracie moved out three days ago. I hit snooze and fall back to sleep until the thing starts blasting again, and then I bolt upright, remembering.

I have to get Stirling to the airport!

I throw on my glasses and tumble out of bed, not bothering with anything except sliding on my shoes and brushing my teeth. I call Stirling as I run to my car. I'm supposed to pick him up in five minutes.

He doesn't answer. I keep calling all the way to his apartment. There are no lights on when I arrive, and it hits me—Stirling didn't wake up.

I run up to the door, banging on it and ringing the doorbell three times. I start calling him again.

My antics must work, because this time he answers. "Crap, I'm coming. I slept through my alarm."

"I'm in the car," I say, trying to stay calm.

I wait in the car, and seven minutes later, Stirling stumbles into the passenger seat. His eyes are puffy with sleep, and his normally perfect hair is a mess.

"I can't believe I did that," he mumbles.

I shrug. "Better you than me."

Fortunately, there's no traffic at this hour. The stoplights stay green for an unusually long time, and I zip through, making it to the airport in twenty minutes.

Stirling is half-asleep when I pull up to the terminal at Eagle Ridge Regional Airport. I park and poke his shoulder. "Stirling, we're here."

He jolts awake, checks the time, and says, "I've still got an hour. Thanks, Cassandra." He gives me a quick hug and grabs his bag from the back.

"Do you need a ride home?" I ask.

"No, Wyatt said he'd pick me up. He doesn't do mornings."

"Which is how I ended up with this job." I scowl, but I'm not really upset. "If

229

anything changes, let me know. I'll come get you."

"You're the best." Stirling gives me a tired grin, pulls a baseball cap over his head, and heads into the terminal.

I pull away from the curb and start the half-hour drive back home.

By the time I get there, my eyes are burning, and my chest feels heavy with a constant ache. It's not even five yet, and no one else is awake. I know I have a busy day ahead of me, preparing my room for my new roommate. But for now, I have nothing pressing. I bury myself under the blankets and fall asleep.

My new roommate is coming on Sunday. I clean my side of the room and pick up anything Tracie left behind. I wish Layne were here because I don't want to be with a new person again.

I don't hear my phone ringing because I have my music playing loudly while I vacuum. The sound catches me by surprise when I turn off the appliance and hear the chiming over the speaker. I pick up the phone.

Monica.

I haven't forgotten last night. But she didn't text me, and neither has Mitch, and the wound has been festering, ignored and putrid, all morning.

It's the second time she's called. I must have missed the first.

I shut off my music and answer. "Hello?"

"Cassandra." She lets out a breathy sigh. "Decided to talk to me?"

"I didn't hear my phone." I don't mean to be rude. I'm stating a fact. But the words come out terse and curt.

"Do you have a minute?"

"I'm cleaning."

"Want me to swing by there or do you want to come here?"

Looks like no isn't an option. "I'll come by there when I'm done."

I hang up and wrap up the vacuum, then drag it to the hall closet. I don't want to stay mad at Monica. In the end, she didn't damage anything. Mitch and I couldn't have a relationship. But I'm still very incensed that she inserted herself in my personal life like that. Like she thought being my ex's sister gave her the right.

We might need to establish boundaries in our friendship. And that sucks.

I make her wait. I finish cleaning and then sit in the kitchen and make tuna and crackers. Then I brush my teeth and put on eye make up so I don't look so tired. But as each second passes, my heart rate increases and my stomach churns with anxiety for the upcoming conversation, and I know it's time to go. So finally I grab my purse and head out to the car.

Ironic that I was supposed to stay the night with her last night. I pull up to the curb and go in the same door to the kitchen as yesterday. I don't wish to catch anyone by surprise, so I call out, "Hello?"

I step into the living room as Monica comes out of the bedroom. Now I hear voices, but they come from the bedrooms. Like all college housing, there's no privacy.

"Let's talk in the kitchen," she says. Her eyes are bare, no makeup, and her face is pale like someone who's sick or didn't sleep well. I push down a jolt of alarm. Monica's cancer is in remission. She would have told me if it were back.

Still, as we pull out chairs at the kitchen table, I have to ask.

"You're not sick, are you?"

"What?" She blinks, momentarily startled. "No. I'm good."

I nod. I can be angry now.

She picks up the salt shaker and examines it, then sets it back on the table. "I'm really sorry, Cassandra. I know I crossed a line."

I bob my head. "Yep."

She jumps to her own defense then. "But you know it couldn't work out, right? Someone had to say something. What if—"

I interrupt her, my indignation rising. "The only person who should have said anything was me. If I felt it was necessary."

"But it was," she says, and I hold up my hand.

"My decision," I say. "You don't get to decide. I was the one dating Mitch, not you. Would you want me telling every guy you date about the other guys you've dated? Or the ones you got serious with?"

She cringes. "No. But that wouldn't be any of—"

"Their business? What makes it different? Because Mitch is your cousin? Or because he's Owen's cousin?"

"That is the difference, they're family—"

"Again, not your decision. What if I decided I was willing to face those consequences? That's something Mitch and I would discuss together. But I never even got that chance because you scared him off before we could."

She looks stricken, her brows furrowing inward. "You would do that to Owen?"

Her words cut me. I take a deep breath and look down at the table. "This isn't about Owen. Or Mitch. It's about you staying out of my love life. I get to decide. Even if you think I'm wrong. I'm happy to listen to you, to hear your opinion, to get your advice. But you've got to stay out." I lift my eyes, putting an edge in my voice. "I'm going to date people, Monica."

She nods. Her eyes are glossy, and when she blinks, tears cling to her lashes. Then she says, "It would tear Owen up if you got serious with Mitch."

She's not getting it. She's still trying to protect her brother. I groan and scrub my hands over my face. Then I lean forward, holding her gaze. "Listen. Mitch and I aren't dating. And we were never going to get serious, because you're right. I can't date someone in your family. But do you understand it was my decision? Not yours!"

I see her start to understand. "Were you going to tell him?"

I honestly don't know if I was. I didn't think it mattered. "Maybe not. Maybe I needed someone to sit down and make me see why it wouldn't work. But you can trust me. You can talk to me."

Her fingers flutter on the table. "I was trying to save you and him from heartache. From having to break it off after getting attached. I thought it was better to do it now."

I clasp my palms and rest my chin on them. "I know. There's a lot of things you might think my future boyfriends have the right to know. You don't get to be the one to tell them."

She gives a slow nod. "I get what you're saying. And I'm sorry. If Mitch is the one you're supposed to be with, and I screwed it all up—"

"You didn't." I shake my head. "Mitch is awesome. But I'm not as ready as I thought I was to get serious. Just promise me the next time I'm dating, you won't sit down and tell them all the reasons they shouldn't date me."

"It's because he's my cousin—" she begins.

"Maybe. Or it might be because you want me to end up with Owen and are willing to sabotage any relationship to make it happen."

She considers that. Then she grins. "I can see your point."

I smile too, and then we both laugh, and I'm conjuring images of her pulling pranks and damaging the property of any boy who tries to get close to me. She gets up and comes around the chair to hug me, and I pat her arm.

I know where she was coming from. But I'm going to date, and even if she doesn't like it, she's got to stay out.

I will steer clear of any of Owen's family, though.

❧

Before I leave Monica's house, we make plans for the evening.

"Let's go dancing," she says. "Introduce you to boys I'm not related to."

It's an olive branch, a peace offering, a show of support for me to live my life. It's also an opportunity for us to strengthen our friendship. To stay on each other's radar.

I want both. "Yeah, sure. Where do you have in mind? Is there a dance on your campus?"

Monica doesn't go to PYU. She's going to the school forty minutes away, which means we have access to the social events happening in both places.

But she shakes her head. "No. But I bet there's a club we can go to."

Not this again.

Monica's four years older than me. She can get into any club she wants.

I have to go the one that takes underage college kids. Because no way am I getting a fake ID so I can sneak into clubs.

"There's one around here," I say, ignoring how my heart rate suddenly ratchets up. "My roommate Abby knows it. I can ask her."

I don't mention how Abby's been trying to get me to go there since we met. Somehow, I successfully navigated my freshman year without stepping foot inside. I just know I'm going to hate it.

But maybe I'm wrong.

"Great!" Monica says, her eyes lighting up. "Invite her along! I'll see if any of my roommates want to go!"

I nod. "She'll be excited."

I'll pretend like I am. I'm good at that.

Abby's hanging with Iris and Camila when I get home. It's only the four of us right now. Abby hasn't had a roommate since June, and I'm by myself until Sunday. I pop into their bedroom but trip over the bras Abby has strung up on a line between the beds.

"What the heck?" I say, and I have a moment of tossing bra straps off of me like spider webs on steroids.

The girls laugh at me.

"I can't put them in the dryer," Abby says. "That stretches out the fabric and ruins the cups."

232

"Ruins the cups?" I repeat, and they laugh again.

I wait for Abby to gather up her special clothing and for the giggles to subside. "What are you guys doing tonight?" I ask, getting comfortable on Iris's bed.

"I've got a concert rehearsal," Iris says.

"I have an evening jog with the cross country team," Camila says. "Nothing after that. Why?"

I turn to Abby. "You?"

"A few friends said they wanted to do something, but I didn't commit."

I lift an eyebrow. "I was thinking of going to the club you've been begging me to take you to for a year."

"The Black Sheep?" Abby says. "You want to go?"

I nod. "Monica wants to go dancing. Want to come?"

"I so do!" Abby laughs. "I can't wait to see you getting it down!"

Iris snorts. "You do know she's still Cassandra, right? There won't be any getting it down."

For some reason I feel affronted. "Hey, now. I might turn out to be a rabid dancer."

"Exactly what I'm saying!" Abby pushes on my forearm, beaming.

I turn to the other girls. "Either of you want to come?"

"I would, but we usually get together after my rehearsal," Iris says.

Camila shakes her head. "I'm out. Early practice in the morning. I need my sleep."

I'm slightly envious of her built-in excuse. "Looks like it's just us, Abby."

CHAPTER FIFTY-ONE

Black Sheep

"We can't get to the club too early," Abby says. "That's not what people do."

I believe her. We make plans to pick up Monica around eight-thirty so we'll be walking into the club close to nine p.m.

My phone rings as I'm laying out my clothing, trying to decide what to wear. I glance at it and I'm surprised to see it's Mitch.

I answer. "Hello?"

"Hi," he says. "How's your day going?"

"Decent," I say. I wonder if he wants to have another real talk or just frivolous stuff. "I took my friend to the airport at oh-dark-thirty and I've been cleaning my room most of the day. Getting a new roommate on Sunday."

"Nice. What happened to your old one?"

"Tracie's getting married." He might not know. Tracie wasn't very social with anyone except her fiance. "She moved out last week."

"Oh."

He pauses, and I think he'll ask about my incoming roommate, but he says, "Did you talk to Monica?"

"I did," I say.

"You okay?"

"I am. I told her my feelings. And we're all right."

He exhales. "I'm glad I didn't come between your friendship. And I'm really sorry about how things went down. I think you're an awesome girl."

"Gee, thanks, I think you're swell also," I say, laying on the thick sarcasm. I'm not quite over it yet. It's hard to believe that a few days ago this was the boy I was thinking of starting a relationship with.

He chuckles. "Have plans tonight? There's a soccer game. We could go watch it."

I lift an eyebrow. He's actually trying to keep the friendship going. I give him props for that.

"I do have plans. Monica wanted to go dancing, so we're headed out to the Black

Sheep. Want to come?"

"Black Sheep? What's that?"

"A club for underage kids. Apparently there's no alcohol."

"Well . . . honestly that doesn't sound like my scene. But let me know if you love it, and maybe I'll go another time."

I'm not surprised. Mitch and I are very similar. It's one of the things that drew me to him. "I will. Thanks for checking on me."

"Yeah, of course. I never meant to hurt you."

"We both got hurt in this one," I say, and I sigh. "And I guess I should have been smart enough to see it coming. So I'm sorry for that."

"You're fine, Cassandra. I'll talk to you later."

I have my doubts about that. I don't feel like Mitch and I can pursue a friendship. It's always going to be weird now. But I appreciate the sentiment, and I hang up feeling closure on the situation.

Abby comes in to check on me a little after eight. Or rather, to check on my outfit. She's wearing blue jeans and a lacy tank top that shows her belly when she moves. But she has thrown an off-the-shoulder sweater over the top.

"Jeans," she says when she sees my plaid pants.

"But these are form-fitting," I say.

"Wear jeans."

I swap out my pants for a pair of dark skinny jeans. "Is my shirt all right?" I ask, not sure if I'm amused or annoyed. I'm wearing a red peasant blouse that ties at the collar bone. The wide neck-line almost falls off my shoulders.

Abby goes through my closet, perusing my clothes. "Nope. Nothing."

I arch an eyebrow. "I've got cute things."

"We're not going for cute. Wait here."

She exits my room and comes back with a tank top similar to hers but light blue and a long-sleeved crochet shirt. The weave is so open it would be scandalous without something worn underneath it.

"Here," she says.

I accept the clothing with hesitation. This is not my style.

"Put it on," she says, as if reading my mind.

I peel off the pleasant blouse and slide the tank top over my shoulder. The long-sleeved shirt comes next. It's more like a swimsuit cover up but skin tight, wrapping around my arms and hugging my torso.

"Now you're ready," she says, satisfaction in her voice.

I step out of the bedroom and into the hallway, where we have a full-length mirror. And I'm startled when I see myself. The clothing suits me, transforming me into a sexy woman.

"You'll need heels," Abby says, coming up beside me. We look at our reflections together. "And I'll do your makeup."

By the time she finishes with my black eyeliner and slicking back parts of my hair, I barely recognize myself.

But that's also totally okay. Now I'm playing dress-up, putting on an act, and I can be someone else entirely for one night.

I lay on the horn when we get to Monica's house, and she comes running out to the car. Abby hops into the back for her. Monica pulls open the passenger door and pops in, then freezes when she sees me.

"OMG," she says, staring at me.

"Like my new look?" I laugh. I know it's extreme.

"Get out so I can see your outfit," she demands.

I shoot an amused smile at Abby in the back, then climb out of the car.

"Oh my gosh!" Monica says again. "Who are you? Strike a pose!"

Strike a pose? I already feel like I'm posing here. I pucker my lips and try looking provocative but think I look like a territorial monkey. Monica shrieks and takes pictures and won't stop laughing.

"All right, enough," I say. I get back in the car. I won't ask her what she plans to do with those pictures.

We pull up at the Black Sheep ten minutes later. It sits over a pot-hole ridden parking lot like a warehouse but with flashing neon lights. The sign out front shows the blinking outline of a woolly sheep in dark blue. I park a few spaces from the other cars.

"At least there's plenty of light," I say. This place already looks sus to me.

The music churns outward over the parking lot, lulling us in like sirens. Monica and Abby chatter excitedly and I try to drum up my playgirl persona a little longer. But I feel like a giraffe in these stilted shoes, and I stumble over a crack in the concrete and pitch into Abby, who gives me an amused look. She straightens me, and we walk into the club together.

A bouncer greets us, but all he does is take our money. He doesn't ask for ID. He ushers us into the darkened building with flashing lights and fake smoke and real smoke.

I hold back a sigh. It's not any different than the club I went to in high school, except it's darker and the kids are older. I cough at the smoke and hold my breath, but I can't do that forever, so I inhale very shallowly.

Monica and Abby move away into the crowd of people and mingle. They're not dancing yet, just talking, trying to get a feel for things. My face stretches tight with my forced smile. Why am I smiling? No one's looking at me. No one cares.

Someone bumps me, knocking me into the dancers, and then a kid in front of me turns to face me. He's holding a cup in one hand and lifts the other over his head, his chin bouncing in some weird parody of dancing to the music. He makes eye contact in one of the bobs and seems to be smiling.

Nope. I'm not here for this.

I back out of the people and head to the bar. I settle behind a barstool and study the non-alcoholic beverages behind the counter.

"What can I get for you, sister?" the bartender asks.

"Soda water, please," I say.

"With lime?"

Now I feel like I'm at a fancy restaurant instead of a wannabe club. "Yeah."

He hands it to me. I turn slightly and see the boys next to me passing around a joint. I study them, sipping on my soda, and think of Owen.

The first time I went clubbing in Arkansas, I bumped into him. We weren't dating.

We weren't thinking about dating. But I think it was that moment that changed things, at least for me. He was smoking, and I teased him about it, and he made a comment about how different we were.

I don't know why that got my mind to think of him in a romantic way, but it did.

Every time I saw him after that, I found myself searching for our similarities, arguing with myself that we weren't that different after all.

I take another sip of my soda and wish life had turned out differently.

Abby bops over to me ten minutes later. "This place is lame," she complains. "No one's dancing."

I'm not sure what she expected. "Maybe not the best place to pick up guys."

She makes a face. "Let's go."

"Go where?"

"I don't know. I'll find Monica."

She returns five minutes later with Monica in tow. Monica looks at me sitting at the bar, and the expression that crosses over her face can only be described as pity.

"Sitting over here by yourself?" she says.

"I'm drinking." I lift my soda.

"We're getting food." Abby loops an arm through mine and pulls me from the barstool. She leans close to my ear and says, "And we never need to come here again."

I grin. "Finally. Monkey off my back."

"Well, I had to see it!" She leads the way back to my car. "Honestly. We need fake IDs so we can get into a real club. This felt like a junior high dance."

I shake my head ruefully as we climb into my car. "You're on your own with that one. This was enough for me."

"But you like dancing!" Abby doesn't stop talking as we drive out to Main Street looking for an open restaurant.

"Not that kind," I say. "I'd rather do something adventurous, like hiking or swimming or caving."

"Have you been caving around here?" Monica asks. "I hear there's a cave nearby the locals like to visit."

"The one that's halfway up the mountain?" I ask. "I took my sister there over the summer."

"No, this one's a wild cave. Out by the lake."

"I've heard of it!" Abby says. "What's it called, the Mud Dauber?"

"Yeah, I think so."

"Let's go there!" Abby says. "It will be so fun!"

"Abby." I laugh at her. "From clubs to caves? Maybe we need a day to do nothing."

"That's what Sunday's for." She pinches my arm as I pull into an Appleby's. "I'll find the info on it!"

CHAPTER FIFTY-TWO

Summer Adventures

Everyone wants to go caving except Monica. She bails after I pull up the website and show the specs of the cave thirty minutes away on the other side of the lake. People have posted videos and photos of descending through the opening in the ground, sliding down a rock, and coming to a myriad of what look like giant ant tunnels. Or a wasp nest.

Hence the name Mud Dauber. That, and it's always muddy.

But Iris and Camila are totally excited.

We work together in the kitchen Saturday morning, packing lunches and filling water bottles. Iris peruses a map on her phone.

"So it's behind some private property by the lake," she says. "It's unmarked on government land but it can be hard to get to. The GPS won't take us there. I'll print this map for us."

"Great," I say.

"Flashlights." Camila dumps them on the table. "I put new batteries in all of them."

Abby comes into the room in shorts and a tank top, and I shake my head at her.

"You can't wear that."

She looks down at her bare legs and light pink tank. "Why not?"

"Seriously?" I roll my eyes. "A, it's going to be freezing in there."

"The website says it stays about sixty degrees," she protests.

I ignore her. "B, some of these tunnels are tiny. You'll scrape your legs and arms all up. You need long sleeves and jeans." I wave my arms at her, emphasizing the fabric covering my skin. "C, this is a muddy cave. You'll get covered in dirt. You'll ruin those pretty little things." I pluck at the lace hem around her shirt.

"Fine." She huffs and turns around to change.

"I think we're ready," Iris says, reappearing in the kitchen with the map in her hands.

"Do we have everything?" Camila ticks items off on her fingers. "Lunch. Water. Flashlights. Do we need helmets? Rope?"

"No," I say. "We're not going spelunking. It's not an expedition. We're exploring a cave that everyone around here goes through. There will probably be tons of people in there."

Abby returns suitably dressed. "Happy?" she grumps.

"You will be," I say.

It takes us another ten minutes, but we finally get out the door. This is far more exciting than going clubbing, and I'm bouncing in my seat as we head south toward the lake. Iris feeds me directions, and all goes well until I get off the interstate. Then the roads split off into gravel and dirt, and things get dicey.

"Turn on this road," Iris says, pointing to a dirt track that winds up a hill.

"Are you sure?" I eye the path in front of me that goes down and then back up. Tire tracks are fresh enough to still kick up dust in the wind.

"I think so . . . Yeah, it's this one."

I turn up it, my car tires spinning in protest as we climb the dusty hill.

It dead ends at the top.

"Sorry, sorry, not this one," Iris says, her face turning pink. She shoves the jet-black hair from her forehead, her eyes pinched.

"It's fine." I hold back any words of annoyance. I drive down the hill carefully because it's quite steep and my car doesn't have four-wheel drive. We reach the bottom, and I scrape over some rocks before I make it to the more obvious road.

"Let me see," Abby says, taking the map from Iris. "Okay, keep going straight. Over that cattle grate . . . Turn left here. This house is on the map, I think."

She points but I don't look. I'm busy watching the cows as they watch me.

"This is someone's yard," I say.

"No, it can't be . . ." she murmurs.

I stop driving. The cows move my direction, tails swishing, big bulgy eyes focused on me. I never thought of the bovine creatures as frightening, but I feel a flash of alarm as they get closer.

"I'm out of here," I say. My tires spit dirt and gravel as I spin around and go back over the cattle grate.

"Okay, I see what I did wrong," Abby says. "Go straight through here, keep to the bottom of this hill."

Sweat beads along my hairline. "I'm starting to think this was a bad idea," I murmur.

"Me too," Camila says beside me.

"What if we can't find this place?" I'm not sure I can find my way back out.

"We'll find it," Abby says, calm and confident as always.

We drive three more minutes through the dust and invisible roads, avoiding potholes, large rocks, and sagebrush. Then Iris points.

"Look, look!"

I see it. A wide, flat expanse of dirt that doubles as a parking lot. A hill rises behind it, and I assume the cave opening is at the top. Two other cars are there, and I laugh in relief.

"We found it."

The girls high-five each other, the anticipation in the car ramping up now that we're not stuck in some farmer's field facing off with his cows.

We get out and sit on the trunk of my car, eating our sandwiches and taking pictures before we begin our exodus into darkness.

"Ready?" Iris asks, tossing the food back into the car.

I down half my water bottle and add it to the food. "I think so."

We climb the hill together, and another group is heading from the cave toward the parking lot as we arrive. I examine them, noting how mud covers their thighs and chests, dust caked to their faces.

"Dirty in there?" I ask.

"A bit wet," the boy says. "Can be slippery. Have fun!"

Abby turns around and watches them descend the hill, a frown on her face.

"Come on, princess," I tease, looping my arm through hers. "This was your idea."

I'm in my element now.

The cave blends right in with the desert ground. No sign marks it, and we wander the hilltop looking for the entrance for five minutes before Camila lets out a cry.

"Here it is!"

She stands at the edge of a hole the size of a car tire. We rush over to join her and peer into the dark. I shine my light and see several rock outcroppings leading down.

It's smaller than I expected.

My heart hammers as my pulse quickens, but no one else makes a move to go down. So I step forward. "Let's go."

My friends come behind me. We don't say a word as we climb down the first steps. I come out into a small chamber tall enough for me to stand, and I exhale in relief when I straighten up. Behind me, the light shines from the opening, and the girls drop into the chamber. In front of me, a giant slab of rock forms a slide away from the cave entrance and down into the depths.

Camila and Iris come to stand next to me, and all three of us shine our flashlights down the granite slide.

"That's the way down?" Iris says.

I nod.

"How do we get back up?" Camila asks.

"There's a rope." I remember this from the website. I crouch down, shining my light until I find the rope that's been tied to a rock at the back of the chamber. It's knotted in several places for grabbing.

"Yikes," Abby says.

Her tone and demeanor express what she doesn't say.

"This is gonna be great," I say, smirking at her.

"You go first," she says, clearly not convinced. "Tell me how it is."

"Fine." I lead the way, sitting on my butt and pushing myself down the rock. And then it gets wetter and slicker, and I suck back a gasp as my momentum throws me down the rock. I clutch my flashlight in one hand, wishing for a headlamp, hoping I'll be able to slow down before I crash into the bottom. Sharp pieces of rock scratch up the back of my thigh, and then my feet hit the ground. I propel forward and land on my knees. Tiny shards jab into my skin, and I hiss as I get back to my feet.

"Okay," I call up, masking my pain. "It's a bit fast. You can either use the rope as you come down or I'll be here to slow you at the bottom."

Camila appears at the top. She takes the rope in her right hand, but her left is holding her flashlight. "I can't do both," she says.

Headlamps. We should have invested in a few.

"No worries," I say. "Put your flashlight in your pocket. I'll shine for you."

Still she hesitates. She ends up placing it in her mouth and scooting down, using one hand for control and the other on the rope. She squeals when she hits the wet spot and the flashlight falls. She releases the rope to grab it, swivels sideways, and crashes into me at the bottom.

I catch her, and somehow we both stay standing. "At least you saved the flashlight."

"Yeah." She gives a laugh.

We turn to the others.

"It's a lot easier now," I say. "Put your light away, Camila and I will guide you."

Iris comes next. Camila shines the light, Iris clings to the rope, and I reach out both hands to steady her as she nears the bottom.

"That wasn't bad at all," she says, bouncing to her feet beside us.

I grunt. She has no idea.

We coax Abby down. She's not thrilled with this. She paces the top of the rock before sitting on the edge. I hold my breath because I sense she wants to back out. But we keep calling to her, encouraging her, and finally she grabs hold of the rock and shimmies down.

We hug her at the bottom, and there's an endorphin high because we made it this far. Abby shines her flashlight on our backsides and scowls.

"You guys are filthy. But you've got it the worst, Cassandra."

I don't tell her how I scraped my butt for her. "Good thing you wore pants."

The cave opens up for us now, and though it's pitch black without our lights, the chamber we've entered is tall and wide. We wander into hallways leading off of it but always end up circling back to the main room.

"There's more to explore," Iris says. "I saw online all these little tunnels that branch off the bigger halls."

"I've seen lots of them," I say. We head down another hallway, and I shine my light on a number of small openings around our calves.

"But not all of them have been explored," Camila warns. "We need to be careful where we go."

"I have a map." Iris pulls it out of her pocket and unfolds it. "The tunnels are labeled. This one here, it's called the Ring of Fire." She points it out on the map. "It's a long and skinny tunnel that leads to a bigger room at the end. Lots of people go through it."

"Why the Ring of Fire?" Abby asks.

Iris smirks. "Because that's what your hoochie feels like when you push out a baby. And we're the babies the cave is pushing out."

"Are you sure it's this one?" I shine my light from the map to the tunnel at my shin. Then I shine the light around the hallway, showing various small openings branching off. "It could be any of these."

Camila holds the map and examines it.

Iris takes her light and shimmies up into another opening, though her feet stay where we can see them. "This one dead ends right here," her voices calls back to us.

"Look at this rock formation." Camila points out an oval-shaped pillar beside us. "The bottom dome looks like a bell, right? It shows it on the map. Right by the Ring of Fire."

Iris pops back out to join us, her black hair coated with a fine dust and making it look like she aged fifty years in that tunnel. "It's got to be it."

I shrug. "Okay, let's do it."

Camila and Iris nod, but Abby hasn't said a word. I shine my light on her. "Abby?"

"Do I have to?"

It's the most uncertain I've ever seen my vivacious friend. "I'm not going to make you," I say. "Do you feel comfortable standing out here by yourself?"

She glances around the cavern and sighs. "I'll come. I'll be last."

It's decided.

Somehow I'm in front again. I push into the tunnel, moving on my hands and knees, clutching the flashlight in one hand. My movements are slow and awkward, the metal light making a clinking sound with each forward motion. The tunnel goes upward, up and up in a gradual slope before leveling off. I pause when I've gone about ten feet and call over my shoulder.

"Are we all here?"

"Here," Iris says at my feet.

"Here!" Camila calls behind her.

"Yep," Abby says, her voice more faint.

So far so good. I can't stand, and I can't straighten up. There's no going backward now. We could turn around if we had to, but it would be difficult. I continue crawling. Ten more feet. Twenty.

The passage narrows. I drop into an army crawl, moving on my elbows and letting my thighs pull myself forward. "How long is this tunnel?" I ask Iris. It feels like we've been crawling forever.

"I don't know," she says.

A smaller tunnel branches off to the side. I examine it with my flashlight, but the downward slope makes me nervous. If I get stuck in there, I don't know how I'll get out.

Our passage gets even narrower, and my heart rate increases. Sweat beads along my forehead as the walls of the cave close in around us. I have to flatten out on my belly. There's no room for my elbows. The flashlight goes in front of me, barely lighting the inches before I get there. I'm shuffling forward, using my whole body, and the thought goes through my mind: what if this doesn't end? Should we stop and begin moving backward?

What if we have already gone too far to get out? My phone is jammed in my pocket, cushioned against my body so it won't break but also bruising my hip with each forward thrust. Do we have signal in here?

Did we tell anywhere where we were going?

CHAPTER FIFTY-THREE

Closing Around Me

I'm breathing faster, sweating more. I'm not sure how long we've been inching forward but it feels like an hour.

It can't have been.

I don't ask how everyone's doing.

The passage tightens around me. I'm surrounded by rock. I can't scrape my way out, dig a new passage, or make it wider.

I'm suddenly terrified we're going to die in here. All four of us, trapped like sardines in this cave. No way back.

I take a deep breath, trying to calm my heart rate.

Does this tunnel ever end? What if it goes on forever? We could end up in China!

And then a black opening appears in front of me. I hardly believe it when the passage opens into a small room. I almost cry with relief as I emerge from the tunnel into a chamber with a ledge around another hole. I shine my light into the hole in the middle, and it's not deep, maybe six feet. I scoot over on the ledge as Iris pops out behind me.

"Oh my gosh," she says, and we hug each other, clutching each other tightly.

"You guys," Camila says, coming out behind her.

I scoot down and we all move over as Abby emerges. Her face is streaked with dirt and her eyes wide, but she's breathing and looks unharmed.

"That was the most awful thing I've ever done," she says.

"There's only one way back," Camila says in a low voice.

None of us respond to that.

I move the flashlight along the chamber and notice another tunnel in front of us. "We can explore that tunnel, see where it goes."

"No," Abby says.

"Are you crazy?" Iris says. "I thought we were going to get stuck in there."

I nod. She's right. "So how long did it take us to get over here?"

Camila retrieves her phone and checks it. "Not sure. At least twenty minutes. Maybe thirty."

I let out a breath. "That's all? It felt like an eternity in there."

"Yeah, it did," Abby agrees.

I look around the chamber again. Twenty minutes of torture for this little room, and now we get to head back in. Twenty more minutes of torture.

It wasn't worth it.

"Who's leading?" I ask.

"I'll lead," Camila says. "We go the way we came, right?"

"Right," I say. "Don't take any of the smaller tunnels branching off."

"What if I miss the exit?"

"You won't," I say. "It's where the tunnel begins." I think. Now I'm not sure.

But Camila nods and climbs back into the tunnel, and I don't share my sudden self-doubt.

Iris follows, and Abby looks at me.

"Are you okay being last?" she asks.

I squeeze her hand. "You've got this. Let's go."

I take one last look around the chamber before climbing up after Abby. I shine my light at the mysterious tunnel across from me, a small part of me disappointed I won't get to explore it.

I won't risk my life for it.

The narrow tunnel challenges my ability to breathe, but going back is easier. I know it won't last forever. I let out a breath as it widens, and I go from a belly crawl to an army crawl, and a few minutes after that I'm able to get back on my hands and knees, bear crawling until I slip out of the tunnel.

We stand in the open hallway of the cave, which feels warm and welcoming after that interlude.

Abby throws her arms around Iris's neck, then we all hug, laughing, and I feel a tickle in the back of my neck.

That was a reckless, foolish thing to do. We could have died.

But we didn't.

We don't discuss the matter as we go back to the rock slide. I send Camila up first, as the most athletic of us, and she uses the rope to get to the top. From the top she's able to help Abby get all the way up, then Iris, and finally me. All of us are intent on one thing: getting into sunlight.

I blink into the bright light of day as I emerge from the cave, and the desert never looked so wonderful. My friends greet me, and we shriek like soldiers who discovered they're still alive after a bombing. Then we snap selfies of our dirty, muddy selves.

"Water," Iris says. She moves away from the cave, heading down the hill to my car.

"That was awful," Abby says.

"Terrible," I agree.

"I hated it," Camila says.

"We could have died," Abby says.

I hadn't wanted to express that out loud. But she's right.

"We didn't, though," I say.

"And now we have an incredible story to share," Camila says.

I think on that. I wonder at all the people who have braved that terrible tunnel. I change my mind on my earlier judgment. "It was worth it."

It starts raining before we reach the car. We stand around and dance in it, letting it wash the dirt from our faces, letting it soak into our clothes and hair.

I'm glad we're not still in the cave. I imagine the rain coating the granite rock slab. Getting out would be a disaster.

☙❈❧

The first day of the semester starts Monday.

I can barely move. I'm aching from our caving expedition on Saturday. Last night my roommate moved in, a pleasant girl with short brown hair and a nice smile. She's my age, named Lauren, and she goes to the community college like Monica and Thomas. But I could already tell after talking to her for a bit that we're not destined to be the best of friends.

Bruises line my hips and thighs and hamstrings. My arms are scraped up, and I wince in each class when I put my elbows on the desks. We went on a crazy adventure and survived, but I'm feeling it.

The population at Preston Yarborough tripled overnight. Where campus felt comfortable and almost empty during summer term, now I can't take a few steps down the sidewalk without having to dodge someone.

Jordan should be back. I make a mental note to call him up.

Even though I tested out of Portuguese 201 last semester, I'm auditing the class this semester. I don't trust my ability. I memorized more than I learned.

As soon as Professor Morales starts talking, though, I realize I shouldn't doubt myself. I understand everything he's saying. Maybe I should have taken Portuguese 202. But it's not offered until next semester, so I don't have any options for this semester except this one or 301. And no way am I ready for a three-hundred level class.

Last year I set a goal to take a dance class every semester, and this time it's ballet.

"There's no need to dress out today," the teacher says. She's an older woman with permed gray hair wearing an oversized sweater over her leggings who speaks in a French accent. I'm not sure if she's actually French or if she thinks that makes her sound more knowledgeable. "But only today. I'm handing out a rubric sheet of expectations. You will be here five minutes before class starts, in your leotard."

I accept the paper when it comes my way and look over it while she speaks. Five minutes before class starts? Sure, we have ten minutes between classes, but I have to change in that time.

"My TA will take role and your grade will drop half a point for every three tardies."

Is she kidding me? That seems ridiculous and unrealistic.

"In addition to the dance moves, you also have to learn the vocabulary and history of ballet as found in the required reading."

This class is half a credit. I don't know if it's worth the aggravation. But I've always wanted to learn ballet. And if I do poorly, that half a credit isn't going to affect my GPA very much.

I glance around the classroom and see it is full of women. There's only one boy. He's tall and slender and must feel like he's the luckiest guy on earth to be taking a ballet class full of girls. It's what I would do, if I were a boy.

I head to work after my English class. The engineering professors keep me busy.

245

We're still getting used to each other. I'm on my feet the entire time, making copies, directing students who aren't sure what classes to take, letting professors know someone's here to see them.

It goes by fast. It's five before I know it, and I close up and head to the bookstore.

I have a list of books to buy, books that weren't listed on the website before school started. My backpack is already so heavy my shoulders hunch when I walk, and I groan as I gather up the new books I need and walk them to the register.

I'm going to need a new backpack also.

❦

"So caving," Iris says as she makes dinner. "That was so much fun."

"I kind of loved it," I admit. "But not at the time."

"No, not at the time," Camila says, and we laugh and groan as we replay the experience of crawling through that twisted, tiny tunnel.

"What shall we do next?" Iris says. She sits down at the table with a bowl of rice and fried onions.

"I don't know." I open my cookbook and begin my own dinner: mac and cheese with breaded chicken. By the end of this year, I should be a cook. "School's started, so it's going to be a lot harder to get away."

"Let's go camping!"

"Camping where?" Camila asks.

Iris shrugs. "I don't know, maybe Moab. It's Labor Day weekend. There's no school Monday."

The front door opens, and Lauren comes in. I'd forgotten she lives here, and the conversation tapers when she steps into the kitchen.

"Hi, guys!" she says, flashing a smile.

"Hi," I say. Iris waves her chopsticks.

"How was school?" Camila asks.

"Great! I think I'm going to like my classes."

Lauren goes into the living room and turns on the TV, and I glance at Iris and Camila. Do we keep making plans for camping? Are we supposed to invite Lauren? She feels like a stranger here.

The front door opens again, and this time it's Abby, laughing as she talks to someone in the hall. Then she steps in, leaving the door open behind her.

"First day of school, in the books!" she says. She joins us at the table, dropping her backpack with a thunk.

"What do you think about going camping this weekend?" Camila asks her.

"Camping?" Abby makes a face. "First you make me go caving, and now you're talking about camping?"

"Caving was your idea!" I protest.

"In theory. I didn't know what it's actually like."

"I went to Black Sheep with you."

"And you said you're never going again."

"Abby, you don't have to come," Camila says.

"Where are you going?" Abby asks, switching the conversation around. "It might be fun."

246

"We were thinking Moab," Iris says.

"Are you going to Moab?" Lauren perks up from the couch. "I love it there! My aunt lives out that direction. I could see if we can stay with her!"

I look at the other girls and see my thoughts mirrored on their faces. We weren't inviting her. But how do we not? She lives here.

"We're still working out the details," I say.

"Yeah, it might not happen," Iris adds.

I turn back to frying my chicken, and we don't say another word.

"Layne's visiting tomorrow," Iris says. "A few more days before her final goodbye."

I meet her eyes, and I know she's thinking what I'm thinking.

We miss our fifth roommie.

CHAPTER FIFTY-FOUR

Ditched

Rain wakes me Tuesday morning. It feels like fall, but it can't be, not even in Colorado. It's the beginning of September.

It rained Saturday also.

I step outside without a jacket but find the temperature dropped. Maybe it is turning into fall. I think of the steamy Arkansas heat and wish I'd spent more time there this summer. But between Brazil and summer term, I barely let my feet touch down in Arkansas.

I grab a jacket and head off to my second English class.

Jordan texts me as I cross the quad.

J: where are you?

I forgot to message him and now he beat me to it. I pause to respond.

Me: living my best college life. Where are you?

J: wondering when I get to see my favorite cousin.

I grin. *Me: we can make it happen. Want to go camping?*

J: tell me more

We work out the details as I pick a desk in the back of the classroom.

I wonder how Camila will feel about this. She and Jordan broke up after freshman year because he thought he'd be leaving, but now he's still here.

I have my other PE class today also. Basketball.

I don't like sports. But I discovered freshman semester that if I don't stay active, I gain weight. That's not what I want.

I step into the basketball gym and smell the age-old sweat clinging to the walls, the rubbery scent that lingers on the wooden floor, and I feel I've made a mistake.

"Welcome, welcome," the teacher says. She hands me a syllabus and directs me to the bleachers. "I'm Ms. Stacy. Have a seat and we'll talk about this class."

I face the other students and recognize Chris from my swimming class. "Chris!" I say, and I scoot up beside her. "You're in here?"

She smiles at me, her short dark hair brushing her shoulders as she shrugs. "Yes. I want to learn how to play." Her English is heavily accented. I know she's from an Asian country but I can't remember which.

"I'm hoping maybe I won't hate the sport so much if I learn to play," I grumble.

Chris gives a teetering giggle.

"I hope you're all in here because you love basketball!" Ms. Stacy says.

No one reacts to her statement.

"That's all right," she says. "I've been doing this long enough to know if you're in here, you probably know nothing about basketball. I'll teach you the basics, all the fundamentals you need. When we're done, you'll be able to play church ball with the best of them!"

Just what I always wanted. I manage to keep my applause to myself.

She takes fifteen minutes to go over the curriculum, the expectations, and the rules of the game. Then she tells us to dress out.

I hoped we wouldn't have to change on the first day of class, but I was prepared in case we needed to. I follow Chris to the locker room, where we change into the school-issued PE shirt and shorts.

I take off my sandals and stop.

"I forgot shoes," I say.

Chris looks over from where she's sliding hers on her feet. "Oops."

"Yeah, oops." I can't fake it in my sandals. I put on socks and follow her back to the basketball court.

"All right, let's have all of you down here on the floor!" Ms. Stacy says as we come out. "I'll put you in groups of three and the first thing you're going to learn is dribbling!"

"I forgot my shoes," I say, interrupting before she gets going.

She pauses and focuses on me. "No shoes?"

I feel the way I did in sixth grade when I forgot to bring my presentation. "Yep."

She points to the bleachers. "You can sit out. But if you miss more than two days of dressing out, it automatically lowers your grade by a letter."

By an entire letter? That's harsh. "I won't forget my shoes again."

I climb to the bleachers and sit back to watch, feeling like a seven-year-old for forgetting something as fundamental as my shoes in basketball. Great start to this class.

⊙ ⚬ ⊙

We make plans for Moab while sitting around the table waiting for Layne to show up. She should be here any second.

We've invited half the apartment complex to go camping with us. Six boys said they could come, including my cousin Jordan.

"We should invite her," Camila says.

"Who?" Iris asks.

"It seems fair," I agree.

"You should do it. You room with her."

"Oh. Lauren." Iris juts out her lower lip.

"What about Layne?" Abby asks. "Will she want to come?"

I clasp my hands in anticipation. There are things I want to talk about with Layne that only she will understand.

"We'll invite her, of course," I say.

"So the first football game is Friday," Iris says. "Are we going? We can go camping after."

"That doesn't work," I say. "We need to leave Friday as soon as we're done with school. It's a three-hour drive."

"Well, we'll lose a lot of people if we skip the game," Abby says.

I consider that and sigh. "I guess we could go after."

"Maybe we change it to Saturday through Monday," Iris says. "Leave Saturday morning."

"I wanted to get out of here earlier," I say. "Spend Friday night there."

"But what if we can't?" Iris says.

I'm not ready to give up. "Some of us can. Those who can't come until Saturday can meet us there."

"All right," Abby says. "So you're going Friday with whoever can go with you?"

"Yes." I brighten when she says it. Now things are happening. "I'll drive. Who can come with me?"

They look at each other.

"I'll go with you Friday," Iris says.

"I want to see the game," Abby says. "So I'll catch a ride with someone Saturday morning."

"Camila?" I say.

"I'm okay missing the game, I think," she says.

"Great! We'll meet here after five. Let's plan to leave at six."

"What about the weather?" Camila lifts a hand toward the window, where it's still raining. "We can't camp in the desert in this."

I open my mouth to reassure her the rain will stop and the sun will come out with full force, but I'm interrupted by a knock on the door, followed by a girl's voice calling out, "Hello?"

It's Layne.

All four of us jump up and hurdle each other to get to the door. Abby gets there first and yanks it open.

"Layne!" she shrieks.

Layne's clutching her pillow, a bunch of bedding, and a backpack. Her blond hair is pulled over to the side and braided in a single twist down her shoulder. She barely gets her things set down before Abby throws her arms around her.

"Hey, guys!" Layne says.

We cling to her, pulling her into the apartment.

"Oh my goodness, I'm so glad you're here!" I say. "I missed you!"

"I missed you too!" she says, and she lets me hug her.

"Come on, come on, let's put your things away," I say, and I guide her to Abby's room, where she'll be staying for the next few days.

❧

I don't get to talk with Layne that first night. She's surrounded by people, first our roommates who want to fill her in on everything, and then half the boys in the complex who want to meet her.

But Wednesday when everyone is gone for evening activities, it's just me and her in the apartment. I make us both a bowl of chicken noodle soup and then we cozy up next to each other on the couch.

I've been dying to talk to her. "How is Brant?" I ask, scooting into the cushion next to her.

"We broke up. He didn't feel like he could focus on his service and me at the same time."

Layne and Brant were having sex last year before he left on a mission trip. It was one of the hot topics in our college dorm.

"I didn't know." I rear my head back to study her. "That's why Owen broke up with me."

I've never told my roommates that. I refused to speak about Owen when I got back from Louisiana. All I told them was we were through.

"It is?" She swivels to face me. "Because you were having sex?"

"No, because he couldn't focus on his mission with me in his life."

"Huh." Layne shrugs. "I guess he thought I was a bad influence or something."

I ponder that. It's not what Owen said, but deductive logic says she's correct. If I were a positive influence on Owen's life, he wouldn't have kicked me out of it so he could serve his mission. "Yes, I suppose that's what they thought of us."

"Jerks."

I laugh.

Now she faces me. "Tell me everything," she says. "Tell me about Brazil."

I take a deep breath.

"There was a boy," I say.

"I knew it," she hisses, her eyes flashing triumphantly.

Not even Camila knows this. I told her only that Tiago and I can't be friends anymore.

"We got pretty involved," I say, and I hesitate. I'm not sure how much backstory I want to give.

Layne leans toward me. "Did you have sex?" she breathes.

I see the anticipation in her dark eyes. She wants me to say yes. She wants to share that experience with someone else.

I shake my head. "No, but . . . I did more with him than I've ever done."

"Even with Owen?"

I nod, and my face burns for the admission.

"What did you do?"

I don't know how to describe what Tiago and I did to each other. So I say, "I never knew how big it is."

"His—" her voice breaks off, and she makes a motion with her hand near her crotch.

"Yes," I say, and I giggle. How mature are we? We can't even say the words.

"Cassandra Jones! What did you do to it?"

I don't answer, I'm giggling too hard now. Instead I make a circle with my thumb and forefinger.

Layne's laughing also. "Yes, it's big! Just wait until it gets inside!"

"Layne!" I cry. I can't imagine it. How can something so big fit inside that little bitty

—

No, I'm not thinking this.

We giggle hysterically like a couple of twelve-year-olds.

"But you didn't go all the way?"

I shake my head.

"Did he want to?"

I nod. "I didn't want to."

She doesn't ask why. Maybe she knows it's a confusing combination of my faith and my feelings for Owen and my uncertainty about myself.

"Do you love him?" she whispers.

I feel like some backstory is necessary, but I don't know how to go about it. I never told my roommates about Tiago. Now it feels too late. "I did love him. But I knew it wouldn't work. So we broke it off before I came back."

She reaches over and hugs me, then pulls back and rubs the space between my shoulder blades. "You've let go of two boys you loved in one year. That's too much."

Unbidden, tears come to my eyes. "It is too much," I agree.

No wonder I'm not ready to get involved again.

"I'm here anytime you want to talk," she says.

"I know you are," I say. "I know you're one person who won't judge me."

"And I'm happy to share my own experiences with you," she says, her eyes twinkling.

"I bet you are." I laugh.

CHAPTER FIFTY-FIVE

Camping Foiled

I pack for Moab on Thursday and load up my car so when I get home from work, I'm ready to go. I tell my roommates to do the same and leave my keys in the apartment so they can get in and out of my car. We invite Lauren, but she can't come, and Layne is leaving Sunday afternoon, so she needs to stay in town. So far it's me, Iris, Camila, Abby, Jordan, and three boys from across the way. It's a small group of us, but it should be fun.

Camila calls me Friday while I'm at work. "Hey, I know we said we'd leave when you get home," she says, "but Iris and I want to watch the game. What if we left after that?"

"After?" I repeat. "Camila, it will be so late. The game won't end until around ten p.m., and then it's a three-hour drive. We'll still need to set up the tent and all that stuff."

"What if we rented a cabin tonight? And set up the tent tomorrow? We're staying three nights, right?"

I feel a surge of frustration. "Are we? No one really tells me what we're doing."

She pauses. "Well, I think this is a good solution. Then tomorrow if we decide we don't want to put up the tents, we can stay in the cabin or come home."

I struggle for a moment as I consider this plan. I want to leave tonight. Two of the boys are bringing tents, so five of us would be there around eight p.m. to set up the campsite. I already pictured myself roasting marshmallows and sleeping out in the open in the desert with nothing but starry skies overhead.

Of course, this plan doesn't work if I'm the only girl going tonight. I can't take two boys with me. So I don't have any choice but to agree.

"All right." I sigh. "I'll see you guys after the game."

I pull out my phone and text Jake and Thomas the news. They send me back a thumbs up in acknowledgment. I scowl and then text Monica my annoyance because I can't vent to anyone else about my roommates.

Me: we're supposed to be going up to Moab to go camping tonight but now my roommates want to watch the football game first! Starting to worry we won't make it.

She gets back to me right away.

Monica: bummer! You'll make it. Moab is so much fun. Come over here and watch the game with me!

Her invite cheers me up. I finish up work and walk home. Lauren is the only one there.

"Still going camping?" she says, glancing up from the TV. "It's supposed to rain tonight."

"Yeah, but we're not going for a few more hours. And we're staying in a cabin tonight," I say breezily, as if that were the plan all along. I hope the cabins don't require reservations. I check the bedrooms for Abby or Iris, but they're not here. Camila must have told them about the change in plans.

The game has already started by the time I get to Monica's. The sight of her makes me smile. Even though we're watching the game at home, she's painted herself in PYU's colors.

"No one can see you except me," I say, accepting her distracted hug before I plop down beside her. "And your roommates," I add, waving to Sandy and another girl.

"That's not the point," she says, handing me a bowl of popcorn. "The point is to ramp up my excitement and get involved in the game. Want some?" She gestures to the paints on the table.

She wasn't there, so she can't know. But this brings back so many painful memories I suddenly find it hard to breathe. When I flew to Louisiana to surprise Owen at his game, his mom painted me in his school colors. It's the one and only time I've done that. He didn't recognize me at first, behind all the paint, but the moment he did was priceless.

That's what I want to remember when I think of football paint.

"No, I'm good," I say.

She doesn't answer me. She's too busy screaming at the game. I turn to watch and realize why: we're already down by seven points, and the opposing team is going in for another touchdown.

By halftime we're down twenty-one points. I'm screaming as loud as Monica when we get the ball in the third quarter. We sit on the edge of the couch, yelling our lungs out as if the players could hear us through the screen. We had such a great season last year. How can we start this year off with a loss?

But then Luke the quarterback scores. The crowd roars his name, and we shout it out as well, cupping our hands to our mouths. "Luuuuuke! Luuuuuuke!"

We're jubilant going into the fourth quarter. We've caught up to them and we're holding our own. They haven't managed to score again, and the clock is running out. We need one more touchdown to make this a win. We can do it.

It starts to rain, but that doesn't stop a football game. Water pelts the people on the bleachers, and I feel a guilty vindictive pleasure that Iris and Camila are getting poured on. The players slip and slide a bit on the turf, but there's no mud on the artificial ground, so they keep right on playing. The timer goes off, ending the game, except we're in a tie. So the game goes into overtime. I'm on my feet now, pacing the living room, and so is Monica. Her two roommates remain seated but hang on the edge of the couch. We're breathless with anticipation.

The play starts. Luke gets the ball. We scoot forward, screaming, cheering, and—he does it! He scores a touchdown! We're ecstatic, and Monica's roommates get to their feet as we hug and cheer. Then we settle down on the couch again, watching with breathless anticipation as the time on the clock runs down, waiting to see if the other team will get the ball and score, put us back at a tie.

They try. But they don't manage it, and I'm energized when the game ends.

"Have fun in Moab!" Monica says. "I hope it all works out!"

"Thanks," I say, waving as I gather my keys and phone. "I enjoyed watching the game with you!"

The rain falls in a constant drizzle. I head back to my apartment to wait for the girls. Lauren either went out or went to bed, because she's not in the living room when I come in. I know it will take the others a minute to get out of the stadium, so I lay down on the couch to wait. I pull out my phone and text them.

Me: hurry home! It's a long drive!

I prop the throw pillow under my head and let my eyes close. I'll hear them when they come in.

❦

I don't wake up until it's morning.

I open my eyes and feel momentary disorientation from where I lay on the couch until my eyes fall on my fishtank. This I recognize, and I realize I fell asleep in the living room.

Why would I do that?

And then I remember.

I bolt upright, feeling a surge of worry. Did my roommates not come home? I check the time. A little after eight in the morning! I jump up and run back to their rooms. I push open the door to Iris's room.

She and Camila are passed out in their beds. I close the door, a rush of relief washing over me. They're okay. I check on Abby next, but I'm less concerned now. They're fine.

They came home from the game and went to bed.

Now that I know they're okay, that knowledge infuriates me. How could they? We were supposed to go to Moab last night! I take a deep breath. We can still go this morning.

I tiptoe into Iris's room and shake her shoulder. "Iris," I whisper.

"Hmm?" She doesn't open her eyes or move.

I shake her again. "Iris," I say again, louder, and I'm half hoping Camila will wake now so I don't have to do this again.

Iris pops one eye open. "What?" she murmurs.

"Camping."

Camila rolls over, blinking, so I direct my words at both of them.

"We're supposed to go camping, remember? I thought we were leaving last night."

"You were asleep on the couch when we got home," Iris says. "And we were so tired. It seemed better . . ."

"Fine," I say. "But it's early still. We can get out there now, have a day of it."

"It's raining," Camila says quietly from her bed.

As if to support her claim, thunder peels outside.

"Still raining?" I go to the window and slide back the curtain.

Sure enough, the same drizzle that fell last night continues to pelt the earth.

I square my shoulders. "It's fine. We don't have to set up a tent. We can be in cabins the whole time."

"What's the point?" Iris says. "Are we going to stay cooped up for days?"

"No," I snap. "We'll get out when it's not raining. Go hiking, start a fire, roast marshmallows. Come on, it's such a beautiful place. We can find something even in the rain!"

Neither of them answer. Iris looks at Camila.

"Cassandra," Camila says, "it's not a good weekend for it."

I shake my head. "We have it all planned out. We can make this work."

"No, we can't," she says. "We shouldn't try. The weather isn't cooperating. We'll drive all the way down there for one night, and then what? We can't start a fire. We'll sit in the cabin wasting our money."

"It's a change of scenery!" I argue. "We can do our homework, enjoy the view!"

"For the same price as one month of rent?" Camila argues.

It's an exaggeration, but I get it. I wilt, letting my breath heave out of me in an exasperated sigh.

"Fine," I say, and I leave the room.

I'm saddened we're not going. But I also know in my heart they're right. It was a half-formed plan and nothing worked out.

I go to my room and call the guys to cancel.

"Camping's off," I tell Jake when he answers. "Will you tell your roommates?"

"Yeah, no problem," he says. "Since we're not going anywhere this weekend, want to do something Monday? It's not supposed to be raining."

"Yes," I say immediately, perking up. Anything to get out of the house, to distract myself. I have to stay busy. "What do you have in mind?" I cross my fingers he won't say dinner and a movie. Not that I'd say no, but I'm so bored with those dates.

"Ever been rock climbing?"

"Rock climbing?" I repeat. "No." My mind conjures images from movies of men climbing red rock faces, dangling from ropes, stabbing picks into solid granite to pull themselves up away from a precarious fall of thousands of feet.

"I love it, and there's a spot in the canyons we can go not far from here. Want to? I've got all the gear."

"Is it safe?" I want adventure but I don't want to die.

Jake laughs. "Yeah. Want me to invite a few more people? I think my roommates are going swimming at the lake after."

"Whatever you want." Jake's funny and easy to talk to. I'm comfortable enough that I don't need a chaperone. "Swimming could be fun."

"All right, let's plan on it. I'll pick you up after lunch and we'll go rock climbing, and then swimming."

"What should I wear?"

"Anything you'd be comfortable hiking in."

"Sounds great."

I hang up, and I'm not upset about missing the Moab trip anymore. I've got something else to look forward to.

CHAPTER FIFTY-SIX

Belay On

The sun comes out Monday morning, shining brightly over the mountains and mocking my failed camping plans.

Jake picks me up at one o'clock. He has Thomas with him, and Jake fills us in on the details for climbing as we drive.

"I'll strap you into harnesses. These rocks already have anchors hooked into them, so that makes it easy. There will be one person on the ground securing your safety rope, so you'll be safe no matter what happens."

"Do you always go rock climbing in pairs?" I ask.

"If you want to be safe. This place we're going is lead climbing for beginners. I'll show you how to do it."

"Are there always anchors set up in mountains for rock climbers?" I ask.

"No. Sometimes you pick a mountain and climb. It's called free soloing."

"Do you do that?" I examine Jake in the front seat. He's average height, maybe five-eight, fair-skinned with dark hair, not particularly muscular. I wouldn't have pegged him as a risk-taker.

"I'm not that crazy. Free climbing is enough for me."

"But is it safe?" Thomas asks.

Jake shrugs. "If you do it right."

We park at the mouth of the canyon, joining several other cars in the lot. I follow Jake around to the back of the car and watch him haul out harnesses and ropes.

"I hope there's not a lot of people here," Jake says. "It can be difficult if we have to share the course."

"I hate waiting my turn for anything," Thomas says, and we laugh.

"Need me to carry something?" I ask. The sun's high in the sky, and I shield my eyes from it as I look back toward the canyon.

"Sure." Jake hands me a harness and loops a rope around my arm.

"Me too," Thomas says.

"Yeah, carry your load." Jake saddles him up also, and then the three of us begin the

257

walk down the path into the canyon.

"Here."

Jake stops us right at the mouth. A cliff faces us, sage brush growing out of the corners, layers of stratified red rock jutting out in uneven layers.

"This is perfect," he says, dropping his harness and unraveling the rope.

I lift my head and peer up at the rock face, towering thirty or forty feet above me. "But how do we do this?"

"I'll show you. We start small. See this?" Jake steps over to the rock and points to a metal hook in the cliff face.

"Yes," I say, surprised. I didn't notice it until he pointed it out.

"These are the anchors, and they're all over the rock," he says. "One here, here, over there."

As he points them out, I start to notice them. They fan out in every direction. Climbers aren't limited to a vertical movement but can go horizontal as well.

"Who puts those there?" Thomas asks.

"Parks and rec, I'm guessing. They machine-drill them in."

"Wow, that's so awesome," I say. "But how do we use them?"

"This rock is absolutely perfect." Jake steps away from the metal loop and sticks his hand into a fissure separating the cliff from the other side. "These cracks are a natural handhold, and the rock is riddled with them."

"It's cracking," Thomas says, and I give a polite laugh.

"Exactly. Each crack here is a chance for you to get leverage."

"With your foot?" I ask.

"Foot, hand, elbow, knee, whatever you can fit in there. And you hook this part of the rope—" he undoes a carabiner and shows how it opens— "and attach it to the anchor."

I watch him connect it to the first anchor. "I don't understand how it supports you."

"Like this." He picks up the harness, threading the rope carefully through the belay loop. "This end," he says, holding up the rope in his hand, "stays with me. I'll belay you from the ground and manage the slack." He points to the other end already tied into a figure-eight knot. "This end is secured to your harness with this knot, and the carabiner clips it in place. Make sure the carabiner is locked before you start." He gives the harness a final tug to check its fit. "Once you're strapped in and everything's double-checked, you're good to climb. Just hook the carabiner into the anchor."

My heart rate picks up a bit as he says this. I picture myself thirty feet up and missing the hook. "If not, I fall?"

"Yeah, there's that chance. But you should be safe. You don't unlatch from one anchor until you get to the next one. So you're always latched in."

"Okay," Thomas says. "So we start at the bottom. Move a few inches and relatch. Move a few inches and do it again. As high as we can go?"

Jake nods, beaming. "Yep. You've got it."

"And how does this work if you're rock climbing by yourself?" I ask.

"You don't have someone to belay you, so you have to use a self-belay system," he explains. "It's called solo climbing, and there are a few ways to do it. One involves using a specialized device that automatically locks the rope if you fall. It's complicated and requires a lot of preparation."

"And what if there aren't any pre-drilled bolts?" I'm fascinated. This sounds terrifying and incredible.

"Then you're looking at traditional climbing. You place your own protection as you go—cams, nuts, that kind of thing—to secure yourself to the rock. Each piece has to hold your weight in case you fall, so you've got to know exactly what you're doing."

"And you've done that?"

He gives a modest shrug. "Yeah, but not in dangerous places."

"As in, if you fell you wouldn't die, just break a few ribs?" Thomas says.

"Yeah, pretty much."

I'm curious and want to know more, but I also want to start climbing. "Okay, let's do this."

"Great. Want to go first?"

"No, I want to see how it's done."

"Okay, then you have to go first." Jake turns to Thomas. "Which is good, since you've done this before."

"Only in a gym. Different stuff."

"Same principle."

"Why don't you go and show us how it works?" I say to Jake. "I'd love to see how you do it."

"I would, but I don't believe either of you has ever belayed before, have you?"

Thomas and I shake our heads, and Jake makes a tsking sound. "Then I'm not trusting you with my life, sorry."

Thomas laughs. "Okay, I'll go first."

I watch Jake help him into the harness, tightening the straps snugly around his legs and waist. Thomas is not a small guy, about two hundred pounds and six foot five, but Jake has no issues securing the harness around him. He secures the rope using a figure-eight knot and reminds him, "This knot stays tied to your belay loop the entire time. Don't mess with it. To open the carabiner, twist the locking mechanism here—never just push it. Always double-check that it's locked before you rely on it."

"And if I lose my balance?" Thomas asks.

"No problem. Just let go of the rock and yell, 'Take!' I'll lock the belay device and catch you."

My pulse races as I watch Thomas step up to the rock face and get into position. He clips the quickdraw into a pre-placed bolt and threads the rope through the carabiner before continuing. Jake stands below, managing the rope with his belay device and encouraging him at every step. "There's a ledge for your right foot above you," Jake says. "And a solid handhold on the left. Keep your hips close to the wall."

It's slow-going. Thomas climbs about fifteen feet before stopping, clinging to the rock face like Spider-Man, his breathing heavy but determined.

"Okay, I think I'm good," he says. "My arms are shaking."

"You can keep going," Jake calls from below, his eyes following Thomas's movements. He keeps the rope taut through the belay device, his feet braced slightly apart for balance. "There's a good hold near your right shoulder. You've got this."

"I'm good," Thomas says, shaking his head. "How do I get down?"

"Lean back and let go," Jake instructs. "I've got you. Keep your feet against the rock, and I'll lower you safely."

Thomas hesitates for a moment, then releases his grip on the rock. Jake shifts his weight slightly, locks the belay device, and begins to feed the rope steadily. Thomas glides smoothly down, using his feet to push off the rock face in controlled, gentle movements until he reaches the ground.

Jake turns to me. "Ready?"

"Yes, I think so." I want to go higher than Thomas. I fixate my eyes on a bolt a few feet above where he stopped.

"All right. Now I need you to trust me, so when you're about five feet off the ground, I want you to let go of the wall. Say, 'Take,' and release your grip."

"Just let go?"

"Make sure your harness and rope are secure first. I want you to feel what it's like to hang on the rope. It'll help you trust me and the system if you fall later."

"Okay." My heart races. Trust.

What if he doesn't catch me?

He fastens the harness snugly around my legs and waist, checking the straps. "Tight?"

"Yeah, it feels tight."

"Good." He double-checks the knot securing the rope to my harness and steps back. "All right, let's see you make your first clip."

I press the gate of the carabiner to open it and attach it to the pre-placed quickdraw hanging from the first bolt.

"Perfect. You're ready."

He steps back, managing the rope through his belay device, and I begin climbing.

The first few feet are easy. There are plenty of footholds, and I feel supported as I remove the rope from each quickdraw and clip it into the next one above me. I'm surprised by how much I have to rely on the rock itself, wedging my fingers into crevices and using my body weight to press against footholds.

"There's a good handhold to your left," Jake says when I pause.

I see it, but where do I put my feet? I clip the rope into the next quickdraw but struggle to move upward.

"There's a ledge by your knee," Jake says. "Try getting your left foot up there."

It's a stretch, but I pull my leg up and press my toe against the ledge. Pushing off, I manage to lift myself above the bolt.

"Nice! There's another hold above your head," Jake calls.

"I see it," I say, reaching to clip the next quickdraw before moving upward again.

"Okay, you're a few feet up now," Jake says. "Let go."

Let go? I glance down, heart pounding. Even five feet looks high. I remind myself it's less than the high dive at the pool.

"Trust me," Jake says. "I've got you."

"He's got you," Thomas adds.

I take a deep breath and release the wall. My stomach clenches as I expect to fall, but there's only a slight jerk before I'm suspended in the air, gently spinning next to the rock face.

"Watch the rock," Jake calls. "You might bump your shoulder."

I open my eyes. "Huh," I say. I'm not falling. I'm just hanging here.

I push lightly off the rock face, gaining confidence as I realize I won't slam into it. I have some control here, and Jake's holding me steady.

That phrase has never felt more literal.

"Ready to climb again?" Jake asks.

"Yes."

"Okay. Swing yourself back to the rock, find a handhold, and keep going."

I swing toward the wall and grab a handhold, pulling myself back into position. Soon, I'm climbing again. Energized and more confident, I focus on the rock, inching upward.

"Keep it up—you're doing great!" Jake says.

I don't respond. My arms are starting to tremble, muscles I've rarely used now groaning with effort. Still, I push on, finding footholds and listening to Jake's guidance when I pause.

I make it a few feet higher than Thomas and stop, clinging to the wall to catch my breath.

"Great job!" Jake calls. "That's awesome for your first climb!"

I'm sweating all over, surprised by how much effort it takes.

"Come on down and take a break," Jake says. "Let Thomas have another turn."

"I want to keep going," I say, eyeing the bolts above me. But my arms protest with a shaky whimper.

"You can, but take a break first," Jake advises. "This is hard work, and resting will help."

I relent. He's right.

"Take!" I call, releasing the rock face. I push off gently with my feet and descend at a steady pace as Jake manages the rope.

"Hey, that was awesome," Thomas says, offering me a high-five.

"Thanks." I remove the harness and grab water, guzzling it and splashing some down my neck and face. "That was way fun."

"You sure you don't want to go?" Thomas asks Jake. "Trust one of us on belay? I can do it if you show me."

Jake shakes his head. "Not taking any chances. But if you want to get trained, maybe next time." He turns to me. "What do you think?"

"This is tons of fun," I say. "I really like it." And it's silenced all my emotional thoughts. My entire focus is on my body.

"We'll get you in that harness again soon. Eat some chips, the salt is good for you." He turns to Thomas and helps him get harnessed, and I munch on crunchy, salty food.

I climb the rock two more times before my arms are as weak as jelly. The second time I get higher, but the third time I tap out around ten feet. I'm shaking so bad I don't think I can lift my body another inch.

"We'll call it a day," Jake says, helping me down. "But we can go again sometime if you want."

"Yes," I say. "That would be awesome."

CHAPTER FIFTY-SEVEN

Footloose

We have a pop quiz in Portuguese Tuesday morning.

It's easy for me. I know how to conjugate verbs. I know everything in this class. I'm bored with it, but it's the only thing I can do to maintain my Portuguese. I finish the quiz and turn it in before pulling up the requirements for a Portuguese minor.

Nothing counts until I get to the three-hundred-level classes. I wonder if I should have skipped ahead and done 301 this semester instead of sitting through 201, which I already tested out of. But I shake off that idea. I might be highly proficient with grammar and writing, but I don't speak the language.

My time in Brazil proved that to me.

English class is an interesting dive into language acquisition, and then it's time for ballet.

I hate my ballet class.

Dread fills me as I stop by my locker before class. Time to change into my leotard and tights and display my skinny, underdeveloped body.

I grumble to myself as I dig through my backpack, looking for the keys to the cheap lock I installed in the PE locker room. Since I have two classes I need to dress out for, I bit the bullet and rented a locker for the semester.

But now I can't find the keys.

I sit on the bench and turn my backpack upside down, emptying out pencils and lead cases and gum wrappers. Even a few coins clatter to the acid-washed concrete floor.

But no keys.

I sit for a moment, weighing my options. I could go to class and not dress out. Ms. Colette is stricter than my basketball teacher, and we can only miss one day during the semester. Today could be that day.

It seems silly to waste it when I'm right here, though.

I head over to the help desk.

"Hi," I say to the girl behind the counter. "I can't find the keys to my locker. Can you help me?"

Her dark hair is pulled into pig tails on either side of her face, and she lifts her head. "I'm not sure what you want me to do. You're the only one with the keys, right?"

"Yeah, but . . ." I trail off and shrug. "You don't have some master key to unlock all locks?"

"No." She smirks as if the idea is stupid. "If you have a combination lock, I can reset it to the default. But not a keyed lock."

"So I'm locked out forever?"

"We can cut it off, if you're sure you're never going to find the keys."

I play it out in my head. I used the keys last week for basketball. I haven't gotten into my backpack since yesterday morning when I did homework, but I didn't take the keys out.

If they're not in my backpack, where could they be?

There's a chance they fell out in my bedroom. I can skip dressing out today and search for them.

"How much was the lock?" she asks.

I shrug. "Eight dollars, maybe."

"We have locks you can rent for fifteen dollars. And we keep the combination up here, in case you forget it."

Why didn't someone tell me that at the beginning of the semester? I give in. "Okay. Let's do it."

"Here, pick one and tell me the number on the back."

She puts a basket of combination locks on the counter. I choose a blue one, and she writes down the number.

"The combination is on the back," she says.

She pulls out what look like a giant pair of gardening sheers. I trail along behind her, feeling helpless and stupid. She probably sees this a lot.

"Okay," she says, getting the sheers around the lock. "Here we go."

She squeezes hard, and the pliers cut through the metal bars, and the lock clatters to the ground.

"There you go, you're all set."

"Thanks." I check my watch.

I'll be late to class. But at least I'll be dressed out.

⟲∽∗∽⟳

Ms. Colette hands out a vocab sheet at the beginning of class. "Our first test is next week," she says. "I'm more interested in how well you know the terminology than how well you can *plie*, but I will be checking both."

I scan the sheet. Most of the terms are French. I recognize words like *releve* and *arabesque*, but I can't define them.

And there's thirty of them. No one told me ballet would be another language class.

"You can earn extra credit in here by attending any of the ballet performances on campus," the teacher says. "There's one in two weeks. Show me your receipt and give me a one-paragraph write up, and you'll get the credit."

I have the feeling I'm going to need it.

"Now everyone line up at the bar. Let's see those *releves*."

I'm not sure what the heck that is. But I line up with everyone else and avoid looking

263

at my reflection.

If it weren't too late to drop this class, I'd be sorely tempted.

I copy the others, lifting my leg and suffering through the teacher coming around to adjust my hips and toes. I can tell from the way she clucks her tongue that she finds me less than satisfactory.

As soon as class is over, I head over to the performing arts center to buy my extra-credit tickets. I'm halfway across the quad when someone calls my name.

"Cassandra!"

I turn around, and there's Mitch, smiling broadly as he walks toward me.

My chest flutters pleasantly. It doesn't matter how much I know I should stay away from him because nothing can develop between us. I still feel attraction toward him. And his friendship made me happy.

"Hey," I say, and I don't fight him when he hugs me.

"How's life?" he says. "What are you up to?"

"Things are going great," I say. "I managed to not die while caving a few weekends ago. And then we almost went camping this weekend and then didn't because of the rain, so I went rock climbing instead, and my arms are very sore today."

"Wow, you're into all kinds of adventures."

"Yeah, I like it."

"What are you doing next Friday?"

Why is he asking? We can't date. I'm not sure we can be friends. "Going to a ballet performance, actually. I'm on my way to get tickets."

"Ballet?" He falls in beside me, and I resume walking. "You like dance?"

"It's for class," I say. "But of all the dance forms, I think ballet's my favorite. Something about the clean lines and classic formations strikes me as very beautiful."

"How long have you done ballet?"

"Oh." I laugh. "I don't do it. I'm terrible at it, actually. I'd drop the class if it weren't too late. But I like watching it."

He laughs with me. "I think watching someone who's awful at ballet would be much more entertaining than watching a real ballet performance."

"Jerk." I shove him. "How's life going for you?"

We step into the performing arts center and the ambient outdoor noise fades away. The clashing sounds of various instruments from the rehearsal rooms fill the hall. Somewhere a cello plays, and somewhere else there's a flute, and also a trumpet. It's like throwing a band and orchestra together and telling everyone to play a different song.

"Good," Mitch says. "I like my new apartment. And the church group is fun."

I step up to the ticket window. "Sounds like it's going well for you."

I'm not sure what else to say. Luckily the boy behind the window comes to help me, and I pay for my ticket.

"Two?" he says, glancing at Mitch at my shoulder.

"Just one," I say, and only after the boy walks away do I wonder if I should have invited Mitch.

No. I should not.

"How are you doing, really?" Mitch asks when the boy comes back and gives me my ticket.

I glance at him as I shove the ticket into my backpack. "I'm good. Really."

Like I'm going to tell him.

"We should hang out more," he says as we walk away from the ticket office. "You're one of my favorites. You're such a fun person."

My heart gives a little tumble. "We had some fun times," I say. "Thanks for being such a big part of my summer."

It's not an agreement. I won't promise to hang out more.

I think he knows it. He gives me another hug.

"Guess I better get to class. Good to see you. If you ever want to do something, give me a call."

"I will."

So he heard what I didn't say about not being able to be friends, and he's put the ball in my court.

Dead ball.

⁓⁂⁓

Wednesday evening a guy from my English class bumps into me in the library.

"It's Cassandra, right?" he says, walking beside me as we exit the library.

"Yeah." I cast him a sideways glance as we walk. He's pasty white, and his eyes are spaced oddly. "You?"

"Rhett."

I catch a whiff of some cologne or something as he speaks, and it's off-putting. I want to put distance between us.

"My sister's in a play in Vail," he says conversationally as we exit the building.

"Oh, that's cool." Why are we still talking? I search the quad for another familiar face, someone who can rescue me.

"My family's going to see her tonight. It's *Jane Eyre*. Have you read it?"

"Yeah," I say. "In high school. I don't remember it, though."

"Want to come see it with us?"

Why didn't I see that coming? I can't think of an excuse quickly enough, so the word that leaves my mouth is, "Sure."

I want to smack my forehead as soon as I've spoken. I don't want to go on a date with this guy.

"Oh, awesome! Are you ready now? I'm parked below campus and we can head out."

I blink. How did this happen? "I haven't eaten dinner."

"We'll get some food. The play's in two hours, so we have a little bit of time."

"Yeah. Okay. I guess."

I follow behind him as he bounces down the hill toward the parking lot below campus, his hands holding his backpack straps, and I text Camila.

Me: what have I done?

She responds quickly. *C: what is it? What's wrong?*

I send back an eye-roll emoji.

I need to learn to say no.

His car has the normal college-kid clutter, pencils, trash, notebooks. He shoves everything into the back, and I climb into the passenger side. I wrinkle my nose because the whole interior smells like him. A slightly musty, woodsy, leathery, astringent scent.

"What theater are we going to?" I ask, holding my phone between my palms. "So I can tell my roommates." In case he has any thoughts about kidnapping me. PYU is a very safe campus, since most of us have the same religious values, but I'm not putting it past someone I barely met.

"The Stead theater. Just inside the city limits."

I text that to Camila. *Me: going to a play in Vail with some kid named Rhett. Here's a photo of his car should I come up missing.*

Now she laughs at me.

"My parents live near Vail, so we'll stop there real quick on the way," he says.

"All right," I say.

The one thing I can usually count on in a date is getting food. And since I'm a poor starving student, I take every meal I can get. I hope his mom's a good cook.

But when we get there, the family is loading up the car.

"Hi, Rhett!" his mom says, giving him a hug. "Jen's already there, and she saved us seats."

"I've got a plus-one," he says, indicating me with a quick hand gesture.

"Oh, hi!" she says, and then she turns back to him. "I'll tell her to save one more seat. See you there?"

"Yep."

And everyone piles back into their cars.

I'm still standing on the driveway in somewhat bewilderment. "I thought you said the play doesn't start for two more hours?" It's been half an hour since we left campus.

"Yeah, but I guess Mom doesn't want to lose our seats. You've got your homework, right? You can study while we wait."

I look back at the house, now empty as his family rolls out of the driveway.

"Do you think we could get something to eat first?" I ask.

"Oh, sure. Let me run in and get you something."

Rhett dashes away, into the house, and then he comes back out with a bag of crackers.

Let me rephrase. A bag of saltines.

"This work?" he says, and he hands it to me before getting back into the car.

I can't believe it. Really? Saltines are good with two things: tuna and soup.

They are not a snack food.

I'm fuming by the time I get back into the car. I want to be back at my apartment with my roommates, cooking dinner. I don't say a word as we drive over to the theater, but I run through my homework assignments, hoping to find something I can fill this time with.

I think my English teacher posted an essay assignment online. I'll work on that.

Rhett parks, and I grab my backpack and follow him up to the theater. We cut through a lobby smelling achingly of butter and popped corn, and my stomach tightens.

I don't even like popcorn.

We aim for the hallway leading into the performance hall, but a security guard stops me in the entrance.

"Sorry, we have a clear-bag only policy. You can't take in your backpack."

"What?" His words don't compute.

He gestures at my backpack. "If the bag is bigger than six inches, it has to be clear."

I lift my eyebrows. "I can empty it for you and show you the contents. I just need my laptop."

He shakes his head. "I'm sorry, we can't do that."

"Here, I'll run it back out to the car for you," Rhett says.

Helpfully.

I stare at him. "I need to do my homework." I have to do something for the next hour. I glance around and spot a bench in the lobby. "I'll sit here and work on it."

"Are you sure?" Rhett looks hesitant. "But my whole family is inside."

"I don't mind."

"All right. I'll make sure your seat is next to mine."

He's not going to stay with me in the lobby? I suppose I shouldn't expect that. "Okay, text me the row and seat."

"Oh, yeah, give me your number."

We step off to the side and exchange info, but I'm already thinking I'll stay in the lobby and study. I don't need to watch his sister in the play.

At least the theater has internet. I tap into it and begin my essay, losing myself in the grammatical theory.

Then the security guard comes up to me. "The play's about to start, so we're closing down the lobby."

"Closing it down?" I blink at him.

"Yes. People can't sit out here during the play."

I cannot understand this. "I'm doing my schoolwork."

"Then you'll have to leave."

I'm incensed. "I can't take my bag into the theater but I can't stay out here working?" I'm so mad at myself. Why did I agree to come here?

He doesn't answer me. I've summed it up.

I stand up and go out to Rhett's car. I'll sit here and work on my homework.

Except when I try to open the door, it's locked.

I sigh. I have no choice now but to text Rhett. I scroll through my recent contacts and find his number. I shoot him a quick text.

Me: need to put my backpack in the car. Come unlock it?

I guess I won't be doing homework in the car.

CHAPTER FIFTY-EIGHT

Binge Dating

Rhett comes jogging out a moment later. "Sorry, I should have left the keys with you!"

"That's all right." I hold back another sigh.

He's not done anything wrong. He probably thinks I'm a horrible date. But this is not what I wanted.

He unlocks the door and I throw my backpack in, and then I follow him back into the theater. He lowers his voice as we get inside.

"We rearranged the seating. I put you next to my mom in the row in front of us."

"I'm not sitting by you?" As much as I don't feel any affinity to Rhett, he's a familiar face. He's putting me next to his mom?

"Do you mind?"

"Well." I pause at the top of the theater. It's round, with the stage down at the bottom and seats in a circular arrangement rising upward. "I don't know her."

"She's really nice. Come on."

He pushes past me, leading the way and cutting off any further argument from me.

I grit my teeth. My stomach growls. Just get through this, Cassandra.

He deposits me at the edge of the row next to his mom, a few seats from the bottom. She gives me a smile and faces front, and the play begins. I'm so annoyed that I want to disengage, pull out my phone and read a book. I can't with his mom beside me, though.

The play is three hours long. It's almost ten p.m. when it finishes. I stand and go to the top of the theater and wait for Rhett. He chats with his family, laughing, standing around, and I descend again to get him.

"I need to get home," I say, pointedly but still trying to be polite. "Can we go?"

"My sister hasn't come out yet," he says. "I need to tell her good job. And don't you want to meet her?"

I'm starting to think this was a dare. He had to bring someone to this play.

"I really want to get something to eat," I say.

"Just a quick minute. She'll be out any moment."

I go back to the top and wait. I'm fuming. I've lost all sense of judgment and I don't know if I'm being unreasonable or if he's an idiot. But finally his sister comes out, and they move to the lobby for photos and more hugs. Rhett gestures me over and introduces me. I fake a smile.

"Well, I have to get Cassandra back to campus," he says. "I'll see you guys later tonight!"

"Are you a freshman?" his sister asks, looking at me.

"No," I say. "A sophomore."

"You look so young."

I'm aware of that. I've heard it my whole life. So I just nod.

Rhett finally extricates himself from his doting family and we make it to his car.

"You're coming back out here tonight?" I ask.

"Yeah, I live at home."

"You live at home?" I suppose if I lived near my family, I would too.

"Saves money. I'm all about that."

He starts driving, pulling toward the interstate. "You sure you want to go home already? We usually play games as a family after one of Jen's performances."

"I'm sure." No more family time. No more Rhett time. Ever again.

"Can we get some food?" I say again. "I'm starving." My apartment is half an hour away, and my stomach is folding in on itself, eating its own corners.

"Oh, yeah, did you finish those crackers?"

For real? They're behind me, untouched. I'm starting to really dislike him. "Yes."

"Well, let's see." He scans the signs on the freeway. "There's an Arby's."

I spot a Taco Bell across the way. If we're doing fast-food, that's my go-to. "How about Taco Bell?"

"I'm not a big fan of tacos." He swings off the interstate and pulls into the Arby's drive-thru. "They have jalapeño poppers here."

My head pounds with the effort not to scream at him. I bite my tongue. "Get me a roast beef slider." And home. Get me home.

He places the order, getting himself a meal with a sandwich and fries. He turns to me before we get to the delivery window.

"Your sandwich was five bucks."

I must be an entitled college kid, to assume he was paying for me. I dig my wallet out of my backpack, find five bucks, and hand it to him.

I don't say another word the rest of the way home.

"Thanks for coming with me!" he says when he drops me off. "It was fun! See you in class."

I want to slam the door on his face but can't bring myself to be that rude. "Bye."

My apartment door is open, the noise of my roommates joking with people inside greeting me before I get to the entryway. I step inside and see Camila sitting on the floor next to Thomas, and Iris talking to James. Lauren's curled up on the couch with a book, and Abby's flirting with Jake.

"So," Camila says, spotting me. "Was it terrible?"

"You guys!" I exclaim, my pent-up emotions spilling out of me. "It was awful! Worst date ever!" And then I launch into it, telling them all about it, and they laugh until they cry.

"Why do you keep going out with these guys you don't like?" Abby asks.

"Well, I don't know if I'm going to like them until we go out, do I?" I say.

"You can't tell?" she says.

I think back on Rhett. "No, I kind of knew that one wasn't going anywhere," I admit.

"Start saying no," Camila says.

I nod. "That's it. No more dates with random guys. From now on."

"How many have you gone on this month?" Iris asks.

"That's the first one."

"No, it's not. You went with that guy to the theater two weekends ago."

"And rock-climbing with Jake," Camila adds.

"Not a date," I say, glancing at Jake.

"The drive-in with Mitch," Abby says.

"Last month," I say. "And also not a date."

"All right, we'll give you a break," Abby says. "Let's say this is the first date of the month."

"And last date of the month," I say.

They laugh at me. They don't believe me.

Iris goes to the white board and writes, "Date #1: 1 of 5 stars." She looks back at me. "Right?"

"Zero of five stars," I say.

"We have to set the bar somewhere. It could get worse."

She has a point. He didn't kidnap me, at least.

❦

I'm grateful not to have my English class the next morning. I resolve not to talk to Rhett when I see him. He's not my friend, I owe him nothing, not even five bucks for a meal. And he smells weird.

I tell Chris all about my terrible date during basketball, and she laughs and laughs. I have my shoes this time and we practice doing point guard. Except I'm terrible at dribbling the ball. It bounces twice and then falls flat, and nothing I do will make it stay alive.

I'm relieved when my school day is over and I head to work. The professors are always kind to me, and they give me constant errands, whether it's making copies or running to the library to pick up books.

Today I'm designing a graph for Professor Stephens. I sit at the computer clicking bars and circles and moving them into place on the screen.

The door opens, and a student comes to stand at the desk. I give it a full two seconds before I swivel my chair with a smile.

"Hi, how can I help you?" I ask.

He puts a stack of books on the desk. "These are for Dr. Lance. And he said there are two packets back here that I'm supposed to deliver to the art department?"

"Let me see." I stand up and move to the mailboxes in the back where the professors stick delivery papers. The engineering and the art department work together a lot, so there are frequent messages going back and forth. I search Dr. Lance's mailbox and find the two packets.

"This what you're looking for?" I return to the counter with both of them in my hand.

"Yeah." He smiles and takes them, then pushes the books toward me.

"Great." I glance down to take the books and notice a sticky note on top. I tilt my head to read it, expecting it to be instructions for me.

Instead it says in the familiar chicken scratch of a boy, "Are you available for a date?"

I'm so caught off-guard that I laugh. "Did you write this while my back was turned?"

I look up at him, and he gives a sheepish grin.

"Yes."

I examine him closer now. He's got thick, wavy brown hair, a pleasant face, and light brown eyes. His shoulders are broad, filled out, but he's trim, and he doesn't smell funny.

But I said no more dates with random strangers.

I stall. "Who are you?"

He holds out a hand, formal and church-like. "Eric. I go to the community college, but I'm trying to transfer here. Dr. Lance is helping me with my transcript."

"Oh." I shake his hand. "My friend goes to that school."

"It's a great school, but I hope to be here by this time next year."

His eyes are bright, crinkle lines forming around them when he talks. He has a natural smile around his mouth as if he's always happy. And he seems nice.

I waver. "I might be available."

"How about tomorrow night? I play in a band, and we're playing this weekend. You should come see it."

"Will there be food?" I may as well lead with that.

"Absolutely! What's a college party without it?"

"All right," I say. "I can do that."

"Great! What's your number?"

I write it down for him on another sticky note, knowing I'll never live this one down once I tell my roommates.

⚬⟋⟋⟍⟍⚬

Iris adds him to the white board as soon as I'm home.

"We knew you'd cave," she says. She writes, "Date #2: __ of 5 stars."

"Let's hope it's more than one this time," Abby says from the kitchen table.

I'm so embarrassed, but I'm also laughing.

Eric picks me up Friday evening, and he wins points right away for taking me to get food. Nothing special, but he doesn't make me wait until nine p.m. And we don't do drive thru, but go inside and eat like people who want to get to know each other.

"What do you play?" I ask him over my chicken sandwich.

"The trombone. I've been playing since the fifth grade."

"What's your band's name?"

"The Iron Lad. You know, as a play off the Iron Maiden."

"I get it." I've heard of the band, though I don't know their music. "Who are you playing for tonight?"

"Oh, a friend. He wanted to have a party and asked us to provide live music on the front lawn to entertain people. But only for an hour. No one wants to play the trombone longer than that."

"That's so cool. Are you from here?"

"California. I've been here a few years though."

I nod. California seems to send half it's population to PYU. "One of my roommates is from CA."

"Yeah? What about you?" he says. "Where are you from?"

"Arkansas."

I expect the usual "oh wow, never met anyone from there" or even "Arkansas? People live there?", but instead Eric's eyes light up, and he says, "Are you really? I love Arkansas!"

I stare at him in somewhat disbelief. "Have you been there?"

"Yeah, I did my mission trip there!"

"No. Way." I put my sandwich down.

"Yep. Lived in Little Rock for a year, then spent six months in Monticello before going up to Fayetteville to finish up."

"I'm from near Fayetteville."

He presses both hands to his chest. "My favorite city!"

I'm warming up to him. He loves Arkansas. "I love it too. That's so awesome how well you know it!"

"Absolutely!"

We spend the next few minutes reminiscing about the weather, the trees, the foliage. He's excited as he tells me how he hopes to get back one day but hasn't made it.

"How long have you been in Colorado?" I ask once we're back in his car.

"It's been six years since I finished my mission trip."

"Six—six years?" I stutter over the words, and I'm glad I wasn't drinking something or I might spew it out in surprise. I look over at him as he drives, at his smiling eyes, his pleasant face. This doesn't make sense. That means he's— "How old are you?"

He glances at me, and his cheeks turn pink. "What? You think I'm old?"

I blink, not sure what to say.

"I'm twenty-seven," he says.

Twenty-seven. Twenty-seven!

I'm nineteen!

I'm floored. He doesn't seem that old. And our conversation is so easy, but—that's an eight-year difference!

He changes the subject, and I force myself to get past his age, but the conversation doesn't feel as easy to me now.

It's just a date, I remind myself. *We're not getting married.*

We get to his friend's house, and Eric finds his band. He introduces me to everyone, and I join the other girlfriends behind the makeshift stage.

"So are you dating Eric?" one of them asks. She looks a few years older than me.

"This is our first date, actually," I say.

"Nice," another says. "Now you get to see what he does."

"He's so nice," the first says. "I'm Jess, by the way. I'm with Dan. The trumpet-player." She nods at him where he stands next to Eric.

"He's your boyfriend?" I say.

She smiles. "My husband."

"Oh." I look at the other two girls. "What about you?"

"With Matt," the second says.

"Dating?" I ask.

"Married." She holds out her hand and shows off a glittering ring.

"Ruben," the third girl says. "We've been married two years now."

"It's just Eric who's not," Jess adds.

And they all look at me like I'm tonight's dinner.

Get me out of here.

The band plays really well. I recognize several of the songs and sing along, but I can't fight the nervous uneasy jumpy feeling in my chest.

As soon as it ends, the band members come back to us. The wives throw their arms around their men and tell them how awesome they did, and Eric grins widely as he reaches me.

"What did you think?" he says.

"You're really good," I say.

"Thanks! Need anything to drink?"

He doesn't try to hug me, to my relief. He's super cute. And it seems everyone genuinely likes him.

But I know what he's looking for. A wife. A woman who will wait backstage while he plays and then greet him with hugs and praise when he finishes.

I'm so not it.

"A drink would be great," I say.

And then I countdown the minutes until we can get home.

CHAPTER FIFTY-NINE

Two Thumbs Down

"How many stars?" Iris asks.

There's an audience in my apartment when I get there. My roommates were waiting to hear about this date. Somehow my love life has become a source of entertainment.

"It was actually a super fun date. Eric is a great guy," I say.

"So four stars?" Iris asks.

I shake my head. "Can't be. I don't want to go out with him again. He's looking for more than I can give."

"Why is that?"

I make a face. "Because he's twenty-seven."

That has my roommates in riots.

"And we thought Stirling was old!" Camila says.

"We'll get him a cane also!"

"But he was so nice. If he were younger!" I feel bad.

"So two stars?" Iris asks. She's still waiting by the white board.

"Three," I say. "It can't go anywhere, but I had fun. One extra star for being a great guy."

Iris writes it down. "3 of 5 stars."

"When's the next date?" she asks.

"I don't have one scheduled," I say. "Looks like I'm by myself tomorrow."

There's a knock on our apartment door, which is closed, for once. Camila opens it.

"Hey, Thomas, come on in."

Jake's roommate comes in. He takes a look at us circled around the white board. "Oh, hey, everyone," he says. Then he looks at me. "Jake says you've been to the Mud Dauber cave and know how to get there. If you're not busy tomorrow, mind taking me? I'll buy you lunch. We can make a date of it."

This is not happening.

I feel every eye on me as I say, "Sure. I'm free in the morning."

"Great! I'll pick you up at ten. Is it okay if we ride in my truck?"

"It's a good idea," I find myself saying. "The roads out there are terrible."

"See you tomorrow, then." He waves at everyone else. "Bye, guys."

He's barely closed the door before my roommates bust up squealing and chortling. Iris writes on the board.

"Date #3: __ out of 5 stars."

"Can't wait to see how this one goes," she says.

"I hate you all," I say, but judging from how they laugh and throw their arms around me, they know I don't mean it.

⚜

Thomas knocks on the apartment precisely at ten. I know what to expect this time, and I'm dressed appropriately, though I still don't have a helmet lamp. He takes me out to his big truck, and it roars to life as we head to the interstate.

"So what do you like about caving?" he asks.

"I love climbing. I like finding new places. I like the adrenaline rush of wondering if I'm going to fit, of not knowing what comes next." I glance over at him. "Although I'm not taking you near the small tunnels."

Thomas laughs heartily. At least six-five, his bulky frame takes up all of the driver's seat. "Yeah, I might get stuck."

"You might be the biggest guy I've ever seen," I say. "I mean, you got nothing on a sumo wrestler, but you could take any of these guys around here."

He nods. "I was an offensive lineman at Georgia State."

That explains his southern accent. "You from Georgia?"

"Yeah, born and raised."

"I have cousins there. We would spend Thanksgiving and sometimes Christmas down there."

"Nice."

I squint, trying to remember what an offensive lineman does. "You played football, then?"

"Is there any other sport?"

I laugh. "I dated a quarterback. I know the other positions but not as well."

"Ah. Everyone knows the quarterback."

"Yeah." I don't say anything else because I'm wounded that I just summed up my entire relationship with Owen as someone I dated.

But it's my fault for mentioning him when I'm on a date with another boy. If this even counts as a date. My roommates think it does.

Luckily I don't have to talk about it again because we've reached the crazy sand dunes outside the cave and it takes all my memory to navigate Thomas around them. I show him where we got lost and ended up in someone's front yard surrounded by cows, and he laughs so loud I think he'll hurt himself. Which makes me laugh.

"Here's the parking area," I say, pointing it out to him.

"That wasn't such a bad drive."

"Much better than last time," I agree.

We get out of the car. There are four other cars, and I hope the cave won't be too crowded. We run into a group coming out, and another is in front of us.

"Suck it in," I tell Thomas as we worm around the narrow opening.

Darkness descends upon us when we hit the inner chamber, and we both click on our flashlights. Thomas shines his light down the giant rock slab.

"Uh-oh," he says.

"No worries." I hobble over to the rope. "This is to help us get up and down."

"Is there no other way down?" he asks.

"I don't think so." I glance around and point my flashlight behind us. "There's a room over there. I don't know where it goes."

"We don't have to go down. Let's explore it."

We head back behind the main entrance. This part of the cave is a smaller room, with tall ceilings and rocks that looked like they peeled off and crashed to the floor. I shine my light above us and hope none of the ceiling pieces are considering a downward plunge at that moment.

"This wraps around." It's tall enough that Thomas only has to duck a little, and he leads us on a downward path around the bell-shaped columns. "Look! Isn't that the end of your rock slab?"

Sure enough, we've come out near the bottom of the slab. We tiptoe around it as more kids come squealing down, as carefully as they can without plunging into the hard rock floor.

"Good job," I say. "You managed to get us past it without going down."

"I think I would break that thing."

Thomas's size makes cave exploration more limited than it was with my roommates. We stick to the bigger rooms, ducking to get into chambers and going through smaller corridors, but he's not willing to squeeze himself into tiny openings. I search along the walls and try to find the space where my roommates and I crawled through, but without Iris's map, I can't recall. I tell him all about it, though.

"I honestly feared we'd get stuck. I wasn't sure how anyone would get us out."

"And you kept going?" Thomas looks at me with something between amazement and disgust on his face. Of course, it's hard to tell in the light of a flashlight.

"Well, I didn't want to believe that could happen. So I told myself if I kept going, eventually we'd reach something worth seeing."

"Did you?"

"We got to a small room where at least we could turn around."

He snorts. "And go through the whole thing again to get back out."

I grin. "Pretty much."

"Want to do it again?"

I consider that and shake my head. "No. It was one of those once-in-a-lifetime experiences. I've done it. Now I don't have to again."

We circle through the cave, but after about thirty more minutes, we've seen all Thomas wants to see.

"I'm not going into any of those tiny tunnels," he says when I point one out. "I'd get stuck, and they'd have to blow the cave apart to get me out."

"Yeah, you might be right." I lead us back to the giant rock slab. "Shall we go up?"

"Let's go up the way we came down."

But try as we might, we can't find the hallway that led us down.

"That's befuddling," I say. "It was right here, behind the slab, wasn't it?" Everywhere I shine my light seems to be a solid wall.

Thomas shrugs. "I thought so." He puts his flashlight in his pocket and grabs the rope with both hands. "Give me a push if I start to fall."

The thought of my hundred-pound frame pushing his several-hundred pound frame up the slab makes me laugh. "You fall, and you're on your own."

"That's not what Jake said when we were rock climbing," he scolds.

I laugh harder.

Luckily Thomas manages to heft himself all the way up the slab without my help, though he grunts a lot and slows down several times. When it's my turn, I use the rope as leverage and climb up with only a little bit of slipping.

"I think that was easier for you," Thomas says.

"Might have something to do with my size," I say.

"That's sexist."

I laugh again. He makes a few more jokes as we wander out of the cave, and I realize I had more fun caving this time than I did last time.

"You know, you should smile more," Thomas says, glancing at me as we get into his truck.

"I thought I smiled a lot," I say, surprised by the comment. "I'm generally a happy person."

"Yeah, but it's like you're faking it. When you think no one's looking, you look sad."

"I do?"

"Are you sad?"

"I—" I shrug. "Sometimes. Isn't everyone?"

"Be happy. Whatever's making you sad, don't let it get you down. We're young, the future's wide open."

"I'll keep that in mind," I say.

There is a lot of sadness in my heart. But I'm trying to ignore it. I'm filling my days with activities and people to lift me up.

I guess it still lingers, though.

"What are your plans after school?" Thomas says as we head back toward campus. "Going to get a masters?"

His words about the future are whispering through my mind, and now he's asking me to think about it. I need to be excited about what's coming, not sad about what I've lost.

"I'm going on a mission trip."

"Oh, yeah? Already working on your application?"

I shake my head. "Not yet. I'm going to do two more years of school so I'm closer to my degree, and then I'm going."

"That's great! At least you know what you want."

"Yep." The next two years are filler time, waiting until I can go. When I get back, my life begins.

None of this matters.

Thomas carries the conversation, and he's easy to talk to. I think I enjoyed our outing more than any other date this week.

But I don't feel any desire to touch him. There's no heady pull of attraction. He's one

I can safely add to the friend zone. Along with Stirling, Jake, and Mitch.

I might not want a relationship, but I would like to find someone to make out with. At least once in awhile.

CHAPTER SIXTY

Given Away

The first snow comes before the end of September.

I see it coating the tops of the mountains as I walk home from school. It hasn't reached us in the valley yet, though the temperature is cold enough that I see my breath.

Great. Winter is coming.

I'm grumpy when I walk into my apartment. We've been busy the past few days and I feel like I haven't done anything fun since I went caving with Thomas last week. Why are all of my evenings filled with homework and library time?

Lauren is in her usual spot in front of the couch when I walk in. Watching TV. Is school at the community college that much easier? It's almost an hour away, and yet she's never gone.

"A letter came for you," she says without looking up. "I put it on your bed."

"Thanks." I move past her down the hall, my heart rate picking up at the thought of a letter.

Only a few people write me.

It's laid face down, a legal-sized envelope. I drop my backpack on the floor and flip it over, and my heart skips a beat.

It's from Owen.

I crawl onto the bed and sit cross legged to open it. I decide not to analyze why it makes me so happy to hear from him. How I'm ready to read and reread his letter and savor every word. I just accept that that's the effect he has on me.

The paper falls from the envelope, along with a few pictures. Him climbing a mountain and grinning at the camera with a bunch of boys. Him eating a street taco and spilling juices all over his shirt. Him squatted down and talking to a child next to a church building.

I trace over his features, the smile and eyes I know so well, the face I see in my sleep. Then I turn to the letter.

Cassandra!

Thank you so much for the pictures. I couldn't imagine you with short hair until I saw it. I'm blown away. You're beautiful, but suddenly you look so grown up. Watch out. The guys out there are going to come knocking.

Ha. If he only knew.

I sent a few pictures also. We spent a few days at a homeless shelter working with the kids. It's sad when you see adults on the outs, with no place to go, damaged by life or in a slump because of negative circumstances. But the kids, it guts me. No kid should ever be on the streets. No kid should go to bed hungry or sleep on a park bench not sure of when the next meal comes. I hate hate that this is their life, and I'm doing everything I can to make it better while I'm out here.

His heart's in his work. He's right where he needs to be, doing what he needs to do, and I'm so impressed with his focus.

Monica told me she sees you a lot. I'm glad you get to hang out with my sister.

I raise an eyebrow. No mention of his cousin, at least.

How's school? What kinds of fun things are you doing? How's your job? At least you're not calling people anymore.

I showed your pictures to my buddies out here and they all think you're beautiful. A few of them asked if they could write you. I gave them your address. I hope you don't mind.

Hold up, what?

I read that paragraph again, my stomach tightening, my brow furrowing.

He gave my address to other guys?

I don't mind having my contact info given out. I don't mind getting mail from strangers and chatting with boys I don't know.

But Owen gave it away?

Owen is willing to have boys contact me?

The implication knees me in the chest.

He doesn't care if other boys are interested in me. I'm so deeply in the friend zone that he's trying to set me up.

The understanding hurts me more than I expected it would. He's accepted that I'm going to be with others and willing to help it happen.

I'm not his anymore.

I knew that already, but the proof of it is in his words.

He ends the letter telling me he loves me, but the words are just words. He loves me. He loves his sister. He loves the children at the shelter. He loves the other missionaries he's working with.

Add me to the list.

I put the letter away. I'll write him back, as his friend, his buddy, but it's going to take me a few days.

And I need to go on more dates.

✦

By the time Sunday rolls around, I've gone through the beginning stages of grief. Anger (who does Owen think he is? He can't give me away), denial (Owen didn't really mean that), bargaining (he only said that to be nice. It's not what he feels), and now I'm stuck in depression (we're really through and I don't know how to keep going).

Thomas sits by me in church. "You have that sad look on your face again."

I roll my eyes. I don't smile. "Been a hard few days."

"Need to get out? Go do something?"

"Yes."

Thomas pats me on the back. "I'll plan something."

Abby comes and joins us. I think she likes Thomas.

The pastor gets up. "Today I feel inspired to speak to you about your futures. Setting goals, seeking guidance to know what's the right step for you, and finding joy in all your endeavors."

It's like he's been reading my journal.

By the time the sermon ends, I feel like I've moved into the final stage of grief: Acceptance. Owen did what he needed to do. Now I need to let him go.

I sit at the kitchen table after church going over my finances. Things are tight. I draw lines in my budget, rearranging things, chopping my grocery bill in half. Even though I'm on scholarship, there are the expenses of books, housing, gas, car, everything. And the money I make at work only covers my rent and groceries. I have some extra in my savings from last year, but it's rapidly disappearing.

I might need to take out a loan. Maybe I can get a second job.

The apartment door is open, but I stay focused on my task as visitors come in and out. Then the table wobbles as someone sits down across from me, and I look up to see Stirling.

"Stirling!" I rise to give him a hug. "How are you?"

"Been a few weeks. Thought I'd drop by."

"So good to see you!"

He glances at my budget sheet. "Things going all right?"

I roll my eyes. "It's tight. I might have to sell the fish."

"You could get good money for that."

I giggle. "It's actually been a hard week. Owen sent me a letter that made me really sad."

Stirling knows a bit about Owen. He's met Monica and there was a phase last year where I wasn't sure if Stirling and I were dating. But we've moved past that. He's another in my friend zone.

My, how I like my friends.

"Let's go for a walk," he says. "You can tell me about it."

"Gladly." I grab my sweater since there's been a nip in the air since Wednesday, and we head out.

"What did the letter say?" Stirling asks.

"Just that he gave my address to a few of his buddies who thought I was cute. So they could write me."

"Isn't that a compliment?"

I shrug. "Probably. From anyone else. From Owen, it's like he's saying, 'in case you thought I still liked you, I don't. There's nothing romantic left between us.'"

"Did you think there still was?"

I consider the question. I look up at the darkening sky, turning deep blue with twilight. The first stars are out. I search for the constellations Owen showed me last summer, but I don't remember them.

"There are still feelings on my part," I admit. "No matter how I try to deny them or hide them, I still feel something for him. And I couldn't help thinking we might get back together in a few years when we see each other. Now, it's like he's closing that door. Telling me he's not waiting for it and neither should I."

"Maybe," Stirling says. He puts his hands in his jacket, his shoulder bumping mine as we stroll along. "Or maybe he feels the same things as you, but since he can't act on them right now, it's easier to pretend he doesn't. And what better way to pretend you don't have feelings than to set up the person you like with other people?"

"I could never recommend other girls to Owen. I'd be too jealous."

"Really? If you thought you were never going to be with him again, you wouldn't want to have a say in what girls he might date?"

"I'd introduce him to the ugliest and meanest girls so he would always long for me."

Stirling laughs. "Maybe these will be the ugliest and meanest guys."

I shake my head. "Owen's better than me. He wouldn't want me to date someone who wouldn't take care of me. He only wants the best for me." I'm sad as I say it. I know it's true. Any guy who Owen's given my info to will be a kind, considerate, awesome guy.

"So you think he's saying he's totally over you?"

"I think so."

Stirling puts his arm around my shoulder and gives me a brief hug. "But you know nothing's over till it's over."

"Which means what?"

He shrugs. "You're not married. Neither is he. Until then, there's still a chance." He smirks. "And maybe even after."

"I couldn't be a home wrecker."

"Maybe he wouldn't mind."

I shake my head. The idea is unfathomable, but it makes me laugh. "Thanks, Stirling."

We do another loop around the block before heading back to my apartment. Stirling walks me up to the door and then digs through his jacket.

"Oh, hey, here. This is for you." He hands me twenty bucks.

I furrow my brow at it. "What's this for?"

"Gas. Because you drove me to the airport."

"I can't take this," I protest.

"Yes, you can. I owe you."

I need the money. I pocket the cash. "Thanks, Stirling."

CHAPTER SIXTY-ONE

Dead Fish

Stirling calls me Monday night. "Want to get some dinner and go to a bonfire? A bunch of my friends will be there."

Is he trying to make sure I get food? I'm unsure of his motives. Money is tight, though, and I'm struggling to make ends meet.

"Yes," I say, if for no other reason than the free meal. "I can brainstorm my English essay while I'm there."

I'm thinking he'll take me to a fast food joint, but Stirling has money and that's not his style. He takes me to a nice burger joint and insists I get one of their fancy drinks. By the time we finish with the food, the sun is setting.

"That's what we needed," he says, driving us into the canyon. "We can't have a bonfire in daylight."

"No, of course not," I say, amused.

"What's your English paper on?"

"*Tess of the Dubervilles*. It's for my British lit class."

"Yeah? What do you think?"

"Thomas Hardy believed in fate and negativity and the book is terribly depressing. I'm supposed to analyze it from the feminist point of view and defend that critique."

"Yikes. Good luck."

"Yeah." I sum up the plot for Stirling, and then we pull into a copse of trees where a fire already roars away. I get out of the car with my sweater on, and yet the heat of the bonfire reaches all the way to us. I take the sweater off and leave it on the hood.

Wyatt, Stirling's roommate, waves at me where he stands by the fire with a can in his hand, surrounded by a dozen other students. I can't tell if it's soda or beer, from the way the light reflects off it. PYU has a no-alcohol-on-campus policy, but once kids get off campus, people do what they want.

He's the only person I recognize.

"This is Cassandra, guys," Stirling says, pulling me over.

Everyone waves and a smattering of hellos call out to me.

"Here's the drinks," another guy says, leading me over to a cooler.

I open it and am relieved to find a can of seltzer.

"Marshmallow?" a girl calls out to me, holding up a stick and a white blob.

"Yes." Never mind that I just ate dinner.

I settle myself on a stump and roast my marshmallow, my can of soda beside me. A guy in a dark jacket and blue jeans sits down beside me.

"Hey." He holds his soda out at me. "Didn't catch your name. I'm Evan."

"Evan." I bump his soda can with my own. "Cassandra."

My marshmallow catches fire. I pull it from the flames and blow it out, then wait for the blackened exterior to cool enough to put it in my mouth.

"Bummer you burned it," he says. "It's so hard to get them brown without turning them to charcoal."

"I like it like this," I say. "The outside is crispy and the inside is gooey. It's perfect."

"Want some chocolate? You can make a s'more."

I shake my head. "Too sweet. I like the mallow by itself."

"Wow." Evan lifts an eyebrow. He's blond, but it's a dark blond, and his eyebrows are as shapely as a girl's, giving his face a sculpted look. He sips from his soda. "You're rather particular about your roasted marshmallows."

"I guess I am. Want me to make you one?"

"Please." He gestures at my stick. "But enjoy yours first. I don't want to cut into your marshmallow time."

I feel self-conscious eating in front of him, but he's staring at me and I have no choice. I bite into the marshmallow, which dribbles all over my chin, predictably.

Evan nods. "Sold. That looked good."

I wipe my face with my hand. "The next one's for you."

We spend the next hour making marshmallows and then talking about other good roasting foods. Turns out several of them are here. Someone brought hot dogs, bratwurst, bacon, and then there's an array of soft candies to roast.

"Let's try all of them," Evan says.

I hold up a hand. "Stirling took me out before we got here. I'm not hungry. But I'll watch you roast them."

"It's a scientific experiment." Evan loads up his plate, and we go back to the fire.

We make guesses about what each food item is going to do and then compare expectations to reality. Evan won't stop laughing. Either he had something else to drink before he got here or he thinks I'm really funny.

"So you and Stirling," he says. "Dating?"

"Oh, no. We're just friends."

"Awesome. I thought so, but can't be too sure."

"Awesome?" I echo. "Why?"

"Well, I couldn't ask you out otherwise."

It's been a week since I went on a date, not counting Stirling. Maybe two weeks. My weekends have been filling up with school-related activities like extra-credit ballet performances.

"Are you going to ask me?" I say.

He laughs again. "Yes. Give me your phone number."

We exchange numbers, and then Stirling comes over. He settles his hand on the back of my neck.

"I know it's early still, but I have to get home," he says. "We have school tomorrow."

"Looks like I'm leaving," I say. "My ride's out of here."

"I can give you a ride home," Evan says.

"It's all right. I have schoolwork to do too." I got my food, and my fun, and now I need to go.

"See ya," Stirling says. The boys fist bump, and then I trail after Stirling to his car.

"Thanks for bringing me to this," I say. "I needed to get out."

"Yeah, I could tell. Cheer up. This will pass."

I sigh as I look out the car window. "I'm so lonely. I feel like I'm going to be alone forever."

"You won't be."

"I want to fill the time with someone."

"I'm here."

"I know." I appreciate Stirling being there. But hanging out with friends is . . . different.

How long has it been since I kissed a guy? Tomorrow is the beginning of October. September, August, July, June . . .

Almost four months.

Too long.

✦

I live at the library for the next few days. I manage to get my English paper done, but then I'm neck-deep in a geography test. When I was a kid, I thought geography meant different countries around the world.

Turns out it actually means wind patterns and climate and rock formations and geothermal activities, and would you believe it, it's got math in it also.

Why does everything have to be complicated by mathematical equations?

I get home and plop myself down in front of my fish tank with a bowl of cereal. I have eight beautiful fish. One of them died over the summer under Wyatt's care, but I don't hold him responsible. They are very finicky creatures to keep alive.

I need to get back to nine.

I stand up and turn to face the four people goofing around in my apartment. It's Thomas and Abby and Iris and Jake.

Jake's over here a lot. I think he likes Camila but she hasn't shown any interest, so he spends his time with Iris instead.

I wonder if Camila still likes Jordan. She hasn't said anything, but she gets very quiet whenever he's mentioned. They dated last year but stopped when the semester ended.

"I'm running to the pet store," I say. "Anyone want to come?"

"What for?" Jake asks.

"I need another fish."

"You have eight," Abby says.

"No, no, don't try to talk her out of this," Iris says. "It's a thing."

"It's a thing?"

Iris nods. "All year last year we watched fish go in and out of our house."

"Like fish trafficking?"

"Yep."

"Hey!" I protest. "I was trying to give them a loving home."

"If you had their best interest at heart, you'd leave them at the pet store," Iris says, straight-faced.

"Funny," I say, but I can't help smiling. "Fine, I'll go alone. See you guys in an hour."

"I'll go," Thomas says, lifting his heavy bulk from the couch.

"You're going?" Abby looks up at him.

"Yeah. Don't want to make Cassandra go alone."

He follows me to the door, and I beam at him. He chose me over sitting here with Abby. I'm honored.

"So what fish are we looking for?" he says as he squishes into my car.

"I'll know it when I see it," I say.

"Lots of history with the fish tank?"

"Oh yeah. It was a big drama last year. I seriously struggled to keep them alive. It took me months before I finally got the right balance of alkalinity and oxygen and protein and destresser—"

"Destresser?" Thomas repeats before I get any more words out. "Like, because your fish were getting stressed out?"

I scowl. "Right? Next I'll be putting them into therapy."

"Are you serious right now?" He can't stop laughing, and Thomas's laugh fills the whole car. He's something of a big guy.

"For real! The pet store guy told me about it. I can get a special therapy light—"

There's no point in saying anything else. Thomas is laughing so hard he's not hearing me.

"Oh, hey," the door greeter says when I come in. "We haven't seen you in awhile."

"Nothing's died in awhile," I reply.

"But we're here to change that," Thomas says behind me.

I scowl at him.

The worker doesn't bat an eye. "Let me know if you need anything."

"Have any of the therapy lights?" Thomas asks.

"Thomas." I hiss and shove him toward the tanks. Or I try, but he's a hundred pounds heavier than me, and all I manage is to push his arm like an annoying fly.

Still, he obliges me and goes with me to the fish tanks.

I examine the beautiful colors but I'm not sure I want another beauty. They're more fickle than the others. "Let's get another algae fish," I say, pointing one out. "They're very good at keeping the glass clean, and I always need that."

"Right. You grab him, I'll bag him?"

"No, Thomas." I'm laughing. "I'll get the worker again."

Ten minutes later we're out the door with the new fish, and I'm more buoyant than I've been in days. I chatter nonstop all the way home.

"You got it wrong about the therapy," Thomas says as I pull into the parking lot.

"What's that?"

"These fish don't need therapy. Buying them is your therapy."

I cock my head. "You might be onto something." I have no money. No need for more fish. But adding another pretty to my tank lifts my spirits.

"Try not to get depressed, or you're gonna need a bigger tank."

CHAPTER SIXTY-TWO

Finish the Job

I plop the fish in the tank and then I'm up half the night working on my Portuguese presentation. And studying for my geography test. Plus I have a vocab quiz in ballet.

I'm exhausted when I get up in the morning, and I'm running late so there's no time for breakfast. But I take a moment to check on my new fish.

He's sort of bobbing around, not latching onto the wall and not swimming either.

I frown at him. He's a new kind of algae eater for me, and I'm not sure what behavior to expect from him. My other one, which is bigger and looks like a relative of a crocodile, doesn't ever leave the sides of the tank unless he's perusing the rocks. Even now his round mouth is suctioned to the glass, his side eyes gazing into nothingness.

Maybe this one has different feeding habits.

I'm not going to spend this semester obsessing over fish like I did last year. I head out the door, my eyes burning with exhaustion, not feeling at all ready for the day.

"Don't forget to turn in your diary entries on Friday," Professor Morales says in Portuguese class. "You should have kept a journal for the past two weeks."

Crap. I have not. I knew this was an assignment, but I keep falling asleep before doing it. I'll have to sit up in the library tonight making up stuff about my life.

I grab a two-dollar sandwich from the vending machine for lunch and curse myself for not making one at home. I can get an entire loaf of bread of two bucks. But I didn't have time, and I'm starving. I sit through two more classes before heading to the office.

The sandwich wasn't enough, and my stomach growls through my work shift. I won't waste money on dinner, though, so as soon as I'm done with work, I book it for home. I run through my ingredients in my mind, coming up with dinner options.

Thomas greets me at the door, his face a mask of concern. "I'm so glad you're home."

"Do you live here now?" I ask, pushing past him.

"I'm considering moving my stuff to the couch." He stands in the living room and swivels toward me. "There's something we need to talk about."

He's being odd. I put my backpack down and give him a strange look, then open the fridge. "Okay, talk. I'm starving. I'm making soup." Not canned soup, either. I haul out celery and carrots and begin chopping.

"There's been a death."

I pause, knife lifted on the cutting board. Then I spin around, and he holds his arms up in surrender when he sees the knife.

"Whoa, whoa! It wasn't me."

My lips purse as I fight a smile. I put the knife down and go into the living room.

The new fish is belly up in the tank.

I sigh. "Not again." I get the net and crouch in front of the tank.

Thomas crouches beside me. "What are you going to do?"

I scoop the fish out of the tank and put it in a plastic baggie. "Take it back to the store and get another." I stand and go to the fridge, then plop it into the freezer.

"So why did you put it in the freezer?"

I run my hands through my hair and give an aggravated sigh. "Because I'm cooking dinner and then I need to go back to campus and finish my Portuguese assignments and I don't have time to deal with the fish today. He's gonna have to wait."

"You're making him wait for a proper funeral?"

"He was never getting a proper funeral. He's lucky he doesn't get a flush down the toilet."

"Harsh."

I can't even joke. I acknowledge his words with an eye roll and turn back to my veggies.

"Tell you what," Thomas says. "Give me the receipt and I'll take him back for you."

I glance up from my chopping. "You will?"

"Yep. It's a small thing I can do for one of my besties."

He smiles wide, and his words warm me.

"Okay, then." I hop back to my room and get the receipt, then bring it to him.

"Cook your food," he says. "I'll drop you off at campus on my way."

I fight the urge to tell him I love him. "You can have some soup too."

"I'll take it."

Half an hour later Thomas leaves me at campus while he runs my errand of death. I sit in the library making up journal entries in Portuguese for an hour and then work on my presentation.

He texts me an hour after that. *T: need a ride home?*

I smile. I text back, *I'll feed you more soup.*

He sends a laughing emoji.

The new fish is already swimming in the tank when we get home. He looks healthy, maybe a little confused but ready to take on his new environment.

"Stay alive," I tell him. "Dying is a cop-out. You have to finish the job."

We'll see if he listens to me.

⌒〜※〜⌒

"It's karaoke night at the Black Sheep," Abby says Saturday morning when I get out of the shower.

"I thought we agreed never to go back there," I say.

"But this is different. There's something fun to do."

I go to my fish tank to check on the new one. He's still alive. If he makes it until

Monday, I'll give him a name. "I've never done karaoke."

"It's three-dollar pizza night also. I already invited Jake and Thomas and Matt, and Thomas said he'd come."

"Who else?"

"You, Iris, Lauren, Camila."

"They said they're coming?"

"I haven't invited yet. Anyone else you want to invite?"

Maybe I'll invite Jordan. And then there's Evan. He texted me two nights ago and asked if I was busy, but I haven't heard from him since then.

"Three dollar pizza night?" I say.

"Yep."

I'm broke and hungry and you can't beat that. "Okay. I'll go."

I call Jordan up for the first time all semester, and he's excited to come along. In the end, it's me, Iris, Abby, Thomas, and Jordan who end up at the pizza place.

The food is terrible but worth the price. The environment is a hundred degrees different from the last time I was here. We're dressed casually in jeans and sweaters, as is everyone else. It's almost family-friendly, with no flashing lights or gyrating music or clouds of smoke. We pay our three bucks and then goad each other on to sing.

"That's why we're here!" Abby says.

"No one said I had to sing," Jordan protests.

My cousin is my complete opposite: almost as tall as Thomas, thick blond hair, fair skin. It's cute to see him looking uncertain.

"Let's do it together," Iris says. "We can all sing a song."

"Like what?" Thomas says. "What song has parts for all of us?"

"'Summer Nights,'" Abby says.

"Say again?" Jordan says.

Abby grins broadly. "'Summer Nights.' From the musical Grease. It has a boy part and a girl part and lots of backup singers."

"I know it," I say. "I used to sing in high school."

"You should sing more," Iris says. "You have a beautiful voice."

"This is your chance." Abby jumps up and runs to the sign up sheet.

"I did not agree to this," Jordan says, tugging on his earlobe. He's genuinely uneasy.

Thomas clasps him on the shoulder. "Accept your fate, man. No one says no to Abby."

There's truth to that. She's suckered me into a lot of activities.

She comes back, smiling so big the dimples show on both sides of her face. "We're on the list!"

"How does this song go?" Jordan says.

Thomas pulls it up on his phone, and the two of them listen to it and then try to sing along for ten minutes before the guy up front calls, "And next we have Abby and friends singing 'Summer Nights'!"

"This is it," she says, grabbing my hand and Iris's arm and tugging us up. It's a given the boys will come. I think she's far too trusting. If I were them, I'd turn and run.

But they don't. They follow us onto the stage. Abby hands Thomas a mic and grabs one for us, and then music starts playing.

Us girls are first. We know the melody, the song, and we deliver our part with no issues.

And then the boys start.

Have they never heard this song? They miss the intro, stumble over the next words, and sing separate notes. They both lean closer to the machine as if seeing the words better will improve their pitch. Iris starts giggling behind me, and I have a hard time keeping a straight face when we begin singing again.

It doesn't get better from there. By the time we're singing back and forth to each other, it sounds like we're singing two different songs.

And then Jordan flat out gives up.

"Twinkle twinkle little star," he sings.

I cut off, not sure I'm hearing right, but Abby elbows me so I come back in.

"Tell me more, tell me more," I sing.

"Up above the world so high!" Jordan sings.

But now Thomas is in on it. He belts with him.

"Like a diamond in the sky!"

I'm dying. I can't sing anymore, I'm laughing too hard. The audience is loving it, cheering, clapping.

It's a total disaster.

We don't stay after we sing, but we don't stop laughing all the way home. And we sing "Twinkle Twinkle Little Star" about a dozen times.

I'm less than a month into my sophomore year of college, but I think I'm finding my groove.

EPISODE 4 :

Roots and Wings

CHAPTER SIXTY-THREE

Lingering Feelings

College is stressing me out.

I spend the first part of the evening taking a geography exam at the testing center. After sweating over it for an hour, I head to the library to write an English essay.

I live at the library. I hate when I forget my food because it means I lose an hour by walking home and getting something to eat.

The other option is to buy food on campus, but even two-dollar sandwiches add up to ten dollars a week.

I'm giving new meaning to the term "starving student."

I'm only three weeks into my first semester as a sophomore, but my British lit teacher is making me work for my grade.

"First thing you're going to do," he told us at the beginning of the semester, "is pick an author and analyze the writer based on their works. Your first assignment is to write an essay explaining why you chose this author."

I think half my class chose Tolkien. So I went with Thomas Hardy. We read one of his books in the first week, and I'm fascinated by his fatalist mentality.

One of his books will be happy, I'm sure of it.

I get the rough draft done, and I heave a sigh of relief when I shut my laptop. I gather my things and trudge over to the elevator.

Countless study evenings with Jared replay through my mind as I stand there waiting for it. At the time, I was afraid to let anything develop between us, even though we both liked each other.

I would let it now, if he were here.

❦

Deep wound in my chest
Compounding my achiness
Yet I know it is not so much him
That makes me empty

But the loss of hope
The chance to make him smile
He could make me happy
And now I am alone
I miss the elation
The wonder of it all
Not so much of him
But of the feeling
Of being needed and wanted
Of wanting and needing someone
For a brief moment
Life was not about me anymore
It was about us
The person known as me
No longer wants to be me
I want to be us
I want to belong to a we

Mr. Monson hands back our geography test scores on Thursday, and I'm so relieved to see I got a 91%. I'm not sure which class I detest more, geography or my environmental biology class.

Add ballet to the running. I'm hating that class also.

I run into Mitch on my way home from school.

Mitch. My almost-ex. Because he was almost my boyfriend.

"Where are you going?" I ask him. We don't live near each other, so I'm surprised to see him walking along my path.

"To visit a friend," he says, and his face turns red.

A girl. He's going to see a girl. I know it.

"Oh, fun," I say.

And then the conversation dies.

"Classes going well?" he says.

"Fine, I guess. I'm not loving this semester. I feel overwhelmed already."

"It can be hard," he agrees. "Make sure to take time for yourself."

"Thanks for the advice," I say sarcastically.

We drift back into silence, and it borders on awkward. Mitch and I nearly dated a few weeks ago until he found out about my high school boyfriend. Who happened to be his cousin.

I come to my intersection, and he says, "Well, enjoy your walk home. See you later."

"See you," I say.

Sadness fills my chest when I walk away. He's the only guy who's made me feel something in months. So of course he's the only one I can't get involved with.

Abby and Thomas are exiting the apartment complex right when I get there.

"Where are you going?" I ask.

"On a walk," Abby says. "Want to come? We have to get our walks in while the weather's warm enough."

I'm so relieved she asked. She's crushing on Thomas, and I thought she might want to be alone with him. "Yes."

"Drop off your backpack," Thomas says. "We'll wait for you."

"No sense in lugging it around," Abby adds.

I don't need to be told twice. I run upstairs and toss it in the kitchen, then grab a sweater before jogging back out to join them. The first week of October brought a chill, and when the sun dips below the mountains, the air will crisp up.

They're talking quietly when I get there, Thomas with his hands in his pockets and Abby standing close to him, her body turned toward him. She obviously likes him.

"You're sad again," Thomas says as I join them.

"Life's kicking my butt right now," I say.

"What's wrong?" Abby asks. We mosy along the sidewalk, strolling, moving at a leisurely pace.

"Classes are hard. I have no money. And I miss having a boyfriend."

"This is a tough stage of life," Thomas says. "Especially if you feel like you don't have any options."

I spread my hands. "I already have a job. It pays decent but not enough, and I don't have time to add another. I'm not smart enough to understand my classes without hours of study time put into it."

"And the boy part?" Thomas says.

I sigh again. "I ran into Mitch today after school. And I felt so sad because there could have been something between us and there's not."

"You need an adventure," Abby says. "You need to go and do something amazing."

"That's what the mission will be."

"But that's two years away. What can you do before then?"

I shrug. I'm feeling dismal. "There's nothing."

We've reached an elementary school with a park, and Abby settles down on one of the swings. I take the other, and Thomas leans on the bar while we talk.

"You should go on a big trip," he says. "Maybe a humanitarian trip somewhere to fill your bucket."

"I could do that," I say. "But when? I still have to wait until school's out."

"Go sooner," Abby says. "Like, Christmas break."

"That's an option." Maybe that's what I need. A change of scenery.

"Why don't you look into study abroad?" Thomas asks. "It's not the same as a mission. But you'd get to go somewhere, do something, and still get school credit."

"Aren't those really expensive?"

"Your scholarship will apply toward it," Abby says.

I imagine myself going to school in another country. Russia, Italy, Spain. "Oh my gosh. You guys might be onto something."

I jump off the swing, anxious to get back to my computer so I can research study abroad options.

I'm in a funk here. I need to get out and do something.

⚥

I stop by the study abroad office Friday after class to see what they have to offer. They have fliers on different locations, different things to study, different prices.

I take them all with me to the library and peruse them in between homework assignments.

They're crazy expensive. My scholarship will only cover half the tuition. But it's worth it, if I can find one that's perfect for me.

But none of them feel right. I read about different adventures in Ireland, Africa, Canada, all the places I would expect. They have fall terms and winter terms, so each one only lasts one semester. The soonest I could go is January.

None of them are for English majors with a Portuguese emphasis. Why aren't there any locations in Brazil?

I want to further my education, not take a bunch of fun classes for a semester that don't get me anywhere.

There must be something for me.

I finish up my English paper and pull out a notebook paper.

I haven't written Owen back. I got his letter weeks ago. It's taken me this long to reach a point where I feel like I can talk to him without being upset.

I'm his friend. That's all I am.

I start the letter.

Hey Owen!

So great to hear from you! I loved seeing your pictures. I feel in your words how much you love the work you're doing. You are changing people's lives, not the least being your own!

School's kicking my trash, but that's not new. I'm actually thinking of doing a study abroad program next semester. I want to get out and experience something different. I'm pretty excited about this. Still looking into it to find the best one for me.

Sure, it's fine if your friends write me! It's so fun to meet new people, even through letters. Only send me the good ones, though. I expect any guy to be fully vetted.

I hesitate, but then I plunge onward. If I'm in the friend zone, I may as well swim in it.

My roommates tease me about how many dates I go on. I haven't met anyone worthy of a second date, but I get a lot of free dinners. Which I need because I never have enough money. College is hard, but it's fun. I'm loving it.

I flinch when I finish the paragraph. We said we wouldn't do it. We wouldn't talk about the people we date.

But that was before. Before he basically told me he was providing a list of boys for me to engage with.

I hope you'll write me again. I get super happy every time I get a letter from you. I love seeing your face. Keep up the good work!

Love, Cassandra

I read it back over and let out a slow breath. It's so platonic I hardly believe I'm writing the boy I thought I'd spend the rest of my life with. I want to rip it up.

But I don't rip it up. I wanted Owen in my life forever. If this is how it's going to be, so be it.

CHAPTER SIXTY-FOUR

Boring Books

I go on three dates the following week. Thursday, Friday, Saturday. Iris loves writing them down on my white board.

None of them stick. I go out twice with Evan, but when he calls a third time, I tell him no.

"I thought you had a good time with him," Camila says when we sit down to eat our fish dinner. Lately I've been making food for both of us, and she's giving me money for groceries. It works well. I waste less, she has food ready for her when she gets home from cross country, and I have more money.

"I did," I agree. "Evan's super fun. But the chemistry isn't there. If we went out a third time, I'd be leading him on."

"It could grow." She uses her fork to chop through the salmon steak. "This is good. You're becoming a good cook, you know."

"Thanks." I beam at her praise. "Thanks for letting me practice on you. But no, it's not going to grow, and I'm tired of saying yes because a guy asks nicely. I'll give them a token date. But if they haven't hooked me by the end of it, I'm not starting the next chapter."

She shakes her head. "They're not stories."

"They are in my book."

We both giggle.

"You're ridiculous," she says.

"I'm an English major."

"Enough said. No more boring books."

I hold out my fist, and she bumps it.

***

Monica invites me to hang out with her and some friends at their cabin Sunday night.

I ride up with her and Sandy, her roommate. We wind through the hills, past civilization into the mountains that border Glenwood Springs. A wood cabin sits at the end of a gravel driveway. Three boys are hanging out on the porch when we get there.

"Hey!" one says. "How are you, girl?"

Monica runs over and hugs him. "Hey!"

I notice how they stand next to each other. She hasn't mentioned dating anyone, but I examine him closer. He's super tall, which is good because Monica is six-foot. And he's muscular. Beneath his baseball cap, I can tell from his eyebrows that his hair is light.

She turns from him now.

"Andrew, you know Sandy, and that's Cassandra, my friend from Arkansas."

"Oh, hey!" Andrew grins at me. "I've heard a lot about you. Nice to finally meet."

"You too," I say, though I've not heard anything about him.

"I'm Mike, that's Larry," the guy beside him says, and Sandy and I wave. "We're getting the four-wheelers out. Up for it?"

"Yes!" Monica says, speaking for all of us.

I've never been four-wheeling. It kind of scares me.

But I'm always up for an adventure.

Andrew pulls a four-wheeler from the adjacent garage, and Larry gets out another. Mike pulls out a third.

"Who's with me?" Andrew says.

"Me!" Monica jumps onto the seat behind him before anyone else can claim it.

Larry looks at me. "Want to ride?"

I nod. He's older than me, but still in his early twenties. I climb on behind him and wrap my arms around his torso. His windbreaker crinkles beneath my arms, and he smells nice, like pines and aftershave.

Sandy gets on behind Mike.

Andrew revs his engine, and away he goes. Larry follows, and I gasp into his jacket at the sudden momentum. My butt scoots back on the seat, and I cling to him, afraid I'm going to fall right off.

That would be embarrassing.

We bounce over small hills and cruise through the woods, following Andrew's trail. After a few minutes, the speed feels more comfortable, and I relax my grip.

"Doing all right?" Larry calls over his shoulder.

"Yes!" I say. The sun hasn't set yet, though twilight colors the sky an indigo blue. I pull away from Larry's back so I can study the trees as they fly by around us. The wind whistles in my ears, my hair spreading out around my head. It's almost to my shoulders but still too short to put in a ponytail.

If I look straight up at the sky, I can't tell how fast we're going. But when I look around me, the trees and bushes are whipping by.

"Having fun?" Larry asks.

"Loving it!" I call back.

Andrew brings us to a stop at a clearing. "This is a great overlook," he says, and we climb down from the four-wheelers. "We can watch the sunset."

A few camp chairs are set up near a cliff. I wander as near to the edge as I dare and peer down. It doesn't drop straight but rolls down into a steep valley. Still not something I want to fall into. I go back to the chairs and settle in next to Larry as the others arrive on their four-wheelers. He's taken his baseball cap off, and I see he's got light brown eyes and similar colored hair.

"It's Cassandra, right?" he says, watching me sit down.

"Yes." I pull out my phone camera and take shots of the sky as it changes to pinks and oranges. The mountains reflect the color, and the trees stretch upward like craggy triangles reaching for the heavens. "It's so beautiful."

"Yeah, it is. You're not from here?"

"Arkansas. No mountains."

"Ah." He nods. "I've heard it's pretty there."

I smile at him. "Most people only have negative things to say about it."

"Have they been there?"

I snort. "Of course not."

"Then they should keep their mouths shut."

"My thoughts exactly!"

We fall silent as the sun continues its descent. Monica says something and Sandy and Andrew laugh, but I'm absorbed in the colors of the sky.

"So what year are you in school, Cassandra?" Larry asks.

"Sophomore. You?"

"Same. But I got a late start. Stayed home and worked for a year, then did a mission trip before starting school."

I try to calculate his age. "So you're . . . twenty-one?"

"Twenty-two next month."

I nod. "What are you studying?"

"Psychology. You?"

"English." I sigh. "But it's getting rather boring. I want to do a study aboard trip, but I can't find one that fits my major."

"No, you don't want to do study abroad. You want to have a cultural experience that immerses you with the people. Like a mission trip but for your education."

"Yes!" I exclaim. "That's what I want! But I don't know how to find one!"

"You're in luck." Larry digs into his pocket and pulls out a wallet, then he hands me a business card. "This is a program that places people around the world teaching English in schools. You can go almost anywhere."

I stare at the card, at the name written across it. Alliances Abroad. "Wait, how does it work? And how do you know about it?"

"I'm going next semester."

"You are?"

"Yeah. It's so much better than study abroad. I get class credit, but I'm also working."

I shake my head. "Explain it to me. Where are you going? How did you find out about this?"

He leans toward me, and I see the excitement glittering in his eyes, reflecting from the last rays of sunlight. "A friend told me about it. And ever since I got back from my mission, I've been dying to get back out and do something again. I can't just sit in school studying, it's not for me. I have to get my hands dirty."

"So where are you going?" I'm enthralled. My heart races. This might be it, what I've been looking for.

"Croatia."

"Croatia!" That's not a country I expected to hear. "Why?"

"I did my mission in Russia. I'm minoring in indo-european languages, and this helps me get class credit while not being stuck on campus."

"Did you pick the place?"

"Kind of. They have a map and you give them your first, second, and third choices. I picked Russia, the Ukraine, and Croatia."

"How do classes work? Will you be attending at a local university?"

"No, that's the best part. Everything I do there, whether it's teaching or learning how to cook or volunteering at an orphanage, it's going to count for college credit."

"How much does it cost?"

"Ah." He shakes his head. "I completely forgot to mention that part. It costs nothing." I lift an eyebrow. "It's free?"

"Not only is it free, but they pay you."

"What?" I gasp out. I picture the study abroad fliers I had in the library, the multiple dollar signs showing how much each program cost.

Can this be real?

"It's a job, Cassandra. You'll be teaching English in schools. They provide a host family for you, and they give you a monthly stipend. In Croatia that doesn't end up being very much, but hey! At least I'm not paying!"

I can't believe it. "This is perfect. It's what I've been looking for."

He smiles wide. The sun is down now, the sky darkening, but his teeth flash white in the darkness. "I thought you'd be interested."

We have to turn the headlights on when we drive the four-wheelers back to the cabin, and Monica convinces me to join everyone in a game of pool. But I can barely contain my excitement. This is it. I know it is. It's why the other programs didn't feel right.

I'm supposed to go to Brazil to teach English.

⁕

As soon as I get a break during work on Monday, I call the Alliances Abroad office.

"I'm interested in your English-teaching program," I say as I peruse the website. I have the country of Brazil pulled up on the screen.

"Great!" the girl on the other line says. Her voice is chipper and cheerful. "Where are you hoping to go?"

"Well, Brazil."

"Awesome. Did you read through the requirements on our website?"

"Requirements . . ." I mutter to myself as I click through. "Oh, found them." I fall silent as I read them. Everything looks good except— "I'm a student. I don't have a bachelor's degree yet." Neither does Larry. He didn't say anything about that. Have they changed their rules?

"Oh." Her voice echoes my disappointment. "That's kind of important. When do you graduate?"

Crap. This is a big snag. "Not for two years. But I'm studying Portuguese and English. So I'm very qualified."

"Hmm." She pauses. "I'm going to put you through to my supervisor and see what he says."

"All right." My heart sinks, and I brace myself for disappointment.

"Hello, this is Alex," a friendly male voice says.

"Hi, Alex," I say. "I'm interested in your teaching program, but I don't have a bachelor's degree. Is there a way around this? I'm studying English and Portuguese."

"Yes, that's what Alice said," he says. "Tell you what, go ahead and fill out the application and send it to us. We'll look over your qualifications and give you a call. Make sure you mention that you're studying secondary ed."

"Oh, it's not secondary ed," I say hastily.

"But it's teaching, right?"

I never said teaching. I said Portuguese and English. But suddenly I know that's about to change. "Yes."

"Great. I look forward to seeing your application."

CHAPTER SIXTY-FIVE

Application Received

The humanities offices have closed by the time I get off work, so I have to wait an entire eighteen hours before I can meet with my educational adviser. As soon as she has an opening, I barrel into her office.

"I need to add a teaching minor," I breathe out, taking my jacket off as I collapse into her seat.

"All right. What's your name?"

"Cassandra Jones."

She puts my name into her computer and leans back to study my history. "You already have a minor."

I nod. "But I need one for teaching."

"Do you know which one you want?"

I give a slow shake of my head. "No, actually. But I want to do this teaching thing in Brazil, and they won't consider me if I'm not studying education."

She pulls out a thick catalog of minors and flips through it. "Of course you can get a minor in secondary ed. But there's also special ed, international education, curriculum and instruction . . . But if you're teaching English to non-native speakers, I suggest you minor in TESOL."

I lean toward her, ready for whatever she wants me to do. "What's that?"

"It's Teaching English as a Second Language. You can use that minor anywhere in the world because it's not part of the secondary education system in America." She hits a button on her computer, and the printer spits out a paper. "One of the requirements is a six-month internship teaching English to English learners. You can do that in the U.S. in some schools, but usually the public schools want a teaching certificate. Your teaching trip to Brazil would fulfill this requirement."

I expected there to be more barriers, more discouragement, something to tell me this wasn't going to work. But instead, she's showing me how it fits together perfectly. "How many hours is the minor?"

She checks a few things on her computer. "Eighteen, just two hours more than your

Portuguese minor. You might need to add another year of school, but some of your English classes could count for both."

I sit back in my chair. Another year of school. I'm on a fast track to finish in three years so I can graduate before I go on my mission.

How much does my life change if I don't do that? Do I cut out the mission? Wait an extra year? Or stop rushing and go before I graduate?

It doesn't matter. I need to do this internship. "Okay. Let's add it."

She hands me another sheet of paper. "Fill this out and sign it, and I'll update your student profile."

I say nothing as I sign and date the form. I'm adding a minor. If I really hate it, I can remove it after my internship to Brazil.

I get tingly when I think those words. An internship to Brazil.

She takes the paper from me and enters the info into the computer. "Done. When you check your coursework requirement online, it will show what you need for both minors now."

"Thank you." I stand up, jubilant. "Thank you so much."

I have another minor.

And now I need to fill out the application for the teaching job.

☙❀❧

The application is more extensive than I expected. It asks for essays like a college application does, but then it also wants references, like a job application. I send out requests to a few professors and focus on my studies.

By Wednesday I feel like I'm going to crash from exhaustion. I make a conscious decision to sleep through my alarm and spend the morning at home. I miss basketball and English and Portuguese and I feel great. There's something deliciously wonderful about being home when I'm supposed to be in school.

Thursday I attempt to do it again. It's a different set of classes, so it's not like I'll be missing two days in a row. But Camila comes in and wakes me up.

"Nope, you're not doing this," she says, pulling back my blankets and sitting me up. "You don't get to start sleeping through classes."

"It's one day," I say, pushing her away. "I'm so tired."

"This is day two. And if you make this a habit, you'll be doing it every day. You'll fail your classes and lose your scholarship and drop out of school. Is that what you want?"

She paints a dismal picture of my future. I let her drag me to the carpet.

I grumble the whole walk to school. "I've already missed my geography class. You could have let me sleep more."

She ignores me. "Let's go study. Get your head on."

We settle at a table in the cafeteria. I check my email and see two professors sent me letters of recommendation. I work on the internship application while she studies.

We've been there five minutes when Iris comes up and settles down beside us.

"Hey, you guys!" she says. "You don't usually study here."

Abby comes along behind her. "Hey, it's a roommate party!"

I perk up with all of them around me. We whisper for a bit before quieting down and settling into our tasks.

Camila's right. I can't slack off now.

I get an email from Alliances Abroad Thursday afternoon.

We received your application to teach through our program and we'd love to talk to you more about this! Please select one of the time slots below for a phone interview.

Oh my gosh. They have my application.

This is happening.

All the time slots are in the morning. I select one that's in between classes and program their number into my phone.

When the calls comes after my Portuguese class the next day, I think I'm going to be sick. I find a quiet hallway and settle down on the ground.

I hope I can wow them.

"Hello?" I say, taking the phone call from my spot on the cold linoleum.

"Hi, is this Cassandra?" a male voice says on the other end.

"Yes, this is her." Is that correct grammar? I can never remember. I shouldn't have said anything at all. Now they're going to think I don't speak English!

"This is Travis from Alliances Abroad. We got your application and wanted to go over it with you! First of all, can you tell me about yourself?"

I take a deep breath and try to think instead of getting nervous. "Well, I'm in college. I love languages and learning, and I enjoy teaching and spending time with kids."

"We usually only take people with a bachelor's degree. Tell me about your education."

I'm prepared for this question. "I totally understand that. I don't have a degree yet, but if your only educational requirement is a degree, I'm more qualified than a lot of your candidates. I'm studying English, but I'm also minoring in Portuguese and Teaching English as a Second Language, so I have more training than someone who finishes a degree in history or biology." I'm thrilled I can plug my new minor in there.

"Excellent. That's very good. It makes you qualified. Did you choose Brazil because of the Portuguese minor?"

"Yes, I love Brazil!" My nervousness goes away as I warm to this subject. "I spent several weeks down there this past summer and a few years ago. I would love to go back and learn more about the country, as well as improve my Portuguese."

"We should be able to accommodate that. We have several schools in Brazil."

"I have one request about that." I take a breath because it makes me nervous to ask for things. "I don't want to be placed in Recife."

I've been thinking about this. I can't risk seeing Tiago. Our separation must be permanent. I can't run into him or be anywhere near him.

"Not a problem, we don't have any schools near there."

"Great." I exhale, relieved not to have to worry about that.

"I'm sure you saw it on our website, but let me tell you a bit more about how our program works. We'll place you with a host family, usually one of the students' families from the school or the school principal. You get paid two hundred dollars a month per class, so it's not a lot of money, but in Brazil that money stretches pretty far. You pay your own transportation, any sightseeing in the country, and eating outside the home. How does that sound?"

"Perfect." It's the only word I have for this. I'm giddy.

"Great! I'll pass this application on to corporate, and if you're selected, we'll reach out to give you more details so you can make your travel arrangements."

If I'm selected. "How long until I know?" I'm crossing my fingers and my toes. I can't sit with this anticipation for too long.

"I'd say a week, two at the most."

Two weeks.

I can wait that long.

⊙↝⚜↝⊙

For the first week after the interview, I check my email daily, hoping for something.

I have to sign up for classes for winter semester at the start of November, and I choose them all with the idea that I might not be here. Alliances Abroad could get back to me and tell me that I'm starting in January.

I make sure to add the intro classes for my new minor.

When another week goes by without hearing from them, my hopes deflate. What if they don't choose me after all? Now that I've picked the TESOL minor, I'm required to do an internship. I could check the local high school . . . but I want to live out of the country.

I spend an hour at work Googling teaching positions abroad. There are lots of programs that do this, but the requirements all differ, the length of time differs, they are not in Brazil, and most of them want a lot of money without offering anything in return.

Alliances Abroad is my best option.

I stop searching and tell myself to be patient.

CHAPTER SIXTY-SIX

Oncoming Winter

Harper texts me while I'm still at work.

H: give me a call. Got something to tell you.

Me: OK

I want to text her again and needle the news out of her. What can she possibly have to say that she wants me to call about? Last year she called to tell me Riley was pregnant. But Riley's married now, so while interesting, it wouldn't be the juicy gossip it was before.

Harper can't be pregnant. There's no way.

I'm so curious.

I call her when I get off work, as I'm walking to the library. My hands are freezing, but I brave the cold with one hand only, holding it close to my ear and burying it in my hair to try and keep it warm.

"Hello?" she answers.

"Hey!" I say. "What's up? Good to hear from you!"

Harper is my best friend. But we only get to hang out and be close when I'm home because I'm absolutely terrible at keeping in touch. I don't do phone calls, I'm bad at texting, and the only person I write is Owen.

Because he's Owen.

"Good to hear from you too!" she says. "What's new?"

I want to skip the small talk and get to whatever she has to say. But we have to do this dance first. "Just school. Wrapping up fall semester. I might do a study abroad program later. I'm feeling the need to travel, to go somewhere and do something."

"Oh, that's exciting! Any idea where?"

Brazil. But I don't tell her. My friends in Arkansas gave me a lot of flack about seeing Tiago when I went back last time, and I don't want to explain how it's not about him and have her not believe me. "Not sure yet. I'm still waiting to see if I get in the program."

"Let me know! I'll have to enjoy it through you. I don't want to go anywhere besides here. Maybe Hawaii one day."

"Yeah, that would be fun," I agree.

And then I don't say anything else because I don't want to make small talk. I want to know what's on her mind.

"Well . . ." she says.

"What's going on?" I say, encouraging her. "Something happening?"

"Actually. . . yes. I'm getting married."

I stop walking, a gasp halfway out of my throat. "You are?"

How is this possible?

"Yep." She laughs, sounding delighted by my reaction.

"But when? How? I didn't know you're dating anyone!"

"I met him a few months ago. September. And it's fallen together. He's perfect for me."

No. Way. September! "Two months, Harper! Isn't it fast? Are you pregnant?"

"No!" She starts laughing. "No, I'm not." She lowers her voice. "I'm still a virgin. We're waiting."

I'm astounded. "But how can you know he's the one? It's hardly any time!"

"How long did it take you to fall in love with Owen?"

It's a painful question. It sobers me. I think on it a half a second. "Two months." I know what she's saying without saying. If I could choose right now who I was going to spend the rest of my life with, it would be Owen. And I knew that within a matter of weeks.

"So I just know. He's the one."

"When's the wedding?" I'm still reeling. I'm excited for her, I think, but I feel like I'm jogging behind, trying to catch my breath while I watch her sprint across the finish line.

"May. I want you to be one of my bridesmaids."

"You do?" I squeal. I've reached the intersection and I pause at the light, waiting for the walk signal.

"Will you? You can get fitted for the dress when you're out here over Christmas. And you'll be home for the wedding, right? Your semester ends before then, doesn't it?"

This changes things. I can't go to Brazil on a six-month internship next semester if I need to be in Arkansas for Harper's wedding.

But it's Harper. It's her wedding. I'll do it.

"Yes," I say. "Of course I will. I'm honored."

"Yay! I'm so glad!"

"Tell me more about him." I enter the library atrium, trying to visualize this guy in my mind. "What's his name? How did you meet? What's he look like? Why didn't you tell me sooner?"

She launches into a description and keeps me occupied as I get on the elevator and head to the fifth floor.

"I'll send you pictures, okay? And the exact date. Come out a few days early, if you can."

"I'm so excited for you, Harper!" My mind is catching up. I feel a reluctance to give my approval to a boy I haven't met yet, but she sounds happy. "I can't believe you're getting married!"

She sighs. "I'll be twenty. I always thought I'd be married by nineteen, but my birthday's in a week. We don't want to rush things."

"No more than you already are," I agree.

She laughs. "Wait until it's your turn, Cassandra. I bet you get married super fast, and then I'll be laughing in your face."

"Right." Marriage feels so out of reach. I can't picture it at all.

"Okay, thanks for calling me back! I'll talk to you soon!"

We hang up, and I re-imagine my future. I'll stay here winter semester because I need to be here for Harper. If I'm accepted to the teaching program, I'll ask to start next fall.

I start to feel a picture of my life coming together.

⌒〜✾〜⌒

I stay at the library browsing through different books by Thomas Hardy. He has several, and I want to read them all. I take two from the shelf and go back to my table and start reading.

Though he's engaging, Hardy is not the easiest to read. The nineteenth-century English vernacular differs substantially from my own. I take notes as I write, logging quotes and ideas in my computer for ease of reference later. It's after nine when I finally decide to pack it up and go home, and that's mostly because I'm starving.

Outside it's snowing. I stop in the quad and spread my arms, then lift my face to the gentle freezing droplets. It's the first snow of the season. I'm not dressed for it, wearing only a thick sweater and tennis shoes, but I don't care. By the time I get home twenty minutes later, my body heat is up from the walk.

"There you are!" Iris says when I come in. "You've been staying late on campus. I made you dinner."

"You did?" I sit gratefully, plopping my backpack beside me as she places a bowl of rice and fried chicken and onions in front of me. Still warm. "It's snowing out there."

"I know. We saw it from the balcony."

Lauren's watching TV and munching on a pizza. Camila sits at the table sipping on a glass of water while she reads a book.

"Where's Abby?" I ask, digging into the food.

"She's out on a date."

"With Thomas?"

Iris shakes her head. "Some guy named Levi. I think she gave up on Thomas."

"I hope Levi likes her."

"Yeah, she deserves someone nice."

There's a knock on the door, and Iris answers it. "Thomas! Did you hear us talking about you?"

His hearty laugh fills the room, and he slips into the apartment. His face is flushed from the cold outside. "All good things, I'm sure."

"Of course. Food?" Iris offers the rice.

"Nah, I came to check on the fish."

I giggle as he goes over to the tank and looks down on them. Then he nods and comes back.

"Yep. Still there."

"I'm thinking about buying another," I say. "A small one. I can fit ten fish in there."

"You need a bright red one."

"Yeah. I do."

He settles down at the table across from me. "How are you doing? You don't seem as down lately."

"I'm doing better, I think." I dig at the last of the rice kernels in my bowl. "I'm still hoping to get to Brazil on the teaching internship. But I haven't heard anything back yet."

"Will they let you know either way?" Camila asks.

"I hope so."

"Give them until December," Thomas says. "If you haven't heard anything by then, call them."

"Good plan." I take my bowl to the sink and grab my backpack. My eyes are already heavy with the need to sleep, but I haven't gotten through my assignments yet. "Gotta go read a little more Thomas Hardy. See you guys later!"

CHAPTER SIXTY-SEVEN

Reservations

I bomb my second biology test.

I stare at the **74%** slashed across the front of my paper, disbelieving. I read all the material, I take notes, I study—I feel like I know what we're talking about in class. So how am I doing so poorly?

I miss a call from Stirling while I'm in class and call him back as I'm leaving.

"Want to get a bite to eat?" he asks.

"I'm just leaving campus," I say. "And I'm beat." Discouraged, too. "We can go somewhere by my apartment."

"Want me to pick you up?"

"Yes." I'll never say no to a ride home.

Stirling is waiting for me at the bottom of campus when I get there.

"What's wrong?" he asks as I climb in.

"Oh." I sigh. "I can't seem to get above a C in this stupid biology class."

"Biology is a hard class. Most people struggle in it."

"I know!" I slap my palm against the dashboard. "That's why I'm taking environmental biology instead of regular biology. I was trying to game the system!"

"Oh." Stirling glances at me, looking mildly amused. "Yeah, then, I don't know what your problem is."

"Shut up," I growl at him.

It's hard to take my grade seriously when someone is making fun of me, though.

Stirling drives us to Taco Bell, and I order a bowl of pinto beans and a seven-layer burrito—practically comfort food for me. I think I lived off Taco Bell in high school.

Of course, Stirling doesn't let me pay for my five-dollar meal.

"Stirling," I protest.

He waves me off. "It's nothing. Pretend like I'm paying you to hang out with me."

In the end, I let him. My budget is tight enough that spending five dollars frivolously on Taco Bell feels like I gouged my grocery budget by twenty percent.

That's only a slight exaggeration.

But Stirling doesn't take me home. Instead, he drives us to a canyon parking lot. The path to hike the Y is here, along with a few other trails that meander through the canyon and around the mountain. He gets out and walks toward the pavilion. I close my car door and shove my hands in my pockets as I join him.

"So, what else is new?" he asks. "Other than you failing biology."

"My best friend is getting married."

"That's pretty huge. How are you feeling about it?"

"All kinds of confused," I admit, venting to him like I can't to anyone else. "I feel like she's so young, she can't possibly be ready to make this kind of decision. She barely knows him. And I don't know him, so I have no idea if he's good for her or not."

"It sounds like you're basing a lot of your feelings off yourself."

"Meaning?"

"Meaning, you're taking it personally. You haven't met him, so you don't want her to marry him."

"Partly. But I could meet him and not like him and still not want her to marry him."

"Do you think it would be easy for him to win your approval?"

My mind scrolls through all the guys I've seen Harper date. "It's not likely. But I don't think that's because I'm a harsh judge. She just hasn't met someone amazing yet."

"Maybe this is him."

"I doubt it."

"Because you weren't there to officiate?"

"No, it's just—" I trail off. "I doubt there's anyone good enough..."

He might be right.

"And let's talk about you thinking she's too young to get married. How old is she?"

"Nineteen. She'll be twenty by then."

"That's a respectable age for marriage. People have been doing it for centuries."

"Yes, I know, but statistics show that people who get married before the age of twenty-two have a higher chance of getting divorced."

"So you're worried about her getting a divorce?"

"I just think it's a bad idea. I don't know him, and she's young."

"I think what you really feel is disdain because you would never make a decision like that."

"No!" I protest. "I don't expect people to make the same choices for their lives that I make for mine."

"Are you sure? Because I think if you were excited to get married right now, your attitude toward her marriage would be different. But marriage, for you, comes with all kinds of anxiety and fear."

Again, I have to think about his words.

"My decision is based on research and logic," I argue, "a sound understanding that should be applicable to everyone."

"Maybe. But not all people are the same. There might be someone who thinks they shouldn't get married until they're done with college, have a stable job, and are at least thirty. And if you got married before that, they'd feel strongly that you were making a mistake."

But Harper is making a mistake, I want to say.

I don't—because it fits right into what he's saying.

I let out a slow breath. "I can try to put my personal expectations aside, be happy for her, and trust that she's making the right decision for her life."

"Bam." Stirling holds his fist out to me. "That's what it's about. Let people live their own lives and assume they know what they're doing." He pauses. "Unless, when you meet this dude, there are some really obvious red flags. Then you speak up."

I laugh at that.

I'll be happy for Harper and trust her decision—until evidence proves otherwise.

⊙━━✦━━⊙

"I got an interesting phone call last night," Iris says the next morning.

I glance at her from where I'm putting my sandwich together. "Yeah? What was it?"

It's just the two of us. Camila is at cross-country practice, Lauren already left for school, and Abby hasn't gotten up yet.

As if on cue, Abby appears in the kitchen, her backpack slung over one shoulder. She joins me at the counter, pulling down a packet of oatmeal and emptying it into a bowl.

"It was Layne's mom," Iris continues.

"Layne's mom?" I ask, slapping cheese, meat, and mayonnaise onto one slice of bread before squishing it next to another. I shove the whole sandwich into a baggie. "That's weird. Is Layne okay?"

"It was kind of weird, but it gets weirder."

Abby and I both turn to her, giving her our full attention now.

"She wants us to come to her house for Thanksgiving."

My eyebrows shoot so high they might disappear into my hairline. "We don't know her."

"Apparently, she's really lonely without Layne and was looking forward to Thanksgiving. She begged us to come stay with her—all of us."

I glance at Abby, who says. "Shoot. I was gonna go home. It's right around the corner."

"What did you say?" I ask Iris.

"That I would ask you guys. But I'm not going home to Canada, so it could be fun."

"I don't have anywhere to go either," I say. "Sure. I'll go."

"Well, I want to go if y'all are going," Abby says.

"I'll talk to my mom about it, see what she says," Iris says.

It could be fun. We haven't had a big adventure since school started.

I leave for campus shortly after. I'm supposed to give a presentation in my English class in a few hours on Thomas Hardy, but I haven't written it yet. I open my laptop at my usual spot on the fifth floor of the library and wonder how I can make this entertaining.

I recall a skit I once saw where the narrator selected two people to act out a script they hadn't seen beforehand. It was hilarious and seems simple enough to replicate.

I get to work writing a script—a somewhat biographical take on Thomas Hardy. My cast consists of one person, but I include action moments like reading a newspaper for inspiration and tapping his head when he gets an idea.

It only takes me half an hour to write it. I print it off at the computer lab and head to class. I start to get nervous when the students ahead of me present slideshows with beautiful visual aids, but I remind myself to lean into my strengths—writing.

When it's my turn, I step to the front of the class. "I need a volunteer to be my main character."

Several hands shoot up, and I pick a tall guy with glasses. As he joins me, I explain, "You are Thomas Hardy. I'll narrate your life, and you'll act out everything I say. Got it?"

He nods, and I begin.

It's immediately a riot. His movements lag a second behind my words, and sometimes he doesn't catch everything.

"When Hardy got the news about his sister, he sat down at a table and put his head in his hand," I say.

The guy quickly pulls out a chair and sits behind a desk, which is impressive quick thinking. But he forgets the last part.

"And put his head in his hand," I add in an impatient tone.

"Oh, right," he says, then dramatically tugs on his hair by the roots.

The class erupts in laughter. It's perfect.

I finish with a brief summary of Hardy's most famous works. The class claps when I sit down, and the professor praises my creativity.

I smile, trying not to look too pleased with myself. That was too easy.

I have to get through my ballet class before work. I sometimes wish ballet were my calling, but I know it's not. I'm more likely to memorize the French terminology than to execute a perfect plié.

When I arrive at the office, my supervisor greets me.

"We have a meeting this afternoon and will be closing the office early," Jan tells me and my coworker. Our shifts overlap by about an hour. "You can leave now, Christina. Cassandra, I'll need you until three."

Until three? That's only two hours.

I don't have to check my watch to know that's not good. An extra two hours would mean an extra twenty bucks, which makes a big difference by the end of the week—especially now that we're planning a road trip to California for Thanksgiving.

I force a smile and nod. "Okay."

I try to find the bright side. I get extra time at the library tonight.

I spend that time studying geography and biology. I'm determined to ace the next test. I take notes, memorize formulas, and study sample questions.

I know the material. I *thought* I knew it last time, too.

When I finally pack up and begin the twenty-minute walk home, the air is cold, a sure sign that fall is settling in. I push open the apartment door and find my roommates gathered around the kitchen table, talking excitedly. I drop my backpack on the couch before heading into the kitchen to grab ingredients for dinner.

"What's for dinner?" Camila asks. She gives me extra grocery money, and in return, I cook for both of us.

"Meatballs and noodles," I say, popping open a cookbook and gathering ingredients.

"We were talking about Thanksgiving," Iris says.

"I'm game to go to California," Camila says. "Sounds like fun."

I glance at her, perking up. "Really? That means all of us—" I cut myself off and frown. Lauren isn't here. I constantly forget we have a fifth roommate. "What about

Lauren?"

Iris and Abby exchange a look before Abby shrugs.

"You room with her," she says. "You should invite her."

Why does this always fall on me?

CHAPTER SIXTY-EIGHT

It's Not the Same

In the end, Lauren thanks me for inviting her, but she's spending Thanksgiving with her family.

I'm quietly relieved but don't express it.

The evening of the last day of school, I go with Abby to Iris's string concert, and I'm blown away by how talented she is. One moment, she's on the violin, the next, the viola, and then she picks up the cello like it's second nature.

When we get home, I make my mom's cheeseballs while Abby regales us with a disaster story from her last date. She has us all in stitches with laughter.

"So you're never going out with him again?" Iris says.

"No, I actually liked him!" Abby says, and we laugh harder.

I put the cheeseballs in the fridge to firm up before our drive to California. Then I head to my bedroom to pack.

❦

I'm exhausted, barely staying awake while studying, so when one o'clock rolls around, I shove my books aside and head to the stadium for the football game.

It's freezing, so I take my car. But once seated in the bleachers, my jacket and hat aren't enough. But then Abby shows up with Camila, Iris, a huge thermos of hot chocolate, and two blankets. We huddle together, cheering for the game, and though the cold bites at my skin, I feel warmth settle in my chest.

We win. I drive us home, and on the way back to the apartment, we stop at the mailbox. Abby flips through the mail as I pull into the parking lot behind our building and turn off the car.

She sorts through the envelopes, then hands me my pile. "Two letters," she says.

"From who?" I ask.

"I didn't look."

I glance down and immediately scan for return addresses. One is from someone I don't know in Chicago. The other is from Owen.

My heart skips. It's been weeks since I wrote back, and I was starting to wonder if I'd ever hear from him again. I hesitate, torn between opening the letter right away and waiting.

By the time I step out of the car, the others are already walking inside, but I'm the first one to the apartment. It's unlocked—Lauren must be home. No one says anything as I push the door open and head straight to my bedroom.

They probably know who the letter is from.

I sit on my bed and open the letter from the unknown sender first. It's from a kid named Dale in Seattle, Washington. He's friendly, complimentary, says Owen speaks highly of me—so I must be awesome.

He talks about missing home, family, and friends. He says he'd love to hear from me if I'd be willing to write back.

I haven't written to many missionaries, but I imagine this is common. They must get lonely. They probably crave connection, even from strangers. It doesn't mean anything that he wants to talk to me.

I set Dale's letter aside and pick up Owen's with trembling fingers. I remind myself that we broke up months ago. *Nine months.*

I slide open the envelope and pull out a single sheet of paper.

Hey Cassandra!

Thanks for writing. It always makes my day to know you took time out of your busy schedule to send me a note.

I hope classes are still going well. Any favorite subjects? Do you still like your roommates? I know you're going to do great at anything you try—you're the kind of person who shines.

Things are really busy here. The holiday season is coming up, and I'm astounded by how many people have so little. It's especially obvious this time of year. While we're at home, reveling in family, friends, and food, others are painfully aware of how much they lack. With the colder weather coming in, we're busier than ever—ministering to those around us, trying to bring cheer, joy, and food to those who don't have it.

I'm exhausted all the time. I'm weary. Bone-weary. Soul-weary. I wish I could fix everything. I'm constantly humbled, constantly ashamed of how much I've taken my life for granted.

Anyway.

I'm sorry this is so short, but I don't have a lot of time today. Write whenever you can.

I love you.

Owen

I stare at the paper, analyzing every word. It's shorter than usual, but maybe he really is busy.

I don't think that's it.

I think he's finally moved past me. Not just *wanting* to move past me—he has.

And yet... those last words.

I love you.

He probably does. He probably always will. Like I love him.

But it's not the same.

⚬⟋⟋⟍⟍⚬

The day before we begin our drive to California, the forecast for Colorado starts calling for snow.

I don't think much of it, but Camila and Abby both look concerned.

"Yes, Dad, we're taking precautions," Camila says into the phone. I glance up from my fish tank, giving the fish their last meal before we leave.

She hangs up and sighs. "My dad is really worried about us going."

"We'll be fine," Abby says. "The snow isn't supposed to hit until we're already out of Colorado."

"It's the Tahoe area he's worried about," Camila replies. "If the storm hits there, we'll be stuck."

"The Tahoe area?" I repeat. I'm not from around here, so I don't know what lies between us and California. "I thought the only concern was the mountain pass between here and Utah."

"No, the Tahoe pass might be worse because it's not an interstate," Camila explains. "My dad wants us to get chains."

I wrinkle my nose. "Chains?"

"For your tires," Iris chimes in, finally joining the conversation.

"You won't need them," Abby says. "We drive in snow all the time without them."

"But new snow?" Camila counters. "Deep snow? Her car doesn't have snow tires!"

"We don't use chains in Canada," Iris says.

"But I bet you have snow tires," Camila points out.

They're using terminology that means nothing to me. "So... should I be worried?"

"Yes," Camila says firmly.

"We've seen you drive in snow," Abby adds, smirking.

I level a glare at her. "Whose side are you on?"

That makes her laugh.

"I'll do whatever you guys think I need to do," I say. "I'm not used to driving in winter weather, and I know nothing about mountains. All I know is it's a twelve-hour drive, and we're leaving tomorrow at four in the morning."

"Let's get chains," Camila says. "Just to be safe."

I nod. "Where do we get them?"

"Any Walmart should have them," Abby says.

"So now we need to leave even earlier to make time for a stop," I mutter, pulling up the Walmart website to check if they have chains in stock.

A hundred and twenty dollars.

"Guys, chains are expensive," I say, lifting my eyes to my roommates. "Are we sure we need them?"

They exchange looks but don't say anything. I wait for someone to offer to split the cost, but when no one does, I say, "Maybe we can all chip in?"

"They're for your car," Iris says.

"And I'm only getting them for this trip. I'll probably never use them again," I say.

"That's fair," Camila say. "Cassandra is chauffeuring us to California. We can help pay for the chains."

"Yeah, that's fine," Abby says.

Iris doesn't say anything, and I can tell she's annoyed. But I don't need chains. And I definitely don't have that kind of money.

We gather our things in the living room so we can load up quickly in the morning. Our new departure time: three-thirty a.m.

Except, when morning comes, no one actually gets out of bed by 3:15. By the time we're fully awake and functioning, it's already four a.m. I'm cranky, tired, and a little snippy as I haul bags toward the door, telling everyone to hurry up.

It's freezing outside, the air crisp and dark. I shiver as I load my suitcase into the trunk, then start the car to warm it up.

Nobody else comes out.

I wait ten minutes. When there's still no sign of my roommates, I leave the car running and stomp back inside.

I find Iris and Camila in the kitchen, making sandwiches.

"Guys, it's four-thirty!" I snap. "We need to go!"

"We'll be glad for the food," Iris says. "This way, we won't have to stop and buy lunch."

She has a point, but I'm still itching to get on the road.

It's 4:45 by the time we finally pile into the car and pull out of the parking lot. I bite my tongue to keep from snapping at everyone. I do *not* want to get to California at nine p.m.

"It's fine," Camila says from the passenger seat, sensing my tension. "Even if it takes all day, we'll still get three full days in California before we have to drive home."

I exhale and loosen my grip on the steering wheel. *Be flexible.*

As we drive, my frustration fades. I head toward Walmart, about fifteen minutes away, but when we pull into the parking lot, everything is dark.

"Are they not open?" Abby asks, leaning forward.

"I thought Walmart was twenty-four/seven," I say, frowning.

Iris is already on her phone, looking it up. Then she groans. "They changed their hours after the pandemic! They don't open until six."

I glance at the clock on my dash. Barely five o'clock.

I'm not waiting an hour.

We sit in silence for a moment. Then I pull up my GPS and program our route.

"Well, I guess we'll have to pray for no snow."

As the route calculates, a red warning pops up above the mileage estimate.

Winter storm could affect route.

I stare at it for a second but say nothing.

I put the car into drive, and we pull away from Walmart, heading west.

CHAPTER SIXTY-NINE

Burning Rubber

I brace for the worst as we leave Colorado, but instead of dropping, the temperature rises. By the time we hit the Colorado-Utah border, it's in the low forties. We relax, taking turns driving, napping, and playing road games.

The hours fly by. By two in the afternoon, we've been driving for nine hours. Since we packed food and took minimal bathroom breaks, we're making great time.

Then we hit traffic as we near the Nevada-California border. We're only five hours from our destination, but as we approach a mountain pass, we're forced to slow down. Camila presses a button on her phone, and a robotic voice announces, "*Weather alert for your area. Low visibility and snowfall expected.*"

"Is that for us?" I ask.

"We're nearing the Tahoe area," she replies.

We exit the interstate and merge onto a winding mountain road. Snow begins to fall. We're not alone—there's a long line of slow-moving cars ahead of us. The snow isn't sticking yet, and I can still see fine as long as I don't go too fast.

Camila points at a side road. "They've already barricaded that one to through traffic."

I glance over and see a metal arm blocking the entrance. A little farther ahead, we pass a sign with lights that reads, *Chains required when lights are flashing.*

The lights are flashing.

Outside, the snowfall intensifies. It starts to stick to my windshield, and I crank the defroster to keep the glass warm. The car in front of me fishtails briefly before straightening out again. I press my lips together and grip the steering wheel tighter. Traffic slows even more as we try to leave enough space between us and the cars ahead.

"Should we put chains on?" Iris asks from the back.

"We didn't buy any," I say, my tone sharper than I intend. I'm more stressed than I thought.

No one responds. We keep climbing the mountain, the temperature on my dashboard steadily dropping. Other cars pull over at designated chain installation spots, and a surge of panic rises in the back of my neck. Why didn't we make more of an effort to get chains?

We creep forward, and I consider asking Camila to take over since she's from here and used to these roads. But stopping to switch drivers would be just as risky.

The GPS guides us higher up the mountain pass. My windshield wipers struggle to keep up with the thickening snow. The road is slick, and I slide once, my stomach dropping before I manage to steady the car.

"Talk about white-knuckling it," I mutter.

Camila chuckles. It's not much, but the humor is enough to make me loosen my grip slightly and relax my shoulders.

The switchback curves are brutal. I slide with every sharp turn. Ahead, a car suddenly loses control, veering into the opposite lane. A vehicle between us slams on its brakes and fishtails. I gently press my own brakes, heart pounding, while watching the car behind me in my rearview mirror to make sure they're not too close.

The out-of-control car manages to correct itself. The vehicle in front of me starts moving again, and before I come to a full stop, my lane is open.

No one says a word. I might've thought no one noticed, but I know our eyes are glued to the road ahead.

Finally, we begin to descend. I exhale. "That must've been the summit."

"I think so," Abby says.

Going down isn't any easier. Signs along the mountainside read *Stay in Low Gear*. I'm already riding the brakes the whole way down. I'm terrified of losing control and careening off the mountain. Nice and slow. Steady. Like the cars ahead and behind me.

The snow thins. Then, at last, the pavement turns back to blacktop.

I finally breathe easy again.

No one speaks for a few minutes as we exit the mountain pass. I merge onto the interstate, our journey to Sacramento continuing under clear blue skies. Slowly, I let out a breath.

"We did it," I say, feeling the weight lift off my shoulders. "And we only added half an hour to our time."

"We did it!" Abby echoes, and Camila and Iris cheer, throwing their hands up triumphantly.

I smile, shifting into the fast lane on the crowded interstate, riding the high of conquering a snowy mountain pass without wrecking my car.

Then—

A loud bang, like a gunshot, explodes around us.

My car jerks violently toward the median as I suddenly lose control of the wheel.

I manage to regain control of the car before we hit the median. The engine is still running, but all I can think is, *Get off the road. Get off the road. Get off the road.*

I have to cross three lanes of traffic. The car is shaking, bumping and listing sideways, but I flip on my turn signal and haul it over as safely as I can. The cars around me must realize something is wrong because they slow down and give me space.

Somehow, I make it to the shoulder.

I kill the engine, and all four of us climb out at the same time. I circle to the front, where the noise came from.

I've blown a tire.

It's shredded. I don't know how I made it to the shoulder in one piece. Scraps of rubber and exposed wire are wrapped around the axle.

"That's bad," Abby says.

"No kidding, Sherlock," Iris says.

"Can you change it?" Abby asks.

I stare in dismay at the wrecked tire, already calculating how much it'll cost to replace. "I can try."

"Let's get your spare," she says.

I pop the trunk, hoping Abby knows more than I do because I can't remember how to do this. We peel back the cover and pull out the spare. It's heavier than it looks, and the two of us stagger under its weight as we carry it to the front of the car.

"Where's the jack?" Camila asks.

I head back to retrieve it. Camila tucks it under the car. "Are you sure that's the right spot?" I ask.

"I think so. I've only watched someone do this."

I groan. I was hoping she had more experience than I do.

"Hang on, I'm looking it up," Abby says.

So, like a bunch of clueless dorks, we stand there while Abby Googles *how to change a tire.*

"Do you girls need help?"

I turn to see a young man standing outside his car on the access road beside us.

"Blew a tire," I say. "Trying to remember where the jack goes."

"Hang on. I can help you."

"I think we've got it," Iris says, apparently offended by his offer.

I'm relieved. I have my roadside assistance card in my wallet and am prepared to use it, but I'd rather not.

He gets back into his car and—drives away.

"What?" I exclaim. "Why's he leaving?"

"We should call Layne's mom and let her know we're delayed," Abby says.

"Good idea," I say, huffy that our savior vanished.

Camila makes the call just as headlights appear behind us. The young man from earlier pulls onto the shoulder and parks, and I realize he had to drive down the interstate the opposite direction before he could get back into the northbound lane and help us.

I feel guilty for misjudging him.

"What tools do you have?" he asks, crouching down to inspect our setup.

I point. "Jack's under the car, we have the spare, and we're about to remove the lug nuts." I feel proud for remembering the terminology—at least, I *think* I remembered it correctly. I probably still look like an idiot.

"Do you work on cars?" Iris asks as he slides onto his back under the car.

"Oh, I did—once upon a time, back in high school," he says, his voice muffled beneath the vehicle.

"Are you in college now?" she presses.

I can tell she's checking him out. I didn't take a good look at him earlier, but apparently, she did—or wants to.

"Yeah, I go to school up here at the local university. What about you girls?"

He jacks up the car and scoots back out.

"We go to school in Colorado," Camila says, her tone almost like a warning. "We're here for Thanksgiving. Visiting a friend."

He kneels by my shredded tire and starts removing the lug nuts. "Nice. The weather's better here than in Colorado."

I grunt, thinking of the snowstorm we just drove through. "That's for sure."

"What's your name?" Iris asks.

"Ian."

I glance at him properly this time—hazel eyes, light brown brows, and a complexion that matches his hair.

"You're our hero, Ian," I say.

He shrugs as he removes the wrecked tire and replaces it with the spare. "You probably could've done it without me."

I have my doubts.

He finishes tightening the lug nuts, removes the jack, and steps back to admire his work.

"Thank you so much," I say.

He holds up a hand. "Don't thank me yet. There's good news and bad news."

"What is it?" I ask.

"The good news is—the spare's on." He gestures to it. "The bad news is—you can't drive on it."

My stomach drops. I look at the tire. It's *flat*. So flat it's practically molded to the pavement.

"What do we do?" I ask, trying not to sound as close to hysteria as I feel.

"I wish I had air to fill it up for you, but I don't. You'll probably need a tow truck. They can take care of it."

I sigh and pull out my roadside assistance card. "Looks like I'm going to need this after all."

☙❦❧

In the end, we're only two hours late getting to Layne's house.

It's ten-thirty at night and pitch black outside when we finally pull into the driveway. Layne's mom, Diane, bursts out of the house, arms open, wrapping us in hugs and exclaiming over our harrowing journey.

We're exhausted but starving, and none of us complain when she sets boxes of chicken nuggets in front of us in the kitchen. As I stash my cheese balls in the fridge, I notice how bare it looks for a Thanksgiving meal.

Diane chatters excitedly about Layne's time in Guatemala, showing us pictures Layne never bothered to send. I smile and nod as I scroll through them, but one thought keeps nagging at me.

How can it be Thanksgiving without mashed potatoes?

"How can we help with the meal tomorrow?" I ask.

"Oh, no," she says, waving a hand. "We don't cook here. The food's catered. It'll arrive at eleven."

I raise my eyebrows. "Well, that's... nice."

No one says anything more about it, but twenty minutes later, when the four of us collapse in an exhausted heap across the bed and air mattresses in Layne's room, Iris mutters, "No wonder she burned the tablecloth when we first moved in."

I remember that incident. And a dozen more—Layne forgetting how to cook rice, not knowing when spaghetti was done, asking if she needed to drain ramen.

"I think Diane explains a lot about Layne," Abby says.

"Abby," Camila scolds, but I bury my face in her shoulder and giggle.

CHAPTER SEVENTY

Red Gate Bridge

The next morning, Diane's boyfriend, Josh, takes a look at my car.

"Yeah, you're lucky nothing else got damaged when your tire blew." He opens my trunk and whistles when he sees the shredded rubber. "You'll need to get a new one before you head back to Colorado."

"Really?" My heart sinks. I knew I needed a new tire, but I'd hoped to put it off a little longer.

"We'll stop by a tire shop tomorrow and get you set up. And you have chains, right?"

"No. The store was closed when we went to buy them."

Josh raises an eyebrow. "You drove through the Tahoe pass without chains?"

I nod, feeling like the most irresponsible college kid on the planet.

"Well, we're not sending you back without them. I'll show you how to put them on so you know what to do."

"Right."

We head back inside just as the food arrives, gathering around the kitchen island as Diane opens the various catered dishes. I eye them with suspicion—they don't look anything like the food my mom makes back home. Instead of creamy mashed potatoes, there's a rosemary-infused potato gratin. Instead of stuffing, there's quinoa salad with cranberries and almonds. The turkey is pre-sliced and covered in some kind of citrus glaze, and instead of pumpkin pie, there's a tray of assorted tarts.

It's fancy. It's well-prepared. But it's not *home*.

Still, in spite of how different it is, the food is delicious. And the warm weather is a welcome change. It feels strange being in someone else's house for the holiday, but my roommates and I make the best of it, spending most of the afternoon basking in the sunshine in the backyard. It's nearly sixty degrees, a far cry from the icy mountain pass we drove through yesterday.

"I think tomorrow we should go to San Francisco," Iris says, scrolling through her phone. "This is my first time in California, and I've *always* wanted to see the Golden Gate Bridge."

"And Chinatown!" Abby chimes in. "That's here too, isn't it?"

"It's only a couple of hours away," Iris says, glancing up at me. "You're the driver. Are you up for it?"

I feel a slight pulsing in my forehead. I'm not sure if it's exhaustion or the weight of my rapidly growing to-do list.

"Yeah, that should be fine. I still have to get new tires, though."

"We can do that first thing in the morning before we go anywhere," Camila says.

I nod, exhaling slowly.

This trip is turning out to be a lot more expensive than I planned.

The pulsing behind my temples increases.

⟳∼🙥∼⟲

"It'll be five-hundred-thirty-eight dollars for both tires, with tax."

I stare at the young man behind the counter of the auto repair shop. "Both tires? I only blew out one."

"Yeah, but if you only replace one of the front tires, you'll throw your alignment off. You'd have one tire that's worn down and a brand-new one, and that would end up costing you more in the long run. It's better to replace both. Plus, we have a deal where you get ten percent off when you buy two."

"Oh. Does the price you quoted already includes the ten percent off?" The headache that never quite went away yesterday is now pounding away at me with a vengeance.

My roommates stand a few feet behind me, muttering together and shooting me sympathetic looks.

I would much rather they open their wallets and hand me some cash.

"Yes, that includes the discount," the guy confirms.

He's so helpful.

"How much for one tire?" I ask.

"Three-hundred and forty-eight dollars, with tax."

I close my eyes and sigh, then pull out my credit card. "I'll take both."

"You also need an alignment and a new filter," he says, punching numbers into the machine.

"Some other day." I can't spend any more.

I watch him swipe my card and acknowledge that I'll have to carry a balance for a few months while I pay this off.

How frustrating.

"Cassandra." Iris beckons me over, and I step toward her.

"Look." She points to several boxes on the shelf. "We can get chains here."

May as well.

I turn back to the guy behind the counter. "Which set of chains will fit my tires?"

"Oh, let me see."

It turns out chains are more expensive in California, where they're not sold in high quantities. I sigh as we add another hundred and fifty dollars to my credit card.

I'm starting to regret this trip.

Twenty minutes later, my car is ready.

"The spare's back in the trunk," he says. "In case you need it again."

I nod and climb into the driver's seat. Heaven forbid.

325

The first thing I notice when we reach San Francisco is how steep the roads are. Iris has written down a few iconic streets to visit, directing me as I drive, and I'm astonished that anyone willingly drives up and down these roller coaster hills every day.

Then we head over to the wharf, and I spend twenty minutes circling before finally finding a metered parking spot that's open. At least Abby pays for that.

As soon as we step out of the car, the sounds and smells of the wharf greet us. Iris squeals in delight at the seagulls squawking overhead and the waves crashing against the pier. We walk through a market where artisans hawk their wares and pass a fishmonger decapitating live fish right in front of us. Abby wrinkles her nose.

"It smells so fishy," she says.

"It's supposed to have the best clam chowder in the U.S.," Camila says.

"Oh, yes!" Iris exclaims, glancing at her phone again. "I found a restaurant that serves it. We *have* to go! Right after we visit the shops along the wharf."

That's decided.

At the end of the wharf, we find sea lions basking in the sunshine. I can't tell the difference between them and a pile of rocks—until they start moving. They've got flippers for hands, whiskers on their faces, and bark and snap at each other as they roll in and out of the water.

"I want to pet one," I say.

Iris grabs my arm like she thinks I'm about to dive straight into the chaos. "Don't! They're *dangerous*."

I give her a look that's halfway between amusement and annoyance. "I'm not *that* stupid."

We wander back along the wharf, admiring the handwoven cover-ups and collected shells, but none of us buys anything. We're saving our money for food.

"There's Alcatraz!" Iris suddenly jumps up and down, pointing at an island with a massive fortress covering most of it.

"Alcatraz?" I squint. "I've heard of that. Isn't it, like, a prison?"

Iris nods excitedly. "They thought no one could ever escape from it, but then some people did! Maybe we can do a tour!"

"So it's not still a prison?" Abby asks.

Iris shakes her head, already opening her web browser. "No, now it's a museum. Dang it." She makes a face. "You have to reserve a time to go, and the next available slot isn't until tonight."

I lean over her shoulder and take a look—mostly to check the prices.

"Sixty dollars *per person*?" I say. "Am I the only one here who's poor?"

Iris looks at me with wide eyes. "But it's *Alcatraz*!"

"I don't care if it's for Alcatraz, I don't have sixty dollars," I say flatly, which makes Abby laugh.

"What if it were a zombie apocalypse and we *had* to get to Alcatraz to hide?" she teases.

"If sixty dollars is the only thing standing between my salvation and death, then I'll fork over the sixty bucks," I say. "But who's going to be collecting money in a zombie apocalypse anyway? It's all gonna be about how well you can use a weapon and whether you still have skin on your face."

"I love how much thought you've put into this." Abby loops her arm through mine, and we make our way off the wharf toward the restaurants along the shore.

Iris has her heart set on an upscale cafe, but I veto it because I have all of eighteen stupid dollars to my name. So we go to a different place a few buildings down, and my bowl of soup is only eight bucks.

We're just settling in at our table when I hear a familiar voice behind me.

"Well, if it isn't Cassandra Jones."

I turn, startled, and then groan when I see my cousin Jordan grinning down at me. "You've got to be kidding me."

Jordan laughs and slaps a hand on my shoulder before plopping down in the empty chair next to Camila. "Nice to see you too, Cassie."

"What are you doing here?" I ask, still in disbelief.

"Thanksgiving break," he says, like it's obvious. "Came out to see a friend. What about you?"

"Road trip."

Jordan shifts his full attention to Camila. "And here I thought San Francisco couldn't get any better."

I roll my eyes. "Oh, please." I wonder if any romantic feelings linger between them. They stopped dating after last semester because he was leaving, but now he's still here. What does that mean for them?

Camila smiles, tilting her head slightly. "Smooth."

"Only when it counts," Jordan says.

The way they're looking at each other answers my question. I focus on my spoon and pretend I don't hear them continue their little back-and-forth while my other roommates exchange amused looks.

As we step outside, we encounter a man covered entirely in bronze paint. He holds perfectly still like a statue, and I circle him twice, impressed by his ability to stay frozen. Then, suddenly, he reaches out and touches my hair.

I yelp in surprise, making my roommates burst into laughter. We take pictures with him, and I manage to dig out a few bills to drop in the box next to him before we continue toward the bridge.

I study it as we get closer.

"We've been swindled," I announce.

Camila gives me a sideways look. "Excuse me?"

I shake my head. "Played for fools. This whole time."

"What are you talking about?" Abby asks.

I grab Camila's arm and point at the bridge. "*Look.*"

"What is it?" Iris says.

"It's *red.*"

Abby looks again at the bridge. "So it is."

I throw my hands in the air. "And this whole time they've been calling it the Golden Gate Bridge! How could they lie to us like that?"

Iris is giggling, Abby can't stop laughing, and Camila is shaking her head.

"You're such a riot," Abby says. "Yes. They tricked us."

Jordan chuckles beside me. "Cassandra, you are never living this down."
I don't tell them I'm halfway serious.
How was I supposed to know the bridge was red?

CHAPTER SEVENTY-ONE

Deceptive Beauty

Jordan leaves us to meet up with his friend when we head to Chinatown for dinner. I want to eat at a food stand, but Abby hesitates, saying it smells fishy.

"What do you expect? It's San Francisco," Iris says, clearly irate.

We walk through the narrow streets of Chinatown, red lanterns hanging overhead, food hawkers on every corner. The air is thick with the scent of seafood—some of it fresh, some of it smelling like it came from the ocean a few days ago. The sidewalks are more crowded than the streets, and I hang onto Abby's belt loop so I don't lose her in the chaos.

Everyone around me is my height or shorter, and I wonder if this is how tall people feel all the time.

We don't stay long. Iris is disappointed—she wanted to eat at an authentic Chinese restaurant—but the rest of us feel like tourists in a foreign land. So, we head back to my car to find something to eat along the wharf instead.

Here, at least, the seafood smells fresher—briny and wet, like the ocean itself, not like something that's been sitting out too long.

"What should we do tomorrow?" Abby asks as we share a dish of fried calamari.

"What if we went to the beach?" Camila suggests. "There's ocean all around us."

I clap my hands, delighted. "Yes! I love the ocean."

There's nothing more peaceful, nothing more majestic. The waves crashing against the shore, the vastness of it—I haven't been to the ocean since Brazil.

That feels like a lifetime ago.

I wonder if that company will ever get back to me, but I remember what Thomas said. We agreed to wait until December before I reach out again.

But I can't shake this horrible sinking feeling that it's not going to work out.

༄

We drive down to Monterrey in the morning so we can spend the day on the beach. I'm picturing the golden-white sands of Brazil, the sparkling turquoise ocean, the waving palm trees with a never-ending expanse of blue sky.

329

"Here," Iris says, directing me to a parking lot on a hill surrounded by giant rocks. "The beach is over that rise."

I hop out of the car, and the first thing I notice is the wind. It whips through my short hair, whispering around my neck and blowing up around my ears. I shiver and pull my striped sweater closer to my skin. Maybe I should have worn a jacket.

But I'm at the beach.

I didn't consider it could be cold.

"Come on!" Iris hops over the rocks and squeals. "Look! I see the ocean!"

My excitement rises, and I climb over the boulders to join her.

Down the studded, rocky hillside, blueish water rolls lazily into a cove. It deposits golden strands of weeds along the shore.

"That's it?" I try to curb the disappointment from my tone.

Iris stands beside me and strikes poses while she takes selfies. Camila and Abby carefully amble down to the shore, sliding on the rocks and clinging to the hillside. I head down after them, longing for the warmth of Brazil, the sunny skies, the roaring ocean.

As if hearing my desire, a large wave thunders toward us. It crashes against the boulders and sprays us with icy sea water, and we shriek. I gasp and spew sea brine from my mouth, my wet hair falling in my face. Another blast of wind follows behind it, combing through my hair and biting through my damp clothing.

Yuck.

"Let's look for shells!" Iris says, climbing down to join us. The water didn't get her, and she's oblivious to my discomfort.

"Sounds fun," Abby says, and together they begin picking up rocks and searching for beautiful discarded sea trash.

I remember examining tiny air tunnels in the sand and picking up shells filled with itty bitty hermit crabs.

I usually don't allow myself to think of Tiago, the boy who I loved and discarded as readily as the ocean spits up unwanted objects, but I think of him now. I had to let him go, and I don't regret that decision for our lives. But I treasure the memories we share, and I hope he's well.

I climb over the boulders and smile for pictures, then search for shells. I pocket a few pretty ones for my fish tank.

I get situated at the top of a boulder and peer out over the horizon. From here I can see the curvature of the earth, and it's stunning. It reminds me of infinity and humbles me at the same time. I close my eyes, feeling the sun's rays as it begins its descent toward the water, ready to disappear for the night. Seagulls cry in the distance, probably looking for the crusts of bread we left after we ate. I inhale, and there's something invigorating about the briny, fishy scent filling the air on all sides of me.

A loud thunderous roar fills my ears, and I open my eyes in time to see a giant wave billowing over my head.

Camila shouts my name, and Abby yells, but the wave crashes over me and knocks me off the rock before I can react. I'm sucked down into the pool of water, scratching my skin and banging my back against smaller boulders. I manage to get my feet under me and come up sputtering, gasping, just as Camila reaches me.

"Oh, Cassandra!" she says, half laughing, half anxious. She grabs me and hugs me and then slops through the water with me in tow.

"I'll get a towel," Abby says. At least we were smart enough to bring some. Mostly because we thought it might be warm enough to go swimming.

I stand on the rocks shivering and shaking, sopping wet, while she towels me off and Iris gives a live play-by-play of my fall into the water.

"Did you at least get it on video?" I ask, my teeth chattering. I wrap the towel around me.

"No," Iris says, looking crestfallen. "I can take a picture though."

"No thanks." I look back over the water, and feelings of misgiving stir in my chest. "I'm ready to go now."

No one argues with me. The fact that I'm soaked to the bone and have the car probably means I get the final say.

⁕

It's a long drive back to Colorado, so we plan to leave at the break of dawn. But when morning comes, we're tired and don't manage to drag ourselves out the door until six a.m. Josh made me practice putting on chains last night in the garage, and they're rolled up in my trunk, ready to be put to use should we hit snow.

There's no snow in the forecast.

My new tires work as expected, and Camila takes a turn driving so I can study for my biology test next week. I go through flashcards, highlight sections in the book, and answer all the questions. I'm determined to get an A on this test.

By the time I put the book away three hours from home, I'm confident the worst I'll do is an A-.

It's a little after ten p.m. when we get back to our apartment. There's no food in the house, and we're starving but too tired to get anything.

I check on my fish and breathe a prayer of gratitude that they're all alive. The fishtank is clean. The sucker fish are doing their job.

I rinse the new shells I collected from the beach with soap and water before depositing them in strategic locations around the tank. I take a moment to admire how beautiful it is before heading to bed.

⁕

I take my biology test Tuesday, along with the rest of my night class. After spending most of Thanksgiving break studying, I'm the most confident I've ever been. For the first time, I leave class with a skip in my step.

"How did you guys feel about the test?"

I hear Aiden's voice, but I don't look up. He's one of those loud kids who knows all the answers and wants to make sure everyone knows he knows.

"It was fine," the tiny girl who sits behind me says, pausing to wrap her scarf around her frame before we step outside. "I spent a lot of time studying, but it seems like no matter what I do, I can't remember everything."

I feel a certain amount of empathy and speak up. "Same. Really frustrating to put so much time into it and not get a better grade."

We share an understanding look until Aiden says, "You guys study? I don't study at all. All of this stuff is intuitive, like breathing. It's not hard."

It's so socially awkward, but I doubt he knows how offensive his words are. I roll my eyes at the girl.

"Are you majoring in conservation management?" she asks.

"No," I say. "I wanted to skip regular biology, and this class was a substitute."

"Yeah, but you have to take Environmental Bio I and II to fulfill the class credit."

"You do?" I almost stop walking.

"That's why most people taking it are conservation majors. We have to take the classes anyway."

She can't be right. Please tell me I haven't taken the class for no reason.

"Interesting," I say. I'm not about to question her on it.

But I'll check as soon as I get home.

CHAPTER SEVENTY-TWO

Dead on Arrival

"A seventy-six?"

I say it out loud and then glance around in embarrassment, hoping nobody heard me. But as I look around my biology class on Thursday evening, I see I'm not the only one reacting. I spin in my seat, trying to catch the eye of Skinny Girl, but before I can find her, Aiden speaks up.

"A ninety-three percent? Come on, I should've at least gotten a ninety-six." He pauses. "No, make it a ninety-four."

My blood boils, and I bite my tongue as I slap my paper face-down on my desk. He didn't even study, and he has the gall to be upset?

"Class dismissed for the evening," our professor says, wiping his face with a tissue. As he hurriedly stuffs his things into his book bag, I get the impression he planned it this way—toss out the tests and run—so he wouldn't have to deal with us.

But I stand up anyway and hurry to the front of the room before he can make his getaway, only to find myself in line behind seven other students.

"Professor, my grade—" a boy begins.

"Can we talk about the answer to number seven?" a girl interrupts, not about to be ignored. "I think you misunderstood my answer."

A chorus of chaos erupts, eight students all trying to get their say in.

The professor lifts both hands. "Sorry, I can't stay to talk about this today. My office hours are posted on the syllabus. You're welcome to come by anytime."

He shuffles past us, ignoring our protests, and I glare at his retreating back.

His office hours are during my work hours.

This time, I don't join in the complaining as we leave the classroom. I'm upset, and I have this pit in my stomach saying I won't be able to fix it. I'll have to talk to him next Tuesday. I have to find a way to improve this grade.

She was right, by the way. This class does nothing for me if I don't take the second half.

I'm still fuming about it when my phone rings on my walk home. My hands are freezing, and I don't plan on taking my gloves off to answer, but when I check the number—it's my dad.

My dad never calls me.

It's enough to make me slide my fingers out of their warm leather coverings and answer. "Daddy? What's wrong?"

"Hey, sweetheart! Nothing's wrong," he says, his voice chipper. "I was checking to see what day you go back to school after Christmas break."

"Christmas break?" I haven't thought that far ahead—I just got back from Thanksgiving break. "Uh, I'm not sure. The second week of January, I think."

"Well, when you get the exact dates, let me know. I'm trying to book plane tickets and want to make sure I get it right."

"Plane tickets? To fly me home for Christmas?" I purchased my own last year, so I'm surprised he'd do this.

He chuckles. "No, no, not home for Christmas. To take us to Colombia."

Time freezes around me.

I stop walking. Everything goes still. I repeat, cautiously, like I'm afraid this is a dream and if I look too closely, it'll disappear, "Colombia?"

"Yes. Would you like to go?"

Everything speeds up again, and I take a slow step forward. My hands are shaking, and I don't know if I'm anxious or excited or super cold. "For real? We're going to Colombia?"

"Your mom's friend reached out and invited us to stay with her family for Christmas. You might remember them—they stayed with us a few years ago. They have a daughter about your age, Rosana? How do you feel about spending Christmas in another country?"

I shriek. "I can't believe it! For real? We're going to Colombia?"

All my questions, all the mystery, all the curiosity, the secrets my grandmother took to her grave—will this be my chance to finally find out?

"So you're in?" He's laughing at me now.

I laugh too, so loudly that a few other students glance over. But I don't care. "Yes! Yes, yes, yes!"

This is fantastic.

Who cares about a stupid biology test?

I'm going to Colombia!!

⟋~⟍※⟋~⟍

I tell my roommates as soon as I get home. "We're going to Colombia for Christmas!"

"Who's we?" Abby says. "All of us?"

"No, you goon, me and my family," I say, swatting at her arm.

"Is it safe?" Iris asks, concern obvious in her furrowed brow.

I wave off her worry. "My dad will keep us safe. He speaks Spanish."

"And your mom's from there, right?" Camila asks.

I nod as I pull up information on my computer about Bogotá, the capital city. "Yeah, but she doesn't speak Spanish, and I don't know how well she knows her family that's still there. We never talk about it."

"It's a big mystery," Iris says. She and Camila heard all about it freshman year.

334

"Oh, I love it." Abby leans over my shoulder, watching as I scroll through pictures and travel blogs.

"Maybe you'll find the answers to your questions!" Camila says.

"And when Layne gets back from Guatemala, the two of you will have similar experiences!" Iris says.

Somehow, I doubt it. Spending a few days in Colombia doesn't compare to spending a semester volunteering in Guatemala.

I hope I get the chance to live in Brazil.

I pause at my fish tank and frown at the colorful swimmers. I don't recall the tetras having red spots on their bellies before. Even the orange guppy has a red blemish. Maybe they have a fungus? I add a few drops of destresser before going to my room.

I stay up way too late, flipping between information about the capital city and travel highlights of several of the smaller villages around it. I don't know how long we'll be in Colombia, but if I don't get to go to Brazil, hopefully this will satisfy at least some of my need to get away.

My alarm goes off too early in the morning, punishing me for staying up late daydreaming about a trip that is far less important than my grades. I struggle to keep my eyes open in every class, cursing myself for not being more responsible. I balance my chin in my palm at work, nodding off several times before the ringing phone or nearby voices jolts me awake.

My head throbs, my eyes burn, and there's a heaviness in my chest that tells me I won't make it home if I don't sleep soon. When my shift ends, I stumble over to one of the couches in the foyer, stretch across it, and pass out.

I wake up two hours later, feeling fully rested—and starving.

I'm not scheduled to make dinner tonight for Camila, so I decide to splurge and grab something from the food court. I sit down with a lettuce wrap and open my computer, pulling up an English assignment to review while I eat.

A pop-up notification flashes across my screen—an email. I almost ignore it until I recognize the sender.

Alliances Abroad.

My heart does a little tumble. I told Thomas I'd give them until December first to answer—which is tomorrow.

I click open the email, my heart lodged in my throat.

Dear Miss Cassandra Jones,

We are so excited to offer you a place of employment in our English teaching program in the country of Brazil.

My breath catches. I grip the table—I can't breathe.

Holy crap.

This is it.

They accepted me.

They accepted me, and I'm going to Brazil.

I clap a hand over my mouth to muffle my excited squeal.

The packet also includes a list of required vaccinations and medical procedures I need to complete beforehand. I add them to my growing to-do list for when I go home for Christmas. At least I've had a TB test before—I know how that works.

I'm so grateful to have this to focus on. Because if I pause to analyze my personal life . . . It's dead on arrival.

⌒∽⁂∽⌒

Justin the fish is belly-up in the morning, his entire intestines dangling down to the bottom of the tank.

I'm disgusted and distressed as I clean the tank of the dead body. I look at the other fish, at the red spots on their bellies, and I feel their lives in mortal peril.

I dispose of the body and wash my hands at the sink. I'm chewing on my lip, trying not to cry, when Abby comes in.

"What's wrong?" she asks.

It must show on my face. "The fish are dying."

She goes over to the tank and takes a look. "Just the one?"

"But it's the way he died." My stomach clenches at the thought.

"What happened?"

"He exploded." I join her at the tank and gesture to the other fish. "Something's wrong with them. All of them have these red spots on their bellies."

She checks her phone. "It's Saturday. Neither of us has work right now. Bag one of the fish, and let's go to the pet store."

I take a deep breath and nod.

Pet store employees should really upgrade their title to *fish doctor*.

We pile into my car. I hold a bag with one of my beautiful neon tetras inside, and I feel horrible guilt and responsibility for their little lives, like I'm playing a game of chess with them, carelessly discarding them like pawns.

I hand the bag over to Abby so I can drive, and she says, "Don't worry about it. It's going to be fine."

I nod and hope she's right.

The same guy I've talked to several times stands at the counter when we walk into the pet store.

"Oh, hey," he says. "It's you."

I can't tell if he's happy to see me or dreading another fish crisis.

I hold up the bag. "Something's wrong with my fish."

He takes the baggie and dumps the fish and water into a small clear container, adding a couple of test strips. "What's going on with them?"

"A lot of them have this red mark on their stomachs. And one of them died. Brutally."

He glances up at me. I know he wants to know how it died, so I whisper, "The intestines fell out."

His eyes go wide, and he turns back to the fish. "It's hemorrhaging. The water's full of blood." He pulls out the test strips and analyzes them. "You've got bacteria in your water. Did you introduce anything new to the tank?"

I start to shake my head—then I freeze.

The shells.

The ones I brought back from Monterey.

"Yes," I say, and I want to slap myself. How could I be so foolish, introducing those shells without considering they might carry bacteria? I washed them with soap and water, but they needed full decontamination.

"Well, there's your problem," he says. I wilt beneath his words, though there's no judgment in his voice. "If you can, take out whatever new thing was introduced." He scans the shelves and hands me a box. "Here are some antibiotics. Give this to them along with some stress treatment, and they should recover. Do you need the stress treatment?"

I shake my head. "I have some at home."

I thought I knew everything about taking care of fish.

I feel like a rookie again.

He puts my fish back in the bag and hands it to me. "Good luck. Contact us if you have any other concerns."

My shoulders slump as we walk out the door, and Abby pats me on the back. "You couldn't have known."

"Maybe." It seems like common sense now.

As soon as we get home, I throw out the shells, change the water in the tank, add the antibiotics and stress treatment, and cross my fingers that no more of them die.

CHAPTER SEVENTY-THREE

Family Secrets

The antibiotics work within twelve hours; by morning, the blood spots on my fish have vanished.

I try to focus on my classes, knowing I need to get through finals before heading home for Christmas. This year, though, I don't feel as stressed as freshman year. I've accepted that I'll get a B in environmental biology. Knowing I still have to take another class to fulfill the credit makes it feel like I wasted my time. I'm resigned.

Just get through it.

I spend a lot of time over the next few days talking to Harper in Arkansas about her wedding plans.

"And then we'll take you to get your bridesmaid dress fitted," she says, listing off everything that still needs to be done.

I remember watching Abby try on a bridesmaid dress when her friend was getting married. I hope I can trust Harper's taste in fashion.

"It's so much to cram in," I say. "Isn't the wedding in May?"

"Yes, but that's not even six months away!" she says. "I'm overwhelmed here, Cassandra!"

"Don't worry," I say, talking her down from what sounds like a potential panic attack. "I'll be there. We'll do whatever you need. You've got me while I'm home."

"Thank you," she says, and I imagine her pinching the bridge of her nose, breathing deep. "Work with me on this, okay?"

"You go it," I say, keeping my tone serious but trying not to giggle.

It's just a wedding. But what do I know? I've never gotten married before.

Sometimes it feels like I never will.

My emotions on my flight home for Christmas are completely different from last year. Last year was my first time away from home, and I missed my family. I was so excited—anxious, even—to see them after four months apart. I couldn't wait to get home.

I don't feel that now. I know their home isn't mine anymore.

Maybe that's part of what fuels my wanderlust. I'm trying to find my place.

The feeling is magnified at the airport when my family picks me up. We laugh, hug, and pose for a family picture.

"Excited for Colombia?" Dad asks.

"Yes, so excited!" I give him a hug and pat his belly. He's looking older—gaining weight around the middle, graying a bit near the ears. "When do we leave?"

"In a week."

"I don't know how I feel about spending Christmas in a foreign country," Mom says, biting her lip.

I glance at Dad. I don't think it's the country that worries her, or being away for Christmas. More likely, it's the fact that she's been hiding her family for decades, and I get the feeling secrets are about to come out.

"It'll be all right, Karen," Dad says, patting her arm.

Mom smiles and shrugs it off, then texts the family picture to all of us while we drive home. I pull it up to examine it.

I'm shorter than everyone now, even my thirteen-year-old sister Annette. And they're pasty white from winter. I'm smaller, thinner, darker-skinned. Dark-haired. I got all of my mom's Latin American coloring. That makes me unique among my family.

I put the phone away.

❦

Winter has a hold in Arkansas as well, but it's manifested in skeletal tree branches and dry, dead grass on every lawn. Not a spec of white snow in sight. The weather is chilly in the high forties and low fifties, but not like the frigid temps I walk to and from school in every day. I spend the first two days sleeping and watching TV and doing absolutely nothing. It feels amazing after the mental grind of school.

Then Harper calls, and it's time to get down to business.

"We have an appointment with the dressmaker at two," she says. "And then next week when the dress arrives, we can make sure it fits."

"I won't be here in a week," I cut in before she can keep talking. "We're spending Christmas in Colombia, remember?"

She pauses. "Shoot, that's right. When do you get back?"

"Two days before I fly back to Colorado."

"All right, we can make it work. Then we need to plan for May. Make sure you're back in Arkansas a few days before the wedding. We'll have a rehearsal, and then a rehearsal dinner—"

"I don't understand," I say, cutting her off again. "We have to practice you getting married?"

She laughs. "Yes. We have to make sure everyone knows their steps, make sure the flower girl walks properly and the ring bearer doesn't miss his entrance. It could take hours."

I wait for her to laugh and tell me she's joking, but when she doesn't, I realize how serious this is.

"Wow," I say. "I had no idea."

"Can you stay the night tonight? We're going out with Colton's family for dinner. I really want you to meet him."

"The sooner, the better," I say.

She's really getting married.

"Great. What time can you meet up? Want to do lunch before the dressmaker?"

I check the time. It's already eleven. I've piddled the morning away. "I actually have to go to the health department. There's a bunch of medical stuff I have to get done before I can start my internship."

"Right! That's so awesome, I'm so excited for you! Okay, I'll send you the address to the dress shop. We can meet at two."

"Sounds like a plan."

We hang up, and I get dressed, finding a large sweater in my closet and pulling it over a pair of jeans that are tighter than I remember. I've gained weight since college.

A mild breeze blows, the sun is out, and there's not a speck of snow.

I scowl as I remember how it thwarted my Christmas vacation last year. Everything colluded against me. I got terribly sick, caught a raging case of pink eye, and the snow piled up between Louisiana and Arkansas and kept Owen from visiting. I'm angry for every moment I might have had with him and didn't.

And now all the moments are over.

Enough of Owen. I shove him out of my thoughts and get in my mom's car.

It's time to find a new love interest.

But not in Arkansas. Or Colombia.

I drive to the health department in Fayetteville, and at least I know what to expect. I know which line to get in, and I have a book to read because I'm prepared for it to take forever. I hope two hours is enough. I need a TB test and vaccinations for yellow fever, typhoid, and malaria.

The fact that I'm headed to a country where these diseases are still prevalent is kind of crazy.

The TB test is the easy one. I watch as the medical worker sticks the needle under the surface of my skin on my forearm. I feel nothing, but I know she left something behind that will cause a reaction if I'm positive.

"Any plans for Christmas?" she asks.

I perk up. I've answered this question with enthusiasm to every person who asks. Perfect strangers are finding out more than they wanted to know about my life. "Yes, actually! My family is going to Colombia."

"Really? Colombia! I don't hear a lot of people heading that way. Do you have family there?"

"Some, but I've never met them. It's the first time for most of us, even my mom." I think. She could've gone back and never told me about it.

"Well, that's exciting! Remember to return to the health center in two to three days to have your test results read."

"But not after that," I say, a little dryly. I missed the window once before and had to redo the test.

She chuckles. "Exactly."

I head back to the waiting room to wait for my next vaccination.

CHAPTER SEVENTY-FOUR

Colton

Three shots and an hour later, I'm out of there. My biceps and triceps ache from the vaccinations, but at least I didn't cry.

I call Harper en route. "I'm almost there!"

"Great! We're here and waiting for you."

I park outside a small shop in downtown Springdale. From the outside, it doesn't look like a dress shop—just a sewing machine in the window and a half-dressed mannequin.

Before I can pull the door open, Harper barrels out, winter coat high around her ears, the door chime ringing behind her. She squeals, throws her arms around me, and squeezes tight.

I rock with her in a tight embrace on the sidewalk.

"How I've missed you!" she says, stepping back. Her eyes are glossy, but she beams from ear to ear. A strand of her long blond hair catches the sunlight.

"You look amazing." I run my fingers over her white faux-fur jacket. "I love this."

"It's so snuggly." She shrugs, looking like she belongs in a winter wonderland instead of dry, brown Arkansas.

"I forgot you cut yours," she says, patting the ends of my short hair. "It's longer now."

I touch the locks. "Yeah, I have to keep trimming it so it grows evenly."

"It's super cute on you."

"Thanks. It's fun."

She leads me into the shop, and the bell jingles again as we step inside.

"Welcome," the seamstress—Ms. Suzy, according to the sign—greets me. She looks older than my mother with her curly gray hair, but she's thin as a rod. Her fingers are cold as she takes my arm and leads me to a stool. "Strip down to your bra and panties so I can take your measurements."

I glance at Harper uncertainly. She didn't mention this. But she smiles and nods encouragingly.

I remove my sweater, then the T-shirt underneath. I'm self-conscious in my bra, aware that I'm mostly padding and no breast. I bend to remove my jeans, then straighten, crossing my arms over my torso to hide myself while trying to look like I'm not.

"So, tell me about school. Met any interesting guys?" Harper starts up a chatty conversation, and I try to focus on her words and not on this woman's cold hands as she wraps a tape measure around my arms, waist, and hips. I don't remember this happening with Abby when she got measured for her dress. I guess I wasn't paying attention.

I tell her a little bit about Mitch, but I leave out the important detail that he was Owen's cousin and just say the relationship didn't work out. She's sad for me but says, "I'm glad you're willing to date other people. I was afraid you wouldn't."

She doesn't explain why she thought that, and she doesn't need to. We both know why.

Ms. Suzy goes over to a rack of clothing and retrieves a few swaths of sparkly purple cloth. I lift one eyebrow. It looks like the material for a junior prom dress. She brings it to me and wraps it around my torso, fitting my arms into pre-cut holes. Then she uses pins to tuck it in place under my breasts, around my waist, and under my shoulder blades.

There's a mirror in front of me. The dress hits my chest oddly, creating a bubble over my breasts.

"Can we fix this?" I ask, patting at it.

She spares me a glance. "It won't be there after the final cutting."

She resumes her work, and I keep my face stoic. The color doesn't flatter me. I want to like it, I want to feel beautiful in this dress. But as long as Harper likes it, that's all that matters.

Ms. Suzy grabs a longer swath of fabric and wraps it around my hips, then scoots it up and does the same routine with the pins. She pinches and adjusts and pulls.

"This one will have a sheer fabric over the top," she says. "But I'll cut it to match the measurements of the bottom piece."

"Okay," I say.

"What do you think?" Harper asks, beaming. "Isn't the color marvelous?"

The purple is deep and royal. It could be beautiful if not full of sparkles. I half expect gold lining on the edges. "I love purple," I say instead. "It's my favorite color."

"I know. That's why I picked it."

Harper might be planning her own wedding, but she also considered me when picking the material for the bridesmaid dresses. I won't say anything negative about it.

"All right," the woman says, finishing her measuring and pulling the material away from me. "You can get dressed."

I put my clothes back on, glad that embarrassing adventure is over. My arm stings where I got the TB test, and I rub at it, but that makes it hurt worse. I smooth my sweater over the site and try not to touch it.

Harper and I exit the small room and find the woman waiting at the front.

"The dress will be done in a week," she says. "You can come back and try it on, and then we can make any additional adjustments."

"She won't be here," Harper says. "She's going out of town for Christmas."

"When she gets back, then," Ms. Suzy says.

They're speaking over me. I'm just the living mannequin for the dress. "I don't live here," I say, asserting myself. "I'll be back a few weeks before the wedding. I can try it on then."

Ms. Suzy's eyelids flutter. "When?"

I shrug. "The first week of May, probably."

"That doesn't give me much time to do alterations," Ms. Suzy says.

"We'll figure it out," Harper says. This little thing doesn't faze her.

"All right, then you'll have to pay for the dress now," Ms. Suzy says, addressing me again.

Pay for the dress? My insides freeze.

I'd forgotten that part.

"Right," I say through stiff lips.

Crap. Crap crap. I just bought new tires . . .

"How much is it?" I say.

"One hundred and sixty dollars."

I want to refuse. To change my mind. But this isn't my decision. I remove my credit card and hand it over, swallowing past a lump in my throat.

Now it will take me six months to pay that card off. Maybe I can double up a few payments. Where can I cut back? I need to be debt-free before I head to Brazil.

Harper loops her arm through mine as we head out the door. "Where do you want to go for dinner?"

I might need to get a second job.

⚮

I meet Harper's fiance at dinner.

We leave my car at her house and ride together to her favorite steakhouse, which luckily is part of a chain and not a super expensive one. I find the cheapest item on the menu and breathe a sigh of relief that it's only eighteen dollars. Harper's parents join us, and I rise to hug both of them.

And then he comes in. Colton commands the attention of the room the way he struts in, wearing a large-weave sea-green sweater and dark jeans. His short blond hair is expertly styled, with no part but a tousle of curls over his forehead. He struts toward us, trim and confident, sharp eyes glancing over me before falling on Harper. His parents come behind him, but I barely notice them. I'm watching him with Harper.

"Hi," he says, his expression softening when he sees her.

"Hey!" She stands, and they embrace. She's his height, maybe an inch or two shorter. Even after he lets her go, she hangs on him, clinging to his waist, her long hair falling over his shoulder.

They look good together.

She turns to me. "Colton, this is my best friend, Cassandra."

He nods at me. He doesn't offer a handshake the way the people at church or my school tend to. "Nice to meet you. I've heard a lot about you."

"Likewise," I say.

I still can't believe she's getting married.

"Shall we sit?" his mom says.

He settles down across from Harper, which makes him across from me also. The

343

parents begin a lively conversation beside us, and he turns to me.

"So why did you decide to go to school in Colorado?"

"I wanted to experience something different," I say. "Needed a change of scenery."

"You don't like Arkansas?"

I'm a little caught off guard by his tone. It's almost like he's challenging me.

I thought I would be the one doing the interrogating.

"I love Arkansas." I fiddle with the napkin in my lap and wonder when the food will arrive. "But I'd been here for a decade. I wanted a change." Pretty sure I already said that.

"Did you feel like you were forced to behave a certain way? Were you trying to get from under your parents' influence?"

"No." I stammer slightly and take a drink of my water. "I wanted to be my own self. Discover me away from other people."

"Which means you felt smothered at home. You couldn't really be yourself."

He's twisting my words. Making me say something I don't mean.

"I could be myself. But I wanted to experience life without my parents right there."

"Because they wouldn't approve of your decisions."

I want to turn to Harper and beg her to get him to lay off. But I don't dare. So I dig in my heels and stand my ground.

"They approve of my decisions just fine. It was time to be independent. To not need my parents for everything. I prepared for eighteen years to be an adult, and I grabbed my chance to try it."

"People who feel like they have to leave home to find themselves usually come from unhappy homes. Or they feel dissatisfied with their lives up to that point and are looking for some way to fill the void."

"And your plan is to live in your parents' basement forever? Are you a gamer too?"

I don't actually say that last line. It's on the tip of my tongue. The skin along my hairline burns and itches, and he is on the verge of getting a verbal lashing from me.

The waitress saves him.

She arrives with our food, and Harper begins a demure conversation with him, telling him how much she loves the color of his sweater, plucking at his sleeve and telling him what a nice day we've had.

I do not look at him. My blood boils.

Is he intimidated because I left Arkansas? Does he think I'm going to sew discontent in Harper's heart and make her want to leave to experience new things?

"I'm going to Brazil in August," I say, loudly, so the whole table hears. "As an English teacher. Because I want to see how people live outside of the U.S. And I want to be fluent in Portuguese."

"Cassandra, that's great!" Harper's mom says.

Colton's parents look at me, their expressions a bit startled.

"Such a bold move for a young person," his dad says.

I shrug. My filter is barely in place. "Not quite as bold as getting married."

That silences any other comments on the subject.

My face flames, and I can barely eat. I should have held my tongue.

I did hold my tongue.

I'll be lucky if Harper still wants me in her wedding after this.

CHAPTER SEVENTY-FIVE

Positive

Harper hugs everyone goodbye after dinner, lingering in the embrace of her loved one. I hug no one. I'm going to her house, and her parents will be there, so no need for a goodbye.

Colton tilts his head at me. "Nice to meet you."

"Likewise," I say.

We're both lying.

I hold my breath as Harper and I get into the car. I expect her to tear into me, to scold me, even yell at me for speaking to him in such a way. I brace myself for tears of exasperation that I could ruin our first meeting.

Instead she says, "What did you think? Isn't he awesome?" She glances at me once, eyes bright, smile wide.

I blink at her, taking a solid three seconds to decipher what she just asked.

It's like she wasn't there. She's oblivious to what went down.

I can't decide if this is good or bad.

"He seems to adore you," I say cautiously, still feeling this might be a trap. "He has strong opinions about things."

"Oh, that he does." She nods vigorously and pulls the car out of the restaurant, heading back toward her house. "He's a mama's boy. They're so close. And everything she thinks, he thinks."

"Ah." Some of his behavior makes sense. "How do you feel about that? Do you worry she'll be in your business?"

"She already is. But when it comes to me, he's good at telling her to back off. She didn't want him dating me. I'm too worldly." Harper winks at me.

"You're too worldly?"

"Yeah. They're super conservative, if you know what I mean."

"I think I get the picture." My skin crawls with apprehension. "How does he treat you?"

"Like a queen. He thinks I'm amazing, beautiful, smart, funny—every moment with him is magical." She beams at the windshield.

"That's great." I want this to be magical for her. "As long as the two of you have everything worked out, nothing else matters."

"Right? That's what I keep telling him."

I fall silent after that. I wonder if I should say more about my misgivings. But I'm sure it's not a character flaw in him, and he and Harper will be fine.

He and I don't get along. But we don't have to. We're not getting married.

⊙ⁿ⸺※⸺ⁿ⊙

Harper and I stay up most of the night. We don't talk about her fiance or any boys from our current life, but we dive deep into the past. We spend hours walking down Memory Lane, laughing over choir incidents, gossip that nearly destroyed our lives, crying over friends we loved who we no longer talk to.

She has to leave for work at ten in the morning, so I'm forced to go home also. But I don't want to. It's so fun to hang out with someone who knows me, who is such a part of my history.

"Have fun in Colombia, if I don't see you before you go," she says, blowing me a kiss as she gets into her car.

"I will! I'll call you when I get back!" I wave as I settle into the driver's seat of my mom's van.

My phone buzzes with an incoming text. I grab it to read it.

Riley: Still okay if I come over today? I'll bring Thea!

The car idles while I put it in Park to respond. *Me: of course!!! We leave for Colombia tomorrow, so today's the day to do it!*

R: Great! See you tonight!

I put the phone down and scratch an itch on my arm. My fingers bump over a hard lump. I roll the sleeve of my sweater up and see a swollen mound of tissue, about the size of a marble, on the inside of my forearm.

Right where they did the TB test.

That's weird. But there's no other reaction, so I cast it from my mind.

⊙ⁿ⸺※⸺ⁿ⊙

All day I intend to get to the health department and have my TB test read, but we're busy packing. My mom needs me to take my sister somewhere in Rogers and then help with cleaning, and driving south to the other side of Fayetteville doesn't fit in my schedule.

"I need you to drive to the post office and drop these packages off," she says at four just as I'm finally finishing up her tasks. She holds out a laundry basket filled with wrapped and labeled packages.

"I'm going to the health department," I say. "I have to go before we leave for Colombia, or my test results will be void."

"Go after you take these packages. The post office closes at four-thirty."

"The health department closes at five! I'm headed there now." I'll barely make it. Everything is at least a half hour drive away from our house out in rural Arkansas.

"Honey, if I don't get these packages mailed today, they won't get there for Christmas!"

"Mom!" I'm frustrated. "Why don't you use mail delivery from the shop like everyone else?"

She completely ignores my line of logic. "You have to go now or you won't make it. They won't close as long as you're already in line."

"I'm worried about my TB test!"

"If you don't make it today, we'll stop by on the way to the airport tomorrow, I promise."

"Fine." I don't see I have much choice in the matter.

I grit my teeth and grab the laundry basket. I know how the post office is at Christmas time. There will be a line out the door and around the stamp machine. I'll be there until five.

I won't let my mom forget that I need to get this TB test read, though.

⟅∕∽❀∾⟆

Riley comes over after dinner with baby Thea.

"Oh my gosh, she's so big and beautiful!" I exclaim, taking her in my arms.

She's a gorgeous combination of Riley's features and Lucas's darker skin tone. But her startling green eyes peer at me beneath a thick layer of lashes.

"Nine months old," Riley says. She looks too amazing to be the mom of a toddler. I reach over and finger her hair, reaching below her shoulder blades.

"Your hair is longer than I've ever seen it," I say.

"It was the pregnancy hormones. It got strong and wouldn't stop growing. It's falling out now, so I'll have to cut it soon."

The baby sticks a finger in my mouth, and I remove it. I bounce her on one hip, but she squirms away and reaches for Riley.

Riley sighs as she takes her from me. "She's a mama's girl. Can't be away from me for long."

"Is it hard?" I study Riley's face. Her skin is paler than usual, with few freckles across her nose, but it is December.

"Exhausting. Never-ending. My mother-in-law watches her a lot so I can work, but then I come home and it's time to make dinner and then she just wants me."

The exhaustion paints a picture across her face, under her eyes. I see it now.

"You're doing so much," I say. "I'm sure you're a great mom."

"I try." She cradles the little girl in her arms. "I want to be there for her every moment. But I can't."

"Someday, Riley. You won't always have to work this hard." I hope, anyway.

"I'm getting out of retail. I applied to nursing school. That should help."

"You'll be great at that!"

"I watched my dad do it. I can do it too."

My arm gives an itchy stabby feeling, and I scratch at it. "Hey," I say. "I want to show you something."

"What?"

I roll my sleeve up and show her the swollen skin. The bump has grown to the size of a ping-pong ball, and the stretched skin both itches and irritates.

"What is that? A bug bite?"

"Maybe," I say. "I thought you might know."

She shakes her head. "When did you get it?"

347

I pull my sleeve back down, a nervous reluctance growing in the pit of my stomach. "It started last night." I hesitate, and then add, "I got a TB test yesterday."

Her eyes go wide. "It started after your TB test?"

"Yes. But that can't be it."

"Maybe it's an irritation. Have you had a TB test before?"

"Yes."

"Did it do that?"

"No." I've had two of them before.

There was no reaction. I never knew what they were looking for when they checked me at the health clinic after each test.

That heavy feeling grows stronger.

I might know now.

⁘

The morning is a harried mess as we load the car with our things for the airport. We each load up a suitcase and pile our bags around our feet. My dad is yelling about turning off the heat and Mom pokes her head in the van.

"Everyone have your passport?"

She's either too trusting or cautiously optimistic, leaving us each in charge of our own. I hold mine up. So do my siblings.

"We're supposed to be at the airport three hours before an international flight," my dad says, hopping in the car.

"I'm not the one holding us up," Mom snips.

"Let's go."

Dad backs the van out of the driveway, and I lean forward in my captain's chair, addressing both parents.

"Health department," I say. "We have to stop there first."

"We need to catch our flight," Dad says.

"Mom promised," I say. "It won't take long. They have to read my test." My palm closes protectively over my forearm through my sweater.

The lump is harder, bigger. Like a mandarin orange under my skin. It itches and burns and something's wrong.

I almost don't want to know.

But I feel like I shouldn't ignore this.

"We—" Dad begins.

"We'll pull up to the sidewalk and drop you off," Mom says to me.

Dad huffs but doesn't say another word as he drives us to Fayetteville. It's entirely the wrong direction. The airport is north of us in Bentonville. This is why I told my mom to let me do this yesterday.

I can't skip it.

Dad pulls up the curb outside the health department and slams to a halt. "Go. Hurry."

Like I have any say in it. I jump out and run into the lobby.

I almost forget what I need when I see how empty it is. Then I remember it's eight in the morning. No one's crazy enough to be here except me.

I step to the window. "I need to get a TB test read," I say, and my stomach turns over as I speak.

"Have a seat," the clerk says, typing away on his computer and not looking at me.

I sit.

The side door opens, and a woman pokes her head out. "TB test?" she says.

I stand up and go with her down the hall, my heart rate picking up with each step. By the time we step into a side room, I'm nauseous.

"Give me your card," she says.

I hand over the card they gave me a few days ago with the timestamps on it. She opens a file in her computer and accesses my chart.

"Going somewhere?" she asks.

"When? Now?" My stomach tightens. Does she know I'm about to leave the country? I feel like a fugitive trying to sneak out.

"For the TB test."

"Oh." Duh. "Yes. I'm going to Brazil to teach English."

She glances at me. "Are you headed somewhere now?"

I nod. "My family's in the car. We're on our way to the airport to go to Colombia for Christmas."

"That's fun." She swivels back to me. "Lift your sweater sleeve, please."

I do so, and her expression changes when she sees my arm. She pulls out a tape measure and makes markings around the lump, then writes them down on a piece of paper.

"One second," she says, and she leaves me.

Alone in that room.

My heart skips a beat, then another. I feel lightheaded.

She comes back in with a man in a lab coat. He glances at the computer and then at my arm.

"Definitely positive," he says.

CHAPTER SEVENTY-SIX

Lifelong Treatment

"Let's do an x-ray."

"Wait, what?" I sputter. My mind is swimming. "I have TB? What's happening?"

"Your test is positive," the woman says, her tone gentle. "We're going to take an x-ray to see if we see any activity in your lungs."

"But—but—" I can't find the words to protest. My face is hot, so hot, and suddenly I burst into tears.

"Is anyone with you?" the man asks.

"My family. They're waiting outside. We're—" I break off, sweat beading on my forehead.

I shouldn't have told her where we're going. What if they won't let me go?

"They're leaving on an international flight," the woman says.

"We need to get that cleared."

"You can't keep me here," I say. "There aren't any regulations saying I can't fly."

"You might want to call someone to join you," he says to me.

I choke back sobs as he leaves the room. The woman comes over and hugs me, then surprises me with a kiss to the cheek.

"You're going to be okay, honey," she says.

I cry harder. And then I call my mom.

"I need you to come in here," I say between sobs.

"What? What is it?"

"Just come in here."

I'm shaking. We're going to miss our flights. I don't know if they'll let me on the plane.

My mom comes in. "What's going on? Why is she still here? Who's in charge?"

She takes over like a bulldog. I take a backseat, gratefully letting her handle it. She has her phone out, checking regulations, searching for rules. The doctor comes back and answers her questions only to have more tossed at him.

"What tests do we need to do?" she demands. "Can they wait?"

"We need to do an x-ray right away," he says. "We have it prepped. We need to know if she's active or incubated."

"We have a flight in two hours. Time is ticking."

"We need to call the Center for—"

"No, you don't." Mom plows right over his words. She waves her phone at him. "TB or no, she's allowed on that plane, and we're going to Colombia this morning."

She's breathing fire, and I'm certain the president of the United States would back down from her if they went head to head.

"The x-ray only takes a moment," the woman says, and she leads me away before Mom can say anything.

Within minutes I'm back in the room with my mom, who's on the phone with my dad, speaking furiously about the flight and tests and important information. She hangs up when I come in.

"We're going to Colombia," she says. "We'll figure all this medical stuff out when we get back. Don't worry about it right now. You're not dying. Medicine and antibiotics exist for this."

To be perfectly honest, I know next to nothing about TB, other than that it stands for tuberculosis, a disease than ran rampant during World War II and killed hundreds of people. And in the eighteen hundreds people called it consumption because it slowly consumed its victims, withering them down to nothing.

What does that mean for me today?

The doctor comes back in. "The x-ray is clear. Her lungs are fine. But as soon as you're back in the States, she needs to go to a doctor and begin a treatment plan."

"I'm going back to school when I get back." Somehow I've found my voice. I speak with a quiver in my words, but I'm gaining my confidence back. "I won't be here in Arkansas."

"Then you make it a priority to get to a doctor wherever you are and go through these steps again. I'll forward a chart, but they'll want to see these results for themselves. Get a TB test and begin treatment. TB is treatable, but it's a lifelong process. You also need to tell everyone you have close contact with. Your whole family needs to get tested."

The words spiral in and out of my mind. Everyone who has contact with me. Lifelong. Treatment.

Forever.

This is forever.

⚮

The health department lets us leave. We promise to get it taken care of, and I think we satisfactorily reassured them we're not going to cause a mass outbreak of TB, either in Arkansas or Colombia.

My dad asks lots of questions in the car, of which I have no answer. Things like, how could I get TB? Was the test really positive? Could it be false? Where did I get TB?

I say I don't know until I get tired of answering, and then I fall silent.

But I spend my time on my phone, searching the internet for everything I can find about the desease.

Here are the generalities:

It's a bacterial disease that affects the lungs.

It's treatable with antibiotics.

It's spread through water droplets.

If it's active, you're contagious. If it's not, you're not.

When active, it usually resolves within months but remains in your body forever.

Symptoms are not good. Coughing up blood, chills, night sweats, no appetite. Death.

It sometimes affects more than just the lungs.

It's super rare in the United States.

Like, super rare. I stare at that fact and then check the numbers. It's not impossible. There are around 200,000 cases every year. But it seems most of those people contract the disease either from someone who just traveled overseas, or from traveling overseas.

I put my phone down and stare out the window. We've reached the airport, and I have to focus as we become a flurry of crazed activity, emptying the van and rushing through the check-in line. My thoughts are elsewhere. I'm an automaton through security, all the way to our gate, where we have forty-five minutes until we board. My parents are ecstatic, and I know in spite of my mom's brave words, she wasn't sure we'd make it to our plane.

Here I am. Traveling to another country.

Again.

And I think of Tiago.

I had to have gotten it in Brazil. Which means he probably has it too.

I pull out my laptop and begin composing emails before we get on the plane. First to my roommates.

Hey guys,

I know this is not the email you're expecting from me. But I tested positive for TB. I'm so sorry. Since you all live with me, the doctor said you need to get tested, but the disease is inactive right now, so I'm not considered contagious.

Get your test taken care of and then I can rest easy. Sorry again.

I feel rotten. I brought this primitive disease back to the U.S.

And then I start another email, reaching out to someone I thought I would never talk to again. Because I care too much about him not to tell him.

Tiago,

Please forgive this email. I'm reaching out because it's important. I tested positive for tuberculosis, and I most likely got it in Brazil. You probably have it. I need you and your family to get tested. I couldn't bear it if something happened to you because of me.

I'm sorry. For this. For everything. Please know that as life moves us in different directions, you, and my experiences with you, will always be a light of joy in my heart.

Cassandra

I don't tell him not to write me back. I know he's going to get tested and then he'll tell me about it, and in truth, I need to know.

But that's it. Our relationship, our friendship, is over. There's nothing more for us to talk about.

I put my computer away and check the marked-up lump on my arm, feeling wretched.

At least there's one person I kept safe. One person I don't have to message and warn about this pernicious disease.

Owen will never know.

☙ ❈ ❧

The flight to Colombia is only slightly shorter than flights to Brazil. It's after nine p.m. when we land, but it's summertime in Colombia. I knew this beforehand but I'm still stunned to see the sun shining overhead when we arrive.

The tiny airport is outside, surrounded by red tile and palm trees. We exit the plane via a ladder and enter a building with only two rooms. One is a bathroom.

My dad has our luggage by the time we come out. I stand at the window and look outside, admiring the tall mountains surrounding us on all sides. They're very unlike the ones in Colorado. These look dipped in green ink and then sprinkled with colorful confetti, rising like mounds of sugar in every direction.

The hot, humid air bathes my skin. I close my eyes and soak it up while my dad speaks to the customs agent. My mom might be Colombian, but my dad is the one who speaks the language thanks to a mission trip in his twenties. I catch a few words here and there, but my mind is steeped in Portuguese. Spanish is less familiar.

"We've got what we need," Dad says. "The taxi will take us to our hotel."

Tropical trees sway along the road when we step outside. It's not as crowded here as I remember Brazil, no honking horns, no cars swerving past each other. We load up the taxi and Dad speaks to the driver.

We travel down from the airport, which is set on a hill. The roads and city becomes more congested as we descend, and soon we're in one of six lanes of traffic. Our driver honks and surges forward and makes U-turns that have my stomach heaving. Other cars cut in front of him, but everyone is honking and yelling and doing the same thing.

Now it feels like Brazil.

I glance at my siblings. Annette has an expression of horror on her face as she clutches her fingers in her lap. Scott stares out the window, head swinging as he tries to take it in. Emily's eyes trail over the scenery to her right.

"The mountains," she says, catching me watching. "They're covered in houses."

I follow her gaze and see what she means. What originally looked like colorful confetti is actually thousands of houses crowded together. Like decks of cards settled precariously on top of each other, entire neighborhoods climb the steep mountainside. I lean closer to her as I peer out the window.

"How? How do they stay up?" I say, enthralled. The roof of one house creates the patio of the next. They climb and climb and climb, wrapping around each thimble-shaped mountain. They share walls. The mountain must be the fourth wall, the foundation.

"It can't be safe," I say.

"I wonder what it's like to live up there," Emily says. "Do they have electricity? Running water?"

I shake my head. "No idea."

We pass mountain after mountain, go around a corner and confront a new array of mountains. The sun begins to set. Dad pulls out his phone and checks something, then begins arguing with the driver. I think that's a bad idea. He might kick us to the curb or pull a gun and take all our luggage.

353

"What's going on?" I ask Mom. I've never heard her speak Spanish, but I can tell from the way she watches my dad and the driver that she understands what's happening.

"Your dad thinks we went the wrong way," she says. "He says we were supposed to turn left a few streets back."

The skin on the back of my neck prickles. I'm tired and emotionally exhausted from this day. I want to sleep. I don't need another adventure. "Are we being kidnapped?"

Mom laughs. She laughs at me, which makes me feel foolish and relieved at the same time. "No. There are two hotels with the same name, and your dad wants to make sure we get to the right one."

"I agree with that." I settle back in my seat.

Dad points something out on his phone. The driver nods and does another U-ey.

The setting sun silhouettes the mountains in front of us. My eyes burn.

It's dark when we pull up to a large hotel an hour later. The name is a familiar chain, one we've stayed at many times in America. The taxi driver brings our bags to the curb and waits while my dad finds him a few bills for a tip. Then he says adios and leaves us to haul our bags into the hotel.

"This better be the right one," I mutter to Emily.

She snorts. "Amen, sister."

We share an eye-roll. She's already eighteen and a senior in high school and hoping to go to PYU also. We won't room together. We did that for most of our lives, and both of us appreciate the space adulthood gives us.

The hotel clerk sends us to the fourth floor, and the room is blissfully clean with beds and white sheets and blackout curtains to conceal the city lights shining from every high-rise building and the myriad of tiny houses blinking at us from the mountains. I close the curtains, remove my contacts, and collapse face down on the bed. I'm asleep before I get my shoes off.

CHAPTER SEVENTY-SEVEN

Missing Toilet Paper

My dad takes a taxi to get a rental car in the morning, and he shows up with a five-passenger sedan while we're finishing breakfast in the pristine lobby. I've logged into the hotel internet, and I'm delighted to see an email from Abby.

Cassandra! I can't believe you have TB. My heart sank as I read those words. I'm so sorry, but I suppose that's the risk of living life as an adventurer.

I'll get tested and we'll get it taken care of. It will all be okay. Have a great time in Colombia and try not to worry!

Her words soothe my heart. If my roommates don't blame me for this, if they're not terrified for their lives, it can't be as frightening as the internet made it seem.

"That won't fit all of us," Scott says around a mouthful of pineapple when my dad enters the lobby.

"They don't rent out bigger vehicles," Dad says, pulling up a chair around the table. "Large families like ours aren't normal around here. Most people only have two kids."

"So we have to squish in there?" I look at the back seat.

"Yep." Dad moves right past our concerns. "We're driving to Zipaquirá. It's an hour from here. We're staying with your mom's friend Anita, who lives across the street from Tia Elba. Tia Elba doesn't speak English, and I'm not sure how the family situation is going to be."

"Family situation? What does that mean?" I glance at Mom. Stress lines furrow her brow, and the hair around her face is parted on the side like she's been tugging on it. She has that look like when she's about to be sick.

Silence meets my question. My dad also looks at my mom, and I sense he wants her to answer.

She doesn't.

"Tia," I say, filling the silence. "Is this an aunt?"

"It is," Mom says. "My tia Elba and Anita's mom were best friends, so Anita is like a daughter to her. When Anita moved to the United States to go to school, Tia Elba made her find me."

"So you and Anita went to college together?" I ask.

"Yes."

"And that's when you became close?"

Mom nods. "Anita told Tia Elba about their visit to our house a few Christmases ago, and Elba begged me to bring the family here. It took a few years and lots of persuasion from Anita, but . . . we came."

I try to remember my mom and Anita talking when the family stayed with us, hanging out that Christmas, but I'd been so absorbed in my own life—torn between two boys, longing for closure from one while falling desperately in love with the other. "Are we welcome here?" I ask.

"Yes," Dad says. "Elba is the one person who's kept in touch with your mom through the years. But don't ask any questions. Just enjoy being here."

Don't ask questions? My curiosity burns almost as badly as the swollen bump on my arm. This is my chance to find out the big family secret! What is Colombia hiding? Why do we never speak of it? Why did I not find out my heritage until I was a senior in high school?

But I don't actually speak Spanish. So I'll have to figure out how to ask first.

"Listen," Dad continues. "We're meeting them at a shopping center first. Tia Elba has a shop and she wants us to see it. But there are a few things you need to know about Colombia. First, never take your cell phones out in public. If you do, you're likely to never see them again. Thieves are watching and will be there so fast, you won't know what happened. Trust nobody. Criminals often pose as policemen. Don't pull out your wallet or passport for anyone. You tell them you need to find a parent first and you come get me. Don't accept any food or drinks from strangers. Don't take pictures of people in costumes or posing for tourists. They want your money. Stick together, never go anywhere alone, not even to the bathroom."

"What about me?" Scott asks.

"You and I get to hang out together, kiddo."

I would laugh, but I'm too busy listening to my dad's warnings, feeling like a second-grader at a Stranger Danger meeting.

Mom is silent through it all. I'm dying to ask her what she thinks, but judging from her expression, she doesn't feel like talking.

"All right." Dad stands. "Let's go."

The four of us kids descend further into childhood when it's time to enter the car. We bicker over who has to sit in the middle and who gets the window. As the oldest, I feel I should get the outside seat, but it's quickly pointed out that I'm also the smallest, and so I find myself crammed into the middle beside Annette, neither one of us thrilled that we're there.

And then we drive.

Mountains ring us on all sides, and Dad finds a road and starts driving up.

"What was the name of the city we're going to?" I ask.

Mom answers. "Zipaquirá."

I mouth the word to myself. I love the way the name feels in my mouth. "Is that where your family is from?" I ask the question timidly. Carefully. I don't want Mom to close up.

"No," she says. "My family is from Manizales. It's a beautiful city in the mountains. I've seen pictures of it, the houses with the red-tile roofs, the old church. Tall trees in front of white-washed houses."

"Why did we wait this long to visit?" I ask. I'm pushing my luck, but she answered my first question, so why not?

"That's not my story to tell," she says.

I feel like it's a cop-out. I look to Dad, but he doesn't say anything either.

The road up the mountain narrows, the concrete disappearing beneath large potholes. It's no bigger than a single-lane road in America, but here we're expected to share, and several times Dad squeezes over to the side to let a bus or wagon loaded with livestock go by. Then we get back to the middle and bump along. Annette's elbow hits me with every jostle, and I try to create more space, but that pushes me into Scott's shoulder. I grit my teeth.

The road changes as we near the city, and the uneven holes become rhythmic bumps as the tires roll over cobblestone. The car clatters along the laid street until we come to a stop in front of a shopping center. It looks mostly abandoned, like an old warehouse, but a colorful banner out front announces "Mercado de Zipaquirá," and Dad parks the car in front of it, so we must be here.

"Come on," Dad says, but he doesn't have to say it twice, we're tumbling from the car like a pack of clowns.

The first thing I notice is the chill in the air. I'm in a T-shirt and shorts, and I shiver, wrapping my arms around myself.

"Oh, right," Dad says, noticing. "It's a lot cooler up here in the mountains."

"Dad!" I exclaim, incensed. "Are we staying in the mountains?"

"Yes, Anita's house is up here."

"And you couldn't warn us?"

"All right," Mom breathes, drawing my attention to her and saving my dad from having to make an explanation. She takes a sip of water and tries to flatten her hair, but it won't lie still with the wind stirring around our heads. "Everyone be polite."

Best behavior.

The market is indoor, but the walls have been rolled up like garage doors to expose the stores to the street. We follow Mom through a narrow corridor, past stores selling pharmaceuticals and jewelry and shoes, and reach a colorful shop in the back with displays of dolls in rainbow dresses touting large hats over their thick black hair. A woman several years older than my mom stands by a register wearing a white, embroidered shirt tucked into a woven skirt. Graying black hair is pulled back into a severe bun at the nape of her neck. She's talking with a younger girl about my age, who looks up at her and nods with every word.

"Elba?" Mom says.

The woman instantly stops talking and turns around. "Careen!"

It takes me a moment to realize she said Karen. She rolled the R and flipped the accent on it's head, and my mom's name doesn't sound American anymore.

Elba bustles to my mom's side and wraps her in a solid hug, then pulls back and kisses each cheek. Ah, the cheek kisses. I remember those.

She rattles off in rapid-fire Spanish, and I'm pleased that I can make out a few words.

How grown up my mom is, how little she used to be, and oh my, these can't possibly be her children!

Smiling bashfully, my mom pulls us over and introduces us, starting with me.

"Cassandra *aqui tiene diecinueve años*," she says, and Elba smashes me in a hug, followed by the chin squish and kisses on both cheeks.

"Cassandra," she says, and she drags me over to the girl at the table. "*Esta és mi vicina Rosana, tiene dieciocho años, casi el mismo idade de ti*," and it's so similar to Portuguese that for a moment I think she switched languages.

I remember Rosana from the family's stay a few years back. But she's grown up in that time, and the placid expression behind her dark brown eyes is less than friendly. Her face is wider than mine, her eyelashes long and straight, and her thick dark hair is parted down the middle and held in place with a clip.

Elba leaves the two of us alone so she can meet my other siblings, and Rosana says, "I speak English now."

Her accent is as thick as her hair, but perfectly intelligible. "Oh, awesome," I say, almost wilting with relief. "I'm afraid I replaced my Spanish with Portuguese."

She doesn't look impressed. I get the impression she's not thrilled we're here.

Emily comes over. "Hi," she says to Rosana, and then she turns to me. "I need to use the bathroom. Mom said you have to come with me."

"Oh, sure." Can't say I mind. "Is it in the corridor?" I ask Rosana.

"The bathroom is near the restaurants," she says.

"Restaurants?" I echo. I look toward the street. "Do we need to go outside?"

She shakes her head. "No, no, the small restaurants inside the shopping."

"Oh, like little cafes," I say, catching on. "Okay, thanks."

I take Emily out of Tia Elba's store with the little dolls and let out a breath. "A little suffocating in there," I say.

"It's going to be an interesting trip, right?"

"We'll finally find out why Grandma left Colombia and why Mom doesn't talk about it," I say.

Emily peers at me. "You think it's some big nefarious secret?"

"Has to be. Why else won't she talk about it?"

"Maybe she doesn't know."

"It's more than that." I remember conspiring with my cousin in Georgia, trying to get answers out of my grandfather. "They're hiding something."

"You think there's treasure somewhere?"

Emily giggles. I glare at her. She's making fun of me.

"No one hides treasure, dufus," I say, elbowing her. "They spend it. Seeing how we're not rich, that's not it."

"Maybe because someone's already spent it," she says, and she's really laughing at herself now.

I ignore her and find the bathroom. I push the door open and survey it quickly. Two stalls, a sink, a tall trashcan. No paper towels or paper towel holder. No soap. I go to a stall and push it open. Standard. White toilet with a toilet paper holder.

An empty toilet paper holder.

"Do you have paper over there?" I ask Emily, leaning out of my stall as she steps into hers.

"Um—no. No toilet paper. You?"

"None here either."

"Well, great, what do I do?"

I open my purse and dig through it. "I have a few receipts in here."

"No thanks." Emily steps out of the stall. "Do you think Tia Elba's shop has any?"

"I bet they do."

We walk back the way we came, noticing how most of the stores are empty in the shopping center. Seems like malls are dying everywhere.

Rosana looks up from her tall stool when we come in, and both eyebrows rise. She almost seems to smirk as she says, "That was fast."

"They didn't have any toilet paper," I say. "So we didn't go. Do you have any here?"

"Oh. Of course." She leans over the counter and comes back up with a roll of paper. "You have to take your own paper with you everywhere you go. Did you think they would give it to you?"

She says this like we're stupid or pampered to expect such a thing. But she's been to the U.S. She knows every bathroom provides paper for you.

She knew we would expect it. She sat here on her stool waiting for us to come back so she could gloat at us.

I take the paper without thanking her and barely make it into the hallway before I hiss to Emily, "We were nice to her when she came to visit."

"Yeah! We liked the whole family."

"I guess things are different now."

We're on Rosana's turf. She doesn't like it, and her true colors are showing.

I'll have to steer clear of her.

CHAPTER SEVENTY-EIGHT

Searching for Christmas

We wait for Tia Elba to close up shop, and then we head into the foothills behind the town to Rosana's house.

These houses aren't like the cardboard cutouts we saw along the side of the mountain earlier. These are square, flat-roofed, and beautiful. Rosana's family has a fenced-in yard the size of a postage stamp, but large green trees and luminous flowers grow from every inch, squished between the fence and the house.

Tia Elba pulls in behind us, and there's a juggling moment while my dad pulls his rental car as far forward as it will go. Elba parks behind, and then a man I recognize as Rosana's dad comes out of the house. They put the cars in neutral and maneuver them around a third vehicle already parked on the concrete. Once all three fit inside the carport like jigsaw puzzles, he closes the gate and locks it.

This reminds me so much of Brazil.

Tia Elba comes inside with us. I stop to take in the layout. A porch encircles the house, but it's got brick walls that come to my waist. It's open to the outside so the garden grows right up to the wall. The house is enclosed within, large windows leaving a view to the porch, but not as much light can get in because of the roof overhead. We enter into a large tiled front room with a few couches on peg legs. I follow the scent of food into a square kitchen, barely big enough for my family to stand in. There's no table.

Anita sees us come in from where she stands stirring a pot of food. "Hello!" she cries. Her English is perfect. She releases her spoon and wipes her hands on a beige apron before coming to hug us. "Oh, you made it!" She holds on extra tight to my mom.

"You're finally in Colombia," she says, releasing my mom to cup her face. "Welcome home."

Mom's face flushes pink. "Thank you."

"Let me show you your rooms." Anita leads us thorough the kitchen to a hallway running the length of the house. "Here is the bathroom," she says, showing us a cubicle with a toilet, a shower, and no roof. I wonder what they do when it rains.

And blessed toilet paper.

"No paper in the toilet, please," she adds. "Here, Karen and Jim, your room."

My parents' room is a kids' room. Two beds have been smashed together to make a full, and soccer balls and dinosaurs decorate the walls. It looks like two little boys sacrificed their space for my parents.

"Girls, you are here, with Rosana," Anita says, leading us down the hall to another room.

Rosana is already in her room. She stands at a dresser removing her earrings and barely gives us a glance. Two beds adorn this room also, as well as a hammock and a mattress.

"Can I sleep in the hammock?" Annette cries.

"If you like," Anita says. "Rosana will take the mattress, and Cassandra and Emily can have the beds."

Rosana leaves the room, and I suspect this is why she doesn't like us. We took over her room, even her bed. "We can sleep on the floor," I say.

"No," Anita says, her expression going stern. "You are guests. You will not sleep on the floor."

I nod. I won't argue with custom.

"And Scott, come with me," Anita says, taking my brother by the arm. "I've put you and my boys in the guest room."

I get my suitcase and lug it into the room, but there's no space to unpack. There's barely room to open it. I sit down on the bed and stare out the window at the jungle around the house. The patio doesn't extend this far, and I can stick my arm through the barred window and grab leaves if I want. Shiny yellow fruit dangles in front of me, and I hope it's mangoes. I hope we eat them for breakfast.

Dinner is boiled chicken and rice and arepas, dough folded over cheese and fried in a way similar to quesadillas but different. I wonder where we will sit, but then Anita unlocks a long slab of wood from the wall, and as she pulls it down, legs extend. She secures a full table to the floor.

"That's cool," I say.

"You have a Murphy table," Dad says.

"I want one," I say.

"It's nice," Anita says. "Doesn't take up much space."

We sit while Rosana gets bowls and the little boys hand out spoons. Then Anita sets the table. Her family eats with gusto, but I find the texture of boiled chicken skin unappealing. Anita passes the broth around to pour over the rice, and I do so in the hopes of flavoring it, but I'm not sure she used salt. I'm hungry enough to eat a large amount, but I'm disappointed there's no spice or zest to the food.

Tia Elba isn't here either. She's already removed her car from the Tetris game in the carport and gone home.

But that's okay. Anita might know about the family scandal also. Maybe I can offer to help make a meal—and slip in some spice while I'm at it.

⟡

Anita's family has internet, but only for a few hours every evening when the satellite is in position, and it's not very fast. I settle into the hard orange cushions of the couch and manage to get my emails loaded. All my roommates have written me now, with varying degrees of concern, and they promise to get tested.

An email from Tiago sits at the top of my email box.

I'm afraid to open it. I'm afraid it will bring a flood of emotions I don't want to deal with. Or it will give me the desire to keep talking to him. Cutting him out of my life was one of the hardest things I've ever done. I shouldn't have emailed him. I should have asked someone else to do it.

The best response now is to not answer his email. Not even read it.

But did he get tested? Did he take care of himself? Does he have TB also?

I tell myself it's none of my concern either way. I close down my email box before opening it.

But I didn't delete it.

Anita has big plans for us in the morning.

"There is a zoo an hour from here that just opened," she says. "They have one of the largest monkey exhibits in the country! And a beautiful market next to it."

"Where are the kids?" Annette asks.

"My children?" Anita says. "They are in school."

"But tomorrow's Christmas Eve!" I say.

"Yes, yes. They have school right until. And Rosana will go help Elba at the shop when she gets out of school. We'll see them at dinner."

I'm not mourning their loss. Rosana hasn't warmed up to us, but Scott seemed to get along well with Tito, her little brother.

"Are you coming?" I ask Anita as my dad tells everyone to get jackets and get in the car.

She shakes her head. "No, I have much work to do here. But go, have fun!"

I hesitate. "I could stay behind and help you," I say slowly, not sure if I mean it. I want to see the monkeys.

She shoos me with her hands. "No, no. This is not your work. Go, enjoy! Go watch the monkeys walk on their tails!"

She's convinced me. I'll stay and ask questions later.

Mom stays behind nursing a headache, and Anita says she'll take care of her. So I get the front seat, which makes the hour drive to the monkey zoo much easier on all of us.

I'm disappointed by the zoo. The animals don't have large enclosures for wandering like in the States and instead look like a dog stuffed into a crate too small for it. The bear lies curled up on the floor with his paws over his nose and doesn't budge even when we call at it.

There are at least a dozen monkeys in their cage, and they climb and chatter at us, their voices full of indignation and repressed rage. I'm thoroughly depressed by the time we leave the zoo.

Shopping cheers me up. We spend the next hour at the market buying gifts. Many are local artisans, but I find enough "made in China" stores to figure out which booths to avoid.

"Tomorrow's Christmas Eve," Annette says. She fingers a shell necklace she bought. "It's strange not to be home."

"Yeah," I say. "But it'll be fun to experience a different culture here."

"Yeah," she says, but I can tell she doesn't agree. She's thirteen and wants to be in her bed, waiting for Christmas morning. It doesn't feel like Christmas. Even though the climate is a bit cooler in Zipaquirá, it's too warm for snow. Too warm for hot chocolate.

I hug her and point out a beautiful pair of leather shoes.

"These are nice," I say.

"Are you offering to buy them for me?" she says, a glint returning to her eye.

"I was hinting that you could get them for me," I say, and she laughs.

I wake in the morning and try to find the feeling of Christmas. Outside birds are yelling, squawking, making noises they don't make back home. Through the window I see the plants waving and trembling in the breeze. Everything is green, so green, so beautiful and alive and so not Christmasy.

"*Buenos dias*, good morning, good morning!" Anita comes into the room and gives us all hugs and kisses. "Feliz Navidad!"

"But Christmas is tomorrow," Annette says, yawning as she throws her legs over the side of the hammock.

"We celebrate it today," Rosana says. "Starting with church." She retrieves a dress from the closet and leaves the room. She doesn't like to change in front of us and prefers to wait in line for the only bathroom in the house.

"Church is in one hour," Anita says. "Please get ready!"

"Christmas Eve," Annette says, a sense of wonder in her voice.

"Christmas Eve," I agree. I pull my dress from the suitcase under the bed and give it a good shake to de-wrinkle it.

An hour later we drive through the open gate to a small chapel tucked into the hillside. I'm disappointed we didn't go to the Salt Cathedral Zipaquirá is famous for, but Anita promises we'll go another day.

"Not Christmas," she said. "Everyone will be there."

Even at this smaller chapel, a large number of people show up.

And then I hear the Christmas carols.

Voices ring out from the pews as we file in, and I know they're singing "Joy to the World" because it's the same melody, even if the words are foreign. I stumble into a bench along with my family. Emily finds a hymn book and searches for the correct page, but I don't wait for it. I belt out the words in English as fiercely as everyone around me sings in Spanish. Annette joins me, and I smile at her even as a few people glance back at us. We launch into "Silent Night" after that, and then "O Little Town of Bethlehem." By the time the preacher has us sit down, my eyes burn and my heart is filled with joy.

I found it. Christmas.

CHAPTER SEVENTY-NINE

Family Names

I can't stop smiling the rest of the day. Anita introduces us to the congregation, and I catch the words, "*La hija de Ruby, se recuerda de Ruby?*"

"*La hermana de Elba?*" one woman asks, placing a hand on Mom's forearm and glancing at Anita.

I'm two steps behind, slowly piecing together the Spanish, but I recognize my abuela's name.

Elba's sister.

I knew, of course, that Tia Elba was my mom's aunt, but only in that moment do I realize they were sisters.

And Elba stayed here in Colombia while my grandmother went to the U.S.

I remember the story my grandfather told me about rescuing my teenage grandmother. He didn't know what he saved her from. She never told him. But he knew she needed help. She never looked back, but she didn't cut ties completely with her family.

Elba always knew where she was. And Elba kept her fingers in my mother's life also.

Which means the problem did not lie with Elba.

Did Ruby have to flee? Was my grandmother forced to run away from something here? Did she end up in America all by herself?

As Anita turns to talk to someone else, I'm certain she knows. I stare at the back of her head as if I can pry the answers from her.

She swivels to us with a smile. The time to ask questions isn't now. But it will come.

When we get back to the house, Anita puts us to work cleaning and cooking. I watch her make tamales, folding the corn massa in giant banana leaves, and it smells flavorful. I hope it tastes good. I don't feel I've eaten a solid meal since I got here.

Rosana's father, Carlos, sets up a tall, skinny Christmas tree in the corner of the room. Family begins to arrive in the early afternoon. Carlos goes out to help with the parking, and I peer out the window to watch as he rolls each car into position. No one will be able to leave without his help, but he knows what he's doing. Tia Elba walks over, since her house isn't far away. She sits in one of the chairs the boys put up in the living room, and Rosana offers her a drink.

No one is sitting by her.

I climb over several pairs of feet, muttering, *"Desculpe, desculpe,"* which is Portuguese, but they seem to understand me, because legs move out of my path to let me by. Then I fall into the seat beside her.

"Ola, Tia Elba," I say.

"Ola, *hija!*" she says, then she kisses my cheeks.

I'm not her daughter, but I'm family, and I grasp her hand, feeling the papery skin and the swollen veins beneath the surface.

"Tia," I say. *"Que es tu nombre?"*

Her name. If I can get a real name—I'll be light years ahead of where I was. The name listed in my family tree is Vallay, but I know Abuela made it up.

"Mi nombre?" she repeats. "Soy Elba."

"Su nombre completo," I say. Did I say that right? I put my hand on my chest. *"Mi nombre es* Cassandra Elena Jones."

"Ah, *sí!*" she says, nodding in understanding. *"Mi nombre es Elba Maria Vasquez Valladares."*

My eyes widen at the long names and rolling consonants. *"Espera,"* I say, and then I stand up and go to my room. I fish around my bag until I find pen and paper, then I return to Elba. *"Escriba?"* I say.

She takes the paper and writes her name down for me. Elba Maria Vasquez Valladares.

It's long and it's beautiful and part of it belongs to me.

But which part?

I tap the last name. *"Este es su nombre de casamento?"*

"No." She shakes her head and then she says something I don't understand. She takes the pen and points to Vasquez. *"Nombre de mi padre."* Then she points to Valladares. *"Nombre de mi madre."*

Ah! That's how it works. That's why she has so many names. I stare again at the names, a shiver running through me.

Valladares.

Vallay.

I look at her again. *"Y el nombre de mi abuela?"* Assuming she remembers my grandmother's name. I'm not sure my grandmother does. Her mind was addled after her stroke.

"Es el mismo," Elba says. "Ruby Beatriz Vasquez Valladares."

I lean over and kiss her papery cheek. *"Gracias,* Tia Elba. *Feliz Navidad."* I fold the paper and shove it into my pocket. I'll examine it later.

We stop talking when Anita's husband Carlos stands up and speaks to all the guests. I can pick up more Spanish now after the few days we've been here, which makes me confident that I'd be able to speak comfortably if I were here longer. He welcomes all the friends and family and then opens his Bible.

Everyone gets out their bags and purses and pulls out a Bible, except the younger kids, who open their phones. I have the Bible on my phone too, but not in Spanish. Still,

I open it to Luke like he instructs, and I read along to the Christmas story in English while he reads in Spanish. The children pop onto the floor at preappointed times dressed in costume, playing the parts of shepherds and camels and wisemen and Mary and Joseph and the angel. One of them even gets to be the donkey. There's laughter and singing, and I'm pleased at how it feels the same as the traditions we do back home, even if the climate and language are different.

Talking and chatter continue for hours after the scripture-reading. I keep wondering when we'll eat dinner, but Rosana brings out appetizer after appetizer, serving us in a traditional red dress with a large red flower in her hair. I would think the appetizers take the place of dinner, except I saw Anita making tamales. I check the time as the hours pass. Already after eight.

It's not until nine p.m. that Anita brings the tamales out to the three long tables filling the kitchen and hallway. She calls everyone to take a seat. I follow my sisters, and one of the banana-wrapped tamales plunks on the plate in front of me with a spoonful of sweet potato salad. I wait until those around me begin opening their tamales, and then I open mine.

I recognize the square shape, the yellow massa, the leaking tomato sauce gathering underneath. I cut off a corner and expose the interior, filled with green olives, raisins, peas, corn, and shredded chicken. The flavors are unusual together, but Mom makes these once a year also, usually for a special occasion, and I've come to enjoy the flavors.

Anita's tamales taste a bit different than my mom's. I don't think she flavored the massa. At least the olives add a nice bite.

We talk and eat and talk some more. I've long run out of things to say, in English or Spanish. It's almost eleven before the plates are cleared and the flan is brought out. The creamy, caramel custard melts in my mouth, sliding from my tongue down my throat, and it's heavenly.

After dessert, people finally begin leaving. It's a long process filled with hugs, kisses, and lingering hand-holding.

After the last person leaves, Carlos turns to the rest of us.

"Merry Christmas!" he says in his awkward English. "Now begins the real party!"

Is he for real? My eyes are burning with the need to take out my contacts. It's almost midnight, and it finally dawns on me that the whole point of these activities was to keep us awake until midnight. Until Christmas day.

His children know what to do. Rosana and Tito run to the skinny Christmas tree, and the parents follow. Sometime in the past few hours, someone snuck a smattering of presents beneath the tree.

Dad already told us going to Colombia was our Christmas gift this year. But Carlos calls my name and hands me a small wrapped box, and he hands one to each of my siblings. Rosana gets two boxes, and Tito gets three.

"Abranlos," he says, or something similar. He nods at all of us.

We tear into the paper at once. Back home we open our gifts one at a time, each person in the family admiring and sharing in the delight of what the other person got. But we also open our gifts on Christmas morning, not at midnight on Christmas Eve.

Not to mention that we receive more gifts than we can count.

Inside my box is a beautiful mug and saucer set, painted with striking red flowers that remind me of poppies. "Oh, it's lovely!" I exclaim.

Rosana exclaims over a necklace and a new pair of shoes, and my sisters got similar cups but different colored flowers. We show our gifts off to each other while Carlos beams.

"*Buenas noches!*" he says. "*Y feliz Navidad!*"

It sounds like the party's over and we're being sent to bed.

"Good night," I say, and I step over to hug him. "*Buenas noches. Muchas grácias.*"

"*De nada, de nada.*"

"Strange how it feels like Christmas is over," Emily says as we walk to the bedroom. "But it hasn't even happened yet."

"Very strange," I agree.

"What will we do tomorrow, since they did everything today?" Annette asks.

"I have no idea." I put my cup and saucer back in the box and pack it into my suitcase. "I guess we'll find out tomorrow."

CHAPTER EIGHTY

Missing Person

The holiday of Christmas itself reminds me a lot of New Year's Day in the States. We sleep in late, probably because no one went to bed before midnight, and even after we climbed into bed, happy revelers set off fireworks into the wee hours outside, and cars rolled down the cobblestone streets honking. I heard singing and caroling as late as two a.m. before sleep finally claimed me.

The morning is lazy. We eat rice pudding for breakfast, and then we drive out to the Salt Cathedral in two cars. I've wanted to see this since we arrived, so I watch with anticipation as we approach the old salt mines. We park in a plaza with tall, beige buildings that remind me of the Alamo in Texas. A tall Christmas tree dwarfs the palm trees beside it, lights dancing even though it's daytime.

Right. I almost forgot it was Christmas.

We walk toward a building with two bell towers, and I assume it's the cathedral.

Anita tells us the history as we approach. Rosana takes Tito and they go on ahead. They've probably heard this story many times before.

"The miners wanted a place to worship," she says. "So they carved a cross out of salt deep down in the mines. And then they added pews. And then, little by little, they carved out a cathedral. But this isn't the original cathedral. It was built in 1801 and closed in the 1950s. This is a new one, built even lower and made safer for public tours."

"It's underground?" I ask. "It's not that building?" I point to the one with the bell towers.

"Oh no, this is the plaza principal. We have to enter the mines to get to it. It's a twenty-minute walk from here, but you should enjoy this beautiful town."

I pull my phone out to fact-check the cathedral before I remember I have no service here. The internet at Rosana's house is unreliable, virtually cutting me off from my social web. I feel crippled without my trusty search engine, usually ready to spit out random facts anytime I get the itch to discover something.

The road begins to incline a few blocks past the plaza. My calves complain with the uphill climb, but I've not had any physical activity since we landed a few days ago, so I tell them to shove it.

A hill looms in front of us. Trees line the walkway, the red bricks around them creating a contrasting image against the green hillside. The walkway narrows and twists and turns as we get close. A tunnel opens before us, like the ones we drive through to get past the Rocky Mountains into Colorado. A large cross sits on top of the tunnel. As we get closer, I see turnstiles for collecting tickets. Dad steps up to a window and purchases our tickets, and then we move into the darkness of the mine.

Except it's not dark in the least. Flashing purple and red lights guide us deeper inside. I sniff, picking up on the rotten-egg smell of sulfur.

Anita begins talking again, giving us a tour-guide-worthy infomercial. "The Muisca people of Colombia were the first to discover this salt mine," she say. "Formed here millions of years ago when an inland sea covered the region."

"The Muisca," I said. "I gave a presentation on them last year in college."

"Did you?" She smiles. "That's good. You know a little bit about your people."

My people. My face flushes. I know nothing about my people.

We pass glowing crosses on the tunnel wall, and Anita says, "Each one of these represents a different stage in the death of Jesus."

"Kind of creepy," Scott mutters.

"I didn't know there are thirteen stages in Jesus' death," I say.

"Because you weren't raised Catolica." She says the word with a distinctly Spanish flair. "But you can still learn about it."

We enter a large dome, lit blue with florescent lights.

"Look at the lights," Mom says.

I lift my head to see giant chandeliers with purple and blue lights clinging to the rock ceiling.

"Wow," I say.

"Over here you can peer down into the temple." Anita leads to a railing and looks over the side. "That is the cathedral. Two hundred and fifty thousand tons of rock salt had to be removed to create it."

We take a staircase, carved of salt, down to the cathedral. The wide room opens up with beautiful salt pillars carved into the walls, as magnificent as marble pillars on a Greek temple. The fact that they could disintegrate with a massive wave of water makes them even more marvelous.

A flashing, colorful cross spanning floor to ceiling attracts my attention at the end of the room. Congregates kneel before an altar in front of it.

"This is the largest underground cross in the world," Anita says.

I move closer to it. Emily sticks by my side.

"How many underground crosses do you think there are in the world?" I murmur to her.

She giggles. "Wouldn't be hard to be the biggest."

"Guessing not."

We keep our cynicism to ourselves.

"There's a theater off the hallway to your left," Anita says. "It shows a movie about the construction of the cathedral."

The cross might not have won my admiration, but there's no question the cathedral is phenomenal.

❦

"We're taking a trip to Manizales for a few days," Dad tells us after Christmas.

We're gathered for family prayer in the room where my parents sleep. I'm only half paying attention, kneeling for prayer but staring out the window. I want to go outside and touch the large pink blossom blooming next to the house. The longer I'm here, the deeper this country gets into my blood. I feel it in my bones, a kinship similar to the love I harbor for Brazil.

I turn to my father when he speaks. "Manizales? Where is that?"

"It's in the Andes mountains."

"Wait, we're not already in the Andes?" I ask.

"No," Dad says.

"Aren't the Andes kind of far?" Emily asks.

"It's an eight-hour drive from here," Dad says.

Hence why I got a B in geography.

And then I picture being squished into the back of the car for eight hours, and I blanch. "And we're going there why?"

Mom and Dad exchange a look, and my spidey-senses tingle.

"There are some historical sites to see there. An amazing teleférico that goes up the mountain. We might even see snow," Dad says.

"So we're sight-seeing?" Scott asks.

"We are tourists, after all," Emily says.

Am I the only one who's picked up on the family mystery? I'm suddenly positive we're going to this city because of it.

"Are we staying in a hotel?" Scott asks.

Dad nods. "We'll drive up tomorrow, stay the night and spend the day there on Thursday. Then we'll drive back here Friday."

"Eight hours crammed in the back of the car?" Emily says, letting out a loud exhale.

I feel her pain. Not a one of us will enjoy that drive.

"Unless someone wants to stay behind," Dad says.

"I volunteer!" Scott says, his hand shooting up.

"I wasn't really offering," Dad says, and Scott lowers his hand.

"What time do we leave?" I ask. I'm dreading the drive also, but I'm buoyed up by the information I've garnered so far on this trip. I finally have pieces to the puzzle, and if I get a few more, I might be able to piece it together.

"Five in the morning."

"Five in the morning!" I gasp. I don't wake up that early, not ever. Not since the days of Bible study in high school.

"Yep," Dad says. "So I suggest you put together an overnight bag and get to bed."

It's not much warning. We go through a rapid prayer and bedtime routine, then head off to pack enough items for a quick trip to the mountains.

I shove a sweater and jeans into a bag while I wait my turn for the bathroom. By the time the line is gone, the house is silent. I brush my teeth and step into the hallway, and then freeze when I hear the murmur of my mom's voice in the dark kitchen.

"We are being careful," she says. "I know it's dangerous."

Who is she talking to? I tiptoe to the corner and peer around it. I don't see anyone. And then I notice the blue glow of a phone, and my mom's silhouette takes shape in the darkness.

"I know, Jadene." She sighs.

Jadene. Her sister. I hold my breath, waiting for more clues to reveal themselves.

"I have to find him," she whispers.

I seize on her words.

Him. She's looking for a him.

She's silent a moment, probably listening to my aunt. "I'm going there tomorrow," she says. "I'm looking for proof."

Proof of what?

The rest of the conversation is murmured affirmations, and then she hangs up. I slip away before I'm spotted.

But I lay in bed staring at the ceiling with my heart racing.

Who is him?

CHAPTER EIGHTY-ONE

History Unraveled

I'm half asleep and dead to the world when we cram into the car the next morning. My eyes burn from putting my contacts in so early, and it's cold outside, so I cuddle up next to Annette and we shiver together in the back seat until my dad gets the heat going. At least there are plenty of places to rest my head when we're smashed together like this.

I sleep until the jostling car wakes me. It's been almost two hours. My body still wants to rest, but my mind is alert now. I watch out the window as we wind through villages and barely get out of the way for bigger vehicles. We go over another pothole, and the car bounces. I yawn and open a book to read.

Two hours later we reach the foothills of the Andes mountains, and that's when things get interesting. The road narrows as we climb, up and up. I shove my body over Scott so I can peer out the window, and it's frightening and impressive to see the mountain fall away beside us.

"Look, the clouds," Annette says, pointing out the windshield.

I duck my head to see. Clouds hover over the mountains, and as we keep winding up and up, we drive through them. For a moment, they block our path.

"Are we that high?" I breathe.

We have to slow down for several animals in the road.

"Llamas!" I say.

"Alpacas," Dad says. "They look like llamas but they're different."

They take their time moving out of our way, long necks bobbing and making me think of camels.

"I need to pee," Scott says.

"I'm hungry," Annette adds.

"I think there's a restaurant a few miles up this mountain," Dad says.

A restaurant, here? We pass through a village, and red-cheeked children watch us from the small houses pressed into the mountainside.

"Their faces are red from the lack of oxygen," Mom says. "They've adapted to it."

We come around a bend in the village and see what looks like a pub. There are cars parked out front as well as donkeys with woven, colorful blankets laid across their backs. Dad parks next to the other vehicles.

"We'll eat lunch here."

"This place was on your GPS?" I'm impressed anything up here is documented.

"Yes. Come on, let's see what they've got."

Inside, the wooden structure is roomy and warm. I feel like I've stepped back in time when I see the fire crackling in the hearth. My dad talks to a man at the door, and a girl younger than me comes and shows us to a table. She smiles but doesn't speak or offer us menus.

My dad joins us. "They'll bring us lunch."

"Do we get to choose?" Scott asks.

"No."

"What is it?" Emily says.

"It's a standard Colombian dish."

The girl returns carrying bowls of soup. She sets two down on the table and disappears to return with two more, until each of us has a bowl. She places a plate of arepas in the middle of the table, which Anita makes every day also.

The steamy green contents teem with vegetables, some I recognize and some I don't. I take a nibble of an orange one and think it might be a sweet potato, but I've never had it in this form, and definitely not in soup. There's a starchy potato-like one that reminds me of mandioca from Brazil. Yucca, I think is the word in English, but I've never eaten it in the States.

Scott pulls a long, off-white cylinder from his soup. "Is this banana?"

"Plantain," my mom says. "Like banana, but more firm and less sweet."

The soup is nourishing and warm. The flavors are interesting, and they please my palate more than what we've been eating. Still, I find myself craving a fat cheeseburger dripping with grease and slathered in mayo.

We use the bathroom before we get back in the car, a single water closet with a trashcan for the toilet paper, but after a week of being in Colombia, tossing my waste in the can instead of the toilet has become a habit. It's not the cleanest bathroom I've ever been in, but the floor has been swept and there are no giant spiders. Maybe too cold up here.

We brought our own toilet paper, of course.

Mom is perusing the small gift shop when I come out. I join her, fingering the soft sweaters made of animal fur and admiring the beautiful woven tapestries. Then we stuff ourselves back into the car and continue our journey.

But now we're headed down the mountain. Somehow this feels even scarier. Through Scott's window I see the face of the mountain, which the narrow road hugs, and our car hugs even tighter on each switchback. We have the inside lane but the road isn't much bigger than a single lane, which is never more obvious than when another vehicle comes from the other side. Emily's window reveals mountains, rising and falling in every direction. They are covered in green foliage and clouds and are breathtaking.

So is looking down, and I avoid it.

A small truck barrels around the bend, loaded with goats. He almost doesn't see us and slams on his brakes before we collide.

But we don't both fit right here in this tight spot.

He can't get around us or he'll go off the mountain, and we can't get any closer to the rock. I hold my breath, my heart racing.

Dad stops driving. No one says a word, but I'm certain we're all pondering how we'll get out of this.

The truck backs up. On this twisty mountain road, with no back up cameras and a bed loaded with bleating goats, he backs up. He wraps himself back around the road until he reaches a wider spot, and then he stops.

Dad starts driving again. I hold my breath, not able to draw oxygen until we've driven past the goat truck and continued down the road. I look behind me to see him resuming his rapid ascent up the mountain.

"Is this the only way in and out?" Mom asks, breaking the tense silence.

"There's the Pan-American highway," Dad says. "But it takes longer."

Mom doesn't comment. She doesn't have to. I know we're all thinking the same thing.

This road is trying to kill us.

⟋⟍ ✦ ⟋⟍

It takes hours longer to get to Manizales than Dad thought it would, mostly because of how treacherous the mountain road is. By the time we finally pull into the small parking lot of Hotel Belén Boutique, it's past nine, and I want to fall to my knees and say a prayer of gratitude that we didn't die.

The warm glow from the windows spills onto the wet pavement, a stark contrast to the cold, misty darkness pressing in around us. The drive was endless—sharp turns with sheer drop-offs, headlights flickering against the damp rock walls, the occasional set of distant taillights disappearing into the fog. I'm pretty sure Dad's fingers are still locked in a death grip on the steering wheel.

Inside, the hotel is small but inviting. The wooden floors creak under our tired steps, and the scent of freshly brewed coffee drifts in from somewhere. The receptionist, a kind-looking woman with dark curls and a soft voice, hands over our keys with an understanding smile, as if she's seen plenty of travelers stumble in like this before—exhausted, shaken, and relieved to be on solid ground.

We have to get three separate hotel rooms because each one only sleeps two people. Outside, the temperature is frigid, since we're still up in the mountains—just not as high as the peaks we drove through to get here.

I'm in a room with Emily. It's simple but clean, with thick blankets on the bed and a window that looks out over the twinkling city lights below. I don't even bother unpacking. I collapse onto the bed, sinking into the mattress with a sigh.

Dad gets a few arepas for dinner and brings them to us with sliced roasted meat and grilled bananas. I eat in my bed with the blankets all around me.

"It's so cold," Emily says, echoing my feelings.

"Dad should have told us to bring winter clothes," I say. "I'm lucky I have a jacket. I only brought it because it was cold when we left Arkansas."

"I didn't know Colombia would be this cold," Emily says.

There's nothing else to do but sleep. We could turn on the TV and watch a handful of Colombian soap operas, but neither of us feels inclined to do that. And we're tired. So

374

we turn out the light and hunker down in our beds, burying under the blankets and trying to get warm.

When the morning light comes streaming in through our window, I'm well-rested and humming with excited energy.

Mom is up to something today, something that has to do with her family, and I'm riddled with excitement to find out what it is.

We meet in the hotel lobby to check out, which is really just a small room with a desk and several plants around tall windows. Outside the sun reflects off red-tiled roofs and the cobblestone street, looking deceitfully warm and inviting.

"Okay," Dad says, joining us. "First thing we're doing is the teleférico up the mountain. It's a cable car that travels to the highest peaks. You'll love this. We'll see snow."

"That sounds amazing," I say. "But that's not why we drove all the way over here, is it?"

"It's something you'll never experience anywhere else," Dad says, not quite answering my question. "I'll drop your mom off first, and then we'll go to the cable car."

"Wait." I latch onto his words, warning bells sounding in my head. "Mom's not going with us?"

"No, she's got something she wants to do here in town."

No way am I letting Mom sneak around, pursuing this mystery without me. "I want to do what Mom's doing."

"And miss the teleférico?" My dad tilts his head and stares at me like I spoke an alien language.

I swallow hard. He knows me well enough to know that this is an adventure I'd give my right arm to go on. A chance to take a cable car up one of the tallest peaks in the Andes and see snow in Colombia? I grit my teeth.

I have to know the answers to my family. Even if I miss the teleférico.

"Yes," I say, forcing the word out.

"Well, it's not an option," Mom says. "You have to go with your dad."

I swivel to her, annoyed she voided my ultimate sacrifice. "Why?"

"Because it will be more fun. You'll be bored with me."

"What are you doing?"

"I'm—" She pauses. She blinks and looks past me, her gaze on my face but her eyes missing mine. "I'm visiting an old church."

"An old church? I want to come!"

"Why?" She furrows her brow.

I latch onto the obvious, something they won't question. "Because it's old and in the mountains and historic! That's even cooler than the Salt Cathedral! Oh, come on, you have to let me see it!"

"You'd rather see an old church than the teleférico?"

"Yes." I sigh. "If I have to pick one, that's what I choose."

She looks at my dad. "Maybe the kids can see the church for a few minutes before going to the cable car."

I hold my breath. We might be able to do both?

Dad shrugs. "Up to you."

Fifteen minutes later we've parked on a steep incline. A small church with a bell in the facade faces us up the mountain, and it's a harrowing ten-minute walk to get to it. I stand in front and take pictures. The colors are faded and the architecture the same as the others we've seen around here, but it's the first church I've seen tucked into a mountainside. I turn around and take a picture of the dips and falls of mountains and valleys behind me.

When I turn back, Mom's disappeared. I see my siblings hanging out by the entrance but not going inside, and my dad's reading something on his phone. I step around my family and peer into the church. It's tiny, with only a few pews, a loft, and a pulpit. The small windows around the top let in very little light, and most of it comes from the open door on the other side of the chapel.

Mom is not inside. I cross the church and exit through the back of the building.

A stunning view of an old cemetery greets me. With the cloud wrapped around the mountain behind it and the faded tombstones lit by any sunlight managing to break through overhead, its picturesque and Gothic-looking.

Mom stands a few yards away, peering down at one of the graves.

CHAPTER EIGHTY-TWO

Poke the Bear

I stumble over my feet in my rush to get to her. I slow when I approach so I won't startle her, but my feet step loudly over the soft dirt and short grass. I join her and look down also.

The tombstone is pressed into the dirt. The words etched into it are covered in lichens and moss and barely legible. I crouch down and wipe at it, my fingers tracing the grooves, searching for the words.

Torres.

I find that one at the end. I scrub and wipe at the rest, but the letters are chipped and filled in.

"Whose grave is this?" I ask, looking up at Mom.

"My grandmother's," she says.

A thrill of delight tickles through my chest. She gave me a real answer. I look back at the tombstone. "What does it say?"

"Aliciane Beatriz Valladares Torres."

"So was Torres her married name?"

Mom shakes her head. "Most women don't take the name of their spouse. Their children get the dad's name. Torres came from her father and Valladares from her mother."

That explains why Tia Elba didn't have a married last name. "Did you know her?"

Mom hesitates in her answer, as if she's trying to decide how much to share. I feel I'm on tenuous ground. "I feel as if I knew her."

How do I interpret that answer? Perhaps Aliciane never left Colombia, and they never met. Or maybe they met briefly but didn't get the chance to develop a relationship.

Either way, it means my grandmother talked about her mother enough for my mom to feel a connection to this dead woman.

I glance around the cemetery plot and push to my feet. I see no other tombstones nearby. "Where is your grandfather buried?"

Mom stiffens. Her face goes still and her body freezes like she's been shot with a stun gun. Then she says, "Stop asking so many questions. It's time for you to go. Tell your dad to take you to the teleférico."

The response is so out of context that I blink in surprise. How did we go from having a conversation to me being sent away? "Do you know where he's buried?" I ask.

Her face changes, her eyes widening and then narrowing, her nostrils flaring, her brow crinkling. "I said no more questions!"

It's an overreaction. I've poked the bee's hive. Angered the sleeping bear.

But I'm a bit closer to knowing where the mystery lies.

Somewhere with my grandfather.

～∞ ☀ ∞～

Dad parks in front of a large rectangular building nestled at the base of the mountain. Giant cables stretch out of one end and lead up. I get out of the car and follow the cables with my eyes up the mountainside. At the very top, as promised, is a plateau of snow.

I shouldn't be so impressed by it. I'm surrounded by the white stuff in Colorado. But I didn't expect to see it in Colombia.

We go inside the rectangular building and wait on benches next to floor-to-ceiling windows while Dad buys tickets. I examine the mountain outside. It's so tall that clouds keep passing in front of it, blocking the view.

Several other people gather around us in the viewing area, and then a woman comes out and begins speaking to us.

I turn to my dad when he joins us. "What's she saying?" I whisper.

"She's saying it's a two-part journey. When we get partway up, we'll stop and rest about ten minutes so our lungs can adjust to the altitude. We can get out and walk around as long as we want before going up to the next part. The cable car comes every twenty minutes. Then we get in the teleférico and continue the journey to the second stop."

"How high is it?" I ask.

"Almost four thousand meters."

That doesn't mean anything to me. "Feet?" I ask.

"Nearly fifteen thousand."

I know it's a high number, but I still can't compute it. "Okay," I say.

We pile into the cable car, a wobbly glass box with windows on all sides. It tilts as we walk inside, and we squeal and cling to the handles on the walls. The last person squishes in. The car starts rolling upward, and I lean up against the glass and watch as the trees, the roads, the cars, the city disappears beneath us.

In a matter of minutes, we reach the first station. The car jolts as it docks. Another employee greets us, and he says something about burros.

I see small donkeys tethered to the fence. "Can we ride them?" I ask.

He hears me and answers in English. "Yes, they are for visitors. Just don't take one off the mountain."

He smiles, so I think he's joking, but I'm not sure.

I'll stay away from the edge just in case.

It's much colder up here. I have my jacket with me, but I'm startled when I see my breath as I speak. I didn't bring gloves, and my fingers are already numb.

We're on a large, flat part of the mountain. The donkey would have to be suicidal to get off. Annette and I claim the last two. The animals are nimble here on the rocks, jumping and running around like goats. My butt gets sore from the bouncing up and down, the jostling, and I last about five minutes before I turn the donkey around and take it to Emily.

"Your turn," I say. "Don't fall off the mountain."

Her eyes go wide, and I imagine that's how I looked when the guy said it to me.

I hustle back into the station and check the time. We have to stay at this point for fifteen minutes so we don't get altitude sickness. I have seven to go.

One by one people join me inside the station, and finally the time is up. We can take the ride to the top.

I watch with anticipation as the snow-covered mountain gets closer. A railing wraps around the sidewalk, and I see people on it, taking pictures, leaning on each other.

The cable car jolts as it reaches the top. Our guide begins talking again, and I pick out enough words to know he's reminding us that the oxygen is much thinner here and to be careful.

My eyes are on the big patch of snow only a few meters away.

The door opens, but before I can rush outside, the air smacks me in the face.

It's shockingly cold. Somehow I didn't expect it, even though there's snow. My jacket feels threadbare, and my teeth chatter as I step out of the teleférico. The oxygen sucks out of my lungs like the mountain is a vacuum, and I cough.

That hurts. I clutch my chest as I step onto the walkway. Everyone moves ahead of me, but no one is running with gleeful anticipation the way I expected to. We move slowly, and I take a deep, rasping breath, then another. My head begins to ache. Each step takes monumental effort.

I see Annette and Scott ahead of me. I catch up to them and hook arms with my sister.

"The snow," she says, pointing at the mound only a few hundred feet in front of us.

It feels like we'll never get there. We shuffle forward, my heart racing as if I'm sprinting for a finish line. My head throbs. My eyes feel heavy, and I want to lie down and rest.

A barrier keeps us from going any closer. The snow sits like a glacier in a bowl, and if we slid down into it, we might not make it back out.

"We're here for a picture," I say, pulling out my phone. "We have to document that we made it this far."

We smile for the camera, shaking in our shoes, shivering and forcing our lips upward. I'm ready to get off this mountain. I want to breathe. We shuffle back toward the station, and this time we're leaning on each other, all three of us. I don't see Emily. The rest of our group is making its way back also, all of us moving slowly like a crowd of zombies.

Maybe this is how to kill zombies. Would a lack of oxygen slow them down also? Or would it only cripple the living?

I'm pondering the end of the world as we step into the station.

The cable car isn't here yet. The timer shows we have twelve more minutes.

Several people sit on the floor, leaning against the wall. I spot Emily and my dad, and we shuffle over to them.

"How long have you been in here?" My words come out slow and slurred. My brain and mouth don't want to coordinate.

"A minute," she says. "I didn't last long. Couldn't breathe."

Annette lays down on my dad's thigh and closes her eyes. Other people sprawl out on the cold floor of the station. I rest my head on Scott's shoulder, and for once he doesn't move away or shrug me off. We're both too exhausted. I shut my eyes and take slow, deep breaths.

Zombies don't breathe. They would have a distinct advantage over the living in areas of high altitude. Best to avoid them.

I clasp my hand around my neck as if it will open my lungs and get me a deeper breath.

My dad nudges me, jarring my eyes open.

"The teleférico is here," he says.

"It came?" My mouth barely moves. I'm not sure the words leave my lips.

My dad pulls me to my feet. We move like slime, slithering toward the open door. Finally we're all in. No one speaks, we barely move, and I don't know who presses against me or who's arm I'm resting on and I don't care.

We reach the second station within minutes, and my eyes pop open when we dock. The worker tells us we'll wait a few minutes if anyone wants out, and the door slides open. None of us make a move to get out. Two people step in. We sit still and wait.

The fog in my head begins to clear. I take a deep breath and feel the oxygen opening up the chambers of my lungs. By the time the the cable car gets moving again, I'm blinking and more alert. The sleepiness fades completely in the next few minutes, and conversation resumes in the cable car.

"Wow," Annette says. "I can't believe how tired I got."

"No kidding," I agree. "I felt wiped."

"That's what oxygen deprivation will do to you," Dad says.

"Fascinating."

It's an experience I won't forget. But I'm glad to be off the mountain.

CHAPTER EIGHTY-THREE

Junk Purge

We opt to take the long way back to Zipaquirá, along the Pan-American highway instead of through the twisting, winding road of the Andes mountains.

I'm brimming with questions. The few answers I got feel like tantalizing bread crumbs, just enough to give me a hint of the right direction but nothing more. Where is my grandfather buried? Is he dead? What is his name? Why did we leave Colombia and why does no one speak of it? Is he the him my mom is looking for?

I'm kind of hoping his name is Bruno.

We traverse a few mountain passes even using the Pan-American highway, but nothing like the day before. There's an official rest area, and I try to ignore the military tank beside it with armed policemen chilling in plastic chairs out front, rifles laid across theirs laps.

I'm certain those are loaded.

We have our own toilet paper. We learned that lesson.

"Look." Annette points to a pipe leading from the toilets through the wall. "The sewage is pumped outside."

"For real?" My curiosity won't be abated, even though I'm disgusted. We head outside and look for the white pipe, and sure enough, waste flows from it into a small ditch behind the rest area. The ditch probably leads to a stream and then a river and hopefully a sanitation plant? I have my doubts. I saw the same thing in Brazil.

"Gross," Annette says.

The police watch us come back around the rest area, and I join my family by the car. The mountains loom to our left. I stand with my hand on the door, admiring their verdant majesty. They stretch up into the sky, disappearing into the clouds.

We drove through that.

"Let's go," Dad says.

I climb into the back seat, no longer bothered by my siblings encroaching on either side of me. I'm sad we're leaving in a few days.

We spend the next day combing through Anita's house, making sure we're not leaving anything behind. Dad stops her when she goes to make dinner and says he wants to treat the family to a meal.

"Where would you like to go?" he asks.

She turns and asks Tito, who's sitting on the couch reading.

"McDonald's!" he says.

Anita looks hesitant, but my dad readily agrees. We pile into our separate cars and drive into town so we can eat at the famous Golden Arches.

As soon as we step inside, I close my eyes and inhale the familiar scent of fried potatoes and melted cheese. A wave of nostalgia hits me, and American fast food never smelled so good.

Or tasted so good. My dad orders enough food to feed twenty people, and I scarf my way through two hamburgers and an entire box of fries.

"McDonald's must be better in Colombia," I say. I swallow and take a sip of soda, which they said was Sprite but doesn't taste like it. My fingers are covered in an orange sauce, and I wipe them off before tackling more fries.

Tito chatters away in Spanish, his face bright as he shows his burger to Rosana.

We finish our food and Anita rises to pick up piles of trash.

We leave tomorrow, and somehow with all the time we had in her house, I never cornered her. I never asked my questions.

I get up also and help clear the tables. When she takes her armload over to the can, I scurry after her.

"Anita," I say, stopping her by touching her arm before she turns back, "can I ask you something?"

She turns large brown eyes on me, blinking in surprise. "Yes."

I take a deep breath and blurt, "What do you know about my great-grandfather?"

"Your great-grandfather?"

I nod and press onward. "Do you know anything about him? What happened? Why my grandmother ran away from him?"

She shakes her head. "I know nothing. Your mother never spoke of him."

"Never said anything? In all the time you knew her at college?"

"No."

I can't tell if she's being honest. I don't know her well enough. I remember how long my mom withheld the fact that she's from Colombia from me. My whole life. "Do you know if he's alive? Know his name? Maybe Elba mentioned something about her father?"

She doesn't stop shaking her head. "No, no, Elba *nunca* say anything. *No habla de él.*"

She's digressing into Spanish, a clear sign that I've made her anxious. I release her arm and take a step back. "Nothing?"

"No, nothing, nada."

Maybe this is typical here, to pretend like a family member never existed. But it's been so many years. Whatever scandal happened, wouldn't it be past injury to discuss now?

"Okay. Thanks for answering me."

She offers a weak smile and scurries past me.

We say our goodbyes that evening. Tia Elba comes over and cries, blubbering in Spanish and clinging to my mom, and even my mom looks emotional. We hug and go to bed, and I can't believe our journey here is over.

I have to find out this family mystery. Someone alive knows the answer. Tia Elba knows, and I curse my inability to speak Spanish. I'll have to learn the language and come back to talk to her.

⟳∿✦∿⟲

The tiny airport in Colombia gets us on our plane in record time. We only showed up an hour before our flight, but at six in the morning, most of South America doesn't remember daytime exists. The stewardess pampers us with drinks and crackers before the flight takes off, and then we watch Bogotá disappear into the distance, watch the snow-capped mountains turn into pinpricks and then barely recognizable blobs.

I'll have one day in Arkansas before I fly back out to Colorado. It's been a whirlwind of a Christmas break, but I've loved it.

It's snowing as we near Dallas, falling on the wings of the plane, and we hit a few pockets of turbulence. As soon as we land, my phone goes haywire. It vibrates and dings with incoming notifications, and I gasp because I'm so startled. After two weeks of silence, it's an unexpected intrusion. We stand in the wicked-long line to get through customs and I go through my texts one by one, sending updates to everyone along with pictures of how amazing and beautiful Colombia was.

Thomas promises to pick me up from the airport. Layne is coming home, and she'll be moving in with us. I'll have a permanent roommate again. Iris will arrive two days after me, but Camila and Abby, who are both from Colorado, will stay with their families right up until school starts.

I open my email and weed through the junk, searching for anything important. School starts in five days. I'm already registered. After how easy Portuguese 201 was, I decided to skip 202 and jump straight to 302. I feel like I'm ready for something more advanced.

And then I see Tiago's email in the midst of my junk purge.

I never opened it.

I almost forgot about it. That was the nice thing about not having access to internet. But I see it, and a surge of confusing emotions spills over me. With hesitant fingers, I tap it.

Cassandra,

Thank you for reaching out. I understand the seriousness of what you're telling me, and I'm very sorry this happened to you, especially if it's my fault. I'll make sure my family gets tested. You don't have to worry about us.

I hope life is being everything you hoped it would be. You are never far from my thoughts.

Tiago.

I close my eyes and let out a small breath. Nothing in the email leaves me feeling guilty or sad or aching. He's cordial. Not quite friendly, but not rude. He's kind, he put my worries to rest, and he did not leave any expectations of continuing the conversation.

He understood the email for exactly what it was.

I compose an email I will never send.

Tiago,

Thank you for not pressuring me. Thank you for not telling me you love me. Thank you

383

for not guilting me or making me feel like a terrible person for loving you and then abandoning you. Guilt plagues me constantly for what I did. For what I allowed to happen between us and then didn't follow through.

I've pushed you far from my thoughts and you will remain far from them. But deep in the depths of my heart, you are never gone. I will always love you.

May life bless you with joy and success and a love much stronger and truer than mine.

I send the email to my draft box as soon as I finish with it so I don't accidentally press a button and send it to him. It's not a nice email, and it would hurt him more than it would comfort him. It's me expressing my thoughts. Venting my feelings. And I do feel so much guilt for what went down between us.

It's done now.

We reach the desk at immigrations to declare our purchases in Colombia, and then we're through customs.

"Our flight's been delayed," Dad says as we meander through the airport. "Let's get to the gate and see what's happening."

I groan internally. It never bodes well when a flight gets delayed. I glance out the window as we walk and see the snow sticking to the ground.

I have the feeling we're not going anywhere.

CHAPTER EIGHTY-FOUR

Layne's Return

My feeling proves correct.

After several hours of delays, our flight is canceled. The airport ships us off to a hotel, but only after arguing with my dad for an hour. The buses aren't running, so we show my dad how to use his app to call a taxi. By the time we get to the hotel, my mind is foggy and I can't think. I don't have my luggage and I didn't put my contact solution or glasses into my carry on. I fall into bed without taking out my contacts.

I wake up in the middle of the night with my eyes aching and burning, feeling as if someone trapped acid between my eye and the contact lens, and now the tiny piece of plastic is trying to eat its way into my cornea. I stumble into the bathroom and squint against the bright light, then peer at my reflection.

Alarm jolts through me when I see my eyes. The veins are swollen, jagged red lines slicing through the whites of my eyes. I look like I'm bleeding. I turn my blurred vision around the counter top of the bathroom, but they don't keep contact cases out for people to use. The best I can come up with are the plastic cups by the sink.

Getting the contacts out of my eyes is the next difficulty. They've suctioned on and then dried out. I wince and hiss and force my eyes to stay open as they tear up, trying to blink, shying away from my finger and the damage I'm doing by prying this hard plastic off my eyeball. It's excruciating, but I manage to get both out, and then I wet the hand towel and press it to my burning eye sockets. Tears roll down my cheeks, both soothing and burning. Without any solution, I have to use tap water, but I pour it into both cups of lenses and guide my blind self back to bed.

"What time is our flight?"

Mom's voice wakes me in the morning. My eyes feel wired shut. Light pours in from a window, I assume, and I massage the corners of my eyes and the lids until I'm able to squint them open. Oh, light hurts.

"The flight was scheduled for ten," Dad says. "But we've been pushed to the two p.m. flight."

I sit up, his words sinking in. "We won't get home until this evening? I fly to

Colorado tomorrow morning!"

"I know, I know. We'll get everything fixed. At least we don't have to leave the hotel early."

Mom stares at me. "Cassandra, your eyes. What happened?"

My eyes. I blink and feel the gritty irritation. I stand up and stumble my way past the beds, all the way to the bathroom.

Even without my glasses on, I can see how bloodshot my eyes are. It's like I have pinkeye all over again.

I stare at the cups with my contact lenses in them. If I want to see the world today, I have to put those back in. But I'm dreading it.

I go back into the room. "I didn't have my contact case or my glasses. I left my contacts in too long."

"Where are they now?" Mom asks.

"In cups in the bathroom. Don't drink them."

She laughs. "Okay."

"They probably sell contact solution in the hotel shop. We can check when we go down to breakfast," Dad says.

I brighten. "That will help."

We wake my siblings and join a disgruntled crowd of displaced travelers in the dining room. The hotel shop indeed sells small bottles of contact solution, so after a breakfast of instant eggs and oatmeal, I return to the room and water my contacts. When it looks like they've soaked up a sufficient amount of the saline solution, I plop them back in.

My eyes don't like it. They sting and burn and tear up in noisy complaint, but I blink several times until they settle into place. I have no choice. Today my eyes have to comply.

The bus comes to take us back to the airport, where we quietly accept our fate.

The two p.m. flight is delayed by six hours. Dad throws his weight around and waves his frequent flyer status and gets us a flight at five. They don't want to give it to us because the only seats left are in first class, but he makes a stink and they do.

I want to get home and take out my contacts.

Our luggage is waiting for us when we arrive in Arkansas. I sit down on the linoleum of the airport and pull out the suitcase, searching for my toiletries bag. Finding it, I remove each lens, sucking in a breath at how they scratch my eyes. Then I put my glasses on and nearly sing with relief. I can see, and it doesn't hurt.

The only thing I have time to do when I get to the house is repack. I find everything I need for school and shove it into my suitcase. One more day of flying, and tomorrow I'll be home.

⚬ ⚭ ⚬

Thomas picks me up from the airport at nine p.m. the next evening and gives me a big hug.

"You're alive!" he says.

"Yes. By some miracle, we weren't kidnapped and we didn't drive off a mountain."

"Was it close?"

"Oh boy. Yes."

I regale him with tales of Colombia, and he gives his deep, hearty laugh before taking me to a 24-hour cafe for food.

Real American food. I appreciate it.

"How's the TB thing?" he asks, and I wince.

"You know about that?"

"Abby told me."

He looks at me sympathetically, but I'm annoyed she said something. Does everyone I ever talked to need to know? I pull back my sleeve and show him my arm, where the lump is still visible.

"It stopped itching. But I'm not coughing, I don't feel sick. I'm going to be okay."

"Yeah, you'll be fine. You just need to be aware. Monitor it. How do you think you got it?"

I shrug. "Brazil, I guess."

"Were you in close contact with someone who had it?"

"I must have been." But I don't remember anyone in Tiago's house coughing or acting sick.

"Your fish are doing great."

Bless him for changing the subject. I spear the last of my pancake. "Thanks for taking care of them."

I check on them as soon as I'm back. They're still alive, mouths bobbing as they flit around, and the sides of the tank are sparkly clean. The sucker fish are doing their job. Nobody lost their guts while I was gone.

At least I averted that crisis.

〇〜⚜〜〇

I still have a few more days before school starts. Work resumes Monday afternoon, but my morning is free, so I walk over to the health department. It's cold enough to need a jacket, scarf, and gloves, and I miss the mild climate of Colombia. Even if it was chilly, it was warmer than this.

"We got the chart from the health department in Arkansas," the doctor says when I'm comfortably seated in a room. He looks over it and pulls up the measurements they took of my arm. "We're going to need to do our own TB test on you so we can record more data, but you have to wait two more weeks. It hasn't been long enough, and your previous results will skew the new test. Let me see your arm."

I pull my sweater up. He swivels my arm and examines the swelling still visible under the skin.

"Make an appointment to come back in a few weeks," he says. "Then we'll do a TB test and make a plan of action."

"All right." My heart sinks slightly. I had half hoped he would say there was no sign of a problem and we could cross that one off the list.

But it looks like I really have TB.

I head to work after. I'm early, but it doesn't matter, there's nothing to do. Only one professor is back from break, and he greets me when I come in and then disappears down the hall to his office. I sit at the computer and check my grades one more time to see if they improved, but they didn't. I scraped by with a 3.57, and as long as I do well this semester, it will even out for the year.

Except my B in geography doesn't make sense. Did I fail the test? That's the only way my grade can be that low.

I debate whether I'm brave enough to go talk to the professor. I'm still scared of adults.

Which is silly, since I am one.

Iris comes home Tuesday night.

Layne comes home Wednesday.

We have a full on screaming/shouting/hugging session when she walks in. Her blond hair is lighter but shorter, falling in soft waves to her shoulders. We go to dinner with Layne's mom and her boyfriend, which doesn't feel odd now that we spent several days at their house for Thanksgiving. Layne and I laugh and giggle and share knowing smiles laced with understanding at everything anyone says.

We help her move her things into my room. Lauren already moved over to Abby's room. She could have made a stink and forced Layne to go over there, but she didn't, and I like her a little more for that.

The three of us have just sprawled out on the couch, legs and arms hanging on each other like we used to do freshman year, when someone knocks on the door.

"Come in!" Iris yells.

The door opens, and Thomas steps in, his large frame filling the doorway.

"Hey," he says. "Jake just got back, and he wants to know if—" Thomas blinks and stops talking as if the rest of the sentence got sucked away from him.

"Yes?" I say, rolling my hand encouragingly.

Thomas's eyes are trained on Layne. "This is your roommate who was in Guatemala?"

Layne smiles at him. It's a seductive, flirtatious, come-hither smile I remember well. "Yep. That's me! I'm so flattered you recognize me!" She presses her hands to her chest like she's been given the greatest honor.

"Your picture's everywhere," Iris points out. "On the message board, the fridge, the wall."

"Yeah, you always said the sixth roommate was moving in this semester," Thomas says. He steps into the room. "The pictures don't do you justice. I'm Thomas."

He extends a hand, and Layne stretches across us to take it, and I roll my eyes.

Why didn't I see this coming? He's totally smitten.

"Want to watch a movie with us?" Layne pats the couch in front of us. "You can sit here."

"Uh." He takes a step forward at the same time that he leans back, as if his body physically wars with itself. "Jake and I are doing something. Going to get ice cream. If you wanted to come."

Layne opens her mouth, and I know she's going to accept, but I clamp my hand down hard on her shoulder and answer for her.

"That's such a nice offer, Thomas," I say. "But it's her first night back. We have so much to catch up on. We really need a girls' night tonight."

Layne smiles and nods like that was what she intended to say all along.

"Yeah. How about tomorrow night?" he says.

I glance at Iris. She shrugs. I suppose if Thomas and Layne are going to hang out, they may as well do it with all of us.

"Sure," I say. "We can do something tomorrow."

"Great!" Thomas points both index fingers at us like he's shooting little guns and says, "See you guys tomorrow," as he backs out of the apartment.

He closes the door, and I make it all of two seconds before I burst out laughing.

"Girl!" I shove Layne. "Can you be here for at least a day before you steal all the guys' hearts?"

She looks back at us, blue eyes wide. "He doesn't belong to someone, does he? Because if one of you is dating him—"

"Nope." I shake my head. "We're just buddies. I think Abby crushed on him for awhile, but she's moved on."

"Okay." Layne smiles. "Because he's cute. We can have some fun."

This time I include Iris in my eye roll. Thomas is never going to know what hit him.

CHAPTER EIGHTY-FIVE

Interloper

Jake texts while I'm at work and invites me and my roommates to go play miniature golf with him and his roommates. I say yes, since this is the plan we agreed upon.

But when I get home, I discover things have changed.

"I'm still adjusting to the time difference," Layne says, drinking a steaming cup of something while she lounges on the couch in her PJs. "I can't go out yet. I need to recover."

"It's miniature golf," I say. "Indoors. There's no pressure. Just come, have fun with us."

"I thought you wanted to get to know Thomas more," Iris adds.

"Oh, I do," she says, and her lips quirk upward in a smirk before she hides it behind her mug.

I almost don't see it. But it's enough to make me suspicious.

Someone knocks on the door, and Iris opens it to let in Jake, Thomas, and Matt.

"Ready?" Jake says.

"Mostly," I say. I gesture at Layne. "I don't think Layne's coming."

"No?" Jake looks at her and lifts an eyebrow. "You're the reason we planned this! We want to make you feel welcome."

She does her best to look abashed. "I know, and it's super sweet. Really awesome. But I'm a bit tuckered out right now. Long international flight."

I snort. I took one a few days before her. It doesn't take that long to recover.

She waves her hand. "But don't worry about me! You guys go, have fun! Tell me all about it!"

"Well, okay," Jake says, looking slightly down as he turns for the door.

"Someone should stay with her," Thomas says. "In case she needs something."

I bark out a laugh. "Are you kidding? Layne's a big girl. She can handle being home by herself."

"But I wouldn't mind if someone stayed," she says, peeking over the tops of her knees demurely.

Thomas is done in. I know it before he answers.

"Yeah, it's cool. I'll stay with her."

Whatever! I leave the apartment, completely annoyed. I stand at the stairs and wait for everyone else to join me.

"I guess it's just us four," Jake says, and he sounds confused, like he's not quite sure what happened.

I know. We got Layne-boozled.

⁂

Playing miniature golf with friends is fun, and my sour mood melts away. Layne's doing what Layne does. If the boys around her aren't eating out of the palm of her hand, she doesn't feel like a whole person. I wonder how many broken hearts she left behind in Guatemala. Probably every boy she met. Smitten by the beautiful American.

Her secret is that she makes each boy feel like he's special. He's the only one. He's been chosen.

I'm envious and disgusted all at the same time.

I'm as bad at miniature golf as I was in high school, but it's a lot more fun with Jake and Matt and Iris than the last time I went. When was that? With Tiago and Inga, I think, and the two of them were fighting, bickering like two wet cats.

We laugh all the way home, replaying my worst swing, where I not only sent the ball flying backward into someone else's game, but the handle broke off, leaving me with nothing but a stick while the putting piece disappeared into the grass. The manager almost made us leave, and it took all four of us to convince him I was simply terribly klutzy and not intentionally vandalizing his property.

The four of us step into my apartment, and my smile freezes when I see Layne curled up into Thomas while they watch a movie. She glances at us, a quick movement of the eyes, but Thomas doesn't look away from the TV. His fingers stroke the edge of her ear, around and around her earlobe, as if she's a precious creature and not some girl he met the day before.

The other three pile in behind me, laughing and eager to share the story of my humiliating folly. Layne sits up away from Thomas, giggling as Iris tells the tale, but Thomas doesn't take his eyes off her. I know because I'm watching him. He stares at Layne as if she's doing the talking, his gaze drinking her in.

I may as well not exist.

I'm pissed and not exactly sure why. I go to my room and close the door, choosing to be antisocial. Eventually I hear the boys leave, and I go to Iris's room before Layne comes to our room. I don't want to see her for the moment.

But she left with Thomas, PJs and all. She must have gotten a shot of energy in the past few hours.

Iris comes in and spots me there, hanging out on her bed. "What are you doing?"

I shrug.

Her expression changes, and she gives me a knowing look. "Are you jealous?"

"No!" I exclaim. Then I tilt my head. "Maybe. A little. But not really of Layne."

"Of what, then? Do you like Thomas?"

I blow air out between my lips and shake my head, crinkling my nose. "No way. He's just a friend." That's it. Right there. I recognize the feelings now, and I seize them. "But he didn't act like one tonight. He didn't even look at me. The only person who existed was Layne."

Her face softens, and she comes to sit by me on the bed. "He's still your friend. He just got a bit blown away."

I snort. "Yeah, and he'll come crying back to me when he needs help picking up the carnage."

"Probably."

I purse my lips. "I still feel abandoned."

"Guys tend to forget their friends—even the female ones—when they get interested in someone else. Maybe especially the female ones."

There's truth to her words. But I hate to lose someone who I consider a genuine friend.

"And it's been two days," Iris adds. "Wait and see. He won't forget you."

I already feel forgotten. I sigh. "I need a man."

"Feeling lonely?" Iris asks.

I nod. "I want to be loved again." I pick up her pillow and hug it to my chest. "I'm ready for someone who cares about me. Who makes me their biggest priority."

"That makes two of us," Iris says. "Maybe we'll both find someone this year."

⁕

Abby and Camila come home the day before school starts, and we throw a taco party. We stand on the balcony inviting everyone we see, telling them the entry fee is a food item, and soon a mob piles in. We provide the taco shells and the meat and cross our fingers the rest of the condominium provides the rest.

They don't disappoint. Soon our table has several selections of cheese, a spring mix, sour cream, salsa, guac, as well as chips, corn, candy, sodas, and whatever people found in their cupboards. My spirits lift, and I'm jovial, because this is what I love about college. Every day can turn into a spontaneous pop-up party.

When Thomas comes in, the first words out of his mouth are, "Where's Layne?"

"Out," I reply, not looking at him as I spoon sour cream into my taco. "She has friends besides us."

He laughs. "I'm sure she does." Then he comes over and towers above me, watching me make my taco. "Keep adding sour cream and that will be taller than you."

I glare at him over the shell and take a bite, but the cream smashes between the shell and goes up my nose. He laughs hard and grabs me a paper towel, and I can't help laughing as I clean myself up.

"Smooth," he says. "Real smooth."

I relent. Nothing's changed between us. We move to the couch and laugh about something idiotic Jake did, and my chest warms. Iris was right. Thomas is my friend.

I'm confident in this feeling until Layne walks in half an hour later. She stands in the entryway, her eyes surveying the crowd, and then a smile spreads across her face.

"Hi, everyone!" she says. "I'm Layne!"

All heads swivel toward her. Thomas jumps up so fast his chair falls backward. "Layne!" he says. He crosses over to hug her, but that's all he gets before half the guys in the room crowd around to introduce themselves. It becomes a smile fest, with her twirling her hair and batting her eyes and telling everyone where she was for the past semester.

I sigh. I should call Stirling. He's well aware of Layne's charms and hasn't fallen for her yet. I haven't talked to him since before Christmas, anyway. And what's Jordan up to? It's funny how someone can go to the same school as you but live on the other side of town, and thus you never see them.

Thomas hovers around Layne and her posse the rest of the evening, doing everything he can to regain her attention. He doesn't talk to me or even glance my way again.

Iris does. She can probably see the steam coming out of my ears.

❦

Classes.

My first class of the day is an editing and linguistics class. I immediately love it. It's the geeky kind of stuff that makes me excited, and I can't wait to learn more about English and how this language works and where it came from.

The next class isn't officially on my schedule. Yet. I feel out of place as soon as I step into the Portuguese 302 class. Like my last Portuguese class, I look like the youngest person in here. I find a seat and pull out the add card. Since I didn't take Portuguese 301, I need permission from the professor to add this class. My heart races as I take one of the syllabus. I don't want to bite off more than I can chew like I did last year, but 201 felt too easy. The 202 class will be more of the same.

As I listen to her launch into an introduction of the class, my breathing evens out. I understand almost everything she's saying. Ironically, I think spending the past two weeks in Colombia helped my understanding of Portuguese. She goes through the class curriculum, the expected books, the tests, and then she asks who in the class served a mission in Brazil.

The hands of the kids in front of me go up. I look to my left, and all their hands have gone up also. Slowly I swivel to see the entire room.

I'm the only person who is not raising their hand.

I'm the only person in this room who is not fluent in this language.

The racing starts up again in my chest. Have I done it again? Is this beyond me?

She tells us to turn to the back page of the syllabus and read the assignment, then turn it in before class is over.

I flip back and read it over. It's simple. Write three paragraphs about me, my introduction to Portuguese, and why I'm taking advanced-level classes.

I blink. Sometimes I forget that three-hundred level classes are considered advanced. They're what I'm taking for my English major, but it feels like the natural progression.

I fill the paper with my thoughts, expounding as much as I can. I reach the limits of my vocabulary when I try to describe things, but I have my dictionary with me. I try not to use it unless I can't think of any other word. When class finishes, I wait behind a line of kids introducing themselves and practice my speech. I have to convince her I'm advanced enough to take this class.

Her eyes land on me, and I know from the way she lifts her eyebrows that she remembers me. The one student who hasn't served a mission in Brazil.

"Yes?" she says.

English. She spoke to me in English. My face burns with the insinuation. Why does she think I'm in here? I begin my speech, speaking as clearly as I can.

"*Preciso de teu permissão para acrescentar a aula,*" I say. I might not be getting every word quite right, but I know I'm doing pretty good as I tell her I need her permission to add the class.

She considers me and says, "*Por quê não fez a registração antes do começo do semestre?*"

My heart pounds a little faster. I feel like she's testing me when she asks why I didn't register before the start of the semester. I know what she said, but I'm nervous. What will she say when I admit I didn't take the prerequisite? "*Porque não fiz a aula de trezentos e un.*" Is that right? 301. Ugh, numbers are so hard for me. Even though I practiced that over and over again, I'm suddenly not sure I said it correctly.

"*E como você sabe português?*"

How do I know Portuguese? My brain is starting to hurt. This is too much Portuguese. I want desperately to switch back into English, but I have to stay strong. I search for the shortest answer that will convey my message. "*Aprendi no Brasil.*" I learned in Brazil.

She shrugs and holds her hand out. "*Tá bom, se tiver certeza que consiga. Mas—*"

I nod along as she says more, but my brain quit on me. I don't know what she's saying.

She's signing my card.

That's all that matters.

I flash her a big smile as she hands it back and say, "*Grácias.*"

"*Grácias?*" she repeats.

Oh, crap! How did I manage to slip into Spanish? "*Obrigada!*"

She starts laughing. "*Não espanhol aqui.*"

"No, no . . ." And I give up on the Portuguese. "Sorry—I just got back from Colombia —I've been speaking Spanish for two weeks."

She smiles and nods, and her whole demeanor seems warmer now. "It's fine. Good luck. Remember what language you're studying."

My face is hot as I leave and head for the registration office.

That was embarrassing. But I did it. I've got the class.

CHAPTER EIGHTY-SIX

So Rightly Wrong

"Hey! It's my favorite short person."

I recognize Thomas's voice at the intersection as I walk home after work. My light turns green, and I cross the street, not waiting for him to catch up to me.

"How did the first day of classes go?" he asks, his long strides reaching me before I get to the other side.

"Fine," I say.

He waits for more, but when none is forthcoming, he says, "Anything good?"

I shrug. "English, Portuguese, Badminton." I keep moving briskly, my breath steaming in and out above my scarf.

"Nice, a badminton class! That will be fun!"

I don't say more, and he picks up on it.

"Are you mad at me?" he asks.

I lift an eyebrow. "Now you decide to talk to me."

"What's that supposed to mean?" His tone goes decidedly defensive.

I should lay off. I sense danger. But I can't back down. "Now that Layne's not here, I'm someone worth talking to again."

"What?" He goes from defensive to insulted in half a second. "You think I only talk to you if Layne's not around?"

"That's what the evidence has shown ever since she moved back."

"That's not true."

"It is."

We've reached the complex, but he stops outside the commons, so I do too.

"I find that very insulting," he says, his eyes flashing, his mouth curving downward. "I've been your friend long before Layne moved in. And you think I'm going to ditch you because I'm dating her?"

"You're dating her?" I can't stop the shocked gasp that escapes. "And you didn't tell me?"

"Well—" He hesitates. "I thought she would tell you."

My blood boils. "Yes, well, apparently I'm not that good a friend to either of you." It's unfair, to both him and Layne. And he seizes it.

"You're my friend, not my girlfriend. I'm not obligated to tell you when I start dating someone. Maybe if I wasn't worried you'd be jealous, I'd feel comfortable telling you."

"Jealous?" My mouth falls open. "You think I'd be jealous? You think I'm interested in you? There's zero attraction between us, nothing! I'm not even sure we're friends!"

He turns around and strides away from me. Through the commons and directly to the boys' side of the condo. I watch him go, a tremble building up in my core.

I'm not wrong. Everything I said was 100% correct.

That's what I tell myself as I march to my room.

Then why does right feel so wrong?

❧

I wake up with that heavy feeling in my chest that I did something wrong.

I try to ignore it.

But I'm upset I argued with Thomas.

I don't have any classes before ten, so I head over to the science center to talk to my geography teacher. That B from last semester doesn't make sense. I must have done really bad on the final. If that's the case, I want to know it.

"Hi, Ms. Jones," he says when I enter his office.

I haven't interacted with Professor Monson before, and he gives me a friendly smile.

"How can I help you?" he asks.

I place my backpack at my feet. "I have a question about my grade, really."

He nods and pleats his fingers. "What do you feel is amiss?"

I lick my lips. "I went through all my tests and scores, and by my calculations, I would have to get a D on the final to come out with a B in the class. Since that would be my worst score ever in your class, I'm confused how that could happen. I'm hoping we can go over my test."

"Okay, let's see." He opens a cabinet under his desk. "What period were you in?"

"Third."

"Uh-huh." He flips through the tests and pulls one out. "This is your final. You did quite well. You got an eighty-seven."

I scan the paper, my eyes flitting over the red markings, and I nod. "But that doesn't explain how I got a B in the class."

"Let's check your other grades." He toggles his computer mouse and wakes up the screen. "So you had an eighty-two going into the final—"

"No, I didn't," I interrupt. "I had a ninety-four."

He pauses and considers me, tilting his head like a bird. "All right. Do you have your grades recorded?"

"Yes." My hands shake as I pull my computer from my bag, and I try to calm my nerves. I open the file where I recorded every assignment and test. He turns back to his computer.

"Let's start with the first test, since those carry the most weight. I have a seventy-seven on the first—"

I can't seem to let him finish a sentence. "Ninety-three."

"Ninety-three?"

"Yes. I got a ninety-three." I remember because I was so pleased by my score. My first test in geography, and I aced it.

He turns back to his cabinet and thumbs through it again before retrieving a stapled packet of papers. He flips through until he lands on one, and I recognize my penciled handwriting on it.

"Sure enough," he says, setting it down on his desk face-up for both of us to see. "Ninety-three. I must have looked at someone else's score when I was inputting."

I don't answer. I'm waiting to see what happens next.

He turns to the computer and edits my grade. "There. That gives you a ninety-one in the class. An A minus. Is that better?"

My face cracks into a smile. "Yes. Much better."

He settles back in his chair. "I'll get the grade change submitted to administration. Watch for it, and follow up with me if it doesn't get changed. Anything else I can help you with?"

I shake my head. This was the outcome I'd hoped for. "That's it. Thank you, Professor."

He shakes my hand and I leave, giddy with success. As soon as the door closes, I lean against it, close my eyes, and let out a long breath.

"Everything go okay in there?"

My eyes snap open to see a short kid with dark brown hair too long to be spiked up, but there's enough gel or spray to make it stay.

"Yeah, great," I say, though it's none of his business. "Just talking to the professor."

He smiles. "You don't recognize me. I'm Sam. I sat behind you in geography."

"Oh." No wonder I don't know him. I didn't make it a habit of turning around in my seat. "Nice to meet you."

"Were you happy with your grade?"

"I think so. I got an A minus for the semester."

"Yeah, that's awesome!"

He sounds so impressed that I'm curious.

"What did you get?" I ask.

"A ninety-seven." He cringes as he says it, lifting his shoulders like he hates having to admit he got a better score than me. But I'm irritated. His earlier enthusiasm feels false.

"You shouldn't be ashamed of that," I say. "Good job." I step past him and head for the exit.

"Want to go out sometime?" he calls, stopping me.

I turn back around. I want someone romantic in my life. I'm feeling the loneliness of not having someone to call at night, not having someone to touch.

But I don't think this guy's it.

Still, I never know. I'll give him one chance.

"Yeah, sure."

"Great!" He smiles again, and I give him my number. He programs it into his phone, then texts me so I have his.

Hey! This is Sam from geography.

"Got it." I hold the phone up as proof. "Talk to you later." I head out the door and attach his name to the text message.

Sam the geography kid. The one that's smarter than me but thinks he has to hide it to keep me from feeling insecure.

Yeah, I don't think this is going anywhere.

◯◞◌◟◯

All day at work I'm bothered by my argument with Thomas. I said stupid things. He's been a true, genuine friend, and I acted selfish and demanding. If I were a better friend, I would be there to encourage and support him while he dates someone new.

Maybe I would have if I'd known he was dating.

No, that's not fair. He doesn't have to tell me. I should be happy for him no matter how I find out.

Him and Layne dating isn't a personal betrayal. It feels that way, but I know it's not.

As soon as I get home, I head to his apartment to talk to him.

"He's not here," Jake says.

My shoulders wilt with disappointment. "Can I leave him a message?"

"Sure."

Jake hands me a spiral notebook, and I pen out a quick apology, saying how I didn't mean what I said and I'm sorry for not being a better friend. I don't say much else because I figure Jake will read this, and I don't need the whole apartment knowing what went down.

"Thanks," I say, handing back the notebook.

I'm certain Thomas will want to fix this between us also.

I've gotten pretty good at cooking chicken, so for dinner I pull out chicken breasts and mustard and honey and broccoli. Camila never complains about what I make, though one time I did notice her throw away half her fish.

I haven't made that recipe again.

I hear Thomas's laugh in the hallway, and I look up, pausing in my beheading of the broccoli. His voice carries down the hall, and I wait for him to come to my apartment. I wait for the knock, and I anticipate his easy smile, what we'll say to make it right between us.

His voice goes back down the stairs, along with the heavy clomping of his footfalls as he leaves the building.

I stand there, dumbfounded. My apology wasn't enough. He's really pissed at me.

And now I want to cry.

EPISODE 5:

The Dating Dilemma

CHAPTER EIGHTY-SEVEN

Stood Up

My roommate Layne comes in late, as always.

I've taken to leaving the small lamp on for her before I go to sleep, so she can come in and get ready for bed and not wake me. She's a bit of a party animal, a socialite, and I'm the opposite, a quiet introvert who enjoys intimate moments with small groups of friends. But we get along well. We've established a good pattern that allows her to live her crazy life without inconveniencing my solitude.

Usually I'm out when she comes home, but tonight all I can think is that she's hanging with Thomas, who is apparently now her boyfriend, and neither of them is talking to me about it.

Thomas, my close friend. And Layne, my man-eater roommate.

I should be chill with them together. But I'm not.

I feign sleep when she comes in. She hums as she changes for bed, then she turns out the light and climbs beneath the blankets. She's asleep before I am.

Why hasn't she said anything about them dating?

And why does this bother me so much?

❧

Sam texts me while I'm at work the next day. It takes me a moment to remember the boy with spiky hair who found me outside the geography professor's room.

S: *want to meet up?*

I text back: *I'm at work.*

S: *oh. Where is that?*

Me: *Engineering department*

I shouldn't be surprised when he walks into my office twenty minutes later, but I am.

"Cool," he says, glancing around the soft chairs and waiting area next to the hallway that leads to the professors' offices. "Are you an engineering student?"

"No. I just work here." I twiddle my pencil. Telling him where I work was like giving him my locker number in high school. Now he can always find me.

"Nice." He comes over to the counter and leans on it. "So want to go to dinner tomorrow?"

I roll my chair back slightly. He has that weird smell, a kind of sweet and musty scent that I find utterly unappealing. I noticed it on Rhett, the guy I went on a disastrous date with last semester.

I want to say no.

I promised myself I'd give him a chance.

"Sure."

"Great!" He smiles, his eyes crinkling up, and I wonder if his eyebrows can go as high as his hair.

No. Nothing can.

"Where do you want to go?" he asks.

Tomorrow's Saturday. We could meet anywhere.

I don't want to go anywhere.

"I have a lot of homework to do," I say. "So I'll probably be on campus all day. We can meet in the cafeteria."

He nods like that's the most sensible thing he's heard all day. "Totally agree. I study a lot also. Is there a certain place you like to go?"

I'm not telling him about my table on the fifth floor of the library. Then he could haunt me there like he's able to haunt me here.

Only Jared was allowed to do that.

"No," I say. "I just wander until I find a quiet spot."

"How does four o'clock sound?"

"That sounds great."

I don't have much else to say. He chats for a little bit, and I make small talk about work.

I wrinkle my nose as soon as he's gone. He left his smell behind. Hopefully one lunch date is all it will take for him to realize there's no chemistry between us, and he'll leave me alone.

I don't tell Iris about my date when I get home. She'll harass me about it. At least she quit keeping count on the message board.

I sit at the kitchen table and do my homework, the whole while hoping Thomas will come by.

He doesn't.

He's either forgotten me or he's still mad at me, and I don't know which is worse.

⌒〜⁂〜⌒

I'm just blinking my eyes open Saturday morning when my alarm goes off, ringing incessantly next to my ear. I grab my phone as Layne stirs. Why did I set an alarm on a Saturday?

I silence it with a few presses of buttons, and then I see it's not an alarm. It's Monica calling me.

Few people can rouse me this early on a weekend, but the sister of my ex-boyfriend is one of them. I pull myself from the bed and slip into the living room, answering before I get to the couch. "Monica! What's up?"

"Hey, lady!" she says. "What are you doing today?"

"Waking up." I glance at the clock. "It's a little after seven on a Saturday."

"I know, and I woke you early!" She laughs. "I have a crazy favor to ask."

"Oh, yeah? What?"

"So, I met this really awesome guy—like super amazing."

"Yeah?" I nestle into the couch. "Keep going."

"And I really want to get to know him, but—he lives in Denver."

"That's a bummer but not a deal breaker. It's only three hours away."

"Right? If you have a car. And . . . mine's broken."

"Your car is broken?" I laugh. "So you're calling me for a ride."

"Yes! But I also want to see you. And I want you to meet him. So it's perfect!"

I shake my head, amused. "I'll take you. But only because I miss you and it will give us a chance to catch up."

"Ha! I knew you loved me. When can you get me?"

I pick Monica up in front of her house half an hour later.

"Here," she says, handing me her phone. "I already programmed the address."

I attach it to my dash and start driving. Even though it's been weeks since we talked, we fall into a comfortable rhythm where we share everything happening in our lives.

"Dating anyone?" she asks. "Met anyone amazing?"

I glance at her to see how she feels about this question, but she's making a kissing face and batting her eyelashes, which makes me laugh.

"No. I wish. I'm incredibly lonely."

"Hence why you jumped at the opportunity to drive me to Denver!"

"I didn't exactly jump at it."

"Yes, you did."

I laugh again. "Okay, maybe I did."

"Hey, you'll find someone. Be patient. When you're alone, it feels like forever, but you don't want to end up with the wrong person because you're so eager to be with someone."

"Sage advice," I say.

"Do you talk to Owen at all?"

There it is, the question I was expecting. And she's brave to ask it. I shake my head.

"We wrote for a while. Then he started giving my address to all the missionaries he was meeting and we sort of fell out of contact."

"He did *what*?"

She screeches in indignation, but I manage a smile.

"It's fine. Some of them were pretty nice, but what's he trying to do, set me up with someone I can't date? I think they're lonely also. And it wasn't all the missionaries, to be fair. Just a few."

She still stares at me. "I can't believe he did that."

I lift a shoulder in a shrug. "I figure I should feel honored. He must think I'm pretty awesome if he's telling other guys to write me. How's he doing, anyway?"

I act nonchalant. Like it's not big deal. But I see from my peripheral vision how she purses her lips together. She doesn't like what he did anymore than I did.

"He's doing great. It's been six months already. Just another year and a half."

"Hey, I got that internship to Brazil!" I brighten and change the subject, artfully steering it in a different direction.

"Oh, wow! That's fantastic!"

We fill the next few hours with talk of home, family, and anything else that comes to mind.

We hit Denver a little after noon and then pull into a bowling alley.

"Bowling?" I say, staring at the sign. "I'm terrible at this."

"Isn't everyone?" Her eyes light on a thick Polynesian man who just walked out, and she ducks out of the car. "Hey!"

I don't watch them make out. Mostly because I'm trying to find my phone. I search my purse, then the console, my frown etching itself deeper into my forehead with each second. I hop out of the car, interrupting their lip syncing moment.

"Monica, can you call me? I can't find my phone."

"Oh, sure." She pulls out her own and pushes the screen. I hop back into the car and wait for it.

Nothing. No ringing. No buzzing to indicate a vibrating phone hidden under a chair.

"Went to voicemail," she says.

I climb back out of the car. "I think I left it at home."

"Dang, that sucks! This is Darren. He's from Tonga. We met playing volleyball."

They have their hands tucked into each other's back pockets. I shrug off my worry over the phone. I'm sure it's at home. I can survive without it for a day. "Nice to meet you, Darren."

I'm as terrible at bowling as I remember. I'm so bad that after one game they allow me to put the bumpers on, and finally I'm able to get a few points. We order fried pickles and mozzarella sticks, and I eat more than my share while Monica and Darren lock lips above the bowling balls.

I think he fits her. Monica's tall, almost as tall as her brother at six-foot.

But Darren is taller. And thicker. She disappears into him when he hugs her.

Of course, it makes me wish I had someone.

I freeze with one fried pickle almost to my mouth. "Crap." I drop the pickle back on the plate and check the time.

It's after two.

My date with Sam.

"Crap, crap, crap!" I jump up and turn around. "Monica, I'm so sorry, I remembered I'm supposed to be somewhere at four!"

"Really?" She looks at her watch and then back at me, and I know she's drawing the same conclusion I just did. "You won't make it."

"I know I won't, but—" I wring my hands. "I should make an effort!"

She gives me a sympathetic look. "You've already missed it."

She's right. Even if we get in the car right now and book it out of here, I'll be more than an hour later.

"What are you missing?" Darren asks.

"I forgot I have a date." I put my face in my hands.

"Can't be that important, if you forgot." Monica smirks.

I don't bother confirming that sentiment. "He's going to think I stood him up! I'm the worst person!"

"Can't you call him and tell him what happened?" she says.

I make a show of checking my pockets. "I don't have my phone!"

"Oh." Her mouth forms a perfect O. She looks sympathetic. "I'm so sorry, honey."

I sigh and slump back in my seat. What a terrible person I am.

We don't stay long after I've realized my blunder. I'm not in the mood, and all I can think about is getting home. And now that I'm thinking logically, I remember all the homework I haven't done. It's time to stop playing and be in the real world.

We clean up and turn in our shoes and head for the car. I get in it, but not Monica. She stands in front with Darren, kissing and hugging and almost walking but then not for ten minutes. I finally lay on the horn. They pull apart, and she gets in the car, giggling.

"Sorry," she says, her face flushed. "He's just so yummy."

"You guys are cute," I say, trying to mask my displeasure at how this day devolved. "I like him."

"Do you? I do too!"

"How did you meet him?" I turn us around and head west, back toward campus. I let Monica do the talking this time.

"Thank you for taking me, and thanks for coming," she says when I pull up in front of her house a few hours later. I check the clock. It's five-forty. "I really enjoyed hanging out with you."

She gives me a hug, and I squeeze her tight, trying not to show my anxiety.

"I'm glad I got to meet him," I say.

"And I'm sorry about your date." She raises her eyebrows. "I guess it wasn't meant to be."

"Apparently not."

She steps back, and I pull away from the curb. I debate going home to get my phone, but I'm right here by campus.

Sam won't still be here.

I have to check.

I park by the music building and head over to the cafeteria. Even though it's Saturday, plenty of kids sit inside studying, goofing around. It's never empty here.

And there's Sam.

Still waiting for me. Even though I'm two hours late.

He sits at one of the round tables studying a book. I cross over to the table and sigh, and he looks up.

"Oh, hey," he says.

I can't read his expression. I don't know him well enough. I plop into a seat at the table. "I'm so, so sorry. I had to take a friend to Denver and I didn't get out of there fast enough to get to you."

I wait for him to say something or give me a sign of emotion, but he doesn't. So I keep going. "I wanted to call you but somehow I left my phone behind. And I don't have your number memorized." I let out an exhale. "I can't believe you stayed and waited."

"I wasn't exactly waiting," he says. "I studied. But I was astonished you stood me up."

I shake my head. "I would never do that. Ever. I felt so terrible when I realized we wouldn't get back in time."

"Was it fun, at least?"

I think I detect a note of humor in his voice. So I crack a smile. "It was awful. I hate bowling. But my friend wanted to see her boyfriend, so I tossed balls at the bumpers while they made out behind me."

That earns a laugh from him. Not a big belly laugh, but enough of a chuckle that I don't feel like such a terrible person.

"I haven't had anything except fried pickles all day," I say. "If you still need food."

"I actually have to go to my sister's house and watch her kids. But you can come if you want."

I balk at the invitation. My palms get sweaty at the very idea. Family houses are too intimate. And I won't get any studying done in a strange place with little kids running around. "I have a lot of homework to do. I better not."

He nods and stands, putting his textbook in his backpack and shouldering it. "I'm sorry we didn't get the chance to talk more. But I'm glad you found me."

I watch him, the guilt over what I did to him gnawing at my chest. "Okay. We can try some other time."

"Good luck with your studying."

He walks away, and I turn my gaze to my backpack, laiden with my homework. I'm hungry and behind in schoolwork. I may as well eat and catch up while I'm here.

CHAPTER EIGHTY-EIGHT

Friendly Ditching

I stay on campus for three more hours. I need a full day of study, not just a few hours, and I have mixed feelings about my day. I can't feel bad about the time I spent with Monica. That relationship is important to me.

But so is my scholarship.

I feel blind without my phone, so I pack it up after eight p.m. and head for my car. At least I don't have to walk home.

My roommates greet me cheerfully. Iris made soup and rice, and I go on a quick hunt for my phone before I let myself eat. I find it, tucked into the couch cushion, right where I sat this morning when Monica called me. I scroll through my notifications, my chest tightening as I see call after call from Sam, interspersed with various text messages.

One of them is from an hour ago, while I was on campus studying.

Sam: Can I come over so we can talk?

Oh heavens. What is there to talk about? I get jittery at the very idea. But I feel like I owe him this much. So I text back, *yeah, I just got home. Eating dinner.*

He replies, *what's your address? I'll come over in thirty minutes.*

I send him the details and then grab a bowl so I can eat Iris's food.

"How was your day?" she asks me.

"Mostly good. I left my phone here, so I screwed up a few things I needed to get done and couldn't fix them. But I think it's taken care of."

"Where did you go?" Abby asks.

"Monica's dating a guy in Denver, and she asked for a ride. What about you guys?"

They fill me on their day, which involved going shopping and eating ice cream. I stand and rinse out my empty bowl, and then there's a knock on the door.

"Come in," Iris calls.

The door slides open, and I turn to see Sam's head peeking around the edge.

"Hi," he says, his demeanor uncertain. "Is Cassandra—oh, hey."

I wave from the sink. "Come on in."

His eyes survey my roommates at the kitchen table. He looks back at me. "Want to go on a walk?"

I don't. It's freezing outside. But I can tell he means to have a serious conversation, which is very hard to do when three other sets of ears are leaning your direction. I'm slightly freaked out by this. What do I owe him, that we need to "talk"? "I'll get my jacket."

We step into the hallway moments later, but to my relief, Sam only goes as far as the last step on the stairs before he sits down. I follow his example, plunking down beside him. I pleat my hands to hide their trembling and try to ignore the twisting in my stomach.

"So what's going on?" I ask. I already apologized. I can't think of much more to say.

He turns to me, and I notice that slightly musty smell again. I'm not sure if it's his cologne or deodorant or negative body chemistry, but it takes all my effort not to shy away.

"I want to know where this is going," he says.

"Where this is going?" I repeat. "Where what is going?"

"You and me," he says, rather boldly. "I really like you, but I'm not sure what you feel for me."

I blink at him. "We met a few days ago."

"But we've known each other since last semester."

"You sat behind me. That doesn't make us acquaintances."

I think I see his cheeks blush in the porch light.

"I guess I should have said hi sooner," he says.

I don't know how to respond to that.

"Every time I talk to you, I'm super impressed by you," he says.

"Even when I'm apologizing for standing you up?" I say.

"Especially when you're apologizing for standing me up."

Now my face warms. "I never meant to."

"I know. I can tell you're sincere. I want to know what your thoughts are. Where you think this can go."

The conversation feels extremely premature. "I barely know you. We've only talked a few times." I wait for him to draw his own conclusion, but he watches me, and I know I have to spell it out. "I'm happy to have a friend. I never have enough of those. But that's all I'm looking for."

He smiles. "That's great. We can be friends. I always need more also."

I lean against the railing behind me. "Awesome. And I won't leave you hanging next time. Friends don't do that."

"No, they don't." He laughs.

But I already know we won't be friends for long. Most guys don't hang around for friendship, and when it's clear it's not going to be more than that, they ditch you.

Like Thomas did.

⟳⟶⟡⟵⟲

After one week in my Portuguese class, one thing becomes very clear: I can speak better than I can understand.

It must be from all the memorization I did in Professor Dennis's class. Words come to mind, phrases, but when my teacher is talking, I struggle to keep up.

I'm faking it again. I regret getting so cocky and taking this class. I should have done 202. It might have been easy, but it would have taught me and prepared me. Then the natural progression would have been 301, and by the time I got to this class, maybe I'd be fluent in Portuguese. Maybe this class would be easy.

Why did I think it necessary to skip a year? I just started learning this stupid language twelve months ago.

I sweat it out in my badminton class and then head to the health department for my TB test.

On my way out of the humanities building, I see a notice plastered to the billboard. There's a painting of Christ exiting the tomb with the words, "Want to sing in an Easter musical celebrating the resurrection of our Lord Jesus? Come try out!" beside it, and little pull tabs with the information.

I take one of the tabs. I love singing. But I never do it anymore.

I need a win somewhere. I feel like I'm drowning in my classes, with friends, with finances. Either this will be a pick-me-up, or I'll have another failure under my belt.

⌒〜※〜⌒

A nurse in the health department takes me to another room and looks over my chart. "Okay, so we have this information from your clinic back home, right?"

I nod. "Yes." My heart still skips a beat as I remember that moment over Christmas break when my TB test came back positive. But even though I was diagnosed with tuberculosis in Arkansas, my doctor here in Colorado wants to see it for himself.

"And you need this for an internship to Brazil?" the nurse asks.

"Yes."

"Push your sleeve up, please."

I push up the sleeve on my left arm. She leans over to do the test and halts.

"Is this from your last one?" She presses her finger into the discolored swollen circle on my flesh.

"Yes."

"Oh man, it's still healing! I can tell you right now what this test is gonna do. Push up your other sleeve, please."

I don't say anything as she puts the needle under the skin of my right arm. The lump in my throat warns me I might cry.

"Can you still do your internship with a positive TB test?" she asks.

"I'm not sure," I say. I haven't told them. I'm still praying for a miracle.

She writes a few things in my chart. "Come back in two days, okay? We'll get this all figured out."

"Thanks."

I exit feeling despondent. I want to go to Brazil. I need this internship.

But I feel like I'm racking up another loss.

⌒〜※〜⌒

Dad calls me when I'm walking home after work. We don't chat a lot. I think he only calls when it's something important. Last time he called, it was to tell me we were going to Colombia. I perk up. Maybe he's got something to make life more exciting.

"Hey, Daddy!" I say.

"How's it going, kiddo?"

408

"Pretty good. Just walking home from work."

"Get that TB test done?"

"Yes, this morning." Speaking of which . . . my arm isn't hurting. Didn't it hurt by now last time? I want to pull off my jacket and sweater here in the middle of the sidewalk, but that's dumb. I quicken my pace. The sooner I'm home, the sooner I can check.

"We're praying for you. Let us know how it goes."

"Thanks, Daddy. I will."

"I have a business trip out to Colorado in three days. You up to going out for dinner?"

"Oh!" I exclaim. "Always!" I've stretched my string-bean budget as tight as it will go.

"Your roommates too. I'll send you my flight info. We can make an evening of it."

"They'd love that!"

"Any boys you want to bring?"

I laugh. The very idea of me introducing boys to my dad is ludicrous. "Not a single one."

We talk all the way back to my apartment, but my mind is on my TB test. I say goodbye when I get home, then rush back to my room to remove my layers. I hold my breath as I peel back the sleeve on my arm.

Nothing. No pink spot, no swelling, no pain.

It's not possible. Is it?

Could the TB be gone?

I check compulsively for the next few hours before going to bed.

There's no sign of anything.

Will they think the test is broken if I go in and it's negative? Will they make me test again?

Could this be the miracle I've been praying for?

＊＊＊

I can hardly sleep. As soon as I wake up, I push back my sleeve and check my arm. I gasp at what I see.

There's no indication of anything there. Just like all the negative TB tests I took last year for work.

I have to wait one more day before I can go back to the health department and get an official report.

But I'm on pins and needles all day.

No lump grows under my skin during the next twenty-four hours. I go to the health department as soon as I'm done with class, and I would run if I had better stamina.

The same woman takes me back to a private room. She checks my arm and says, "Negative. You don't have TB."

She makes the announcement without fanfare or excitement. Just fact.

The breath whooshes out of me. "How is it possible?" I ask. "I still have the mark from the last test."

She shrugs. "I don't know. But we'll send these results to your clinic back home. You're fine."

I can't believe it. I'm shaking with joy and disbelief. I make it a few steps outside before I collapse on a bench. I call Camila because she's the only I know who doesn't have class right now.

"I don't have TB!" I shriek into the phone.

She gasps. "You don't? But how? Was it a false positive?"

"It must have been!" Those don't usually happen. I spent a decent number of hours of my life scouring the internet for cases like mine and didn't find any.

But it happened to me. Maybe it happened to other people, and there was no documentation.

"I'm so happy for you! You get to go to Brazil!"

"Yes!" I do a wiggle dance on the cold metal bench. "Yes, yes!"

"Let's celebrate! There's a volleyball game tonight. Come with me and Abby!"

At this moment I'll do anything anyone asks. I feel like I was given a brand-new lease on life. "Absolutely!"

My enthusiasm can't erase the chill of the frozen metal under my butt, so I eventually stand up and head back to campus. And then I park myself in the library and send all the required documentation to the English teaching company.

I'm going to Brazil.

CHAPTER EIGHTY-NINE

Monica invites me over Saturday to help her scrapbook. Now that the TB scare is over, I tell her all about it while I help cut flowers from construction paper and create frames to layer over her pictures.

"Oh my gosh," she says, handing me another pattern to cut out. "I can't believe you went through that."

"I'm so relieved nothing came of it. I was prepared to spend the rest of my life monitoring this disease."

"That's so crazy." She pulls out a shoe box of pictures. "These are all from last year. I have to get them scrapbooked before I get too behind. Weed through and take out all the blurry ones or pictures with no people."

"Okay." I sit at the chair and take out the photos. "How's Darren?"

"Oh, Cassandra, I really like him. He's coming over tomorrow and going to church with me."

"Have you seen him since last week?"

"No, but we talk every day."

"That's awesome." I make a pile of the good pictures on the table and toss the others in the trashcan.

And then my heart stops because she has pictures of Owen's departure for his mission.

I forget to breathe as I stare at him in his missionary suit, standing with his brother Richard, hugging his mom, grinning broadly as he punches the air. His family is there, a bunch of people I don't know, maybe friends, kids from church.

I'm not there. I should have been there.

The deep chasm in my heart yawns wide, reminding me it's not been filled in. It still exists, even if I've built bridges over it, covered it up the best I can. I suck in a breath, the ache as tangible as if someone punched me in the chest.

"You okay?" Monica asks.

I quickly school my features, going for calm and stoic. "Yeah." I sift through the pictures quickly, adding the good ones to the table as if they mean nothing to me. "Just sorting."

She doesn't ask. She's not dumb. She'll know it affected me.

But neither of us points it out.

"There's another reason I asked you to come over," she says, so casually that my spider senses tingle.

I look at her, but she's still cutting, not making eye contact. "What?" I say.

She doesn't answer a long moment, long hair falling over her face as she makes a precise circular cut around an object, pausing to poke out tiny indentations. Sweat beads along my hairline, and I wait, not daring to speculate.

Finally she puts the scissors down and looks at me. "The cancer," she says, and my heart skips a beat. "It's back."

"Shut up," I whisper. A chill runs down my back, and I stare at her, willing her to smile, to crack a joke. "It can't be."

"It's not a big deal," she says hastily. "I'm okay. We found it early. But I have to do a few more tests, maybe radiation again."

"Do you have another tumor?" Last time she got a tumor in her back that turned out to be malignant.

"Yes." She hesitates. "This time it's in my stomach."

My own stomach clenches at her words. "And they know it's cancerous?"

She shakes her head. "There's a chance it's not but . . . considering my history, we're assuming it is."

"So what's next?"

"I need surgery." She says it calmly. "So I'm going home. Again."

Just like last time. She left school before so they could operate on her tumor. I put down the pictures and go around the table to hug her.

"I'm so sorry," I say.

"I'm okay," she says, patting my arm. "I'm really okay."

I don't respond as I squeeze her tight.

None of this feels okay.

⚮

Abby gets it in her head that she wants a plant. She pounces at me when I get home and begs me to drive her to the garden center and pick one out. I'm still reeling from Monica's news, and Abby's exuberant enthusiasm is a welcome distraction.

"You're going to kill it," I say. "You want a plant, we can go dig one up from outside."

"I'll be a better plant parent than you are a fish parent, wait and see."

I shake my head. I can't wait to watch this play out. But if she wants something to mother, I can help her out with that.

She ends up buying a small green plant with orange stalks.

"I love the color," I say. The leaves spill out from the central stalk like miniature banana leaves.

"I love the name. Spider plant? Who doesn't want one?"

"I wonder how long it will stay alive," I say, straight-faced.

She elbows me. "Forever!"

Of course she wants a special pot for it. We peruse them until she finds a bright blue one that compliments the orange of the stalks quite nicely.

I tease her as we walk up the stairs to the apartment. "You're carrying that plant like you're afraid it will crumble in your hands. It's in a vase, you know."

"This is my baby. Stop mocking."

"What have you named it?"

"Philo."

"Philo? Like, the Greek dough?"

She glares at me as my lips twitch in a smile. "You're still mocking."

I push open the door, laughing, and step into the living room.

Thomas is there, sitting on the couch talking to Camila. I give a start. I haven't seen him over here in two weeks. I look around for Layne, but she's not here.

"Hey," he says when he sees me.

I bite back the acerbic response on the tip of my tongue. That's what got us into this mess in the first place. "Hey."

Camila stands up and leaves the living room. Abby follows her, chattering about her new spider plant the whole way.

Thomas and I are alone, and I feel like that's intentional.

"Layne's not here," I say, pointedly.

"I know. I came over to talk to you."

I approach the couch and sit down in the large chair across from it. I'm glad to see him, but he hurt me, and I want to lash out at him. But I fear anything negative I say will make him withdraw. So I go the opposite direction. "I'm sorry for what I said, Thomas. The last thing I wanted to do was drive a further wedge between us."

"I know. And I shouldn't have waited this long to come over and see you."

I pleat my fingers over my knees and keep very still as I feel the heat building behind my eyes. "I didn't think we were friends anymore."

He scoffs. "Of course we are. We were friends having a disagreement."

I don't argue because I don't want to fight, but I don't agree. Friends try to rectify any hurtful behavior. Thomas did the opposite. "Have you been mad at me this whole time?"

"No. I quit being mad like two days after we argued."

I furrow my brow. "So why didn't you say something?"

He hesitates. "Because you were right."

I lean toward him, confused. "I was right?"

"You were right that I dropped you for Layne. And . . . I felt bad about that."

I lift a shoulder. "It's what people do when they like someone. I shouldn't have been so needy. No one wants a friend like that."

He sighs. "It's more than that. I like Layne. I like her a lot. But . . . I don't think my feelings are safe with her. I need your friendship, now more than ever."

I want him to need my friendship. I need his. "Why do you say that?"

"What do you know of Layne, Cassandra?"

I give a short laugh. "A lot. I lived with her all last year."

"Is she someone I can trust?"

Warning bells go off in the back of my head. This is thin ice. How can I warn Thomas without betraying Layne? "Sure, you can trust her. She was in a committed relationship last year." I don't feel I'm being totally honest, though. "She does have a tendency to act more attached than she actually is. So be careful."

He nods. "That's what I was afraid of. She acts so involved, like I'm the only person on earth, but sometimes I see her with other guys and wonder, does she act the same with them?"

She absolutely does. But I won't say that. "You're smart to keep one eye open."

He stands up and gestures to me. "Come here."

I stand also, and he hugs me, and Thomas is easily twice my size. Anyone looking probably wouldn't even see me enfolded in his arms.

"You're my favorite girl," he says. "Maybe my best girl."

His words warm my heart. I take a step back. "Same. You're my best guy."

He holds out his fist. "Friends again?"

I bump his fist with mine. "Yes."

I know he won't spend as much time over here with me, not when he has a girlfriend to hang out with.

But I have my friend back. That's enough for now.

⁂

The musical tryouts are on Sunday. I'm a nervous wreck as I drive over to the music building on campus. Abby rides along with me for moral support.

"I haven't tried out for anything since my senior year of high school," I blabber. "I thought the part was made for me. It was Maria from *West Side Story,* and I felt the story in my soul.

"The tryout went so well. I knew the song, I knew my part, but I went a little sharp on the last note. Nothing too bad, I still thought I nailed it. But then we had to do a dance routine."

I pause, and Abby fills in for me, "And you can't dance?"

I shrug. "I don't know if I could or not. I'd just had foot surgery and was in a cast. I didn't even make callbacks."

She gives me a sympathetic look. "That's rough."

"It crushed me. Totally stole my confidence. I haven't tried out for anything since."

"You'll nail this one."

"I hope so."

About a hundred other girls are present in the tryout room. The musical is about the women who Christ met during his mortal ministry, and the tryout requirements are simple. Pick a song we're familiar with from the hymn book that shows off our range and vocal flexibility, and sing it as an audition.

I sit next to Abby on a padded chair waiting my turn, and I flip through the green hymnal in my lap. None of the songs seem adequate. Most are too low. I'm a soprano, and I want something that climbs and moves and breathes life to my voice.

Seven people later, I find the song. I step out into the hall and warm up on a scale, putting a finger in my ear to drown out the other girls around me doing the same thing. Then I run through the song several times.

I think I've got this.

I go back inside and sit on my hands to keep them from fidgeting, though they do it anyway. I bounce back and forth like a kindergartner.

The coordinator comes into the room with a clipboard. "Next."

It's me. I'm the person at the edge of the row. I grab my hymnbook and follow her out, glad I didn't eat anything after church because I want to throw up.

She leads me into a smaller room with a piano and a pianist.

"Name?" she asks me.

"Cassandra Jones," I say.

"What song are you singing?" the woman behind the piano says.

"'The Lord is my Light,'" I answer.

She flips through the hymnal in front of her until she finds it. "Ready?" she asks.

I take a deep breath and nod.

She play an intro, and then I launch into the music. I sing two verses, and I forget to be nervous as I relax into the song. My voice floats up on the high notes and trills through the rapid exchanges. I don't watch the other woman with her clipboard even though I know she's making notes about my performance.

"Thank you," she says when I finish the second verse, and I cut myself off before I launch into the third. "Did you write your phone number on the sign in sheet?"

I remember the yellow pad in the waiting room and nod.

"Great. We'll be in touch if you get a part in the musical."

That's it. I thank them and back out of the room.

Abby is waiting for me in the hallway.

"I could hear you," she says, joining me as we walk toward my car. "You sounded fantastic. I bet for sure you'll make it in."

I take a deep breath, hold in, then let it out very slowly. "I don't know," I say. "But I enjoyed trying. I'm glad I did it. It's been a long time since I put myself out there."

Abby pats my shoulder. "I'm proud of you."

We step into the apartment and find the usual crowd of neighbors and strangers hanging out. I'm surprised when I see Sam sitting at the kitchen table.

"Hey," I say. "I didn't know you were coming over."

"Surprise." He shrugs. "My afternoon was open, so I thought I'd pop over."

"Well, hi," I say, but I'm uneasy with him here. We said we're friends, but I pick up a vibe around him. Something about the way he looks at me makes me think he wants more than that.

Or maybe it's his smell.

CHAPTER NINETY

Becoming a Habit

No one calls back about the musical Sunday night.

Did they say when we should expect to hear from them? The more I try not to think about it, the more it's all I can think about.

Nothing Monday either.

Tuesday Harper calls me. I'm in class so I can't take the call, but as soon as I get out, I call her back. I head up the stairs in the humanities building and sit in one of the oversized chairs, gazing out the large windows at the students walking around campus.

"Everything all right?" I ask.

"There's been a change of plans," she says, and I tense up. If Colton did something to screw things up between them, I might have to rough someone up.

"What's going on?" I ask.

"Well, we're changing the wedding date."

"You are?" I'm disappointed and relieved. I don't love who she's marrying, but I don't want her to get her dreams crushed. "To when?"

"March."

"March?" I sit up in my seat. "But that's in two months."

"Yeah. We feel like it's better timing than May. And we're ready."

"Harper, that's the middle of the semester."

"Is that a problem? You'll still come, won't you?"

I close my eyes. I don't want to fly home and miss classes and fly back out. That's a waste of money, and I'll get behind in all my classes.

But I force the selfish thoughts back. It's Harper's wedding. She gets to decide when it's going to be. The rest of us are lucky to attend. "Of course I'll be there. I'll do whatever it takes to make it work."

"I knew you would!"

Another call comes through, and I pull the phone away to check it. It's a local number but I don't recognize it. Probably spam. I ignore it.

"Send me the new dates," I say. "I'll start looking for plane tickets." A fist of worry tightens in my belly.

Money money money money money. It's on my mind all the time.

"I will, I'll email you all the new info."

"Okay. I gotta go. I have another class to get to, and it's a good seven-minute walk from here."

"All right, get your steps in. I'll talk to you later."

I forget about the other call until I'm in my seat in English class and see the voice message they left me. Class hasn't started yet, so I play it back.

"Cassandra, this is Ms. Young with the music program. Please give me a call back at this number at your earliest convenience."

Ms. Young. Wasn't she the one with the clipboard on Sunday during the auditions? I try to call her back right then, but now it's my turn to get an answering machine.

"Hi, this is Cassandra, returning your call. Sorry I missed you. I'm in class until noon, and then I'll be free the rest of the day," I say.

She wouldn't call me to tell me I didn't get into the musical, would she?

Maybe she would?

I'm so not sure. But I spend the rest of class checking my phone, hoping she'll call again.

She doesn't, but I get an email from Alliances Abroad while I'm at work.

We received all of your paperwork! We'll contact you soon to set up a placement interview. We're excited to work with you!

Oh goodness! Now comes the hard part.

Sam comes over again as I'm making dinner. I think this is weird. Why doesn't he call or text beforehand? But I suppose that's normal for friends.

"You hungry?" I ask. I open another can of corn and thicken my soup to make it go further.

"I can always eat," he says.

Sam isn't a big guy. Rather short, actually. Maybe five-five, only a few inches taller than me. I wonder if that's why he's interested in me. Hard to find girls shorter than him.

Abby comes in, Thomas behind her.

"Knock knock," he says.

I favor him with a smile. He doesn't need permission to come in. "Hey! Good to see you. Soup? I'm making a bunch."

He spots Sam and holds out a hand in greeting. "Thomas. Come for dinner?"

Sam shakes his hand. "Sam. Apparently there's a bunch of soup."

I lift an eyebrow, ready to empty another can of corn into the soup. It's rapidly becoming corn chowder.

"Can't stay," Thomas says. "Just came to say hi."

"You don't have to go," I say. Begging him to reconsider.

He doesn't pick up on my tone and gives my shoulder a squeeze. "You've got company." He waves at Sam and heads for the door.

"Thanks for coming by," I say. He's only leaving because Sam is here.

Why is Sam here, anyway? I hope this doesn't become a habit.

Sam doesn't get the chance to come by the next day because my dad arrives in town. He takes me and my roommates to an Indian restaurant, except Layne, who is out with Thomas. I'm not thrilled she chose not to eat with us, but at least Thomas is talking to me again.

Dad jokes and teases my roommates. They think he's hilarious, and I'm tickled because this fun guy is not the one I grew up with. He was angry and cross and demanding.

"I might be traveling a lot more," Dad tells me while we wait on the check. "I'll come see you every chance I get."

"I'd love that," I say. "And not for the free dinner. Though this was great." I gesture to what's left of my rice and lamb. I have enough food for tomorrow.

My phone rings, and I check it to see the same number as yesterday. Ms. Young. "Excuse me," I say, jumping up. "I've got to take this." I scurry into the hallway and hold the phone close to my ear so I can hear. "Hello, this is Cassandra."

"Cassandra, hi! This is Ms. Young. You auditioned for the Easter musical, is that right?"

"Yes," I say, my heart suddenly galloping in my neck.

"We'd like to offer you a part, if you're still interested."

Oh my gosh! I want to scream and jump up and down and cry. Instead I bury all my feelings deep in my chest and say, "That's wonderful. Yes, I'd love a part."

"Great, I'll mark you down. Practices start next week. I'll email you the place and time. If there are any scheduling issues, please let me know."

"Okay, thanks."

I hang up and walk calmly back to the table, where my dad is paying the check and everyone's standing up.

"I got in!" I shriek, giving into my need to shout. "I made the musical!"

My roommates crowd around to hug and congratulate me.

I'm in bed when Layne gets home but not asleep. I look up from the book I'm reading.

"How were things with Thomas?" I ask.

"Oh, fun." She shimmies out of her clothing and pulls on a pair of pajama bottoms with a matching button up. "We ended up at a dance performance with super awesome costumes. I loved it."

"You guys go out a lot," I say. "Must be getting serious."

"Serious? No way. We're having fun." She climbs into bed.

"Does Thomas feel the same as you about things?"

"We haven't talked about it, but I'm sure. Why would we get old and boring when we're young with so much to do and try? He's on this journey with me right now, but there's no telling what tomorrow brings."

Typical Layne. It's about what I'd expect from her. But I'm not sure Thomas is on the same page.

"Did you have fun with your dad?" she asks.

"Yeah. We had great Indian food. We get along better now that I'm an adult."

"Isn't it weird that parents are like that?" She hits her lamp. "Night, Cassandra!"

"Night," I echo. I put my book away and turn out my own lamp.

⊙〜᪥〜◎

"Cassandra."

I'm sleeping. The world in my mind is hazy, out of focus, but the fog has a hold of me and won't let me go.

"Cassandra."

The world jostles, bouncing me, and I grimace, but I cling to the fog. I can't go. I'm not ready. Let me sleep.

Someone giggles, and the fog snaps away with alarming speed. I open my eyes to see Camila and Abby peering down at me, their heads tilted as they watch me. Behind them rises row after row of bookshelves, and I see a blinking exit sign.

I sit up as I merge reality with my dream state.

I'm in the library.

"Oh, crap," I say. "I fell asleep."

Abby smirks at me. "Yeah, you did."

"We came to get you," Camila says. "We're headed home and thought we might find you here. Ready to go, or should we find you a pillow?"

"Ha ha." I check my face for drool, but luckily I slept with my mouth closed. "Let's go."

They wait while I load up my bag, and then we head for the elevator. We descend five floors and come out in the large atrium.

"Cassandra!"

I turn at the sound of my name. Waving wildly from across the atrium is Jordan. "Jordan, hey!" I call to my cousin.

He disappears from view and reappears on our side. He gives me a crushing hug, something that's easy to accomplish because he's a good foot taller than me. Then he gives one to Camila and Abby.

"Hi," he says to Camila.

"Hi," she replies.

"Where are you going?" he asks.

"Headed home." I move toward the exit, and he stays with us. "You?"

"Going to buy tickets for the medieval festival, actually. You going?"

"Medieval festival?" I picture a Renaissance fair with long cleavage-revealing dresses and sleeves to the ankles. "When is that?"

"Tomorrow. It's a dinner celebrating the new year the way the pagans did it. Want to go?" He includes Camila and Abby in his question.

"Who else is going?" I ask.

"My roommate."

"I'm in," Abby says. "Sounds like a blast."

"How much are tickets?" I ask.

Jordan pulls out his phone and checks something. "Twenty dollars a person. But that includes your traditional medieval dinner." He grins at me.

I bite my lip. "Sounds like so much fun." It's right up my alley. Strange foods, historic cultures, different lifestyle.

But I'm so broke it's not funny.

"Come on, take a look and you can decide," Jordan says, and he hustles me along to the billboard plastered with signs.

"All right," I say. It can't hurt to look at the promotional fliers.

We read through the activities at the dinner. It's a reenactment of the medieval Twelfth Night festivities, complete with music, storytelling, singing, dancing, eating, and hiding a treasure in the cake for one person to find.

"Let's do it!" Abby says, already pulling out her wallet.

"Yes!" Jordan says. He leans into the box office. "Two tickets, please."

"Get one for me too, Abby," Camila says, nudging her. "I'll pay you back."

Abby gets the tickets, and they both look at me.

"I'm still deciding," I say.

"No, you're not," Jordan says. "I got you a ticket."

I turn to him in surprise. "I thought you got one for you and your roommate."

"My roommate already has one. This one's for you."

"Jordan." I can't even be annoyed. I give him another hug. "Thank you."

He hands me my ticket. "See you guys tomorrow."

I wait until he's gone before I turn to Camila. "Well?"

"Well what?" she says.

I wave my hand after him. "You guys clearly still like each other. Why aren't you dating?"

Her face warms. "Because nothing's changed. He's still leaving."

"But he's not gone yet," I say. "And we don't know when he's going."

"Which is even more reason why I shouldn't start something with him."

Her voice is quiet, but it doesn't leave room for argument. So I say nothing in return.

I understand her desire to keep her heart intact, to protect herself from as much pain as possible. But every relationship right now is transient.

And I want one. Even if it's just a fling.

CHAPTER NINETY-ONE

I Need a Guy

Saturday is errand day.

My to-do list keeps growing, and I need to check things off before midterms get here and try to kill me.

The biggest thing glaring at me is buying a plane ticket for Harper's wedding.

It's at the end of March now. Just six weeks away. I've been watching prices like a hawk and they're holding steady, but I know that's about to change. If I wait much longer, they'll go up.

I sit at my computer and pull out my credit card. My heart begins to pound as I put in the information for my flight. I thought about flying out of Denver, but it's only a hundred dollars cheaper. Not worth it for the extra six hours of driving.

I try not to think of all the other big ticket items I'm paying off. Car tires. Bridesmaid dresses. Chains.

I go back and forth between the refundable and the economy ticket. The price difference is a hundred and fifty dollars.

I can't bring myself to spend the extra money.

I click the basic ticket and hit Purchase.

Harper better not change the date again.

Then I text her. *Tickets bought! See you in March!*

She sends back happy hearts and smiley faces, and I know I did the right thing. The money won't matter to me later, but being there for her will.

I move from online tasks to household tasks. Iris's birthday is next Saturday, and we decided to hold a big barbecue at the park and invite everyone we know. I told her I'd start the grocery list and she could look it over to make sure I didn't forget anything.

"Iris," I call down the hall, "how many people are coming to your birthday party?"

"Um. I don't know. How many people should I invite?"

"Not my party," I yell back. "You decide."

"Let's invite everyone we know!" she says.

"So, fifty people?"

"Sure!"

It's a lot of people. We'll feed everyone hot dogs and chips. College fare.

My phone dings with an incoming text from Monica. My heart skips a beat when I see it. I haven't forgotten about her. I answer quickly, my heart in my throat.

"Hey. You all right?"

"Yes." She gives a laugh. "I wanted to let you know I'm flying home next week."

"Any updates?" I ask, trying not to sound anxious.

"I'm scheduled for surgery the day after I get home. Then we'll plan next steps. With any luck, I can setup a treatment plan here in Colorado and finish the semester."

My insides are all twisted thinking about what she's going through. I study the green water of my fishtank in front of me. Have I cleaned it since the contaminated shells? "You let me know if I can help with anything, okay?"

"I will. And Cassandra? Don't say anything to Owen about this, please."

My eyebrows rise at the request. "He doesn't know?"

"I don't want to distract him from his mission if I don't have to. Remember how he handled it in high school?"

"I do. And he didn't take kindly to me keeping it a secret then, either," I remind her.

"If you don't tell him you're keeping it a secret, he's never going to know, is he?" she says cheerfully.

It's true. When do I talk to Owen? We barely even write anymore. "I won't say anything," I promise.

"All right."

"What about your new man?" I ask, trying to find his name in my memory and pulling up blank. "Does he know?"

"Not yet. I'm going to tell him—but not until I'm home."

I don't question her logic. She's been through this before. "I'm praying for you."

"Thank you. I'll see you soon. Love you."

"Love you too, tell your family I said hello!"

And then she hangs up, and I'm left staring at the fishtank and trying not to worry.

She's going to be fine. She has to be.

"Everything all right?" Iris asks, coming into the kitchen.

"Fine," I say. I don't want to discuss this.

I abandon Iris's birthday list to clean the fishtank. I change out the water and lean back to peer at it. No one's died since the fiasco with the shells. The sides are clean. We have nine beautiful fish swimming around.

But they're the same nine fish as last month.

"I need something new," I announce to whoever is listening. I glance around and see only Iris.

"What do you need?" she asks.

"A guy." Layne comes down the hallway, running a hand through her blond hair and yawning. "Cassandra needs a guy."

"Yeah, that too," I say, and they both laugh. "But I'm thinking of something I can get from the petstore."

"Oo, you gonna bring one of the workers home?" Layne settles onto the couch and grabs a pillow.

"Another fish?" Iris asks, ignoring Layne.

"Something." I study the tank again, then grab my car keys from the hook.

"Surprise us," Layne says.

"I think I will." I'll be surprising myself as well.

Thomas is right. Fish are my therapy.

⟡

I return an hour later with a newt. He's a beautiful bluish-black creature with a spotted gray underbelly. I arrange his new castle in the water so he can bathe at the surface and catch his rays from the artificial light installed, and I put his brine shrimp in the freezer.

We creatively name him Mute because he doesn't say much. And it rhymes with newt.

We're so clever.

"I absolutely love him," Layne says as everyone gathers around to admire him.

"Isn't he fun?" I'm excited to have something besides a fish. I pull the top off the tank and stroke his back. His slick skin flattens under my finger. "He's like a real pet."

"Dogs are better," Camila says. "But the newt is pretty cool."

Iris shakes her head. "You'll get bored and have to decide which animal you'll torture next."

I scowl. "That's not true." There's a hint of truth to it. But I wasn't bored, I was anxious. And I'm not going to torture this amazing little guy.

Abby bursts through the front door, clapping her hands like a herald announcing a royal decree. "Medieval night! Let's go, ladies!"

"Oh goodness, I forgot," I say, my stomach twisting with a mix of excitement and mild panic. "I better find something to wear."

My wardrobe is woefully lacking in long medieval gowns, which I find deeply tragic at a moment like this. I settle for a velvet top with a square neckline that at least hints at medieval fashion. I pin up the sides of my short hair to mimic the elegant styles of the era, though I suspect I look more like a lady-in-waiting than an actual lady.

I take pictures with my roommates, laughing as Camila pulls out a cheap masquerade mask and declares herself a mysterious noblewoman. We march through the crisp January night toward the history building, where the festivities are in full swing. Outside, torches flicker in the cold night air, illuminating the stone pathways leading to the main hall. A few students dressed as jesters skip past us, ringing bells and tossing confetti in the air. Others are dressed in elaborate medieval gowns and tunics, their breath visible in the winter chill. Jordan and his roommate Shane meet us at the entrance, both of them looking questionably medieval in tunics that resemble thrifted graduation robes.

The building has been utterly transformed. The moment we step inside, it's like entering another century. Flickering candlelight casts golden shadows over long wooden tables, draped with deep red and gold fabric. Evergreen garlands laced with holly berries and golden ribbons hang from the ceiling, and thick beeswax candles sit in iron sconces, making the whole place smell faintly of honey and pine.

A trio of musicians—one with a lute, another with a drum, and a third with a recorder—fill the space with merry, lilting music that makes me want to twirl in circles.

Long wooden tables stretch the length of the hall, each adorned with goblets, candles, and platters of bread and cheese. Students chatter excitedly, waiting for the festivities to begin.

"This is incredible," Camila whispers, her eyes wide as she takes in the scene.

Jordan, less impressed, nudges my arm. "Did people actually have parties like this in medieval times?"

His roommate nods and launches into full geek mode. "Twelfth Night was a *huge* deal back then. It marked the end of the Christmas season and was all about role reversals, mischief, and feasting." He motions toward a group of students dressed as jesters, their hats jingling as they prance through the room. "The idea was that for one night, the world was turned upside down. Peasants could become kings, fools could rule over lords, and general chaos was encouraged."

"General chaos," Jordan repeats. "I like it."

We find our assigned table and sit, and the music swells as a woman with flowing golden hair—her dress impossibly elegant, embroidered with gold thread—steps onto a platform at the front of the room. She raises her arms, silencing the crowd.

"Good evening, merry revelers!" Her voice rings through the hall. "Welcome to our grand feast! Tonight, we honor tradition, revel in mischief, and embrace the spirit of Twelfth Night!"

We erupt into cheers.

"To begin," she continues, "we shall partake in a sacred and time-honored tradition... the bean and the pea!"

She gestures to a side table, where a massive cake sits, decorated with sugared fruit and a thick layer of icing.

"And now we eat cake!" she declares.

As if on cue, several servers dressed in minstrel hats and pointed shoes dance around us to a strumming lute and plop plates of cake in front of each person.

"But we haven't had dinner yet," I say.

"Don't question it," Jordan says, his fork in his hand. "We eat cake."

"Forks hadn't been invented yet," Camila says. "We should be using our fingers."

"We're taking creative license," Abby says, stabbing her fork into the cake.

"I know this one," Camila says as she takes a bite. "One slice has a bean, and one has a pea. Whoever finds them gets to be king and queen for the night!"

I pick up my fork, but Jordan is already tearing through his like an archaeologist hunting for treasure.

"There's a pea in here? Sweet," he mutters, crumbling his cake into a pile of sugar.

I sift through mine more delicately. "I don't see anything."

"Did anyone find the bean or the pea?" the golden-haired woman calls, her head swiveling like a hawk.

"Me."

We all turn as Abby raises her hand, holding up a small, cake-crumb-covered object between her fingers.

"At least, I *think* it's a pea," she says. "Right now, it's mostly cake."

"And you are?"

"Abby," she says, her face coloring as red as her hair.

The woman practically dances toward her. "All hail Queen Abby!" She takes her hand and pulls her to her feet.

"All hail Queen Abby!" the minstrels echo, and as the chant ripples through the hall, we join in. "All hail Queen Abby!"

With a dramatic flourish, the woman pulls a crown from her waistband and places it on Abby's head.

"Thanks," Abby says, adjusting it with an awkward laugh. I pull out my phone and snap pictures, giggling.

Then Abby tries to step back, but the woman tightens her grip.

"Oh no, my queen," she says with exaggerated solemnity. "You are royalty now. You must sit at the head table with us." She gestures toward the honored guests, all dressed in elaborate medieval attire.

Abby looks over her shoulder at us, eyes wide. "You mean—I won't sit with my friends?"

"Tonight, you dine in high places," the woman declares, leading Abby away as she gives us one last, betrayed look.

I watch Abby at the head table as a jester pours her a goblet of something dark and mysterious. Her expression is pure horror.

Jordan grins. "All hail Queen Abby."

The feast begins in earnest, with trays of roasted meats, spiced cider, and strange medieval dishes like "figgy pudding" making their way down the tables. Some of it is delicious, some of it...not so much. I poke at a mysterious meat pie and decide I don't want to know what's inside.

Halfway through the meal, jesters take the stage, performing skits full of exaggerated gestures and ridiculous jokes. One of them juggles flaming torches, while another reads out humorous "predictions" for the new year, declaring that Jordan will "fall madly in love with a fair maiden" and that Camila will "discover a hidden treasure, probably in the laundry room."

As the night wears on, the festivities grow even more raucous. There are riddles and songs, a few clumsy attempts at medieval dancing, and a ceremonial "banishing of mischief," where a student dressed as a mischievous spirit is playfully chased out of the hall. Jesters weave through the tables, playing tricks and challenging guests to tongue-twisting riddles. At one point, Jordan gets dragged into a game of blindfolded apple bobbing, which he loses spectacularly.

Through it all, Abby reigns over the event with a bemused smile, occasionally glancing over at us as if to say, "How did this happen?"

The evening ends with the *Wassail Toast*, a traditional blessing for health and prosperity. We raise our cups of warm spiced cider and shout, "Wassail!" in unison, the word ringing through the hall like an ancient spell.

I sigh and sip my cider. The night is ridiculous, the food is terrible, but I can't stop smiling. Traditions like this remind me why I love this school.

Abby finally rejoins us, plopping into her chair with a dramatic sigh. "That," she announces, adjusting her crooked crown, "was a *lot* of pressure."

"Welcome back to the peasants," I say, raising my goblet.

She clinks hers against mine. "Glad to be here."

CHAPTER NINETY-TWO

Non-Consensual

I have my first practice for the musical on Sunday.

"There's a list on the door," Ms. Young says to me when I arrive at the music building. "Find your name and room number, and the pianist will be in there waiting for you with your music."

"Thanks." I work hard to conceal my excitement. I hope it's a beautiful, challenging piece, one that will stir the emotions and the spirit as well as showcase my voice.

I head down the hall and hear voices coming from the room. I push on the handle and step into a small studio with three women inside. One sits at the piano, but the other two swivel to stare at me when I walk in.

"Oh, I'm sorry," I say, backing out, my hand still on the door. "I thought this was my room." I pop my head in the hallway and frown. It's the correct number.

"It's the right room," the pianist calls.

I step back inside. "Oh. Um . . . What are we doing?"

"It turns out we're a trio," one of the other girls says. Both are tall and blond and much larger than I am.

"A trio?" I repeat.

The one at the piano nods. "Yes, they thought this song would sound better with several voices."

"Is it arranged to be a trio?"

The third girl sits in a chair and separates sheets of music for me. "No, but the parts were separated for us by the director. She said we can write in a harmony unless we all want to sing melody. Here, this is your music. Your part is highlighted."

I take the sheet music, still mentally trying to catch up. I look over the paper, following the song, turning the page. "So it's a song written for one person, and we've divided it into three people?" Frustration mingles with disappointment in an unpleasant tumble.

"Not us," the girl sitting says. "Ms. Young. She had an idea of what she wanted, so she did this."

"And these highlighted parts, they're mine?"

"Yeah." The tall girl leans forward and runs her finger along my paper. "Some of these parts we all sing. Others we break off."

My heart sinks further as I read the notes. "Why was this part assigned to me?"

The two girls look at each other, and I know why before they say anything.

"We picked our parts when we came in," the tall one says.

And I was last. So they gave me this one. I shake my head. "I can't sing this." The disappointment creeps all the way to my toes, and I'm afraid I'll cry. I was so excited about this.

The one sitting frowns. "Why not?"

"Because I'm a soprano and half off these notes are below middle C. I can't go that low."

"Oh," the tall one says. "So . . . do you want to drop out?"

I feel a flash of anger. She doesn't offer to change parts with me. She wants me to leave. Then she'll have more to sing, anyway.

The pianist just watches us. Probably waiting to go report on our drama.

"We can transpose the notes," the girl sitting says. She, at least, looks sympathetic. "We'll move them around in the chord so it's in your range. I'm Erika." She waves.

"Nat," the tall girl says.

"Cassandra." I don't care about their names. I care that they've stolen my solo.

"Let's run through it," the pianist says, speaking for the first time. "Maybe it will feel different once you've sung it."

I suck in a breath and hold it, then let it out very slowly. "I'm sure it will."

The song is beautiful and incorporates a wide range of notes, from high soprano all the way down to notes a tenor would be proud of. Hebrew words are interlaced in the song, and my hand goes to my neck, clutching at the necklace I wear there.

A virtuous woman has the value of pearls.

The song brings tears to my eyes. Or maybe it's the thought of the other Hebrew words engraved around my neck. Either way, after we've sung through it once, I know I won't quit.

"We'll move those notes for you," Erika says. "It won't be hard."

I nod. We have to, because my voice disappeared on every note that dipped below middle C.

I'm a tumble of emotions by the time I get home. The practice didn't go the way I wanted, and my heart is aching. I want to fall into bed, close my eyes, and hug my pillow as I slip into the blissful, mindless state of sleep.

But when I walk into my apartment, Sam is there with Abby at the table.

"Sam. I didn't know you were coming," I say.

"Yeah, I was in the area."

He's making a habit of this.

"Well, I'm . . . going to bed soon."

"I won't stay long. How was your day?"

I should have said I was going to bed now. But I didn't. I sit down at the table and oblige him, telling him and Abby about the disappointing practice. They make noises of sympathy and outrage, but all I want is to be alone.

"I'm so tired." I stand up. "I'm going to bed now, guys." There. I said it.

"Night, Cassandra," Abby says.

Sam stands. "Can I get a hug?" he asks, holding his arms out.

And how do you say no to that? I step into his embrace and give him a half-hearted pat on the back. "Good night."

"Night."

I don't wait for Sam to leave but head down the hall to my room. I hear his voice talking to Abby while I change into pajamas, and then she comes into my room, smirking.

"Where's my hug?" she says.

"Oh, shut up," I grumble.

She only laughs.

Mitch calls me when I'm in class Monday morning. I find that highly unusual. It's been months since we almost dated and nearly that long since I've thought of him. I should call him back but I don't feel like it. So I don't.

I walk over to the post office between classes and work and get visa photos taken. Since I'll be in Brazil for several months, I need a special visa. One that will allow me to earn money, not just be there as a tourist. Tourist visas are only good for thirty days.

I'll be there six months.

Six months! I squirm with excitement. I can hardly wait to start this adventure.

I stand in front of a white wall, and the machine takes four photos. The worker hands them to me. They're terrible. I wasn't allowed to smile and I look like I'm terrified of something, my eyes wide and unfocused. I hate them. I still pay for them. I doubt the Brazilian consulate cares how I look.

I put the photos together with a notarized transcript when I get home and write the address to Alliances Abroad on the envelope.

Someone knocks on my apartment door, and then they call out, "Cassandra? Are you there?"

"Come on in," I call. We leave the door unlocked as long as there are at least two of us at home.

Thomas comes in. He sees me at the table, and I know from his face that he's not okay. His mouth trembles, his eyes are red, and he can't quite focus on me. I put the envelope down.

"What's wrong?" I ask.

"Can I—Can I talk to you?"

"Yes, of course."

He sucks in a shaky breath. "Can we go on a drive? In my truck."

"Yep." I put the envelope down and follow him out. Thomas stays two steps in front of me, but I have an uneasy feeling I know what this is about.

He still holds my door open when we get to his truck, which is kind, because I need both hands to climb inside. Then he gets in and barrels out of the complex. He doesn't speak as we drive toward the canyon, and I let him lead. He pulls into a park near where we went rock climbing over the summer, and then he parks. He rests one arm on the steering wheel and stares out into the night.

"What happened?"

He swallows hard. "Layne—" His mouth trembles, and it's shocking to watch this big giant of a man crumble like a sand castle when a wave washes over it. "Layne, she—she really hurt me."

My heart clenches, and I sympathize with his pain. I knew it. "Thomas, I'm so sorry."

He nods and spares me a quick glance, and then he's staring out the windshield again. "I thought she really cared about me. We've been dating for four weeks now. She acted like everything was great, like I was all she needed."

I don't say anything. I'm here for when he wants comfort, and if he wants to trash-talk my roommate, I'm here for that too. But at the moment, I'm just listening.

"She said she liked me. She said I'm the one she wants to be with." He breaks down and starts to cry, hanging his head so the tears fall toward his seat.

I place a hand on his arm, just enough to let him remember I'm here. "What happened, Thomas?"

He lifts his head and uses his sweater sleeve to wipe his face. "I asked her yesterday if she wanted to do something today, and she said she couldn't, she had to TA one of the Spanish classes. So I went up to her class to bring her some food because I thought she might be hungry . . ."

I know exactly where this is going. But I let him finish it.

"And she was sitting on the desk making out with one of her students." Anger colors his words, flashes in his eyes. "She never cared about me at all."

"She cared about you," I say, not because I'm trying to defend my roommate—I hate this quality about her—but because it's important for Thomas to know not all of it was a charade. "She cared about you a lot, Thomas. But for Layne, trying out different boys is as fun as trying different kinds of pizza at a buffet. Why order one kind when you can taste so many varieties?"

He exhales sharply, shaking his head. "I just—I don't get it. How do people do that? Act like you mean something to them, say all the right things, then turn around and throw you away like it was nothing?"

I think about that for a second, watching him as he grips the steering wheel so hard his knuckles turn white. "I don't think she sees it like that. Layne likes the thrill of something new, but she doesn't think about what happens when the shine wears off. It's selfish. And it's wrong. But it's not about you not being enough."

Thomas lets out a humorless laugh. "That's what it feels like, though."

"Yeah. It always does."

He turns his bloodshot eyes my direction. "You warned me about her. And deep down, I knew it too. But she made me think we were different. What she felt for me was different."

I give a wan smile. "She's very, very good at that."

"How can you be friends with someone like that?"

The question makes me slightly defensive. "I see Layne for who she is, and who she isn't. I can still love the good qualities about her without loving the bad ones. And I'm not trying to date her, so the worst qualities don't affect me."

He snorts. "Word to the wise. Don't ever date her."

The comment is so unexpected that I laugh. "Okay. I'll keep that in mind."

He tilts his head back against the seat and lets out a slow breath. "I feel like such an idiot."

"You're not an idiot, Thomas. You just have a heart. And you're going to make some girl really, really happy one day. Someone who actually deserves you."

He looks over at me, his expression softer now. "You think so?"

"I know so."

For a moment, we sit there in the quiet of the truck, the only sound the faint rustle of wind through the trees outside. His breathing evens out, and I can see the tension in his shoulders slowly start to fade.

He gives a half smile and sighs. "Thanks for coming out here to talk to me, Cassandra. You're a real friend."

"I'm here for you. Anything you need."

He huffs a breath. "You wanna get out of here? Go do something stupid to get my mind off this?"

I raise an eyebrow. "Define stupid."

He rubs his chin like he's considering. "Midnight pancakes at that 24-hour diner? Maybe way too many milkshakes?"

I grin. "Now you're speaking my language."

He finally gives me a real smile—small, tired, but real. "Then let's go."

CHAPTER NINETY-THREE

The Right Reasons

After my talk with Thomas, I feel bad for blowing Mitch off. We're supposed to be friends, right? There was something between us when we almost dated.

But it's still slightly awkward now, and I'm not sure I want to talk to him. So I call when I know he's at work and won't be able to answer, and then I leave a message.

My job is done. I reached back out.

I don't expect him to call me back, but that's exactly what he does. I'm alone in my room, getting ready for bed and wondering whose heart Layne is screwing with tonight, when my phone rings. I see his name and groan. I don't want to talk. I want to sleep.

I answer anyway. "Mitch. What's up?"

"Cassandra, hey!" he says. "How are you? It's been a moment."

"Yes," I say. "It has." I climb into bed and hold the phone to my ear. "What's going on?"

"Not much, really. I haven't talked to you in weeks."

"Months."

"Yeah." He laughs. "Months. And you're pretty cool, and I kept thinking, you know, I should call Cassandra."

For a moment, I thought he might be calling because he heard about Monica, but he doesn't mention her at all.

"Well, we kind of went different directions," I say.

"We did, we did. But it was for the right reasons."

Is it my imagination, or is there a ring of doubt in his tone? I'm probably just tired. "Yep. The right reasons."

"Yeah."

The conversation drifts into a pause, and I search for a topic of conversation before it can get weird. "So are you dating anyone?" Yikes. Why did my mind go there?

"No, but there's this girl I like. I just haven't asked her out. Sometimes I'm afraid I'm chasing after all the wrong things and that's why it's not working out."

"Hmm." I'm not sure what to say to that.

"You?" he asks.

I sigh. "No, unfortunately."

He laughs. "Feeling lonely?"

"Extremely. I have a dozen guy friends and all I want is one boyfriend. Is that so hard?"

"Why don't you pick one from those dozen guy friends?"

"Because they're only friends for a reason. They're not boyfriend material, not for me."

"What excludes them?"

I run through the list of guys in my head. "No chemistry, no attraction, dating my roommate, already tried, smells funny—"

Mitch laughs at that one. "Related to your ex," he says.

"Yep. That gets someone on the friend list."

"As long as I'm on that list. I still consider you a friend."

"Friends hang out. They talk. We don't do either."

"Ouch. So we're not friends?"

"Well . . ."

"Tell you what. Let's hang out on Friday. As friends. I'll get a few people together and we can watch a game, go out for ice cream."

"Better idea. We're throwing a birthday party for Iris at the park on Friday. Come."

"Will she care?"

"Oh, no, it's an open invite. We'll play soccer before the party, too."

"I'll come. It'll be great to see you."

"Yeah," I say. "Yeah, it will be."

We chat a few more minutes and then I go to bed. It must be a testament to how lonely I am that I'm wondering if it's possible to date him after all. I don't think Monica would throw a fit anymore. The more time that passes, the less relevant dating Owen seems. So what if his cousin and I fall for each other? Owen and I are just friends now.

So why can't I take off that necklace?

⚘

I know as soon as I wake up that I'm sick.

My nose won't stop running, and the pressure makes my head feel like it's going to explode.

But there's no time for sickness. I drug myself with over the counter meds and haul myself to school. I text back and forth with Iris for most of the day, ironing out plans for her birthday party in two days.

My aching head. I take my scarf off at work and wrap it around my head. I'm trying to conceal the fact that I'm sick. So far none of the professors have noticed. I almost got through winter without getting ill.

The office door bangs open, and I lift my head as a student comes in.

"Hey, do you have a—" he pauses when he sees me, and then he starts to laugh. "A turban, by any chance?"

I think of the scarf wrapped up around my head and laugh with him. "Yes, but you can't have it."

"Darn it." He snaps his fingers. "How about a pen, then?"

"Yes." I open the drawer and hand him one. "We have paper too, if you need that."

"No . . ." He ducks his head, giving me a good view of his wavy, dark hair while he combs through his messenger bag. "I've got paper. Do you know what else I need?" He lifts his head and flashes me a brilliant smile.

"No, what?"

"Your phone number."

I feel both eyebrows lift up into the lining of my scarf. "Really?" Here I am, nose running like a faucet, eyes droopy with exhaustion, all of my hair tucked up in a turban, and he's asking for my number? "Do you mean the office number?"

"No, I mean yours. Because anyone who can pull of wearing a turban without caring what anyone else thinks is someone I want to get to know."

His words are rather flattering. I'm astonished at his confidence. He didn't ask for my number so much as explain that he needed it. He hasn't worried about if I have a boyfriend or something, but I suppose if I did, I would tell him.

I take a sticky note and give him one more quick glance before I write my number on it, careful not to tilt my head too far and lose my turban. He has brown eyes streaked with gold, and his face is pleasant, although he looks several years older than me.

"Now I need your name," I say, offering the sticky note to him.

"I'm Jessie." He gives me that bright smile again and takes the note. "And you are?"

"Cassandra."

"Cassandra." He salutes me with the note. "I look forward to discovering what color your hair is." He goes down the hall to the professors without asking me to call any of them, which means he's expected. He walks with an air of confidence and certainty I don't often see in college kids.

I find myself hoping he calls.

⊙↣✦↢⊙

Sam is sitting on the steps of my apartment when I get there. My scarf is back around my neck where it belongs, and my head throbs with each step.

"Do you live here?" I tease, moving around him to unlock the door.

"Yeah, and I got locked out," he says, joking back with me.

I unlock the door, but I block him before he can enter. "Sam, I'm sick. It's not a good day to be here."

"Oh." He raises his eyebrows, drawing my gaze back to his tall hair. "Can I get you anything?"

I shake my head. "No. I'm going to bed. But I hope you have a good night." Then I can't help adding, "And, maybe you should call before you stop by."

It feels harsh. I quickly amend, "For your own sake. So stuff like this doesn't happen."

He shrugs. "It's not a big deal. I don't live far."

"Yeah. Okay." I begin closing the door. "Good night."

"Night."

At least I didn't have to entertain him tonight.

⊙↣✦↢⊙

I'm at the park as soon as I get off work on Friday evening, helping set up for Iris's birthday bash. I get the grill going with Jake's help, and then I stand on tables and string streamers under the pavilion. I feel woozy as I do so, my head heavy and pounding, the world spinning around me. I'm still so sick. But I'm heavily medicated and I have to fake it. Tonight I'm hosting Iris's birthday.

Camila sets up the flag football game over at the field, and Abby sets out precut slices of cake on paper plates. I check on Jake to see how the grill's going, and he's got it under control.

"Just give me the hot dogs," he says.

Layne pops over dragging a green cooler behind her. She wears slimming capris and a cute pink blouse, and I wonder if she knows it's still winter. I'm grateful it got above freezing so we could hold the barbecue outside.

"I brought the drinks!" she announces, dropping the cooler next to the grill. She shivers and looks toward the fireplace. "You're going to get a fire going, right?"

That's the plan, but I'm cranky and not in the mood to placate her. I grab the lighter and fire starter and hand it to her. "The wood's stacked beside it. Be my guest."

She eyes me, probably picking up on my mood, but before she can say anything, the guests begin to arrive.

"Iris!" I call.

She's putting paper Chinese dragons on every table, and she turns to me now. I incline my head to indicate the arriving people, and her face lights up. She climbs down from the table and bounds over to them.

"Hi, hi!" she says, giving hugs.

I go and help Layne with the fire. I shouldn't be anywhere near the food right now.

"Need any help?"

I turn from my crouch and look over my shoulder to see Sam approaching. That uneasy feeling stirs in my chest, and I shove it down. "I think we got it," I say.

He crouches beside me, a little too close. "Are you feeling any better?"

I weave my hand back and forth. "Good enough to be here."

He presses the back of his palm to my face, and I scoot back, not comfortable with the touch.

"You don't feel warm," he says.

Layne watches us and says, "That's because it's freezing out here. Cassandra, can you bring the lighter over here?"

I shift away from him, getting closer to Layne. When Sam doesn't move, she says, "Sam, will you see if Camila needs help getting the football game going?"

He squints out toward the field and looks back at me.

"You good here?"

I nod. "Yes."

He stands and leaves, and Layne says, "Tell him to go away, Cassandra."

"He's not doing anything. We're friends."

She grunts. "He wants to be more than that."

"No, he doesn't," I argue. "We already had that talk."

She gives me a look. "He might not have been listening."

I don't want to believe her because it makes things more uncomfortable. So I don't answer.

We get the fire going and Layne goes off to socialize. I stay next to the fire, letting it warm my back, and survey the pavilion. Guests are arriving, but no one needs my help.

Everyone is self-sufficient and able to entertain themselves, get their own food, find the football game. I hear Layne's high-pitched giggle and see her snuggling into a borrowed leather jacket from some guy. Maybe not wearing a jacket was intentional on her part.

"You should go warn him."

I turn and grimace as Thomas approaches, looking fluffy in a large down jacket. "I should, huh?"

"Yeah. Or put a sign on her back that says, 'man-eater.'"

I laugh and accept his side hug. "You really think they don't know? It's fairly obvious."

"They all think they're going to be the one that's different."

I shake my head. "I can't save stupid." And I do think they're dumb, Thomas included. Boys trip over themselves to get Layne's attention, hungering for her affection, all the while knowing she's a vampire.

But I still feel sorry for them.

"How are you feeling?" I ask him.

He shrugs. "I'm still pretty hurt. But talking to you helped. I realized I fell for something that doesn't exist anyway."

"Cassandra, there you are!"

I focus on the approaching figure, and I can't help the smile that spreads across my lips when I see Mitch. "Mitch? You actually came?"

I pull away from Thomas to accept his hug, and I'm startled to remember how short he is. He backs up and looks me over while I do the same to him.

"I told you I would," he said. "You look great."

"I do not," I say, and I know I look like death warmed over. I wear jeans over long-johns and a long-sleeved shirt followed by a bulky sweater and then a jacket over the whole ensemble. A black beanie is pulled low over my head, and I saw my face before I left. It's pale and lined with dark circles. "I've been sick."

"You look pretty good for sick."

Thomas moves away from me. "I'm going to check out that football game."

"Go help Camila," I tell him. "I sent Sam her direction."

"Sam," Thomas says, and then he's gone.

I turn to Mitch. "Well, how are you?"

He sits down on the hearth in front of the fire, and I do also.

"Not much changed since our phone call," he says.

"School's going well, then?"

I study him as he answers. I'm trying to assess my feelings. He's still attractive, but not like he was to me over the summer. I don't feel a pull toward him.

"I'm competing a lot. Which is great because it takes me warmer places, and I don't love the cold."

"Me neither." My eyes flick over his arms, and while I can't see the additional bulk from here, I remember from our lake trip that his muscles have muscles. "So tell me about this girl you're interested in."

He leans back and sighs. "I think I have a problem. Every girl I meet I immediately begin evaluating as a future wife."

I arch an eyebrow. "What do you mean?"

"Like, I want to get married, and I'm beginning to think it's a major character flaw. I can't just date and have fun. I'm looking for a companion, a partner."

I furrow my brow. "How old are you, Mitch?"

"Twenty-two. See? Way too young to be obsessed with this."

I bob my head. "Total agreement. Plus if that's what you're doing every time you meet a girl, you won't get to know her for her. And people can change, they can grow, we don't even know who we'll be in a permanent relationship like that. It's rather unfair to place such high expectations on every acquaintance."

He rests his hand on my leg, his eyes reflecting the firelight behind us. "Right? I think the same thing. But I can't seem to stop. It's a problem."

I shrug. "Just don't miss a good thing because you're so focused on the future."

"Like you?"

The comment startles me. So I was right. We've both been wondering what could have been.

But as I look at him now, as I talk to him, I feel nothing. No spark, no chemistry, no interest. Maybe it could have been there, if we'd nurtured it. Maybe it would have grown. But we didn't and it didn't.

"It's possible," I say. "We'll never know. That ship has sailed."

He looks down and then back up and nods. "Yeah. Yeah, I guess it has. I should stop worrying and analyzing so much and see what happens."

I lean forward, resting my elbows on my knees. "I have the feeling, Mitch, that when the right girl comes along, she'll knock you so off-balance you won't be able to have a logical thought about the future or what your family thinks or if it's going to last. You'll be swept along for the ride."

"I want that," he says. "Maybe that's why nothing lasts. I'm waiting for something like that."

"It will happen."

His old roommates spot him then, and they come over to do the guy-handshake and talk about old times. I sit back and watch and I'm so glad he and I did not get serious. He's not who I want.

I'm waiting like him. Waiting for someone to come along and make me feel something so strong that I have no choice but to fall.

CHAPTER NINETY-FOUR

Free Orbit

Unknown text number: is this Cassandra?

Me: yes

It's Monday night and I'm at school still because I won't get this essay written if I head home. My classical civilizations class started out fairly easy, as we learned history and analyzed philosophical writings. But now we've moved into the art portion, and I have the hardest time recognizing styles and artists or even agreeing that something is art.

I welcome this distraction from the unknown texter.

Stranger: this is Jessie

That name does not ring a bell anywhere.

Me: Jessie. How do I know you?

Jessie: we met at your work. You were wearing a turban and wouldn't let me borrow it.

I remember now, and I laugh out loud.

Me: you can borrow it now

J: can I? I was hoping. Want to meet up tomorrow?

Tomorrow.

Tomorrow is Valentine's Day.

I've tried not to think of it because there's a serious ache in my heart when I do. My hand closes over the necklace under my shirt, the one that I take off every time I shower and swear I won't put back on but then I do.

I release it under my shirt and text him back.

Me: I can't tomorrow. How about another day?

J: oh, so sorry, I should have asked. You already have a date.

I grimace. I don't have a date. I'm single and lonely and I'm choosing to be alone on Valentine's Day rather than go out with someone I barely know.

That's probably more insulting to Jessie than pretending I have a date.

Me: yeah.

I'm interested, though. People who make me laugh suck me in like a planet to a star.

I want to be around that joy.

Me: but I'd love to some other time.

J: cool. Have a great evening. I'll let you know when I want to get that turban from you

Me: OK, have a good night

I save his number in my phone, but something about the conversation felt off.

He thinks I have a date tomorrow. He either thinks (incorrectly) that I have a boyfriend or thinks (correctly) that I date a lot.

Somehow I don't think I'm going to hear from him again. And that makes me a little sad. I'm still waiting to be swept off my feet, and he could have been the one.

Now I'll never know.

❦

I'm back at the library as soon as my badminton class finishes on Tuesday. I'm neck-deep in midterms, and even though I have work in an hour, I can't waste any time on lunch, plus I'm out of money and forgot to pack any food. I'm constantly on the verge of a panic attack, trying to keep all my tests and papers lined up so I don't miss one.

I finish my English essay with minutes to spare. I email it to my professor, slam my computer shut, and fly out of the library to the Engineering department. I flatten my hair after I clock in, take a collected breath, and enter the office.

No one's here. No one saw my mad dash, no one's waiting for me.

Christina is standing by her computer, closing out her folders.

"I'm leaving," she says. "But look what came for you!"

She points to a small bouquet of flowers on the counter next to my computer.

"For me?" I'm flabbergasted. Who would send me flowers?

"Happy Valentine's Day!" She waves and hurries out.

I go around the desk and drop my backpack behind the counter. I take the time to wake my computer, drawing out the suspense, before I turn to the flowers. Who? Could it be Jessie, who I turned down for tonight? Surely not Mitch. I suppose it could be Sam, but this would be a serious red flag to our friendship.

Who else knows where I work?

I pluck out the card in the center and open it, heart racing with anticipation.

To Cassandra. Love you, roommie! Abby.

Abby. The breath whooshes out of me, and I try not to feel disappointed, but it's impossible. I love that she thought of me, that she wanted me to feel loved today.

But this doesn't do it for me. I want romantic love.

I glance up when the door opens, and a kid walks in. He doesn't look up from his phone, and I sit down at my desk and swivel to the computer.

"Excuse me."

I turn back to the counter when he leans on it, and I catch my breath.

He might be the most beautiful boy I've ever seen.

I can't tell his ethnicity. Dark, Latino, maybe Mexican, but his eyes are large and almond-shaped. His jet black hair tumbles around his face, as straight as mine. And the moment his gaze catches mine, something knocks in my chest.

I can't tear my eyes away.

I want to take a picture of him and paste it on my wall. He's gorgeous. But he looks so young. "Hi," I say.

He smiles, and his eyes crinkle, his face lighting up like a ray of sunshine bursting through storm clouds. The effect is magnificent. I wonder if I can make it happen again.

"Could I see Professor Stephens?" he asks.

His voice is deeper than I'd expect from such a youthful face. I turn to the phone with automatic precision, trying to hide my awe at the fact that this beautiful person is standing at my counter. I call the professor.

"There's a student here to see you," I say. "Are you open?"

"It's my office hours," Professor Stephens says. "You can send anyone back."

Right. I know that. "Thanks," I say, and I'm flustered, the back of my neck hot. I hang up and look at the kid, who is still watching me. A little closely. Can he tell he has me rattled? "You can go on back."

"Thanks." He smiles again.

I sit down and try to understand what just happened. I feel like I was watching a lamb at a petting zoo and suddenly a T-Rex bent down and ate me. What? Where did that come from? I wasn't expecting it.

I pull out the list of tasks the professors have left for me. I'm transcribing the notes from a meeting when the kid appears again, backpack strung on both shoulders, his hands in the pockets of his loose pants. He strolls toward me and stops to examine my flowers.

"Did your boyfriend send these?" he asks.

I shake my head. I don't stand. I'm afraid of what will happen if I get any closer to him. I have a good view of his profile from here, anyway. "No."

He looks at me, dark brown eyes framed by black lashes, and I feel he's trying to read my soul. "That's too bad. He should have."

He strolls out of the office without another word, and I stand up to watch him go.

My heart pounds much harder than it should for a small interaction with a handsome stranger. I put it from my mind. I'll probably never see him again.

⟡

Abby got flowers for all of us. I get home and add my bouquet to the three others on the table, and I laugh and hug her.

"You're so good to us," I say.

"You poor thing." She pats my face. "I can tell you're still sick."

"I'm doing so much better." I open the fridge, but it's bare. Maybe that's why I forgot to pack a lunch. I search for lunch meat, cheese, something. I'm out of food.

"So, volleyball game?" Iris pops into the kitchen.

I turn to her. "What?"

"There's a game tonight," Abby says. "Camila can't go, Lauren went to a friend's house, and Layne's got a date."

I roll my eyes. "It is Valentine's Day, after all."

"I can't believe you don't have a date," Iris says.

"I turned one down."

"You did?" She gapes and doesn't quite hide the envy that flashes across her face. Iris goes out here and there, but she often jokes/not jokes about how unfair it is that I date so much.

"I didn't want to spend today with a stranger," I say. "This night is for being with loved ones."

"Like us!" Abby says. "So let's go to the game!"

"Yay!" I throw my arms up. "That's why I left my evening open!"

Someone knocks on the door, and I brace myself. "Please don't let that be Sam," I breathe out.

Abby glances at me and strides forward. "If it is, want me to tell him to go away?"

"Yes," I say. "Tell him we're leaving."

She cracks the door, and then throws it wide. "Thomas! We like you. You can come in."

"Oh really?" He laughs as he enters. He carries what looks like a pizza box with him, and my mouth waters. I haven't eaten all day. "I come bearing gifts." He drops the box on the table and opens it to reveal a giant chocolate chip cookie.

"Oh my goodness, you're my favorite," I say, snatching a piece.

"So do we tell him to go away also?" Abby asks.

"Tell me to go away? Am I in trouble?" Thomas looks back and forth between us.

I roll my eyes. "No, he can stay. He's not someone I'm trying to get rid of."

"That got dark. Glad I'm not on that list."

We laugh around cookie bites.

"We're about to go to the volleyball game," Abby says. "Seeing as how you're not on a hot date, want to come?"

"Yes. Yes, I would. I can now say I had a hot date with not one, but three beautiful girls on Valentine's Day."

That earns more laughter from my roommates, but I see how the flattery butters them up.

Thomas drives us, since he fits in his truck a lot better than in my car. My favorite part about these games is watching the volleyball players. Not only are they tall, but many of them are dark and handsome as well.

Which makes me think of the dark and handsome stranger who walked into my office this afternoon.

"Did you bring the cookie?" Iris asks, squeezing into the row near the front beside me and Abby.

"I've got all the treats I need right here," Abby says, her eyes glued to the players.

"Agreed." I laugh, but I hold up the plastic bag where I brought several slices of Thomas's giant cookie. "We're well equipped."

I don't understand the point system of these games, but they move very fast. The players slam the ball over the net, then volley from the other side, and then do it all again. If you blink, you miss an important play.

The ball skids off the court and bounces over a row to land next to our feet. Thomas leans over and picks it up, and then surprises me by shoving it under his shirt.

"What are you doing?" I ask.

In front of us on the court, the players are trying to find their ball.

"Keeping a souvenir?" Abby asks.

Thomas shrugs.

"Excuse me." A kid, maybe thirteen or fourteen, scrambles over the risers to us. He stops in front of Thomas. "I know you took the ball."

The three of us swivel to stare at Thomas.

"You do?" Thomas says.

"Yeah. I see it there." He points to it under Thomas's shirt, and I bite my lip to keep from laughing.

"How do you know I'm not just fat?" Thomas asks, straight-faced.

"I saw you put the ball under your shirt."

"You caught me." Thomas releases it and hands it to the boy, who gives Thomas the strangest look before returning the ball to the confused players.

We bust up laughing so hard I can't breath. My stomach hurts. I want to replay that moment again and again.

CHAPTER NINETY-FIVE

Trapped

On Sunday I have my third rehearsal for the musical. Erika helped me transpose the notes so they fit my range, and I don't feel so jipped now. I still wish I'd been given a longer musical number, but it does come together beautifully when the three of us sing at the same time.

Erika and Nat don't agree on their parts, though.

"I thought we said you were going to come in right here," Erika says.

"My paper has it marked here. So that's the part I've been practicing."

"Yes, but last time we decided together that entrance wasn't working and you should start at this measure."

"I wouldn't have said that."

They both turned to me to mediate, a position I'm loathe to be in. But I try to be fair and honest. "You guys did talk about moving your entry."

Nat huffs over this, and we go through it again, but it doesn't feel resolved.

"We have three more weeks until the performance," Erika says as the three of us walk out. "Think we'll be ready?"

"We have it already," Nat says. "We need to make sure we have the words memorized."

It's a direct jab at Erika, who didn't know the words to the chorus as well as we did.

She bristles, and I redirect. "We almost have the words," I say. "It won't be a problem. Three weeks is plenty of time."

Nat nods, Erika rolls her eyes at me, and I get in my car and drive away from all the drama.

I see Sam's car parked out front as I pull into the complex and groan. At least I recognize his car now and can prepare myself.

He's sitting at the table by himself. Abby, Layne, and Lauren are watching TV. They pay him no attention and barely glance at me when I walk in.

The message is clear: he's your friend, take care of him.

"Hi," I say, smiling, trying to drum up some excitement.

"Hi." He stays sitting. "How's your day been?"

"Nice. It was a good Sunday." I don't move to the table. I don't want to sit with him.

He reads my body language and stands. "Want to go on a walk?"

Not with him. But at least we won't be sitting in my apartment. "Yeah, sure."

We head outside, where the sun shines but doesn't do much to warm the air. I'm ready for spring. Nothing else is, judging by the bare tree branches and the naked bushes lining the streets and walkways.

I don't talk. I'm drained and still getting over my cold and making small talk with Sam is past my abilities right now.

"Did you have a church meeting?" he asks.

"Rehearsal for the musical."

"Oh, right! How's that going?"

"Fine, I guess." I punctuate my words with a shrug. "There are three of us, and we don't always get along or agree on how we should perform the piece. But it's coming."

"When's the performance?"

"In a few weeks." I keep it vague. If I tell him when or where, he'll show up.

And I don't want him there. This friendship is getting uncomfortable.

We walk along in silence for several more minutes. I run my hands over the tops of bony bushes and stare up at the mountains in the distance. They're covered in snow. The trees are begging for a color that isn't a shade of brown. I'm ready for it.

"How's school going?"

It's hard, I'm drowning, I challenge myself and then I regret it. I start out strong in the semester and then fall by the wayside and have to catch up.

I don't say any of that. Too many words. "It's fine. I like it."

"Yeah."

He doesn't say anything either. There's nothing. We don't connect. His company doesn't light me up. He can't make me laugh.

I'm so relieved when we get back to my place.

"Thanks for the walk," he says.

"Sure, anytime," I say, and I think there might be joy in my voice. But only because I'm glad it's over.

He opens his arms for a hug, and I try not to grimace. Great. Apparently he expects it now.

I oblige him, trying not to shudder when we touch.

"Good night," he says, turning for his car.

"Night." I take the steps to my apartment two at a time.

Ugh. I feel like I need to shower.

◎〜·⋇·〜◎

I spend six hours on Monday studying for midterms. I get a lot done, but I feel my brain breaking.

Iris texts on the roommate thread.

I: church talent show in two weeks. Are we doing anything?

Layne: TOGETHER?

I: why not? It would be fun

Lauren: sure. But what?

Me: Iris, you should play your cello. It's so beautiful.

I: I want to do something together. When are you home? We could practice a song.

Abby: I don't sing

Camila: me neither. But I can sprint a fast 800

Layne: BORING

Me: I can't think about this right now, I'm studying. Just tell me what you decide.

My phone rings, and I expect it to be one of my roommates, begging me to stop studying long enough to consider this so important matter.

It's Sam.

I click over and answer. "Hey."

"Hey, are you still on campus?"

I sigh. "Yes. So much work to do."

"When did you get there?"

"Seven this morning. I needed to finish an essay before my nine o'clock class."

He whistles. "It's time you left. Need dinner?"

Of course I do. I always need dinner. There's never enough food in my apartment. "What do you have in mind?"

"My brother's visiting and he wants to take me out. Want to come?"

Sam and his brother. At least it won't be the two of us.

"Yeah, okay."

Sam's brother Allan picks me up in front of the music building. Sam is sitting in the back of the car, which leaves me in the weird position of sitting up front with his brother, or sitting in the back with him.

I opt for up front.

"Sam says you're an English major," Allan says as he drives us to a steakhouse. "That's awesome."

"And fairly generic, if we're being honest," I say. "Fifty percent of kids choose the English major because it has so few credits, and all they need is a degree so they can apply to a masters or doctorate program. They're not actually interested in anything literary related."

Allan laughs. "Sam said you're witty also."

"I'm not. Just blunt. And maybe a little hangry."

He laughs again. "I see why Sam likes you. I like you too."

It's a weird statement. I let it slide. He's getting me dinner.

I find Allan much easier to talk to than his brother. He's not so serious, he smiles and laughs and teases. I warm up to him. I can't finish my steak so I get it to go, and Allan goes up to pay.

"My brother's pretty nice, isn't he?" Sam says.

"It was nice of him to take us out."

"He lives in California. He'll be flying back tomorrow."

"I'm glad you got to see him."

He doesn't say anything else, and I run the tines of my fork over my napkin.

I don't like complicated.

This friendship is feeling complicated.

By Wednesday I've taken two midterms and turned in an essay. Three down, two to go. I'm finding breathing room.

I settle in at work, putting together the packages that need to go out to the mail and writing down what books Dr. Lance wants me to get from the library. The door opens, and I look up as a student walks in.

It's him. The beautiful boy.

I'm not as shell-shocked at the sight of him this time. I keep my wits about me. So what that he has a pretty face?

"It's you again," he says.

Oh, but his voice is nice. Deep, with a very subtle accent.

"It's me," I say. "I work here."

"I know." He comes over to the counter and leans on it. "No flowers today?"

"People don't realize you're supposed to send flowers every day of the year, not just Valentine's Day."

"Massive oversight. I wonder what it will take to change that."

"Someone more important than me."

"More important than the secretary in the engineering office?" He widens his eyes. "How far up the food chain do we need to go?"

I've run out of witty comebacks. I shake my head. "Are you here to see Professor Stephens?"

"Technically."

"Technically?"

"Yes. He's my reason for coming over here. But I'd say I had a secondary reason."

"That being?"

He tilts his head and looks at me and he's almost smiling but not. It's something I see in the quirk of his lips and the squint of his eyes.

"An important reason. You're nosy, aren't you."

He startles a laugh out of me. And that delights me.

Professor Stephens appears in the doorway. He's a balding older man with glasses and red hair. "Oh, you're here. I've been waiting for you."

The kid turns away from the counter and goes down the hallway without another word. But I know I'll see him when he comes back out, and I'm waiting for it.

He returns fifteen minutes later. Professor Stephens follows him out and stands in the doorway.

"Let me know if you have any other questions," the professor says.

"Thanks." The boy's steps falter by my desk, and his eyes fall on me. Then he picks up his pace and leaves.

"Looks like he wanted to say something to you," Professor Stephens says, a teasing note in his voice.

"Did he? He didn't try very hard."

"That's teenagers for you."

"Is he a freshman?" Please don't say he's in high school. It happens sometimes that high school kids take college classes.

"Yes. As fresh as they come."

Whew. At least he's in college. "A bit young for me."

"Only a year younger. You're a sophomore, aren't you?"

"Yes." I turn back to my computer, pretending like I have no more interest. But then I look up. "Did he say anything about me?"

There's a twinkle in Professor Stephens' eyes. "He asked your name. I told him he'd have to get it from you."

Flutters of delight erupt in my chest. "What's his name? And don't tell me I have to ask him."

"He goes by Kai. But that's a nickname."

Kai. I immediately attach the strong consonant to the mental image I have of him, as if my mind conjured a contact card and put his face and name together. "What's his given name?"

"Malachi."

Malachi. A smile pulls at my lips, and I turn back to the computer. "Thanks for sharing."

We barely talked, but the interaction left my buoyant and giddy. Who cares about midterms?

Professor Stephens pushes off the wall. "Robbing the cradle. Want me to pass any messages along?"

"Oh, hush!" I call after him. "I can send my own messages!"

He laughs as he disappears down the hall.

CHAPTER NINETY-SIX

Different Vibe

Sam calls me Wednesday night. I've seen too much of him this week and I don't answer. He calls again Thursday after school and I can't ignore him forever, so I answer. He wants to go out again.

He's suffocating me.

I don't know how to get out of this relationship without breaking off the friendship entirely.

"Who else is going?" I ask.

"I don't know. Did you have someone you want to invite?"

"What are we doing?"

"Let's go to the international cinema tomorrow night, there's a historical Chinese film playing."

"I'll invite Iris," I say. "Maybe it's something she'll enjoy."

"Okay, sounds fun."

Abby texts me before I get to Iris. *Let's go to the volleyball game.*

Yes. A perfect, mindless activity with beautiful men I can objectify in my mind. I'm in.

But we aren't the only people wanting to sit and drool over the volleyball players. The line wraps through the hallway. It will be standing room only by the time we get in. We abort and begin the long walk home together, but with my friend cracking jokes and making fun of Sam the whole way there, it doesn't feel long.

"You've got to give him the boot, Cassandra," she says. "There's more expectation on his side than you realize."

"I think you might be right." I sigh. I don't want her to be right.

We walk in the door together, and I step over to Iris, who's chopping carrots.

"Want to go the movies with me and Sam tomorrow?"

"No." She makes a face at me. "No one wants to hang out with you and Sam."

"Is he so annoying you guys can't stand him?" He's not that bad.

She considers the question and shakes her head. "It's just that we know you don't want him around, so that makes us not want him either."

I don't know how she knows that. But it warms me to know my roommates feel that for me. I give her a hug. "Will you come anyway? It's a Chinese historical film."

She hands me the cutting board and knife. "If you cut the rest of these carrots."

"Done."

I get to work chopping, and Camila strolls into the kitchen with sweats on.

"Anyone get the mail today?" she asks.

I glance around but don't see any piles.

"No," Iris says.

Camila plucks the key from the board and heads out the door.

I wonder when I'll hear back from Alliances Abroad. They got my paperwork. Things should be moving along soon, right?

Camila pops back in and drops the pile on the table. "There's a letter for you, Cassandra."

"Is it from Alliances Abroad?" I peer over the cutting board, searching for the letter.

She pushes it toward me.

It's from Owen.

I hear her laugh as I put down the knife and grab it. She knew. I shoot her a glare and go to my room so I can read it in privacy.

The single page spills out on my bedspread. I nestle into my pillow and read the few words carefully.

Cassandra Jones!

Sorry it's taken me so long to write you. Things are busy, and I'm tireder than I've ever been in my life. I fall asleep in my food, at prayers, any time I hold still.

Let me tell you, winter in Chicago is terrible. Brutal. It wants to kill all living creatures, and missionaries are no exception. My mom had to find me a new coat, but I sure miss the warmth and humidity of Louisiana. Or Arkansas. But come summer, I know I'll be cursing that same sunshine. I remember how we melted here last summer.

Spring will be here soon. We're organizing a housing project that will start as soon as the weather's nice. The homeless population here is huge, and so many of them are families. I want to cry every time I see a little kid with no place to go, no shoes, no jacket. We can't give all of them everything they need, but this housing project should provide roofs for a lot of people.

I love my work here. I love helping people. Sometimes I miss home and people, but I know my time here is temporary, so I try to throw myself into it.

Write me when you have the chance, I love hearing from you.

Love, Owen

I get goosebumps when I finish the letter. The whole vibe is different. I'm his friend, his buddy.

Whatever we had is gone and over.

I put the letter down and take deep breaths. My throat aches, and I feel a burning right behind my eyelids.

It's not going to change. I will always love him.

But I'm going to live my life without him.

Iris meets me at the international cinema so I don't have to wait for Sam alone. He shows up right on time, and I'm so grateful for her because the conversation is easy with her there. I talk to Iris, she talks to me, and Sam jumps into the conversation whenever he feels like it.

Which isn't often.

He sits next to me and Iris takes the other side. I'm so aware of him beside me, but not in a good way. We're like opposing magnets, and every time he moves, I shift away. I keep an empty space between us at all times.

The movie might be the worst I've ever seen. Everyone dies, and I feel dismal and depressed when it's over.

"Really?" I say, incensed as we make our way out of the theater. "If we'd paid money for that, I'd want my money back!"

"China has a dark history," Iris says. "They tried to show it realistically."

"I don't go to the movies for realism!" I huff. "If I want depressing and sad, I'll read my journal."

That makes Sam laugh. "Your life hasn't been that bad."

"Not as bad as the people in the movie, that's for sure! I'll go write an uplifting entry for tonight!"

"You keep a journal?" Sam keeps pace with me and Iris, and I sure hope he doesn't intend to follow us home.

"Yes, but I don't write in it as often as I used to. I print a lot of pictures these days and put them in albums and let that be my journal. I got prints back from my trip to Colombia, and every time I see them, I'm reminded how much I loved it there."

"Sweet! I'll come over after church, and you can show me."

My mouth opens and closes like a fish, but I find no words. Iris looks at me. I'm at a loss.

"We might not be home," she says.

I recover and latch onto that. "I have rehearsal tomorrow."

"I know. I'll come over after that."

"Um. Okay," I squeak.

He turns toward the parking lot in front of the music building. "See you Sunday!"

Iris watches until he's out of sight, and then she rounds on me. "You have to tell him, Cassandra."

"Tell him what?" My heart's racing. He's intruding on my life. Planting himself in it and wedging his way in and trying to make himself a part of it. "What do I say? We're just friends."

"Then you break off the friendship. This isn't normal."

I one-hundred-percent agree.

But the thought of doing this makes me want to vomit.

⌒〜✿〜⌒

I'm distracted at church. My mind is on my upcoming rehearsal, my floundering grades, my need to rid myself of Sam.

My letter from Owen.

I'm not sure I should write him back. I remember how I blocked him last year, how I deleted his number, precisely so I wouldn't go through agonizing pain every time I heard from him.

If I were over him, if it didn't hurt every time we talked, maybe I could write him. Maybe we could be nothing except pen pals.

But that's not the case.

I go from church to my rehearsal, and for two hours I concentrate only on the music. I have my words memorized, and with my transposed notes, the music fits my range. But Erika and Nat changed their music so they'd both be happy with it, and our accompanist can't keep up.

"We need to meet again," she says. "Text me and tell me when you're available next week. We perform in two weeks, and we need to have this perfect."

We nod in agreement. At least Erika and Nat didn't argue through the whole thing.

My heart sinks when I arrive home and see Sam's car out front. I sit in my car and text my roommates on the group thread.

Me: we need to get Sam out of the house

Abby: yep. What can we do?

Iris: if we tell him you're not coming home, he'll leave

Me: no, I told him I'd be home and he could see pictures of Colombia. But then he's got to go

Iris: you didn't technically tell him he could. He invited himself

Layne: GET HIM OUT

I chortle. They're funny, and they've got my back.

Camila: Aren't we supposed to be practicing our skit for the talent show?

Me: yes!!!

Abby: OK he can look at pictures for fifteen minutes and then we're giving him the boot

Layne: THE BOOT

Lauren: ROFL

I grin and head up to my apartment, not nearly as anxious as I was a minute ago. I enter with a fresh smile.

"Hi, Sam!"

"Hi," he says, grinning back at me.

"Cassandra," Abby calls from the living room, "don't forget we scheduled to practice our skit in fifteen minutes."

"Oh, right!" I say. "Okay, let me get my pictures from Colombia and I'll show you what I can."

"I don't have to leave while you're practicing. It would be fun to see."

Oh, no no no, and if I'm not careful, he'll invite himself along to our talent show.

"Nope." Abby pops into the kitchen. "This is a roommate-only activity. No one is allowed to see."

"Sorry, Sam," Camila adds, coming out of her room.

I go down the hall to get my photo album, trying not to giggle.

We zoom through the pictures. I enjoy reliving every moment, from the Salt Cathedral to the teleférico to the zoo with the monkeys.

And then Layne comes home and says, "I'm ready to practice, guys!"

It's the first time she's shown any interest in our skit, the first time she's shown herself on a Sunday afternoon in as long as I can remember. She's here for one thing only: to make sure Sam gets out.

And I love her for it.

I beam at her and turn to Sam. "Sorry such a short visit!"

He stands up. "Hey, it's okay. I enjoyed your pictures. Looks like a fun trip. I'll have to put Colombia on my bucket list."

"Yeah, you need to." I nod and follow him to the door. I sense my roommates closing around me, making sure he exits.

He looks over my shoulder and sees them also. He looks slightly uneasy when he says to me, "Hug?"

This isn't awkward or anything, not with everyone staring. But I allow him to hug me.

I don't breathe with him that close. That smell nauseates me.

"All right, bye!" I say, ushering him out. Then I close the door and turn around, leaning against it. I press my finger to my lips to keep my roommates quiet and listen to his footsteps clanging down the stairs. Iris runs to the balcony and looks out the window, then turns around.

"He's gone!"

I burst out laughing, and so do they, and then we have a group huddle before we split apart and work on our skit.

CHAPTER NINETY-SEVEN

Arrow in the Gut

Someone from Alliances Abroad calls while I'm in my religion class. I have the number saved in my phone, and I stare at it as it lights up silently in my bag. The phone is facing me so I can see who calls even while it's tucked safe in the netting of the backpack.

I can't miss this call. I've been waiting. Anxious to hear what's happening.

I slide the phone from my backpack to my pocket and slip out of class. I'm in college; no one asks for permission to leave and no one asks for an explanation.

I still feel odd leaving in the middle of class.

I answer the call as soon as I'm in the hallway. "Hello?"

"Hello, am I speaking with Cassandra?"

"Yes," I say.

"This is Kathryn from Alliances Abroad. We got all your paperwork, and we'd like to set up a phone interview to make sure everything is finished with your placement. Are you available Friday at eight a.m.?"

"Yes, I am," I say, an anxious and excited bubble rising in my chest.

"Great, I've got you down. The interviewer will call you from this number and ask you a few questions. Just answer honestly, all right?"

"All right," I say, and nervousness adds itself to the bubble.

My boss throws a big luncheon at work for the professors because they have meetings to attend to all day. I'm required to be there also because I have to take the minutes.

"Here's your food," Jan says, setting a huge salad in front of me.

I've never seen such a beautiful salad. Apple slices and cranberries are tucked around walnuts and blue cheese, all over a bed of spring greens. "This is for me?"

"Yep."

"I'll take minutes any time you need."

She laughs and leaves to take care of the front office, since I'll be in this meeting all day.

I'm glad for the salad as I head to the music building for practice after work. I still have a little bit of it left. I won't have time to go home for dinner today because I go straight from practice to the church talent show.

We couldn't find a time for all three of us to meet with the accompanist during the week, so Erika and I go by ourselves.

"I can sing Nat's part," she tells the pianist. "Then at least you can get the rhythm and stuff right."

"That's perfect," she says.

We go over the song five times, but each time it's flawless. The music moves me, and I'm honored to sing this song about the death and resurrection of Christ.

"Okay, I think we have it," the accompanist says. She stands, folding her sheet music and putting it in her bag. "As long as it goes that way at the dress rehearsal this weekend, we're set."

"That sounded really good," Erika says as the two of us walk out. "It would be a lot easier if it were just two people."

"Truth," I say. "It's hard to match our schedules."

"And it sounds better. Just the two of us."

I agree with that. We'd be able to sing more of the song. But I don't say anything.

My church group is meeting in the humanities building, using one of their auditoriums for the talent show. I head that direction, and my phone vibrates with incoming texts. I pull it out and grin as I read through my roommates' commentary.

Iris: remind me again who's mama

Camila: I'm mama

Layne: I THOUGHT I WAS MAMA

Abby: Layne, stop yelling

Layne: I'M NOT YELLING IM MAMA

I laugh out loud and quicken my pace. We're putting on a skit that's been in my family as long as I can remember, and my dad said he learned it from his family. It's called, "Arrow in the Gut." There's very little acting involved. It's a lot of impromptu, and the more you mess up, the better it is.

I step into the auditorium and find my roommates all in a row.

"We said I would be Mama," Iris hisses.

They're still bickering.

"Then who am I?" Layne asks.

"The ambulance," I say.

"You should be Mama," she says.

"I'm the director," I say.

"Who am I again?" Camila asks.

"The doctor."

"And me?" Lauren says.

"You ride in the ambulance with Layne."

"And I'm the son," Abby says.

I giggle. This is going to be hilarious.

We have a lot of talented people in our congregation, and I'm impressed with every singer and musical instrument I hear.

Our act is different. I hope they're ready for comedy.

Abby has our box of props, and I hand them out right before we go up. "Broom. Steering wheel. Stethoscope. Arrow. Okay, let's go, let's go." I pull a visor on.

We already get a few giggles as we walk up to the stage with our strange ensemble of costumes.

Oh, they have no idea what's coming.

I gather my roommates together and speak to them in a loud voice, with all seriousness. "Positions, everyone. Mama, start sweeping. Son, left stage. Doctor and paramedics, right stage. *Arrow in the Gut*, take one." I clap my hands to start the scene and back away.

Iris sings loudly as she sweeps the stage. That's new. I didn't tell her to do that.

Abby comes running onto the stage, crying, "Mama, Mama!"

"What is it?" Iris cries.

Abby holds out her foam arrow and waves it. "I've got an arrow in my gut!" She promptly collapses, holding the arrow to her stomach.

"Oh, no!" Iris cries, dropping the broom and pressing her hands to her face. "My son has an arrow in his gut!"

People are already laughing. My roommates are dramatic and ridiculous and we're just getting started.

"Someone call a doctor!" Iris continues. "Doctor, doctor!"

Layne comes onto the stage, turning her steering wheel (which is a plastic plate) and making a siren noise with her mouth. Lauren and Camila come with her, holding onto each other's waists like they're doing the Locomotion.

We didn't plan that either.

Camila comes running out from behind them when Iris calls, and the two of them have an urgent, brief conversation about the arrow in Abby's gut before I step in.

"Cut, cut!"

They rise, sighing, looking bored, giving the expected looks of exasperation.

"Hey, it was pretty good," I say. "But a little slow. Can we speed it up just a tad? This is an urgent matter."

They nod sullenly back at me.

"Back in positions."

Everyone returns to where they were. Iris holds the broom center-stage, ready.

"*Arrow in the Gut*, take two." I clap my hands and step back.

Immediately Iris begins sweeping in fast-forward speed. Abby streaks out, shrieks a few words, Iris does it back and then she collapses on the ground.

And now the audience can't stop laughing. It's nothing but frivolous fun, and we go through the short script three more times, slow, sad, and finally happy.

Everyone cheers and laughs and claps for us when we finish. I laughed so hard I cried. I grin at my roommates as we gather our props and head back to our row.

"That," Layne whispers as we sit, "was the best act ever."

Total agreement.

⁂

My Classical Civ teacher hands back our midterms in class Wednesday, and I'm pleased to see I got a 97% on the exam. But he only gave me a 92% on the essay. I'm annoyed. He subscribed to the myth of twenty years ago and counted me off for using contractions and starting sentences with conjunctions. I feel like someone should tell him those things aren't wrong.

It won't be me.

My grade is a solid A. With two months left to the semester, I hope I can keep it that way.

I check my notifications after class, skim through the text messages and glance over my emails.

There's one from Sam.

That's rather unusual. If he needs something, he generally texts me. And he's at my house so often, there's not a need to communicate more than that.

I open the email while I'm walking but have to slow down to read it, and eventually I come to a complete halt.

Hey Cassandra,

I hope this email doesn't feel completely out of left field. I think some things are easier to say in an email than in person, and when I try to approach this subject, it seems you close up a bit. So I'm coming at it this way, hoping I can keep you from feeling intimidated.

We've been seeing a lot of each other for a few months now. We've gotten pretty close. The more we're together, the more it seems we enjoy the same things. I think we have the right personalities and the right chemistry to turn this friendship into something more. And we've been inching that way very slowly.

I'm hoping you're ready to make it a more solid relationship. I've been patient, I've respected your need to take it slow, and I've been kind and attentive. I've earned your friendship, I think, and I think I deserve some respect and commitment also.

Hopefully this doesn't frighten you. I know relationships scare you and you can be skittish. But they don't have to be scary. They can be safe and beautiful. You're someone I want to be with, and I'm ready to guide you, ready to show you how wonderful it can be.

Just tell me you'll let me.

Sam

By the time I finish reading it, my mouth is hanging open.

What.

The.

Freak?

Relationships scare me? I'm skittish? He wants to GUIDE me?

I want to shove this email down his throat.

I resume walking, marching, really, fuming as I head home. I compose a dozen angry responses in my head. I'm not afraid of dating, I just don't want to date YOU. I'm not skittish. I'm not INTERESTED. There's no chemistry, that's your body odor! You DESERVE my respect? You DESERVE commitment?

Oh, no.

My roommates were right. I let this go for too long. I let a "friendship" brew into something else, and one of us is confused about what is going on in this relationship.

It's not me. I know exactly what's going on.

It's going down.

I fume over Sam's email for the rest of the night. I share it with my roommates, and we have a collective gasping party where we dissect every word and mock his assumptions. It's cruel and I feel a bit guilty but I'm so angry that I also take comfort in it.

"You've got to end this," Abby says.

I nod. "I'll call him tomorrow."

But that thought fills me with apprehension, and I can't sleep as I compose my words, mentally delete them, and try again. I don't want to hurt him. I want to make it clear this is not progressing the way he wants, and in fact, we should stop being friends.

Friendship with him comes with an agenda.

That seems to be true of most guys, actually.

I'm exhausted when my alarm goes off. I bat at it, hitting the snooze button and giving myself ten more minutes.

Except when I open my eyes again, it's nine-thirty in the morning, and I realize I must have turned it off.

I leap into panic mode. I have an English midterm at ten.

I change my clothes in one minute and run to the bathroom. "Is anyone here?" I yell before I slam myself inside.

"I'm here." Camila's voice comes from the kitchen.

I finish in the bathroom and wash my hands, then brush my teeth as I run into the kitchen. "I slept through my alarm and have to be to campus in thirty minutes can you take me?" I say around my toothbrush.

"I don't know what you said," she says.

"Argh!" I run to the sink and spit and rinse, then spin back around. "I slept through my alarm and I have a test in—" I check the time. "Twenty-four minutes! Can you drive me to campus?"

"Yes, let's go."

I slump with relief, then run back to my room and get my backpack.

It's nine-thirty-five when we get in the car. From the moment I woke up to the moment we got in the car, it was a whole five minutes.

Camila drops me off at the music building and shouts, "Good luck!" as I race out the door. I wave back at her.

I get across campus in a record seven minutes. I'm still panting when I reach the classroom door, but I'm impressed with myself. It's nine-fifty-two.

Twenty-two minutes ago, I was in bed sleeping.

Ha.

My professor strolls in with several books under his arms. "Morning, class," he says.

I grab my backpack and search around for the testing booklet I bought yesterday. My fingers close on it, but I stop and stare at my bag.

My empty bag.

I forgot every book I need for today.

Crap.

CHAPTER NINETY-EIGHT

False Alarm

I have my laptop, at least, and the testing booklet and a pencil. I can worry about the rest later. I breathe deeply to calm my racing heart.

"So I had a bit of a rough morning," he says, opening a notebook and setting it on the podium. Then he leans his arms on it, letting the podium take his body weight as he looks out at us. "And I didn't get the tests printed. Are there any qualms about waiting until tomorrow to take it?"

My breath catches.

"I'm good with that!" someone shouts from the back.

I sit there, stunned. After all that effort to get here, and the test isn't even today?

"Great." He closes his notebook. "Then you have today to study and prepare. You can stay in class or go somewhere else. See you tomorrow."

I'm annoyed. I mutter under my breath as I pack everything up and head to the library. If he'd made this decision last night, I could have showered this morning. Made sure my backpack had what I needed. Maybe even eaten breakfast.

There's plenty I can work on with my laptop.

And there are other important items I need to attend to.

I study for Portuguese while trying to decide the best way to contact Sam. I could email him back, but I'd prefer not to make that another avenue of communication between us. Plus what I have to say, I need to say in person. He needs to know how serious I am.

I could call him, but then I'd be tempted to say it all over the phone and get it over with.

In the end I text him. *Me: you busy tonight?*

S: not too. What time?

Me: late. I've got a night class. Maybe 9?

S: what are you thinking?

Me: just come over for a bit.

S: sure.

I stop texting, but my stomach is in knots.

I know what he's thinking. He sent me a fairly presumptuous email yesterday requesting we make our relationship more official and date, something he thinks I'm wanting also but have been too timid to follow through on. And now I've asked him to come over. So naturally he's probably assuming I'm going to make good on his request.

I'm so anxious I'm sick to my stomach. I dread this conversation with every part of my being.

They need a sub in the technology office across the street, so Jan sends me over there for work. The office is in the basement, but at least there are a few windows. Beverly is a nice old lady with graying hair, and her office is separated from the front desk by a movable wall. Not exactly private.

"You'll be here all week," she tells me. "Seth went out of town. He's my right-hand guy."

"Sure." I nod. I've met him several times when I dropped papers over here. The technology and engineering departments work well together.

But there's not nearly as much for me to do. There are no professors down here, no office hours, no students coming in every moment. Beverly is an adviser, and a few kids come in wanting to go over their schedules or classes or graduation requirements. For the most part, though, it's very quiet. I do the filing tasks she has for me and type up course maps for students.

It's going to be a long week.

First I have to get through this long day.

I get more and more anxious for the upcoming conversation as I sit through my classical civ class. It's hard to concentrate. I want to skip what's likely to be an uncomfortable confrontation entirely.

Maybe he'll react quite well. I remember the talk we had months ago when I told him I only wanted to be friends. He was agreeable.

But now I'll be telling him I don't want to date. Not only do I not want to date, but I don't want to be friends anymore.

What am I saying? We aren't friends. I've come to dread his company, dread his phone calls, dread when he wants to hang out. He might have thought he was pulling me closer, but he was pushing me away.

I need to stay strong and be clear.

Still, I can't bring myself to hurry home. My teeth chatter with nerves as I make my way up the sidewalk, moving toward my apartment. My phone dings, and I stop to read the message, delaying my walk up the stairs.

Iris: he's here.

I didn't tell my roommates what I have planned for tonight. But I'm sure they know, especially now.

I text back, *it would be great if you guys could make yourselves scarce.*

How they rise to that challenge. I pass Iris and Abby on the stairs, and they wave as if it's not a big deal that they're leaving the house at nine p.m. I hear them giggling as they cross the commons to the boys' side.

Lauren's next. She goes down the hall to hang out with other people she's friends with.

Layne texts: *I'M NOT THERE ANYWAY*

Camila: I'm staying in my room but I'm here if you need me.

I appreciate that. I won't be alone. But I'll have privacy.

I have no idea how to begin this conversation.

Sam sits on the couch messing with his phone. He has the whole front living area to himself. He looks up and smiles at me when I come in, something quizzical in his eyes.

"Hey," I say, heart racing.

"Hey," he replies.

Out with it. I can't make small talk. Let's get this done. "I got your email." I sit in the oversized chair to his right.

He swivels to face me. "You didn't respond."

He probably expected me to. There's a lot I didn't realize about Sam, but now I see he's been expecting me to fit into a role he made for me. He's been waiting for me to come around to it. Since I haven't, he's prodding me in that direction. Helping me get there.

I have to make him see it's not working.

"Intentionally," I say. "The email was a wake up call for me."

"Yeah?"

He's hearing me wrong. I grit my teeth. "Sam, I told you from the beginning I only wanted to be friends."

His expression softens. "I know. And we are. I appreciate all the time we've taken to get to know each other without any romantic pressures. It's been really great. But—"

I speak up again before he can steal this conversation. "Sam, you need to stop talking and listen to me. I'm not interested in you romantically. I feel nothing that way. I got on this boat willingly with you, but I don't like the direction you're steering, so I'm getting off."

"What do you mean? What boat?"

My clever analogy is lost on him, but no matter. "Let me speak plainly. I don't want to date you. Not now, not ever. We can't be friends, either, because you want more than that and as long as you're on the boat—as long as you're steering—you're going to keep trying to convince me that we need to be more. You need to stop coming over to my house. You need to look for a girl who feels for you what you feel for her, and you can't do that if you're trying to get me back on the boat."

He looks confused. Like my words don't register. Like he can't comprehend that he's being rejected. Was it the boat analogy?

"But all the time we've spent together, the talks we've shared—"

I'm getting frustrated. I don't want to hurt him, but he refuses to believe me. "Sam. I was being nice. You're a nice person. But we are so not compatible."

He shakes his head. "I don't believe it."

"Listen to me. I don't want to date you. Please don't make this any harder than it is. I'm not trying to hurt you, but we need to part ways. You need to stop calling me and stop coming over."

"Listen, I know it scares you, the thought of getting close to a guy—"

"I'm not scared!" I finally explode. "I don't like you! I feel nothing when I'm with you and—you stink!"

Oh heavens. Oh crap. I can't believe I said that. I suck in a breath, wishing I could suck those words back in.

His face goes pale. He heard me. I got through to him. "You dislike me?"

I close my eyes and rub the bridge of my nose. I'm going to cry, and that will give him the wrong impression.

I hear a door open, and a moment later Camila's in the living room.

"Sam," she says, her face quite firm, "Cassandra likes you as a person. We all like you as a person. But that's not what you're asking. You're asking for her to like you as a boyfriend. She's said no. A lot. Quite clearly. You're pushing her, and what you want is non-consensual. Now I'm asking you to respect her. That means, now is when you leave, believing she's smart enough and intelligent enough to know her own feelings. And if you continue to believe she doesn't, if you try to convince her she feels something else or you try to manipulate her in any way, I'm going to have to call the police."

"I'll go." His eyes are wide, and he stands. He turns to me, his expression one of absolute torture. "You hate me this much?"

I'm trapped. If I disagree, he'll hear something else. If I agree, he'll think the worst of me.

He moves toward the door. "I'm a nice person, Cassandra. You know this. We've spent months together. It's not fair that you treat me this way." He presses the palms of his hands together likes he's praying. "Please, this isn't right."

I turn around and go down the hallway to my room.

"Go now, Sam, before you make things worse," Camila says.

"But if she'd just listen to me—I want what's best for us—"

I pull out my phone. I'm shaking as I text Thomas.

Me: help. I need you now. Come quickly

T: OMW. What do you need?

Me: GET SAM OUT

"But you see it, don't you, Camila? And what did she mean—Cassandra, what did you mean? I stink?"

He's calling down the hallway after me.

I hear the apartment door swing open, and then Thomas's deep voice echoes in the kitchen.

"Hey, Sam. It's good to see you, but it's time to go."

I wilt in relief. Thomas will take care of this.

"Thomas, it's all a big misunderstanding." His voice catches, and then he begins to cry. The sound is pathetic and it tears at my heart. I press my hands over my ears. I hate myself. How did this happen?

"I know. Come on, let's go."

Then they're gone. Camila comes into my room and climbs onto my bed, and then she wraps her arms around me.

I break. I cry into her embrace. I picture Sam's bewilderment, his confused face, and I hate that I had to do that.

But what was my other option? Pretend to like him? End up dating him because I didn't want to hurt him? End up marrying him because I'm afraid he'll be sad if he learns how I feel?

The front door opens again, and I hear Thomas's voice. "Cassandra? Camila?"

"We're back here," Camila calls.

Boys are not allowed in the bedrooms, but Thomas doesn't hesitate. He's in the room in an instant, and he comes right over to the bed and enfolds us in an embrace. Then he steps back.

"Now I was kind to him," he says. "I let him down easy. But you tell me right now if he hurt you or did anything disrespectful to you, and I'll chase him down. I know where he's going."

I laugh and wipe at my eyes. "No, he didn't. He really is the nicest person. I don't think he'd ever hurt a fly."

"But he wasn't quite normal," Camila says. "If you hadn't come, he'd still be in that doorway, trying to convince Cassandra that she doesn't mean it because she doesn't know her feelings."

Thomas pats my shoulder. "You did the right thing. And even nice types can be scary. So don't be alone with him, all right? If you see him come around, you call me. I don't want you girls with him by yourselves." He includes Camila in this mandate.

I nod. I feel that in my bones. How did things get out of control? The helplessness of the situation frightens me. It was like reasoning with a wall. I grab Thomas's hand and give it a squeeze.

"Thank you so much. I knew I could rely on you."

He squeezes back. "Us Southerners have to stick together."

<hr>

My roommates come back one by one after Thomas is gone, and I tell them the whole story. Then Camila says, "We should pray. Cassandra has her interview to go to Brazil tomorrow, and this has rattled her heart. We need her to have peace."

"And we need to express gratitude for Thomas," Iris says. "Thank goodness he came over."

I'm moved by their compassion, by their faith, by their love for me. We pray together, and my soul is lighter when I go to bed.

<hr>

Somehow, we've slipped into March.

Both Erika and Nat cancel on our next rehearsal. The accompanist asks if I want to meet by myself, but I don't. I can't begrudge the fact that I get my evening back, but I would rather make sure our song is perfect.

Alliances Abroad calls me right before I walk in the door at home.

"We're going to have to reschedule your placement interview," the woman says. "There's a snowstorm in Houston, and the interviewer can't get to the office."

That seems like a lame excuse to me. It's a phone call. Can't it be done from anywhere?

"Oh, okay," I say, caught off guard. "Can't he call me from his house?"

"I'm sorry, we don't have our employees work from home. We require them to come into the office and clock in if they're working."

That's fair, and I understand, but...

"Sure. Just let me know when we'll reschedule."

"Thanks for understanding. We'll be in touch."

I step into the apartment to find Iris and Camila circled around the fish tank. They both spin toward me, and I already know something's wrong.

"What is it?" I ask, dropping my backpack and rushing over to join them. "What's going on?"

"Mute is missing," Camila says.

That's what we named our silent newt. Seemed so clever at the time.

"What?" I gasp, kneeling beside the fish tank.

There's no sign of him sitting on his rock, basking in the light. No sign of him swimming near the bottom with the fish.

He has, indeed, disappeared.

CHAPTER NINETY-NINE

Mute Miracle

We search all evening for Mute.

We move furniture. We lift up the air-conditioning vent. We pick up dirty laundry. We even move all the dishes drying on the counter, even though we're certain he didn't get up there.

We cannot find the newt.

It's both frustrating and hilarious.

"Maybe he got outside," Camila says, eyeing the sliding glass door to the balcony.

"If he did, he's a goner," Iris says.

This is all true. I hope, for his sake, the little critter didn't make a getaway.

<hr/>

Erika and I manage to get together for rehearsal on Saturday, but Nat can't come. Miss Young gathers everyone into the big room and hands out costumes. We've got prayer shawls, headscarves, and wraps—everything to make us look like Middle Eastern women from the first century.

I try on several different costumes, and I love how they transform me from an American college student into a Jewish girl from 35 A.D. With my dark hair and features, I look the part.

We run through our song, and it's much smoother this time. This would be so much easier if it were two people instead of three.

There's still no sign of the newt.

"He'll starve soon," Layne says after dinner.

It's a very unappealing thought.

<hr/>

I wake up Monday with a surprisingly giddy feeling in my chest.

It's my birthday.

I didn't expect to feel so happy about that. There's no party. I still have to go to school, work, and do my chores. Nothing special.

But today, I'm twenty.

I've crossed over the rainbow bridge from teenager to . . . well, something else. Legally, I've been an adult for a while.

A shriek from the living room interrupts my thoughts, followed by Abby's voice yelling, "Cassandra! Come here!"

I pull myself out of bed and hurry into the living room. "What is it?"

She turns to me and points at a little water bowl by the balcony.

Nestled inside is Mute.

"He's alive?" I stare in disbelief. He's been missing for three days.

Abby bursts out laughing. "I can't believe it!"

I pick up the bowl and dump him back into the tank. "Now you stay where you belong," I scold. Then I go to the freezer and scoop out a tablespoon of brine shrimp. He must be starving.

"How do we keep him from getting out again?" Abby asks.

I eye the small opening in the lid meant for oxygen. "If I cover it up, will he still be able to breathe?"

"We could poke holes in it or something."

It's worth a try.

We search the apartment and find a roll of duct tape in Iris's room. I stretch it over the opening and poke small breathing holes in it.

"Let's hope he's not smart enough to widen those holes and escape again," Camila says.

The newt sits happily on his rock. "I don't think he's that smart," I reply, then I glance at the clock and jump. "Crap, I gotta go! I'll see you later!"

"Oh! I almost forgot!" Camila jumps up and hugs me. "Happy birthday!"

I laugh, happiness swelling in my chest. "Thanks!"

It's my birthday.

It's a quieter birthday than last year, when my mom flew in to see me and went to my classes with me. She told everyone it was my birthday. This time, I keep it quiet, sharing it around like a delicious secret in my heart. But my phone lights up with notifications throughout every class as dozens of friends from various places reach out to wish me a happy birthday.

Somebody at work knows, because there's a frosted cookie on my desk when I come in that says, "Happy Birthday!"

I smile at the thoughtfulness and tear off a piece. Just as I take a bite, the door opens and a student walks in. I nearly choke when I see him. I put my hand to my mouth to keep from spewing cookie crumbs everywhere.

It's the boy. Kai.

"Is this the time you always get here? You work every day?"

He approaches my desk with his hands in his pockets, backpack slung over both shoulders, gliding on sandals that slap the floor with each step.

I'm still trying to get the cookie crumbs down the right pipe. He raises an eyebrow, his expression a mix of amusement and concern.

"Do you need some water?"

"No, no. I'm okay." I look around the office, wishing I had a water bottle with me. When I look back, he's still watching me, that same quizzical look on his face.

My gosh, he's beautiful.

Stop staring.

I clear my throat while he watches. I feel like the biggest idiot. "Can I help you?" I finally blurt out.

"Not sure. It seems more like you need help."

He's not wrong. I'm still coughing, but now I'm laughing, too. He grins.

"You always get this flustered when someone talks to you?"

There's no graceful way to save this. My eyes are tearing up. I lift one finger and say, "Excuse me," then dart around the desk, out of the office, and down the hall to the water fountain. I stand there, guzzling water and trying to cool the heat on my face. Then I straighten up and take a deep breath.

I don't know if I should hope he's gone or if I want him still in there.

I step back into the office, and he's still there, smiling.

"So sorry about that. I was eating a cookie." I shrug helplessly. "And I choked."

He nods solemnly. "Cookies are a choking hazard. I'm pretty sure they come with warnings on them."

"This one didn't."

His eyes peek over the top of the counter and spot the aforementioned cookie. "It's your birthday?"

I feel my face getting pink again, and I nod.

"Happy birthday. How old are you?"

I get the feeling this isn't a random question. I already know how old he is, and I'm a little reluctant to tell him my age.

"Twenty."

His eyes go wide. "Twenty! Wow. You're, like, old."

His assessment makes me laugh. "I guess."

He shakes his head. "Congratulations. On . . . getting old. I mean, staying alive this long."

I laugh harder. "Thanks. It took a lot of effort."

"Well, I'm going to see Professor Stephens now." He jerks one hand from his pocket and waves, then disappears down the hall. I can't help smirking. Our interaction was fun, and it leaves me happy.

But now he knows the difference in our ages, and I'm certain that will be the end of it.

I go through the task list from the professors, and when I have a moment, I check my email.

There's a message from Alliances Abroad. They've rescheduled my interview for tomorrow morning.

"Yes!" I breathe. I send a quick email confirmation telling them that works for me.

"See you later."

I look up as Kai walks out. He waves from the door, and I wave back.

He still doesn't know my name. And he doesn't know I know his.

Professor Stephens appears in the doorway. "He thinks you're cute."

I turn to him. "He say that?"

"He came in last week when you were working at the other building—and asked where the receptionist was. I can only assume he meant you." The professor's eyes twinkle.

I smile. "Well, he knows how old I am now, so I guess we can admire each other from a distance."

"Does that mean you think he's cute, too?"

My face goes hot again, and I'm grateful I don't have the tendency to blush. I tap my phone. "You could say that."

In reality, I want to take a dozen pictures of him in different poses and make a collage to put on my bedroom wall. I can't think of better eye candy to distract me when I'm supposed to be doing homework.

I don't say that.

✧

There's a box waiting for me at my apartment. My family sent it. I open it up and go through it, excited that they thought of me.

I look up when the apartment door opens, and Iris comes in.

"You're home early!" she says.

I smile big. "It's my birthday!"

"I know! And we're taking you out for dinner."

"You are?"

"Let me text Camila and tell her she doesn't need to get you at the library." Iris grabs her phone and then sends a message to the group chat: *Cassandra's home early! Let's go to dinner.*

It takes another hour to round everyone up, and then we head to the little Italian place downtown. I order gnocchi and pesto, something I always get when it's available because it reminds me of the Italian restaurant I worked at in high school.

Then each of my roommates gives me a little gift. Layne gives me a box of chocolates, Iris gives me rabbit fur-lined gloves, Camila gives me a fancy pen, and Abby gives me colored eyeliner.

"Thanks, you guys!" I say, hugging them. I sit back and admire my gifts.

It's funny how each gift says something about the personality of the giver.

"No dessert," Layne says. "I baked you something at home."

It's just us when we get back to the apartment, gathered around the cake Layne made. She shows off the two-tiered caked with tiny pink rosettes piped around it.

There's a knock on the door, and Abby opens it to find Thomas.

"Thomas!" I say. "Did you come for cake and ice cream? Because there's no ice cream."

He laughs, that deep, hearty sound that makes me grin, too. "I didn't even know there was cake. I came to tell you happy birthday. But if there's cake..."

Layne cuts him off. "I've got you right here." She plops a huge slice of cake for him onto a plate.

He eyes her suspiciously, like he's not sure if he wants a piece, but he takes it. Then he comes over and gives me a big hug.

"Happy birthday, Cassandra. You're old now."

I grin. "I'm twenty."

It feels like the top of the world.

CHAPTER ONE HUNDRED

The Kid

I get an email from Alliances Abroad ten minutes before my interview time.

Here's the link for your video call.

Video call! My heart skips a beat. They're going to see me!

My last class is almost over, but I planned on taking the call in the hallway. Now I need to book it somewhere quiet and calm.

I'm still panting when I get seated at my table in the library. It's usually quiet here and I hope no one shoots me for having a video call. I set up my computer and click the link for the call.

"Hi, Cassandra, good morning!" The woman on the other end of the call looks about five years older than me. "How's it going?"

She smiles brightly, and I swallow back my nerves. She can't see my hands tremble. "Good, good." Crap. Was that proper grammar?

"Great! So, Cassandra," she says, glancing down. "No need to be nervous, we already approved you for our program. This is to figure out the best placement for you. Are you still thinking Brazil?"

I nod vigorously. "Yes! I love Brazil and I'm studying Portuguese, so it's perfect for me."

"And you're still a student. You're okay with missing your studies? For how long?"

"Yes, I've already cleared it with the school. Six months would be perfect. Or one full semester here."

"Fantastic." She asks a few more logistical questions, such as how many hours a week I want to work and whether I prefer a big city, the beach, or a rural community, and before I know it, the interview is over.

"Be sure to email me your availability date, and we'll be in touch," she says, smiling. "You're going to be great in this program."

"Thank you! Thank you so much!" I hang up the call, totally jazzed, and equally pleased no one in the library tried to eviscerate me with evil looks while I talked.

I'll be late to work if I don't hurry. I shoulder my backpack and beeline it for my office.

I'm still waking up the computer when the door opens and in walks the cute kid—Kai.

I lift an eyebrow. "Back so soon?"

He flashes a grin at me, his eyes bright, his energy infectious. "You know, gotta have my daily meeting with the professor."

"You have to meet with him every day?"

"No, but I like to."

"He must be an awesome instructor."

"Going to his office always cheers me up."

I tilt my head. Is he complimenting me? His tone is light, but there's a seriousness lurking in his eyes that I can't ignore. "Glad to brighten your day."

He grins again. "Anyway. Don't let this place eat you alive."

"I'll try not to."

For a moment, it's just us, the two of us in this quiet space. It's a nice distraction, a fleeting moment of fun in an otherwise serious day.

"You know," he says, "I never did catch your name."

I can't help the smug smile. Finally. "Cassandra."

"I'm Kai," he says. "In case you wondered. Since you didn't ask."

Because I can't have him thinking I'm not interested, I say, "I know."

"You do?" His face brightens. "Wait, how did you—"

"Professor Stephens is in his office," I interrupt. "You can go now." And then I add, "Malachi."

His face wreaths in an exuberant smile, making him look years younger, and yet somehow the youthful energy draws me closer. I want to surround myself in it, soak up the rays of his joy.

He pats the counter. "Take care of yourself, Cassandra," he says as he turns to leave.

"Will do," I reply, watching him go.

It was nothing. Simple. Frivolous.

Yet my heart sings like he left something behind.

❦

Now that I'm officially going to Brazil, I head back to my advisor's office to formalize the internship credit.

But it's a different advisor this time. And she's not nearly as helpful.

"You can't get credit for this internship," she says, like it's obvious. "We already have established internships—you have to pick one that fits our parameters."

I frown at her. "That's not what I was told last time."

She shrugs. "That's how it is. The only credit you'd be able to get is if you do an independent study class while you're in Brazil."

"It won't even count as my internship credit?"

"Requirements are requirements. You don't *have* to do an internship. We prefer students stay at school and finish their degree on time."

"But that's not what I was told last time," I say again, fingers of frustration and anxiety starting to claw at my throat.

"I'm sorry. It might not be what you were hoping, but you'll have to make it work. Or

. . . don't go."

Her message is clear: *This isn't my problem.*

"Okay," I say, even though what I really want to say is *thanks for nothing.* I hitch my backpack over my shoulder and leave the room.

It's definitely not going the way I expected. I thought I'd be able to get class credit for the internship. I thought my advisor would be at least a little excited for me.

I fight back the disappointment. I'm not canceling this trip to Brazil. So I'll have to be satisfied with what I can get.

⟨∾⟩

There are a bunch of guys over at my apartment when I get home. As this is fairly normal, I ignore them and start making dinner—even though it's after eight p.m. Also fairly normal.

"Cassandra, have you asked anyone to the dance yet?" Abby asks.

I turn away from the package of noodles I'm opening. "What dance?"

"There's a girl-picks-guy dance this weekend. Weren't you paying attention in church?"

I give a sheepish shrug. "Somewhat."

"Remember last year?" Iris says. "You walked up to some random guy and asked him."

"I do remember. Adam." I turn back to the noodles and dump them in the pot. "It was here at this apartment complex, actually. We had just signed our contract."

My roommates laugh at the memory.

"So who are you going with this year?" Jake asks.

"I don't know," I say. "Do you want to go?"

"Someone already asked," he says.

I turn around and scan the room. Thomas, Trent, Matt, Mike. "Who doesn't have a date?" I ask.

None of them raise their hands.

I jut out my lower lip in a pout. "Well, I guess I can't go."

"With that attitude, you won't," Abby says.

I shrug again. "Let me know if you hear of someone who needs a date."

"Do you even want to go?" Jake asks.

"Sure. I love dances."

But the point isn't to go with a guy friend. It's to go with someone you're actually interested in.

I don't know that such a guy exists for me right now.

I turn my attention back to cooking my pasta.

⟨∾⟩

On Saturday, we finally manage to get all three of us in the same spot to go over our song. It's dress rehearsal, and since we're performing tomorrow, I'm more than a little nervous that we haven't practiced together yet.

"It's going to be fine," Erika tells me as she adjusts the multicolored woven wrap around my head.

Except—it's not. Erika and Nat keep singing over each other's parts, and then they argue in front of everyone about who's supposed to be singing what.

469

My part goes smoothly, thankfully, but the frustration is obvious on everyone's faces —especially when we have to go through it six different times. Eventually, Miss Young focuses only on the two of them.

My face is flaming when we finally step off the stage to let the next group go. We're the only ones who didn't have our music fully put together.

We're also the only group of three. The other performers are in pairs or solos. I try not to be envious.

Miss Young claps her hands to get our attention after we finish running through the pieces. "Be here three hours early tomorrow," she says, clearly frazzled. "Run through your parts ten times tonight! We need to be ready."

She doesn't think we'll pull it off. I share her doubts.

Camila calls me as I'm heading home, and I remember—I was supposed to pick up tickets for the dance next Friday. The one I still don't have a date to.

"I forgot," I say when I answer.

"Forgot what?"

"The tickets."

"That's all right, I'm on campus. I'll get them," she says. "How was practice?"

"Oh, terrible! The performance is going to be awful."

"Maybe you guys will pull it off."

I find my car—since the performance isn't on campus, I didn't feel like walking the mile and a half to get to the art center. I open the door and sigh. "That's what Miss Young said too. 'Do we believe in miracles?'"

"It could happen," Camila says, and I can hear the shrug in her voice.

But I know she didn't call to check on me.

"What's up?" I ask.

"I saw Sam and Trent on campus. They were talking about you."

I frown. I told Sam not to come around my apartment anymore, but Trent lives in our complex. "How do they even know each other?"

"Because Sam was always coming over," she says.

True. "What were they saying?"

"Sam was saying all this stuff about how you don't like him, and you were really mean to him, and anything you say about him isn't true because you made stuff up."

My mouth drops open. "Seriously?"

"He didn't see me. Trent said, 'Wow, that really surprises me.'"

I'm still shell-shocked. "I've never said anything about him!" I'm stunned—and rapidly becoming angry.

"Oh, I know," Camila says. "I barged in on the conversation and told them, 'Actually, I was there, and I was the mean one. Some people don't take no for an answer.'"

I gasp and then laugh. "No way. You said that?"

"Yep. You could tell he didn't know I'd been there, and whatever impression he was trying to give got completely wrecked by my words."

I can't help laughing.

But the weight behind Camila's words goes deeper than that. It's not about setting the record straight—it's a warning.

"I'd say something before he says anything else about you," Camila says. "I'm giving you a heads-up in case you see him around campus."

"He probably regrets the day he met me."

"Not your problem. He's the one who went and turned this ugly."

She's right. But as I hang up and put my phone away, I still feel sad that it turned out like this.

I know Sam well enough to know he didn't mean any harm.

But he still caused it.

CHAPTER ONE HUNDRED ONE

Out of Control

We meet at one o'clock to get ready for our performance on Saturday. I'm a bundle of nerves in the dressing room, but I'm not the only one. Around me, I hear the bubbly noises of vocal warm-ups, long sighs, and scale exercises.

"We're going to go through the whole thing one time," Miss Young says, coming into the dressing room.

I sit on a stool beneath the bright lights in front of the mirror, carefully applying black eyeliner, the kind women in the Middle East have worn for thousands of years.

"Now is the time to get all your mistakes out," she says.

I don't look over at Erika or Nat. I've been praying for twenty-four hours straight that the three of us will get our act together. I'm afraid to look into their eyes and see doubt there.

We sit in the chairs meant for the audience, watching the others perform, and then go through our parts, act by act.

Finally, it's our turn. We go on stage and take our places as if we've arrived at the tomb after the death of our Lord.

The music begins. The narrator speaks, and Erika starts singing. We're holding our microphones—great for recitals, but not so much for musical performances. The voices echo off the back of the performance hall, and I have to count the measures to my entrance because I can't hear them very well.

But I come in on time, and I don't forget any of my words. Erika and Nat sing their respective parts correctly without fighting, and for the first time, we sound like a unit instead of three individuals singing similar lines. Miss Young whistles, cheers, and claps enthusiastically when we finish.

"Bravo! Bravo! That was fantastic, and so much better than yesterday! Thank you for working on your song together."

My face flushes with warmth. The three of us exchange smiles, basking in our shared triumph, but also sheepishly aware we didn't practice as much as we should have.

We sit together, and Nat leans over and whispers while the next soloist takes the stage.

"Oh my gosh, I can't believe we pulled that off!" she says.

"We did amazing!" Erika squeals.

The two of them giggle and squeeze each other's hands, their faces flushed—just a day after nearly being at each other's throats.

I don't remind them.

"It was perfect," I say. "Now we have to do that again."

Even as I speak, though, I feel a stab of worry. No one ever gives the same performance twice.

We listen to the rest of the music, then head back to the dressing room to wait as the audience begins arriving. I know some of my roommates are coming, but I don't know who else. I wish my mom could be here. She hasn't seen me perform in a while.

We hear Miss Young's voice on stage, speaking through the microphone. She and her assistant come back to the dressing room.

"Okay, everyone follow me. Just like we practiced. We'll be offstage, watching for your turn."

We're as quiet as church mice, tiptoeing behind the curtains to wait in the wings. There's a smattering of applause. I take a deep breath and slowly let it out, my nerves firing in double time, reminding me of so many recitals and vocal performances in high school.

But I haven't done one in so long.

Each performance before ours goes beautifully. I feel the music in my heart, a stirring in my soul as one after another sings about the life of Christ.

Of course, my group gets the section about his death and resurrection. We might have the most emotional part in the whole musical.

The narrator begins her speech to introduce our song, and the three of us step onstage. I carry linens in my arms. Erika has a pot of oil. We step over to the bench set up as a prop and go through the motions of searching for something. Then I kneel at the bench and press my face into my hands while Nat begins to sing. Erika comes in on her part, and I stand for the chorus.

The three of us wear expressions of sorrow and despair as we sing about the life, the death, and the missing body.

Then it's my verse—the one that sings about the resurrection, about joy and hope and new life. My voice is strong, anticipation heavy in my words.

From out of nowhere, the meaning behind the lyrics hits me right behind the eyes. I feel such gratitude—for my life, for how many second chances I've been given, for my family, for getting to go to school here. I'm struck by so much love that my voice stutters and tears spring to my eyes.

No, no, no, no, no! Not now!

I try to get control of my voice, but the tremors won't stop. I eke out one more trembling word and then stop singing.

The tears keep flowing down my face, and I suck in a breath to hold back the shuddering gasps. I wait—half a second, five seconds—then try again. My voice is brassy and shaky. I shake my head and stop again.

I'm so embarrassed. But I can't get a hold of myself. So I smile through the overflow of emotion and listen as the other two girls carry the chorus.

The audience smiles back at me, many of them mirroring my emotion. I manage to get myself under control enough to sing the final chorus, even though my voice is trembling and shaking—and then our piece is over.

Miss Young grabs me in a hug when we come backstage.

"That was so beautiful! We could all feel what you were feeling when you sang!"

"I wanted to sing the song," I say, still flustered.

"I know. But everyone's remembering Easter and why it's important."

Her words make me feel a little better. Still, I'm the only one who had an emotional breakdown during the entire musical. I would've preferred to let the song deliver the message for me.

✦

It's a blessedly slow day at work, which is good because I'm very behind in Portuguese. I have an essay due tomorrow that's making me want to pull my hair out. I mumble to myself as I try to stick in an idiomatic phrase—the direct translation won't be the same as what I'm trying to say, but my dictionary is failing me.

A shadow falls over my counter, and I lift my face, customer service smile already in place. Somehow, I was distracted enough to not notice the door opening, and I missed anyone walking in.

It's Kai, and my heart does a little somersault at the sight of those dark eyes peering down at me, his lips curved upward in his perpetual grin.

"So, when are we going out?" he says.

I give a startled laugh, which I think is an appropriate response to someone asking a question like that. "I didn't know we were," I say, my mind tripping over itself as it tries to find something witty and flirty to say.

"Well, I hope we are. I've been working up the courage all week to ask you out, so if you turn me down now…"

I lean back in my chair, pressing my pen between my index fingers. "You didn't exactly ask me out."

He takes a deep breath, bobs his head, then opens his backpack and pulls out a folder. "Let me see. Yeah. I can do this better." He pulls out a piece of notebook paper and begins writing on it. I lean forward in my chair, but he covers the paper with his arm and gives me a stern look.

"You can't see it yet."

A smile presses itself to my lips, and I look down.

"Okay," he says. Then he waves the paper, and I lift my head again. He clears his throat and reads:

"This contract states that I, Kai Tanaka, have asked you, Cassandra Jones, to officially go out with me. By signing on the line below, you accept that you will come on a date with no preconceived expectations and a good attitude to have a nice time."

He slides the paper toward me. "Sign below if you agree—and date it."

I lift an eyebrow and take the paper from him, reading over his words for myself. "I don't know . . . I feel like there's a lot of pressure on me here."

He nods. "Yeah. It's a lot."

We look at each other with all seriousness, and then I return the paper and sign my name. "I think I can do it."

I don't miss the fact that he knows my full name.

He takes the signed paper from me and slips it back into his notebook, but the corners of his eyes are crinkling mischievously.

"So . . . when?"

I shrug. "Friday?"

"I have a soccer game. Hey! Want to come?"

"Oh, I love soccer players." I don't mean it the way it sounds, so I quickly clarify. "Soccer. In general. I love soccer games. And soccer balls. And . . . soccer players."

He laughs, and I love the sound of it. It's kind and genuine, but not overbearing.

"Then you'll love my game."

I grin, my face hot, but I'm delighted. "It's a date. See you Friday." Now I'm incredibly grateful I never got a date to the dance.

He arches both eyebrows. "Oh, no. Friday's not our date. That's just a soccer game."

"Okay," I say, slightly off-guard.

"Let's go out Saturday. Are you busy?"

I shake my head. "No. I'm not." My schedule is remarkably open right now.

He holds his fist out to me. "Saturday is a date."

I meet his fist bump with my own. "Looking forward to it."

"Let me get your number."

I write it down on a slip of paper, and he gives me his. Then he waves and heads for the door.

"Wait," I call. "Didn't you want to see the professor?"

He looks back at me and cocks a smile. "I got what I came for."

And then he leaves, and I settle back in my chair with a strange feeling in my chest that I'm quite unfamiliar with.

He's just a kid. But this is fun.

CHAPTER ONE HUNDRED TWO

Study Buddy

I don't remember the last time I felt this happy.

I mean—of course I do. I *remember*.

But it's been so long . . . I don't really remember.

I don't expect to see Kai again on Thursday—after all, I saw him yesterday, and we have a date on Saturday, and I'm going to his soccer game tomorrow. But I can't help the little flicker of hope every time the door opens.

But he doesn't come into the office, and I admit my disappointment as I clock out.

So I'm surprised when he calls me shortly after I've left campus.

"Hi!" I say. "I didn't expect to hear from you."

"Should I not have called?"

He sounds like he's laughing.

"You're fine," I say, laughing too. "What's up?"

"Well, I don't know what you're doing tonight, but I thought I'd see if you want to study together for a bit."

"Oh! I'd love to, but . . . I'm already headed home."

"Cool. I can meet you there."

"Where do you live?" I ask. Unless he lives near me, it'll be a hike from his house.

"Tower dorm."

"Oh." I giggle. "I forgot you're a freshman."

"Hey now. Don't hold it against me."

"I don't live close to campus. I'm not a freshman. It's almost a two-mile walk from the dorms."

"Walk? I can drive, thank you very much."

"You have a car?" That's unusual. I'm one of the only people I know with a vehicle—and that was especially true when I was a freshmen.

"Not only do I have a car, I know how to use it."

He makes me laugh. "Let's hope you have a good sense of direction."

"My GPS does."

"I'll text you the address."

A white truck pulls up to the apartment as I'm arriving. It honks and pulls to a stop in front of me, off to the side of the street and blocking the mailboxes. I notice a blue Adidas sticker on the back window and walk over to the passenger side.

The window rolls down, and Kai grins at me from the driver's seat. His dark eyebrows lift, causing his brow to furrow into the straight black hair around his face.

"This you?" he says.

"This is me," I reply, gesturing to the brownstone condos behind me. "Home sweet home."

"Nice. Where do I park?"

"Here is fine." I glance at the street around us. "You're lucky you found a spot. Sometimes I have to park here when the lot is full, and it's never easy."

"That sucks." He turns the truck off and comes around to the front, somehow managing to lope despite being only a few inches taller than me. "One of the benefits of the dorms, huh."

"Oh yes." I walk with him through the commons, guiding him to my apartment. "I never fought for parking when I lived there."

"Were you in the tower dorms?"

"No, the apartment ones."

"So you know how to cook."

"Well . . ." I weave my hand back and forth. "I got sick of ramen and canned soup last year, so I've been teaching myself."

"My mom—she's the best cook. Her flautas taste better than anything you'll get in a Mexican restaurant."

I stay quiet as we walk the stairs and he tells me about his mom's cooking. His voice is rich and deep, just slightly accented. I love listening to it.

I push open the apartment door and spot half of my roommates inside.

"Hey, Cassandra!" Camila says. Then her eyes dart to Kai as he steps in behind me, and there's no mistaking the surprise.

Iris looks up from her textbook, and Abby turns around from the stove. Somehow, they all sense something unusual.

My face warms. I brought a boy home.

"Guys, this is Kai," I say, touching his arm to pull him inside. Just as quickly, I yank my hand away. "Kai, my roommates. Abby, Camila, and Iris."

"Hi," Kai says, jerking a hand from his pocket to wave. "We're going to—" he glances at me. "Study."

"Do you want dinner?" I ask. "I can make some food."

"Yeah, Cassandra's an excellent cook," Camila says. "She cooks for me almost every night."

"Sure, if you're eating. I have a meal plan, so I won't go hungry." He wanders over to the fish tank. "Hey, you've got fish!"

"I do." I join him and lift the lid. "We have a newt, too. But we keep this opening covered because he tries to escape."

"Ah." Kai nods sagely. "My tree frog does that too. You have to get a special tank for them."

I tilt my head. "You have a tree frog?"

"Yeah, I brought him from home."

"Oh, that's awesome! Where's home?"

"California." He faces me. "You?"

"Arkansas." I'm vaguely aware of the silence around me. I glance at the couch, but my roommates haven't moved. They sit there, watching us.

"Arkansas!" Kai lifts those expressive eyebrows again. "Wow. I've never met anyone from there before."

"Good thing you didn't say anything negative about it," Camila says. "She would have been showing you the door. I've watched her do it."

Kai's eyes flick toward her, but his grin is aimed at me. "Thanks for the warning. That was on the tip of my tongue. Guess I dodged a bullet."

I laugh. "You lucked out."

Kai shakes his head. "Too bad no one warned the other guys."

"People shouldn't make negative comments about someone's hometown. That's just how it is."

"A lesson I shall commit to memory." Kai sits down at the table and hauls his backpack onto it.

I open the fridge, but the ingredients stare at me like they're turning into non-food items. I can't think of what to make.

Iris jumps in. "I can cook tonight, if no one minds Chinese food," she says. "Then you two can study."

"I love Chinese food. I love any food, really. My mom's Mexican and my dad's Japanese, so everything I eat is a mix."

"Really?" I sit across from him and study his features. "That explains it."

"My amazing good looks?" he says, smirking under my scrutiny.

My face warms, but I don't look away. "That's one way of putting it." My boldness surprises me, but I don't take it back.

He laughs. "And you? Where do you get your coloring?"

"My grandmother is Colombian."

"That explains it," he says, mimicking me, and stares at me as unabashedly as I stared at him.

But I can't meet his gaze anymore. My heart races, and I feel like things are getting intense. I open my backpack and slide out my homework. "Study time?"

"Yep," he says, and I let out a breath of relief at the silence that falls over us.

Iris feeds us rice with some kind of onion noodle soup, but I don't touch it. My stomach is in knots thanks to the boy across from me. I lift my eyes from my homework several times to look at him, and one time when I do, he's already looking at me. He grins, and I look back down.

After an hour and a half, he stands up. "Hey, thanks for the study session," he says, holding out his fist. "And for the food," he adds to Iris.

I stand and meet his fist, then hug myself as I walk him to the door.

"Thanks for wanting to come over." I stay two feet away from him the whole way to the door. I feel the need for space.

He pauses in the entryway. Maybe he expects me to walk him to his car. Or maybe he's hoping for a hug. Either way, he doesn't get it.

"Still coming to my game tomorrow?" he asks.

I nod. "Yes."

"All right." He shoulders his backpack. "Night, Cassandra."

I stand in the doorway as he walks down the sidewalk and disappears from view. Then I step back inside and close the door.

Just as I expect, my roommates burst into twenty questions.

"Who the heck was that?" Abby asks.

"Study buddy?" Camila adds, raising an eyebrow.

"You haven't mentioned *anyone*," Iris says.

I flop onto the couch beside Camila and lift my legs to rest on her lap. "There's not anything to mention."

Camila snorts. "Then how did he end up at our house?"

I shrug, trying to play it cool. "I met him at work. He asked if we could study together."

"Oh, right," Camila says. "And you brought him over. That's something that happens all the time with you."

My cheeks burn. "Well—"

"I mean, it has before," Abby says. "Sam was over here all the time."

They all lean in, inspecting me, waiting to see if Kai is another Sam.

I shake my head. "Kai isn't like that."

"The difference is, you *want* this guy to come around," Abby says, and she's not wrong.

"Do you like him?" Camila asks, eyes narrowed.

"I don't know… maybe," I say. "He's funny, and he's super cute. He's only eighteen, though. It's not like something's going to happen between us."

Immediately, my roommates laugh.

"Girl!" Abby says. "You were supposed to get dating freshmen out of your system *last* year!"

"I know, I know!" I say, my face burning. "I'm not planning to date him! I just like hanging out with him."

Camila levels her gaze at me. "Don't let him be another Jared."

Silence. Her words settle deep, and I contemplate them. I know what she means. I didn't let myself build a relationship with Jared for many reasons. And now he's gone. He was an amazing person. I can't say I *regret* not having a relationship with him, but I do feel a sense of unfulfillment.

If I get the chance to develop something like that with Kai, will I take it?

I'm not sure.

But I go to bed with her warning ringing in my ears.

⁕

I wake up thinking of Kai.

The day is drizzly and gray. I pull out the red rain jacket I bought at a thrift store and grab an umbrella. This kind of weather is the worst—clingy, cold, and impossible to dry off from. I trudge through each of my classes, shivering under the overzealous air conditioning, wondering why no one has turned the heat on. By the time I get to work, I feel like a soggy, shivering dog.

Christina is still there, so I stand by her desk, complaining for five solid minutes while I dab at myself with paper towels. She makes sympathetic noises and smiles at me, clearly amused.

"I'm guessing you don't love the rain?" she says.

"Not this kind." I grab another paper towel from the back room and return to my desk. "I like rain with drama—thunder, lightning, hail, wind. Something with energy. Something climactic. And then it's over in twenty minutes."

She laughs. "That's not the kind of rain we get in Colorado."

"Oh, I know. I've been dealing with this drizzly, damp, not-quite-rain, not-quite-sleet nonsense for the past year and a half." I toss the paper towel in the trash can, but it floats down statically, without even the satisfaction of a good swish. I reach up and run my fingers through my hair—wet, matted, frizzy.

"At least it's not snow," she says. "That's just one cold front away."

"You're right, you're right," I mutter. "I'll stop complaining."

The door opens behind me. I drop my hands from my hair and turn to smile at whoever walked in.

My smile freezes.

It's Kai. And he brings a girl with him.

She's cute—adorably cute—in a red blouse, her blonde hair twisted into a messy bun. She looks young too, probably a freshman. Maybe someone from his dorm?

"Hey," he says, not bothering to introduce her. "How's your day going?"

"Fine," I say, trying not to sound stiff. But I'm caught off guard, the wind knocked out of me. I've thought about Kai nonstop since last night. And now I feel like I showed up to a wedding in my pajamas. This is not what I expected.

"Other than the rain," I add. "Not loving it."

"Yeah, me neither. It doesn't rain like this in California." He glances toward the hallway. "Is the professor in?"

"Let me make sure he's not with a student." I pick up the phone, trying to ignore the prickly twist in my stomach as the girl leans in to whisper something to him.

Why do I care?

Why did he bring another girl in here? Is he trying to say something?

I'm totally bothered.

The professor picks up. "There's a student here to see you," I say.

"All right. Send him in."

I hang up and look at them. Is she going with Kai? Is she an engineering student too? She doesn't look like one. She looks like she'd be really good at painting. Or modern dance. Or something that doesn't require a lot of brain power.

Why am I being so judgy?

"You can go back," I say.

Kai turns to her. "I'll see you later."

"Okay."

She waves and turns to walk out. He heads down the hallway. They don't hug, they don't touch. Nothing.

And still, I'm overanalyzing. I'm annoyed with myself for feeling this way.

"I'm out of here. Catch you later," Christina says.

"Yeah," I say.

I sigh and chew on my lower lip.

I need to not be here when Kai comes out.

I put up the *Be right back* sign and slip out of the office. I'll hang out in the bathroom for a few minutes and hope Kai is gone by the time I get back.

At least I have his soccer game to look forward to tonight.

Unless she's there too.

CHAPTER ONE HUNDRED THREE

One Dance

My plan works like a charm. Kai has already come out of the office and gone by the time I get back, and I'm disappointed. I chide myself for being so fickle and concentrate on my work.

The blast of drizzly rain is still coming down when I leave the office, and it's not pleasant. I tighten the hood around my face and open the umbrella.

It's raining so hard I don't feel my phone buzzing in my backpack, but when I get inside my apartment and shake off the rain, I find three missed calls from Kai. Anticipation fires through me, followed by dread. I'm excited to see his name, but I'm anxious it's bad news.

And that's when I know I have somehow gotten more emotionally involved than I intended to.

I press the button to call him back.

"Cassandra," he says, like he's surprised to hear from me, like he wasn't the one who called.

"I missed your calls," I say, lightly and nonchalantly.

"You were gone when I came out from talking to the professor."

"I had to run to the restroom," I say breezily. As if it wasn't him I was trying to avoid.

"I waited, but you didn't come back."

Crap. Does that mean he realized I was avoiding him? How long did I take, anyway?

"Sorry," I say, because I'm not sure what else to say to that comment.

"I wanted to let you know, in case you were still planning on coming, they canceled my soccer game."

"Oh, that's a bummer." I sink down onto the couch, the disappointment heavy in my chest. I won't see him tonight after all. "Not surprising, really, when you see the rain outside."

"I know. But at least your Friday evening is free now!"

"Uh-huh." My mind tumbles along, trying to think of something else. "Are we still on for tomorrow?" The question blurts out without my permission, and I wince. What if he doesn't want to go out with me tomorrow?

"Yeah, of course! I'll call you tomorrow."

"All right. Talk to you later."

I hang up and sit on the couch, holding the phone, feeling a little lost. Slightly overwhelmed by the intensity of my disappointment.

Camila comes down the hall. At first, she turns toward the kitchen, but then she sees me and redirects.

"What's going on?"

I lift a shoulder like I don't care. "It's raining. The soccer game was canceled. I'm not going to see Kai tonight."

She didn't know my plans to begin with, but that doesn't matter. She reads my face. "I'm sorry. Why don't you guys do something else?"

My shoulder goes up again. "We're going out tomorrow." So why am I so bummed about tonight?

Has to be because of that girl he brought in.

The front door opens, and Iris comes in, bouncing on the balls of her feet, wiggly with excited energy.

"Time to get ready for the dance!" she says.

I stand up, not in the mood to join their celebratory joy. "You guys have fun."

Camila gasps. "I have an idea!"

"What's that?" Iris asks.

I've already started down the hall when I hear Camila say, "We can ask Kai to go to the dance with Cassandra!"

I turn around and come back into the living room. "No, you can't. He doesn't want to go with me."

"Did you already ask him?" Iris asks.

"No, but—"

"So you don't know."

"I know. He brought another girl in when he came to my office today," I say in a rush, all my insecurity and hurt feelings erupting in those words.

Iris looks sympathetic, but Camila says, "That doesn't mean anything! Boys follow you around everywhere and it doesn't mean you're interested in them."

I can see her point. And he didn't act overly affectionate with her—just friendly.

"Is he busy tonight?" Iris asks.

"No!" Camila shakes her head. "His soccer game was canceled! He has nothing!"

"He may have already filled his schedule," I say.

Camila has her phone out. "What's his number?"

I hesitate.

She lifts her face and stares me down. "Girl. Do you want to go to the dance with him?"

I cave. "Yes," I admit.

"This is the only way you have a chance. His phone number."

I give Camila the number and then hold my breath as she dials.

"Hello?" His voice answers on the other end.

"Hi, Kai?" Camila says.

I hear him answer, but I don't make out the words.

"This is Camila, Cassandra's roommate." She pauses. "Yeah! Anyway, I heard your soccer game got canceled. I don't know if you're interested, but there's a dance tonight, and Cassandra wasn't going to come because she was going to your soccer game."

Oh, Camila. I have to hand it to her. I wondered how she would avoid making me look desperate.

"Since your soccer game is canceled, I thought maybe she could come to the dance with us now—if you came too. She doesn't want to go by herself." There's a pause, then she says, "Seven o'clock! Come over here in about an hour? We can all go together. Great! See you then."

Camila puts the phone down and squeals. "He said yes!"

I squeal too. I jump up and hug her, then run to my room, more nervous than I remember being in a very long time.

I have the hardest time deciding what to wear. I finally settle on a short-sleeve yellow sweater with a pink skirt. But as I stand in front of the full-length mirror, with my shoulder-length hair, I worry I look more like an Easter egg than a dance partner.

"You look great," Abby says, cuddling up beside me and grinning at our reflection.

I don't get the chance to argue, because someone knocks on the door. We both swivel, wondering which of our dates has arrived.

It's Abby's. She curls up next to Levi on the couch, and Camila checks the time. Iris goes into the kitchen, and I stand there, squeezing my fingers and smiling hard, wondering if Kai will actually come.

There's another knock on the door. Iris opens it, and I catch my breath.

It's Kai. He's wearing black pants and a button-up collared shirt with a wool sweater over the top, the sleeves of his long-sleeve shirt rolled back. He looks classy and comfortable all at the same time.

His eyes meet mine. "Hi," he says, stepping into my kitchen. He brings with him an intoxicating, masculine scent. It has the effect of a pheromone on me, and I want to throw myself into his arms and inhale his neck.

Somehow, I refrain.

"Come on inside." I step out of the way, gesturing for him to come to the couch. He sits down across from Abby. I flounder for a moment, unsure where I'm supposed to go, but the most logical place is right next to him. So I sit, keenly aware of the proximity of his arm the entire time. I grab a throw pillow and hold it in my lap to help with my nerves. Holding the pillow makes me feel more grounded.

There's another knock on the door, and Iris answers it again. It's her date, but I don't pay much attention, glancing over at Kai instead. I almost laugh when I see he's also grabbed a pillow and clutches it in his hands. Somehow, it makes me feel better. We're both nervous.

"Thanks for coming, especially so last minute," I say.

He shrugs and glances my direction, his eyes meeting mine for a quick second before looking away again. "I'm glad it worked out. This'll be fun."

I sure hope so. If we're both too nervous to look at each other, I'm not sure. The normal ease with which we joke and play in my office seems to have vanished.

Jake arrives for Camila, and Abby says, "Okay, we have two vehicles. Cassandra and

Levi. Who's riding with who?"

"I can drive too," Kai says.

"I mean, if you want to," Abby says. "Otherwise, you can ride with one of us."

All eyes are on him, and I can almost feel his uneasiness. He looks at me and says, "I'll ride with Cassandra."

"I'll let you have shotgun," I say, going for comic relief.

"Oh, that's nice of you," he says, and I smile.

It's decided that Camila and Jake will ride with me. I take the lead, and Kai keeps up with me.

"I have to be one of the drivers," I say, still apologetic he didn't get to drive. "My car."

"Yeah, that makes sense." His hand comes out and touches my arm lightly, just beneath my elbow. His fingers trail downward, and I think he might try to take my hand. My whole body freezes in anticipation, but then his fingers drop.

I feel an overwhelming sense of disappointment. There's something electric between us, something that makes my flesh tingle where he touched it.

Or maybe it's been a very long time since anyone touched me.

We pile into my Camry, and he says, "This is a nice car."

"I'm fond of it," I say.

"We're all fond of it," Camila says from the back. "We seriously rely on Cassandra to get us from B to A very frequently."

"I'm happy to help," I say, feeling like a lame customer service agent.

It's a short drive up to the music hall on campus. I park, and Camila and Jake jump out and rush to the sidewalk to join everyone else. I lock the car and drop the keys into my purse, then wait for Kai.

"You didn't have a date, huh?" he says as we follow behind everyone else on the sidewalk.

"Apparently, I took too long to ask, and everyone was taken."

"But maybe that's how it was meant to be, so you could come to my soccer game, which got canceled, and now I can come to your dance."

I give a short laugh. "Yep. I'm sure that's exactly what was supposed to happen."

We enter the dance hall and hang up our jackets and purses. There's a band, and the music is lively—nothing like the Top 40 or the oldies I used to dance to in high school. I stand against the wall next to Kai, more uncertain than ever.

"Do you like dancing?" I ask him.

"Yeah. Pretty bad at it, though."

"Me too."

"Well…" He takes a step back and holds out his hand. "Let's give it a whirl."

I slip my hand into his. He might not be tall, but his hand is warm, and heat travels from my palm to my arm. He pulls me into the center of the dance floor, takes my other hand, and begins spinning me. Not in a circle, but like we're swing dancing.

I don't know how to dance like this. I've had other kids play around with me at dances, pretending to swing dance, but nobody knew any real steps like Kai does. For a moment, I freeze up, but Kai pulls me in close, close enough that I'm held against his chest, and whispers, "Relax. I'll lead you."

I exhale and let the tension fall from my shoulders.

Kai takes a step back but doesn't release my hand. He applies slight pressure to the joint between my thumb and my index finger, and I respond by moving in the direction he's pushing. I forget technique or to over-analyze my movements. If he pushes me left, I go left. If he pushes me right, I go right. I miss one time and go left when he's trying to send me right, and I laugh awkwardly, my face burning as we bump into each other, but he just smiles, and there's nothing mocking in it. I keep my eyes trained on his, letting him be my home base.

We dance three songs before he takes me off the dance floor to get water. A sheen of sweat clings to my face, and my feet are burning. But I feel exhilarated and alive, and I've never had so much fun dancing.

I slap his arm. "You didn't tell me you could dance!"

He doesn't even look ashamed. "I can't. But I watched my parents do it. I know the steps."

"No, you can dance," I say, shaking my head. "You seriously underestimated your ability." I reach up and touch my hair. It's slick from sweat. I move slightly away from him, afraid I might stink.

"You're not bad either," he says. "You let me lead you."

"You're a good leader," I say.

We rest for a few more minutes, and then he takes my empty cup and tosses it in the trash. "Ready to go again?" he asks, his eyes glittering.

I slide my hand into his, feeling my heart rate quicken at the very idea of the cardio I'm about to go through.

At least, I think that's why my heart is racing.

"Let's do it."

CHAPTER ONE HUNDRED FOUR

Terrifying Turn

It's one in the morning by the time we get back to my apartment. I say goodnight to everyone and then walk Kai out to his truck, the white one with the Adidas flower in the back window. I recognize it now.

"Thanks for coming with me tonight," he says, opening his truck door and leaning against the armrest. "I had a lot of fun. I'm glad you invited me."

If I didn't feel so stinky and gross, I'd step closer to him. I'd want him to hug me. But I do feel stinky and gross, so I take a step back.

"Do you need me to follow you home, make sure you get there?"

He laughs. "I might be younger than you, but I've stayed out after midnight before."

"Of course." I feel stupid.

But then he surprises me by stepping forward and wrapping his arms around me. For a moment, I stiffen, awkward and self-conscious, imagining my hair smells like sweat and my skin feels slimy.

But then I forget that, because his chest is warm and solid, and he still smells like boy and aftershave—the scent I've been dying to breathe in all evening.

He releases me and gives me a soft smile that crinkles his eyes. "See you later." He climbs into the truck and closes the door.

"See ya," I echo, stepping out of the street so his truck can pass by.

I don't know what he feels for me. But there's this warm, gooey, buttery feeling melting inside me that says I could like him.

And that terrifies me.

⁀⊙↗↘↖☀↙↗⊙↖

Kai doesn't call me the next day.

I didn't expect us to go out again today after we went out last night, but I'm still disappointed not to hear from him.

When I still haven't heard from him by Sunday night, I feel wounded. I thought we connected at the dance. Was it just me? Maybe I'm the only one who felt it.

By Monday, I'm downright discouraged. I head into work a few minutes early, and

Christina is there.

"Hey!" she says, giving me a hug. "How was your weekend?"

"Oh my gosh, Christina, I had so much fun." I sit on the edge of her counter and proceed to tell her all about the soccer game that didn't happen and the subsequent dance and how I felt being near him. Her eyes grow wider with every word.

"So, are you guys going to, like, date now?"

I make a noise in the back of my throat. "I'm not even sure if we're going to talk. We haven't spoken since Friday."

"He hasn't texted?" She presses a hand to her mouth, like this is a big deal.

I stand up, my fingers fluttering with nerves and anticipation. "I haven't heard anything. I'm going to call him." I pull my phone out.

"No." Christina puts her hand on mine before I can do anything. "It's his turn. Don't call him."

But now that the idea's in my head, I want to hear his voice. He'll make me laugh, and I'll feel safe in our friendship, like I did Friday. "It's not a big deal to call and say hi," I say. "It's been three days since we talked."

She shakes her head. "Do not be the one chasing. If he wants to talk to you, he'll call you."

"But—"

My words are cut off by the door to the office opening, and I stand up because I'm on the clock, so I should be prepared.

"I thought I would get here before you," Kai says as he steps into the lobby.

I stare at him. Christina giggles behind me. He's here, in my office, again.

"I came in a little early," I say. "Are you here to see the professor?" I move off Christina's counter and go to my computer. There's a pile of handwritten notes with a message from Dr. Lance on top, asking me to please transcribe his minutes. I sit down at the computer and open a Word document, trying to focus, even though I'm acutely aware of Kai hanging out at the counter to my left.

"He doesn't need to see me every day," he says, sounding mildly amused by my question. He rests his elbows on the counter and leans forward to watch me. "You're a fast typist."

The observation makes me laugh. "That might be part of why they hired me."

"So if I learned to type faster, would they hire me?"

"They'd have to fire me first, so that wouldn't work out well."

"No, probably not, since I'm only coming here so I can talk to you."

It's not funny, but everything he says makes me want to laugh. "Yeah, so I don't think that would work."

"Did I tell you you looked really pretty at the dance?"

"Thanks." My face is getting hot again, and I can't maintain eye contact.

"What are you doing tonight? Want to go out?"

It's all I can do to keep from gasping. He's asking me out again—in front of my coworker!

"Well..." I open my phone and check my calendar. "I'm getting together with a bunch of friends to play volleyball." Inspiration strikes. "Why don't you come?"

"I'd love that. I'm more of a soccer person, you know, but I can do volleyball."

"Great!" I smile, because suddenly there's sunshine pouring through my veins, and I can't stop grinning. "I'll text you the location."

"See you later, then."

He turns around and walks back out. I put my face in my hands and squeal. Christina actually stands up and pats me on the back.

"You didn't have to call. Don't chase him." She puts her arms through her backpack and gives me a stern look.

"I'm not going to chase him. We're not going to date. He's a kid."

"Well, have fun then. And don't chase him."

I groan and try to smack her backpack as she walks by. She gets away from me, laughing.

⁂

I've never been more excited for a volleyball game.

I head home quickly after work, anxious to find out exactly how tonight's going to play out. Thomas, Jake, and Trent are at the house talking with Iris and Abby when I walk in.

"Hey," I say. "Who's playing volleyball with us?"

"I'm actually not going to be able to," Jake says. "It turns out I have another commitment."

"And Nate can't make it, he has to work," Trent adds.

"Well, then who's going to be there?" I ask, a spurt of worry flashing through my limbs.

"I reserved the volleyball court for seven-thirty, but it looks like we're down to just a few people. It's not really enough to play," Abby says.

"We can see who's by the courts and maybe invite other people to join us," Camila suggests.

"It's actually not a great night for me, either," Iris says. "I have a big test tomorrow. If we end up postponing it for some other time, that would be better."

My heart sinks. I wanted this to be a fun and easy activity for Kai to participate in, but it doesn't sound like it's going to work out that way. "I invited Kai," I say.

Abby looks at me, eyebrows raised. "We can still do something fun, you, me, and Thomas."

"Yeah," I agree, feeling significantly more lame now. "I'll give him a call and tell him volleyball's off." I don't think he's going to want to hang out with us, especially when we don't have anything planned. I keep those negative thoughts to myself.

I go to my bedroom to call Kai. He answers on the second ring.

"Hey!" he says.

"Hey," I reply, relieved to hear his voice. "So, everyone decided to scratch volleyball tonight."

I hesitate before inviting him to do nothing with us, and he speaks into the silence.

"That's a bummer. Want to get together and study instead?"

My heart skips a beat. He still wants to do something with me? I don't have to come up with an interesting alternative? I answer before he can change his mind. "Yeah. That sounds good to me."

"Great. The business center is right next to my dorm. I study there a lot. Want to

489

meet there?"

"Sure. I'll see you there." I hang up, feeling animated and happy again as I bounce out of my room.

"So, are we doing something with Kai?" Abby asks.

I grab my backpack and my car keys. "I am."

CHAPTER ONE HUNDRED FIVE

Swept Along

It's after hours, so finding parking at the Tatter building is easy. I pull into a spot and look up at the seven-story glass structure. It doesn't look like a college building, but I guess that's why it's for the business students. I've never been inside.

Kai told me to meet him on the first floor. I enter at ground level and pause. There's a terrace set up like a café, with a little coffee shop and round tables and chairs. It would be a great place to study, but lots of other people have claimed it.

Kai is not one of them.

He said the east side of the building. Thanks to the mountains of Colorado, telling my east from west is much easier than in Arkansas. I wander through the terrace café and down the hall toward the other entrance. I pass a large auditorium with wide open doors and a presentation happening inside. I ignore it and keep going.

I reach the end of the building and pause. There's no entrance here, which makes sense because the building was built into the hillside. Level one is ground level on the west side, but not on the east side.

I pull out my phone, and then I groan. I have no signal down here. I'll have to go back outside and message Kai—unless he changed his mind and didn't tell me. Or maybe he's been trying to reach me and I'm not getting the messages.

My anxiety starts firing, and I make my way toward the terrace.

And there he is, strolling down the hall. He wears khaki board shorts, a striped blue polo, and flip-flops. He looks utterly casual and adorable, with his black hair falling around his face.

"Hey," he says, and the hint of a smile appears around his eyes.

"Oh, hey! I thought I was lost," I say, quickly masking my inner turmoil.

"No, you're just finding my secret spot. Come on." He gestures with his head, and I follow.

He leads me around the corner to a quiet alcove beneath the stairs. There are three small tables and a bench, and no one else is there.

Kai sets his backpack on the table beneath the stairs, and I join him.

"This the place?" I ask.

"Yeah. It's where I come when I want some quiet study time."

He pulls out a giant graphing calculator and a notebook, and I pull out my anthology of American short stories. He watches me for a moment, then says, "You must like to read."

"I love it. I think reading is the only thing I'm actually good at."

"I like a good book too. What are your favorites?"

"I'm into science fiction and fantasy." I grin because thinking about the books I enjoy makes me happy. "I know, I'm nothing but a big nerd."

He shrugs. "A little fantasy is good for everyone. So, what are you majoring in?"

I gesture at the anthology in front of me. "Isn't it obvious? English."

"I had my suspicions, but I didn't want to jump to conclusions."

"I suspect you're majoring in engineering," I say, smirking.

"How on earth did you figure that out?"

I laugh, then pull out the essay I printed earlier and read through it. Satisfied it's ready, I get out my tiny stapler so I can fasten it together before I turn it in tomorrow.

"Wait. What is that?" Kai leans over the table toward me.

I pause, essay in one hand, stapler in the other. "What is what?"

"That." He points to the little blue stapler.

I raise an eyebrow and rotate it to him. "It's a stapler."

He takes it from me, rolls it between his fingers, and says, "It's a baby stapler. I've never seen anything so cute."

"It's pretty cute."

He hands it back. "What do you call him?"

"You're making assumptions again. How do you know it's a boy?"

He looks slightly chagrined. "I did make an assumption because it's blue. Is it a girl?" He raises both eyebrows.

I'm struggling to keep a straight face. "He does happen to be a boy, and I call him—" I suddenly can't think of anything original. "Blue."

"Blue," Kai says with an unexpected reverence in his tone. "I never would have assumed that."

I can't help it. I laugh.

He grins too, but not too widely, like he's willing to let this be my joke. "Azulito," he says.

"Little Blue" in Spanish. My interest is piqued. Does he speak Spanish? I respond, "Azulinho," in Portuguese.

His eyebrows go up again, an expression of interest and surprise, and I find I like surprising him.

"What language was that?" he asks.

"Portuguese," I say.

"Portuguese! You speak Portuguese?"

"I'm learning it."

"Why?"

There's no way I'm explaining anything about Tiago to him. "I keep finding myself in Brazil, so I decided to study the language. I'm actually going back in July."

His eyebrows rise even higher, disappearing into his hairline. "Are you going on a mission?"

"Someday. Not yet, though. It's an internship."

"Wow, you are—so cool."

"I am?"

"Yeah. That's amazing."

"How do you know Spanish?" I ask.

"Do you speak Spanish too?"

I wave my hand back and forth. "Not really. But I know a little."

"I grew up speaking it. My mom's Mexican."

And his dad's Japanese. I haven't forgotten. I study him for a moment—the straight, shiny black hair, the dark eyebrows, his almond-shaped eyes, the shape of his face. He blinks, and I realize I'm staring. "Uh," I say, almost apologizing, but that would only make it more obvious.

And he laughs. It's higher pitched than I expected, almost like a giggle.

"Say something in Portuguese," he says.

What can I say that he won't understand? The languages are so similar. "*Meu cabelo é liso e preto.*"

"Argh." He bites off a piece of his notebook paper. "It's like listening to someone speak Spanish with rocks in their mouth."

"So you took a bite of paper?"

"Yeah. Now I have a rock in my mouth too."

"Well," I shrug a shoulder. "We say Spanish sounds like children learning how to speak."

"Say something else."

"*Há um fogo na mesa.*"

"Ugh." He takes another bite of paper. "You're making my ears bleed."

"Do you know what I said?"

"It's a bit harder for Spanish speakers," he says. "I think you have an easier time understanding us."

"Yeah, I think you're right." I glance down at my homework. It's been open on the table in front of me since I sat down, but I haven't read anything. "I should do some of this."

"You should."

His tone is serious, but I know he's mocking me.

"You're a bad influence," I say. "You said we'd study."

"So study. What's stopping you?"

I give him a glare that falls flat and focus my eyes on my book. Silence descends upon us, and I try to remember the points of the story I'm analyzing.

I manage a total of four lines before Kai says, "So what do you think is the most important quality to look for in a spouse?"

I lift my eyes, startled by the question. "A spouse?" I sputter.

"Yeah. You know, the person you'll marry someday."

I tell my heart rate to slow down. He's not asking me to marry him. It's a philosophical question.

But it's so weird to ask a girl he's just getting to know.

I lean back in my seat and try to play it cool. This is a normal topic of conversation for two nearly strangers. "Humor. I have to be able to laugh. That'll make the good times better and the bad times—tolerable."

He nods. "Yeah. I can agree with that. I like to laugh."

I shouldn't ask, but I'm curious now. "And what do you think is the most important quality?"

"Friendship," he answers immediately, like he anticipated my question. Like maybe he started this whole conversation so he could tell me. "I want my wife to be my best friend. Friendship is the most important relationship to me. This friendship I've started with you—let's say it grew into something more. The friendship would still be what means the most to me. That's what I would nurture. And then if things didn't work out, if the relationship fell apart, I'd make sure we stayed friends. I wouldn't want to lose that."

I'm tangled in his words. I'm trying to decipher them and trying not to read too much into them, but I'm carried away in a current of possibilities and maybes and potential. It feels very premature to be having this conversation, and yet it also feels like he's laying down a foundation of intention, and he wants me to know it.

And I can feel myself being swept along.

"Yes," I say. "I would want to keep your friendship too."

That doesn't begin to describe the rollercoaster of emotions he just took me on, but it's the simplest response.

"Cool," he says.

Like something's been decided. But I'm not sure what.

We spend the next four hours together, just talking. Laughing. Building that friendship, I suppose. A janitor comes by after eleven and tells us they're closing the building down, so we start packing up.

"Need a ride home?" he asks as I shoulder my backpack. He walks beside me down the hall, only a few inches taller than me, our shoulders nearly bumping.

"I brought my car," I say. "But you can walk me to it."

He grins. "Of course. I wouldn't leave you to the vultures at this hour."

He follows me out, holding the door for me as we exit the building. His hand touches my forearm as I pass, and I'm not sure if it's intentional. But it brings back memories of holding his hands while we danced, of him holding me close, and I want to go dancing again so that he'll touch me.

"This is me," I say, unlocking the light blue car as we approach.

"Can I get a ride to my dorm?"

I look at him and then look over to his dorm. I can see the lights of the tall structure from here, under the bridge and a seven-minute walk at most. "For real?"

"Yeah." He grins, and this time it's a little sheepish. "I like spending time with you."

I smile back and climb inside. "Let's go, then."

He gets in beside me, and I back us out of the parking lot, then swing a right toward the dorms.

"What are you going to do in Brazil?" he asks.

"Teach English."

"By yourself?"

"The company will place me with a host family. I'm still working out the details."

"I think that takes a lot of bravery."

I shrug. "I love the country. And traveling and adventure."

I park the car, but he makes no move to get out. He squints out my windshield and says, "I'm leaving on a mission soon."

"Oh, cool." Of course he is. The university has a mission program in place, and it encourages us to take advantage of it. "When do you go?"

"I don't know yet. I've put in my application. So I should find out soon."

"Hey, that's awesome." One more reason to keep my distance.

The last thing I need is another heartbreak.

He looks at me again. "So we'll both be going our separate ways, huh?"

"Me to Brazil and you to . . . Who knows?"

"Who knows," he echoes. "Thanks for the ride."

"Sure," I say, and in spite of everything, in spite of what he just told me, I wish he'd hug me. I wish he'd pull me in close.

My heart and my mind are warring against each other.

He puts his hand on the door handle and it seems he's having a similar war about whether to get out of my car. Then he laughs and says, "Okay. Good night."

"Night," I say.

He steps out and closes the door and I watch him walk away and I wish I knew what the heck was going on in his head.

CHAPTER ONE HUNDRED SIX

Sneak Attack

There's a bounce in my step when I go into the office on Tuesday. I've never been more excited to work—or at least, to be here.

I couldn't stop thinking about Kai last night. Just remembering his face, the way he would smile, the jokes he made—I'm giggling as I replay them in my mind.

I hope he'll ask me to study with him again tonight. But I know it's too much, too many days in a row together. Things need to go slow, especially since I don't want to date him.

There's a list of things for me to do when I get to the office, so I dive into it, starting with making coffee in the kitchen. The coffee machine gives me trouble, and I grumble while I deal with it.

The door rattles, indicating a student has stepped in. I step out of the kitchen into the office, smiling, my heart racing in anticipation.

I'm not disappointed.

My smile widens when I see Kai, and I force myself to stay calm. He might not be here for me.

"Hi, Kai," I say. "What can I help you with today?"

He smirks at me like I've done a terrible job of hiding my emotions. "I'm here to see Dr. Lance."

"Of course," I reply, dropping my eyes to the laminated sheets on my desk. "He's got office hours right now, so you can head on in."

"Thanks." He pats the top of my desk and goes down the hall.

I return to the coffee, skin tingly with anticipations of the banter we'll engage in when he comes out. A few more students walk through the lobby, and I attend to them. Then I take the coffees around the corner to the professors' rooms.

There's a different student with Dr. Lance, which means Kai finished his appointment while I was making coffee and left without staying to chat.

I let out a sigh. So what if that means he's not into me? He's still turning out to be a good friend.

I sit down at the computer and start working on the mailing list Dr. Lance requested, pretending I'm not feeling glum. I must be attention-starved.

I type addresses into the correct fields, pausing to answer the phone every time it rings. A student comes in, and I look up from the phone to smile and gesture for them to wait. But instead, my eyebrows shoot up when I see it's Kai.

I finish my call and hang up.

"Did you forget something? Need to see Professor Stephens this time?"

"Oh, yeah, I forgot something." He pats down the sides of his shirt and pant leg. "I can't seem to find my pencil."

"Did you check your backpack?"

"My backpack?" He slides it from his shoulder and opens the back pocket. "Right. I should've checked there."

I'm mildly amused. "Was there anything else you needed?"

"Haven't seen any baby blue staplers around here, have you?"

I can't help but laugh. I grab the giant stapler from my desk and place it on the counter. "I've got the mother stapler right here."

His eyes widen. "No, that's the dad, and I'm a little frightened."

I grab the stapler and hold a hand out. "I can help you. Give me your paper."

He looks at the stapler in my hand and shakes his head. "You're a little too familiar with that thing. Like you've handled him before."

There's just the right amount of distrust in his tone, and even though we're talking about a stapler, there's enough innuendo in his words that my face warms. I put the stapler down, feeling like I've been caught doing something inappropriate.

"Only when necessary," I say, not sure why I feel defensive.

"Oh, I'm sure," Kai says. "You don't seem like the kind who would handle him when it's not necessary. Still, I'll pass."

"Is there anything else I can help you with?" I ask.

He shakes his head. "I don't think so," he says, lifting his shoulders to his ears and shoving his hands in his pockets. "I guess I'll wander out of here again."

I give a little laugh and lean forward to watch him leave, but that floating feeling stays with me.

This time, he did come to see me.

I barely sit back down at my computer when the door opens again, and Kai comes back, carrying something in his hand.

"They were selling cookies out there," he says, his tone apologetic. "I had to get one."

He places a piece of wax paper with a gooey chocolate chip cookie on my counter. My stomach clenches at the rich aroma of sugar and chocolate.

"I can see why," I say. "Are you going to eat it?"

"For you." He says the words confidently, but there's a bashfulness behind them. "I hope you like cookies."

"I do, and I'm starving, and it smells amazing. But what about you?"

He shrugs. "I'm gonna go out and get one for me too. But I thought you should have one first."

He slides the cookie toward me, and my feelings go from giddy to emotional. I'm touched. "Thank you. It's so kind of you. I'll enjoy this."

"Great. Then I'll see you later." He heads for the door, then turns back. "Are you doing anything tonight?"

I shake my head. "No. Just homework."

"Same," he says.

I expect him to ask if I want to study together, but instead, he says, "Enjoy your cookie," and leaves.

I hold the warm cookie in my hand and tear off pieces of chocolate, savoring each morsel.

☙ ❧

I have more homework than I realized. I got behind when I spent yesterday playing with Kai instead of doing schoolwork. I stay on campus so I can focus, hunkering down in the library, wondering if Kai is at his usual spot in the business building. I'm tempted to go check, but that feels borderline desperate, and I'm not desperate.

That doesn't stop me from checking my phone every ten minutes to see if he's called.

At nine o'clock, he still hasn't, and I remember I need to do laundry before I go to bed, or I won't have clean underwear tomorrow. I pack up and head home, acknowledging as I walk away from campus that I'm not going to see Kai tonight.

It's for the best. I got a lot more done.

I keep telling myself that the whole way home.

☙ ❧

My eyes are sticky and heavy when I pry myself out of my warm bed in the morning. I was up until after midnight doing laundry and working on English papers.

I don't remember my Portuguese assignment until after I shove my contacts into my tired eyes. Crap. I never finished it, and it's due this morning. I skip breakfast, cutting my morning short so I can leave fifteen minutes early and try to finish it. The weather's nice, and I slide my feet into my black sandals.

I wonder about my choice as soon as I start walking. The elastic band around the top of my foot snaps the bottom of the shoe against my sole with each step. Snap slap snap slap. Great. I'll make an entrance everywhere I go today.

Somehow, I get the assignment done in the hallway outside my classroom right before my professor arrives. But I'm so tired I can barely keep my head up in class. My eyes burn. How many more hours until I can go home and sleep? Maybe I should start drinking coffee.

I wake up a little at lunch when I eat the cheese and onion sandwich Iris prepared for me. The flavors remind me of my mom's Thanksgiving cheese ball, and I'm grateful for Iris's thoughtfulness.

Dr. Lance is standing at my counter when I come in for work. He swivels to face me.

"Oh, good, you're here," he says, holding a large textbook out toward me. "I need this run back to the library, and I have a book waiting for me to grab. Here's the pickup slip. Can you do that?"

"Sure." I go around to my desk, aware of how my sandals slap loudly in the quiet office. I pull out the "Be Right Back" sign, then drop my backpack behind the counter and take the textbook from Dr. Lance.

"I'll be back in a moment," I say.

"Thank you," he says, turning back for the professors' hall.

498

I walk down the silent corridor, glad that it's carpeted so my sandals aren't quite as loud. They still make a slapping sound every time I lift my foot, but it's not as noticeable here.

"Cassandra."

I turn at the sound of Kai's voice calling out behind me, and I pause, waiting as he catches up to me.

"I was about to go into your office to see you, but you're here," he says.

I give him an amused look, hoping he doesn't see how much I've been looking forward to seeing him today. "Do you ever go to class?"

"I only have one class in the afternoon, which means I'm free to come and bug you the rest of the time."

"You don't bug me," I say, the honesty escaping my lips before I can hold it back. My face warms, but he doesn't make an issue of it.

"Good. Then I'll keep coming around. Where are you off to?" he asks.

"The library." I wave the inter-library loan book Dr. Lance gave me. "I have to turn this one in and pick up another."

"Mind if I come along?"

"No, of course not."

We keep stride, matching each other's pace as we exit the building and cross the quad. The library isn't close to the engineering department, and I'm glad we have this time to walk together.

"So, what's it like back in Arkansas?" he asks.

"A lot greener than here. More humid."

"Is that a good thing or a bad thing?"

"Good thing for sure. Here I have to bathe in lotion, and I always get nosebleeds."

"Yeah, I know what you mean. California isn't dry like this either."

I glance at him. "What's home like for you?"

"Well, we lived in a small suburb, lots of houses around us. I spent my time playing soccer and trying to shake off the racial attitudes."

I raise an eyebrow. "You encountered that in California?"

"Yeah. There were a bunch of kids at school that called me a Mexican beaner. I pretended like I wasn't Mexican so they wouldn't call me that."

"But you are Mexican?" I ask, not entirely sure.

"I am. I was born there."

"That's so cool. I'm American, but my grandmother was from Colombia, and there were some kids that made fun of me for it."

Kai looks at me, his brow furrowed. "How? You're like one of the most beautiful girls I've ever seen. So it doesn't matter where you're from."

I want to tell him how I think the same of him, that he's one of the most beautiful boys I've ever seen, but all I say is, "Some people think of color before anything else."

"Yeah, I guess that's true. But it's still weird."

We enter the library, and immediately I notice the sound of my sandals flapping as we cross the atrium. Even though there are voices from students congregating and lingering, the noise echoes through the open room. Kai glances at me, and I shrug.

"I could take my shoes off," I say.

"Let's just get in and out."

"Agreed," I say.

The slapping sound diminishes slightly as we exit the tile floor of the atrium and approach the carpeted reception desk. Kai stands behind me, a silent companion, while I turn in the book for Dr. Lance and hand over the paper for the next one.

The employee takes the paper and tilts her head as she reads it. "Oh, this one's at the checkout desk at the end of floor five. Take the paper all the way down the hall, go up two flights of stairs, and you'll find it on the south side of the building."

"Oh, okay," I say, slightly taken aback.

We have to cross the entire library. In my noisy sandals.

I turn to Kai and gesture with my head. "This way."

We start down the hall, passing the computer room where fingers clack on keyboards and voices whisper as students converse. We reach the section with tables for studying, and silence descends upon us, other than the clacking of my sandals.

My shoes continue to slap against the floor with each step. I keep my eyes forward, my face burning, not daring to look at anyone even though I feel the eyes of each student on me as they glance up to watch us go by. We get past most of the study areas, and then we're in an unoccupied corridor with rooms on either side. My shoes keep clacking, and Kai looks at me. He inhales a big breath noisily and holds it in as if that will silence my shoes.

I have to laugh, but still, he doesn't breathe. The only sound is the slap of my sandals until we reach the stairwell, and then he lets out his breath with a woosh.

"That was intense," he says.

My sandals are even louder in the stairwell, echoing off the linoleum steps and against the brick wall.

"It's not over," I warn. "We still have to get the book and then walk back."

He gives me a very serious look, his dark eyes wide and somber. "I think maybe you should take your shoes off."

CHAPTER ONE HUNDRED SEVEN

Ready for More

We make it out of the library without me removing my shoes or getting escorted out, but as soon as we're outside, we both collapse into fits of laughter, so hard that we have to stop walking. Kai, his hands on his knees, shakes his head, and I clutch my stomach.

"Are you ever going to wear those shoes again?" he asks.

"They're going straight into the trash," I say.

We start walking again, and my shoes still make a noise as they cross the concrete blocks of the quad. It's not as loud now that we're not in the echoey silence of the library. We walk side-by-side, our arms nearly brushing with every step. He could take my hand so easily.

"I want to go dancing again," he says. "That was a lot of fun."

"Yeah, it was." We've reached my work building, and we slow our pace as we approach my office.

"What are you doing tonight? Want to study?" he asks.

"Yes," I say, so quickly that I'm embarrassed.

He doesn't seem to notice. "But I don't know if we can stay on campus with you wearing those shoes. Want to study at my dorm? It's close."

Now I laugh at the idea of sitting in the common room with a bunch of freshmen. "Why don't you come to my place?"

"I can do that. I'll pick you up after work."

I won't say no to a ride. "Sure."

We stop outside my office. "See you in a few hours," he says.

"Yes," I reply.

He waves and turns around, walking away, and I'm left feeling lonely.

"Get a grip," I scold myself as I open the door and walk in. "He's leaving on a mission. He's not looking to form attachments right now. And you're in no mood to say goodbyes."

Been there, done that.

Kai picks me up in the white truck I've come to recognize. I climb into the front seat and press my hands against the heater he has going.

"Your apartment?" he asks.

"Actually, I need to drop off my rent check." I bend over and rummage through my backpack.

"You don't mail it in?"

I withdraw the envelope and wave it theatrically. "I forgot to drop it off at the post office, and it's due tomorrow. So do you mind if we drop it off?"

Kai shrugs. "Lead the way."

We pull out onto the main street, and I give him directions. The light in front of us turns red, and Kai slows down. A car with three big dogs hanging their heads out the window pulls up beside us.

"Look at those dogs," Kai says.

"They look big enough to eat me," I say.

"Probably," Kai agrees. And then he rolls down his window and talks to the dog, the big black one that's turned toward us.

"Hey, buddy," he calls. "You wouldn't eat her, would you?" He tilts his head toward me.

The dog looks at him, pulls in its tongue and closes its mouth, as if considering his words carefully. Then the mouth drops back open, the tongue falls out, and it resumes panting, although this time it's looking at Kai.

"I see you're not much of a conversationalist," Kai says, and I start giggling.

That's when Kai starts barking.

The dogs' ears perk up, their tongues retract, and they freeze, staring at Kai as if they've unexpectedly encountered a friend. Or maybe a foe?

"Now it's going to eat you!" I say, laughing.

The light turns green, and the car pulls away from us, and I'll never know if the dogs' owners were aware of what was happening.

"Turn right here," I say, and Kai responds with a bark.

So, I do the only logical thing when someone barks at you: I bark back.

A big grin spreads across his face, and I'm reminded that he's only eighteen—high school wasn't even a year ago. We carry on the rest of the drive barking at each other, so I have no idea if we're actually saying anything or just goofing off.

It doesn't matter.

We reach my landlord's dropbox, and I spring out of the car, shivering in the breeze as I drop my rent into the box. Then I come running back. He shoots me a smile, then turns us around and drives back to my apartment.

We head up through the commons, and I feel the distance between our hands like magnetic charges.

But I'm starting to wonder if I'm the only one who feels it.

We step into my apartment, and he sits down on the couch. I hesitate, suddenly unsure if I'm supposed to sit next to him or if that's assuming too much. Am I making things weird if I sit at the table?

Camila comes into the kitchen. "Hey, guys. Cassandra, Kai."

She sits at the table, and I take that as an excuse to sit on the couch—on the opposite side of Kai, of course.

"Hi, Camila," I say. I open my backpack and pull out my homework. Kai does the same.

"Study session?" Camila asks.

"Yeah, we needed a change of scenery from the business building," I say.

"And she didn't want to hang out at my freshman dorm," Kai adds.

It's the truth, but I didn't know he read me so easily.

Camila laughs. "I won't distract you then." She gets a glass of water and leaves the kitchen.

We fall into silence. Now that we're alone on the couch, the ease with which we interacted earlier has vanished, and I'm full of apprehensive thoughts. What does he think of me? Am I really just a study buddy? Why are we hanging out?

Kai clears his throat after about twenty minutes. "I hate to ask this, but do you have any food?"

My head jerks up. I cast a quick glance at the oven and see that it's after six.

"Of course!" Why didn't I think of that? I jump up. "I'll make us something to eat."

"No, no, I don't mean for you to make me something," Kai says. "I thought maybe you have, you know, a piece of cheese or something."

"I've got dinner plans." I start pulling out ingredients more frantically than I normally would, filled with an anxiousness to satisfy his hunger and prove my ability to cook.

But as I look at what I planned to make for dinner tonight, my heart sinks. I want to impress him, and I don't think my cracker casserole is going to do it.

It's all I've got.

Camila comes back into the kitchen. "Are you making dinner tonight?" she asks.

"Yep. I'm on it," I say.

"Okay, making sure I didn't mix up our dates," she replies.

She's being polite. Camila doesn't take a turn cooking. She gives me money, and I cook for both of us.

"Nope. Working on it right now," I reply.

She turns and flashes a smile at Kai. "Cassandra is a great cook. I pay her to make dinners for me."

"I'm excited to try her food," Kai says.

I wince. I hope he's not too excited—maybe he'll be so hungry that he'll think it's amazing.

Dinner takes forty-five minutes, thirty minutes of in the oven baking. I try to study during that time, but all I can think about is Kai sitting beside me, probably starving, and how he's going to be so disappointed with my food.

The timer goes off, and I haul it from the oven, then call down the hall, "Camila, it's ready!"

"Smells amazing," Kai says, coming to the table.

I look at the 8x8 pan that I intended to feed me and Camila for two nights with a sinking fear. I didn't plan on feeding a third person.

"Thanks. Do you like to cook?" I ask.

"Actually, I do," Kai says. "My mom is an excellent cook. I love when she makes flan.

Next time, I'll cook for you."

That makes me smile as I pull out three plates and divide the cracker casserole among the three of us.

"Where, in your dorm?" I ask teasingly.

He smirks at my tone. "You think it's funny that you're older than me?"

I raise my plate to him and sit down. "I'm twenty, and you're eighteen. Yeah, I think that's funny." *But dang, you're cute for eighteen,* I add to myself.

"I'll be nineteen in . . ." He checks his phone. "Twenty-one days. So we're really only a year apart."

Twenty-one days until his birthday. I clock that away for further notice.

"But I have a whole year's worth of college experience more than you."

"This is true," he says.

My roommate pops out of her room and joins us at the table. "This smells amazing. What is it?"

I hold up the box of saltines. "The recipe I found on the box. It looked good."

We both giggle, and I turn to Kai.

"Sorry it's nothing fancy. I didn't know I was entertaining."

"No big deal, I like crackers. And I didn't expect you to cook for me."

"Oh, I know. But I was going to make dinner anyway." I dig into the casserole.

"Hey, this is good," Kai says.

"Thanks," I say. I watch him get a second helping, almost as big as his first, and then I watch Camila do the same. It hits me: the food is almost gone.

I don't want to take any more, but my stomach growls, telling me I'm still hungry.

There's only a little bit left.

"All right if I take the rest of this?" I ask.

Camila gestures at me. "You made it. Of course."

"This is already my second helping," Kai says.

I take it, feeling pacified.

Kai is done with his food two minutes later. He picks up the cracker box and plays with it, and I watch him with a gnawing feeling in my gut.

"Can I get you anything else?" I ask.

He lifts his eyes and meets my gaze. "Oh, that was great."

"You're not still hungry?" I ask.

He hesitates. "Maybe a little."

I'm mortified. My face flames. "Let me see what else I've got."

"Oh, no, you already made this food. I feel really bad for taking it."

Kai stands, and I feel all kinds of awkward.

"I should probably go home now. I can get more food at the dorm; I have a meal plan."

Of course he does. But I hate that he's leaving like this. I wrap my arms around my torso and follow him to the door as he grabs his bag.

"Are you sure? I can find something else to eat."

"No, I don't want to put you out anymore." He gives me a grin, but I wish he would release his backpack and hug me. He doesn't, so I just hold myself tighter.

"Okay. Sorry about that."

"Stop saying sorry," he admonishes. "You didn't do anything wrong. I'll see you tomorrow. We'll do something together Friday or Saturday."

I nod and exhale.

He leaves, and I close the door. I hear Camila saying something, but I'm a bit moody. I thought I was the one going slow, but I'm ready for more.

At least he left me with the promise of tomorrow.

CHAPTER ONE HUNDRED EIGHT

Just Friends

I watch for Kai every time the door opens at work, and I berate myself for turning into a lovesick schoolgirl. But I want to see him, especially after the weirdness of last night. He said he'd call me.

But my phone is silent.

He finally comes in when I'm highlighting test scores for Dr. Lance.

"Hey," he says, drumming his fingers on the counter.

"Hey!" I say, and I can't help it. My whole face pulls into a smile when I see him. "What's up?"

"Not much," he says, and he turns his body sideways so he faces the hallway instead of looking at me. "Do you know when Dr. Lance's office hours are today?"

Of courses I do, but I check anyway. "Right now. You can go on back." Is it just me, or does he seem a bit distant? I tuck a stray piece of hair behind my ear, but I've pulled it into a messy bun because I didn't have time to shower.

The movement attracts his attention, and he glances at me. "I like your hair," he says.

I laugh. "Thanks."

And then he's gone.

Did he smile at me? Make eye contact?

I shove down the paranoid feelings of anxiety. He clearly had something on his mind. I'm sure he'll talk to me when he comes out. He said we'd do something this weekend.

I move from highlighting to sorting papers and stapling them, all the while watching the hallway, barely concealing my anticipation. Kai finally comes out, and he gives me a wave before heading to the door.

"See you later," he says.

That was it?

I work myself up into a quasi-frenzy based on what I'm beginning to interpret as a rejection. If he's not interested, he needs to say so.

Wait a minute. We're not supposed to be interested in each other. We're just friends. He doesn't have to say anything to me.

But the way we talk to each other, it's more than just friendly, isn't it?

I facepalm my forehead. Why am I so confused?

The door opens, and I haven't had the chance to lift my head before a student voice says, "Hello, is Dr. Lance here?"

I lift my head. I knew from the accent that the boy wouldn't be American, but as soon as I look at him—with his smooth, dark skin and curly black hair—I have a sense of his origin.

"Yes. Do you have an appointment?"

"Kind of. He told me to come by."

"What's your name?"

"Patrick."

"Patrick?" It's a very American name, but he doesn't look or sound American.

"Well, in English," he says with a smile.

I can't help myself. I blurt, "Are you Brazilian?"

He blinks dark lashes over dark eyes that stir up nostalgic feelings in my gut. "Yeah. How did you know?"

"Your accent." I leave out the reminiscences of Tiago. "I have a couple of good friends who are Brazilian, and you remind me of them. And I've been to Brazil twice."

"You've been to Brazil?" He raises his eyebrows. "That's amazing. I don't meet a lot of people who have been to Brazil."

"Yes, I kind of love the country. I'm going back at the end of summer."

"Are you really?" He rests his elbows on the counter and leans over, clearly about to engage in conversation when he jerks upright. "Oh, I have to see the professor, but I'd love to talk more when I come out."

"I'll be here," I reply.

He goes in, and it makes me happy, remembering Brazil. It helps me forget, or at least not dwell on, the fact that Kai wasn't overly friendly and I have no idea where I stand with him.

Patrick comes back out twenty minutes later.

"Would you like to go out tonight?" he asks, jumping straight to the point. "I'm going to a concert for a friend, and then we can go to dinner."

For a heartbeat, I think of Kai, but I push that thought aside.

We're just friends.

"I'd love to! That sounds fun."

"Great! Let me get your number, and I'll pick you up tonight."

We exchange details, and he leaves.

I let out a relieved exhale. I need to stop thinking about Kai. Other boys exist, mature boys, boys my age, boys ready to commit.

Maybe Patrick is who I need.

◎⌒◟※◞⌒◎

Patrick picks me up a little after seven and drives me to the concert hall near campus. It's a beautiful orchestral performance, but I haven't eaten anything since a sandwich before work, and as my stomach twists and turns, all I can think about is how hungry I am. I enjoy the concert—at least, the first twenty minutes.

But when we rise for the intermission an hour into it, I lean over and whisper, "I'm going to find the concessions."

"Oh," Patrick says, placing a hand on my arm, his dark eyes wide as they look at me intently. "Do you want to leave? We don't have to stay for the whole concert."

I exhale, and I'm sure my relief is visible on my face. "We don't have to leave. I'm just hungry."

"So . . . let's go to dinner." He puts an arm around my shoulders. It's comfortable, like a warm jacket, but not exciting. No sparks or magnetic pulses. But I barely know him, so what do I expect?

We head to the Olive Garden. I'm in my element as I place an order for eggplant parmesan and a salad with the waiter. Patrick takes a little longer to decide, and I know from experience that the Italian food in America is nothing like the Italian food in Brazil.

The waiter leaves, and I begin, "So tell me how—" just as Patrick says, "So why were you—"

We both stop talking, and then we laugh.

"You first," he says, gesturing. "Ask your questions."

"Where are you from in Brazil?" I ask.

"I'm from Salvador, the capital of Bahia. Are you familiar with it?"

I shake my head. "No. I've only been to Recife, up in the northeast."

"Recife! Yes, that's way up there—farther north than my city."

"But you speak English so well. How did you learn it?"

"I was an exchange student in the U.S. in high school."

I give a smile. That makes sense, and it brings back so many memories. "Where did you stay in the U.S.?"

"Nevada. But a small town, not one of the big ones you're probably familiar with."

"And that's how you speak English so well?" Even Tiago didn't speak this well.

Patrick lifts one shoulder. "Well, I spent the last two years here in Colorado, so that helped. But I've only been home from a service mission for about six months, and I'm afraid my English is a bit rusty."

"You did a mission?" This is helpful information. He won't be leaving. He's here to stay. He's someone I can form an attachment to.

"Yes."

"Where did you go?" I unfold my napkin.

"Mozambique. It's a country in Africa where they speak Portuguese."

I tilt my head. "They speak Portuguese in Africa? I didn't know that."

"Yes, the Portuguese accent is a little bit different from what we speak in Brazil, but we can understand each other."

I'm absolutely fascinated and add Mozambique to the list of places I want to visit.

"Now you," Patrick says. "Why are you going to Brazil in a few months?"

I lean in, warming to the subject, excited as I think about this adventure I'm about to go on. "I'm doing a teaching internship. I'll be working at an English school."

"Oh, we have those all over Brazil. Did you choose the country?"

I nod. "I'm minoring in Portuguese, so it made sense for me to go to Brazil."

He raises both eyebrows. "Do you speak Portuguese?"

I wave my hand back and forth. "So-so," I say in Portuguese.

"*Que legal!* You have a pretty good accent. How did you learn?"

I stutter, trying to find the right explanation. "I went to Brazil in high school to spend a week with our exchange student." Crap, now I've said too much. He's going to figure out our exchange student was a boy. "Then I went back last summer and stayed another month. I fell more and more in love with the culture each time."

"Wow, I love that! How long will you be there this time?"

"Five or six months, I think."

"You'll be fluent by the time you get back. We could speak in Portuguese to each other."

He flashes a grin, his teeth white against his brown skin, but I don't really hear his words because his smile makes me think of Kai's smile, and suddenly I wish it were Kai sitting across from me, talking to me about places we've been and languages we can speak to each other.

The food is fantastic, and Patrick and I have no difficulty finding things to talk about. But once I get Kai in my head, I can't get him out.

There's a chemistry that exists between Kai and me. And I realize, as I walk back to my apartment after Patrick drops me off, that there's no point in going on dates with other people right now. Somehow, I've fallen for Kai.

CHAPTER ONE HUNDRED NINE
Pivotal Moment

I have a lot to work on Saturday. I've got three tests next week and papers due in both English classes, plus a paper in my religion class. For the first part of the day, there's no room in my head to think about anything except homework.

But then the afternoon rolls around, and my phone is suspiciously silent, and my mind starts talking.

Kai hasn't called me. Or texted me. I don't remember the last time I spent so much time feeling insecure and doubting myself.

Oh, except maybe when I was almost dating Mitch.

Dating is for the dogs. I hate it.

By five o'clock, I'm frustrated. It's a Saturday evening, and I have no plans. Who's fault is this? I'm tempted to blame myself, but instead, I blame Kai. He could've straight up told me that he wasn't going to call, that he had no interest in me, but he didn't. I should have made plans with other people and not worried about him.

Boys are the worst. Especially young boys who haven't even turned nineteen and are barely out of high school and still act like—

My phone rings.

It's at the foot of my bed, where I tossed it in frustration. I slam my laptop shut and scramble over the blanket to get to it.

It's Kai.

"Hello?" I hope I don't sound too breathy. I lean back against my bed, legs stretched out in front of me.

"Hey," he says, casual and chill. "What are you doing?"

"Studying." I try to keep my voice cool. *I thought you were going to call yesterday,* I want to say, but that sounds desperate, like I'm nagging. "What about you?"

"I'm hungry, but I don't want dorm food. Want to get something to eat?"

Yes! I want to scream. *I've been waiting twenty-four hours to hear from you!* But somehow, I keep calm. "Yeah, sure. When were you thinking?"

"Does now work? I can come get you."

"Okay. See you in fifteen."

The moment we hang up the phone, I jump off my bed and race into the hallway to check my reflection. I don't look terrible, but I do look like I've been sitting around doing homework all day. I change out of my T-shirt and put on a cute button-up blouse.

The jeans stay. I can't look like I tried too hard.

I've barely finished applying lip gloss and mascara when there's a knock on the apartment door.

Abby answers. "Kai! Come on in." She yells down the hall, "Cassandra, Kai's here!"

I close the mascara wand and jab it into my pocket, then saunter down the hall all casual-like, flashing a smile. "Hi."

My eyes scan him over, taking in his appearance. Kai wears jeans and a long-sleeve T-shirt, both comfy and incredibly adorable. I cross my arms over my waist and hope he finds me as appealing as I find him.

"Ready to get some food?" he asks.

"Yes," I say. "Want me to drive?"

He rattles his car keys in his hands. "No, I've got it." He steps out into the corridor.

I grab my jacket, just in case it's cold, then hurry out after him.

We walk side by side, our shoulders almost brushing. We keep our hands in our pockets, like we always do. Two good friends.

I wonder what it would feel like if he held my hand.

"How was your Friday?" he asks.

"Fun. I went to a concert and then out to dinner."

"That's cool. With who?"

"A friend." I don't offer any more info, and he doesn't ask. I'm sure he's smart enough to realize it was a guy. But we're not exclusive. Are we even dating?

Yes. Yes, we are.

It's time I acknowledged that.

But for all I know, he was out on a date with another girl last night too.

I'm not asking.

We get into his truck, and he asks, "Do you like tacos?"

"Love them," I say.

"Me too. The ones from the street vendors in Mexico are by far the best, but I'll settle for just about any taco."

"I'm not picky. I haven't had any from the street vendors in Mexico."

"Oh, that needs to be rectified. Maybe I can show you around sometime."

I don't say anything in response to his words, but a warm, anticipatory feeling bubbles up in my chest.

If he's imagining a trip between the two of us to Mexico one day, he's thinking into the future. We're not likely to make such a trip in the next few weeks before the semester ends and he leaves on his mission and I go to Brazil.

I like the thought of seeing Kai in my future, and that surprises me. I haven't been able to think seriously about anyone in a long time. Not since . . . well, I don't want to analyze it.

Kai pulls into Taco Bell, and I give a short laugh of surprise.

"This okay?" he asks.

"Of course. I love Taco Bell." I get out of the car, my feet hitting the pavement as he comes to my door. "I think I lived off Taco Bell my senior year."

"Me too."

As much as I frequented Taco Bell in high school, I haven't really gone in college. It's near my apartment, but stepping inside floods me with memories of all the meals eaten with various people, various boys. I stand behind Kai in line, pressing up on my tiptoes and resting my chin on the back of his shoulder. I pretend to do it so I can see the menu better, but really it's so I can inhale his scent.

"What's your favorite?" he asks, glancing slightly over his shoulder at me.

I straighten up, stepping back from him. He didn't act weird about me touching him, but I have this terrible paranoia that he'll pull away from me if I get too close.

"Can't go wrong with a seven-layer burrito."

"We speak the same language."

He steps up to order for us—seven-layer burritos and a few Gorditas. I grab our drinks, then find us a table while he waits for the food.

"Is all of this all right?" he asks when he comes to the table with the tray.

I grab one of the burritos and start unwrapping it. "Everything looks great to me. I'm easy."

"Yeah, you don't seem like someone who'd be high maintenance. It's another thing I like about you."

"Are there multiple things you like about me?" I tease.

"What's not to like? I'm still waiting to find something negative about you."

They're flattering words, and yet I suspect he means them. I fall silent, any witty response dying in the wake of his pronouncement.

"So, tell me everything about Arkansas," he says.

"Oh, that's gonna take more than an evening."

"We'd better get started, then." Kai takes a bite of his burrito. The opposite end opens, and sour cream and liquid cheese spill on his pants.

"Oh, shoot!" he says, dumping the burrito and grabbing a napkin to wipe his pants. "Dang. That was graceful."

I purse my lips to keep from laughing, but the dark stain on his light pants is undeniable. "Might not have been your finest moment."

"I don't know. It depends on your definition."

"Here. Let me get you more napkins." I stand up.

"No, I got it." He swivels as I pass him, grabbing my arm and stopping me.

I catch my breath because there is a momentary kinetic energy between us when he touches me, where I feel like I'm moving toward him and he's pulling me in.

But I'm not, and he's not. In fact, neither of us moves. He lets go of my arm, but it's not a hurried motion. He looks at me carefully, like there's some calculation going on behind his eyes, and I wonder what his engineering brain is coming up with.

"You don't need to clean up after me," he says. He doesn't seem eighteen anymore, but older than me—mature, compassionate, understanding.

"Okay," I say, sitting down. I try to pretend like I didn't have an earth-shattering moment at Taco Bell.

He glances down and continues cleaning his pants. "Tell me about Arkansas."

Focus. Stop watching his hands. "Well, it's very hot and very humid. We do get snowy days, but not often."

"Is it flat?"

I shake my head. "There are no mountains like out here, but it's not flat. Lots of rolling hills. And very green."

"Sounds like you miss it."

I give a wistful smile. "I do. I'm cold here all the time. And I miss the green."

Kai nods. "You've mentioned the green a few times."

"It's just so alive. I feel rejuvenated and energized when I see the color."

"I hope I see it someday."

There it is again—talk of a future. Not even necessarily *our* future, but the possibility of our lives intertwining in the future.

He finishes the burrito.

"How did your parents meet?" I ask.

"California. It's a big melting pot. Everyone goes there for better opportunities, more jobs, expensive housing..."

I laugh at the last part. "Do you like it there? What part are you from?"

"I like it, it's home. My family's still there. I'm from a small town near San Jose."

San Jose. That name sounds familiar. "Oh, one of my roommates is from there. We went to her house for Thanksgiving."

"Cool. If we'd known each other, we could've met up."

It's such a weird thought, that a few months ago I didn't know Kai.

"That would've been fun," I say.

"Who else is in your family?"

"I'm the oldest of four. Two younger sisters and one younger brother."

"Three girls, yikes. That must've been stressful for your father."

"Stressful for my brother, maybe. It's not like my dad was worried about marrying us off. We're lucky we don't live in the *Pride and Prejudice* time period."

"*Pride and Prejudice*," Kai echoes. "That's one show I've never seen."

"To be honest, neither have I," I admit. "But I've heard a lot about it."

"Let me guess. You've read it?"

"I actually haven't. I've read other works of hers as an English major, but I've never picked up a Jane Austen book for fun."

"Here I thought for sure Jane Austen was your favorite author."

"And now you're stereotyping me."

"Dang it! I hate it when I do that."

I smile and gather up the trash.

"Anything else you want before we go to the movies?" Kai asks.

"No, I'm good."

He picks up the trash I've gathered, crumbling the paper into individual balls. "Watch this. I'm not just a soccer player."

I lean back in my seat as he takes a shot at the trashcan. He misses.

"That was a trial run," he says, holding up a hand, as if to wave away my argument. "Okay, for real this time." He takes the next one and tosses it. He misses again.

I start laughing.

"Blah," he says.

"Blah blah blah," I reply, with a tone that implies I was almost impressed, even though he missed his shot.

He shrugs one shoulder. "Blah blah."

Somehow I know he said, "Oh well." When he turns back to me and says, "Blah blah blah?", he's asking if I'm ready to go.

I pick up my purse. "Blah blah."

CHAPTER ONE HUNDRED TEN

Slow Burn

It's silly and immensely fun, but we get into his truck, and the only words we say are nonsense. He changes the song on the radio and then says, "Blah blah," which I understand as permission to commandeer his radio and find my own music. I change the station, look at him and say, "Blah blah?" He shrugs again and says, "Blah."

We drive to the peppy tune on the radio, but I'm barely hearing it. All I can think about is how happy and carefree I feel sitting next to him.

We both get out of the car at the theater. As we walk away from it, I notice he didn't lock it, and I say, "Blah blah?"

"Oh, blah," he says, and goes back to lock it.

Delight bubbles up in my chest. We understand each other, even when speaking nonsense.

We really do speak the same language.

We sit beside each other in the theater, and I think for sure he'll take this opportunity to hold my hand. But he doesn't. I flex my fingers on my leg, annoyed at the actors in the movie because they're ridiculous, the movie is ridiculous, and I don't know why we're watching it. We should be sitting together, laughing and talking. Maybe even touching. Maybe even more.

A shiver runs through me, tightening in my chest, and I know I'm wanting it. This feels different than the crush I had on Mitch at the beginning of the year. More intense. Like if we let this fire burn, we might not be able to control it.

I wonder if Kai feels the same way.

This is all for fun, I remind myself. *He's leaving.*

"Well, that was a dumb movie," Kai says when it finishes, and we head around the theater toward his car.

I have to laugh.

"Yes," I agree.

"Really bad acting," Kai continues. "And the plot was dumb. I wasn't engaged with the characters at all."

"I was thinking the same thing."

He unlocks the truck and starts it up, and the time flashes on the dash: 11:43. It's late.

"Did you want to go home or . . . are you okay going somewhere else?"

The question throws me, considering the hour, but I bob my head. "I'm game. We can do whatever you want."

"Great. I know just the place."

We pull out of the movie theater parking lot, and I'm along for the ride, curious where we'll end up. He drives to campus, then turns left before we get there and takes a road up to the canyon.

I know where we're going now.

He takes one of the narrow roads that leads to the hiking path high up on the mountain, but before we get to the trailhead, he pulls off into a small parking area.

I haven't been to the overlook since I came here with Layne last year. Most people come here to make out. Somehow, I don't think that's what we're doing.

He turns off the car, and we stare out over the valley, at the twinkling lights of campus beneath us.

"It's pretty," I say, but what I really want to ask is, "Why are we up here, Kai? Just to look at lights?"

The front seat of his truck is a bench seat. There's nothing but empty space between us. And yet, that space might as well be a black hole. I don't know how to bridge this gap, and I don't want to be the one to take the lead.

"Yeah, it's pretty," he says, then falls silent, and for the first time all evening, things feel awkward.

"You know," he says, breaking the silence, "your friendship is really important to me."

Uh-oh. Here it comes. I brace myself, staring at him in profile while he looks out the windshield. This is where he'll tell me I've misread him, and he's only interested in being my friend. If he says that, I'll laugh and pretend that's all I want too.

What else can I do? Throw open the car door and run crying down the mountain?

"Yeah, I feel that," I say.

"The thing is," he continues, "when I think about having a girlfriend, it's not even that I want a romantic relationship as much as I want a friendship. Someone I can talk to about anything, someone who's going to support me and be there for me, someone I can laugh with. I just want a best friend."

So far, he hasn't told me to back off.

"I agree. That's exactly what I want," I say.

"I worry sometimes maybe I'm expecting too much," Kai says, and he finally shifts in his seat to face me. "Maybe I'm being too idealistic. Maybe I'll never find someone who meets all of my expectations."

"I think it's important to be realistic in your expectations," I say. "You're not perfect, so you can't expect perfection."

"Of course, I know that."

"Awesome," I reply, "but remember our expectations are usually idealistic. We create people in our minds based on what we want, or maybe past experiences, but we're dealing with real people, not figments of our own creation. We have to allow for the unexpected deviations that an actual human being might bring to the table."

"Whoa," he says, holding up both hands and cracking a smile. "Are you still speaking English?"

I give a self-deprecating laugh. He doesn't know that I'm counseling myself. I'm giving myself a pep talk and self-soothing at the same time. "Keep your eye on the goal, and you'll find what you're looking for."

"Thanks for telling me that," he says, as serious as I've ever seen him, his eyes steady on me. "It's reassuring."

Voices come from outside, and we both look over to see a group of boys walking near the trailhead. One of them grins suggestively at Kai and makes a crude gesture with his hands. Kai nods, acknowledging the greeting but saying nothing. It's probably for the best not to engage with them, but I feel like I should cover myself up from the insinuation behind the gesture.

"Some guys are creeps," I mutter.

"Yeah, some are," Kai says. "I hope you don't spend a lot of time with the creepy ones."

"I make it a habit not to," I reply.

"You're one of the smarter people out there."

We drift into silence again, and he faces the windshield. I do too, staring at the pretty lights and bright stars. I wonder if I can find Cassiopeia...

The air has gotten cooler. I shiver and wish Kai would put his arm around me, but then I remember that moment with Mitch in Chris's car, when I was cold and Mitch put his arm around me.

The universe has no originality. It's the same thing over and over again with different faces, different boys playing the lead role.

The silence grows too long. I'm either going to fall asleep or ask him to take me home. So, I take a chance and ask, "Do you mind if I rest my head on your shoulder?"

Kai looks at me again, and even in the dim light, I can see he's regarding me curiously. "Of course I don't mind."

His tone of voice makes me feel stupid for asking, like I should've had the confidence to do so from the beginning, but he's done nothing to give me that confidence.

"Thanks," I say. I slide closer, but I feel all kinds of tension now. There's a tightness in my chest that makes me feel like I missed something somehow.

Kai shifts slightly, and my head rests on the soft spot of his shoulder as he moves his arm around me. "I'm going to assume you don't have a lot of experience with guys," he says. "When a guy likes a girl, he doesn't mind if she leans on him."

It takes me a full two seconds to finish processing and analyzing every word he said.

When a guy likes a girl = he likes me?

He doesn't mind if she puts her head on his shoulder = he likes me?

You don't have a lot of experience with guys = I'm trying really hard not to laugh?

I give myself a moment to settle into the emotional implications of his statement and then say, "There was a guy over the summer that I really liked, and I thought he liked me too. So, I was comfortable with him, hanging on him, touching him. And then he sat me down and explained that he didn't have any feelings for me, and I needed to back off."

It's kind of a simplified summary of my relationship with Mitch, but it should explain my hesitation.

I feel the shift as Kai looks at me. "That happened to you?"

I sit up enough so that I can meet his eyes. "Yup."

"Sorry," he says, and he pulls me into his arms again, this time without the awkwardness. It's comfortable and warm, and a feeling of delight unfolds in my chest as he embraces me, holding me against him.

"How could anyone not like you?" he murmurs.

It's such a beautiful statement that I want to laugh, and I want to kiss him.

I refrain from both. "It happens," I say.

I don't mind staring at the lights in the valley beneath us, with his arm around me and his fingers making tiny circles on my skin. I give a soft sigh of contentment, and my frustrations with him slowly melt away.

This was worth waiting for.

"I think our friendship is developing nicely," I say, and that prompts him to laugh.

"Yeah," he says, and his finger pauses for a moment before he wraps his hand around my arm, pulling me in closer. "I like the direction it's going."

It's a nice feeling. I want to hold onto it.

"If something became of you and me," he says, "and you ended things for any reason, I'd still want to stay friends. That's the part that lasts."

Goosebumps ripple across my skin at his words. *If something became of you and me.*

CHAPTER ONE HUNDRED ELEVEN

If

I don't call him out on the "if." Not today.

It's a lovely sentiment—naïve and idealistic, spoken by someone who's never had their heart broken.

I force myself to keep my head still, resting on his shoulder, eyes fixed on the windshield, even though I want nothing more than to turn my chin and find his mouth with mine.

But I won't push this relationship. It needs to move slowly. Because he's going to leave me, just like everyone else has.

And I know how that story ends.

The thought sends a fresh wave of pain through my chest, and I can't push it away. So I stay silent, hoping he doesn't pick up on the change in my mood. I close my eyes and rest my head on his shoulder, breathing deeply.

Kai shifts beneath me, and I blink my eyes open, fighting the stickiness of my contact lenses. "Oh," I murmur. "I was falling asleep."

"Yeah," he says with a quiet laugh. "Let's get you home."

I sit up, and he moves his arm from around me to grip the steering wheel. I try to stay awake on the short drive to my apartment, but my eyes keep drifting shut, my head bobbing.

"Almost there," he says, amusement lacing his voice. I glance over and catch him sneaking a look at me, a smile playing on his lips.

He pulls into the lot behind my apartment and parks. "Let me walk you in," he says.

I glance at the time. "It's after three in the morning. No one's going to be out here kidnapping me."

"It's after three in the morning," he repeats. "It'd be irresponsible of me *not* to make sure you get inside safely. My mom would insist."

"Well, I'm certainly not going to argue with your mom," I say.

"Me either."

We get out of the car and walk side by side, hands in our pockets, shoulders and elbows brushing. The closeness we shared in the car dissipates now that we're back in the real world. I want to reach for it, but I'm timid all over again.

He stands behind me while I unlock my door. I turn to face him as I push it open.

"Thanks for taking me out. It was . . . tons of fun."

"Thanks for agreeing."

I hesitate, then ask, "Do you want a hug?"

I feel ridiculous for asking, but Kai's the one who's keeping this distance between us. I'm trying to respect his boundaries.

Kai gives a small laugh. "Remember what I said earlier?" he asks, then adds, "Sure."

I step into the space between us and wrap my arms around his chest.

His arms go loosely around my back, hesitating like he's not sure what to do or like I'm a sister in need of comfort.

But then they tighten around me, pulling me close. He holds me like that, and I breathe in deep because his cologne is warm and woodsy and delicious.

"This is nice," he says.

"It's very *friendly*," I say, and we both laugh, and I feel closer to him than I ever have. Not just physically.

I pull back before I get carried away. Best not to scare him.

"Good night."

"Good night," he says.

I step into my dark and quiet apartment, locking the door before tiptoeing to my room. I hope Layne's left the bedroom light on for me like I do for her when she's out late.

This dance with Kai—coming close only to pull back, watching him lead, following carefully—feels familiar. I know my steps, even though I've never danced this particular choreography before.

And then I realize: I *have*. Only I was the one leading.

It's the same dance I did with Jared—keeping him at a distance while he watched and carefully made sure not to cross any boundaries, because he knew I'd bolt like a spooked deer if he got too close.

And now Kai is doing the same.

For the first time, I understand how frustrated Jared must have been all the time.

⚬⟞⟝⚬

Kai doesn't come to see me at work on Monday.

I'm already flustered because the morning didn't go well. I have two tests today, and my plan was to knock out the Portuguese exam before classes and take my Humanities test tonight after work. But when I got to the testing center this morning, they didn't open until ten a.m. Ten! Doesn't everyone have classes by then?

Now I'm on my way back to the testing center after work to take both tests back-to-back. I'm starving, frustrated, and a little sad.

I have that feeling in my gut—the one that tells me I need to back off. That I should get uninvolved before this gets harder.

But all of my thoughts revolve around Kai, and every part of me wants to see him. I don't know how to stop that.

The Humanities test goes all right, but the verbs on my Portuguese exam kill me. I sweat bullets over the paper and I'm reminded, once again, that I don't speak this language fluently.

I sure hope that changes after living there.

It's a little after seven when I leave the testing center. Two tests done in a row. My spirits are low.

I want something to lift them.

I want to see Kai. I want to laugh with him and bask in his friendship—and the kind things he says about me. But I hesitate. He hasn't called in two days.

Stop being such a fool, I tell myself. *He's your friend. If he wants to hang out, he will, and if he doesn't want to, it's no big deal.*

Feeling a little more assured, I give into what I want and dial his number.

"Hey," he says, answering on the first ring.

"Hey," I say back.

So profound.

"What's up?" he asks.

I don't have any subtlety left in me. "Just finished taking a couple of tests. I was checking to see if you wanted to get together and study before I head home?"

There's a pause. Then he says, "Yeah. Meet you at the business building?"

"Usual place?"

"Be there in ten."

I hang up—and suddenly, I'm smiling. Floating. Skipping as I exit the testing center. I try not to break into song as I walk toward the business building.

Kai's already there, standing under the stairwell, scrolling on his phone with one hand, the other resting casually in his pocket. He's wearing those khaki pants and a sweater that fits just right—casual and sexy all at once. He looks up when he sees me, his dark eyes landing on mine, and he gives one of those smiles that only shows in his eyes.

"Have you been waiting for me?" I ask.

"Not really. I found another place to study," he says. "Come on, I'll show you."

I follow, not about to argue.

He leads me to the elevator and presses the button for the sixth floor—two flights up. We stand there in silence, not touching, for the two minutes it takes to rise. I thought we crossed that barrier.

We exit the elevator and walk down a quiet hallway. This part of the building feels more like a corporate office than a college campus. Kai turns a corner and leads me into a foyer with two couches, an end table, and a potted plant.

"Wow," I say.

"Unexpected, right?" He grins.

"Very." I sit down on one of the couches. He settles next to me.

We're sitting close. That's a good start.

I open my backpack and pull out my homework. He does the same. But I haven't even grabbed a pen before he asks, "How was your Sunday?"

I look over to see him watching me.

I shrug. "It was fine. Nothing exciting. Unless you count painting my nails." I flutter the red fingertips at him. "Abby said my cuticles were cringy."

"Let me see." He takes my hand, and I hold it steady as he studies the color. His touch sends little sparks of hypersensitivity along my nerve endings.

"She may have exaggerated the problem," he says.

He doesn't release my hand. Instead, he takes each individual finger, bringing them close to his face.

"I'm not noticing any deficiencies."

I'm in on this game. I turn my hand around and take his, turning his wrist so I can examine his cuticles.

"I'm afraid Abby would have the same complaints about your fingers," I say. "You should steer clear."

"Or maybe we should have a nail-painting day at your place."

I laugh. "I suppose we could."

"What color are you thinking?"

"I think you'd look great in pink." I continue turning his hand in mine.

"Not pink. Maybe purple."

I can't picture Kai with painted nails, and I smirk. "Now I won't be able to rest until this happens."

"Tell me when. I'll put it on my calendar."

I can't tell if he's serious. I don't know if *I'm* serious. But somehow, we're playing with each other's fingers, and then we're holding hands. And even after we turn back to our books and pretend to study—after we let go—he keeps one hand resting lightly on my thigh.

Maybe we'll graduate to full-on handholding before he leaves next month.

EPISODE 6 :

Taking Flight

CHAPTER ONE HUNDRED TWELVE

Same Song

Kai doesn't come into the office on Tuesday, and I don't call him. As much as I love spending time with him, I get significantly less homework done when we're together. And tomorrow, I've got a Portuguese presentation I need to nail. I curse myself for once again biting off more than I can chew with the language class.

I spend the evening putting together slides, and then I head to the Portuguese lab so they can double-check the grammar on my presentation. They correct so many things I feel like an idiot for even trying to take this class. Why was I so prideful I thought I could skip Portuguese 301?

But I have to get through a few more days before I head home for Harper's wedding.

I'm super nervous Wednesday morning as I set up my Portuguese presentation before class. No one in here knows I don't actually speak Portuguese, and this class would be so much easier if I did. I pull out my drive with the presentation and plug it into the projector.

"*Pronta?*" Vanessa, my Portuguese instructor, asks.

I nod, and she dims the lights. Total darkness. I wait a moment for the first image of my slide to show up, but nothing happens. Shouldn't something be showing on the wall?

My heart thumps faster, and my stomach does somersaults. It's not working. Why isn't it working?

Vanessa flips the lights back on and joins me at the desk, fiddling with the projector.

"*Não está funcionando,*" I stammer—one of the only phrases I can say with confidence.

She unplugs the projector and plugs it back in. Still nothing. No light, no hum. She makes a sound in her throat, somewhere between frustration and disappointment.

"I'm sorry," she says in English—probably because I look too flustered to understand anything else. "Can you give your presentation without the projector?"

"No..." What about my pictures? My stories?

I printed them. I can still do this. "I mean, yes. I can." My fingers shake as I pull out the folder with my printed pictures. The slideshow made everything easier. But I can do it this way.

She leaves the lights on and takes a seat in the back. I turn to my classmates, paste on a bright smile, and recite my Portuguese speech.

"Unlike most of you, I have not lived in Brazil," I say, sticking to my memorized Portuguese. "But I did spend one month in Recife, and I want to tell you about this beautiful city."

I'm careful with every word, because if I lose my place, I'm not sure I'll be able to find my script again. The pictures help. I hold up each one and tell a story around it, watching their faces for reactions. When I get to the story about blowing farofa all over the table, their polite expressions break into laughter—exactly what I'd hoped for.

Everyone claps when I finish, and my heart rate starts to level out as the adrenaline drains from my system.

"Why did you go to Brazil?" my professor asks, this time sticking to Portuguese.

The question is not unexpected, and I've got a response ready. "My family had an exchange student from Brazil, so I went to visit."

"That's nice. What a great introduction to the country. You must've been very close to her."

I could just nod in agreement, let the assumption hang there. But I can't. My face flushes as I say, "Him. And yes, I was."

She arches an eyebrow, but I don't wait for her to ask. I gather my things and slip back to my seat, trying to decompress while the next student takes the front—also without the projector.

⟲⟳✴︎⟲⟳

It's Professor Stephen's open office hours, and I'm relieved when the door to my reception area opens and Kai walks in while I'm working. I'm in the middle of the glorifying task of un-stapling test packets so I can re-staple them a different way. Glamorous, I know.

I look up, and I can't help the smile that spreads across my face.

"I missed you yesterday," I say. And as the words leave my mouth, I realize something: I'm feeling more confident, more secure in our relationship. I'm willing to be vulnerable with him. I'm trusting him with my feelings.

"You didn't even call me," he says, and the way he says it fills me with delight. It makes me want to laugh. I picture him in his dorm room, sitting there all evening with his phone in his lap, waiting for me to call. I raise an eyebrow.

"You have my number," I point out.

"Yeah, I know, but..."

And I *do* know. He might not even realize it, but he's determined not to chase me. Because chasing me would mean admitting he wants something serious—and he's getting ready to leave, so that's not the impression he wants to give.

But I also know he *does* want something serious. He just doesn't know how to let it happen.

Quite the Catch-22. And I get it.

"I had a big presentation to work on last night," I say. "I was afraid I wouldn't get it done if I spent the evening hanging out with you."

"Your fears are legitimate. I know my good looks and charming personality would be too much of a distraction for you."

He's not wrong. But the way he says it makes me laugh.

"Maybe we shouldn't see each other anymore," I say.

Kai squints at me. "Are you trying to break off our friendship? Because I already told you I wasn't gonna let that happen."

I finish with the stapler and tap the pile of packets against the counter. "I'm counting on it."

We share a smile, and that familiar warmth rises in my chest again.

We're more than friends, and we both know it—even if we're pretending otherwise.

"Here to see Professor Stephens?" I ask.

"If I need an official reason, then yes."

"Go on in. It's office hours."

"Thanks." His fingers tap a soft double-tap on my counter. He pauses before turning away, his body already angled toward the hallway. "Want to go out tonight?"

It's a Wednesday. I'm exhausted. I'm behind on all my homework.

"Yes," I say without hesitation.

"Great. I'll figure something out and call you later."

He comes back through the lobby ten minutes later and gives a wave before leaving.

Professor Stephens appears in the doorway, an amused expression on his face.

"That young man is taken with you," he says.

I suck in a breath. "I really like him," I admit, tiny fingers of ice stinging my cheeks just from saying the words out loud.

"I can tell. I think the feeling's mutual."

"I don't know how it happened. I tried so hard not to. He's just a kid, getting ready to leave, and I'm not going to see him for years." I bury my face in my hands. "This was a foolish thing I've done."

"Be patient with him. His head's in a different place right now, knowing he's leaving."

I lift my face. "I already know this song. He's not the first one I've said goodbye to."

Professor Stephens gives me a sympathetic smile. "Life still has surprises in store for you."

"I know."

But I don't want to do this again. Am I doomed to always be the girl who falls for someone just in time for them to walk out of her life?

Professor Stephens heads back down the hallway, but he calls over his shoulder before he disappears, "Engineers make a lot of money, you know."

I laugh. I laugh for a good twenty minutes.

⁂

Kai calls me the moment I finish work.

"Are you still on campus?" he asks.

"I just clocked out," I say, stepping out of the office. "Just getting off work."

"Oh, good. There's a movie showing on campus tonight, and I thought it would be fun to go. But I didn't want to make you walk back—I was hoping to catch you before you left."

"You did." I walk down the hallway toward the foyer and entryway of the building.

"Awesome. So, do you want to get something to eat and then go to the movie?"

"Sure. What are you thinking? Want to do Taco Bell again?" I'm only half-teasing. There's one on campus, and I enjoy their food—and his company.

"Tonight, I was thinking we live on the wild side. How do you feel about wings?"

"Wings?" I echo. "There's a place on campus that sells wings?"

"No, but there's a place nearby that does—if you're willing to walk a little."

"I think I can handle that."

Wings wouldn't have been my first choice for a date. I give up after three, then carefully clean my hands and use the wipes to try to remove the lingering garlic chicken smell. It seems embedded in every crevice of my skin.

"You have a busy week?" he asks.

"Lots of school, as always. I didn't realize that coming to college meant doing *more* schoolwork."

He laughs and polishes off the last wing. "I don't think any of us knew. I knew it would be harder, but I also thought it would be stuff I was good at."

I nod. "Instead, I'm discovering that I'm not good at anything."

He gives me this look like I've missed something obvious. "I hope you don't believe that. Everything about you is amazing."

I pleat a napkin on the table. "I'm afraid the people paying for my scholarship might not agree."

"I'm not worried about you. I don't think it's possible for you not to succeed."

His praise flatters me—but it also makes me uncomfortable. I look away from his probing gaze.

"What are you doing Saturday?" he asks.

Saturday. I think about it for a moment, just as Kai keeps talking.

"Some kids from the dorm are going to hike the mountain behind the canyon. Apparently, there's a hot spring on the trail. Do you want to go?"

"Yes," I say immediately, because the idea of being in a swimsuit in a hot spring on a mountain with Kai sounds delightful. "But I can't. I'm going out of town."

"Oh." He leans back in his seat and frowns. "Hot springs don't sound as fun anymore."

"You should still go," I urge. "Have fun with your friends."

"Maybe I will. Where are you headed?"

"Arkansas. My best friend's getting married."

"No way! Do you like the guy?"

"Funny you should ask. I'm not sure what to think of him. I've only met him once, but I'm sure she's a better judge than I am."

"Maybe. Sometimes our friends see things we don't. When do you leave?"

I check my watch as if it'll tell me. "Tomorrow, actually. That's why I was so stressed with schoolwork yesterday and today—trying to get everything done."

"Do you need a ride to the airport?"

I lift a shoulder, heart fluttering at his offer. "I was just going to park my car, but sure —I'll take a ride."

"Great. I'll take you and pick you up when you get back."

I wave him off. "I come back Monday, in the middle of classes. I'll take the shuttle.

No reason for you to skip class to get me."

"I'll be awfully disappointed if I show up at the airport when I'm supposed to be in engineering class and you took the shuttle home."

I laugh. "We can talk about it."

We finish our food and stroll back to campus together. We don't touch, both of us with our hands in our pockets, but as we walk side by side, our arms brush now and then. It feels natural. Comfortable.

Kai leads the way to the international cinema, and I raise my eyebrows when I see what movie is playing.

"*The Letter*? I love this movie."

"You've seen it? Should we go somewhere else?"

I shake my head. "It might be my favorite movie. I saw it freshman year. I bawled my eyes out."

"Great. So, you're telling me I'm going to cry?"

"Only if you're the sensitive type."

"Do you like the sensitive type?"

I smile and poke his ribs. "Maybe."

He smiles back but doesn't react to my touch.

We sit next to each other in the theater. The movie begins just as I remember it—a Korean school teacher, a chance encounter on a bus, and the marriage of two strangers. The first half is them getting to know each other, fighting, bickering, slowly falling in love. I don't overanalyze. I just *feel* it.

By the time she realizes she loves him, he's sick. Dying. His death derails her, and I don't even try to hide my sobs as she falls into a mind-numbing depression.

Kai glances at me, then puts an arm around my shoulder and pulls me close.

I cry again when she finds out she's pregnant, but those tears are joyful—hopeful. A new reason to get up every day.

The story is beautiful. I remember watching it with Abby. The two of us bawled and hugged and cried some more. I have my tears mostly under control when the lights come on and we stand up.

Kai brushes a hand over my cheek. "Did you cry as much the first time?"

"I'm not crying."

"You can't hide it."

I make a face. "You didn't cry at all. You're heartless."

"There was a tear. Right here." He points to the corner of his eye. "I had to work really hard to hold it back."

I laugh, and it comes out a little garbled because I'm still sniffling.

He laughs too, and then he wraps his arms around my waist and pulls me close.

My heart immediately starts racing like I'm running a marathon. I rest my head against his collarbone. There's only a few inches of height between us, and I very much want to tilt my head up and kiss him.

I want it so badly I can *feel* the press of his lips against mine, the way his grip around my waist would tighten, the slow give-and-take of our mouths as they open against each other.

I'm so physically aware of him that every nerve in my body is pulled tight—ready to snap.

But we do nothing.

And then he steps away, and my heart plummets. The warmth drains from my limbs, leaving me cold. I lower my eyes so he won't see the mix of want and disappointment in them.

He clears his throat. "I guess it's time to get you home."

"Yeah. It's about that time."

We walk out together, and I wish he would take my hand. I wish he'd prolong the moment. But he doesn't. He won't. Maybe he's already uncomfortable with how close we've gotten.

I want it to grow.

But he's pulling away.

CHAPTER ONE HUNDRED THIRTEEN

Desire

Kai takes me home after the movie. It's after ten, but I'm not quite ready to say goodbye when we reach my front door.

"Want to come in for a little bit?" I ask outside my apartment.

"Sure," he says, so readily that I know he didn't want to say goodbye yet either.

"Grab your backpack," I tell him. "We can study a little."

"It *is* a Wednesday," he says with a smirk, and turns around to go back down the stairs.

I head into the apartment and find Iris and Camila hanging out in the living room. As rarely as I see Layne, sometimes I think she doesn't actually live here.

"Hi, guys," I greet them. They parrot my greeting back at me, and I drop my backpack on the couch and go to the kitchen for a snack. A moment later, Kai knocks on the door.

"Come in," I call, and he joins me in the kitchen, perusing the cupboards. "Are you hungry?"

"I consumed about five chickens' worth of wings earlier," he says. "But if you have anything to drink, I'll take it."

I pull down two glasses. "I can do that. Your options are water or milk. Which do you prefer?"

"Water sounds awesome," he says.

I turn on the tap and pour us both lukewarm, unflavored, uncarbonated water. Then I grab the ice tray from the freezer so it's at least cold. He stands directly behind me the entire time—so close I can feel the warmth of his body.

When I spin around, I nearly collide with his chest. A nervous giggle escapes me.

"Water," I say, offering him the glass.

"Thanks." He takes it from me, his eyes never leaving my face. I can't tear mine away from his either, and my breath catches.

Iris laughs in the living room, and I quickly turn my head away. Here we are, having a moment in my kitchen, with my roommates just ten feet away on the couch.

"Want to sit here or in the living room?" I ask.

"Here is good. The living room looks occupied."

"It does," I say, and I'm more than a little disappointed. I'd rather be on the couch with him, studying—or more likely, cuddling.

Instead, we pull out chairs at the small kitchen table and spread out our textbooks. And for once, we actually study. The only sounds are the quiet rustle of pages turning and the scratch of my pen against paper. Iris goes to bed. Camila turns off the TV and starts reading a book.

Kai props his head up with his hand and closes his eyes. I look down at my paper, but when I glance back up, his head is on the table.

I reach over and poke his shoulder with my pen. "Kai."

He startles awake, lifting his head and blinking.

"You okay?" I ask, laughing a little. "I think you fell asleep."

"I'm good." He takes a sip of water and hides a yawn behind his hand. "No, I'm good."

I check the time. It's after eleven. "You can go home if you're tired."

"No, I have to get through this assignment." He pulls out some graphing paper, resets his textbook, and gets back to work.

Camila stands up. "I'm headed to bed. See you guys later."

"Night," I say.

I glance at Kai, but his eyes are focused on the graph he's drawing. I'm starting to get sleepy too. I stand up and poke around the cupboards, looking for chocolate or something sugary. Nothing.

When I turn back, Kai's head is bobbing again.

"Kai," I say, chuckling.

"Hm? Oh. Yeah. I'm good."

"Maybe I should be looking for caffeine instead of sugar," I tease.

"But then I wouldn't sleep tonight."

"Couch's open now."

Kai glances at it and says, "That looks more comfortable."

We gather our things and move to the sofa. He sits in the corner, and I fall in next to him. We rest our homework in our laps, but it doesn't take long before he sets his book aside and drapes his arm around my shoulder.

I pretend not to notice, even though I'm secretly relishing the touch. I snuggle into him but keep jotting down answers.

Kai presses his face into my hair, then leans back against the armrest. After a moment, his hand slips down to rest in the crook of my elbow, sandwiched between me and the couch.

I glance over and, unsurprisingly, he's asleep. Poor guy must be exhausted.

I let him rest while I finish outlining my essay. Then I lean over, putting my head lightly against his chest, and whisper, "Kai."

His eyelids twitch, but he doesn't move.

I feel bad waking him. Maybe I should let him sleep here. But then he'll have to go straight to school without changing his clothes or anything. Not to mention, the couch isn't that comfortable. And I *know* there's a rule about boys not sleeping over.

Still... I'd be willing to break it.

I sit up and gently tug on his arm. "Kai."

His head jerks up, eyes bloodshot as he blinks rapidly, trying to focus.

"It's almost midnight. You should go home."

"Yup." He stands, and I stand with him, helping him gather his things.

"Will you be all right driving?" I ask.

"Yeah, I'll be fine. It's only a five-minute drive." He shrugs on his backpack, then pulls me into a hug, wrapping his arms around my shoulders and pressing his face to my hairline.

My heart flutters. It feels like we've finally—*finally*—crossed that invisible line from awkward uncertainty to... something real.

He releases me and steps back.

"I'll meet you here before noon to take you to the airport?" he says.

I nod. "Thanks. See you then."

"Good night." He gives a little wave and heads out the door.

"Night," I call after him.

I watch him descend the stairs, my whole body aching with the desire to hold him close, to kiss him, to feel that physical connection.

This might be all we get.

And I need to be satisfied with it.

☙ ⁂ ❧

Kai is at my house promptly at eleven A.M. the next morning. I'm still submitting homework assignments, standing at the table with my laptop open, trying to make sure I won't be behind when I get back.

"Come in," I call when I hear the knock at the door.

He opens it and stands in the doorway. "You should at least verify who I am."

"I knew it was you." I close my laptop and shove it into my backpack. That, and a small carry-on, are all I'm taking.

"But you can't be too sure," he says. "You don't actually know everyone around you."

I find his concern cute. I sling my backpack over one shoulder and roll my suitcase toward him, then grin up at him impishly, flirtatiously. "Kai, is that you?"

His pupils are large as he focuses on my face. His eyes drift to my mouth.

"It's me," he says, his tone slightly husky. One hand slides around my waist, pulling me in close.

Just when my heart begins to pound and my throat tightens in anticipation—he lets go. He grabs my carry-on.

"This is all you're taking?"

I'm absolutely captivated by him—and by the growing chemistry between us—but I force myself to look away as I step out and close the door behind me.

"Yep."

I step around him and start down the stairs, feeling his eyes on me. I can feel his internal struggle, the way he wants to be close to me but also feels like he's supposed to keep his distance.

I'm hoping I can tug him over to my side of that struggle. To hell with distance.

The tension between us eases as we walk out to the truck—his white truck. My eyes catch on the blue Adidas flower decal in the back window.

One more month, and he'll be gone. We'll separate.

That's how every relationship goes, until someday, maybe, you get married—which isn't happening anytime soon for me. So I give myself permission to settle into relationships and enjoy them for as long as they last... even if they break my heart at the end.

Owen crushed me when he broke it off. It took me months to recover. But now that I have, I'd go through that pain again just to experience the joy and closeness we had.

I try to keep that same perspective with Kai.

"You excited for the wedding?" Kai asks as we pull away from my apartment and head toward the highway.

"I think so."

"Pretty close with her?"

"Yeah. She's been my best friend since I was fifteen. We've been through a lot together."

"That's cool. I don't really have a best friend from high school. We kind of went different directions last year."

"We almost did, too, senior year," I say. "I wanted more of her time and got jealous of how much she spent with her boyfriend."

"You don't seem like the jealous type."

"I don't know if 'jealous' is the right word. Maybe more like... needy? I just wanted her time. I like to feel important to people."

"So if someone doesn't make time for you, you feel like you don't matter?"

"Exactly."

"Well... I'll try to always make time for you."

I laugh, even as a voice in my head says: for the next thirty days, anyway. "Thank you. I appreciate that."

We fall into a comfortable silence while he navigates traffic. I check my phone—everything looks good for my flight.

"What's the first thing you're gonna do when you get home?" he asks.

"Well, my other best friend got married last year and had a baby over the summer. We're supposed to meet up at the airport right after I land."

"A baby? Sheesh. You're not that much older than me."

"It definitely wasn't planned. She got pregnant and had to get married."

"She happy?"

"That's the golden question," I say. "She wasn't, last time I saw her. I'm hoping her relationship's improved."

"Ouch."

"Your birthday's next week, right?"

Kai glances at me, chewing on his lower lip. "How do you know that?"

"You told me."

"And you remembered?"

I lift a shoulder. "It's an important date."

"Yeah. I'll be nineteen."

"Catching up to me," I tease.

"You don't act older than me."

That makes me laugh. "How exactly am I supposed to act?"

He shrugs. "I don't know. More mature. Serious."

"Definitely not me," I agree. "Wanna do something for your birthday?"

"Yeah, for sure. I know this really great study spot."

We both laugh.

"I'm sure we can find something more exciting than studying to do," I say, and I can't help throwing a teasing note into my voice when I say it.

Kai glances at me, and I'm certain I see a blush rise on his olive-toned skin. "Uh, yeah," he says, suddenly fumbling with his words.

I laugh. He's just a kid, and I doubt he's as experienced in relationships as I am. But for some reason, I don't want to admit that to him. I like that he sees me as fresh and innocent.

He gets me to the airport an hour and a half before my flight. He helps with my carry-on, then hugs me beside his truck.

"Okay." He shoves his hands into his pockets and takes a step back. "Call me if you need anything."

"Yeah, because there's so much you can do for me from Colorado," I say.

"You never know. I have connections."

"In Arkansas?" I smirk. "Nobody has connections in Arkansas."

He surprises me by grabbing me again, placing both hands on my hips and tugging me closer. "I do now."

"Yeah, you do."

Delighted by his sudden affection, I drop my bag and wrap my arms around his neck. He presses his jaw and cheek against my temple. Just when I think he might kiss me, he lets go.

He's not going to do it.

I can't stop the small sigh that slips out that somehow he continues to resist my charm.

He picks up my bag and puts it on the curb. "Have a great flight. See you when you get home," he says.

"Bye."

I turn and walk into the airport without looking back, not wanting him to see the disappointment and frustration I'm feeling.

I'm not checking any luggage, so security goes quickly. I get to my gate and settle in, bags at my feet, to wait out the next hour.

A notification buzzes on my phone. I glance down at it, then click it open.

It's an email from my airline. My flight has been rescheduled.

"What?" I murmur. "How can they reschedule a flight that's leaving in an hour?"

I look up at the gate counter, and my heart sinks when I see the new departure time: four P.M. I was supposed to leave at one.

Now I won't have time to see Riley before she goes to work. We were supposed to meet up when I landed.

I let out a long sigh and open my backpack.

Nothing to do for the next three hours... except work on my essay.

CHAPTER ONE HUNDRED FOURTEEN

Maids of Honor

My flight leaves right on time at four. The airlines rescheduled me but left me a very small window to catch my next flight, and I have to run to the gate in Dallas. There's nobody in line when I arrive, and I assume the flight must be gone. But as I come huffing up to the counter, the young man behind it says, "Are you Cassandra?"

I nod. "Yes. Is that my plane?"

"We saw your flight just landed, so we held it for you."

"Really?" I blink. "Nobody does that!"

"And here." He picks up a piece of paper from his side of the counter. "Your dad left this note for you. He wasn't sure you'd make the flight."

"My dad?" I take the note and hurry down the walkway to the plane, reading it as I go.

Hey sweetie,

I thought I'd surprise you by being on your plane when you got here, but it looks like you're going to miss your flight. See you in Arkansas!

It would've been a fun surprise, seeing my dad on the plane. I board quickly and stow my carry-on in the first available overhead bin before continuing to my assigned seat.

I'm shocked when I see my dad sitting there.

"What are you doing here?" I ask.

He looks up at me and smiles. "When I saw you got rebooked on the next flight to Arkansas, I decided to skip mine and try to get on yours. They even gave me the seat next to you."

I drop into the seat beside him. I'm almost done with my English essay, but I'm not the least bit tempted to pull out my laptop. I already spent the last two hours working on it. "That's awesome!"

I'm chatty after hours of being by myself in an airport. We talk about school, Harper, the wedding—and I even tell him a little about Kai.

"Is it serious?" my dad asks.

I shrug. "How can it be? He's about to leave, and I'm only twenty. This isn't the time to settle down. I'm just enjoying myself. Having fun."

I only half believe my own words, but my dad nods like I've spoken a profound truth. "That's right," he says.

It's not a horribly long flight, but I'm three hours behind schedule by the time we land. My dad's car is parked at the airport, and I text my friends while he drives. Riley's sad we won't be able to meet up tonight, but we'll see each other at the wedding. I message Harper next.

Me: Just landed! Anything planned tonight?

She doesn't respond right away, so I call Kai.

"Cassandra?" he says when he picks up, like he's not sure it's really me.

"It's me," I reply with a laugh. "No one stole my phone."

"Are you sure? What's the password?"

There's no password between us, but I play along. "Wings."

He exhales. "It really is you."

I laugh again. "Yup. I made it to Arkansas."

"I thought I'd hear from you hours ago. Been busy?"

"Busy catching airplanes. I just landed."

"What? I dropped you off before noon!"

"They changed my flight. I didn't leave until four, and then I had to catch a different connection to Arkansas."

"Why didn't you call me? You just sat at the airport for three hours by yourself?"

"You would've been in class. And what were you going to do—sit on the phone with me for three hours?"

"Oh. Yeah, you're right. Still... I hate that that was your day."

I love that he worries about me. "It's fine. I made it."

"Yeah. Have fun with your best friend. Call me anytime."

"Thanks."

I hang up, pleased by the tone of the call—and even more pleased that he's not out with some other girl tonight.

A moment later, Harper finally responds:

Harper: I'm so glad you're here!! Tonight is busy, but we will get together tomorrow for sure! I have your bridesmaid's dress!

Yes, we *have* to get together tomorrow—because tomorrow's Friday, and the wedding is Saturday.

⌒〜✦〜⌒

I meet up with Harper Friday at the dress shop.

"I'm so glad you made it!" she says, throwing her arms around me in a tight hug. "Oh —here's your dress!"

The dressmaker comes from the back carrying something long and shimmery purple over her arms.

"Let's see how it looks. The dresses look wonderful on everyone, but I think purple will look best on you, with your dark skin tone." Harper brushes a hand over my shoulder like she can see my skin, even though I'm wearing a long-sleeve T-shirt.

My skin isn't dark right now. After four months of Colorado winter, it's more of a sickly yellow—at least that's how it seems to me.

"Are you excited?" I ask, shimmying out of my jeans and pulling my sweater over my head so I can put on the purple skirt and matching top.

"I can hardly believe it. I'm getting married tomorrow. It's surreal. Are you spending the night tonight?"

"Am I?" I ask as the seamstress starts pinning the waist of my skirt and making a few quick notes before telling me to take it off. I stand there in my underwear while she works on the alterations, but I know Harper too well to feel self-conscious.

"I want you to," she says. "We're having the rehearsal tonight, followed by the dinner. Things are going to be so busy—I'm not going to get another chance to sit and talk with you. So it has to be tonight, right?"

I nod, still not sure how she's holding it all together. I feel overwhelmed just listening.

"Tomorrow's the wedding. And then you're off on your honeymoon," I tease, shooting her a sideways glance. "You're finally going to lose your virginity?"

Her eyes dance, and she presses her hands over mine with a mischievous grin. "Finally."

We both giggle, and I lean toward her, soaking in this moment of friendship.

The seamstress returns and puts the altered skirt back on me.

"This is done. Now, the top—I'm not totally satisfied with this area," she says, pinching the loose fabric beneath my bust. "But I don't have time to fix it right now. Leave it with me, and I'll bring it to the wedding tomorrow."

I lift my eyebrows, a little startled. "So I won't try it on again until the wedding?"

"Right. It'll be fine. I'll have it ready," she assures me.

I glance over at Harper, who gives me a confident nod. "Right," I echo.

I change back into my clothes, and we leave the shop together.

"What are you doing right now?" I ask. "Want to get some lunch?"

Harper shakes her head and checks her watch. "I can't. I've got a meeting with the florist at one, then the bakery at two-thirty. The rehearsal's at four, and somewhere in there, I have to pick up the napkins for the reception."

That panicky, breathless feeling hits me—like I've been plunged into cold water. I'm anxious, and it's not even my wedding. "Do you need help? I've got my mom's van. I can pick something up for you."

"No, I've got this." She kisses my cheek. "I'm so glad you're here. I'll see you later."

She waves, and then she's gone—a whirlwind of energy. Of course she's nervous, but keeping busy with her endless to-do list is clearly helping her stay grounded.

I have nothing to do for a few hours, and when I glance down at my hands, I realize how terrible they look. Abby's attempts to rectify my cuticles fell short.

So I call Riley.

"Hey! What are you doing? Want to get manicures before the wedding?"

⌒⌒※⌒⌒

It takes some finagling because Riley has a child, and I don't feel like babysitting the nine-month-old while we get our nails done. But eventually, my mom agrees to watch her. So, almost two hours later, after picking up Riley and dropping the baby off at my house, we finally land at the salon. We pick up a few burritos, and then Riley tells me about motherhood, keeping me distracted while we get our nails painted.

"It's exhausting," she says. "I always knew I wanted to be a mom someday, but I didn't imagine it being now. I don't feel ready."

"Ready or not, here it is," I reply.

"Here it is," Riley agrees. "Don't get me wrong, I love my daughter. But I feel so alone all the time. Lucas and I—we're not compatible. We're not even friends. I'm doing all of this parenting with his mother. I definitely don't recommend trapping yourself the way I did."

Her words make me sad, and I feel the sincerity in my core.

"I'm so sorry it's not what you wanted."

"I didn't know what I wanted; that's part of the problem. And now I do, but it's too late, isn't it?"

Is it?

Her words stick with me as we sit in the salon.

At what point does it become too late to change your path? It feels like an important question. One I'm not sure I have an answer to.

After that we head to the wedding rehearsal. It's at a church I've been to many times before, but never for a wedding. I feel a flutter of excitement when we step into the chapel because I see so many friends from school. I hug Betsy and Janice, who has become Harper's closest friend in my absence. We stand close, reminiscing, laughing brightly.

A woman comes in and begins handing out orders, calling people by name. I assume she's the wedding planner. I've only ever seen one on TV.

"Be sure to check the order," she says. "The flower girls will go first, exiting out the back. The men are already at the stand..." She grabs Harper's fiancé and positions him at the front of the row. "Stand here, staring at the front, and do not turn around until we give you your cue. Understood?"

He nods, and I catch his profile. He's handsome, with the expression of someone who likes to laugh. That's an important quality. I didn't get warm fuzzies when we met, but he's not marrying me. As long as he treats her well, that's all that matters.

The wedding planner lines up the rest of the groomsmen, then turns to the bridesmaids.

"Go to the room in the back," she instructs.

We follow her down the aisle as she checks the order.

"Bridesmaids, there are six of you. Where are the maids of honor?"

Janice steps forward, and I hesitate until Harper elbows me, saying, "You're the other one."

I step forward too.

The wedding planner nods. She glances at a paper in her hand. "Janice, you follow Cassandra."

I'm second to last. Janice is last. My heart gives a little twinge. If there's a hierarchy, I'm not at the top, but that's fair. I don't live here, and I don't get to be part of Harper's every day life like Janice. I'm glad she wants me here at all. It's not like I've been a great best friend from afar. I love her, but I'm not there for her.

"The rest of you..." The wedding planner squints and points to Riley, Betsy, and Harper's two cousins. "That's your order. When the music starts, bridesmaid number one starts down the aisle. Ready? Go."

Betsy and Riley hold their bouquet of flowers carefully as they march down the aisle to the music. The wedding planner doesn't like their timing and stops them just as the third bridesmaid comes out.

"That's okay, that's okay, ladies," she says, clapping as she sends them back. "That's why we're practicing it."

The music starts again, and this time we make it to my turn. I hold fake flowers in my hand because we won't get the real bouquets until tomorrow. There are only a handful of people watching. I'm supposed to move with the beat, and I hope I'm doing it right. I join the other bridesmaids at the front and turn to watch as Janice makes her way down the aisle. Next, Harper's mom steps out, escorted by her fiance's father. Then, the music changes, and Harper steps out, her father by her side.

It's just a rehearsal, but I feel this tingly sensation inside, watching my beautiful friend come down the aisle, knowing that tomorrow it's the real thing.

She's getting married. Her life will no longer revolve around her friends. The friendship we have now will change.

It's a lot to swallow. Of my two best friends from high school, I'll be the only one not married.

I'm only twenty. I don't want to get married yet. But I'm envious—envious that they've found that person, their best friend, the one who will stand by their side and share everything with them for the rest of their lives.

Harper and Colton go over a summary of the vows they'll say tomorrow. She glows with excitement, a smile playing on her lips as she stares at him. He doesn't take his eyes off her face. I notice how his hand twitches, like he wants to touch her.

When the rehearsal ends, Harper claps her hands and announces, "Okay, let's head to the restaurant for the wedding dinner!"

We step down from the podium, all of us moving in Harper's direction. As she passes me, she catches my eye and smiles, but someone else intercepts her, wrapping her in a hug.

I head over to her parents instead, and her dad puts an arm over my shoulders.

"So great to have you here."

"I'm honored to be here," I say.

Colton has a hold of Harper's arm, and he pulls her closer as he whispers in her ear.

"I don't know if he's good enough for her," I say, my eyes on the two of them. Instantly my face grows hot that I spoke out loud. "But I'm glad she's happy," I amend.

Her dad laughs. "Oh, I feel the same way. But I doubt anyone would ever be good enough for my little girl."

Of course he gets it. I exhale, my shoulders relaxing. "That's probably it. No matter who she ends up with, I wouldn't approve."

And maybe it has to do with the fact that a part of me will always be a little jealous, just like I was all through high school—someone else has her attention now.

CHAPTER ONE HUNDRED FIFTEEN

Wedding Day

I spend most of the wedding dinner with Betsy and Riley. Harper is busy, surrounded by friends and family, with Janice next to her. I fight back the silly feeling of being left out and enjoy the fact that I'm sitting next to two of my high school friends.

It's almost 9 o'clock when the dinner ends. I'm tired, and the thought of going home crosses my mind, but maybe Harper senses it, because she turns to me before I can get out the door.

"You're coming over to spend the night, right?"

I can't deny her. "Of course. I'll see you at your house."

She gives me a broad smile and kisses my cheek, then she's off again, talking to someone else, and I leave for her house.

So many memories rush back when I park my car in the grass out front. I spent almost as much time here as I did at my own house in high school. I remember slumber parties in the living room, sleepovers in her bed, early mornings when I would come and see her. Prom, fights, crises, and makeup hugs in the living room.

I have the sudden urge to drive out to Owen's old house and see if it brings back the same feelings. I want to step in the front door with the spare key I still have and let the memories wash over me, as solidly as if I've stepped back in time.

I take a deep breath, hold it, then slowly release it. There's an ache of nostalgia in my throat. So many things I miss from that time.

The house is dark. I'm the only one here. I go to Harper's room and make myself comfortable.

What is Owen up to? I never wrote him back after the last letter, and he hasn't written me either. I've pretty much closed the door on that chapter of my life, but no one else fits in my memories here, and I miss him.

I brought my backpack just in case I got ambitious and decided to do homework, but now I decide to write Owen back. I pull out one of my notebooks. *Keep it friendly.*

Owen,

Hey! I'm back home in Arkansas, just for the weekend. Harper is getting married. It's so fun to be here, but I also feel this sadness that I'm losing my friend. She won't really be gone, but our relationship will change as her life revolves around her husband. I miss her already.

I'm surrounded by memories here, and so many of them include you. It makes me want to laugh and cry at the same time. I hope you're doing well. There's a sweetness in my heart whenever I think of you, which is often, even though I don't write. Tell me how Colorado is. You've been there for nine months now. Does it feel like home?

I wonder where home is for him. Not Arkansas, where he only lived for a year and a half. Louisiana, where he grew up and where he moved back to?

I don't like school any more than I did the last time we talked about it. I'm always stressed out and feel like I'm drowning trying to keep up with my classes. But I'm getting through them, with high enough grades to not lose my scholarship.

Did I tell you I'm going back to Brazil? I got an internship teaching English. You know I fell in love with that country and want to learn Portuguese. This will be a good taste of what it would be like to do a mission trip. When I get back, I'll decide if it's something I really want to do.

I hesitate now. I haven't told him one of the biggest pieces of my life, that I'm dating someone. Should I? The fact that he tried to set me up with other guys is a good indicator that we've moved past the time in our lives when seeing other people was taboo. Am I ready to bring it up in casual conversation?

Yes, I am. Because it still hurts me that he tried to set me up with other people as if I were a candy bar on the grocery store shelf. So I add:

I've been dating someone for about a month now. He makes me laugh. You know how important that is to me.

I pause, wondering if I'm crossing a line. I'll never forget what I wrote in Owen's Valentine's Day card.

I want to laugh with you every day for the rest of my life.

Maybe it's too much, but I won't erase it. I continue as if it's merely a continuation of that thought.

But it's all just for fun. I'm only twenty. I feel like you have so much more life experience than me, even though we're the same age. I want to have that life, too.

Anyway, miss you! Hope you're having a fabulous time working and serving with the people in Chicago!

Love,

Cassandra

I don't have any issues signing it with *Love*. The letter is so clearly platonic.

I close the notebook just as I hear the front door open, followed by Harper's voice calling out, "Hello!" Her parents voices murmur in the background.

"I'm here!" I call.

I step out of the room and run into Harper in the hallway, where she throws her arms around me and hugs me so hard we collapse into the wall. As she lets go, a big grin breaks across her face.

"It's tomorrow. Tomorrow! I'm getting married tomorrow!" She beams at me, her eyes sparkling, her face flushed as she breathes a little too fast.

"Yes, you are," I say, extracting my fingers from hers and patting her hand.

We just had a fairly extravagant dinner, but Harper wants to snack, so we end up in the kitchen, sitting on the counter, spooning marshmallow cream onto crackers. She wants to recount every moment of the day, critiquing everything from the way the bridesmaids walked to how the groomsmen shifted their weight while they waited.

"They better hold it together tomorrow! It's not like they have to wait that long!" she says.

"I'm sure it's just that they knew this was only the rehearsal," I say, mentally reminding myself to watch each step carefully when I walk down the aisle in the morning.

"I'm sure you're right." She smiles at herself. "Isn't my fiancé dreamy? Tomorrow, we'll be married!" She gives a sigh.

"Well, I certainly hope he's dreamy to you," I say, neatly sidestepping the question.

She doesn't let me avoid it. She leans forward on the counter, catching my eye. "But don't you think he's cute?"

"Yeah. He's cute," I say. There really is no other acceptable answer for me to give in a situation like that.

She nods in satisfaction and presses her back up against the counter. "What about you? Are you still seeing that high school kid?"

I laugh at that. "He's a freshman, not a high schooler. And yes, we're still seeing each other."

"Pictures?"

"I have a few." I'm doing better about taking pictures. College is going by fast, and I want to have a memory of it I can hold onto. I pull up a picture of me and Kai waiting to go to the dance. I didn't know him well then, and his smile looks shy and uncertain, something I didn't pick up on at the time.

"Oh, I see why you like him. He's a pretty boy. Latino." Harper winks at me.

"He is very nice to look at." I scroll through my photos and find another one, this time of us sitting at my kitchen table, taking selfies when we were supposed to be studying.

"You guys are super cute. Is he a good kisser?"

"We haven't kissed," I admit. "He's putting in his application for a mission trip right now, and he doesn't want to start anything."

"He probably shouldn't have asked you out, then."

I wince slightly. "I think that goes through his head every time we're together."

"So nothing's going to happen between you?"

"Whatever happens between us will be temporary. But I really like him."

"Like, not love?"

I shake my head. "I don't love him. But I really, really like him. I could see it becoming love if given the opportunity."

"Where does he rank on your scale of boys?"

There've only been a handful of boys who mattered in my life. I tick them off. "I don't love him like I loved Tiago, but I feel the possibility of more, someone I could be with long-term. Just for that, Kai ranks above Tiago. Jared was amazing, a super good friend, but it never became more than that. We could have had a relationship similar to this, but we didn't. So he also ranks above Jared."

I hesitate, but Harper doesn't let me deliberate. "And Owen?" she asks, not batting an eye.

I try to remove Owen from his pedestal in my heart, but he won't budge. "Owen is still at the top," I say. "I can only hope someday I'll love someone as much as I loved him."

She pats my thigh. "You will. Who knows? Maybe it will be this Kai."

⁓⁓⁕⁓⁓

Harper is out the door early in the morning, despite how late we stayed up talking. I'm filled with so many nerves that one would think it was my own wedding. Her parents are gone, so I don't spend much time alone in her house once she's gone. I curl my shoulder-length hair and throw on some clothes. The seamstress will meet me at the chapel with my dress.

The activity of so many people bustling about overwhelms me when I arrive. Harper's dad is at the door, directing traffic, and he sends me upstairs to a dressing room. I find the other bridesmaids and Harper inside. The seamstress is busy with Harper, slipping her into the silver wedding gown and pinching and pulling fabric.

"Cassandra!" Riley calls me over. She and Betsy hug me when I reach them. Both of them are wearing their purple bridesmaids' dresses.

"Do you know where the other dresses are?" I glance at Harper and the seamstress, but they're occupied.

"Dresses?" Betsy leads me to a hanging rod and rifles through the plastic-covered clothing. "Cassandra. Here."

She removes a dress with my name pinned to the plastic, and she and Riley help me get it on. It fits like a glove thanks to the personal alterations the seamstress made, but it keeps riding up on my waist.

"Great," I grumble as I tug it down. "By the time I get down the aisle, I'll be wearing a crop top."

My friends giggle, but then Harper says, "Cassandra," and I quit fussing because it's not my day.

I hop over to her. She's wedged into the dress, and her mom stands behind her, pinning the veil into the immaculate updo of blond curls falling around her face and neck.

"I think I need more mascara," she says.

Black lashes frame her blue eyes, and black eyeliner sets them off against her fair skin. She doesn't need anything. But I see the anxiety behind her expression. I grab the wand and move in front of her.

"I got ya," I say, and she holds still while I carefully move the wand through her eyelashes. My mind flashes back to hundreds of mornings in her bathroom before school or in the hall between classes, fixing each other's hair or lip gloss or trying on each other's concealer and laughing at the difference in our skin tone. A lump fills my throat, my eyes burn, and I swallow hard.

Those days are behind us.

I blink several times, forcing back the tears. I can't cry. It will set her off, and all the hard work we've done on this makeup will be for nothing.

Her mom finishes with the veil, and I step back to examine her. "You look fantastic,"

543

I say.

She exhales and fans her face. "I'm so hot. Am I flushed?"

Pink splotches dot her cheeks, and a sheen of sweat glistens on her neck. I grab a tissue and dab at her skin, then I lean in and blow, moving the tiny neck hairs with my breath.

The other girls see what I'm doing and gather around. We blow on her skin, trying to cool her off.

Harper laughs. "I have my own personal entourage!"

"Today you are the queen," her mom says, beaming at her. "They are your attendants."

Harper turns around, her gown rustling as she moves to a gift bag sitting in a chair. "I have something for each of you to wear." She reaches into the bag and pulls out several slender silver bracelets. "Thank you for being here with me today. It means more to me than you can know."

I accept my bracelet and fasten it on my wrist along with the other bridesmaids.

The wedding planner pops into the room. "Are we ready?" she asks.

We turn to Harper for our cue. She exhales and nods.

"Yes," she whispers.

I squeeze her hand.

She's really doing this.

We follow her down the stairs to the foyer behind the chapel. The planner hands us bouquets and whispers instructions as the music plays. Harper's mom and the groom's party have already gone down the aisle. The bridesmaids go next, with Riley followed by Betsy, then Harper's cousins, and finally me. I keep my eyes focused straight ahead, knowing my family is in the audience but not daring to look. I doubt Harper's watching, but I don't want to fumble this for her.

I take my place at the front with Harper's cousin and wait for Janice to come last. The ring-bearer and flower girl come next, and I bite my lower lip, knowing what's coming.

The music changes, the organ playing out the opening chords to a march, and the entire audience rises to their feet. A moment later, Harper appears on her father's arm. She smiles radiantly, beaming from ear to ear, her eyes glistening with unshed tears.

She doesn't see me. Her focus is on her fiancé, who stares back at her with unabashed excitement on his face, his smile as broad as hers.

All I can hope is they will be good for each other.

They go through the vows, and I see the quiver in her lips as he speaks to her. She can't hold it back when she says, "I do," and she cries when he kisses her.

She's not the only one.

They turn and face the congregation, and everyone cheers and claps, then Harper and Colton go back down the aisle, leading the way to the reception.

She did it. She's married.

I join the receiving line at the reception, but I want the chance to talk to Harper. She's mobbed with people for every minute of the next half hour before she and her fiancé—husband—break away. I chat with Betsy and Riley and Harper's parents until the newlyweds return in street clothes, and we follow them out to their car, throwing rice and wishing them goodwill. They get in the car, waving, smiling, and drive away for their honeymoon, and I feel this strange emptiness in my chest.

I never got to say goodbye.

CHAPTER ONE HUNDRED SIXTEEN

Crazy Paranoia

My mom drives me to the airport Sunday morning, and I set my expectations for the rest of school. I only have a month until my sophomore year of college is over.

I don't know what to expect from the next few weeks, but I know I hope Kai will be a big part of them.

I call him from Dallas to let him know I'm on my way home—and to see if maybe I can get a ride—but he doesn't answer. So I call Thomas instead, who was already my backup plan.

"I'll see you at the airport," he says.

As soon as the plane lands in Colorado, I check my messages, hoping there's something from Kai.

There's nothing.

I consider calling again, but he already knows I called. He knows I'm coming back today. If he wants to talk to me, he'll reach out.

I keep up a constant barrage of conversation with Thomas the whole way home so I'm not just staring at my phone, wondering about Kai. But as the day turns into evening and there's still no response, I feel more and more put out.

And I can't help this crazy paranoia—maybe all it took for Kai to forget about me was three days apart. Now he remembers his objectives for the next few months, and spending time with a girl isn't part of the plan.

If he never wants to talk to me again, he can make that happen.

I don't hear from Kai all day Sunday.

I try not to be frantic about it as I go to class on Monday. I already have a lot to worry about with school, since I got behind during the wedding. But no matter how hard I try to focus, there's this nagging fear lodged in the back of my throat. I feel nauseous and short of breath.

My hopes are high when I go to work, because I frequently see Kai there. But as the hours slip by, my hopes dwindle.

He's not coming to see me.

I'm moody and depressed when I clock out. Somewhere between taking me to the airport and now, Kai must've reevaluated our relationship and decided not to pursue it. Maybe the distance gave him what he needed—the strength to finally do what he's been trying to do this whole time.

But there's a lump in my throat and an ache in my chest, and I'm just... sad about it.

I have an overabundance of homework, but I lack the motivation to go to the library and do it. I want the comfort of my own home and my own bed. I head down the long hallway toward the stairs that lead out of the building.

My phone rings just as I step onto the sidewalk, and I pause to pull it from my pocket, hoping—

It is.

It's Kai.

My heart flutters in my chest, anticipation firing through my veins and chewing away my despondency. But I'm cautious. This doesn't mean anything.

"Hello?" I say, not taking another step.

"Hey," he says, his voice warm and friendly. "You just got off work, right?"

"Yes," I say. "I'm walking home."

"Oh. Where are you?"

I glance back at the building behind me. "Not far from campus."

"Want to study together? I can come get you."

I should draw this out, make him work harder to get me to come along. But I haven't seen him in days, and I want to be near him. "I can just walk back."

"You sure?"

"Yeah, it's fine. See you at the usual spot?"

"I'll be there in fifteen."

I turn back toward campus, an energetic skip in my step now. I want to fist pump the sky, but I contain myself. I hum as I walk, touching the emerging leaf buds on the trees, running my hands over the bark.

A brown leaf on the ground catches my eye. "You're out of place," I tell it. "Your season has passed." But something about its lonely defiance strikes me as beautiful. I bend to pick it up and study it the entire way to the business building—its veins, its pointed edges, its dry prickliness.

I'm still studying it when I step off the elevator in our little foyer. I look up and see Kai standing in front of me with his hands in his pockets, like he's about to get on.

"Hi," he says.

"Hi." My smile wants to break across my face, but I restrain it. I hold the leaf out to him. "I brought this for you."

He lifts an eyebrow and stares at it. "A leaf?"

"A dead leaf. None of them should be falling right now, but this one did."

"You brought me a dead leaf." Now he looks at me like I'm crazy.

I can't help but smile as I stroke the edges. "It's beautiful. So I brought it for you."

He finally reaches out and takes it, the corners of his mouth pushing upward. "Thanks, I guess."

I step around him to the couch and sit. "Did you have a good weekend?"

"Really great, actually. My parents came into town." He takes off his backpack and places it by the couch, setting the brown leaf on top.

"They did?" I turn to him, surprised. "Did you know they were coming?"

"No. My dad called me from the airport and said they were on their way."

He drops onto the couch beside me, bouncing slightly, and when he stops moving, he's leaning against me, our shoulders touching. He doesn't adjust his posture.

"So you didn't make it to the hot springs?" I say.

"I went on Saturday. It was so fun. We had to climb like twenty minutes to get there." He gestures as he talks, jostling me with every motion. "It was night, and the stars were out, and there were lots of people there."

"Your parents went too?" I picture a typical college hangout spot—elderly folk don't quite fit the image.

"No, just my sister and some friends from the dorm."

I reach over and pluck at his dark hair, trying to sound joking as I say, "Any cute girls?"

He pauses, tilting his head toward me so more of his hair falls between my fingers. "Some."

It's honest—and it makes me jealous. I want to yank my hand back and scoot to the other end of the couch. But I don't want him to know I feel that way, so I keep running my fingers through his hair like it doesn't matter. "Nice."

"Yeah, one of them invited me to go out tonight. We were going to get dinner, but I changed my mind."

Now I can't help it. My hand freezes, and my mind rifles through his words, sorting them, trying to make sense of what he just said. "So, like, you were going to go on a date?" In spite of my attempt to sound casual, my words come out stilted, and my body stiffens. I'm cognizant that it's not fair of me to feel this way. Just ten days ago I went on a date. But things have solidified between us since then.

At least, they have for me.

"Just, like, an outing between friends." He straightens and looks at me, and I quickly school my expression. If I make a big deal out of this, he'll know my feelings have gotten too strong, and he'll make a bigger effort at backing away.

Crap. When did my feelings get this strong?

"Friends like we are?" I ask. I'm terrible at keeping my voice steady. I drop my gaze.

"I think we're more than friends," he says, then puts an arm around my shoulder, pulling me close.

I push aside my insecurities and remind myself—this is a short-term relationship. Whatever it is, it's not meant to last.

His fingers drift down my arm, stroking the bare skin, then wander up to comb through my hair and back down again. "How was the wedding?" he asks.

I wonder if the reason he didn't call me was because he was at the hot springs with other hot girls, but I don't voice it. "It was beautiful. My best friend looked amazing. I can't believe she's married. It feels like we closed a chapter of our lives."

"Well, you did. But not in a bad way."

"Except only one of us has moved onto the next chapter," I murmur. "I'm still here, stuck in the book she already left behind."

He laughs. "Not for long."

I eye him. "What's that supposed to mean?"

He gives me an amused look. "I think you'll figure it out."

I know what he thinks. That some guy will sweep me off my feet and I'll be married before I even know what happened.

It annoys me. There are too many things I want to do with my life before I get married. I lift an eyebrow and dig into my backpack to retrieve my homework. "Not happening."

"You're against marriage?"

He's teasing. I open my English anthology and bat at his hand with my notebook. "No. But I'm very against it *right now.*"

"What are you waiting for?"

"I'm about to leave on an internship to Brazil. Then when I get back, I want to finish school, maybe do a mission trip. So we're talking four more years before I'm ready to get married."

"You want to do a mission trip? I thought your internship was one."

I shake my head. "No. There's so much life to live while I'm single. Things I can't do if I'm attached to another person."

"There's some truth to that. So is that why you don't do serious relationships?"

The question makes me laugh. "Who says I don't? I've done a terrible job avoiding relationships. I always tell myself not to get involved, but my heart is louder than my head, and suddenly I *am* involved." Like now.

"How many have you been in?"

I squirm and avoid his gaze. "That's on a need-to-know basis."

"Touché. And I haven't reached that stage yet?"

I give him a look. "You're still going on friendly outings with other girls."

He chuckles, and I smile and turn to my English book. His words left my brain stirring, but I force my thoughts to focus on my schoolwork. We fall into that peaceful space that comes when we're both concentrating. But my eyes grow heavy as I read essays from the nineteenth century. My head droops. I fight to stay awake, but it's no use. I slide into the corner of the couch and drift off.

I'm not sure how long I sleep—probably just a moment—but I wake when someone gently shakes my arm. I blink through blurry eyes and see Kai leaning toward me.

"I wrote you something," he says.

I sit up, blinking, trying to produce enough tears to unstick my contact lenses. "You did?"

"Let me read it to you." He clears his throat.

"Clinging to life on its tree, it held on through the cold rain and wind of autumn, defiant, like a victor as all the other leaves fell to the ground to be trampled or blown away.

Winter came, with heavy snow and freezing temperatures, but still the leaf clung to its branch.

The remaining leaves fell off, and when the snow melted and the sun came out, the leaf thought, I'm the victor. I've succeeded where no one else has. I alone have life.

But then the temperature began to rise and the tree stirred with life, and the leaf watched as new buds unfurled. Green spread. Flowers bloomed, popping out along the branches. The leaf trembled in anticipation.

Here it had survived the hard winter and was the only original leaf left on the tree. But as it basked in the glory of the sun shining on it, it noticed something strange.

People passing by didn't smile or sigh and marvel at its beauty. Instead, they ignored it, or sometimes even made comments about the ugly leaf clinging to the beautiful tree. And finally, the leaf realized: it didn't belong. It should have let go in the fall when the rest of his brothers fell off the tree.

So with a sigh, it released its grip and fell to the ground, preparing to be trampled underfoot and erased from existence.

But to its surprise, a girl walking by picked it up and held it in her hand. She laughed and marveled at the nearly extinguished life remaining in the leaf, and the leaf quivered with joy at the smile it brought to the beautiful girl's face.

And it finally felt content to let go."

Kai stops and looks at me. I stare at him, mesmerized.

"You wrote that just now?" I ask.

He nods. "While you were sleeping."

"Can I have it?"

He offers me the paper. I take it and carefully tuck it inside my folder.

The story is poetic. "You never told me you're a writer."

"I'm not," he says. "You inspired me."

I smile and look down, hiding my face.

He called me a beautiful girl.

I will treasure this forever.

CHAPTER ONE HUNDRED SEVENTEEN

Bad Timing

I don't see Kai during the day Wednesday, and he doesn't text me. But I don't expect him to. I feel like I understand him, and the closer we are in the evening, the more he distances himself from me the next day. I feel him trying not to get attached.

Too late, my brain whispers. It's too late. We weren't supposed to get attached, but we did.

I head to the student bookstore after work because I know what I want to get him for his birthday tomorrow. A writing journal and a fountain pen. It might not be the best gift he ever got, but I'm certain it'll remind him of me.

I find the journal I want easily enough, but a search of the bookstore reveals no fountain pens. I flag down an employee and ask if they sell any.

"No," she says, "the ink dries out and we don't sell enough of them, so we don't keep them in stock. But you can buy one from our catalog, and it will be here in three days."

I deflate somewhat, because it means I won't have Kai's gift here in time. I don't know what we're doing tomorrow, but I wanted to give it to him then.

I shrug it off. This is what I want for him. "All right."

I spend ten minutes analyzing ink nibs and cartridges and then choose one. It's only a few more bucks to get it personalized, so I have it engraved with his full name.

Malachi Tanaka.

I pause to stare at the name I've written in the squares. "Malachi Tanaka," I whisper out loud. His name is beautiful and majestic on my tongue. I close the order form and hand it to the woman, a little frightened at the depth of my feelings. "Thank you."

"We'll call you when it arrives."

I nod and leave, but I keep picturing his name engraved in gold on the fountain pen.

I decide to take a page out of Kai's book and not call him. We need some space.

⚬━✷━⚬

By six o'clock, sitting in my apartment studying, I'm going nuts. I check my phone every three minutes to see if I've heard anything from Kai. Is he doing the same thing? Determined not to contact me because he knows we're getting too close, but wishing I would contact him?

I give in at 6:22. My heart hammers in my chest as I squint at my phone, pull up Kai's name, and type out a message.

Me: what's up?

There's no waiting to see if he'll respond. The three dots appear immediately.

Kai: where've you been?

Me: school. then my apartment

Kai: you're home?

Me: yeah

Kai: call me

My lip twists, and I roll my eyes. This is him finding a loophole. He can't be the one to call, but he wants to talk to me.

I'll play.

He answers on the first ring. "It's almost seven," he says.

"It's a little after six," I say. "Is it past your bedtime?"

"I thought you'd call earlier."

"You can call me," I point out.

"I did yesterday."

Ah. So that's the game we're playing. "All right." I laugh. "I called you."

"Finally. Let's study."

"Want to come here?"

"I'm lazy and don't feel like driving. Meet at the business building?"

"What if I'm feeling lazy too?"

I expect him to say, *then we don't study together*, but he says, "Then I'll get off my butt and come to you."

I smile, and it's enough to motivate me. "I'll be there in fifteen."

Kai is already sitting on our couch when I step out of the elevator. He pulls his legs up so I can sit next to him and gives me a warm smile. "Hi."

"Hi," I say, and I tap his hand in greeting. I pull out my Classical Civ book. "Excited for tomorrow?"

"Why? What's tomorrow?"

I glance at him to see if he's joking and see the smirk playing at the corners of his mouth. His gorgeous, perfectly kissable mouth.

"Oh, I don't know. This kid I know is moving a little closer to outgrowing his teen years."

He laughs and leans forward to grab me. He squeezes me tight before releasing me. "It's mostly just another day."

"What did you want to do? Something more than sit in the business building and study, right?"

His brow furrows, and this time his perplexity looks genuine. "What do you mean?"

"Tomorrow. What do you want to do?"

"I don't—quite know—" He seems more at a loss for words than I've ever seen him. "Do when? Where?"

I tilt my head. "This isn't that hard. For your birthday. What do you want to do?" I say the words slowly, enunciating each one. "We can't just treat it like another day."

"Well, a few friends are making me dinner, and I'm going over there. And then I think they wanted to watch a movie or something."

Now it's my turn to look at him like we're speaking different languages. "What?"

He shrugs. "Some girls from church invited me over. We set it up awhile ago."

"Wait." I hold up my hand. "You made plans to celebrate your birthday and didn't include me?"

"Well, it's not your birthday," he says, but his eyes flit away from me, examining the corners of the room.

"No, it's not. It's yours. And you didn't want to spend it with me?"

"I told them I would before—before you and I—"

He's nervous, I see it in the way he licks his lips, the lift of his eyebrows. I interrupt his excuse and shake my head.

"You told me a week ago we'd do something for your birthday. Am I not—" I cut myself off. I can't bring myself to ask if I'm his girlfriend.

I'm clearly not.

I take a deep breath, trying to school my emotions. He's going to think I'm a spazz or a jealous, possessive girl.

What I am is confused. Trying to figure out where I fit in his heart. "It's fine. We can do something Friday."

He pulls his hands into his lap. "I have plans Friday, too."

"Wow, that's great." I'm wounded. "Have fun celebrating your birthday." *With everyone else.*

I overestimated my importance in his life. When he doesn't call, it's not because he's trying to stay away from me. It's because he freaking doesn't care what I'm doing.

But I can't say this. I can't say any of this. Because I know the last thing he wants is a clingy, sobby girlfriend begging for more of his time.

So I turn back to my textbook and pretend to be studying, but the words blur before my eyes and I don't blink because I'm afraid if I do I'll cry.

I want to get up and leave. Cut the cord between us because I just got a glimpse of our future, and it's going to be bloody and jagged. He's going to wound me and he won't know he did it, and if he does know, he won't care.

I can't cause a scene. I'll study another ten minutes, then politely excuse myself and leave and never talk to him again—

"Are you mad?" he says, his voice cutting into my thoughts.

I shake my head, but that almost dislodges the tears, so I hold still. "Nope," I say, carefully, concealing any tremor in my voice. I still don't look at him.

"Are you sure?" he asks. "You're acting funny."

"I'm fine."

"Look at me, Cassandra."

It's unfair to command someone to look at you. If they refuse, they're being rude and you know something's wrong, and if they comply, you see their distress.

Ugh.

I take my time, pretending to read the last line of the page, then turn the page over and lift my face to his. "What's up?" I say, and I'm proud at how calm I remain.

He gives a half-smile. "You're mad at me."

I can't lie to his face. "I'm a bit upset," I admit.

"What did I do?"

Does he really not know? "It's your birthday, Kai. I thought—never mind."

"What?"

My lip twists, and I throw his words from a few weeks ago back at him. "I'm going to assume you don't have a lot of experience with girls. When a guy likes a girl, he wants her at his birthday celebration. If that's not a priority to him, it says something about how he feels about her."

He gets it. I see the way the understanding crosses his face. "Oh."

"Oh?" I repeat.

He holds his hands out, palms up. "Of course I want to spend my birthday with you. But I spend all my time with you. I can't neglect my other friendships."

"Of course not," I say. "I just don't understand why I couldn't be there too."

He sighs and reaches over, taking my arm and pulling me into him. "Saturday. We can do something Saturday."

"I'm not asking you to sacrifice your life—" I begin.

"Oh, shut up, now you're being argumentative. I want to spend Saturday with you. Come to my soccer game, and we'll hang out after."

I relent. How can I hold onto my hurt feelings when he's holding me in his arms? "What if I'm busy?"

"Then you can have my Sunday."

I turn into him, curling into a ball and pressing into his chest. "Saturday's open."

He hugs me. "I'm sorry if I made you feel unimportant. It's not that. I'm just— juggling a lot of things. People. There are a lot of relationships I'm trying to maintain."

"And I'm just one more. And a rather new one." My words ring true, and I sigh. I need to accept where I fit in his life.

"Let me rephrase. There are a lot of friendships I'm trying to maintain. There's only one relationship—and it perplexes me a lot. To be honest, I've never been in one before."

I pull my hand out and run my fingers up his arm. "They're confusing, aren't they?"

He digs his fingers into my hair, massaging my scalp, pulling the hair at the roots in a way that wakes up my body, reminds me I'm female and he's male.

"I didn't see this happening right now," he says.

I smile and pull away enough to look at him. "Bad timing, huh?"

Our faces are inches from each other. He pushes my hair out of my face with one hand, the other hand firm on my back. His deep brown eyes are serious as they study me, and I memorize his expression, his face. I don't move, I don't breathe. I'm waiting to see if he'll close the distance between us and kiss me.

"I'm leaving," he says. "I put in my mission application today."

I nod. "I know you're leaving."

"It probably was poor judgment on my part to get involved with you."

I slide away from his chest. Putting more distance between us instead of closing it. Nothing he says surprises me, but it stings to hear the truth from his mouth.

"You should probably stop touching me."

"Probably." He watches me move away from him. "But it feels so nice."

A thrill jolts through me at his admission. I shrug. "I won't make you stop."

"No." He laughs. "You are not helping things."

Some of the tension eases between us. I give a small smile and turn back to my Classical Civ book, and he turns back to his mathematical equation. But there's something heavier in the air between us, even though it feels like we had a necessary conversation.

We're still sitting beside each other, but there's a fair amount of space between us now. I think that's how it's going to remain—until Kai reaches over and pokes my rib cage.

"You don't have to sit so far away," he says.

I swat at his hands. "I'm just trying not to be such a distraction."

"You are not a distraction." He pokes my ribs again, and I swat at his hand again. "I like spending time with you."

He pokes me again, and this time I grab his hand and push it away.

"Why do you keep pushing me away?"

Because that's what you want. That's what I want to say. But what good will that do? So I say, "I'm ticklish."

Immediately, a big grin splits his face, washing away any visible emotion. "You are?"

"No," I say too fast, already knowing what I've opened myself up to. "I'm not ticklish. Not at all."

His grin grows more mischievous, and then he pushes his fingers against my rib cage. I didn't think I was ticklish—but he finds a spot on my side that suddenly has me squirming away from him.

"Kai!" I shove his hand back, but he pushes his textbook off his lap and goes at me with his other hand.

I'm not helpless. I can't hold both of his hands in mine, but I can tickle back.

CHAPTER ONE HUNDRED EIGHTEEN

Falling Too Fast

He gives a yelp when my fingers wiggle against his ribs, and then it's all out war. He grabs my hands and I pull them free, finding an advantage in my smaller size. It's much easier for me to get him. He tries to trap my hands with his knees, but I evade him, and then he even snaps at my fingers with his mouth, which makes me squeal with laughter.

Somehow we tumble from the couch to the floor, laughing, gasping for breath, as he holds up both hands.

"Truce."

"You're calling for peace?" I say.

"Yes."

"Okay." I give him a slightly suspicious look and then haul myself back onto the couch.

"I lied, I was—" he says, and then grabs my ankle and begins tickling the back of my knee.

"Kai!" I can't stop laughing, and I accidentally kick his shoulder trying to get him off. It doesn't deter him.

I climb off the couch and push him with both hands, knocking him onto his back, and then, before I think it through, I straddle him—and he's merciless as I tickle him. He keeps grabbing at my hands, trying to hold both of them in one of his while he tickles me, but I break free every time.

"Okay, okay, I give," he says finally. He reaches his arms up and hugs me, pulling me against him.

The way we're sitting could be sexual. But he makes no moves to kiss me, or to reposition my body so it touches his just right, and I'm struck by the reminder that he's just a kid. I have more experience than he does.

I do not try to seduce him.

I lie with my head against his chest, breathing hard, feeling only light and joy where an hour ago I felt discouraged and frustrated.

Nothing shakes your confidence like uncertainty in a relationship.

He releases me, and I sit up, gripping his hand to help him sit as well. We move back to the couch, but there's no pretending like we're not touching. I crawl up to his side, and he puts one arm around my shoulder, taking notes with the pencil in his other hand. That joyful hum is in the back of my throat—the one that fills almost every moment I'm with Kai.

At ten to eleven, the lights go out. We're used to this—it happens every night we're here. We put our things away without saying a word. Kai stands beside me, then helps pull me up. We tuck our hands into our pockets and step into the elevator together, standing apart as if we don't know each other.

Our dynamic is so strange.

"Well, I guess I'll see you later," I say as I fish my car keys out of my backpack.

"Your car's here?"

"Yes." I stop at the back door.

"Can I get a ride?"

I bite my lip so I don't giggle. It will take longer to drive to his place than to walk there. "Of course."

He goes through my things in the car. Picks up the pile of receipts and sifts through it, grabs my makeup bag and examines the contents, finds my dance shoes under his seat.

"Ew," I say when he picks them up.

"What are these for?"

"My dance class."

"You dance?"

"Horribly."

We both laugh. I slide into a parking spot beside his dorm.

"I'll walk you in," I say, turning off the car.

I can't go up to his room, so we stop in the common living room. I wait for Kai to say goodbye, but instead he leans up against the wall.

"Hey, thanks for wanting to get together tonight," he says.

"It was kind of an interesting evening," I say, thinking of the emotional back and forth of being upset with him and then feeling closer to him than ever.

"My life's been more interesting since I met you," he says.

"I'm that kind of person," I say.

"Yeah, you are," he says, his eyes crinkling as he smiles. He pushes off the wall and hugs me.

We stand there holding onto each other for a moment, and then he pulls away. "I'll walk you to your car."

The silliness isn't lost on me, but I'm not going to argue. "Okay."

We stroll outside, back into the night, back to my car. I open my car door and say, "Good night."

"Good night," he says, and he grabs me again in another hug.

I close the car door and cling to him.

"Hugging's nice," he says, his voice just above my ear.

"I like it. You know someone cares when they hug you." At least the way we're hugging, our arms wrapped around each other, holding on tight.

He starts to sway, stepping sideways, still holding onto me. I slide out of the embrace when I lose my balance, but I keep my hands on his hips, and suddenly we're dancing in the parking lot. The music is in our heads, but we match each other's steps.

"I said I wanted to dance with you again," he says.

"Now you get your chance," I say.

Other students walk past us, but they barely spare us a glance. We're just two more kids enjoying each other's company and not wanting to let it end.

My heart soars with each step, from the effect of his hand holding mine.

"Have you been in love before?" he asks.

I miss a step in our dance because the question catches me off guard. I squeeze his hand to ground myself. "Yes."

He pulls me closer and slows his steps, so now we're slow dancing to an inaudible song. I wait to see if he'll ask more questions, my heart hammering with sudden nerves. How much does he want to know?

But he doesn't ask. Just holds me close, and then stops moving, halting our dance and wrapping his arms around me. I lay my head on his chest and listen to the pounding of his heartbeat beneath his sweater.

I could fall in love again.

It's an astonishing thought, but I feel it happening, and I'm amazed, because I don't have a say in the matter. Feelings happen on their own. I can't even say I don't want it to happen because the euphoria of falling is exquisite.

"More than once?" he asks, and I know our conversation from earlier hasn't ended or been resolved in any way.

"Yes," I say again.

I don't tell him I'm about to add him to the list.

He takes my hands in his and moves us into a silent swing dance, spinning me and dipping me before pulling me against his body, holding me so we both face the mountains. I mold myself to him and he presses his cheek to mine, his hands clasping mine in front of my stomach. His breath is warm on my skin, and I imagine turning my head, making it impossible for him not to kiss me.

But though I want him to kiss me, I don't want to be the one leading.

I should ask him if he's been in love before. Reciprocate the interest. But somehow I don't think there were girls before me.

He releases me, letting me go and taking a step back. I turn around to face him.

"It's after midnight," he says. "I need to get to bed."

We've been saying goodnight for an hour. I run a hand through my hair and nod, though I want to pull him back to me, I want to feed this emotional energy, I want it to capitalize on the physical draw between us.

I open my car door and step back, using it as a shield to keep me from launching myself at him.

"You're coming to my game Saturday?" he blurts out.

I don't hesitate. "Of course."

"See?" He gives a brief smile. "Told you we'd do something."

I smile back. "Good night, Kai."

"Good night, Cassandra," he says, his hands already back in his pockets.

He doesn't go inside, but stands there watching as I reverse from the parking spot and drive away from his dorm.

I'm on a high. But reality rears its ugly head and sneers at me as I drive.

He's leaving.

I'm leaving.

I absolutely cannot let myself fall in love with him.

I exhale and clutch at the steering wheel, stopping at a red traffic light. I'm only twenty. If this relationship continued, it would go somewhere. And I'm not ready. It's not time for that.

Now I need my mind to communicate with my heart.

⌒〜※〜⌒

I can't drag myself from my bed in the morning. My alarm goes off and I slap it silent. My head aches and my eyes burn. The bedroom door opens and closes several times as my roommate gets ready for the day. I'm usually up by now, making noise, being a part of the commotion.

I flop my wrist in front of my face and check the time. A quarter to nine. I won't make it on time to my Portuguese class even if I hurry. So I roll over and shove my face in my pillow, intent on getting a few more hours of sleep.

The murmur of voices in the kitchen and living room increases in volume. I think I hear my name but I ignore it, until someone shouts, "Cassandra!"

What? What could they possibly want? Maybe they'll go away if I don't respond.

My bedroom door opens, and Lauren pokes her head in. "Cassandra, you have to come out and see this!"

"What is it?" I say, lowering the pillow.

Camila comes in behind her. "You won't believe this. Come on, come on, come see!"

I can't imagine what would cause this much excitement, but then, I'm too tired to be very imaginative. I stumble out of my room, half dragged by my roommates.

Iris and Layne stoop in front of the fish tank, staring at it. They spin when I come in, and Layne says, "Did you know about this?"

"About what?" My feet are working now and I push away from Camila. "You made me get out of bed to examine my fish?"

"She doesn't know." Layne exchanges a smile with Iris and gestures me forward. "Look."

I join them beside the fish tank, ready to be annoyed, and then I see what they do: two tiny red fish swimming around the plastic plants we have decorating the tank.

"What?" I gasp, bending forward.

"Moby had babies!" Layne crows.

"How is that possible?" I wrack my brain. "We've had that fish for over a year!"

"He—" Iris begins.

"She," Camila corrects with a giggle.

"She must have been pregnant when we got her."

"And the babies were just now born?" I press my palm to my forehead, mind-blown. "This isn't possible!"

"I'm looking this up," Camila says. "What kind of fish is Moby?"

"Oh, goodness." It's been a long time since I bought him. But I remember the fish type was similar to the name we gave him—her . . . "A molly, maybe?"

Camila gasps. "So get this. Mollies can reproduce asexually!"

"Meaning they don't need a guy?" Layne says.

"Exactly!"

We stare at the little fish. I'm enthralled. I've never seen such tiny critters, no bigger than the tip of my pen.

"There are only two," I say.

"There might have been more," Iris says. "The other fish could have eaten them."

"Or the newt," Layne says, pointing him out where he sits on his rock, basking in the aquarium light.

"How do we protect these two?" I say, trying not to think of the other babies that didn't make it.

"The plants," Camila says. "They have to hide in the plants. That's probably how they've made it this far."

"I wonder when it happened," Layne murmurs.

The two little fish flit about near the tall plants, completely unaware of their mortal danger.

"I can't believe she had babies," I say. Then I swivel away from my roommates. "All right, excitement's over. Time to get ready for the day." May as well get ready for my English class.

A shiver of anticipation shimmies down my spine, and for a moment I can't remember why. And then I do.

Today's Kai's birthday. He's nineteen.

I can't wait to tell him he shares it with my fish.

CHAPTER ONE HUNDRED NINETEEN

Hot then Cold

I resist texting Kai. I want to wish him a happy birthday in person.

I brought his notebook with me so I can give it to him when I see him. I know he's eating dinner with friends tonight, but I hope he'll come see me at work.

I spend my English class dedicating the book to him, writing a short note about how happy he makes me and how I like to record every moment we spend together.

The book is so he can too.

I wonder what he's doing, what class he's in. I don't know his schedule. We mostly see each other after classes.

I head to work a few minutes early so I can check the online forum for my Portuguese assignment. If I get it done before class on Friday, I won't feel like a slacker for missing today.

"Hello," Christina says, looking up from her computer when I come in. She doesn't remove her fingers from her keyboard but watches me come around.

"Hi," I say. "I came in early to get some schoolwork done."

"Cool," she says.

I round my desk and pause.

A single daffodil lays across my keyboard.

"What is this?" I ask, picking it up and turning to face her.

She's already smirking. "Someone came and dropped that off for you."

My heart gives a little leap in my chest. "Who?" I ask, though it can only be one person. I hope.

Her grin widens. "Who do you think? Kai."

I pick up the flower and bring it to my face, inhaling the fragile fragrance, touching the tender petals. I love that it's not a rose.

I get a cup from the kitchen and fill it with water, then place the daffodil in it. I keep looking at it as I type up my assignment, and bubbles of joy burst in my chest every time I do.

He really does like me.

I can't text him and thank him for the flower and not say happy birthday. But I want so badly to message him.

I have to thank him for the flower. I don't want him to think I didn't get it or that I wasn't appreciative.

I'll wait as long as I can and then say happy birthday at the same time and ask what time he's free.

Christina leaves with a cheerful goodbye, and I smile and hum to myself and look over at my flower every few minutes.

Things are going very well.

<hr />

I stall as long as I can. I walk my flower home and set it up on the counter on the desk in my bedroom. Then I make myself a quick dinner, all the while wondering how Kai's dinner is going. Who are these girls he's always hanging out with? I'm jealous, which comes from my insecurity. I know he's not spending his time studying with these girls, or holding them in his arms, or dancing with them in the parking lot. But they have some part of his mind that supersedes me, and I fear at any moment they could replace me.

How long should I wait?

I give it until eight p.m. I'm antsy because I don't want him to think I've forgotten, but I also don't want to appear whiny or needy. I pull out my phone and shoot off the text.

Me: Thank you for the flower! I love it.

I send it off and wait.

It's not five minutes later that he responds.

K: You're welcome. I know it can't compare to dead leaves but I tried.

His response draws up the feelings from when he wrote me the beautiful story. I sit back in my chair at the table and cradle my phone in both hands while I respond to him.

Me: It's pretty close. Happy birthday!

I'm assuming he's done with his dinner, since he answered me so quickly. So I dial his number.

It rings twice before going to voicemail.

K: I'm with my friends, I can't answer right now.

He's texting me, at least, and I try to take that as a good sign.

He brought me a flower, after all.

Damn this insecurity.

Me: I wanted to say happy birthday in person. What time will you be done?

K: not for awhile.

Me: like, ten?

K: I didn't make a schedule.

The response feels rude, and irritation replaces my euphoria. I text back, *OK. Happy birthday.*

That will have to do. I put my phone in the other room to charge and to avoid any further correspondence with him.

I'm sitting on the couch, eating ramen and watching a movie with Iris, when I hear my phone ringing in the bedroom. I check the time. It's almost eleven.

The phone has stopped ringing by the time I get to my room, but I'm not surprised to see the caller was Kai.

Did he just now remember me? I consider going back to the couch and not responding, but that would be cutting off my own nose to spite my face. So I dial back.

"I'm home," he says when he answers.

"Yay. Was it a nice dinner?"

"Yeah. It went late."

"Apparently," I say, and some testiness enters my voice, even though I don't want it to.

"Well, you can come over for a few minutes if you want."

I can come over for a few minutes if I want? That's a weird way to extend an invitation. Like he's doing me a favor to come say hi on his birthday. My skin prickles, and I'm picking up all kinds of weird vibes.

Silence follows, and then Kai says, "So, are you coming over?"

How petty am I feeling? Do I want to be snide or just politely disinclined?

I go for the more mature option. "I don't want to keep you up."

"Oh. Good night, then."

For real? I pull the phone away, ready to hang up, when he says, his voice tiny through the phone, "You could just come for a minute. We don't have to study or anything."

I bring the phone back to my ear. I say, as carefully as I can, "If I want?"

"If you want."

"What do you want?"

He hesitates. "I mean, I'd like to see you."

Why were those words so hard for him to say? "Okay. I'll be there in fifteen."

I wrap his gift in a brown grocery bag, apprehensive and unsure how the visit will go. I didn't get encouraging vibes from him over the phone.

Did something happen at dinner?

I park at his dorm twelve minutes later and send him a text.

Me: I'm here.

K: Come on in, I'm chilling in the common room.

I grab the bag and head in.

Kai is sitting on the couch with a bunch of other kids who all look fresh out of high school. They're laughing at something on a phone and passing it from person to person.

I sit down on the couch across from him, perching on the edge, clutching my purse with his gift inside to my chest.

I didn't like the high school crowd when I was in high school. I definitely don't like it now.

Kai doesn't even say hi. He barely glances at me.

Oh, he's in cool guy mode. I've never seen it on him, but I've seen it on others. He shows virtually no reaction to my presence.

"Hey," I say. Something inside me is trembling, shimmering, a thin curtain trying to hold back an emotional response.

I didn't imagine the weirdness.

He nods at me, then goes back to talking with his friends, inclining his head and pointing at the phone and laughing. It's like I'm not here. I give myself three minutes, and then I interrupt them to say, "I'm gonna go."

He finally looks at me when I stand.

"You just got here," he says.

"And I'm not waiting here until you have time to talk to me," I say, an aggressive edge to my words.

I see a subtle shift in his eyes, and I know whatever he's doing here is intentional. He's got other people, and he wants me to know he doesn't need me.

And I hate him for it.

His friends look up too. They stare at me. I'm making a scene in front of a bunch of barely-older-than-high-school kids.

I turn around and walk out.

Kai catches up to me before I've made it to the exit. "That was rude."

I turn around, reminding myself yelling and screaming and crying will not solve anything.

You've learned that lesson, girl.

"I'm sorry, but I didn't come to sit on the couch and be ignored. I hope you didn't rush home from your dinner to meet with me." I don't offer him the gift in my purse. For all I know, I'll go home and burn it. "I hope you had a nice time."

I'm angry and hurt and I really mean, have a nice life. But as I turn around again, Kai's fingers close around my forearm.

"I wasn't ignoring you. I was just finishing up a conversation with my friends."

"Don't lie. We both know what's happening. You were going to cut me out sooner or later."

Kai's cheeks flush pink, a stunning color against his olive tone. "I didn't mean—that's not what was happening—" he begins, but I interrupt him.

"Listen, Kai. This isn't my first rodeo. If you don't want to hang out with me, don't hang out with me."

"It's not that, Cassandra. It's just, I have to prioritize my life."

He may as well tell me I'm not a priority. "Then let's stop pretending our relationship is important to you, because it's not," I say.

In spite of his words, he flinches slightly. He wants to be the one to draw the hard lines. He doesn't like it when I do.

I change my mind about burning his gift. Let him stew in this moment for the rest of his life. I pull the paper bag from my purse and thrust it at him. "Here."

He takes it gingerly, like he's afraid it will explode. "What's this?"

"Your birthday present."

I swivel again, intent on my exit. But Kai calls me back.

"I wanted to see you."

I turn around, leaning against the wall, bone-weary and fighting tears. "I'm sure you did. After you got done with your friends at dinner and after you got done looking at photos with your friends in the dorm. Thanks for making time for me."

He's been called out, and the grimace on his face shows he knows it. So I add, "I'm too old for games, Kai."

A small smile graces his lips. "You're only a year older than me now."

"Then act your age," I say sweetly.

His eyes fall back to the gift in his hands. "Can I open it?"

I lift a shoulder. "Sure."

I don't move as his fingers fumble with the brown paper, the same fingers that ran through my hair yesterday, that held my hand and spun me in circles as we danced in the parking lot, and my chest aches.

He's hurting me.

He gets the paper open and pulls out the dedicated notebook. He turns it over in his hands, letting the paper fall to the floor. He opens the front flap and pauses to read what I wrote, and a lump forms in my throat. I wish I could take back those words, but I have unfurled my heart right there.

He lifts his gaze from the book, not moving his head, though his eyes find mine. "It might be the nicest thing anyone's ever gotten me."

If it's an olive branch, he'll have to try harder.

"I'm not going to call you again. If you want to meet up, you'll have to call me," I say.

"And if I don't?" he says.

I lift an eyebrow. Is he calling my bluff?

Bring it.

"I guess we don't see each other," I say.

He studies me from the three-foot distance between us. "Are you still coming to my game tomorrow?"

I'm not sure I want to. But I told him I would. And suddenly I'm not strong enough to put an end to this relationship right now, tonight. So I sigh and say, "Yes."

"Okay."

Kai doesn't say anything more, and neither do I. I turn around and go out the door, straight to my car, and I swallow back the angry tears and my hurt feelings.

It's just as well.

CHAPTER ONE HUNDRED TWENTY

Backing Off

I don't attempt to contact Kai all day Friday. I don't text him, and I definitely don't call him, although I'm not able to refrain from checking my phone every half an hour to see if he gives in and contacts me.

He doesn't.

He doesn't miss me. He doesn't need me in his life.

And that grates on my nerves.

It's cold outside. I wear my tennis shoes and a heavy jacket as I walk to school, and I'm glad I did because by the time I go to work, it's snowing.

Saturday is the same. It snows as I walk to the library, and I'm freezing.

Maybe they'll cancel the soccer game.

I finish my homework around three. I have some time before the game, so I head home. I check my phone again to see if Kai has messaged, but he hasn't, and I have to assume he'd tell me if they canceled the game. But I wouldn't put it past him to not tell me—just to make sure I got the message that I don't matter.

I grab my hat and a blanket. I can't believe I'm going to a soccer game in the snow. In April.

What kind of a place is this?

I head out to the soccer field behind campus—the same ones where I played intramural over the summer. Only a few people sit on the bleachers. I stand on the cold metal step, wondering where I'm least likely to be sprayed by the wind, and then someone calls out to me.

"Cassandra!"

I crane my neck back to see who it is, and I'm surprised when I see Mitch and his brother John sitting near the top of the bleachers, waving at me. I climb the bleachers to join them.

"Mitch!" I say, giving him a hug, and then I give his brother a courtesy one. "It's been a long time!"

"Yeah, it has."

I haul out my blanket and get comfortable beside them. "Cheering for someone? Or just felt like a little soccer in the snow?"

They both laugh.

"It's a beautiful day for it, isn't it?" John says.

"Define 'beautiful,'" I say, smirking.

Mitch points toward the team warming up on the sidelines. "That's our roommate. He begged us to come."

"Oh." I spot Kai. He might be the shortest one on the team. He jogs with the others, and even from here, I can see the seriousness on his face. "You're very supportive."

"And which one are you watching?" Mitch asks, amusement in his tone.

I exchange a smile with him. There are no residual feelings between me and Mitch. In fact, I can't believe I felt something for him once. What was I thinking?

I nod in the direction of the team. "The short Hispanic kid out there."

"There's a couple of them," John says.

"The cute one," I say, which makes them laugh again.

"What's his name?"

"Kai."

"Oh, I know Kai," John says. "One of the freshmen."

"Yeah."

"He must be pretty good, playing on the team with the older kids."

I shrug. "It's my first game."

"How long have you guys been dating?" Mitch asks.

"About a month." Odd how certain I felt about that two days ago. Now, I feel a twinge of guilt, as if I'm lying.

"I talked to Monica the other day," Mitch says.

"How is she?" I ask immediately.

He hesitates, as if unsure how much to reveal. "She's back in Louisiana for a bit."

I nod. "Doing treatments. Do you have any updates?" I should text her. I pull out my phone and shoot off a quick hello.

"She seemed well, but I don't know anything official. Her boyfriend was visiting her."

"Oh, that's great!" At least someone's looking after her.

"Seems like Owen is doing well."

Owen. "I miss him." The words leave my mouth before I even think them.

But it's true.

My heart squeezes painfully when I think of my relationship with Owen. My hand comes up to clasp the necklace I wear, the one I've given up attempting to remove. It's my own form of permanent jewelry.

Mitch gives me a knowing look. "I'm sure you do."

I don't say anything else, and we drift into game mode, cheering and booing when necessary. I sit up straighter, my attention drawn to the field as the coach yells something, and suddenly Kai is jogging across it. "Oh, Kai's playing!"

We're twenty minutes into the game, and it's the first time he's gone out.

Mitch and John join me in yelling for him as he gets the ball and passes it to another player. His team loses possession, but Kai gets another chance to touch it.

He plays until the end of the first half, but he doesn't score any goals. And I know him well enough to tell—just from the way he walks off the field—that he's discouraged.

He sits on the bench with his teammates, his brooding expression visible from here, and I'm struck by another memory.

Owen's first football game at LSU—when the coach brought him in but only let him play for a few minutes before sending him back to the bench. Owen was pissed.

It was our first long-distance fight.

The memory brings a smile to my lips.

Thanks, Mitch. Owen is on my brain again.

Kai doesn't play the rest of the game. I fold up my blanket and brave the cold to cross the soccer field and greet him when it ends. He's still sitting on the bench, changing his shoes, and his eyes lift when I approach.

"Hey," he says, but he doesn't smile.

I offer one. "Hey. Good job out there."

"I barely played. I barely did anything." He stands.

"You got some good touches."

He grunts in response.

I poke his arm, playfully, trying to bring him out of his despondency. "It was the best soccer game I've ever seen. In the snow."

He doesn't crack a grin.

"Kai!"

I swivel and turn to see four girls walking across the field. They don't even look at me—like me standing there doesn't register.

Kai's brow furrows. He takes a slight step sideways, putting just enough space between us that it's like we weren't talking.

"Hey," he says, his tone different, his expression lighter.

They close around him, all of them talking at once.

"You're such a stud!"

"I was freezing!"

"They should've had you play more!"

He does for them what I couldn't get him to do: he smiles.

He laughs.

And the action is like a knife twisting in my chest.

I take a step backward. Then I turn and walk away.

His every word, his every gesture, his expression only confirms what I realized last night: he's pulling away from me.

Perhaps the time has come for me to pull away also.

❧

I'm just backing out of the parking lot when my phone rings. I don't have to look to know it's Kai. Probably just noticed I left.

I shouldn't answer. Why subject myself to this pain? But I swipe the phone.

"Hey," I say.

"Where are you?" he asks.

I don't want to tell him how I'm hurting and that I'm headed home. So I say, "Oh, I had to run to Walmart."

"I'm going to shower and change. Meet me in the commons in twenty minutes."

He doesn't ask, just assumes I will.

"I don't want to," are the words on the tip of my tongue. But they're such a lie. I can't even avoid him to save myself.

"Okay," I say, giving in.

Now I need to follow through with going to Walmart. I turn my car around and head to the store. I can't think of anything I need, so I buy a pack of gum. Dumb purchase. I have to hurry if I'm going to make it to Kai's place in time, though.

I'm five minutes late when I park in front of his dorm. I rush inside without my jacket, snow clinging to my hair and face. I shiver and scan the students sitting in the common room.

Kai's not here.

Just to be sure, I wander around the chairs, pretending not to check out every person sitting in the corners. People glance at me, and I feel a few eyes lingering on me. My skin prickles. They recognize I'm not a resident.

I take myself back out to my car and scan the parking lot. His truck isn't here.

It's been forty minutes.

Is he just late, or is this another message I need to pick up on?

My wounded feelings are too tender. I feel raw and damaged on the edges. I put my car in reverse and start backing out of the parking lot just as his white truck rumbles into the lot.

I might have left anyway, except he comes to a stop right behind me.

He doesn't get out of his car, and I can't back into him. So I climb out and go to his window. He rolls it down.

"Are you leaving?" he asks.

I want so badly to take my anger out on him. But I feel so defeated. "It's been forty minutes."

"Sorry. Showering took longer than I expected."

I wrap my arms around my torso and shiver. It's still snowing. "That's fine. But I should go home."

His eyes scan my face. "Stay. I'll just hop in your car for a bit."

He has to know he's hurting me. I shrug. "Okay."

I pull my car forward and turn it off while he parks his truck. A moment later, he hops into the passenger seat beside me.

"I'm going to get something out of my room real fast," he says. "That okay?"

I nod.

My body won't stop shivering. I don't think it's entirely the cold. I'm emotionally distraught, and it robs me of my body heat.

He returns a moment later and ducks in beside me, the notebook I gave him for his birthday tucked under his arm.

"Hey, you're freezing," he says. "Want to go somewhere and get a drink?"

I shake my head. "I don't feel like peopling right now. I had enough at the game."

"Here." He slides his arms out of his dark gray sweater and pulls it over his head. Underneath he wears a long-sleeved blue T-shirt. "Wear this."

I take the soft, fuzzy material in my hands and can't help inhaling his scent from the fabric. Tangy and masculine and clean. "Thanks." I slip the sweater on and close my eyes as the warmth embraces me.

"I'm teaching Sunday School tomorrow at church. Can I share my lesson with you?"

I open my eyes and swivel my body so I lean against my door and face him better. He's watching me, his dark eyes wide and studying.

Waiting to see if I'll say something. Waiting to see if I'll break.

I won't let on. Three more weeks until I never see him again. I won't show him my pain.

"Sure," I say.

He smiles and lowers his gaze as he opens the notebook. He starts reading the material he's written down for his lesson, but the back cover slides open, revealing the last page.

He's written on it. One line, at the very bottom.

Cassandra Elena Jones

April 5th

My heart gives a tiny pulse. I didn't know he knows my middle name.

The gift meant enough to him that he memorialized it with my name and date.

I mean enough to him.

I lift my eyes back to his face, watching his mouth move as he reads. He's put a lot of thought into this lesson, what he's trying to convey, but he uses the euphemisms and language of someone who's afraid to get straight to the point. Someone who is new to this adult arena.

He's so young. I want to stroke his face, run my fingers along his cheek.

He finishes and meets my gaze. "Well? How is it?"

"It's good," I say. "I can tell you understand the subject matter."

"I do. I hope I'm able to convey it."

I clear my throat, unable to avoid the elephant in the room any longer. "Kai, if you don't want to spend time together, we don't have to."

His eyes flick over my face, and for a heartbeat he doesn't speak. Then he says, "I do want to. Or I wouldn't be. The thing is, and I don't mean this to be rude, but girls don't matter right now. Only God. That's where my mind needs to be."

At least he didn't say *I* don't matter.

And I hear something else. His mind *needs* to be there.

But it's not.

He's in a tug-of-war with himself.

"Right now I'm just a distraction," I say.

I'm parroting back his own sentiment, but he furrows his brow.

"No. You're not a distraction."

My soul latches onto his words. "What am I?"

"There's a scripture that says it's not good for man to be alone."

"So I'm keeping you from being lonely?"

"Cassandra." He closes the book and presses against his door, keeping the maximum amount of space between us. "I only have a few weeks left to choose who I spend my time with. So when I choose to spend it with you, please understand that it's because I *want* to."

Spend time with me, but keep me at an arm's length.

He doesn't understand this situation any better than I do.

"Okay," I say.

I believe him.

But I don't feel any better.

CHAPTER ONE HUNDRED TWENTY-ONE

Diversions

I sleep in Kai's sweater.

I don't want to wake in the morning and I nearly miss church, but at the last minute I drag myself from bed and get dressed. Since it's snowing again, everyone piles into my car and we begin the laborious drive to campus.

The sermon is uplifting and positive, about finding joy where we are, and recognizing the value of good friendships. I look around at the people besides me, Iris and Camila, Abby and Layne and half a dozen other kids from my apartment complex who I've become close to over the past year.

Jake comes over after church and asks for help on a service project he's doing. But I've noticed the way he and Abby keep making eyes at each other, and I suspect the service project is a ruse.

He's doing volunteer work for kids, in the trauma ward of the local hospital, and in the end, we decide on care bags filled with fun activities for the children. Camila suggests we cut out hearts to put in the bags, and Layne provide construction paper.

I move over to the fish tank to check on the baby fish. They're both still there.

"Don't eat them," I tell the newt, but he sits back on his rock and stares at me, as immutable as a statue. Since he hasn't eaten them yet, I have hopes he won't.

I check my watch. A little after six. I tap my foot against the carpet, trying to shove down the desire growing in my chest.

Call Kai.

No, I reply to my inner desire. *He's pulling away. He hurts my feelings every time we're together. Leave him alone.*

You only have a few weeks left.

I shake my head, still warring with myself. *If he says no or acts distant, it might ruin what's left. Besides, I'm tired of being the one to call.*

But you want to see him. What if he says yes? He could be over here right now.

I glance over at my roommates. Abby and Camila are cutting out hearts and giggling at Jake, Iris is cooking, and Layne's stretched out on the couch, talking on the phone.

Lauren disappeared the moment we got home.

There's room for Kai here.

I give in and pull my phone out, then give a sigh as I press the button for his number. A pressure lifts out of my chest, and I realize I would have spent the rest of the evening anxious if I didn't call him.

"Hey, Cassandra," he says, answering almost immediately.

I'm reassured. Anytime I don't get sent to voicemail, it's a good sign. "Hey," I say. "How did your lesson go?"

"Good, I think. Sometimes it's hard to get class participation."

"Yeah, it's like suddenly you're speaking a different language."

"Yeah." He laughs. "Maybe I should have tried Spanish."

"If you really wanted to earn bonus points, you could have tried Portuguese."

"My Portuguese is worse than my English."

"It needs improvement," I agree. "What are you doing?"

"Studying and drawing."

"Well, come over here and do it."

"Man, I'd love to. But I can't. I won't study, I'll just talk and laugh with you."

His words warm my heart. He wants to. I can work with that. "No, you won't. I'll make you study."

"You have this skill and you haven't used it before?"

"Okay, I'll leave the room and you can study."

"And I'll be like, Cassandra, come here, and then I won't."

I laugh, giddy that I have the same effect on him he has on me. At the same time, I know how sometimes I've avoided him precisely because I had something I needed to do. "Half an hour," I say. "Come over for half an hour."

There's a long enough pause that I know he's considering it, then he says, "I really want to, but I can't."

I've almost got him, I know it. "I'll kick you out, I promise."

"Promise?"

Got him. "Yes."

"Okay, I'll be there in a minute."

He hangs up, and I can't help it, I give a fist pump and crow, "Yes!"

Camila and Iris both laugh.

"We didn't think he was going to come," Iris says.

"It took some work," I say. "But he's coming." Now I'm jubilant. I skip back over to the table and grab the scissors. I get three hearts cut out before the knock comes on the door.

Layne gets there first. She opens it and says, "Kai! What a surprise. Fancy seeing you here."

"It's been a few days," he says.

"Yes, we've missed you." She gives him a friendly pat on the shoulder, and I really appreciate that she doesn't try to flirt with him.

He's probably too young for her.

"Kai!" I exclaim as if I didn't know he was coming. I drop the scissors and skip over to him, then grab his hand and haul him over to the fish tank. "Look at this!"

"What?"

I release his hand so I can point to the fish, and immediately I miss the warmth of his flesh against mine. "My fish had babies."

"What?" He leans over, bending beside me, and I point out the tiny fishlings. "No way! How did it do that?"

"Apparently mollies can reproduce asexually."

"Well, that doesn't sound like much fun," he says, and it's the first time he's ever said anything remotely sexual, the first time he's given any indication that sex interests him at all.

"No, it doesn't," I say, and I start laughing because my thoughts have taken a downward turn.

"What are you laughing at?"

He turns to face me, and I keep my gaze steady on his face to avoid letting my eyes wander over his body.

I remember what Layne said last year. That sex is *fun*.

My relationship with Kai is the most chaste I've ever had. But all it took was one slight innuendo from him, and my body is hot with desire.

"Nothing," I say, composing myself. "Just thinking how that doesn't sound like fun. The sexual way is . . . definitely more fun. Poor fishies," I add, just in case he thought I was thinking about sex with him.

Because I wasn't.

Of course I was.

His cheeks turn that lovely pink hue, warmth creeping over his olive skin. I've managed to make him blush twice now, and heavens, I want to drag him back to my room and make out with him on my bed. I want to corrupt this innocent kid.

Cassandra! I mentally chastise myself for my profane thoughts.

"Uh—yes—I'm sure it is," he says, and he can't take his eyes from me, and I know he's thinking, wondering, seeing me in a different light just like I'm seeing him now.

I'm not just his friend/possible girlfriend. I'm a woman.

Who needs the birds and the bees? Just bring in a couple of mollies.

I stand up and move away from the fishtank before either one of us does or says something more to expose our thoughts.

"We're helping Jake with a service project for kids at the hospital," I announce, settling myself down at the table and picking up pieces of construction paper. "Want to help?" I shoot him a flirty smile beneath lowered lashes. "Or study?"

"Service is good," he says, and I know as he comes to sit by me that I've summoned him to me like a siren's call.

It thrills me that I can do that.

Abby and Jake tease each other and the rest of us laugh at their antics. Kai cuts out hearts beside me, and I feel him glance at me several times.

I check the time and hop up. "It's been half an hour, Kai. Time to go."

"All right, if you insist," he says, pushing away from the table.

"Bye, Kai!" Abby says, and my roommates take up the chant. "Bye, Kai!"

"Let me get your sweater," I say, and I leave him in the kitchen while I grab it.

"Thanks," he says when I return.

"See you soon, guys," I say, and I step out the door with him.

It's stopped snowing, but the air still has a bite to it. I rub my arms as we walk to his truck, and he holds his sweater out to me.

"Maybe you should keep this," he says.

"I won't be out here that long."

He's parked down the street, just a hundred meters from my apartment. I walk with him to the driver's side.

"Thanks for sacrificing your study time to come see me," I say.

"It wasn't much of a sacrifice," he says.

There's so much he's not saying. So many words and emotions in the depths of his dark brown eyes, but I don't know if he can express them.

I take his hands and squeeze his fingers. "Thanks for diverting yourself with me, then."

He laughs and tugs me closer, then pulls me against him. I shiver into his sweater, letting his body warmth wrap around me.

"Let's get out of the street," he says.

So we can keep hugging? I think, but I keep my amused thoughts to myself. I don't want him to change his mind. A moment ago we were saying good night, and now we're . . . not.

We step onto the sidewalk, and he hesitates, as if afraid to resume our hugging session.

"You can hug me anytime you want, you know. I like hugging you," I say.

"You are strange," he says, but that doesn't prevent him from pulling me into his arms.

"Strange?" I step back. "Says who? Maybe I'm normal and everyone else is strange."

"Yeah, that's it," he says, grabbing me and tugging me close again. "It's not you, it's everyone else."

"That's what I've been saying." I snatch his hands and pull at his fingers, then weave them between mine. "Your fingers are big."

"Fat? Are you calling my hands fat?"

"No." I laugh and press my palm up to his. "But your hand could eat mine."

"Because you have the hands of a first grader." He snatches me around the waist and pulls me back into a hug.

I giggle. He doesn't want me away from him. "My hands are freezing."

"I've got pockets."

"Which ones are appropriate for me to put my hands in?" I tease.

He gives a strange cough, and I wish it weren't dark because I'm certain he'd be blushing again.

"Well, I guess my hands will have to do," he says, wrapping my hand up in his.

"Didn't your time expire?" I grin up at him.

"I'll just put another quarter in."

I step away and point up at the sky. "Hey, look at the moon. It's got this reddish orange glow to it tonight."

"So?" He hugs me back to him. "Who wants to look at the moon when they can look at you?"

"Kai." I melt against him. Why isn't he always like this?

Because he's leaving. Because this is temporary. Because things are so confusing between us.

Kai pushes my hair away from my face, and his eyes are on me, his gaze so intent that I freeze.

Will this be the moment that he finally kisses me?

Then he lifts his eyes and looks at something over my shoulder. "Is that Abby? I think that's Abby."

I turn around to see Abby's blue and white jacket jogging away from us down the sidewalk, going toward my apartment. "Abby!" I call after her.

She doesn't stop. But she does glance over her shoulder and laugh before running off.

I arch an eyebrow. "What was that?"

"Maybe it's because she saw us hugging."

"So?"

"Well, maybe she's never seen you hug anyone before." Kai doesn't let me stay out of his arms for long before he hauls me back.

I laugh and dig my hand through his straight dark hair. He ducks his head, pushing his face against my neck.

Just kiss me, already! I scream at him in my head.

But he doesn't. He holds me close and sways with me there on the sidewalk, and I don't feel the least bit cold anymore.

I slide my hand away to check the time. "I don't want to make you leave," I say, "but I don't want you to be upset with me later when you realize you were supposed to leave an hour ago."

"I know." He sighs and ever so reluctantly slides away from me, though his hands stay on my hips until the distance forces him to release me. "I knew this would happen."

"Sorry not sorry?" I say.

"I know that too."

He takes a step backward and I take one forward. I'm moments away from leaping back into his arms, but when he takes another step back, I stay where I am.

"I'll see you tomorrow," he says.

"Good night," I say, my body humming with happy euphoric energy.

"Good night, Cassandra."

He gets in his truck and pulls away from the curb, throwing a wave my direction as he turns the vehicle around. I wave back, and then I run home.

I burst into my apartment and exclaim, "You guys!"

The four of them stand there in a circle, Abby, Camila, Iris, and Layne. They each swivel toward me when I come in and break into peals of laughter.

"Did you kiss him?" Layne exclaims.

"No!" I say, laughing, my face hot. "Why?"

"Because I was outside walking," Abby says, "after Jake left. When I walked by, I was like, oh, there's a couple making out, so I'll walk on the grass. Wait, I know those people —it's Cassandra and Kai!"

"So then she comes running in here," Iris says, jumping into the narrative. "And she says, you won't believe what I just saw Kai and Cassandra doing!"

"And we had to see!" Camila says. "So we snuck outside to spy on you guys!"

"You did what?" I press my hands to my chest, but I'm laughing so hard I can't stand up straight. "You snuck out to see if we were making out?"

"We did!" Layne's laughing too, her face red, her words gasping as she tries to speak. "We snuck up and stood on the sidewalk watching you guys for like six minutes!"

"I never noticed you!" I say.

"You were busy—not kissing," Abby says.

I can't catch my breath. I collapse in a chair in the kitchen, gasping because my side aches. "I can't believe you did that!"

They fall in around me also, and we wipe tears from our eyes. Every time I picture them tiptoeing down the sidewalk to spy on me and Kai, I start laughing all over again.

"You sure you didn't kiss?" Layne says skeptically.

"I'm sure." I shake my head, but the smile won't leave my face. "I would remember."

CHAPTER ONE HUNDRED TWENTY-TWO

Define the Relationship

Kai does not contact me on Monday.

I'm not surprised. I'm beginning to recognize his MO. We get close, super close, maybe too close for comfort, and he backs away. Puts space between us. Then he reaches out, just a little, just to see if I'll reach back, and I do. So he tiptoes back in, then he gets closer, and then we get too close, and it starts over.

Except there's been a change. He's not reaching out anymore.

I won't let it bother me. I take advantage of the time to study. I stay on campus as long as I can but I forgot to make a lunch and I didn't bring money for dinner. When I reach the point where I feel like I'm going to faint, I pack up my books and head home.

By Tuesday, I'm missing Kai fiercely. It's only been a day. How will I handle it when he leaves?

I set up my studying in the engineering building, praying he'll walk past me in between classes. But I've only been there half an hour before I get an email from the registration office telling me I'll lose my scholarship if I don't sign up for fall classes.

My heart skips a beat. My adviser told me I could defer for a semester without any trouble.

I send another email off to my adviser.

"Yes, you can defer," she says in her email. "Come by my office to fill out the official form."

Well, fine. Forget waiting for Kai. I sigh and pack up my things. Maybe I'll get lucky and Kai will come by my work.

She has the form waiting for me when I get there, and I sit down to fill it out. I pause when I read one of the lines I'm supposed to initial.

I understand I can only defer my schooling once during my academic career.

"Wait a minute," I say, trying to make sure I do understand this. "If I defer now, I can't do a mission trip later?"

"You could do one over summer term, but not during a semester."

Now the panic rises in my chest. "Then I can't defer."

She takes the form back from me. "So you won't be doing the internship?"

"Doesn't it count toward my education?"

She shakes her head. "You take a form with you and have your boss sign off on it, but that's just an internship credit."

My heart stutters. "There's nothing else I can do?"

"You can check with the registration office to see if they have another solution, but you can only defer once."

I find her less than helpful. She clearly doesn't care about my situation. I stand up again and shoulder my backpack. "Okay. Thanks for letting me know."

And then I'm off to the registration office.

The girl in the office doesn't look much older than me. She pulls up my classes on her computer and nods as I explain my situation.

"So the study abroad office didn't help you with classes in Brazil?" she says.

"The study abroad office?" I repeat. "I went to my adviser. She acted like there's nothing I can do to get class credit."

"She won't know," the girl says. "You need to go to the study abroad office. They'll help you get the credit you need through classes you design."

"Oh! I had no idea. I thought I could only use them for one of their planned programs."

"Nope. They'll work with you. Go chat with them."

"Thank you, that's great!" I check the time. I have an hour before work.

And this keeps me from thinking about Kai.

"Sure, this is easy," the guy in the study abroad office says. He turns his computer around and shows me my class requirements. "We do this with our programs all the time. You need three classes to be considered full-time, but you have to build them through our office to make them count."

"Build them?" I repeat.

"Yeah. We already have a few classes in place for situations like this. You can get credit for a religion course, a teaching course, and a Portuguese course. Then you won't have to defer."

"That's great!" A huge weight lifts off my shoulders, and I exhale. "Let's do that, then!"

"All right." He hands me a few forms. "You get started on the leg work, and we'll get you set up in the system."

"Thank you!" I'm so grateful I want to kiss him.

Or maybe I want to kiss someone else . . . and I just haven't heard from him.

Nor do I hear from him the rest of the day.

⚬⚬⚬

By Wednesday afternoon, Kai is all I can think about. I'm sick to my stomach over the fact that we haven't communicated. He told me days ago that if I didn't reach out, neither would he. But does he really not miss me? Has he pushed me so far from his mind?

This time I plant myself in the engineering building for two hours after my classes. But Kai doesn't walk by.

I head to work early to distract myself, but I'm a mess. I'm fighting tears, swallowing against an ache in my throat, my head pounding.

Christina looks up when I walk in. "Are you sick?" she says, her brow furrowing. "You look awful."

And then I burst into tears.

Her eyebrows go up in alarm, and she half rises from her chair. "What's wrong? What's happening?"

"It's nothing," I say, waving her off. I come around the desk and grab a tissue. "I'm just stressing over Kai."

"Why? What did he do?"

"He did nothing! And that's precisely the problem!" My eyes well up again, and I plop down cross-legged on the floor beside her chair.

She looks down at me, clasping her hands in her lap, her lips pursed and her eyes serious. "Cassandra, I think it's time for you to tell him how you feel."

"He already knows how I feel. We have this conversation every time we're together."

"No, you tiptoe around the subject. You need to tell him what he's doing to you."

I wipe at my eyes. "What is that?"

"This." She gestures at me. "How do you feel for him?"

I give a choking laugh. "I like him."

"Does he know that?"

"Yes."

"Have you told him?"

"Not in that many words."

"So it's time. It's time to define the relationship."

Define the relationship. Those words are tossed around with mock horror in college social groups. The running joke is that if you have to sit down and define the relationship, it wasn't much of a relationship to begin with.

I balk at the idea. "I don't want to do that."

"Your other option is to let him keep jerking you around like this."

"I haven't talked to him since Sunday," I murmur, twisting my fingers around each other.

"Did you guys fight?"

I shake my head. "The opposite. We spent over an hour together, and it was amazing. It's the closest he's come to kissing me."

She gazes at me with the utmost pity. "So his next response is to cut communication with you. Cassandra, that's messed up."

"Yeah, it is."

"You deserve better."

"I deserve better." I believe her words when she says them. Not so much coming from me.

"So are you going to let this go on?"

"No." I stand up, fisting my hands on my hips and pretending like I'm filled with confidence. "It's time he and I talked. For real."

Christina smiles. "There you go, girl! Don't you feel better?"

I nod. "Yes. Ready for action."

She stands up and grabs her bag. "I can't wait to hear how it goes!"

Then she leaves, and I take her place behind the computer screen.

But now it's all I can think about.

Words play themselves in my head on repeat. *I like you, Kai. I like you a lot. You're important to me. I thought I was important to you too but now I'm not sure.*

That's what it boils down to, isn't it? I need to know I'm special to him. That I'm important.

I used to feel so confident. But now his talk of girls not mattering—prioritizing his life—makes me feel like I've dropped off his radar completely.

Christina's right. If that's the case, I deserve to be told in so many words.

What do you hope happens between us in the next two weeks? Because I sure as heck want to spend at least five hours of it having a heavy make out session in your car. Or on my bed. I'd even take the couch where we study.

That makes me giggle. And it makes my body hot and tingly.

I scratch those words from my mental rough draft. But I keep the others.

It's literally all I can think about, but I force myself not to try calling him the moment I leave work. I head to the library first and throw myself into my studies. I have a creative narrative due in Portuguese, and I don't feel like being creative, so I write a story about me and Tiago, except I change our names and make it fictional. The story ends with my fictional character saying goodbye to her fictional boyfriend and never seeing him again, except she's okay with it because they broke up on good terms, and she knows he's not the one for her anyway.

I sigh as I end it, an old familiar feeling of longing welling up in my chest. If Tiago had broken up with me when I left Brazil, set me free instead of breaking my heart, would Owen and I have gotten together sooner?

I don't usually let my thoughts go down this rabbit hole, but they are tumbling away from me now. Kai has left me wounded and vulnerable, and it's made me think of Owen more often than I want.

My stomach is all twisted now. I try to concentrate on editing the narrative I just wrote, but my thoughts are wrapped around Owen.

I never wanted to date again after him. I never wanted to be in the position of trying to find someone else.

But here I am, and this is the result. An immature kid who has wormed his way into my heart and hurt me badly enough that I regret taking a chance on dating.

Casual dating isn't a thing.

It's almost seven. I pick up my phone and consider texting him, but texts are too difficult to read. I won't feel his emotions and I'll be super sensitive to his response, thinking he's being rude even if he's not.

We need to meet, and I need to extend the invitation via a phone call.

I take a deep breath and step into the hallway of the library so I won't disturb the other studying students. Then I press the button for his number.

The phone rings four times and goes to voicemail. I don't bother leaving a message. Kai will know it was me. I return to my desk and sit in front of my computer, but my toe taps out an anxious melody. I just need to wait for him to call me back, and then we'll talk.

Half an hour passes. I'm getting more anxious, checking my phone every two minutes to make sure it's not on silent. He saw my call. He hasn't texted or anything.

What if he doesn't call me back?

Then that says something about where he places you, I tell myself. *And you should let it go.*

I can't.

I give it thirty more minutes, and then I try again.

Still no answer.

Now what? If I leave a message, this immediately goes from a casual, "let's get together" to, "something's wrong."

But if I don't leave a message, he might not know it's important to me that he call back.

The fact that I've called twice should tell him that.

I hang up, and now I don't know what to do. If I call again, I've showed my hand. But if I don't, I might not get to talk to him.

And I won't sleep tonight if I don't get these words out of my head.

CHAPTER ONE HUNDRED TWENTY-THREE

Dead Last

I try to study, but I'm sick to my stomach with nerves. I give it a solid twenty minutes. It's almost nine now. I stand up and put my things away. I don't have a plan. But I can't stay here.

I head outside, but instead of going straight to begin the walk home, I turn left, moving toward the business building.

Maybe Kai is already there.

Maybe he's there with another girl.

I dismiss the thought. He likes me. He's trying not to get more involved with me. He won't solve the problem by getting involved with someone else.

My heart begins racing as I approach the building, and I grip my backpack straps tighter as my anxiety ratchets.

I pull my phone out.

I'm still not thinking. I'm not planning. I'm letting my body decide what to do. But as soon as I hit his phone number, my heart rate slows, my breathing calms, and I know he's going to answer.

"Hello?"

His baritone voice carries through the line, and I can't tell what he's feeling from his tone.

"Hey," I say, trying to sound calm and friendly. "I've been trying to reach you."

"I saw your calls."

Don't read anything into that, I tell myself, but it's too late.

He intentionally didn't call me back. He didn't want to talk to me. I forced his hand by calling a third time, finally triggering him to where he felt he couldn't ignore me.

"Awesome," I say, attempting levity. "Would it be possible for me to see you tonight?"

"No," he says. "I'm too busy."

This time there's no missing the coldness in his tone. Something breaks in my chest. A lump forms in my throat, and my eyes tear. I swallow hard. If this is going to end, it's going to end nice and proper, dammit. "Could I just see you for half an hour? I need to talk to you." My voice quivers on the end, all appearances of false cheer vanishing.

"Yeah," he says, changing his mind so suddenly I'm caught off guard. "Yeah, I'll come."

"I'm at the usual place," I whisper, and I hang up.

Great. Now he knows exactly what he's walking into.

I take the elevator up to our spot. My hands shake as I unload my backpack, putting text books out on the table and opening notebooks to create the facade of studying.

The elevator dings, and Kai walks in. He has his hands in his pockets, and the expression on his face is guarded, wary. It makes my stomach pitch.

But it also gives me courage.

He comes over to the couch and sits down on the edge. As far from me as can be. "What's wrong?" he asks.

At least we're not beating around the bush.

I take a deep breath and search for my rehearsed speech, but it's fled my mind. Traitor. "It's been three days since I've heard from you."

"I've been busy."

"We've always been busy."

"Yes . . ." He drifts off.

I go for the jugular. "Your feelings for me have changed."

He tilts his head, fixing his gaze on me. "No."

Fierce hope ignites in my belly, and I bite my lip. "Then why are you ignoring me?"

"I'm not. You didn't contact me either."

"I called you three times today before I got a response from you."

"Well—I answered the third time."

I give a short laugh. "Kai, I get where your priorities are. You've got God, school, your friends . . . and then me. Do I have to be last?"

"What do you want me to do about it?"

He doesn't deny it. Doesn't try to convince me otherwise.

I am last.

I shake my head, defeat rising like bile in the back of my throat. "I don't want to be last. I deserve more." I begin gathering my books, tears hot behind my eyes as I shove them into my backpack. "This was fun." I'm choking on my words, papers blurring in front of my vision. *Finish it.* Find the words for this to be done, once and for all.

Kai puts a hand on my arm, stopping me. "You're not last."

I freeze, my fingers still grappling with my notebook. I don't look at him. "I feel like I am."

"I don't know what to do to change that."

I lift my eyes without moving my face. "A text would do it. Stopping by to see me. Just letting me know you care, that you think of me."

His solemn gaze arrests me. "Of course I think about you. Of course I care. You have to have faith in me. I have faith in you."

"I don't have faith in you," I say shortly. "You're hot, then you're cold. You're attentive and then you ignore me. You don't want to hang out with me anymore."

"I never said that."

"No, you didn't say it." My words are biting. I'm hurling them at him.

He lets go of my arm. "Finish your thought."

I do. "But you don't do anything about it. And that says a lot."

He lowers his gaze. "Yeah, I suppose it does."

I resume putting my books away, but my head is more clear, and I remember parts of my speech now. I string the words together as I gather my things. "I like you, Kai. I like you a lot. You make me happy, and I want to be with you. I miss you when I'm not. I knew I'd have to get used to you not being here when you left on your mission. I guess I'll just do it sooner than later."

"Cassandra, if I could, I'd be with you every minute. I'd give you all my attention. But I can't do that."

I look up, frustrated. "I'm not asking for that! I just want some of your time, some consideration! Some effort on your part!"

He pleats his fingers, steepling them and pressing his index fingers to his chin. "Listen to me. I'll say this once and I need you to remember it, because I won't say it again, and you're going to have to trust me, to believe in me, through whatever may come in the future."

I stop moving and focus on him. He has my attention.

"I care for you very much. You might not understand it, but I love you. I love you a lot. How you take that is up to you."

I blink at him, not sure at all how to take that.

It feels very serious, and that's not what I expected.

"You're not treating me like someone you love," I say.

"I don't know how I'm supposed to treat someone I have to say goodbye to in seventeen days," he says.

Seventeen days.

He knows the number.

I'm not the only one counting.

My emotions do a sudden one-eighty as I understand what he's grappling with. He's not handling it the way I would, and he's not handling it the way Owen did.

He's handling it in his own way.

I lean back on the couch, abandoning my backpack. "What do you want out of our relationship?" I hold my breath, waiting to see what he'll say.

I'm not sure what I want him to say.

He shakes his head. "I don't want anything more than what it is right now. I'm not going to ask you to wait for me, I'm not going to ask you not to see other guys."

I exhale. That's probably the best I could expect. I'm not prepared to put myself on a shelf until I see him again.

And I can't promise my heart would be available.

"So what is this, then?" I gesture between us. "Just a fling for the next seventeen days, and then it's over, done with, forgotten?"

He looks away from me, staring at the carpet, and doesn't answer for what feels like a very long time. "No. There's more to it. I don't want to lose your friendship."

Friendship. That's what we're reduced to.

I snort and roll my eyes. "Then you better do something now to preserve it."

He meets my eyes and gives a small smile. "All right." He gestures at my backpack. "Did you want to study?"

I turn my gaze to everything I've put away and heave a sigh. "I'm done for the night. I think I just want to go home."

"Come here."

Kai takes my arm and tugs me over to him, and then he folds me into a hug. I lean into him and blink rapidly, taking shallow breaths and swallowing hard to keep from crying.

I understand that this is a consolation hug. The relationship as it was has ended.

My heart is swollen and raw like I scrubbed it with a pumice stone until it bled.

He's not the first boy I've said goodbye to.

I suspect he won't be the last.

⌒⌒✳︎⌒⌒

I don't study. And we don't make out, so it feels like a lose-lose to me. But at least he holds me close for half an hour, an hour, until my eyes grow heavy and I know I need to go home.

"I'll drive you," he says, and I accept the offer.

We don't talk in the car. I'm emotionally drained. But he walks me to my front door, and he grabs me and hugs me tight before I go in. Then I pull away.

"Good night," I say. "Thanks for talking to me."

"Night," he echoes. "You can talk to me about anything."

I nod. He's my friend.

That's all he can be. He's not available for more.

I need to put myself firmly on this side of that line.

I slip inside. It's almost eleven, but my roommates and a few neighbors are over watching TV and goofing around. I murmur good night and go to my room.

The door opens as I'm changing for bed, and I turn to see Camila stepping inside.

"You okay?" she asks.

I give a toothy grin. "Don't I look great?"

She gestures around her eyes. "Yeah. Like you've been crying."

I sigh and sit on the bed. "It's just Kai."

She climbs up beside me, sitting cross-legged in front of me. "Did you guys break up?"

I shake my head. "Not officially. But every time we're together it feels like it's going that direction."

She takes my hand, smoothing the skin on my fingers. "What it boils down to, Cassandra, is Kai is already in missionary mode. He's pushing you and all thoughts of you away. You don't get to be in his mind or heart right now."

"I know." I squeeze her fingers, accepting her touch. "I don't know if he realizes how hard this is on me, though."

"I bet he does. He's probably kicking himself for starting anything with you."

That thought stings, and I frown. "I don't want him to regret dating me."

She doesn't say anything, and I consider how I'm making this harder on Kai.

I slide my fingers from Camila's and pat her hand. "I need to make this a positive experience for him."

586

I don't want him to look back on us, wincing at how we got too involved.

Camila leans over and hugs me. "You'll get through this."

"I know."

She leaves, and I finish getting ready for bed.

Being with Kai has enriched my life.

The past few weeks have been filled with joy.

I won't let our impending separation sour that connection.

I climb into bed with an attitude change.

CHAPTER ONE HUNDRED TWENTY-FOUR

Untouchable

I don't have class in the morning, and the extra sleep is a balm to my wounded heart. I wake feeling more at peace. Kai is pulling away, and it's time to let him go.

It was never supposed to get serious.

I shower and head to the kitchen, where Iris is standing by the balcony doors, backpack slung over one shoulder, staring outside. She swivels when I come in.

"Cassandra, it's snowing," she says.

I give a short laugh. "Of course it is. It's April. That's what it does here."

"Do you think you could give me a ride to school?"

Ah. So she was waiting for me. I join her at the doors and peer at the fat white flakes drifting down. "Sure, I have time. I need to get milk anyway."

Her face breaks into a smile. "Thank you! I don't feel like walking in the cold this morning."

We jump into my car, and I slip and slide down the road, but I'm more accustomed to driving in snow now. I don't love it, but I can do it.

We pass Jake on the way, and I slow down.

"Want a ride to campus?" I ask.

"Yes!" He doesn't hesitate before opening the car door and jumping in. "Brrr! Not fun to be walking in!"

He holds his hands up to the heater, and I keep driving.

"That poor girl looks soaked," Iris says, pointing out another student.

"Yeah, she does," I say, and I pull up beside her. "Need a ride to campus?" I ask.

She takes one look at my car filled with other kids and says, "I'd love that, thank you!"

Soon she's in my car also, and Iris and I chat with her and Jake like we're all old friends.

But now I have a new mission: find walkers who need rides.

We find two more people before we reach campus, and we cram us into my car that doesn't legally hold six riders. We're laughing and the atmosphere is jovial as we introduce ourselves, and then I deposit my load of students on campus.

I do this two more times in the next hour, driving around the streets and offering rides to students trudging onward in the snow. No one turns me down, and I'm delighted to feel so much joy that has nothing to do with Kai.

I finally make it to the creamery and get my milk, and then I head home because it's time for me to go to work. The snow has stopped, but it's frigid outside. I grab a set of dress pants to change into at work and stay in my sweats for the walk. As I lock the front door and begin the walk to campus, I wish someone would offer me a ride.

No one does, of course, but a speedy car drives by as I'm near an intersection and sends a cascade of water over my whole body as they race through a puddle.

"Unbelievable," I say, looking down at my mud-splattered, wet clothing.

But I don't really care. Nothing can ruin my mood today. I happen to have a dry set of clothes in my backpack.

Christina lifts her head when I walk in, and her eyes go wide when she sees me. "What happened to you?" she exclaims.

"Dangerous walk to school," I say, and I laugh, which gives her permission to laugh also. "I came in early change before my shift starts."

"Use the back office, I'll keep an eye out."

I step into the copy room and close the door, then shimmy out of my wet items as fast as I can.

"You look like a different person," she says when I come out.

"You just had a rare glimpse of my alter ego," I say.

She laughs, then says, "You're in a very different mood from yesterday. Good talk with Kai?"

"Good enough." I come over and slide my bag under the desk. "It's ending between us, but it's fine. The sooner I extrapolate my heart, the sooner I'll be over him."

She giggles. "You're such an English nerd."

"That I am."

Her smile dissolves. "But you're sure you're okay? Yesterday you were in tears over him."

I sigh and shove down the twinge of sadness that attempts to take root.

"Yes, I'm sure. It was a wake-up call. I got way too invested for a relationship that's going nowhere. And we both knew it from the start."

"You fell for him."

"I did," I admit. "At least I didn't fall all the way."

I don't love Kai.

But I know from the strength of what I do feel for him, it wouldn't have taken long to fall hard, deep, and in love.

"Well." She stands up and gathers her things, then offers me a hug. "I'm glad you're in a better place today. Let me know how things go as you navigate this with him."

"It's strange," I say. "He's the third boy I've sent off on a mission trip. But each experience has been completely different."

"That's boys for you. And, word of advice? Maybe you should stop dating boys who are leaving on missions."

"Period," I say, and I can't help laughing. "Need to get that through my thick skull!"

It's a quiet afternoon. I gather the mail for the professors and deliver it to their classrooms. Professor Stephens stops me before I leave his office.

"How are things going?" he asks. "I think of you every time Kai walks into my classroom."

"Funny you should ask," I say. "We're kind of in a confusing place. He's getting ready to leave on a mission, and he goes back and forth between pulling me close and pushing me away."

"I still can't believe you're dating." He smiles. "I teased you about saying something to him, but then I never had to because you did it all on your own."

My face warms. "I've never been so drawn to someone so quickly. I go on a lot of dates, and usually by the end of the first date, I know there's nothing between us. So to have this happen... it surprised me, to say the least."

"I can tell his mind is elsewhere. His schoolwork has felt hurried lately—when he bothers to turn it in."

"He's already gone," I say. "He's going through the motions with us here."

"That must be hard on you."

"It is." I nod, not letting myself get emotional as I admit my feelings. "I like him a lot."

"Well, that much is obvious." The professor chuckles.

"But this is it. What we have now is as far as it will go." My chest twists with a painful twang.

I'm never going to get that kiss.

"You never know," Professor Stephens says. "Time goes by. Things could change in the future."

"The future is completely invisible to me," I say. "But I think the chances of he and I being in the same place and in the same position in a few years is very unlikely."

I hear the swoosh of the door in the reception area, and I step out. "I better go."

"Nice talking to you," he says. "Best of luck."

"Thanks." I smile.

I am untouchable.

Nothing's changed except my attitude. I haven't heard from Kai. He doesn't come by the office. And I'm okay with it. I understand, to a certain extent, what's going on in his head and in his heart.

But that doesn't mean I don't want to see him.

❦

I get my homework done and take my essay to the Portuguese lab so they can look it over. Elizabeth doesn't work there anymore, and I wonder how she's doing. She helped me mentally last year when I was suffocating in my Portuguese classes.

With the corrections from the Portuguese TA, I sit down at a computer and correct my essay. Then I check the time.

It's a little after eight o'clock.

I have held strong all day. I feel like it's acceptable if I call Kai, for the sake of our friendship.

I don't expect him to answer, after the drama I put us through yesterday. But he does. Maybe he's feeling guilty for ignoring me.

"Hello?" he says.

"Hey," I say breezily. "I'm about to head home and it's freezing outside. Can I get a ride?"

"Sure," he says, and I smile.

"Great. I'm headed your way. Be there in fifteen."

"See you."

I hang up, but now a goofy grin won't wipe from my face.

There's a lot of crazy going on between us. But there's something else also, something strong that finds us together even through the crazy.

I call Kai as I step into the lobby of his dorm. "I'm here."

"I'm almost there."

I sit on the couch and read a book on my phone. I don't even know which room is his. He's never invited me to see his dorm.

He appears a moment later, and his straight dark hair is mussed like he just woke up. I smirk at him and say, "Did you have a good nap?"

"Huh?" He blinks, and his hand flies to his head. A slight flush colors his cheeks. "Dang. I guess I should've looked in a mirror."

"Because 'bedhead' is all the rage," I say, shoving my phone into my backpack and standing up.

"I guess it depends who you're asking," he says.

"So probably don't ask me."

It takes him about half a second to get my joke, and then he laughs. "Not impressed?"

"I've seen better."

It's a total lie. Even with his hair a mess, Kai has to be the most beautiful person I've ever seen. I have a hard time tearing my eyes away from his face until I finally step in front of him and lead the way out the door.

"You've seen better?" He keeps up the teasing, moving in front of me to unlock his truck. "Like who?"

He unlocks the passenger side first, and then turns around to face me—except I don't think he expected me to be right behind him. I stumble slightly as I try to step back, and his hand shoots out, grabbing my forearm to steady me.

And for a breathless moment, our eyes lock. The air grows thick between us, and I swear I can hear our hearts beating.

His gaze moves over my face. When it lands on my mouth, he sucks in a breath and lowers his nose slightly.

And I think, *Oh my gosh, he's going to kiss me.*

It's going to happen now.

And then—like someone slapped him—he jerks back, crashing against the car.

If I weren't so disappointed, I would laugh. It's actually comical.

"You can get in now," he says, opening my door and stepping away from the car.

"Why, thank you, Kai. You're ever the gentleman." I say it with a joke in my voice, but there's bitterness behind my words.

I wish he wasn't quite *this* gentlemanly.

But I don't let on. I refuse to bring negativity to our space.

So instead, I regale him with tales of picking up snow-walkers and arriving at work completely soaked. I'm patting my hands, laughing, acting carefree and light, exactly how I want to be.

Neither of us mentions our discussion yesterday.

I hop out of his truck with a cheerful smile. "Thanks for the ride," I say.

"No problem," he says. He squints at me. "If it's not too much trouble, since you're in the habit of taking people places, could you give me a ride to the airport tomorrow?"

"Of course I can," I say immediately. Whatever he needs, I'll do it. If there's something else on my Saturday morning, I'll clear it.

"I need to be there at six." He grins at me.

"Well, if I'd known that going into it . . ."

"If I hitchhike in the snow will you feel sorry enough to take me?"

I mock scowl at him. "See you at four-thirty."

"Whoa, whoa." He holds up both hands. "Let's not be hasty. Five is early enough."

I laugh. "See you then."

I close the passenger door, expecting him to leave me there, but he doesn't. He parks his truck and follows me up the stairs to my apartment.

I glance at him as I unlock the door.

"Want to come in?" I ask.

He shakes his head. "I have to go. Trying to study for finals."

I wrinkle my nose and roll my eyes. "Don't remind me. I always think I'm going to die from a stress attack when it's finals."

"I'm not fond of them either," he says. "Especially right now. Grades don't feel important."

"I wish I could have that attitude." I give him my sweetest smile. "Good night."

He tilts his head like a little bird, and says, "Do you want a hug?"

I bite my lip to hold back my delighted laugh. This is where I want him—asking me, instead of me begging. "Yes."

He flaps his arms like wings, and I step into his embrace.

"Are you going to fly away?" I say.

He flaps his arms again. "Yes." Then he wraps them around my back, and I hug him tighter.

"Take me with you," I whisper into his chest.

"I can't. You're too heavy."

I step out of his embrace and take his hands, and he threads his fingers through mine.

We don't say anything.

It's better not to acknowledge this physical connection between us.

I turn my hands over so that his palms are face-up, and then I pull my fingers free and run them over the lines in his skin.

I want to remember him. I want to remember *this*.

He says nothing. Then he closes his fingers around mine and pulls me into another hug before saying, "I really gotta go."

I step away as if it doesn't matter to me. "See you."

I turn around and go into the house before I can beg to be back in his arms.

It's so crazy to think that was me last year. Nineteen and thinking I had my head on straight.

I was so young.

CHAPTER ONE HUNDRED TWENTY-FIVE

Delete Him

I'm not a morning person, but being someone's ride to the airport gets me up better than any alarm ever could.

I pull up to Kai's dorm promptly at five a.m., just like we planned. I try the door to go inside, but the lobby is locked. It's freezing, so I circle back to my car and climb inside, then call him.

No answer.

I check the time. His flight isn't until seven, and the airport is only thirty minutes away, but I'm getting antsy. I like to get to the airport two hours before I fly.

Then I remember the dorms have landlines—and they're listed publicly.

I spend the next few minutes digging through the university directory and searching for Kai's name. I find it. Address, email, phone number.

The student directory is weirdly helpful.

The phone number listed isn't Kai's cell, so it must be his dorm's landline. I take a deep breath, heart racing, and dial, praying I'm not about to wake up his mom and dad.

It rings. Once. Twice. Three times. My heart sinks as the voicemail kicks in—

—but then it cuts off, and a groggy male voice says, "Hello?"

I don't recognize the speaker. His voice is rough, thick with sleep, and very much not thrilled to be woken up.

I try to sound confident, but it comes out a little squeaky. "Oh—uh, I'm so sorry to wake you. I was looking for Kai?"

The voice clears his throat, softening a little. "He's here. Let me get him."

I exhale with relief. Must be Kai's roommate. I've never met him.

Odd, considering how close Kai and I have gotten. Why has he kept me out of his personal life?

A moment later, Kai is on the line, and he doesn't sound much more awake than his roommate.

"Cassandra?" he mumbles.

"I'm here," I say, bright and helpful.

"I'm coming. Just a sec."

I settle back in my seat and wait.

Kai strolls out the door a minute later, face puffy with sleep, hands jammed in his hoodie pocket, flip-flops on his feet, a single backpack slung over one shoulder. He looks like he hasn't worried about anything in his life.

He climbs in. "Sorry. I overslept."

"Yeah, you did." I shift into reverse and pull away from his dorm. "You're dressed for summer."

"It's not cold in California. Gotta get myself out of Colorado."

"I'm a bit envious," I say. "It's wrong to live somewhere where it snows in April."

He makes a noise between a grunt and a laugh. "I agree with that."

"Why are you flying home now? Aren't your parents coming to see you in two weeks when school's out?"

"Yeah, but my dad had these miles he wanted to use, and we're not sure when I'm leaving for my mission trip, so we figured we'd get in some extra family time."

A pit opens in my chest at the mention of his mission trip. "No sign of your assignment yet?"

"Nope. Not yet."

"It's gotta be soon."

"Yeah. I submitted my application over a week ago."

I merge onto the highway. He yawns and leans his seat back.

"I'm so tired..."

"Even though you slept till five?" I say dryly.

He grins faintly. "I was out late last night. We hiked up to the hot springs on the mountain."

"Oh—the one you told me about last month?"

"Yeah, it was fun. Except I'm sitting there talking to these girls from my dorm, and I can't help feeling lonely. Even surrounded by people."

If he's trying to make me jealous, it's working. My chest tightens like someone set a boa constrictor loose around my ribcage.

"Well," I say, aiming for glib, "you better get used to it."

He glances over at me, but I don't meet his eyes.

"I want to take you there sometime," he says.

There are so many things I want to say. *Did you think of me while you were there? Why didn't you invite me there when you drove me home? When exactly were you planning to take me—before or after you disappear for two years?*

But I settle on: "I was free last night."

"They invited me, you know? Didn't feel like I could ask you."

That's BS. If he wanted me there, he wouldn't have waited for permission. He'd have told them he was inviting someone, and they would've said, *Cool. It's a public place.*

My goal between now and his departure is to be positive and cheerful. He doesn't get to see how much this hurts.

"Well," I say, "you can't blame me this time for being tired."

"I don't blame you when I'm tired. Honestly, it's the best reason to be tired—because I spent my time with you."

The words are sweet. But this guy doesn't act the way he used to. Even now, I feel a space between us—a wall that keeps me from reaching over and touching him while I drive.

The sooner he leaves, the sooner I can start getting over this.

And maybe start looking for my next heartbreak.

Great.

I pull up to the airport terminal and park. "I guess you don't need help with anything," I say, nodding at his tiny backpack.

"Nope. My parents have everything I need at home."

"Have a good flight. Call me if anything changes. Otherwise, I'll be back here Tuesday."

"I will." He grabs his backpack and pauses, looking at me across the passenger seat as he opens the door. "Thanks for the ride."

I wave. He gets out, closes the door, and walks away.

I don't watch him go. I delete him in my mind before he even disappears through the doors. I leave the terminal and head back toward campus, already shifting focus. I've got church ahead of me, and I want to be in the right frame of mind.

Time to lift my spirit.

❧

Shut the door behind you,
Throw away the key
Lock me here inside
Do not return
Nobody can come in
Nobody is allowed
"Do not disturb"
Says the sign
Hang it on the wall
Seal it in your heart
Feel it on your lips
You will not isolate me
If I should be alone
It will be my own choice
Nobody can come in
Do not disturb

I only have three more days of classes before finals. It's easier to buckle down and study now that Kai's out of town. No distractions.

It also helps me think more clearly about him. He's so young. So immature. He has a lot of growing to do. Honestly, it's good for us to be apart.

In Portuguese, my teacher hands back our stories. When she stops by my desk, she says, "I particularly enjoyed this one. I wanted to know if there's an ending."

My face warms. I fictionalized my experience with Tiago—wrote about a girl who fell in love with her exchange student. I gave it a better ending than it had in real life, but it probably still feels like it's missing closure.

"That's all there is to the story," I say. "It ended."

She smiles, and I get the feeling she knows it isn't entirely fiction. I'm left with a weird sense of déjà vu.

It ended.

Story of my life.

I spend the evening goofing off with my roommates. Camila comes with me while I do laundry, and we hang out in the basement, eating ice cream from the carton and talking about our futures while the clothes spin.

"I'm thinking of going on a mission trip," she says.

It's the first she's said anything, but I'm not surprised. Camila's always struck me as the kind of person who would love serving others and would be amazing at connecting with people.

"Me too," I say. "Maybe after I get back from my internship in Brazil."

"I'm thinking of doing it instead of school next year."

That one catches me off guard. I peer at her over the carton, swinging my legs where we sit. "That soon?"

She nods. "I'm excited about it. It's what I want to do."

She's not just thinking anymore—she's decided. I suspect she's been sitting on this longer than I realized.

"It'll be amazing," I say. "You'll be a fantastic missionary. I can't wait to see how it goes for you."

A part of me feels jealous. Maybe I should skip the internship and just go on a mission.

But no—I'm not ready for that. I want to do this for me.

As soon as my laundry's done, I head to the airport to pick up Kai. I pray he's in a good mood and that he enjoyed being home.

I text him when I get to the curb. A minute later, he walks out, smiling as he climbs into the car.

"Thanks for coming to get me," he says.

"Of course. We're good at giving each other rides."

He laughs. I'm ready with questions—anything to keep the space between us from stretching too wide.

"Did you enjoy your time with your family?"

"Yeah. The weather was nice, it was comfortable. I'm still trying to wrap my head around the fact that I'll be living there again soon, even if just for a little bit. Not just visiting."

"It's weird, isn't it?" I say. "When you move out, home stops feeling like home."

"Exactly. My mom keeps reminding me that my place is with her—first and foremost."

"Moms do that."

"How about here? Any more snow?"

I shake my head. "Thankfully, no. I got a lot done. I think I'm going to get As in all my classes—though some of them just barely. I feel ready for finals."

"I wish I cared about my grades like you."

"No, you don't. I'd be less anxious if I didn't either."

"How's Portuguese?"

I wonder if we're both doing the same thing—keeping the conversation going so there are no gaps. "I got a good grade on a short story I wrote."

"You wrote a short story in Portuguese? Can I read it?"

My face flushes. My story about me and Tiago? "I don't think so. I'm not that brave."

"Come on."

I don't want him to keep needling for it, which I think he'll do if I say no. But what will he think if he reads it?

I can't pretend I don't have it—my backpack's sitting at his feet.

"Okay, but don't make fun of me," I say, as if the only thing I'm worried about is my grammar. "Open the top flap. You'll find my Portuguese binder."

He pulls it out and flips it open. I'm suddenly grateful everything in the binder is in Portuguese. I've written a lot about him in the pages, but I never use his name, referring to him simply as "the kid" or "the boy."

"This one?" he says, pulling out the typed paper.

"Yes."

"Well, good job. Ninety-seven?"

I nod. "It helped raise my grade."

He starts reading, and I hold my breath. How much will he understand?

After a couple minutes, he gives up. "It's hard. I see a lot of familiar words, but there are too many I don't know."

I almost sag with relief. "If you heard them, you'd probably understand. Some of them sound the same."

He puts the essay back and slides the binder into my backpack. "What's it about?"

"A romance," I say. "One that doesn't work out."

"Couldn't write a happy ending?"

I laugh. "I don't know how. I've never seen one."

There's just enough sarcasm and amused bitterness in my voice that he glances over at me. I feel his eyes but don't look back.

"Someday," he says quietly. "Someday you will."

I don't respond.

CHAPTER ONE HUNDRED TWENTY-SIX

Expired Time

There's a dance on campus Wednesday night to commemorate the end of classes.

Abby and Iris convince me to go. I haven't been to a dance since the one Kai and I went to for our first date, and I can't help being filled with nostalgia now that I'm here. I barely knew him at the time, and I certainly couldn't have predicted how much he would influence my life.

I don't feel like dancing, and I hang out along the wall like a wallflower, wondering how long I have to stay before Abby and Iris will let me leave.

"Well, well. Cassandra Jones."

I turn when someone says my name, and my jaw drops when I see Stirling—one of my closest friends.

"Stirling!" I throw my arms around his neck, laughing as he hugs me back.

I step away, already feeling guilty for not doing a better job of maintaining our friendship. "Oh my goodness, how are you? It's been so long!"

He shoves his hands in his pockets and grins at me. "Yeah, it has. What are you up to these days?"

"Same as everyone, I guess. Getting through the semester. I'm going to Brazil in August."

His face lights up. "Doing that study abroad thing?"

"I am. I'm still working out the details, but I should be gone all semester."

"That's amazing."

"And you? What are you up to?" And because it's the question everyone really wants to know, I ask, "Dating?"

"Funny you should ask." He leans against the wall beside me. "I've been dating this girl for about three months now. I think she's the one."

My eyebrows lift. "Wow, that's amazing!" Somehow I never pictured Stirling in a serious relationship. "Is she here?" I glance around, like I expect to see her hiding behind him.

He shakes his head. "No, my roommate dragged me to this."

I groan as I picture his roommate. "Wyatt. He doing well?"

"As well as a socially awkward rich kid can be doing." Then he says, "What about you? Did you get over Mitch yet?"

The question makes me feel like a pathetic, lovesick schoolgirl. I move from one heartbreak to the next. "Oh, months ago. I'm dating someone else now." Was. I was dating.

"You are?" Stirling's eyes go wide with delight—or surprise—or both. "Tell me about him! Is it serious?"

I laugh at the idea of my relationship with Kai being serious. I shake my head. "You won't believe this. He's just a kid, barely out of high school."

"But they're so fun that way," Stirling says, which makes me laugh harder.

I spend the next ten minutes telling him stories about Kai, sharing the silly things he does and his idiosyncrasies, and it's great fun—and a little bit healing.

"I want to meet him," Stirling says.

"Good luck," I say. "He's leaving on a mission and barely makes time for me anymore."

"Of course," Stirling says, rolling his eyes.

"You know what? Let me see if I can get him. I'll ask him for a ride home from the dance."

"Oo, I know! Tell him I need a gallon of milk. Everyone wants to to look helpful."

We step out into the hall where it's not so loud, and I'm giggling as I dial Kai's number.

He answers on the second ring. "Yeah?"

"Hi!" I'm already goofy with the energy of the dance and talking with Stirling, so I don't even have to force the energetic/happy vibe. "I'm on campus at a dance. My friend needs a gallon of milk. Can you take us to the creamery and then take me home?"

I meet Stirling's eyes over the phone, and he winks at me.

"Yeah, sure. Where should I get you?"

"Meet me outside the food court."

I hang up, and Stirling says, "You didn't tell him your friend is a boy."

"Does it matter?"

"Of course it does. It's always good to keep someone doubting. When people get secure, they don't try hard."

I mull that over as food for thought, but I'm not good at that. I wear my heart on my sleeve and overshare whatever I'm feeling.

Kai's truck pulls up a minute later. I go running out and open the passenger door. Stirling strolls out behind me, lip twisted in a smile, hands in his pockets.

I spin around to Stirling as he gets in the back seat. "All good?" I ask him.

Kai turns around, and I can't read the expression on his face in the dark.

"All good," Stirling says smoothly. "You must be Kai."

"I am," Kai says, and again, I can't tell from his voice what he's thinking. "And you are?"

"The friend who needs milk," Stirling says, and I burst out laughing.

He's playing this well.

"Oh," is all Kai says.

I have to intervene. "Kai, this is Stirling. We met during my freshman year, so we've been friends for a while."

"That's nice."

Kai starts driving, and I can tell from his emotionless reactions that he's not sure what to think.

Stirling comes to the rescue. He leans between us on the console and says, "Cassandra says you're getting ready to go on a mission. She says you're one of her favorite people. What did you do to get rated so high?"

Kai's eyes crinkle as he smiles. I see some of the tension go out of his shoulders as he realizes Stirling's not competition. "I gave her a stapler."

I turn to Stirling, all smiles, running with the joke. "It's a baby. We named it Blue."

"A stapler?" Stirling gives me an amused look. "Only English majors. I don't think it would go over well if I gave Miranda a stapler."

"Is that your fiancée?" I ask.

"Girlfriend," Stirling corrects. "I haven't popped the question yet."

Kai jumps on this too, glancing at Stirling in the rearview mirror. "Getting serious?" he says, like he's known Stirling and Miranda his whole life. "Can't stop thinking about her?"

Stirling nods. "There's something special about her. I've never met anyone like her."

"Better not let her get away then," Kai says, and now I can read his body language. He's totally at ease.

"That's what I'm thinking," Stirling says.

We pull into the creamery and hop out of the car so Stirling can go get his milk. I wander over to the pens and pencils in the school supply section, and Kai follows me.

"Look, Kai!" I say, grabbing an unopened package of a blue stapler. "Baby staplers!"

He glances at them, and a smile creases his lips. "They haven't been born yet."

My heart swells—an emotional reaction that makes me want to throw my arms around his neck and say words I can't take back. Words I refuse to say. Words I refuse to *think*. I cannot fall for him.

"You guys ready?" Stirling appears with his gallon of milk, and his eyes fall on us where we're examining the stapler. "Or are you thinking of having more kids?"

I laugh and glance back over to Stirling. "I think we're good to go."

I want to loop my arm through Kai's, but I can't.

Stirling and I walk out of the creamery together with Kai behind us. Then we separate to climb into the car. Stirling directs Kai to his apartment, and then it's just the two of us again as we head to mine.

"Well, he seems nice," Kai says.

"He is. I like my friends."

"As you should," he says.

We pull up to my apartment, and Kai turns off the truck and follows me up, just as I expect him to.

My roommates are home, celebrating the end of classes. I grab three cookies and a bottle of Martinelli's and take Kai, and we sit on the stairs outside. I'm in a goofy mood, and I can't stop teasing him and making fun of him as we share the bottle of soda and the cookies.

But the only touching I do is poke him mercilessly in the ribs every time he takes the bottle from me.

"Next time—" he says, batting my hand away for the fifth time. "Next time, get two."

"I would've if I'd known you were going to drink it all," I say, snatching it back from him.

"You brought me two frosted cookies and thought I wouldn't get thirsty?"

All I can do is laugh as I take another swig.

And then the food is gone and it's just the two of us, and I've run out of things to say —because what I *want* to do is lean my head on his shoulder and wrap my arm around him and cuddle.

And I know that's exactly what I shouldn't do.

I stand up and brush the cookie crumbs off my jeans. "Thanks for the ride."

He stands too. "Is this where you send me home?"

"I'm afraid our time together has expired," I say, straight-faced.

But I pretty much mean it. I have to get out now before I get in deeper.

"I'm fresh out of quarters," he says.

I take a step back. "Then you better go."

He shoves his hands in his pockets and doesn't attempt to bridge the distance between us. "Good night."

"Night."

I turn around and go back into the apartment, and I know I did the right thing—but I'm aching.

Longing.

Wishing I'd given into temptation and fallen into his arms.

⁂

Finals.

It's where my entire focus is for the next two days. I hardly eat, I'm so anxious. I over-prepare for each exam and then sit there with my stomach twisting and turning. I can't think of anything during the tests, the pencil shaking in my fingers.

I just have to get through this.

I don't hear one word from Kai.

On one hand, this wounds me terribly. On the other hand, I thrust it from my mind and try not to think of him. He's basically gone.

The bookstore calls me Thursday morning to say his pen arrived. I pick it up and remove it from the case to make sure they spelled his name right. It makes my heart tighten to see his full name embossed in gold across the pen. I trace my fingers over it, mouthing it.

I wonder if I'll get the chance to give it to him.

In spite of all my studying, I only get a 78% on my Classical Civ test. I scowl as I examine the score before leaving the Testing Center Saturday afternoon.

I'm almost done. Just two finals to go, and my sophomore year of college is over.

My phone rings as I walk through the quad, vibrating in the pocket against my lower back. I stop outside the engineering building to answer it, hoping it's—

It's not Kai. But I forget to be disappointed when I see Monica's name across the screen.

"Monica!" I say. "How are you?" I resume walking, but slowly this time, because my office is only a few minutes away.

"Doing all right," she says, and I strain to hear if her voice is weak, if she's more frail —but she sounds fine.

"Long time no talk," she says.

Guilt slashes through my chest. "I know. I've been so busy with school! But I think of you often!"

"What are your summer plans?"

I lift my shoulder even though she can't see me. "I'm staying for spring term, then I'll take a break and go home, see my family, before I head to Brazil for my internship."

She gives a squeal. "I'm so excited for you! What do you think of coming here to spend a few days with me?"

I lift my eyebrows, startled. "To Louisiana?"

"Yes! I miss you! And I know my family would love to see you."

I'm hesitant, imagining the dynamics of spending time in that house where so many memories and heartbreaks occurred.

"You don't have to, of course, if it makes you uncomfortable," she adds.

I put aside my misgivings. This is Monica, and she's sick, and she needs me. "Of course I can come. What's the plan?"

"You could come out after spring term. Some time in July, spend a week with me."

A trip to Louisiana.

The championship game. Meeting Owen's roommates. The way he kissed me. Going to his parents' house, that night—our night together.

My mind is tripping, and it's taking my heart with it. I can't let myself fall back into those memories. They were so long ago now. I was just a kid.

"Absolutely. I'll make it happen."

"Oh, I'm so glad! I love you. I'll see you in a few weeks!"

"See you," I echo. One more thing to look forward to.

I put my phone away and step into my office, and I stop short when I see Kai at the counter talking to Christina.

CHAPTER ONE HUNDRED TWENTY-SEVEN

Out of my Hands

He catches my eye, and I say cautiously, "Hey."

Why is he here now, before my shift? Was he hoping to get out before I arrived? Or is he here to see me?

I hate how uncertain I am.

"Hey," he says. "How are you?"

"I'm fine." I go around the desk and raise my eyebrows at Christina, who turns away with a smirk.

"Here to see Professor Stephens?" I ask as I scoot my chair into the computer desk.

"I already saw him. Just on my way out."

"Oh." I focus on the computer screen in front of me, logging in.

"Finals going okay?"

I make a face, sticking my tongue out at the computer. "Terrible. I can't wait for them to be over."

"I don't love them either."

His pen is in my backpack. I could give it to him now, and then we'd be done. No reason to see each other again.

But I can't do it. I don't want to end everything between us right here in my office.

So I say, "When do you head home?"

"Early Thursday morning. Wednesday's my last day here."

Wednesday. In five days.

My chest squeezes like someone's got a hold of my heart and is tightening their fist.

"Do you think I can see you before then?" I say, keeping my eyes on the computer screen, and I'm pleased at how calm and even my voice is.

"Yeah. I've got a final to take Monday, but you could come over Tuesday afternoon. I'll just be packing up."

I nod, a warm rush of relief. "Yeah, that works," I say.

I'll give him his pen then.

And officially say goodbye.

"I have a soccer game tomorrow night," he says. "If you want to come."

"Yeah, I'd love to." I want to spend as much time as possible with this boy before he's gone.

"Okay, great. I'll see you tomorrow." He taps the top of the counter with the palm of his hand and starts to leave. "Oh," he says, turning back. "I almost forgot to tell you. I got my mission call."

It takes a moment for the words to sink in. I lift my gaze from the computer and blink at him. "You did? Did you open it?"

"Yeah. I'm going to Neuquén, Argentina. Leaving in August."

I hear the words, but I'm still stuck on one thing: He didn't invite me to be there when he opened it.

"That's great," I manage to croak out between dry lips. My mind buzzes. My eyes burn.

He cut me out.

Don't say anything, I tell myself. *Pretend like it doesn't phase you, you don't care.*

But I can't. "I thought—" I lick my lips and tell myself not to say these words, but they tumble from my lips anyway. "I thought you would want me there."

Something flashes in his eyes. His eyebrows furrow—and then it's gone.

But I recognized the expression: guilt.

My absence was a deliberate choice. One that he knew would hurt me. But he did it anyway.

"I only had a few people there. My roommates. Friends from church."

Not you.

My smile is too bright, the crinkle around my eyes too tight as I say, "Of course. The important people."

He presses his lips together. It takes him a moment to find a response that isn't a lie. "No. Just... people."

I feel a moment of victory—he's defenseless.

But it's short-lived.

Back off. You're not his girlfriend anymore.

You're not even a close friend.

"You'll be a fantastic missionary," I say. The words are diplomatic, delivered with the precision of an unbiased phone operator.

I turn back to my computer, eyes on the screen, and begin typing.

I'm done talking to him.

And he knows it.

He leaves without another word, and I swallow hard. My emotions are digging into the back of my throat, and it's all I can do not to cry.

I exhale and turn back to my work.

I shouldn't go to the soccer game. I should finish studying for finals and stop letting my heart grow attached to him.

But it doesn't matter what I *should* do.

I know what I'm *going* to do.

⁘

I head to Kai's soccer game by myself Saturday evening. I don't tell my roommates, because part of me is ashamed that I'm going. I'm pathetic, going just so I can catch a glimpse of him—this boy who has no time or consideration for me.

I don't even intend to talk to him. He might not know I'm there. But my opportunities to see him are numbered.

It's beautiful weather for a soccer game. I sit in the bleachers next to a few other people, my hair pulled back under a baseball cap I borrowed from Abby. I don't want him to see me.

He plays almost the entire game, and I'm so proud of him every time he gets the ball. I take my phone out and snap a few pictures.

When the game ends, I step away from the bleachers with the intent to make it to my car without talking to Kai—but then I see him stop and scan the spectators. I know he's looking for me.

I know that, even as he pushes me away, he wants to pull me close. And I can't bring myself to hurt him, even though he's hurting me.

So I stand still and wait until his head turns almost in my direction. Then I wave— just enough of a motion to attract his attention.

I'm still not sure he knows it's me, because I'm so far away and wearing my disguise.

But he lifts his hand in a wave.

And I turn away.

That will have to do.

◦◦◦※◦◦◦

I spend Monday morning taking the last of my finals. I'm pleased with my scores, and then I'm on air the whole way to work—because I did it! I completed my sophomore year of college!

I can do this. Next year, I'm spending a semester in Brazil, and then I'll have a year and a half of school left. The end is in sight.

Work has me training in the academic advisement center across the street. My supervisor said that's where they'll place me when I get back from Brazil, since they have to fill my position in the engineering department. They already know the employee at the advisement center is leaving after the fall semester, which leaves an opening for me when I get back from Brazil next year.

I'm dubious. I like the professors I work with, and the advisement center feels like a basement—but I don't complain. I'm grateful to have a job.

The afternoon drags and doesn't provide enough distractions. My mind drifts frequently to Kai.

Tomorrow we'll officially say goodbye. Emotionally, it happened weeks ago.

Abby is in the middle of hauling boxes out of a van when I get home.

"My parents are here," she says. "I'll be off tonight."

I grab her and hug her hard. "Will I see you before I leave for Brazil?"

She shrugs. "Maybe. I don't live far from here."

I nod, but there's a lump in my throat.

Things are changing. Camila's put in her mission papers, Abby's leaving now, and I won't be here next semester.

Life feels like it's spinning out of control, away from me—but maybe I never had it in my hands to begin with.

I go upstairs to help her move her things to the car.

❧

I head to the advisor's building Tuesday morning to train a little more and get to know the professors. This is where I'll be all summer, and I need to get used to it. Since classes are over and I'm not in a rush, I can drive to school. I put on a dress and take the time to curl my hair, which is longer now, hitting the edges of my shoulders. My supervisor, Beverly, always wears pantsuits and exudes a no-nonsense exterior, which makes me feel I should dress fancier for work. The professors on this side of the street teach the technology side of engineering, and they look at me like they aren't sure if they trust me.

That's all right. The feeling's mutual. I miss Dr. Lance and Professor Stephens.

I keep waiting for Kai to call me. We planned to get together but didn't set a time, and he doesn't know my new work schedule. He doesn't even know I'm working at the other building.

At two o'clock, Beverly comes in. She's spiked her short pepper gray hair up today, but it doesn't make her look any younger.

"You can go, Cassandra," she says. "You've put in enough hours today. I think you're getting the hang of it."

"Thank you," I say, gathering my things and resisting the urge to curtsy.

As soon as I step out of the building, I call Kai. My heart races as I do so, and I hate the trepidation I feel. Everything between us has changed in the past two weeks, and I'm not sure how that happened.

"Hello?" he says.

His lack of enthusiasm sets me on edge. "Hey. Did you still want to get together today?" The pen with his name engraved on it is burning a hole in my backpack. I want to give it to him in person.

"Yeah."

I wait, but there's no more. "Okay. I'll drive over to your dorm."

"All right."

He hangs up, and I almost change my mind. Maybe I should just mail the pen to him.

Stop being such a coward, I scold myself. *Just give him the pen and say goodbye.*

That will be the end of it, and I admit I feel a sense of relief at the thought of having it done.

Kai meets me on the sidewalk. "I was just on my way to get lunch," he says. "Want to eat something?"

He doesn't reach for me, shows no sign of touching me or being close, but he's not scowling at me either. "Yeah, sure."

He turns around and leads me to the cafeteria next to his dorm. I've eaten here before, back in the summer before freshman year when I took the Honor's week.

"Kai!"

As soon as we enter, a flurry of kids hurry over, a mixture of boys and girls dressed in casual summer clothes. They look like high school kids to me, but I remind myself they've just finished their freshman year of college.

"Hey." Kai's face transforms into a smile as he fist bumps the boys and accepts hugs

607

from the girls, and my heart clenches. That's the smile I'd hoped to see when I arrived.

These are his real friends. Not me.

One of the boys is studying me, and when I glance at him he says, "Hey, I'm Peter."

"Hi, Peter," I say.

"Are you Kai's sister?"

I glance at Kai, nodding his head along to a girl who's engrossed in telling an engaging tale, complete with exaggerated hand motions.

"Yeah," I say. It's easier than trying to explain what I am—and what I'm not.

"You guys look alike."

"Huh. How interesting."

"I haven't seen you around here before."

I shrug. "Kai keeps me hidden."

"Older brothers can be protective that way."

Older. Kai's more than a year younger than me.

Kai looks over at us, and he moves a half step in my direction. "You've met Cassandra," he says.

"Kind of. She's nice." Peter looks at me again, and I hide a smirk because he's clearly interested in me but apparently afraid of what my "brother"'s reaction will be if he hits on me.

"Yeah, she is," Kai says, and he puts a hand on the small of my back and steers me over to a table, away from everyone else.

Stirling was right. If you want to keep a guy's interest, make him think you might be into someone else.

"Want anything?" he asks as we sit.

His friends have dispersed to other tables. "I'm not very hungry," I say. My stomach twists with nerves over our impending goodbye. "I'll just get a drink of water."

"You sure?"

"Yeah."

"All right."

While Kai goes through the food line, I head to the fountain. I fill a water cup and sit down, then wish I had something to munch on because I feel silly sitting at the table sipping water.

Kai returns with a burger and fries, and I take a fry so my hands aren't empty.

"Peter thinks I'm your sister," I say.

His brow furrows. "Why does he think that?"

"I may have said I was." I smile behind my cup.

Now he directs the frown at me. "Why?"

I shrug. "I couldn't think of how to define us."

He lets out a sound like a snort. "Definitely not siblings."

What am I, then? I want to ask. Definitely not girlfriend. Not feeling like much of a friend, either.

An old acquaintance?

Gosh, I hate those.

"All done with finals?" he asks around a bite of burger.

"Yes. Didn't fail any, so." I lift two fingers in front of my face. "Peace out, PYU."

"Same. You're done with work early."

Ah. He probably expected me to finish around five. "I'm working at the other building now."

"Really? So if I went to see Professor Stephens, I wouldn't see you?"

"Did you go to see Professor Stephens?"

"No, class is over." He smirks. "And I don't care what grade I got. Just glad to be done."

I shrug. "Yeah, you wouldn't see me, should you happen to go over there."

"Where are you now?"

It's a polite question. I know his interest isn't genuine. He's out of here, and he's not going to hunt me down at my office to see me. But I can politely answer. "The advisement center."

"Oh. Cool." He takes another bite, I steal another fry, and then he says, his mouth full of food, "You look nice."

I pause and lift my eyes to his face. And then I start giggling because his words were difficult to interpret, and why did he wait to say them until they'd be unintelligible?

"Thanks," I say. "You look nice too."

That warm pink color creeps up his face. I turn my gaze away and dig through my backpack, finding the pen. Is this the moment? Should I give it to him now?

He swallows and takes a swig from his cup of juice. "I have to help a friend move out. Benefits of having a truck, of course."

"Of course," I say, my fingers closing over the gift box. My heart pounds a little harder, my throat closing.

This could be goodbye.

CHAPTER ONE HUNDRED TWENTY-EIGHT

Save Tonight

My stomach churns, and I want to vomit. I'm not ready for goodbye.

"Want to come help me move her?" Kai asks. "It might be boring."

I exhale, my fingers loosening their grip on the box. Not yet. He bought me a little more time. "Sure."

Kai leads the way to his white truck, the one with the blue Adidas flower in the window, and it feels me with such nostalgia that I already miss him. And why not? He put distance between us days ago. I've lost my friend.

He drives over to another side of the dorm, and a moment later a small girl with short blond hair comes out, her arms loaded with boxes. I pop out and take one from her.

"Looks like you could use a hand," I say.

"Or two," she says, shooting me a smile. She glances at Kai. "Thanks so much of the help!"

"Hey, no problem," he says.

His shoulders relax, his mannerisms less restricted.

I'm the one who makes him uptight.

"I'm Megan. Who are you?" she asks me as we load boxes into the bed of Kai's truck. "I haven't seen you around before."

"I'm Kai's on-again-off-again friend," I say.

"Oh, one of those," she says, giving me a knowing smile.

Yep. She gets it.

"One of what?" Kai asks.

She rounds on him. "Boys are all the same," she says with an eye roll and huff of breath. "Can't you ever make up your mind?"

She stomps away to get another box, and Kai turns his wide eyes on me.

"What did you say to her?"

I shrug. "Nothing. She figured you out."

"Figured me out?" he echoes.

"Wait." I narrow my eyes and tap my lip. "Were you dating her also?"

"What?" he exclaims. "No! I wouldn't do that!"

His response is so scathed that I believe him. But that lovely blush has crept up his cheeks again, and I can't help but keep teasing him just to see it last longer.

"Well, why not? She seems like a perfectly nice girl."

"Date her? You think I should have dated her? But you—" He cuts himself off.

I hook my arm through his. "We were never exclusive. Half the time I wasn't sure we were even dating." I pull back to look at his face. "Were we?"

He's so red, like a beet before it's been cooked. "Yes," he manages to croak out. "Yeah, we dated."

"And then we stopped." I pat his hand and release him.

I head back into the dorm to help Megan, and I keep up a steady conversation with her while we empty her dorm. Every time Kai tries to enter the conversation, I cut him off with a teasing comment, and she picks up on the momentum. We tease him mercilessly, but he takes in stride, teasing us right back whenever he gets the chance.

I'm lighter than I've been all week. *See?* I want to tell him. *We can be friends too. I'm fun. I'm energetic. I make you laugh.*

I don't say it because that would ruin it.

Megan turns to Kai when she's done loading the truck. "My parents parked their van by the stadium. Mind if we drive over there so I can unload?"

"Here." Kai pulls out his keys and hands them to her. "Take it. Just make sure to bring it back."

"Don't you have to go somewhere?" she asks.

He inclines his head at me. "Cassandra can take me."

Oh, I can?

Gladly.

Megan gives him a hug and thanks me for my help and then drives away, honking her horn.

"You're brave," I say as we begin walking to the other side of the dorm, where my car is. "I'm always afraid to let people drive my car."

"It's a car," he says. "I'll have it back if I need it. I'm not worried about something happening to it."

It's a more generous attitude than I have.

We reach my car, and he says, "Can you drive me to soccer practice?"

"Sure." He could walk if he wanted. The soccer fields are just a block away.

"I need to get a few soccer balls from my room. That okay?"

I shrug, then sit in my car and let the AC do its work while I wait for him. Hard to believe two weeks ago it was snowing.

Kai comes back ten minutes later with a net full of soccer balls. I pop the trunk, and he drops them in, then climbs in beside me.

"You're the ballkeeper for the team?" I say, putting my car in reverse.

"Yeah. Big responsibility. They trust me."

"As long as you're not asking me to keep your balls," I say, straight-faced. Intentionally lacing my words with innuendo.

He groans and puts his face in his hands, but his shoulders shake with laughter. "You did not just go there."

"Oh, I did." I grin.

He pulls out his phone and messes with it. "Hey, I want you to hear this song."

I stay quiet while he presses the buttons and connects the phone to my car stereo. I arrive at the soccer fields before he's got it hooked up, and he says, "Just park," while waving a hand at me.

I do so.

The music starts.

"I know this song," I say as soon as I hear the chords of the guitar. I remember hearing it when I dated Tiago and seizing upon the words because of what they meant to me then. My throat closes as I think of all the losses I've had since then.

Save tonight . . . Because tomorrow I'll be gone.

"I heard it the other night and it made me think of you," Kai says.

We descend into a quiet moment, only the lyrics of the song and the strumming of the guitar filling the car cabin. We don't look at each other, both of us staring at the car stereo as if the sounds coming out of it are doing the speaking for us.

I should give him the pen now. This is a good moment to say goodbye.

But I don't move. I don't want to break this stillness.

Someone slams both hands down on the hood of my car, and our heads jerk up.

"Kai!" A grinning redhead peers into the car at us, his eyes glinting with mischief. "You got the balls or what?"

Kai grins back and gets out, all evidence of the earlier mood between us vanishing in a split second. "Oh, I've got them."

I laugh and pop the trunk and get out also, but I'm shaking because I lost the best chance I had. How do I say goodbye now, here, at the soccer fields with his idiot friend laughing and sneering at us?

Kai hands over the net of balls and turns to me. "Thanks for the ride."

I lick my lips. "Of course. It's what we do."

Crap. Crap crap crap. This is it.

I stall for time. "Do you need a ride home?"

He shakes his head. "Nah, I think I've got it."

"You sure?" My face is growing hot. I'm panicking. This is not how I want to end it.

"Yeah." He turns away from the car, glancing out at the soccer fields. "I'll see you tomorrow."

My heart stops its mad racing. "Y-you will?" I stutter.

He turns back to me, a small smile gracing his lips. "Yeah."

I narrow my eyes. Two days in a row? This feels suspicious. Is he blowing me off because he doesn't want to say goodbye? "When?"

He shrugs. "I don't know, when can you?"

I flip through my schedule in my head. "I'm off work at five."

"Cool. Come over then."

He holds out a hand, and I clasp it. Like the college buddies we are.

"All right. Until tomorrow."

He moves away without a second look, and I have to believe he plans to see me tomorrow, because if that was our goodbye, it sucked.

I spend Tuesday evening helping Layne move out. She hugs all of us before getting in the car with her parents and driving off. Camila, Iris, and I stand at the curb watching her go.

"Three down, three to go," Iris says, and we turn back for the apartment.

"I barely saw Layne this year," Camila says. "Often it felt like we didn't have that sixth roommate."

"Or fifth," I say. "First it was Tracie, then Heather, then Lauren . . ." I tick off the names of our sixth person.

"You forgot Crystal," Iris says.

"She only lived with us for a hot minute," Camila says.

"A hot weekend, you mean," Iris says, and we can't help cackling.

"That one was boy crazy if I ever saw one," Camila says.

"Worse than Layne," Iris agrees.

"Layne wasn't so bad." I open the door, and we step into our apartment. "She honored our wishes." I glance around the quiet kitchen, the gurgling fishtank in the corner the only thing making noise.

"And now it's just us three," Iris says. "Until the landlord fills the space with strangers."

"Just you two, you mean," Camila says, and we look at her.

"I put in my mission application," she says. "A week ago."

I keep my eyes steady on her. I knew this was coming. "When do you go?"

"I don't know." She gives a sheepish smile. "But I'll get the call in May."

And then she'll leave. I turn to Iris. "Then it will be just me and you . . . Until I leave for Brazil in August."

Iris's eyes go wide, and I think she might panic, but then she relaxes. "Yes, but the same time you leave, Abby and Layne will come back. So I won't ever be alone."

"This is true," I say, and then I put my arms around both of them.

Camila won't be here when I get back from Brazil. I can't picture college without her. But this is happening.

I'm jittery at work all day Wednesday like I downed a gallon of caffeine, except not really because that would probably kill me. My heart pounds in my chest, in my throat, in my lungs, choking me, suffocating me.

Today we'll say goodbye. It has to be today because tomorrow he leaves, he gets in his car and drives back to California and then goes to Argentina and I'll never see him again and that sucks.

Kai got under my skin.

I decide my favorite part of working in between semesters is getting to drive my car to campus. I get a special sticker that lets me park in the faculty lot, since most of the teachers are gone in between classes. Spring term starts in a few weeks, and that will keep me busy, but July is full of fun. My parents want to do a family trip to Mexico, and I'm going to Louisiana to see Monica.

I don't text or call Kai. I'm afraid to confirm with him for fear he's changed his mind. If he wants to cancel on me, he'll have to contact me.

And he won't.

So as soon as work ends, I hop in my car and beeline it over to his dorm.

Even more people are out and about than yesterday. It's like someone stepped in an anthill. Every parking spot is full, and parents and kids go from car to dorm to car, emptying out the room that held their entire lives for one year.

Oh, I remember it, even though my dorm life was quite different.

I toss the gift box with the pen into my purse and hop out of the car.

I'm not sure where to find Kai. But the rooms are unlocked and visitors are allowed on every floor and in every room right now, since so many families are here helping kids leave. So I stop one of the RAs as he walks by and ask, "Do you know which room is Kai Tanaka's?"

"Kai? I think so." He steps into another corridor, and I follow him. I watch him read down a clipboard on the wall, then he says, "Yeah, third floor, room three-twelve."

"Thank you." I flash him a smile and then take the elevator.

I should have called. What if Kai isn't in his room? He could be in the cafeteria, or at the soccer fields . . .

I step out of the elevator and wander down the hall until I find the open room. Laughter comes from within, and my stomach tightens in apprehension as I knock on the door frame.

"Hello?" I say.

Three boys cluster around a table, and they turn as one. Kai is among them. His brow furrows when he sees me.

"What are you doing here?" he says.

I arch one eyebrow, my heartbeat slowing as reality descends. "You told me to come."

He blinks, still staring at me, and I realize he didn't expect me to show up. Maybe he forgot what he said, or he didn't think I'd come. Humiliation burns up my cheeks. I misread this situation, again.

"I'll just go," I say, and I turn around. Never mind the gift, never mind goodbyes. I'll mail this to him. He won't care.

"No, wait," he says, and he comes after me in the hall. "It's just, I don't have time for you right now. I would just be ignoring you."

I bob my head and say, "You do that anyway."

"What?" he says. And then he grins and says, "Okay, maybe I do."

I laugh even though my lungs feel like they're caving in.

This will have to do. I pull my purse up to rest on my hip and dig through it, searching for the gift box.

"I'll call you tonight," he says.

I stop my digging and lift my eyes. "You will?"

He rolls his eyes. "Yeah, if I said I'll call, I'll call."

"Like you remembered you said we'd meet when I got off work?" I say, a bit dryly.

"I didn't forget—I did forget."

I nod, but my face stings like he slapped me. Saying goodbye to me wasn't on his list of priorities.

Everything I'm feeling must show on my face, because he says, "I didn't forget you. I forgot what time it was. I forgot we said five. I was thinking later, for some reason."

If he's lying, he's good at it, and I'd rather not explore that possibility. "You don't have to call me later." I can say goodbye right now.

"Maybe I want to," he says, petulance entering his tone.

My lip quirks upward. "If you want to, then definitely call."

He bobs his head and says, "Okay, leave it at that. I'll call."

"Okay." I turn away again, and Kai says, "And give me a hug."

I swivel back, immediately suspicious. Kai hasn't hugged me in days. "Won't I see you later tonight?"

He shrugs. "Yeah, but you can still give me a hug."

I step up to him and wrap my arms around his waist, and his arms go around my shoulders, and he clutches me close like he just ran a marathon and I'm the finish line. It's desperate and starving and exhausted.

"You're a strange kid," I say, stepping out of his embrace.

He gives a short laugh. "I know."

"See you later, then," I say, and I turn around and walk out.

He better call. I need to have that closure.

CHAPTER ONE HUNDRED TWENTY-NINE

Skilled Seductress

The sun is setting and soon
Darkness will prevent our sight
As an image serves for light
The weak mirror of the moon
But I will never feel dismay
I saw it as down it went
Lighting, for a brief moment
In a beautiful array
It won't be the same again
But anon the sun will rise
Each day a marvelous prize
And none shall be forgotten

Kai didn't give me a time, and I don't know how long he'll need, but I leave my evening open.

Camila comes into the living room a little after seven. I'm seated in front of the fish tank, watching my beautiful swimming colors and journaling.

"My friend got married yesterday and is having a reception half an hour from here in Vail. Want to come?" she says.

I shake my head. "Kai said he'd call."

She nods and grabs her purse. "Okay, good luck! I know tonight's important to you."

"Thanks," I say, not acknowledging the truth of her words.

By eight I've abandoned my journal and I'm curled up with a book on the couch.

"Mind if a turn on a movie?" Iris asks.

I shrug. "Isn't your family it town?"

"Yeah, but I'll see plenty of them over the next few days."

Her movie is mindless and distracting. My phone rings and I jump, but I sigh when I see it's my cousin Jordan.

"Hey, there!" he says enthusiastically when I answer. "My mom and dad just got in town and we're going out for ice cream. Want to come?"

"Oh, Jordan, I'd love to!" I say. "But I already have plans tonight." Do I? It's after nine p.m., and there's no word from Kai.

My heart sinks to my toes. He's not calling.

"Okay, if you change your mind or something comes up, just let me know!"

"I will," I say, blinking hard.

I should tell Jordan I'm free.

I stand up and go to my room, so hurt and angry I can't cry. I pace the carpet, wanting to call him and yell at him and tell him hateful things before hanging up on him and never talking to him again.

Why didn't he just tell me he wasn't going to call me? Why the charade? Oh, right, because I don't *matter* to him.

I pick up my phone, ready to call Jordan back, when it rings. I scream, startled, and throw it like a snake across my room. And then I drop to my hands and knees and scramble after it, because I saw the name on the screen.

Kai.

I sit under the window and pull my knees up as I answer. "Hello?" I say, breathless.

"Hey. You ready?"

Every ounce of anger and hurt melts way with those three words. He remembered me. He wants to see me. His last night here, and he wants to spend it with me.

"Yes," I say. I have no plan, no idea what we're doing, but I'm going to give him that pen, doggonit.

"Great. I'm at a friend's house. Can you come get me? I'll text you the address."

"Okay."

"The door's open, just walk in."

"Sure." I hang up and wait for his text. Was I sitting here all evening, waiting at his beck and call so I could do something with him?

Yes. There's no way to sugar coat that.

The address comes through a moment later. It's not far from here, in a cluster of apartments south of campus. I sail out the door of my apartment, singing goodbye to Iris.

Parking is usually allusive around campus, but with so many people gone for the semester, there's plenty of spots. I pull in and head around the corner for the apartment. I find the open door and step into the living room just as a girl inside says, "Kai, did you call your woman?"

I start laughing, and the four girls on the couch turn to look at me just as Kai comes out of a bedroom in the back. He sees me and laughs also and says, "My woman, huh?"

"There she is!" The girl on the couch beams at me and gestures me over. "I'm Esther. We've been waiting to meet you."

You have? I keep the question to myself and join them on the couch.

"This is Cassandra," Kai says. "That's Esther, Amy, Josie, and Lars."

"Hi," they say in unison.

"Hi," I say back. I study them, but it's okay because they're studying me. They're older girls, older than me, junior or seniors. "How do you guys know Kai?"

"From back home," Amy says. "I promised his mom I'd look after him when he came to school here."

"So we all take turns babysitting him," Josie says.

"Ha ha," Kai says. He sits down in front of a big box and looks up at me. "Want to help me with my Legos?"

"No," I say. "You left me sitting by my phone all night waiting for your call without the courtesy to tell me it would be this late. Do your own Legos."

That makes the girls beside me hoot with laughter. Esther pats my thigh. "Oh, I like you already."

Kai grins. "Fair. I'm very inconsiderate."

"The worst," I agree, fired up and rolling.

"Not the worst," he protests.

"That might be harsh," I say. "But you could definitely learn better communication skills."

"She's so right," one of the other girls says. "Remember when we invited you ice skating and you couldn't come but didn't tell us? By the time we gave up on you, we'd missed fifteen minutes of our scheduled time."

"Or when you said you'd come to my birthday but showed up a day late," Esther says.

I lean over my thighs to peer at them. "You mean it's not just me he does this to?"

"Oh, girl, you're just one of us," Esther says, putting her arm around my shoulders and hugging me to her.

"I've never done that to you," Kai protests.

"No, different scenarios," I say, waving him off.

His eyes swivel over us on the couch. "One of you is supposed to defend me."

Josie raises her eyebrows, and I join in as the five of us look around at each other.

"Not it," Lars says.

Esther heaves a dramatic sigh. "Kai has a lot of growing up to do."

"I'll say," I say, and it feels so *good* because I'm venting my anger but in a healthy, joking way.

Kai might not even know I'm being honest.

"I like her, Kai," Esther says.

"She's a funny girl, isn't she?" he says, grinning at his Legos.

I look down at Kai on the floor and take pity on him. "I'll help you with your Legos."

"I don't need your mercy," he says, but he's smirking. He scoots over as I plop down next to him.

They are big chunks of Legos but I can't tell what they used to be. "What was this?"

"I had a Lego table in my dorm." He separates several blocks and dumps them into a plastic bin. "This particular one was a village from an anime."

He likes anime. I add that to the mental list in my brain of all things Kai. So many things I still don't know about him. "What did it look like?"

"I'll show you." He pulls out his phone and swipes through pictures before he finds one.

I take the phone. "I'm impressed." The village covered an entire card table with several buildings and a multi-story tower. "I didn't know you do Legos."

"Me and my brother. I'm giving these to him while I'm on my mission."

I have his phone in my hands, and I can't help taking advantage of that. I pull up his camera and lean into him. "Smile."

He does, automatically, and the resulting selfie shows two carefree young people enjoying each other's company. It doesn't show any of the uncertain, negative emotions that have swirled around us lately.

I text it to myself and hand his phone back.

"You could have just said you wanted a picture," he teases. "You didn't have to sneak my phone."

"Oh, if I wanted a picture, I would have taken one," I tease right back, snapping off a few Lego pieces and adding them to the bin. "I knew you wanted one, though, and I knew you lacked the courage to ask."

He laughs.

"Where's your frog?" Esther says. "It's time to get that out of here."

"The frog isn't hurting anything," he says, waving her off.

"Your frog is here?" I turn to him, excited. "Where is it?"

"In the bathroom," Esther says.

"I'll get it." I stand up and find the hall bathroom. Inside is a small plastic aquarium with a bright green tree frog clinging to the walls, peering at me with large eyes behind his suctioned fingers.

"Oh, he's adorable!" I squeal as I come back with it.

"Better warn your roommates," he says. "Next you'll want a frog in your fish tank."

I scowl at him. "Oh, hush." I sit down with the aquarium between my hands and stare at him. "What's his name?"

"Green."

I shove his arm. "It is not."

He laughs. "Why not? That's what you named your stapler."

"I named it Blue!"

"Exactly."

"You named your stapler?" Lars says.

"We share custody of it," I say.

"I almost bought her another one, she likes it so much," Kai adds.

Josie lifts an eyebrow. "Is a stapler a euphemism for something?"

I roar with laughter at the very idea. Kai grins also.

"She likes my staplers," he says.

"Kai!" I shake my head, but I can't stop laughing.

He leans toward me and whispers, loud enough for everyone to hear, "You can have as many as you want."

"Should we give you guys a room?" Esther asks, lifting an eyebrow.

"Yes," I say. "You probably should." Because I'm ready to put this frog down and seize Kai's face between my hands and kiss him silly. I wipe at my eyes, where moisture gathers from laughing so hard. "So definitely don't."

"Or staplers," Kai says.

That does it, I'm laughing again. Kai shakes his head and takes the aquarium from me.

"You're scaring him."

I work hard to wipe the smile off my face. "Can I hold him?"

"Instead of Kai's stapler?" Josie says, and even my face grows hot as the laughter starts up again. I glance at Kai, and my thoughts have taken such a downward turn, which is incredibly ironic, considering we've never even kissed.

I've given up hoping for it.

Kai's cheeks are pink too, and he meets my eyes and smirks, and I'm delighted he's comfortable enough with me to joke this way.

I bump his shoulder with mine. "Is that a yes or a no?"

"You want the stapler or the frog?" he says.

I catch his gaze and wonder how far I can take this before it becomes inappropriate. "I'd be happy with both."

He sucks in a breath, and then I see it too, that same desire I feel in my navel, churning in the depth of his dark eyes, and I think, if we can just be alone for a moment, I might be able to make something happen.

I have proven to be a skilled seductress.

A skill I should not use on this virginal young man getting ready to leave on a mission.

CHAPTER ONE HUNDRED THIRTY

Fight the Break of Dawn

I hold my hand out and whisper, "We'll settle for the frog."

"The frog it is." He turns his gaze from mine and reaches into the aquarium. "Here you go."

He places the little green critter in my palm, and I hold it up to my face, cooing at it.

"I love you!" I say. His fingers and toes tickle as he jumps around my palm.

He jumps again. But this time instead of landing cutely in my hand, he lands directly on Esther's chest.

"Ahh!" she shrieks, thrusting her chest out and waving her hands. "Get it off, get it off, get it off!"

Her reaction would be comical if it weren't so genuinely distressed. Kai jumps to his feet immediately and reaches for the frog, and then stops.

"I'm not going there," he says.

"I've got it," I say, and I scoop it off.

"Oh my gosh," Esther says, and she takes several deep breaths, pressing her hands into her chest and gasping for air.

"I'm sure you scared him more than he scared you," I say.

"I don't know about that," she breathes, eyeing the frog like he tried to eat her. "Get that thing out of here, Kai!"

"I'm getting, I'm getting," he says. His face is serious, but I see how his lip trembles and know he's trying not to laugh. "Cassandra, put Green away."

He holds out the aquarium, and I drop the frog inside. Kai turns to his friends. "We're taking our frog home, thank you very much."

"Oh, the frog belongs to both of you now?" Josie says, and she doesn't hide her smirk.

Kai ignores her. "We're taking the Legos too."

He tucks the other bin under his arm and puts his hand between my shoulder blades and guides me out. As soon as we're out of earshot, they start chattering, and I want to slip away and go back so I can eavesdrop. But Kai's hand on my back keeps me moving forward.

"So what's the frog's real name?" I ask.

"His name's Green." Kai stops by my car.

"No, for real."

He cocks his head at me over the top of my car. "From now on he shall be known as Green."

I grin to myself as I unlock the car and get in.

Maybe Kai won't forget me after all.

We drive back to Kai's dorm, and I say, "Why was the frog at your friends' house?"

"We had cleaning inspections and I wasn't allowed to have him. They hid him for me every time."

"You just have to claim science experiment. That's what I did to keep my fish."

"Ah. Look at you, skirting the rules. I didn't know you had it in you."

"I'm not that much of a goody-two-shoes," I say, face hot, but I kind of am.

He glances over at me. "I'm noticing."

"Hey!" I protest. "You can't judge me based off anything I said or did back there! I was under the influence!"

He laughs. "Influence of what?"

Influence of lust. "You have no idea," I mutter.

He falls silent, but I know he's wondering about me now.

"Want me to come in?" I ask when we pull up at his dorm. The whole time, the question is there in my mind: is this it? Is it goodbye?

"No, I'll be back," he says, and I have my answer.

He takes Green up to his room and then returns to my car and says, "Mind if we go for a drive?"

My heart skips a beat, and my blood races hotter. "Not at all."

We'll be alone. His last night here.

The lyrics from the song he played for me yesterday dance through my head. *Save tonight and fight the break of dawn.*

"There's a canyon I know just south of here about twenty minutes. You game?" he says.

"Are we going hiking?"

"Do you want to?"

I shrug. "If you do."

"Not hiking. It's got a nice view."

"Lead on."

We drive south, and he has me turn off the main road and go up a road off the beaten path. I wonder if this is where his hot springs are. He directs me to a grassy area up on an overlook. I park the car and he opens the door.

"Come on," he says.

"We going hiking after all?" I say.

"Just a bit." He takes my hand and pulls me up a small incline. The grasses here come up to my thigh, and then he lays down in them. He tugs me down beside him. He lets go of my hand but he drops it onto my arm and tugs me closer so I'm tucked in next to him.

I can't see anything except grass around us. If I look straight up, I see the stars. I squint and try to remember the constellations Owen taught me, but all I remember is the Big Dipper.

Will I never get him out of my mind? I don't want him here between me and Kai.

"The stars are beautiful," I say, opening my eyes again and staring up at them. "Do you know the constellations?"

"No. Just the North Star."

"Everyone knows that one." I smirk at him.

"True that." He pulls me closer, close enough that I'm half on him. "Keep me warm, Cassandra."

I lean my head on his chest and wrap my arms around his torso. I can't see the stars now, but it doesn't matter, because his hand is in my hair, stroking me, holding me close, giving me the touch I've been craving. I sigh and close my eyes and snuggle closer. I don't care about the stars anymore.

We don't talk. We've said everything, I think, and the only thing left is goodbye. I sense he's no more ready for it than I am.

"Hey," he says, and I lift my eyes, propping my chin on his chest to peer at him.

"You know you were my favorite thing about this semester," he says.

For some reason my eyes tear up, and I sit up, putting space between us. "You didn't act like it most times."

"I know." He doesn't move from where he lays in the grass.

"You did at first," I say. "You always said nice things to me and made me feel good. But not lately. To be honest, I'm glad you're leaving. I can't take the way you're hurting me."

"I know that too," he says, quietly. "I don't know if we were supposed to meet right now. I didn't plan on getting involved with anyone, but I met you and I couldn't help myself. So I'm sorry . . . I should have left you alone."

His words are a balm to the stings he's left on my heart the past few weeks. I take his hand and squeeze it. "You touched my life, Kai. You enriched it. You made me a better person. And I'd take that over and over again, even if it meant I had to hurt when it ended."

"Everything has an ending, doesn't it?"

I nod. "And you and I had an expiration date before we started. We knew it. We did it anyway."

He tugs on my arm and pulls me back to his chest and holds me. "You don't regret it?"

I snort. "Honestly? My only regret is that we didn't get more serious."

He laughs, his eyes flashing in the moonlight as they study my face. "I would have liked to see where things went."

I say nothing more but snuggle up to him. I won't make any promises I can't keep.

Eventually Kai stirs, and I lift my face.

"You should go home," he says with a sigh. "It's almost two in the morning."

"And you have a busy day tomorrow." I stand and take his hand, pulling him up also. I turn for the car, but his hand snakes out to grab my wrist, and he pulls me back, surprising me by how he yanks me against him. Then he wraps his arms around me and buries his face in my hair, inhaling.

My heart pounds in my throat. It's now or never. I whisper, "I would let you kiss me if you tried."

He releases me and takes a step back, and then he cups my face in his hands. He doesn't say a word, his eyes flicking over my face, his breathing heavy. He runs his thumb over my lips and exhales. Then he lets go and puts another three feet between us.

"Time to go," he says.

He heads for my car and my body flushes hot and then cold with his rejection. I feel like an idiot for saying anything, for ruining the moment between us.

What moment? I laugh at myself. Nothing happened.

We say nothing on the drive. I think he's asleep, but when I glance at him, Kai's awake, eyes focused out the windshield just like mine.

Then he says, "You've had a serious boyfriend before?"

Ah. I wondered if he'd bring that up again. "Yes."

"More than one?"

"Yes."

"Where are they now?"

"Living their best lives."

"Why did it end?"

"Distance and wanting different things."

He's quiet, and then he says, "Well, Cassandra, it seems you've lived a lot longer and seen a lot more than I have. I've never even had a real girlfriend."

I look over at him. "You've had me. Whatever I was."

He takes my hand and weaves his fingers through mine.

We pull up at his dorm, and I park the car.

It's time. This is the moment I was waiting for.

"I have something for you," I say, and I lean over the console to dig around in my purse for the gift box.

"Let's get out of the car," he says.

I follow him out to stand under the street lamp next to his dorm. It's quiet other than the crickets, and my eyes sweep over the bushes along the wall, the sidewalk we danced on, all the unexpected things about this dorm that will always make me think of Kai. I pull out the box and hand it to him.

He opens it without a word and withdraws the pen. I take the box from him as he holds the pen up to the light, turning it back and forth. I admire the way the colors burn in the reflection, the way his engraved name looks like fire etched into stone.

"This is beautiful," he says. He looks at me and pulls me to him and pushes his nose into my cheek.

I cling to him. I will not cry. "Can I write you?" I ask. "Not often. I don't need a pen-pal. But just, sometimes, if I have something to say."

He lets me go. "Cassandra," he says, "I hope you won't take this wrong. But I don't want you to. You'll be a distraction."

I knew he'd say that. I'm perpetually distracting boys from their true purposes. "Can I at least write you when I go on a mission? Tell you where I'm going?"

He tilts his head and considers that, then nods. "Yes. You can also write me if you get married."

I snort and roll my eyes. "I'm not getting married."

"You could."

I level my gaze on him. "There are too many things I want to do first. Marriage can wait."

He grins. "All right. Then . . . I guess this is it."

I ache to step up to him, to touch his face, slide my fingers along his jaw. The pull is so strong that I have to get away. He doesn't want it, or he would have done it. I hand the gift box back to him, and he slides the pen into it. "Good night," I say, shoving my hands in my pockets and taking a giant step back.

"I guess I'll see you later," he says. "In a few years . . . Maybe . . ."

"Maybe." I take another step back, out of touching distance, closer to my car. "Goodbye, Kai."

He remains rooted to the spot. "Goodbye."

I turn and get in my car. I put it in reverse and drive away. I don't look back. I don't check to see if he's watching or if he went inside.

That is probably the last time I will ever see Kai Tanaka.

❧

I wake up in the morning feeling surprisingly refreshed for having such a late night out. And also . . . clean. Like I shook off a heavy load.

I'm untethered. Kai is gone. And there's no denying the aching in my heart that says I miss him, I care for him, but it was getting too complicated, too confusing.

I'm free again.

I work at the advisement center in the morning, still learning the ropes. It's quiet and boring with most students and professors gone already, and I spend my time reading.

Jordan calls as I'm leaving for the day.

"All right, you blew me off last night, tell me you don't have plans today."

I grin. "No plans."

"Great. Get your roommates. My parents want to take everyone out to dinner."

"I'm not going to argue with free food."

"I knew you wouldn't."

My cousin and I have always been close, but never closer than last year when we both lived in the dorms. This year we've seen less of each other because of class schedules and proximity, but he's still one of my closest friends.

I call Camila and Iris to tell them, and they're game. I start my car and turn the AC on full blast, because Colorado decided it's time to get hot.

My phone rings again, and I pick it up, my heart lurching in the hopes it will be Kai. Foolish thought, and I need to stop wanting that. He didn't even call me when he was here. Why would he now?

It's Monica. I answer, a warning ping tightening in my chest.

"Monica. Hey, what's up, girl?"

"Cassandra." Her voice is ragged, stuffy, and she sniffs. I tense.

"What is it? What's wrong?"

"It's the cancer," she says, her voice shaking. "It took a turn. Can you come sooner?"

The cancer. I close my eyes and grit my teeth.

This wasn't in the plans for right now.

"Yes," I say. "I'll come. Just tell me when."

"Can you come now? I'm headed to Utah for a special treatment tomorrow. We're flying. It's just for one day, and then Sunday we fly home. My mom said we could plan a stop in Colorado and get you from the airport."

My mind races, trying to absorb what she's asking. School just got out, I'm training at work, it's Thursday afternoon, classes start on Tuesday . . .

"Send me the flight itinerary," I say. "I'll plan on it."

She lets out a sob. "Thank you. I'm just so . . . scared."

"It's all right," I say. "I've got time." It's the money I'm lacking.

"Thank you," she says, crying. "I'll see you soon."

"See you soon," I echo, and I hang up, my heart squeezing.

Guess I better talk to my boss.

Coming soon!

Sneak peek of the cover of Episode 1!

PSSS. You. Yeah, you.
Did you know I have a reader exclusive club? My own private syndicate?
And if you join, you get not one, but TWO exclusive ebooks??

Join the Syndicate here to get the links to your free ebooks! (https://tamara-hart-heiner.kit.com/4d7889b1f5 in case the button doesn't work)

You can even join my Discord channel here and become a part of my own book community!

Find me on social media! Join my Cassandra Jones fan club on Facebook. Here we can theorize together on what's going to happen, talk about past events, dive into character feelings, and even give me ideas for upcoming books! Find it on Facebook at "All About Cassandra Jones." And follow me on Instagram @tamaraheiner, where I post all kinds of sneak peeks, do fun giveaways, and enjoy interacting with you! Say hello and

I'll say hi back!

Follow me on TikTok for video updates on all my writing activities! @Tamara_writes

Don't miss any of Cassandra's exciting adventures! Get the entire Cassandra Jones Series now!

Did you find a typo?

Even though I have a critique group, an editor, a beta team, an ARC team, and a proofreader, errors still slip through, and I want to know! If you find one, email me at Tamara@tamarahartheiner.com and let me know which book and what it is, and I'll send you your choice of one of my ebooks for free!

Thank you for helping me make my books better!

Enjoy this book? You can make a huge difference!

If you enjoyed this book, I'd be honored if you'd leave an honest review on whatever book haunt you frequent.

Reviews are indie authors' bread and butter, and we couldn't do it without readers like you!

About the Author

I live in beautiful northwest Arkansas in a big blue castle with two princesses and a two princes, and several loyal cats (and one dog). I fill my days with slaying dragons at traffic lights, earning stars at Starbucks, and sparring with the dishes. I also enter the amazing magical kingdom of my mind to pull out stories of wizards, goddesses, high school, angels, and first kisses. Sigh.

I'm the author of several young adult stories, kids books, romance novels, and even one nonfiction.

You can find me outside enjoying a cup of iced tea or in my closet snuggling with my cat. But if you can't make the trip to Arkansas, I'm also hanging out on Facebook and Instagram but usually TikTok as @Tamara_writes. You can also visit me on my website, tamarahartheiner.com. I look forward to connecting with you!